FIRE-HAIR WOMAN

Fire-Hair Woman

The Epic Story of Lucinda Eubank

Gina Ellis & C.J. Pierce

PRAIRIE SPIRIT, LLC
Firestone, Colorado
2022

PRAIRIE SPIRIT, LLC

FIRST EDITION
FIRE-HAIR WOMAN
by Gina Ellis & C.J. Pierce

Copyright © 2022. All rights reserved.
Printed in the United States of America.
ISBN 979-8-218-01221-2

Note to the Reader

During their research the authors discovered many interesting quotes and documents which are inserted throughout the book. Because the language of the nineteenth century was stilted and opaque, in the interest of historical accuracy, they have chosen not to correct spelling or grammar, and otherwise edit, abridge, or modernize the prose. Quotes, newspaper articles, letters, dispatches, depositions, affidavits, proclamations, and speeches are written in their original form with no efforts made to correct grammar, spelling, and punctuation. In regards to grammar and punctuation errors and omissions, the authors hold sole responsibility.

Dedicated
to
Lucinda

For her perseverance, strength, and faith she maintained for the love of her descendants. This story followed the Eubank generations until it settled in our hearts. As we give it voice, may her story find us worthy.

———•———

*She was of sweet disposition and kind to all who
met her, even those who had done her harm.*

Mrs. L. A. Atkinson
Niece by Marriage
St. Paul, KS

I've seen in my mind that sometime after I am dead they will come. Light-skinned, bearded men will arrive with sticks spitting fire. They will conquer the land and drive the Indian before them. They will kill the animals who give their flesh that Indians may live, and they will bring strange animals for them to ride and eat. They will introduce war and evil, strange sicknesses and death. They will take the Indians' land little by little, until there is nothing left. You must be strong when that time comes, you men, and particularly you women, because much depends on you, because you are the perpetuators of life and if you weaken, the Cheyenne will cease to be.

Sweet Medicine, Prophet and Teacher
Traditional Folklore

The Overland Trail

Along the Little Blue River

NEBRASKA TERRITORY

WILLIAM EUBANK, SR
SECTION;6
TOWNSHIP: 3
RANGE:5

JOSEPH EUBANK, SR
SECTION;7
TOWNSHIP: 3
RANGE:5

◄ TO FORT KEARNY

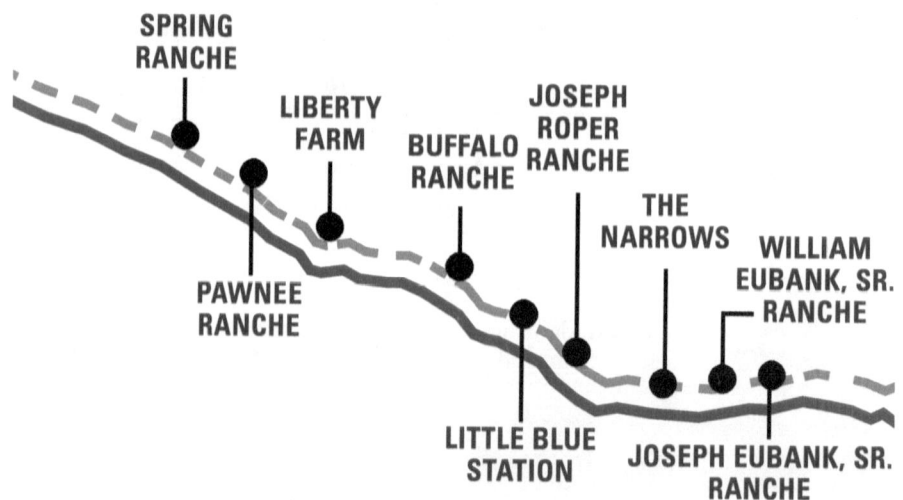

SPRING
RANCHE

LIBERTY
FARM

BUFFALO
RANCHE

JOSEPH
ROPER
RANCHE

THE
NARROWS

WILLIAM
EUBANK, SR.
RANCHE

PAWNEE
RANCHE

LITTLE BLUE
STATION

JOSEPH EUBANK, SR.
RANCHE

- - - OVERLAND TRAIL

▬▬▬ LITTLE BLUE RIVER

KANSAS

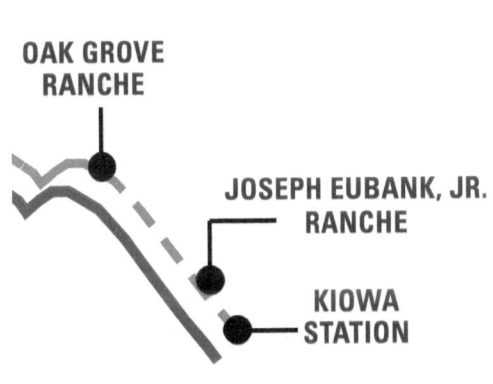

OAK GROVE RANCHE

JOSEPH EUBANK, JR. RANCHE

KIOWA STATION

TO ATCHISON, KS ▶

Eubank Family Tree

GENERATION ONE & CHILDREN

Joseph Eubank, Sr. & Ruth Adamson Eubank
1802 - 1864   1810 - 1874

Mary Eliza	1834 - 1869
Joseph, Jr. (Joe)	1835 - 1864
William (Will)	1837 - 1864
Hannah	1838 - 1915
Sarah	1843 - ?
Fredrick (Fred)	1845 - 1864
George	1847 - ?
Medora (Dora)	1848 - 1864
James	1851 - 1864
Henry	1852 - 1864

GENERATION TWO & CHILDREN

William Joseph Eubank, Sr. & Ruby Lucinda Walton Eubank
1837 - 1864   1840 - 1913

Isabelle Eubank, (Belle)	1861 - 1865
William Joseph, Jr. (Willie)	1863 - 1935

GENERATION THREE & CHILDREN

William Joseph Eubank, Jr. & Sarah Jane Frogge Eubank
(Willie)   (Jennie)
1863 - 1935   1871 - 1937

Ruby Lucinda (Lucy)	1897 - 1968
Virgil Francis	1898 - 1956
Arthur Lowell (Art)	1900 - 1965
Ollie Mack	1902 - 1974
William Joseph Noel	1904 - 1904
Beatrice Evelyn (Bea)	1905 - 1977
Blanche Elizabeth	1907 - 1958
Daniel Loren (Loren)	1909 - 1987
Kenneth Charles (Kenny)	1913 - 1998

Preface

Ruby Lucinda Walton Eubank is the great-great grandmother of C.J. Pierce and Gina Ellis. FIRE-HAIR WOMAN, The Epic Story of Lucinda Eubank, follows the 1864-1865 Indian captivity of Lucinda, her daughter Isabelle, and her baby Willie. C.J. and Gina have delved into extensive research through the preservation of family documents, photographs, and oral accounts to undertake the telling of their story in historical fiction form. This is an alternative western saga—unique in its feminine character and rich in the details of Lucinda's role in an American historical conflict. She and her family were unwilling participants in the Great Indian War of 1864.

In 1964, C.J. accompanied her mother and grandmother, Beatrice Eubank Ellis, to the site of the Eubank Ranches near Oak, Nebraska. Several family members met there, including Willie's sons, Loren and Kenny Eubank. C.J.'s interest was sparked by stories of Lucinda shared by her grandmother.

The Oak-Angus Centennial Celebration and 103rd Anniversary of the Indian Raids was held in 1967, and C.J. returned to the Eubank Ranche to play the part of great-great grandmother Lucinda during the Oregon Trail Tour and Reenactment. She remembers running for cover as Lucinda did under the hot, August sun along the same harrowing ground in a prairie bonnet and long, pioneer dress. Renegade actors hoisted her on and off the backs of sweating horses as hundreds of cars drove to the site to witness the tragic story.

Throughout the years, photographs and memories of lost ancestors sprang to life. Tattered, yellow newspaper clippings lovingly stored in the authors' grandmother's trunk surfaced like sand, covered and uncovered through time. C.J.'s mother lovingly protected two of the most treasured items in the Eubank Historical Family Collection—the photos of Lucinda and Will Eubank.

Family members conducted research at the National Archives in the Library of Congress, Washington, D.C. Xeroxed copies of depredation claims, depositions, affidavits, and eyewitness accounts were obtained and stored. Bits of Lucinda's story were found in dozens of books, newspaper articles, letters, depositions, and archival collections. The firsthand accounts of fellow captives, Nancy Morton and Laura Roper, and the writings of native women from generations past were particularly enlightening. Piecing the story timeline together was often interrupted by periods of paralyzing grief as the grand-daughters labored over descriptions of torture, mistreatment, and death. Original sources were valuable and yielded glimpses into Lucinda's and

Willie's captivity. Many finds were thrilling in nature and provided tiny snapshots into nineteenth century frontier life. Using this information, Gina and C.J. resolved to write Lucinda's story from her first-person perspective.

Lucinda's captive journey carried her through Nebraska, Kansas, Colorado, New Mexico, and modern-day Wyoming, then known as part of the Dakotah Territory. The authors have personally visited these places and other significant family locations, such as the grave of her daughter, Lottie Bartholomew, in the Deepwood Cemetery, Nevada, Missouri. Lucinda's grave in the Frogue/Frogge Cemetery near McCune, Kansas, is of special importance. The family is grateful to those who faithfully tend to the burial site of so many family members.

The authors started a quest for a connection in Oak, Nebraska. They wanted to know if the re-enactments were still taking place and yearned to return to the former Eubank Ranche. Finally, a contact was found who said, "We've been waiting for you!" The trip to Oak in 2018 was met with warmth and graciousness from the residents. Together the authors walked the same path along the Narrows their great-great grandparents and their children took in 1864. In the serenity of the moment, they felt the wind grace their cheeks in the valley of the Little Blue River.

Over the years, Great-Grandfather Willie lamented the loss of his sister Isabelle. In 1930, newspaper articles were written about his story of captivity in the hopes a woman would come forward and identify herself as Belle. He died without certain knowledge of his sister's fate. In 1990, Belle's post-captivity story was found in Mollie Sanford's pioneer diary and the mystery was solved.

The mission of this book is to wrap the retelling of the Eubank story within the framework of a more informed position yet include Lucinda's nineteenth-century perspective—especially of her captors. The authors wish to be respectful of all people who lost their homelands one hundred and fifty years ago.

Lucinda Eubank's encounters with hardship, deprivation, pain, and loss at such a young age were eclipsed only by the miraculous survival of her young son Willie—the authors' great-grandfather, William Joseph Eubank, Jr.

Introduction

The Hebron Champion
July 28, 1911

E. M. Correll

Earliest History of Thayer County

The attention of the whole nation was occupied by the great war of the rebellion in 1864, so that the Indian raid of that year, the most carefully planned and skillfully executed known in the history of the Western frontier, received but little attention and seemed in comparison of so little importance as scarcely to deserve a place in National history. "Yet the military strategy and precision, and the secrecy and success and the cool butchery and cruelty of the attack, make it as Napoleonic in its design and execution, and should place it on the pages of history alongside of other great and bloody butchery by savages. At this time, many ranches dotted the great military road at intervals of a few miles. These ranches had become in many cases valuable farms, with substantial improvements, graced by woman's presence and ornamented by woman's tasteful care. A number of such ranches were in Thayer County upon and contiguous to the Government road. The Indians had been peaceful and quiet for a long time, and the settlers along the road were prosperous and happy. Without a single note of warning the crisis came. From Denver City to Big Sandy, a distance of over six hundred miles, near the middle of the day, at precisely the same time, along the whole distance a simultaneous attack was made upon the ranches. No time was given for couriers no time for concentration, no time for the erection or strengthening of places of defense, but, as the eagle swoops down upon his prey, the savage warriors attacked the defenseless white men. No principle of kingly courtesy actuated the breasts of the painted assailants. It mattered little to them that they were in vastly superior number and their opponents in part women and children. All alike were made to feel their cruelty or their lust. No mercy was shown. No captives were taken but women, and death was preferred to the captivity that awaited them. Could the Eastern philanthropists who speak so flatteringly of "the noble red man of the West" have witnessed the cruel butchery of unoffending children, the disgrace of women, who were first horribly mutilated and then slain, the cowardly assassination of husbands and fathers, they might, perhaps (if fools can learn), be impressed with their true character. On the morning of the 7th of August, Indians must have been secreted in the ravines (of which ere were many) adjacent to the military road, and, at a given hour, rushed forth and commenced their work of destruction. At morn, the Government road was a traveled thoroughfare, dotted with prosperous and happy homes; at night, a wilderness, strewn with mangled bodies and wrecks, and illuminated with the glare of burning houses."

Hoofbeats

11 August 1864
Solomon River, Northern Kansas Territory

In the Platte Valley, on the other hand, was the great Overland Stage Line with stations every ten or twelve miles and daily coaches carrying the mail passing both ways, east and west. This was also the great emigrant and wagon-freighting route, and you could often see wagon trains extending unbroken for miles along the valley, the huge freight wagons with their white canvas tops looking from the distance like fleets of ships at sea.

George Bent

Plunging across the vast ocean prairie, the war horse's hooves pound relentlessly. The jolting rhythm carries me through woven patches of consciousness. Cringing with every powerful movement of its muscular form, my body aches from days of travel and the abuses heaped upon it. Blood pulses through the veins in my neck, and my head throbs. Days in the hot August sun have left me blistered, and I suffer an unquenchable thirst.

Propelled forward, I am transported to an unknown distant land—despite my contempt of its direction. Stunned senses cease to function as shock permeates my being. Unsure of my own identity, I question if I am still Lucinda Eubank. Can this be? Where am I? Engulfed in a dark abyss of fear, my body and mind are overwhelmed. The horse's trampling feet are inconsequential. I hear nothing. Numbness creeps upward from my dangling feet and spreads to my brain.

The animal beneath exudes strength and stamina. Hand-painted images on its hips and shoulders glow vividly in the sunlight. Its dark chestnut coat is accented by iridescent white blotches and adorned with colorful circles, slashes, and handprints—all in motion. The gay colorful ribbons woven within its mane and tail whip in the wind.

With deep-throated grunts, the dragon flies to freedom from gravity's pull. Stretching its neck, the animal charges forward with increasing speed. Angrily snapping its yellow teeth at invaders, it pins back its notched ears. The horse transforms into a shapeless phantom gaining flight on huge amorphous wings. Flapping wildly, it is a moving mystical creature of war.

My will is in defiance of every stride, yet, I am resigned. I can do nothing to change course. With fingers wrapped in the twisted vine of the horse's mane, my other arm shields the babe. I desperately cup Willie's round, smooth head and press it to me. The jostling has taken a toll on the child who is slumped nearly lifeless in the sling across my chest. Apprehension increases as I search for my three-year-old daughter amid the melee.

Isabelle!

Swiveling my head, I strain to see her small, pale face among the storming warriors surrounding us. I cling to the thought that Laura holds her in a covetous grip while astride one of the thundering beasts—shielding her from the blazing globe. Is my nephew Conrad with them? Mile after mile, the ground rolls past, and I cannot calm the inner dread. I imagine Belle's fair hair shining like a beacon just beyond my line of sight. Oh, for it to be so! Where is she? At our last encounter, she wore the burdensome air of one who has endured much. Thrust into a nightmarish world of frightening strangers and violence, her face speaks to the horror, fear, and sorrow.

Hordes of mounted warriors charge across the grassy, open plains in a controlled stampede of men and weapons. Tomahawks, knives, rifles, pistols, clubs, sabers, lances, bows and arrows are brandished among highly decorated shields. So many painful ways to die.

Large war bonnets of spiked crow feathers distinguish the fiercest chiefs. The war party displays silver armbands, quilled breast plates, buckskin leggings, and beaded moccasins. Fur skins sail and flap about the shoulders as surreal images of bobbing stuffed birds, buffalo skulls, and grimacing wolves snarl and threaten with malevolent intent.

The renegades are equally prepared for victory, or death—whichever is required. Rattling weapons, hoofbeats, and regalia blend into the jarring discord of my pounding heart. Ornaments on bridles gleam and flash while the hair of those recently vanquished spins in the wind. The fresh scalps of my murdered loved ones call to me amid the shrieking of the infidel.

As the raiders stream across the green expanse of rolling hills, I strain to see behind me. The dust kicked up by such a large contingent obscures my view. My little girl....

Sunlit clouds rise thousands of feet into the sky behind us. Their dark, bulging underbellies, tinged with a green hue, portend a fury unimaginable. Lightning splits the sky followed by a thunderous shaking of the earth. Darkness descends, and the light of the sun is blotted out. The towering wraith above rotates and boils—ominously matching the swirling mayhem at the horses' feet. I am desperate to escape the storms behind and within, yet, our charge continues unabated. The wind carries the scent of rain.

A relentless, sleepless journey into a faraway land is about to claim its first casualty. I teeter on the edge and lurch toward the smoking hellfire below. The black-faced marauder behind me grips my rib cage hard. He shakes me, and my head snaps up. My sense of hearing gradually returns as the dimness around me subsides. I shake the hair out of my eyes and breathe deeply, trying to calm the panic that claws at my life force.

Long, lean arms glistening with sweat cross over my body and that of my boy. Strong hands grip my sunburned wrists and pin them down. Long tendrils of my hair fly wildly about, sticking to the shoulders of the painted banshee behind me. With rampaging speed, our impending doom is colliding with an evil unknown.

I long to erase the experiences of the past several days. The memories tug at my bleeding heart—its fragmented shards torn by sorrow. I can see them vividly—it is futile to force my mind from those moments which led to our dire circumstances.

Will, my husband, my anchor. I wish to strike down what has occurred, place it in a lock box, and possess my loved ones forever. Our family has suffered unimaginable tragedy on this newest frontier. I beg God to keep its tattered remnants together.

Ultimately, each lonely soul desires to eradicate such unspeakable events from the record of human existence; but this cataclysm will not be forgotten. In fact, this day, and those to follow, will haunt me for the rest of my life.

chapter one

Captivity

Four Days Prior
Sunday, 7 August 1864
Little Blue River, Nebraska Territory

The attacks along the Little Blue River were even more severe than those made along the Platte. There was no telegraph line through this country to warn the settlers of the Indian outbreak. These attacks centered on the Overland Stage Company's route along the Little Blue River in what is now Thayer, Nuckolls and Clay counties. On the first day of the raid, August 7, the Indians attacked the Eubank family. This attack constitutes the most horrible tragedy perpetrated in all the history of the Indian outbreaks upon the Nebraska frontier.

Leroy W. Hagerty

A dozen renegades pillaged and burned our home, then departed. They headed southwest of the Eubank Ranche—with five captives in tow. A final glance over my shoulder laid bare a chilling scene. Our ranche was in flames, its contents scattered across the valley. The mutilated bodies of my loved ones lay mangled and alone. The safety and peace we once treasured were destroyed in a blinding instant.

Leaving stony structures barren inside, my bones drained of their marrow. By force of will, I connected to the cold, logical center of my brain. Its icy touch penetrated the truth. Shivering despite the heat, I wiped my tear-soaked face over and over trying to cleanse it from the unbelievable facts.

My hand throbbed, and I examined the swollen knuckle of my ring finger. The ring was gone. The man was gone. Nothing but a pale shadow lingered in their former resting places. Love still flowed from heart to finger, but its pulse slowed with the dying. The wedding band had been wrenched from my finger—nearly breaking my hand. I rubbed the sore appendage and recalled the struggle.

A young, repulsive warrior attacked me in the yard of my home like a vicious dog. Noticing the gold ring, he grabbed my wrist and twisted my finger to the point of exploding pain. I kicked him in the groin, and his face turned purple. Doubling over, he sank to his knees. I managed to pull free from his grasp and without thinking, swallowed the ring. The thief staggered to a standing position and lunged toward me. I backed away, flinging my arm in a feigned effort to draw his attention. The invisible ring soared into nearby shrubs.

The warrior was distracted as his companions leapt upon their horses and charged out of our yard. Willie and I were swept upon a horse in front of a hideously painted raider, and the ring was forgotten. There would be a price to pay, but the symbol of my union with Will was still in my possession—to be retrieved later.

Hooves splashed softly across small channels of water only inches deep. Clear, clean, and cool, the Little Blue River flowed through our verdant and peaceful valley. Crossing it left me shaken, as though transgressing a boundary of sanity.

Our home sat on the edge of a vast wilderness in a slim crescent of civilization, primitive but adequate by most standards. Beyond the rim of our homeland lay millions of square miles held within a continent filled with wilderness, danger, and the unknown. The Eubank ranche established a tiny foothold in this great land—a comforting and soothing place of promise. Until now.

The setting sun lit the evening—so contrary to the dark misery inflicted upon my soul. Rays of light cascaded across the prairie and created golden paths beckoning me toward heaven. If only I could join my loved ones who embarked upon their final journey today. Yet, I remained waist deep and drowning in fright and sorrow.

Along the south side of the river, we rode silently through the light-tinged oaks and cottonwoods. The sparkling towheads of the river's sand bar winked at me.

Then I saw him.

The beautiful man was prone and still among the shadows. Fixing my weeping eyes upon his form, I struggled to remain upright. As we passed, my ringless hand lifted of its own accord and reached back to my husband. Come with me, I begged. Do not allow this separation. Will. I shook my head and bent my chin to my chest. Suffocating in loss, I wavered in and out of consciousness. Nothing could force out the nightmare.

Will had been my native guide full of courage and resolution. He never faltered. No matter how daunting the task or difficult the conditions, he was industrious, independent, and brave. I blinked hard and swallowed to quash the panic. I was in mortal danger, alone and adrift in a black sea. Without the strength and presence of my foundation, how would I survive? Did his abilities abide within me? Would they rise to meet this threat or crumble to ash?

Trapped between the thighs of the predatory rogue behind me, my head lolled and drooped on the stem of my neck like a wet reed. Hours passed.

Stunned by a glancing blow to my shoulder, my awareness snapped to the forefront. The warrior who tried to steal my ring kicked his pony around mine and glared at me. Smiling maliciously, he lifted his lance high. Fresh scalps dangled. He shrieked with glee before galloping off. The dripping tokens of my family's sacrifices strengthened his heart while tearing out my own. Stranded in grief, I willed my eyes to unsee, my memory to erase the images. But it was impossible to staunch the dread and loss. The tears were unrelenting as I left the final vestiges of my homeland. I wondered if I would survive or if I would ever return. There would be nothing left....

Hours later, I rode through the darkness in an exhausted state of shock. The trauma of the day's events were exacting their payment. My heart pounded erratically against my rib cage. Adrenaline was waning. Weakness permeated my limbs and left me feeble. My ability to speak or scream was gone. I fumbled with the baby's sling in a mindless attempt to ease his discomfort.

The frightening enemy were but gray figures in the gloom. Jagged, white stripes stood out on their painted faces, the blood-red and black portions hid the evil behind.

Silently, we crossed a final familiar landmark, the Republican River. A measureless and unknown country lay ahead. Faintly, I asked, "Where are we going?"

No one answered, and I slipped into oblivion.

Startled from my stupor, I heard a strong voice speak to me in English! Jerking my head up, I located its source. A strange man had ridden up next to us. "The other white woman is behind you. I spoke to her. I am not sure what will happen to you. I told her that if they were going to kill you, they would have done so already."

I stared unbelievingly.

He said, "I don't think they will murder you."

The warrior in front of me turned his head to look at the man but seemed unperturbed by the intrusion. He continued to guide his horse through the tall grass of a buffalo trail.

I peered at our rugged companion in the dim light. To my surprise, he was a white man dressed as an Indian. His accent was unfamiliar. My focus sharpened at the mention of my neighbor Laura. My little girl must be with her! I remained quiet but alert. Now he had my attention.

"These Indians are Sioux, Arapaho, and Cheyenne Dog Men. I think they will give you up soon or trade you to other Indians."

Trembling, I found my voice and croaked, "Who are you?"

"Joe Beralda." Tilting a chin toward my captor, he added, "That is Heap of Birds."

"Is my daughter with the other white woman?"

Without responding, Mr. Beralda turned his horse around and trotted away. I was left with new questions and worries. I knew of these kinds of men who lived with the Indians. Sick, confused, and angry, I wondered. Had he been part of the attack? My thoughts returned to the man's message.

"Give up or be traded."

Our lives were balanced on the thin edge of a blade. For the first time, I processed the motives of our captors. We were a commodity to be bartered, traded, or ransomed. Or...were we sacrificial lambs kept to avenge a grievance?

Merciful God, help us....

The day's staggering fever gave way to the smothering embrace of night. It held a terrible beauty. The gleam of the half-moon painted the grassy plains with a velvety, smooth shimmer. It was a place of pure desolation—which matched my heart perfectly.

chapter two

Wolves

8 August 1864
Republican River, Kansas Territory

It was a land of vast silent spaces, of lonely rivers, and of plains where the wild game stared at passing horsemen.

Theodore Roosevelt

The Indian ponies plodded through the night, carrying us further into the wilderness. It was cool and overcast. A gray mizzle of thick fog cloaked us within feathery shadows. The dawning presence of morning lit the cottonwoods growing along the river. Light flickered through the leaves as my eyes adjusted to its pale mantle. The fresh earth held the scent of an unsullied existence. Not a wrinkle or a bump, no gaping wounds or rocky intrusions interrupted the landscape of grass. Its blanket extended beyond the river like an endless emerald sea as far as the eye could see.

Willie was asleep in my arms. The only sound to break the silence were hooves softly beating their slow cadence as we walked through damp leaves on the wooded path. My bare feet were bound together tightly under the horse's belly, and I longed to stretch my legs to relieve the unrelenting cramps. I turned my head repeatedly to find Isabelle and Laura. Were they still behind us?

Instinctively, I pressed Willie closer to my chest. With eyes screwed tightly shut, he mewed slightly and insistently nudged my breast. I comforted him the only way I knew how.

This land had been the happiness of our life. Now it was a curse. Desperation resided deep in my gut, and I tasted its sour bile. I continued to search for landmarks or evidence of people. I scanned the distance for a place to hide, a way to escape.

Riding through the shadows, the cool leaves filtered the sun. From this enclave along the Republican River, I peered at the dazzling light beyond. Drawing my sight back to the path, I noticed a doe standing motionless in her shady hiding place. Head up and ears forward, her moist nostrils flared to meet our scent. Tranquil eyes stared placidly between delicately-fringed lashes. Our eyes met, yet, she seemed unconcerned by my plight. In her wild innocence, she was unafraid, and I envied her. Our passage through her home was but a moment in her day; yet, my sojourn was never ending.

By afternoon, five Indians intersected our path and joined the procession. Their frightening appearance must have alarmed Isabelle, for I thought I heard her cry out. Despite the continuous movement, I assessed our situation and forced myself to notice the surroundings. Insane dread, fueled by numerous assaults upon my person, left me with the sobering fact—there were no breadcrumbs to lead me home. I needed to get my bearings in a hurry if I hoped to ever find our way back to civilization.

I struggled to free my legs, but they were clamped into place with no choice but surrender. Within a state of semiconsciousness, my thoughts slowed as tiny physical discomforts magnified. My focus selected different painful sensations which grew and became insurmountable. I shook off the manifestations of pain, but my mind would settle upon a new source of twinging spasm.

Soon my derangement was in full swing. I swatted wildly at the swarming gnats, mosquitoes…so many flying tormentors. My callous captor answered my pleas with a hard slap across my cheek, arresting my mind to focus, and the cycle began again.

Another full day's ride produced a shrunken woman barely breathing. I watched as the horizontal light of the sinking sun glittered across the prairie. The ocean of grass swayed in its purity, untouched by the human or his plow. Monotonous, yet, ever-changing, the wild and shaggy expanse heated to a quiet bake.

Finally, the motion stopped. The Indians gathered near a brook gurgling with cool water. I stared down at the tiny riffles of water that purled over the colorful rocks in the streambed. The binds that held my ankles fell away, yielding to a knife's blade. Unceremoniously, I was pulled off the horse and plunked onto the grass. My non-functioning, stump-like legs were useless. I crawled into the water, grasping Willie to my chest. Kneeling, I leaned and drank deeply—not bothering to cup the liquid with my hands. Swallowing, gulping, I dipped my mouth repeatedly into the cooling rivulet.

Willie struggled to free himself from his sling. He was coughing and gasping. He needed air. I lifted the baby to my shoulder and pounded his back. Once normal breathing resumed, I plunked his bottom into the shallow water. We revived as I swished water and bathed our hot faces and necks. The hair on top of his head spiked crazily like a long-haired baby goat. I stared at my constant companion as though seeing him for the first time. Using both fists, he rubbed water from his eyes and sneezed a glob of snot from his wrinkled nose. A sigh of relief escaped my lungs as I hugged the child. It was time for him to eat, but I was reluctant to remove our scraped and blistered bodies from the brook. So, we sat in the water, and he nursed. Willie suckled his meal like a piglet.

"Thank you, Lord," I whispered.

Scanning the nearby fringe of trees, I spotted a gray head pointing its snout between willow saplings. The lifeless body of a rabbit hung from its mouth. I dared not move as a huge wolf stepped forward sniffing the air. It paused a moment and looked at me with golden eyes framed in black. Hackles rose along its ruff, and its ears lay back threateningly. With a quick shake of its coat, it slipped back into the shadows, the evening meal dangling from toothy jaws. The utter silence of its disappearance was replaced by the empty wildness of its hiding spot. The wolf was gone, but I shuddered at the encounter.

Quickly, I made my way to a spot along the bank where I could step out. Holding Willie, I stood unsteadily as water drained off our soaked clothing. I noticed a large warrior watching us over the sweat-soaked back of his horse. Like the wolf, his nostrils flared, and his face expressed a sinister interest. The hairs on my neck stood on end like frozen grass. I glanced back toward the saplings, searching my surroundings for danger. Looking back, the Indian was gone. I held the baby closely and hustled in the opposite direction—away from both watchers.

The braves dismounted, stripped the burdens from the horses, and hobbled them. Heads down, the animals stumbled to the grass-rimmed stream. Ripping and tearing at the sprouts, they grazed ravenously, for their journey had been arduous as well.

I needed two things—to relieve myself and to find Isabelle.

Lifting my dress, I squatted. Hovering above the ground, a violent kick launched me onto my stomach. My face was thrust into the dirt as ravenous human wolves assaulted me. My agonized cries produced only harsh slaps and kicks. Fearing the children might hear, I bit my tongue to squash the terror-filled screams. Struggling met with curses and laughter.

True fear, my constant companion, overpowered reason. Rattlesnakes! Crawling over and around me! Hissing! Biting! I cannot get away! Thrashing about, I could do little to stop the ruthless, repeated attacks. Pain-filled moans escaped into the oppressive air. The disjointed quiet of lunacy offered relief, but it was elusive. Fading in and out of consciousness, the defilement of my body continued...then blackness.

———•———

Barely breathing, I was alive. Staked to the hard prairie ground, my wrists and ankles were secured tightly by leather thongs. The skin on my thighs was covered with blood. Oblivious to my surroundings, I lost consciousness again.

Hours later, I opened my eyes to the sight of millions of stars chastising me from a black sky. I pulled on the stakes. Firmly bound, I searched frantically for my baby! Willie! Where is he? My engorged breasts told me he needed another feeding. Gripped by the urgency to find my child, I realized the hunched bundle pressed against my thigh was breathing. Alive, he crawled next to me like a helpless fawn. Unreachable, yet, near.

But...Belle, Laura, Conrad. Where were they? Afraid to call out, I tossed from side to side and searched in vain for sight or sound of them. Nothing.

So, I waited....

chapter three

Calamity

9 August 1864
Republican River, Kansas Territory

The second night we went down a deep ditch and my saddle came off and the pony, in trying to get up, hit me with his hoof and broke my nose. The Indians took a sheet they had gotten at Mrs. Eubank's home and wiped the blood from my face, and nearly whipped the pony to death.

Laura Roper

Gulping wildly, I swallowed water from a rusted coffee pot. No food was offered as our captors mounted quickly in the predawn light. I noticed Heap of Birds ride into the lead without me. Suddenly, Willie and I were tossed onto the back of a large paint horse. This time my raw, bleeding ankles were not bound under its belly. The Indian spoke to me. His white teeth flashed in contrast to his black and red painted face.

Two Face.

While trading at stage stops along the Little Blue, he stopped at our station for a meal on occasion. Noticing the flash of recognition in my eyes, he did not disguise his amused expression. Leaping up behind us, he squeezed the horse into a lope. I seethed with anger and fed the urge to stab him. The fiend had betrayed our friendship. Reaching a boil, I spat on the ground. Two Face was oblivious to my rage. In fact, he was one with his horse, relaxed and untroubled.

Two Face's free hand rested on his thigh. He stretched his fingers, repeatedly opening and closing his fist. Finally, it rested palm up on his leg. I stared at the maze of crisscrossing lines and scars. Did they simply foretell his fate, or was my life woven into the pattern as well? Perhaps I could end his lifeline....

The day wore on and the lack of food left me light-headed. My famished state was amplified by waves of weakness. Worry washed over me. The misery increased as I thought of my little girl's hunger. I had to find a way to help her. Hearing the grumbling from my stomach, Two Face reached into his bag and handed me a large strip of dried buffalo meat. I ripped off a piece and began to chew rapidly. As the meat softened, I placed a small piece in Willie's mouth, and he busily gummed the offering. I tucked the remainder of the meat into my satchel, hoping to give it to Belle at some point during our day's trek.

Later that afternoon, other riders joined the group. After serious discussion, the newcomers pointed to the north. I noticed their general mood was solemn. The Indians were watchful and alert as we rode quietly through the hills. I never got a close look at our new companions as they linked themselves to the rear of our moving chain.

Suddenly, out of the hills to my right, a dozen braves rapidly rode toward us shouting, "Winnebago!" Scouting the area, they had spotted a cause for alarm. A large, buckskin-clad scout and a military detachment of blue coats were poised at the top of a rise overlooking our trail. I recognized the leader. It was Mr. O.P. Wiggins, and behind him were more than thirty Winnebago Indians. It was a well-known fact they were employed by the United States government to increase security along the Overland Trail. The Winnebago Indians were outfitted with military jackets and American horses. My heart lifted. Our rescuers had come!

The stream of warriors turned as one and kicked their ponies into a dead run down through the valley. My hair whipped across my eyes as we tore through rolling prairie knolls. I tried to keep the military in sight. Two warriors fired their rifles at the soldiers. They turned their mounts from the lead position to pass us and form a rearguard. As our fleet Indian horses picked up speed, we pulled away from our pursuers. Their horses slowed despite the urgings of the soldiers. To my consternation, the horses played out quickly and were soon out of sight. Perhaps they had ridden hard out of Fort Kearny to search for us. I managed one last look. I knew they had seen us, but our rescuers were left behind with but a taste of freedom left in our wake.

Twilight gave way to night when the path turned down into a deep gulley. Darkness swallowed rider after rider. Horses stumbled under the loose footing. The cinch on a saddle carrying several riders snapped. I turned and watched as a trio of shadows flipped and somersaulted with the horse. The whole entangled mass of splayed arms, legs, and bodies slid down the loose dirt and rocks on the side of the ravine. To my surprise, it was Laura, Isabelle, and their captor who had pitched forward over the neck of an unbalanced horse. The horse struggled to stand in the ruckus. Its hoof kicked Laura in the face. She rose to her feet as blood poured from her nose. A gash on her cheek created a stream like thick black coffee down her bodice. Near the top of the incline, Belle wailed.

Two Face did not have a moment to react before I was off his horse in a swirl of skirts and bare feet. Clutching the baby to my chest, I ran frenziedly to comfort my daughter. Embracing the child, I held her tightly, then extended her at arm's length for a full inspection. She was bruised but whole.

Grateful for the moment to hold my whimpering, trembling child, I thanked God! Kisses on her soft brow and motherly reassurances calmed her. A sheet from our family bed was dug out of the bags of loot, and a young Cheyenne wiped the blood from Laura's face. I tore a strip of fabric to treat Belle's scrapes. She clung to me like sheep's wool.

The entourage took several minutes to gather itself; the strewn items were dusted off and shifted onto other ponies. The offending horse was whipped without mercy for the mishap and eventually pulled into line with only baggage strapped to its back.

A fierce-looking Indian strode over to the rock where I sat with my arms wrapped protectively around both children. As he marched closer, I shook my head vigorously and shouted, "No!" Without breaking stride, he stripped Belle from my arms. Then he unleashed a torrent of unintelligible scolding directly into my face. Cowering, I dropped to my knees. The shrieking child was carried away, her little legs kicking frantically. She was plopped on the pony with Laura, who tried to shush the inconsolable child. Her cries went unnoticed as the brave mounted behind them and turned the horse away. My arms ached for my girl. Helpless to rescue her, I prayed….

Two Face rode up to my side. Reaching down, he pulled us up. Limp and depleted, I yielded to his tight embrace. Every few minutes, I twisted my neck and strained to see Belle. Soon she was out of sight. I willed my eyes to remain open, but darkness lay like a blanket and the prairie was quiet. We passed deep purplish-blue rocks, each one casting a sharp shadow in the moonlight. I prayed for her safety and willed that I would soon have another chance to hold her. A heavy shadow of sadness ground my spirit to dust and scattered it to the wind.

Unrelenting

10 August 1864
Western Kansas Territory

Dear Pioneer,
If we could live the old days over again. Only the difference would
be...There would be no fear or hatred burning within us.

M.A. Alexander
Letter Written to William Joseph Eubank, Jr.
June 21, 1930

The procession stopped to rest a couple of hours before daylight. I collapsed like a rag doll onto the ground. My essence rose above its prone form. I looked down at the tattered and bloody dress covering my body. Hovering above, memories merged with the presence of Will. I extended my fingers. Solace and safety were within reach. I joined him.

"Laura! Dora!" I call. "Come, look at these grapes! We can pick over here! The bees aren't nearly as pesky in the shade!" We quickly fill baskets and burlap sacks with the sweet beads of treasure.

I look over at Will, who is grinning at me. Holding Belle's hand, his bare feet scuffle through the sand. Together, they pick wild grapes from the lowest vines.

I am pleased that Will announced he would not be joining his brothers, father, and young nephew in the hay fields! Nor were we needed at the Little Blue Station. We are free to spend our Sunday together.

Willie rests in his sling on my back. His toe dangles near my waist, and I squeeze it. My sister-in-law Dora and our neighbor, Laura Roper, link arms and walk our way. Hitching up their long skirts, they giggle—amused by their rhyming names.

My gaze shifts to the open pasture nearby. The cattle are grazing peacefully among sunflowers. Tails switch back and forth to mark time as they wander at will in the tall, lush grass. Their glossy-brown hides reflect the afternoon sunlight.

Will planted two and a half acres of corn in the bottom land near the river, and it is nearly ready for harvest. He boasts this year's crop will yield thirty-five bushels an acre. The rich soil in this new land supplies sustenance for our family. We are thankful for its bounty.

Our youngest was born the prior October on our Nebraska ranche. We named him William Joseph Eubank, Jr., after his father. He is robust and very heavy. He squirms, grunts, and pats me urgently on the shoulder. I sit on a fallen oak tree. It once grew along the sandy bank of the Little Blue River. Pulling the babe from his sling, he nurses gustily. The contented and muffled sounds of vigorous sucking bring a sense of contentment. The mantle of motherhood is an easy one. Our children bestow pride and pleasure upon us.

A scrub of wild roses catches my eye. Its tendrils of shiny foliage extend and pulse toward the sun. Such a contrast to the twisted trunks of the ancient bur oak trees surrounding this spot! I reflect on the human story—not so unlike the natural one. The little, unruly rose bush appears so sprite and gloriously new. The remains of past stories are apparent in the deadfall of trees and leafless shrubs that once thrived here.

A rustle brings my attention to Will, who sits down beside me. His manly smell blends with soap from a fresh shave and the sweet grass he has gathered all summer. I lean my face into his neck and inhale deeply. I stare at his hands, which hold Belle's. They are long-fingered, strong, and elegant—and so very capable. Belle snuggles between my legs and caresses her brother with sticky fingers. The little red bow of her mouth dribbles grape juice.

"There is freedom here, Lucy!" Will declares. "The Eubank hay and cattle operations are in full swing. With you and me running the Little Blue stage stop and Joe managing Kiowa Station with Hattie, the potential is unlimited. More stages, freighters, and settlers pass by every day! Now, with my pa's family here, we will all prosper! It is a wonder to behold! Days like today make me want to reach out and seize the future."

He tilts his head up to take in the sky, then gently kisses my cheek. I look deeply into his shining face and see my image mirrored in his eyes. A contented sigh escapes his lungs as he slides off the fallen tree trunk, arms spread as wide as his smile. He collapses into the soft leaves. His legs dangle next to me, and we laugh together—his kiss lingers on my face.

I recall how I wanted him. I would forsake all others. As a married eighteen year-old girl, I possessed nothing but the knowledge that this man was mine alone. Our new life led us away from all that was familiar.

Someday, I will drop my final petal and my life will be just a memory. Yet at this moment, in this time, I am thankful for our union. This family is where it belongs, and it is our turn to bloom....

Reality crashed into my consciousness and bashed the sweet dream to bits. With a bone-cracking thud, I found myself untethered and prone in the shade of a tree—dropped like a sack of potatoes. I shook my head, and the memories dissipated. My body, no longer light as air, seemed heavily immaterial.

Was it possible for a heart to perish yet, leave its hapless host to carry on? Alone. I was alone with four children whose sufferings I could not soothe. The children! Where were they? I sat up to find Willie asleep at my feet. "Belle! Laura! Conrad!" I called out.

Nothing. Ready to dash at the first answering cry, I jumped to my feet. Unsure which direction to head, I faltered. My disreputable captors dismounted while others wandered about in the brush. I grabbed the baby and rushed haphazardly through the tangle of bushes.

As I hacked and shoved, Two Face stepped onto the overgrown path and blocked my progress. With the sun at his back, his large form and face were silhouetted, hidden in shadow. Disoriented by the heat, hunger, and exhaustion, I squinted up at him, trying to focus. Reaching toward me, he spoke, but his voice was muffled. I jerked back in alarm.

Holding a bunch of wild grapes in offering, he commanded, "Eat!"

I shook my head no. Although he had not attacked me, Two Face had not interfered with my painful mistreatment, and I was acutely aware of my vulnerability. My refusal did not seem to ruffle him.

"You hungry. Child, too." He pointed to Willie in my arms.

Still connected with my husband in my dream state, I was confused by a different man holding different grapes. My eyes sought his in a moment of weakness. His language skills betrayed my better judgment. Hungry for my people, the familiarity of his words momentarily overrode caution.

I stared at him. This was the first time I dared to look closely. The warrior smiled broadly, revealing sculptured, high cheekbones and a long straight nose. His coal-black hair was plaited in two thick braids neatly encased in furry moleskin sleeves. Bits of hammered silver coins and a single feather tilted at an angle adorned his head. His presence was too near, too alarming.

"You eat, you live."

I raised questioning eyes to his. What did he mean?

"You not be killed," he added in response to my confusion. "You traded soon, but no freedom today."

I felt my cheeks flush in anger.

"I see fire behind sky eyes," he said as he extended the fruit to me.

Still frightened and distrustful, I hesitantly accepted his offering. The sweet, juicy pulp slid down my throat like a slippery secret. I touched Willie's lips with a crushed grape, and he quickly slurped it into his mouth. I reached for another.

17

Soon we were on the move again.

Relief came mid-afternoon. We stopped at the edge of a small tributary where the water was calm. My back ached and my inner thighs were raw from straddling the horse's wide back. Laura's face was swollen and had turned red, blue, green, and purple. Her nose was clearly askew. The skin on my sunburned face, arms, and shoulders was pulled taut like old tree bark, and it tingled with painful intensity. My hunger was only superseded by concern for the famished, tired children. I fed Willie as often as possible, but the emptiness in my stomach left me shaken and nauseous. My mouth was parched as a dry well, and the blood from my split lips supplied little moisture. I licked them anyway.

Grateful to stop, I cautiously watched braves unsaddle their horses. Buffalo robes were spread on the ground. Two Face motioned for me to sit. I slid off the horse and unsteadily tried to restore some dignity to my torn and dirty skirts. It was then that Belle and I saw each other. From the robe she shared with Laura, my daughter reached her arms toward me and cried out, "Mama!"

My rush to embrace her was abruptly interrupted as I was roughly jerked to the ground.

"Two Face," I insisted. "Listen to me. The child is mine! Not Laura's! I must go to her. Now!"

I tried to pull away from his grip.

Curtly, he explained Belle and Laura were the property of another warrior. With a shrug of indifference, he walked away. I stared in disbelief as a brave forced Laura and Belle to stay on their robe. Our captors were intent on maintaining control.

With our reunion blocked, I softened my tone and used my voice to calm my sobbing child. Belle must not attract unwanted attention. Maternal instinct, tinged with apprehension, left me anxious and helpless. I tried to quiet my distraught daughter. This could mean life or death....

"Belle," I called sweetly. "Lie down, baby. You are okay. Mama is okay. Baby brother is okay."

I blinked back the tears. Disguising the fear that gripped me, I implored her in my most motherly voice, "Sleep for a while, Belle, and then we will eat." I smiled wanly at her in the hope she would find comfort in my demeanor.

Inside I was a jangle of nerves. My ears were ringing from the lack of sleep, and the heat rising from my skin seemed near to combustion. I positioned my body as I would in our bed at home, then peeked over at Belle. She had quieted. Thumb in her mouth, she succumbed to her own pain and depleted condition; but she was alive...just beyond the reach of my aching heart and yearning arms.

18

Sometime later, I woke to the smell of wood smoke and something else. I sat up to locate the campfire. A turkey on a stick was roasting over coals. The fat dripped in spatters. I counted fourteen of us and knew the bird would be picked to the bone. I hoped the children would be given a generous portion.

Needing to relieve myself, I hesitantly motioned to a nearby warrior who allowed me to slip into the willows. After cleaning myself, I caught a glimmer in the grass below. Picking up a stick, I lifted my ring and wiped it with a leaf. Glancing around, I slipped the treasure into my pocket.

As we sat eating, three young braves strode over and sat down in front of Laura, Belle, and me. We stopped mid-chew and drew back. Suddenly, our hair was yanked, and our heads tilted back. Terrified, we gazed into the dark eyes of the aggressors. They reached to touch our faces. Squeezing my eyes shut, I braced for the strike.

Fingers touched my forehead as the warrior stroked my face with something like oily red paint. It smelled like bear grease mixed with fishy red mud. The stench was overpowering.

In moments, the pain from sunburn eased, and I realized the purpose of the confrontation was medicinal. Belle stared wide-eyed at Laura and then at me. Her thumb still in her mouth, she was not sure of this new development. I stared at Laura and she at me—our faces smeared and sticky red.

It was time to mount up once again. Belle and I were cruelly separated as Willie was shoved into my arms. I complied and stumbled toward the horse.

Resigned to the hoofbeats of another dying day, I feared the enormity of the prairie, which spread out in all directions. Staring at the long shadows of diminutive figures far in the lead, I recognized how truly small we were in a land of grass and sky.

Two Face disrupted my musings by draping a deerskin, soft as a baby gosling, across my blistered arms and shoulders. The thin cotton cloth of my torn bodice offered little protection. After tossing us lithely onto the horse, he leapt behind us. Startled by the act of kindness, I wavered. Instead, I chose silence.

Head bent to adjust the hide over Willie, I heard a panicked scream. Glancing around furtively, I discovered Isabelle and Laura enmeshed in chaos.

Belle!

Carried by a sneering savage, Belle arched her back and shrieked in fear. He pulled his hunting knife from its scabbard and grabbed her by the hair. Glaring at Laura and relishing the torment, he held the blade to Belle's scalp.

"Stop!" I commanded and sprang into action. Throwing my leg over the neck of the horse, I dropped to the ground. Laura leapt forward and grabbed the hand with the knife. I stopped in my tracks as the mutually-held weapon pointed at my head. The Cheyenne Dog Soldier laughed like a crazed maniac and pushed Laura to the ground.

"Brave Whe-Ho!" he hollered.

Filling the air with war whoops, he reveled in tormenting Laura. Trying a new tact, he grabbed her arm and the rope of a wild mule. Swinging her onto the back of the protesting animal, he struggled to hold his grasp on Laura. Dirt flew from feet and hooves, swirling like an angry dust devil. Eventually, he succeeded in restraining the young woman and the unruly mule, then he changed his mind. Placing Laura and Belle on a docile pony, he nonchalantly swung up onto his own mount, amused by the entire affair. Meanwhile, Laura huffed in indignation and turned her horse into the departing line-up.

I knew both of us had suffered the same indignities. I heard Laura's screams as the filthy heathens ravished both our tired and sore bodies at every opportunity. This warrior was certainly a frequent perpetrator. I sorrowed at the thought of our shared, yet, unspoken, misery.

chapter five

Regalia

11 August 1864
Solomon River, Kansas Territory

The Dog Soldiers did not wear the common war bonnet of eagle feathers, but a peculiar round bonnet of crow feathers, without a tail; that is, without the string of feathers hanging down the warrior's back.

George Bent

Nearly fifty mounted Dog Soldiers were rapidly approaching. I scanned the group with apprehension. Their arrival was met with friendly shouts and shoves as the gathering spread out across the grass. I was disturbed when they pointed to each of the captives while conversing excitedly.

During our time with friends and travelers at the station, I heard tales about the ferocity and reputation of the Cheyenne Dog Soldiers. These warriors stood their ground even to the death, sometimes by tying themselves to a lance thrust into the earth. These accounts seemed unbelievable. Yet here they were—in the flesh. I recognized these new arrivals as the absolute danger they were. Face paint amplified their powerful aggression in manner and word. The black paint, I learned later, stood for victory without the loss of one of their own. Their battle tactics were legendary, but it was the tales of mistreatment endured by unfortunate captives, Indian or white, that frightened me most.

Members of this most terrifying and feared of all tribal societies were now our captors, and we were vulnerable in their midst. It was all I could do to not run screeching across the prairie until an arrow brought me down. I needed to restrain my impulsive instincts for the sake of the children, so I kept a cautious eye on them. Relieved that the attention was not on me or Laura, I watched as they dug through the contents of their baggage.

The warriors adorned themselves with feathered headdresses and ornamentations pulled from rawhide cases. Prior to placing an item of significance atop his head, each Indian would lift it, speak sacred words, then turn—repeating the ceremony in each of the four directions. Blood-red paint was applied to the top half of their faces and black paint added to cover the lower half. White, vertical stripes of lightning added a jagged effect to the chin—as if split open. Some added a green stripe across the bridge of the nose.

Medicine bundles containing coveted roots, stones, charms, and oddities were fastened around the necks of their horses. Their ornamented bull-hide shields were removed from buckskin covers and swept toward the earth four times. Each shield was raised and shaken toward the sun four times. Once the ritual was complete, each warrior slipped the shield onto his left forearm. Mounting up, they held a weapon of choice in the right hand.

As war whoops shattered the air, I worried if an attack on unsuspecting victims was imminent. The joint mood of the aggressors was expectant and full of discourse. I understood nothing.

Were we to be their tributes? Gifts to the tribe? Oh, my dear God! What did this new development mean? I scanned the empty stretch of horizon for clues. A sense of paralyzing dread, like the silent pull of quicksand, immobilized me. What was to come?

Two Face was deliberate and commanding in his speech to those in our group, and I asked if he was a chief. He nodded and explained that five of his Spleen band were with him. Oglala Sioux and their lodges were in the north country.

A nearby warrior spoke to him in jest while pointing his lance at me. A fresh scalp dangled from the shaft of the spear. Two Face glanced at me once with a solemn nod of his head. Finishing his attire, he carried paints to his horse and applied fresh emblems with swift strokes of his fingers.

The final leg of the journey was brief, an hour or so. The large party of warriors quieted as we rode across the open prairie, avoiding the mosquito-filled stalks of rushes and cattails along the river.

I squinted into the distance and saw nothing more than the repetition of what I had seen for five days—a vast expanse of open range with few trees and no signs of human occupation. The terrain progressively heaved into gently rolling hills. In the distance, the illusion of peaks disappeared into obscurity with only a doubt left as to their existence. I was quickly falling into a disorienting fuzz. Gasping for air like a trout out of water, I struggled to keep my balance by staring at the horizon.

Then it appeared. Ominous columns of smoke rose in the distance. The warriors charged forward, urging their horses into a run. Apparitions from a thousand campfires spiraled upward in the calm afternoon air. My mouth produced a soundless scream, and I began to flail wildly. It was time to run. No! I must get off! Wait! I will jump, then run!

Nightmarish images sank into my numbed brain as I succumbed to panic. Despair grew into maddening fear. I realized our next interaction would be of enormous proportions. Squirming to slide off the loping horse, reason took flight. Two Face grunted something threatening and squeezed his body around mine. The horse responded to the pressure, snorted, and surged off the path near the river. Its long mane lashed my face as it bolted down a bend in the river.

Our captivity was torturous and brutal, but a new and unexpected foreboding crept into my mind. The withered hope of freedom shattered. We were so far…so far…from anything or anyone. Would we be ripped into tiny pieces, our remains scattered for the buzzards? Dry heaves shocked my rib cage.

Approaching the huge encampment, hundreds of cone-shaped lodges encompassed the village, expanding along both sides of the river's winding blue thread. I was startled and horrified by its menacing size. The village vibrated with an ominous rhythm.

Large pony herds wandered along the outskirts of the camp, which teemed with life. Thousands of inhabitants were going about their daily lives. I never imagined such a large gathering of Indians. Announcing our arrival, dogs barked in the distance.

Herds of grazing ponies popped up their heads to sniff the air. Galloping, kicking, and bucking, they stampeded toward us, their high-pitched squeals reminiscent of Scottish bagpipes.

Two Face's horse flew on its invisible serpent wings and crowned the top of a rise in the terrain. We summitted at a full-out run. Recognition dawned as vision connected with my brain—my attention riveted to the scene below. Escape was impossible. Tremors banged uncontrollably within my torso, like a grizzly shaking its prey. Through watery eyes, I peered into an uncertain future.

My captor directed the horse down an embankment with a confusing urgency. The animal leapt forward at a frantic speed as the warriors burst into frightening war whoops, shrieks, and blood-chilling yells.

Willie startled and began to cry. A good sign, I thought. He had been so wide-eyed and quiet for days. Now jostled and tossed by the charging animal, his high-pitched cries rivaled those of the wild men racing near us.

The days of dread, hunger, and weariness dulled my senses, but now adrenaline surged through my body, nerve endings signaled high alert. A quivering mass of organs plunged into the pit of my stomach, and I buzzed with apprehension. Eyes straining at the sight, I searched for a way off the dipping, diving force. Now! Giving no thought as to which direction to flee, I leaned to dive off the huge war horse. Behind me, Two Face clamped invisible chains around me. Strong arms. So heavy. So impossible.

New thoughts shot through the fog of panic as I envisioned details of what was to come. Our children! I would not give up! My brain searched for a plan, for a way out, but no answers came.

Innately, the claws of life's power dug deeply into survival mode. Whatever lay ahead, I could not take flight. The remnants of the Eubank family were caught in the wake of destruction, but I would fight this formidable new foe. I would not go down without defending those I held so dear.

Oh, my God, help....

Wild imaginings ceased as darkness crept in around the periphery and pressed up out of the fiery depths to regain a stranglehold on my deliberations. I slammed the lid down on the tangled, wicked vines invading my lock box.

Whether long or short,
certain death or tenuous life,
fight or flight,
I would trade my life for the children.
My personal war had begun.

chapter six

Fire-Hair Woman

11 August 1864
Solomon River, Kansas Territory

They had saved the woman for a purpose worse than death. She was a blonde, with complexion so fair that the prairie sun had freckled her somewhat, and the hair that waved around her head was the prettiest reddish gold I have ever seen.

Oliver P. Wiggins

Guns blazing, the war party fired into the air as they charged full speed into the Indian camp. Chaos erupted, amplified by explosive howling and bellowing shouts. A great chief slammed his white stallion to a stop, and the animal reared wildly to the thrill of the crowd. Eagle feathers on the chief's war bonnet floated to the ground. Men, women, and children rushed from all sides to greet the riders with excited leaps and yips. Dust swirled, blurred my vision, and clogged my parched throat as Two Face's horse halted and reared. The crowd pressed in as the horse spun frantically, backing away from the frenzy and clamor.

Two Face loosened his hold as a group of women reached through the throng and jerked me off the horse. Willie was wrenched from his wrap and my chest felt the cool void of his abrupt absence. I spun my head in the chaos searching for him. A cry reached my throat; but if I released it, I would never have heard it amid the shrill trilling of the women and the roar of the crowd.

A blow to my shoulder dropped me to my knees. Another struck my head, and I was pushed roughly to the ground. I lay on my side as the attack from the stick-wielding women landed on every part of my body. Yanked upright, I was inspected from top to bottom. My hair seemed a fascination to the squaws. An old, hunched woman painfully pulled a hunk of hair from my head and held up the prize. Their pinches and scratches were punctuated by a few well-aimed slaps. I dodged and whirled in futile attempts to avoid my attackers.

Just as the pain intensified, the cruel blows subsided. Stunned by the raw outburst of violence, I was dragged to a smoldering campfire in the center of the main village and left standing with arms hanging uselessly at my sides. The crowd's attention shifted to the Dog Soldiers, who were busy illustrating recent feats of bravery.

I could not breathe. Ominous flashes of light and a spinning sensation plagued my vision. An ashen curtain fell around me. My feet anxiously sought purchase from the ground...the earth spun wildly.

A baby's screams seared into my consciousness. Mama bear roused. My baby! Dodging past my surprised captors, I pushed toward the cries. Finding him alone behind a lodge, I scooped him up and held him with firm maternal possessiveness. I scrutinized his frightened face. We locked eyes. Oblivious to the rough hands that pushed me back to my place, our warm bodies crushed together— squeezing out the fear and pain.

I braced my stance and proclaimed this babe *would* survive! A granite-like determination rose from the deepest recesses of my being. I would not surrender this young life. The child blinked his dark eyes twice more, clenched them shut, and nudged my breast. The familiar tug produced a fervent desire to envelop my other offspring. She must be nearby! But the village was so large! I had to find Belle. Left with no true direction to follow, I sank to the ground.

The beating of drums and chanting of voices were terrifying. Young bucks sauntered past me in a steady stream as afternoon turned to evening. I grew increasingly apprehensive. The grand scalp dance continued into the night as bloody trophies were hoisted high to the admiration of all. The foe was slain.

Unarmed and unprepared for the slaughter, our family was gone. Massacred. I turned my head from the scene. The agonizing memories of loved ones cut down rushed uninvited to the forefront. Unlocked and surfacing from the depths of dark places, grief detonated once again. Head pounding, I covered my face with my hands.

Later, as the bonfires rose higher and higher into the night sky, I sat near a lodge entrance and tried to control the rising bile in my throat. Fear was a constant companion, for I was the intruder, the interloper. My attempts to be as innocuous as possible were thwarted by the curiosity of the camp's dogs that continued to sniff and growl around us. I shooed them away with a stamp of my foot, but they continued to circle.

Sounds of the camp were altered by the joining of purpose in ceremony and custom by its inhabitants. The Indians gathered around a huge fire in the center of the village. The teepees flickered in the fire's light, causing dark red geometric shapes on their sides to move in a dance of their own.

I noticed the full eagle feather headdress of one of the older men as he pushed aside a flap and entered the largest tent followed by other moccasin clad feet. I dared not look at their faces.

Incapacitated by hunger, I listened to the thrum of the drums and the chants of the people growing in intensity. Dusty feet pounded a circle around the fire as they danced with odd gyrations, hawkish winged arms outspread.

The celebrations crept into the early morning hours. I wavered and slumped from dizzying fatigue. Unexpectedly, a warrior grabbed Willie by one leg and pulled him out of my protective hold. My feet were in motion before I was upright. I followed his screaming. The child was lifted high above the warrior's head, then swung jerkily toward the fire. I exhaled as though belly punched, then roared with a primal fury at this senseless violence! My baby twirled as the threatening devil swung him again towards the edge of the fire, his black eyes gleamed defiantly at me.

I grabbed Willie as the frenzied ghouls burst into hilarious laughter. Sneering insults and gnarly fingers pointed at our helpless condition.

A tiny, haggard, old woman appeared and shoved us into a lodge. Lines zigzagged like rough canyons across her worn face. She forced us to lie on a buffalo robe.

"Down, Fire-Hair Squaw," she muttered.

My dry throat and cotton mouth prevented words of protest. Lying prone, my eyes quickly closed, and I drifted into a fitful place. I recalled the first time Two Face attributed that name to me. Fire-Hair Squaw.

The nightmare began as it had so many nights before. The memory of my capture would leave me weak and terrified each time it replayed in my mind....

Painted warriors pull us from our hiding place among the roots of a large tree. Laura clamps her hand over Belle's mouth, but her muffled screams reveal our location.

The marauders gallop back to our home, and I quickly scan for survivors. We pass my dear sister-in-law Medora. She lies in a pool of blood streaming profusely from her head. Stripped of her clothing, a lance protrudes from the middle of her body, pinning her to the ground.

"Dora!" I cry.

The young woman lifts an arm as if to touch me, then covers her face. She pleads weakly, "Help me."

"Oh, Dora...."

Panicked by the gruesome sight, I slide off the pony into my yard. Along its perimeter, I see Laura and Belle pulled off a pony and pushed to their knees.

Willie swings to and fro in his sling as I turn and run to Dora. Mid-stride, the butcher jerks me to the ground—tomahawk poised at my forehead. Horrible yells and war cries fill the air. I tear myself free from his grip and scramble into the yard, calling for Henry, for Laura, for Belle. I hear the piercing screams of my little girl. Laura holds her several yards away. I dash to the helpless children and collide with Laura. Huddling together we smash the babes between us.

A crashing sound explodes inside the house amid deafening whoops and maniacal screams. We shudder in terror. Pots, silverware, furniture, and clothing are tossed out the door. Our tick bedding is dragged and slashed to pieces as feathers fly in directionless wafts. Covered in down, some of the raiders wear the hats and jackets of family members. Their heartless indifference adds to the surreal scene.

I whirl my head around. Flee! We must get away! But which way? I witlessly scream, "Run!" into Laura's face. She is frozen in place, as if time has stopped. Grabbing her hand, I leap forward, head bent, ready to find refuge in the trees behind our home. I catch a glimpse of young Henry crawling into the scrub brush, his head matted with blood. We lurch and stumble to follow him.

Without warning, I am pulled off balance from behind and thrown to the ground. Laura and Belle lie sprawled next to me, their faces masked with terror. I look into the fierce face of my attacker. Malice and murder stare back. The maniac holds my thrashing infant by his ankles and prepares to dash his head against the corner of the house.

A primitive growl rises from my throat. It fills the air as I transform into a raving lunatic. Gnashing my teeth, I am airborne and violently seize the devil by the arm. The failed momentum of his swing and the unexpected loss of impact cause him to lose balance. He topples over with the baby on top of him. I grab Willie and run for our lives.

The attacker is on his feet at once. Knife drawn, he enters the chase. I am tackled from behind and we fall. Willie tumbles from my arms. The warrior and I roll together across the flattened earth, thrashing, and fighting. I gash his cheeks and eyes with my fingernails. Tangled skirts render my kicks useless. The warrior is under me but with a lithe twisting of his powerful leg muscles, I am flung face down in the dirt. Straddling me, his entire weight presses down on my back. Seizing my head by the hair, a glint of steel flashes above my brow. Arms extended, I scrabble in the dirt for anything to use as a weapon. My fist closes upon a stone just as the sharp scalping knife presses in. Squeezing my eyes shut, I brace for searing pain....

Instead, the weight lifts off. A deep voice mocks my assailant. "You not so big warrior. Thrown by Fire-Hair Woman. I take her! Heap of Birds, you go!"

Hefted onto my feet, I am pulled to the center of the yard by Two Face, his black hair streaming behind him.

I turn away and look down at my closed fist, then open it slowly. I hold a smooth river rock of the deepest blue. Its unique heart shape startles me. I place it against my pounding chest.

In shock, Laura and Belle stagger to me, and we embrace. Tears stream down Belle's soft cheeks. She is traumatized and inconsolable.

Bruised and shaken, the world expands. Instinctively drawn to the peril of my loved ones, I must help! First, I head in Dora's direction. She needs me! What about Will? I must reach Will! Run to the river!

Two Face is on me in a flash. He snags my arm, spinning me to face him. Scowling, he orders, "No!" He shoves me roughly back to the house.

At that moment, Heap of Birds dashes by. With blood-curdling yells, he holds high Dora's blood-soaked locks. We must escape!

With the children in tow, Laura and I head for the brush behind the house. Henry must be hiding! He was with Dora during the first moments of the raid. Where is the boy?

Suddenly, a forlorn little figure steps out from the shadows. Six-year-old Conrad! Grandfather Eubank's black and white dog Butch stands protectively by his side. I gasp and quickly cover my mouth lest I alert the Indians to the presence of another hapless victim. Flinging myself toward the frightened boy, I land on my knees in front of him. Gripping his shoulders with my hands, I croak, "Conrad, are you hurt?" I look around frantically. "Where is Grandfather?"

His large, blue eyes stare vacantly past me. He says in a flat voice, "They killed, they killed him in the wagon and jerked him out by his hands. They took off his clothes...and shot the oxen...and took the horses...and burned the wagon."

"Who, Conrad? Who did they kill?"

"They killed them," he repeats softly. "My Grandpa and Jimmy and Henry, too, I think. He is not here." His lip trembles as he rubs his dirty tear-streaked face.

The grandson of our patriarch is alive but lost to the world. The vision of his beloved grandfather's violent death is crushing. I gently pull the boy to me. On our knees, we rock back and forth as I try to soothe the terrorized child. Pressing Connie's sweaty head against my shoulder, I see Willie soberly pat his cousin. Laura and Belle join us in the dirt. Arms wrapped tightly around each other, sobs come in waves.

Fearing discovery and retaliation for wandering too far, we stand and clasp hands. A sniffling Conrad grips my hand with man-like strength. Glancing around, no threatening figure approaches. We cautiously walk to the corner of our precious home. The ransack, like a cyclone, is thorough.

I pick up my embroidered satchel, which was thrown into the yard. Realization dawns. The renegades plan to take us away!

Shaking the stricken Laura, I shout, "Quickly, Laura! Think! What might we take?" I gesture urgently around the yard. "I think they will take us with them. Oh, my Lord, Laura! What do we need?"

With renewed desperation, Laura and I gather baby items from the ground. Clothing, bedding, broken china, and furniture lay strewn about the yard. All of it jumbled in piles and covered with dirt and feathers. After minutes of confused sorting, I realize the futility of trying to carry the children and a load of supplies. I find their sun bonnets, nappies, and two little dresses. I stuff these into the satchel. Laura fills a pillowcase with random items, including her slippers, hoping to hide them from the Indians. I notice she removes her locket and drops it down her bodice. Then she picks up her trampled sunbonnet near the waiting horses.

I stuff Willie's jacket into the last available corner of my bag. My fingers touch the tiny metal box holding the photo of my husband. The mere presence of the image of handsome, young Will stops my heart. I glance toward the river but cannot see him. I drop the blue stone into the bag.

Within moments, a dozen warriors surround us, shoving and pushing us toward the waiting horses. Standing in stunned silence, I resist the impulse to shove back. Many of our belongings are loaded onto horses.

Suddenly, Conrad is jerked from my side, and Willie is pulled from my arms. Grabbed by the waist, I am tossed onto an immense horse adorned with feathers and paint. Ears pinned back, the animal stares menacingly through its red-circled eye. Willie is held up to me, and I pull him into the safety of my arms. I point to Belle and demand she be lifted up as well. Ignoring my pleas, I watch another warrior lift Laura and Belle behind an old Indian.

My captor effortlessly swings up behind me, rolls his horse back onto its hind legs, then spins around in one smooth motion. Destruction is everywhere. Smoke billows and rises from the interior of the house.

I spot Conrad—splayed on his stomach across a pony's back, tied like a slain deer. His arms and legs are looped with thongs, his upper torso stretched. His arms are tied around the neck of the horse and his legs secured beneath its belly. He is still and quiet—eyes closed tightly against the scene.

Two Face approaches on his horse. He pulls my leather sling from his belt and tosses it to me. It was lost in the tussle. I adjust Willie into his pouch.

Two Face turns his prancing war horse away from the devastation. In passing, he looks directly at me. I hear him say,

"Fire-Hair Woman."

chapter seven

Cola Smoke

3 August 1864
Four Days Prior to the Raid on the Eubank Ranch
Near Gilman Ranch, Overland Trail, Nebraska Territory

> *I really am not capable of advising you whether, in the providence
> of the Great Spirit, who is the Great Father of us all, it is for you to
> maintain the habits and customs of your race, or to adopt a new
> mode of life. I can only say that I can see no way in which your race
> is to become as prosperous as the white race except by living as they
> do, by cultivation of the earth.*

Abraham Lincoln

Two Face tucked the strand of hair behind his ear and absent-mindedly fed a twig into the small cooking fire. Rabbit bones smoldered in the flames. His Sioux name was Ite Nunjpa. He was leader of the Tapisleca, or Spleen band, of the Oglala. His name and clan lineage identified him as one of "The People" of the great Teton Sioux. The oral stories of his ancestors always started with the introduction of this lineage, so the young ones would know their connection to those living on the sacred ground of the Black Hills.

Earlier that day, Two Face and the dozen braves in his band rode east along the trail the white men called Overland. His people called it the Holy Road. The Cheyenne called it the Medicine Road. Its broad width scoured the Indians' once prized hunting grounds. The wheels and feet of so many created a divisive and festering scar across the plains. Continually filled with wagons, livestock, and all manner of the human condition, it was a source of conflict.

Two Face's band met these westward invading caravans of stage-coaches, freighters, military columns, and wagon trains filled with pioneers fresh from the east. The increasing presence of Indians along the road was designed to appear safe and "routine." Simple nods of acknowledgement or indifference disguised their intentions.

Military mastermind, George Bent, instructed the raiders not to alarm the feckless travelers along the trail, who viewed their passing with interest and caution. When questioned, the warriors were to say they were "headed to St. Joe." George's brother, Charley Bent, would lead the attack on the Gilman's Ranch.

Earlier that evening, Two Face and his band moved off the rutted trail and dropped out of sight into a crack in the landscape. They quietly guided their ponies down through the tall, dry grasses that shimmered in the August heat. A small, spring-fed stream lingered and straggled in the bottoms of the sandy gulch like a small, errant child of the great Platte River from which it drained. Two Face frequently camped in this ravine a couple of miles southwest of the Gilman Ranch. Red cedar trees grew tall in these canyons and provided cover for men and animals alike.

The talk that night was solemn as his companions discussed the raid which would begin in four days. In preparation for a coordinated assault, hundreds of different tribal warriors sifted into camps near road ranches, settlers' cabins, and stage stations. The word Minnehaska was spoken in their conversation. The word applied to the white race and meant "long knife." All agreed the whites were unprepared; the element of surprise was to the warriors' advantage. Two Face pondered all the broken promises and betrayal, which lay like jagged sores across the vastness of his homeland.

The night turned black as his warriors slept scattered on the ground. Their muffled snoring, combined with the singing of crickets and cicadas, was enfolded in the late summer heat. Two Face was a tall and strongly-built man with prominent features. He shifted his cross-legged sitting position slightly to adjust the breech cloth hanging draped across his lap. He could not sleep. His mind was troubled, just as it was the prior spring when the Brulé, Oglala, and Cheyenne united in plans to push the flow of emigrants back off their ancestral hunting grounds.

Months earlier, Two Face and Blackfoot, as concerned leaders of their bands, traveled to Fort Laramie to speak with the garrison's commander. Two Face's English language skills developed over the past few years of trading with the whites. He stood in front of Lieutenant Fleming's desk to explain that his people were "good" Indians come from the north. They did not attack the whites.

"I want words on paper," requested Two Face. "We hunt. Soldiers find our camp, we show "Good Paper." They know we good Indians. We go east on Platte River. Much trouble there. We follow buffalo. I protect my people from soldiers. They know we not fight." Two Face finished with an emphatic shake of his head.

Lieutenant Fleming listened, then leaned back quietly in his chair. With hands clasped in front of his waist, he locked eyes with the chief. He seemed to measure his response to the unusual request. Two Face waited.

"Yes…. Yes, I can do that for you, Two Face."

Two Face remembered a glimmer of admiration in the soldier's face as he quickly wrote the directive on a piece of crisp, white paper pulled from his desk. The dance of the feathered quill across the page held the chief's focus as he thought soberly about the strength, numbers, and outright military advantages of the whites. It would be an unmatched conflict, with Indians suffering great losses. He must do what he could to preserve his small band of five lodges in the fighting time to come.

Blackfoot, sensing the advantage, quickly asked for supplies: food, tobacco, and ammunition for hunting. The young Lieutenant looked over at the other chief as if just noticing his presence. He suggested they see the quartermaster. They departed from the fort with a false confidence. That confidence would be tested in ways they could not have predicted.

Two Face looked into his heart at that meeting. He intended to stay out of the fray, for he desired peace. He was happy and satisfied with the business arrangements made with the residents of the stage stations, trading posts, and road ranches along the Platte River. He did not expect his heart to change, but so much had happened. He was drawn into the impending war despite his conflicting personal attachments.

While conducting business with the Brulé Sioux earlier that spring, a Cheyenne chief displayed a sergeant's cavalry jacket, a watch, and other items taken during a recent skirmish. The chief admonished the Sioux for not addressing the plight of the Cheyenne as the white men from the east traveled through their conjoined hunting grounds and drove the game away. He warned the Sioux lands to the north would soon endure the same fate.

The Brulé were stirred by the warning and held council. Raids against the whites had taken place in the vast region between the North Platte and Arkansas Rivers, resulting in stolen livestock, torched homes, killings, and captives. To launch random attacks under individual leaders was not effective. The unified might of all the tribes would be required in a concerted effort to drive the whites out.

The next strike would lay waste to the elements of molten change flowing across the plains. The foreign interlopers would be left with no stations, no feed for their livestock, no supplies, no telegraph lines, and most importantly, no security.

A plan was forged, and the warring factions left the council teepee with a common aim—destroy the invaders, their animals, their forts, corrals, and buildings. Their intrusions would not be tolerated any longer. The massive, debris-strewn road would fade back into the pristine hunting grounds of memory. Smoke signals and fire arrows lit the sky for two nights after the council ended. War was imminent.

Two Face left the Brulé with a heavy heart. He saw firsthand the increasing numbers of whites and their resources. He knew defense of the homeland was imperative, yet, he sensed it was futile. His people would fight and win a few battles, but the open grasslands, flowing rivers, and mounded sand hills were changed forever. The steady stream from the east would continue long after the Indian peoples were subdued.

However, he was now a warrior—no longer a trader. He stretched out and leaned back onto the blanket beneath him. The stars blinked in the inky depths of the night sky. Two Face reflected on the source of his mind's discomfort. He closed his eyes, thinking of John Gilman. He remembered the day when John saved his life.

———•———

The injured Indian stumbled through the door into the gloomy light of the Gilman's sod-built store. Thirst forced his throat closed and the pounding in his head clouded his sight.

A stocky, black-haired man in a white shirt approached the counter with indifference. The man's bushy eyebrows drew together as he noticed the Indian in the dirty torn breechcloth. His dark skin gleamed with sweat. The relaxed smile in the man's black beard disappeared. He leaned closer to inspect the stranger.

Two Face motioned desperately for water. The man turned to the barrel sitting on a bench. Two Face, squinting through double vision, watched the raised ladle drip. It was attached to a muscular arm. He heard a thump, as his body collapsed onto the dirt floor. The white trader, known to him as a Minnehaska, hustled and knelt next to his burning body.

The man's cool hand lifted his head. Two Face noticed the concern on his face as feverish heat emanated from his forehead. Two Face's straggly hair fell back from his shoulder. Gilman was confronted by the staggering sight of a swollen and infected collarbone wound.

Two Face's last memory was the sound of John Gilman swearing under his breath.

Dreams for the next two days were filled with images of the Pawnee hunters who jumped him, the fight, and the flash of a club. The red-

35

bearded men with white faces appeared as phantoms as they gently ministered to him. His misery seeped up out of his bones through his burning flesh.

When Two Face finally awakened, he was aware of morning light in the dimness of the white man's lodge. He slowly raised his head and placed his fingers gently on the oozing bandages tied around his shoulder. The remnants of a smelly, sticky poultice ran in rivulets down his ribs. He held the substance to his nose and sniffed. The repulsive tobacco and herb odor reminded him of his mother's wound treatments. Two Face's head dropped back, and he lost consciousness again.

Later, a man with dark whiskers raised a spoon to his mouth, and he heard the soft voice entreating him to drink the bone broth. He tried to listen to the voices in the background but understood few words of the white man's language.

Within days, the thin offerings were replaced by more substantial, yet, strange food. Two Face was relieved to notice a positive turn in his condition. He began to eagerly await the sustaining food which was so freely given.

Regaining strength, he spent time sitting outside on a fallen log near the corral. He watched multitudes of travelers in constant motion along the trail below the station. He was most curious about the mysterious riders who would arrive on a lathered horse amid shouts of greeting. A leather mochila filled with white man's papers was quickly thrown over the saddle horn of a fresh horse. The rider rode off in a flurry.

Later, Jeremiah Gilman explained with words and signs that their road ranche was a Pony Express "swing station." The recovering patient looked forward to these exciting exchanges. He soon helped in the care and saddling of the swift horses that bolted to the east or the west.

Two Face increased his workload at the station and quickly learned the white man's language. John and the station employees were intent on teaching English to the red skin. John was just as committed to learn the Sioux language. The first word caught by the whites was "cola," which meant friend.

Two Face remembered another member of the Gilman Ranche operation. The cook. How confusing to see an elder male attending to squaw's work. But he smiled as he recalled the cook's coffee and flap jacks. There was always plenty of both.

In time, he was whole again. One night, Two Face simply walked away. He carried nothing with him but a strong sense of grateful appreciation for these men who chose to shelter and restore a stranger.

Later that summer, Two Face returned to the Gilman Ranche bearing gifts. He carried with him the finest buffalo robes lined with red flannel. He obtained these from the industrious Sioux women of his northern homeland. This quality merchandise was beyond compare to the local offerings of the bands living near the trading post. The raucous and joyous greetings which accompanied his arrival were mutual.

The Gilman brothers learned from prior interactions with the Sioux that gift-giving was an esteemed ceremony. They gathered their men together and accepted the gifts with proper solemnity and respect. This was followed by enthusiastic handshakes and expressions of "Cola! Friend!"

A mutual business arrangement began at that visit. The Gilmans loaded Two Face's travois with copious quantities of coffee, tobacco, sugar, cloth, metal items, and trinkets. He was entrusted with the storehouse items and rode away days later with an expectant spirit. He envisioned the potential for years of trade profits for himself, his Sioux and Cheyenne kinsman, and his new enterprising Minnehaska partners.

Within months of successful trading, he made the acquaintance of John Smith, who spent his own time healing from an illness at the Gilman's place. He and Two Face practiced the English, Cheyenne, and Sioux languages together, becoming fluent.

John was encouraged to join Two Face on his trading travels. The Indian liked him. Others said this white man was educated at a particularly important school called "Yale." It was back East where many whites lived in large villages.

By fall, Smith integrated into the Cheyenne way of life. He married the daughter of the Red Willow band chief. A new name was bestowed upon him. Gray Blanket. His pack horses were seen less frequently on the trail. Gradually, John Smith was absorbed into the culture of the plains.

These memories of happier times haunted Two Face as he listened to the night sounds, always alert for animal or human threat. His thoughts lingered on the faces of his family. He mused about his name. It reminded him of his dual ties to the Cheyenne, his father's people, and the Sioux, his mother's tribe. Yes, he was a member of two respected clans. But now he recalled the years of trading and friendship with the whites. His two-sided name applied to both societies. His Indian world entered a conflict-filled destiny with the white world. And Two Face had made his choice.

He sipped the warm, bitter-tasting water from the buffalo bladder replenished from the nearby stream. The taint of it hung in the back of his throat. Through the darkness, he swallowed hard and looked with unseeing eyes toward the Gilman ranche. He remembered the cold, clear water gulped from a tin cup tied to the pump. He thought pensively of his working relationship with the Gilmans and recalled the shared benefits of their strong and successful business.

John Gilman was known by the Indians as We-Chox-Cha, the Old Man with a Pump. Two Face marveled at the red iron pipe and handle that protruded from the ground. Early in their acquaintance, John showed him the hole dug into the ground and lined with cedar posts from the canyons to the south. Water from an underground lake filtered up through the sandy soil.

Last spring, Two Face returned to the post from north of the Platte. The reunion took on a serious tone as he delivered alarming news. The Cheyenne smoked the war pipe with the Sioux and Arapaho.

Now he wondered if the Gilman brothers heeded his words of warning. Soon the coordinated attack would begin. Two Face knew each station along the road would be destroyed. Joint forces of Sioux, Arapaho, Cheyenne, and Kiowa were positioned along the Overland Trail. The young men listened carefully to Two Face and agreed to the plan's details with one deviation.

To honor the Gilman family who saved his life, Two Face planned to leave six braves, including Charley Bent, at this camp. Their sole purpose was to follow John and Jeremiah Gilman's families once the attack began. He instructed them to intervene and preserve them when the killing began. He wondered if Charley would follow through. Of all the Bent brothers, he was the most volatile.

The Gilman station would be destroyed, but the lives of the friends who had fed him, healed him, and partnered with him would be spared. There was no guarantee his small, hidden group of protectors could oversee his white friends' escape. The Gilmans would suffer, but it was the best he could do.

Two Face sighed, rolled over, and rested his head on his bent arm. A solution of friendship and compromise was like the smoke of the war pipe. It could be offered and snuffed out in the same generation. The Minnehaska were here to stay. He could not imagine where his chosen path led, but he was sure that "Cola" would no longer be spoken the next time he encountered the whites. His friendship and fellowship with the Gilman brothers would be rendered as deceitful quicksand in the changing channels of unfolding events. He closed his eyes as "cola smoke" evaporated into the night sky.

Two Face was relieved his lot was not tied to the Gilman's part of the trail. His thoughts turned to the woman. She was beautiful, strong, and good. Her family lived three days east. She was the woman of the Little Blue Station manager, Will Eubank. He would position himself there, near the station, near the Eubank ranches. He would intervene. The woman's family would be caught in the raid to come. He knew the plans were unchangeable; and great injury was inevitable, but this was personal.

Two Face drifted off to sleep. He could not know the extent to which the coming tempest would engulf him and the woman…the one called Lucinda Eubank.

chapter eight

When Lean Bear Fell

4 August 1864
Overland Trail, Nebraska Territory

*The Cheyenne were so stirred up...over the killing of Lean Bear
that the chiefs could not control the young warriors.*

George Bent

L ean Bear! Two Face woke the next morning from a dream. It plagued his thoughts. Mounting his horse, he silently turned toward the Little Blue Valley; his companions followed. Six braves were left behind to join a Southern Cheyenne and Arapaho war party. Hopefully, the Gilman families would safely escape.

--------◆--------

Avoiding the main road, Two Face followed game and buffalo trails through quiet canyons and grassy plains south of the Platte. The others rode at a respectful distance. Two Face continued to think. He recalled the events that occurred in the Month of the Mouse's Ears.

Two Face and his band camped with Black Kettle on Ash Creek. Reports of recent attacks by the military concerned both chiefs. The village of two hundred-fifty lodges needed to move to the larger Cheyenne camp on the Smoky Hill River. After days of travel, the tribe stopped to rest and hunt at one of their favorite sites, Big Timbers.

The sun shone brightly on their teepees that day, but a fury was stirring to the west. Two Face spotted the anvil-shaped clouds of a thunderstorm about midday. He watched a distant squall as its dark-blue broom of rain swept across the plains. Bolts of lightning split the distant sky, but all was quiet in the village. He would keep an eye on its direction.

Then Two Face spotted clouds of dust stirring up from the ground. He concentrated on this phenomenon, which seemed unrelated to the storm. It was headed straight toward the camp. He stood up and pointed it out to Black Kettle, who immediately sent a mounted warrior to investigate.

Within minutes the brave, accompanied by the tribe's hunters, raced back into camp. Soldiers with cannons were marching toward them. The village criers sounded the alarm. People scrambled to find their children, their weapons, their horses. The hunters' report of advancing soldiers, wagons, and howitzers signaled danger.

Young bands of warriors continued to raid the stage roads and area settlements; horses and mules had been stolen. The battles escalated with loss of life on both sides. Now the consequences of their unrestrained raids extended its tentacles into the peaceful village.

Rumors from Denver circulated among the tribes that Lieutenant George Eayre intended to "kill Cheyennes whenever and wherever found." The people fled in terror from burning villages to the north—abandoning their belongings. Those who escaped to the safety of Black Kettle's village were now once again under threat.

Chiefs Black Kettle and Lean Bear quickly went into action. The year before, both visited the Great Father in Washington, D.C. They knew what to do. Emerging from their lodges, the chiefs carried white parlay flags and wore presidential medals prominently displayed on their chests. The village should not be mistaken for a war party. The medals would grant immunity to the chiefs, who wished to clear up the misunderstanding before violence broke out.

Lean Bear and his right-hand man Star prepared to meet the soldiers. They hoped to stall the soldiers while women, children, and elders scattered in nearby hills. The remaining braves of Black Kettle's village acted quickly to join Lean Bear and Star. A show of strength and the white flag of peace would surely dissuade the troops from their intended target.

Two Face's thoughts were interrupted by the morning insects buzzing around his face. He checked his surroundings in the dawn's dim light. A half-risen sun lit up bits of steel on his rifle. Its bright reflections revealed his position. He slid the weapon deep into its leather scabbard. These tools of the white man, once called fire sticks or long knives, instilled confidence in a hunter and fighter. But he knew they would not be enough against the full force of the United States Army—and their big guns. The back of his neck tingled as he remembered what happened next.

A sharp trumpet report echoed across the prairie. The double column of trotting soldiers divided ominously at the top of a rise like one magical snake becoming two. As the soldiers split ranks, they spread out across the hills to the right and the left. With one concerted movement, they stopped and turned to face the approaching Indians. Their horses stood shoulder to shoulder; a strong wind blew behind them. The building storm clouds rose and churned as they rolled over the conflict on the ground. Red, white, and blue flags whipped and snapped toward the Indian village as if straining to possess the land and people below. The feared cannons were quickly positioned on two rocky knolls above the camp.

Chief Lean Bear and Star courageously trotted forward while communicating the message of parlay. To prove their good-faith intentions, Lean Bear held high his medal, it caught the sun and flashed directly at the troops. Carefully guarded reference papers, obtained in Washington, D.C., were retrieved from his medicine bag. He waved these in the direction of the waiting troops as well. Lean Bear instructed Star to remain behind as he proceeded forward alone. Pulling his horse to a stop forty feet from the battle line, he waited for an invitation to talk.

Lieutenant Eayre faced the Indians and raised his sword in the air— Lean Bear responded with a hand raise. Suddenly, the officer barked a sharp order, "Take no prisoners! Charge!" He whipped his arm down and the troops opened fire.

Shots rang out and Lean Bear fell—his peace medal struck the ground. Struggling to rise, another bullet knocked him face down onto the prairie sod. The valued papers fluttered away in the wind.

Star charged forward to help the wounded chief and was instantly shot off his horse. The incensed Indians returned fire, arcing their arrows into the line of soldiers. Several were hit and fell from their mounts.

Within moments, two howitzers began to pound the village. From a distance, bits and pieces of teepees, pots, people, and dirt were flung in all directions—as if jumping to the clouds. Booming sounds of the cannon explosions followed claps of thunder, splitting the air directly overhead. The front line of troops rode down upon the dying Cheyenne leaders and pumped more bullets into their bodies.

Lean Bear, who had personally agreed to peace with President Lincoln and was one of the original six to sign the treaty of Fort Wise, breathed his last. Lightning flashed and struck the ground near the body. The soldiers fled the scene, unwilling to take on nature's wrath.

Upon seeing the unjust killing of their leaders, the full force of mounted warriors screamed in defiance and attacked. Rain and hail unleashed its full fury from the skies. The braves ran past the artillery in their furious lust to engage the cavalry. Another contingent of warriors headed toward the unguarded wagons in the rear. The army was too spread out to defend its position. They repositioned the howitzers and attempted to fire upon the fleet Indian ponies as they dashed through the smoke and rain, but it had little effect.

The full force of six hundred Arapaho and Cheyenne warriors was closing in. The Indians, sensing their advantage, raged toward the goal of total annihilation. Chaos increased as the fight spread across miles of open prairie.

Two Face remembered the look in Black Kettle's eyes. His hair had come loose from their binds and whipped across his wet face as the storm pounded the battlefield. He used his booming voice to outshout the rushing wind. Today they would not fight! The thunder and rain would intervene for the Indians and give them a chance to gather their dead!

"Get your families to safety!" he boomed.

The old chief worked his mount from skirmish to skirmish as he repeatedly commanded his braves to pull back. Unbelievably, his intervention worked. The warriors turned away as the vastly out-numbered soldiers stampeded a hasty retreat in the direction of Fort Larned. Dozens of warriors followed in hot pursuit.

The blood of Lean Bear soaked into the damp earth, the storm moved on and the sun reappeared. His body was recovered, and the grieving began. Women, children, and the elderly returned to what was left of their camp. The incensed Cheyenne warriors captured fifteen fully tacked American horses complete with saddle bags—but they were not done for the day.

Two Face remembered their drumbeats and war dance; it continued through the night. The next morning, a war party angrily raced off. The stations along the road between Fort Larned and Fort Riley would be burned and plundered; many whites would die. There was no stopping them, for the momentum had changed.

The need to avenge the deaths of the ones lost that day drove a stake into the heart of peace. The needless death of Lean Bear sparked the Indian revolt led by his brother, the fierce Dog Soldier, Bull Bear. The words of Black Kettle temporarily held back the wave but could not stop the tide of fear, hatred, and injury.

Two Face opened his eyes and surveyed the braves around him as they rode peacefully along the familiar path. He sighed. In three short months multiple plains tribes had joined forces. The long-awaited retaliation was about to come full circle. The steady heartbeat of the earth beneath him was reassuring, yet, his mood was dark. He could not free himself of the image of Lean Bear shattered and blown to bits on the open prairie.

The Cheyenne War began in earnest at that moment—the moment when Lean Bear fell.

chapter nine

Four Chiefs and a Rebel

6 August 1864
Little Blue Valley, Nebraska Territory

The Indian saw in the westward march of civilization his rights diminishing; the settlements along the streams meant the loss of water. He saw his hunting ground broken up and game going west before the white man's advance. He is a reader of signs, and in these signs he read "the beginning of the end."

Julia S. Lambert

T wo days later, the assemblage of warriors was in place along the Little Blue River. Reconnaissance complete, the ranches of the Ropers, Eubanks, Uligs, and Comstocks were unaware of the impending storm. The Overland Trail was filled with unsuspecting travelers: stagecoaches filled with people and mail, freighters, settlers, and gold seekers. The movements of the unsuspecting throngs were seen and noted by the infiltrators.

Two Face sat astride his large paint horse of black, brown, and white, blending seamlessly into the shadows of the oak trees that rimmed Nine Mile Ridge. Summer's cool fragrance crept up out of the Little Blue Valley and spread across the overheated meadows. Insects buzzed as birds flitted from tree to shrub, chirping instructions at one another as they sought shelter for the coming night.

Soundlessly, others appeared through the trees. Each warrior pulled his horse up next to Two Face. Sitting quietly, they surveyed the scene below. In the shadow of the ridge sat a corral filled with horses, a milk cow, and a couple of calves. Smoke rose from the chimney of the log home and the enticing aroma of baking cornbread wafted up to the watchers. The small corn field situated in the lowlands to the east rustled softly in the breeze; the golden leaves revealed ripening ears.

A woman stepped out of the cabin below and hustled into her garden, filling her apron with its bounty. A little girl, bonnet dangling, ran after her mother. Chattering indistinctly, she stopped intermittently to

45

investigate each bug and flower along the way. Several boys tussled and shouted as they ran barefooted between the shallow channel of the river and the corral. An old man with long white whiskers fed the stock. The nickers and whinnies of the horses blended with the lowing of the cattle. It was dinner time. In the doorway stood a man holding a baby. He gazed after the woman in the garden, then spoke to her with a hearty laugh.

The Arapaho, Chief Left Hand, sat motionless next to Two Face and grunted in the direction of the woman with the fiery blonde hair. Two Face nodded, then said quietly, "Yes, the woman. And her two children, the girl, and the papoose."

Black Kettle nudged his great white horse nearer to Two Face. "No papooses. No young children. Slow travel. Same with child you show me at Roper house. No. They die with men."

Left Hand waited respectfully until Black Kettle finished his words, then replied. "Two Face knows these people. It good he decide captives we take," he said diplomatically. "He wants fire-hair woman and her two papooses."

Sitting next to Black Kettle, George Bent stretched his legs and patted his horse. The son of the trader William Bent and Owl Woman would be the tie breaker. His relationship with the old chief extended beyond familial ties. Bent's mother was the daughter of the Cheyenne Sacred Arrow Keeper. He was married to Black Kettle's daughter Magpie. More importantly, the old chief bestowed upon him the mantle of leadership.

Black Kettle was pleased when Bent returned from the white man's school and army to train in the Cheyenne way. The chief recently initiated him into the Crooked Lance Society. Bent's training in the ways of war among the whites was beneficial to the overall strategy of amassing Indian strength to coordinate a surprise attack.

Black Kettle was always a bit edgy on the eve of battle. The Dog Soldiers would strike. However, he knew firsthand the great strength of the white foe; it should not be underestimated. He trusted George Bent and Two Face, for their knowledge of these things was extensive. He tipped his head toward Bent and said, "I will listen. You know whites. Your plans are good. You speak truth. Captives bring ransom. We trade prisoners for supplies. Help our people through winter." He paused, then continued regretfully. "We hide truth. We capture their women and children. We tell soldier chiefs we buy captives with our own ponies. They ready to trade when time comes."

George nodded and swept his hand across the Eubank Ranche.

"Two Face knows this road and the settlers who live here. Let him decide."

Blackfoot, a Sioux chief with Two Face's band, grunted in agreement with the former rebel. He liked the woman, too. He said, "We take her. We take young Roper squaw. Children, too. Older boys fight. Take small ones. White hearts will burn."

Behind the four chiefs, young warriors watched. Gall, Heap of Birds, Big Thunder, Doc Billy, and Roaring Wind waited. The great council of tribes on the Solomon River combined thousands of warriors just like them into unstoppable fighting units. The huge gathering was spoken of as a great forest filled with the strong and mighty. They were pleased with the leaders and anxious for the raids to begin. It was difficult to hold back an attack on the settlers below them this very night.

Black Kettle, sensing their excitement, turned to the Dog Men and said, "You understand who to kill and who to take?" They nodded. "Return to big camp with Two Face. Two Face will honor us with his tribute to our tribe. We stay and fight along road. Go! Tell others."

Leaving the chiefs with their thoughts, the Dog Men smoothly turned their horses and disappeared down the bluff. Within hours, the war would begin. Each chief knew the spear would pierce the white man's trail for many miles, but the results might bring new threats to their way of life. What choice did they have? A warrior defending his people is not deterred by the size and strength of the enemy. The merging of the tribes with a common purpose was their last hope, but how long until the white man's long knives and wagon guns retaliated?

Each watcher sat in solemn contemplation. Their hunting grounds were diminishing as the natural trails of game migration were disrupted. Sweet water streams were poisoned. Their homeland was hemmed in by settlers and livestock. The westward advance of those who brought with them sticks and viewing glasses to measure the earth must stop. As wisdom and caution rose within their breasts, each chief mulled over a common but unspoken concern. They were certain their united forces would win tomorrow's battles. But at what future cost?

The four chiefs and the rebel, George Bent, would not remember the bucolic scene before them. None gave a thought to the Eubank family's idyllic presence—the last to occupy this burgeoning ranche along the banks of the Little Blue.

The following day, it would be gone. Forever.

chapter ten

Proclamations

11 August 1864
Governor's Office, Denver City, Colorado Territory

Kill and destroy, as enemies of the country, wherever they may be found, all such hostile Indians…

Governor John Evans

The trader, Elbridge Gerry, sat uncomfortably across from the massive, wooden desk belonging to the governor of Colorado. Gerry was a simple man of simple tastes. His eyes wandered to the crystal decanters placed perfectly on the credenza. The sun beam striking their amber liquid threw tiny golden lights onto the wall. He looked down at his dusty boots jutting out at the end of stocky legs. His barrel chest was restricted in the confining jacket he wore specifically for this meeting. He recalled the garment provided a better fit years before when he carried it west.

Straightening his posture and buttoning his jacket, Gerry prepared once again to field the governor's inquiries into the "Indian Problem." The trader had hidden sympathies and regretted his decision to come. He decided it would be their final meeting.

Gerry held a copy of the handbill which contained the governor's proclamation sent out in June to the Indian tribes. He was one of those instructed to distribute the message. The trader scanned it again.

Proclamation
June 27, 1864

To the friendly Indians of the plains:

Agents, interpreters, and traders will inform the friendly Indians of the plains, that some members of their tribes have gone to war with the white people. They steal stock and run it off, hoping to escape detection and punishment. In some instances they have attacked and killed soldiers, and murdered peaceable citizens. For this the Great Father is angry, and will certainly hunt them out, and punish them. But he does not want to injure those who remain friendly to the whites. He desires to protect and take care of them. For this purpose, I direct that all friendly Indians keep away from those who are at war, and go to places of safety.

Friendly Arapahoes and Cheyennes belonging on the Arkansas river will go to Major Colley, United States Indian agent at Fort Lyon, who will give them provisions and show them a place of safety.

Friendly Kiowas and Camanches will go to Fort Larned, where they will be cared for in the same way.

Friendly Sioux will go to their agent at Fort Laramie for directions.

Friendly Arapahoes and Cheyennes of the Upper Platte will go to Camp Collins, on the Cache la Poudre, where they will be assigned a place of safety, and provisions will be given them.

The object of this is to prevent friendly Indians from being killed through mistake. None but those who intend to be friendly with the whites must come to these places. The families of those who have gone to war with the whites must be kept away from among the friendly Indians.

The war on hostile Indians will be continued until they are all effectually subdued.

John Evans
Governor of Colorado Territory, and Superintendent Indian
Affairs

"Governor, I want to let you know that two bands of Indians moved to the safety of Fort Collins per these instructions," Elbridge began as he held up the proclamation.

"Who are they, Gerry?" asked a surprised Evans.

Attempts to communicate with the tribes had proven unsuccessful. The natives lacked attention and obedience to the Governor's requests. Frustrated by their nomadic tendencies and independent leadership clans, Evans could not understand why there was no supreme tribal leader. The hierarchy was loosely controlled within the roving bands. The position which he held as governor of the territory held little authority in their minds.

"The followers of the Arapaho Chief Friday left the Poudre River area and came in. Spotted Tail and his Cheyenne plan to spend the winter in the vicinity as well," answered Gerry.

The governor grunted as he received the news. His overall dissatisfaction with the persistent Indian troubles along the Arkansas and

Platte Rivers was creating a blight on his executive record.

The trader was brought in to discuss the failure of the prior September's council. The Cheyenne, Arapaho, and Sioux never arrived on the Arickaree Fork of the Republican River, just as Gerry knew would happen. Their refusal to meet the recently appointed governor stung. Now Evans' hopes of unifying and confining the various tribes to the Arkansas River Reserve were vanishing.

The overall peaceful year of 1863 was followed by the eruption of an all-out Indian war. Evans decided to adjust his strategy before he lost the governorship. The new developments along the Overland Trail in Nebraska magnified the warlike abilities of the natives. The recent coordinated attacks between Julesburg and Nebraska City confirmed that a war with the Indians, particularly the Cheyenne, had begun. The safety of the Denver citizenry was at risk.

"Mr. Gerry!" exclaimed the exasperated governor. "Your wife is a Cheyenne, and you are trusted by the Indians. Why were you not able to persuade them to meet with me? Their refusal did not play well in the Rocky Mountain News. I was confident of achieving success through negotiation! Now it is chaos! What do they want?"

"As you know, Governor Evans, my relationship with the Indians is based on family and trade, not my political skill."

The governor bristled at this jab but held his tongue. The overheated office was unbearable. Gerry unbuttoned his jacket before continuing to school the governor on diplomacy.

"Last winter, Robert North warned you of his observations regarding the Indians. There was stiff trading for arms and ammunition to build up sufficient fire power to start this war. As you know, they attacked freighters for plunder all summer. Now they are focused on closing the only means of supply for all the settlements. They plan to drive out the white man once and for all."

"Yes, yes," replied the governor. "I cannot fathom how they plan to succeed, considering the size and scope of western expansion." He chewed his lip. "Now, I know that the Indians are still smarting from the death of Little Heart last year. That was an unfortunate event." Evans shook his head in disgust. "The Indian was drunk! Riding over a fort sentry could easily be mistaken as a hostile act. What was he doing there anyway?" Evans was determined to place the blame where it belonged.

Gerry cleared his throat and decided to hit at the heart of the matter. "The Indians refused to meet with you because they were hunting, making lodges, and trying to strengthen their ponies for the coming winter. The Fort Wise Treaty was never agreed to by all the chiefs. In fact, most who signed were members of the smaller bands. The shrinking boundaries of their homeland are certainly unacceptable. Attempts to keep the young braves peaceful is undermined by your actions. Sending soldiers to attack villages is stirring up war parties."

Evans opened his mouth to defend his position, then closed it as he pondered the potential causes of the current mess. Gerry took advantage of the pause to press on.

"Governor, surely you knew the unprovoked attacks on Cheyenne camps by Lieutenant Eayre's troops would add fire to an already volatile situation. Lean Bear was a man of peace and his unjust murder by the soldiers was certainly the turning point. I hope you understand negotiations are no longer an option."

The governor scowled and leaned back in his chair. The trader's summary of recent attempts to corral the tribes and force them onto the reservations was hard to digest. He stroked his wrinkled brow with the fine uncalloused fingers of a politician.

"Hmph! A lot of good the treaty accomplished," snorted the governor. "The Indians' lands along the South Platte will never be legally settled by whites until the tribes are contained."

Gerry pressed on. "The Cheyenne and Arapaho refused the war pipe offered by the Sioux last summer. As I was saying, they seek revenge for recent attacks. The actions of your military leaders have amounted to a flagrant persecution of the tribes, Governor," the tough trader concluded.

"Persecution!" sputtered Evans angrily. "Just days ago, every road ranch, stage stop, wagon train, and settler's home was attacked along a four-hundred-mile corridor! The merchandise destroyed is incalculable. Denver will starve! Now, that is persecution!"

Gerry narrowed his eyes and spoke with deliberate calm as he tried to control his rising temper. It was time to finish this conversation.

"I will no longer serve at the pleasure of the governor."

He stood abruptly and threw the proclamation handbill on the governor's desk. Without another word, the informant strode out of the office leaving the door wide open. His cooperation with the power brokers of Denver City had reached its end. Gerry lamented that his efforts had only set the tribes up for open betrayal. Now he worried about the security of his own ranche along the South Platte.

Watching the squaw man leave, Evans sat stunned. He realized it was folly to use these independent frontiersmen to report on the Indians' activities.

The governor's thoughts turned to the war against the Confederacy. He was concerned the rebels were recruiting Indians to their cause. This was indeed a serious complication to their increasingly dire situation. He stared out the window at the passersby who choked the crowded overheated streets.

General Curtis was warned of Indian trouble by numerous telegrams. Ignoring Evans' pleas, the general committed his troops instead to the violent, armed bushwhackers roaming Kansas. Evans knew that soon the troops of his own First Regiment would be called upon to bring order to the southern border of Kansas. The entire Colorado Territory would be left defenseless. There were not enough troops to subdue the rabble in the city, let alone the multitude of tribes in the surrounding region.

Prior to this summer, the tribes were peaceful. Military action was difficult to justify.

Now, however, that may change....

Evans raised one eyebrow as he refused the caution that accompanied this new thought. The land would never be settled until the tribes were subdued—or eliminated.

He called into the adjoining room. "Elbert! Bring the clerk! We have work to do."

The Secretary of Colorado Territory quickly appeared in the governor's office.

"Sir?" he questioned.

"Sit down!" barked Governor Evans. "I have a new proclamation to write."

Proclamation
August 11, 1864

Having sent special messengers to the Indians of the plains, directing the friendly to rendezvous at Fort Lyon, Fort Larned, Fort Laramie, and Camp Collins for safety and protection, warning them that at all hostile Indians would be pursued and destroyed, and the last of said messengers having now returned, and evidence being conclusive that most of the Indian tribes of the plains are at war and hostile to the whites, and having to the utmost of my ability endeavored to induce all of the Indians of the plains to come to said places of rendezvous, furnishing them subsistence and protection, which with a few exceptions they have refused to do:

"Now, therefore, I, John Evans, governor of Colorado Territory, do issue this my proclamation, authorizing all citizens of Colorado, either individually or in such parties as they may organize, to go in pursuit of all hostile Indians on the plains, scrupulously avoiding those who have responded to my call to rendezvous at the points indicated; also to kill and destroy as enemies of the country wherever they may be found, all such hostile Indians; and further, as the only reward I am authorized to offer for such services, I hereby empower such citizens, or parties of citizens, to take captive, and hold to their own private use and benefit, all the property of said hostile Indians that they may capture, and to receive for all stolen property recovered from said Indians such reward as may be deemed proper and just therefor.

I further offer to all such parties as will organize under the militia law of the Territory for the purpose, to furnish them arms and ammunition, and to present their accounts for pay, as regular soldiers, for themselves, their horses, their subsistence, and transportation, to Congress, under the assurance of the department commander that they will be paid.

The conflict is upon us, and all good citizens are called upon to do their duty for the defence of their homes and families.

In testimony whereof, I have hereunto set my hand and caused the great seal of the Territory of Colorado to be affixed this 11th day of August, A. D. 1864.

John Evans

By the governor: S. H. Elbert, Secretary of Colorado Territory *chapter eleven*

Smoking Ruins

12 August 1864
Eubank Ranch, Nebraska Territory

I went up there with a company of men to help get away men who were surrounded by the Indians on some of the ranches along the Little Blue river, and while we were there we buried the dead that the Indians had killed. We got to the ranch on August 13th, It had been burned down; all the buildings were burned; they were still smoking and burning when we reached there. We buried the Eubanks family about three-quarters of a mile from Roper's ranch on the 15th of August, 1864, We were unable to bury them before that because the Indians were all around us, and we had to get re-inforcements.

Daniel Freeman

Smoke purled above the ruins of the two dwellings. Lieutenant Henry Palmer's hand shaded his gray eyes as he surveyed the scene. The smooth exterior of his face concealed inward turmoil—for he saw something else entirely. The past did not match the present, and he squinted suspiciously at the carnage before him. Sitting motionless on his tall cavalry mount, he could not force himself out of the saddle onto the ground. All was quiet save for the buzzing of flies and the songs of birds along the river. Their cheerful singing belied the destruction confronting him.

Palmer's eyes slowly scanned the surrounding area. It was littered with all manner of destroyed household items…and bodies. High in the sky, flocks of vultures and ravens rose and wheeled, circling the scene below. After several moments, he realized he was holding his breath and pulled his neck scarf up around his nose. The stench was overpowering.

His gaze followed the trail of discarded items from the cabin to the dusty patch of ground next to his sorrel's front foot. Then he noticed it. A broken piece of her china teapot. The blue flowers winked cheerily against a white background. The young lieutenant swallowed hard as panic threatened to trample reason.

The 11th Ohio Volunteer Cavalry halted respectfully just outside this hallowed ground upon which a massacre of human life had recently occurred. The enormity of the horrid event silenced the entire company. Sixty men, every one of them a seasoned Confederate war veteran, sat motionless.

After signing an oath of loyalty to the United States, the rebel soldiers were released from a Union prison and coerced into Federal Service. They pledged to fight Indians. Palmer took command of them at Fort Leavenworth and, by orders of General Curtis, was en route to transport these Galvanized Yankees to Fort Kearny.

The day before, near Big Sandy, Lieutenant Palmer met a party of freighters, stagecoach passengers, and ranchers fleeing the Little Blue Valley. They reported multiple bands of Cheyenne, Sioux, and Arapaho Indians raiding and leaving mayhem in their wake.

One westward-bound couple shared details of their narrow escape. The day before the coordinated attacks, Jim Green and his wife Elizabeth were concerned about the rumors of Indian trouble. Deciding to turn back at Cottonwood Springs, they planned to wait until the following year to make the trek to the mountains. Henry Palmer recalled their conversation.

"Well, sir," said Jim, "Mrs. Green and I turned our team around and we'd driven east about twelve miles. Passing the Gilman Ranche by about a half mile, we decided to rest awhile. We unhitched the oxen and settled in along a shallow channel of the river. I was sittin' on the tongue thinking about movin' on when suddenly and silently, nine of the biggest, blackest war-painted Indians I ever saw appeared out of the river, all riding good horses. I will never forget the vision of such imposing human specimens rising out of the tranquil waters." Jim Green paused to reflect on his experience. "My wife has not slept a wink since!"

The poor woman nodded and said, "Nine of the biggest, blackest, baddest...."

Without thinking, Lieutenant Palmer shifted his pistol in its holster— a subconscious response to threat, real or imagined.

Green continued, "They began to parley, some of them talking pretty good English. They wanted to trade ponies for my "squaw." While my wife sat on the wagon in plain sight of them, they raised their bids from one to four ponies for her."

His wife covered her eyes with her hands, trying to dislodge the memory.

Shocked by their badgering brazenness, Palmer asked, "How did you evade them? Such harassment was surely alarming!"

"I'll tell you, I wasn't sure how we were going to get out of that fix! But all at once the whole party struck out for the bluffs on a full run, which for the moment was a puzzle to me. But the mystery was soon solved."

Green paused in the telling as more galvanized soldiers arrived to hear the tale. "I looked down the road, and what do you suppose was coming our way? A troop of cavalry on the march from Fort Kearny to Cottonwood Springs!"

"It's a wonder those Indians didn't wipe you out then and there," commented a young soldier.

"Yes, sir! We narrowly missed the raiders as we proceeded along the trail. It must be Providence! Since hearing the reports of all the people massacred to the west, I have concluded they could not have harmed us at that point in time. That little squad would not have dared start the scrap before the appointed time. It was all premeditated, I tell you!"

Lieutenant Palmer had to agree. Nervously, he and his company had gone ahead to Kiowa Station. The ruins of freight wagons, the station house, and buildings in the vicinity all spoke to a frightening fight for survival. It was here they were joined by members of the recently formed 1st Nebraska Civilian Militia. The reports of women and children captured by the raiders spurred the desire to take matters into civilian hands.

Bill Dunn of the hastily gathered militia introduced himself and suggested they ride west together. Surveying the hills for possible attackers, the veins on Dunn's neck protruded and his Adam's apple bobbed up and down as he talked. Quick bursts of coughing revealed the tension in his voice.

"We plan to give those Indians a run for their money!"

The Lieutenant knew it was going to take more than bluster to counter the actions of an aggressive and well-armed foe, but he said nothing.

———◆———

Ordering a halt to the civilians and soldiers behind him, Lieutenant Henry Palmer sat at the Eubank Ranche—gaining a potent firsthand knowledge of what had taken place. Not a man stirred. Each was quiet within his own imaginings of the nightmare which unfolded days earlier. The beautiful Little Blue Valley was invaded, and all were struck down— nowhere more viciously than the Eubank place.

The lieutenant quietly ordered a dismount. Bits and spurs jingled as the troops slowly stepped to the ground and secured their horses nearby.

Palmer ordered twenty of his troops to spread out and assess the situation. The remaining men along with the citizen militia were to stay near their horses, weapons ready, should the Indians return to engage them.

Lieutenant Palmer inhaled sharply, secured the brim of his hat to shade his face, and continued on foot. An increasing dread accompanied his every step. It seemed impossible that his friends had survived the surprise attack on their home. The identification of the dead would be difficult. Near the smoking remains of the house, several bodies were found. It was a grisly sight, and Palmer wondered if Lucinda was among the victims.

A week earlier, on the eastward portion of his mission, he briefly met Will's father. Sitting outside his recently-built cabin just yards from Will and Lucinda's home, Joseph Eubank and family had arrived that spring. He spoke of his pleasure in joining his sons and looked forward to expanding their ranching operations.

Close to the cabin was the body of the elder Eubank. His gray whiskers were cut off and his body most fearfully mutilated. Due to the baldness of the elderly gentleman, the Indians left his scalp intact. However, the body of his young son, a boy of twelve years or so, was so mangled it was unrecognizable.

Approximately fifteen rods from the ranche house, Bill Dunn hollered and waved the lieutenant over. Lying face-up on the ground was Will's sister Dora. Staked to the ground, tied by her hands and feet, she was naked. Her body, lying in pools of sticky, fly-covered blood, was full of arrows, and she was horribly violated. Captain Palmer turned away.

Calling his sergeant over, Palmer said softly, "Wilkes, I know this family. Search carefully for the remains of a young woman, the lady of the ranche. Her husband and their two children should be near." Palmer watched as Wilkes turned to begin the search, then added, "I believe there are two more boys who should be accounted for as well."

His next words caught in his throat. "The woman. She has strawberry blonde hair. Let me know if you find her."

"Yes! Sir!" the sergeant replied in a soft southern drawl. Then under his breath, "May God protect her."

The Indians, intent on wiping out the immigrant flow through their lands, calculated that intimidation through fear would turn others away. The bodies were frightful in appearance. Palmer quickly glanced around the woods and hills nearby. Raiders could descend upon them at any moment to deliver a similar fate.

Soon the body of another of Joseph Eubank's sons was found. The young boy was dead in the bushes up a draw behind the house. Injured by a tomahawk blow to the head, it appeared the fellow lingered for days.

An hour later, there was still no sign of Lucinda, Will, or their children. It was time to continue their march to Fort Kearny. The civilians would bury the dead. The Eubanks were their neighbors and friends. A hasty burial was expedient due to the summer heat, but all agreed to provide as much dignity to the burials as possible. There was still the ever-present danger of another attack, so Dunn's men quickly began the task of digging graves as the soldiers mounted up.

Leaving the scene of devastation, the young lieutenant wondered which Indians were responsible. After years of travel along the Overland Trail, he personally knew many of the individuals who belonged to the trading tribes in the area. It was unthinkable they could perpetrate such violations on human souls.

Trotting through the yard and around the debris, Henry's thoughts remained on his friends. They, too, could be dead in any one of the hidden places along the trail. Or…Henry cringed at the equally frightening possibility…or Will was murdered and his family taken captive by the raiders.

Current duties prevented him from riding out in pursuit of Lucinda and her children. He knew he could track her. Time must not be wasted in these circumstances. However, leaving the rebels to their own devices would be a dereliction of duty and the evidence pointed to hundreds, if not thousands, of Indian raiders spread about the area. It would be an effort in futility. Admittedly, he might never know their fates. Heart heaving erratically in his chest, Henry struggled to breathe. This was one decision he would always regret.

As the detachment moved out, Henry Palmer tugged the brim of his hat down to shield his eyes from the sun—and to hide his distraught face from the men.

Spurring their horses, the soldiers galloped behind the lieutenant through the Narrows. The weight of each heart heavy with the burden of the innocent. The seasoned veterans of the current war between the states had seen it all before, but their experiences did little to change the rawness of this new reality. The sobering truth was the galvanized southerners were leaving one war to join a new one. A war directed at a new adversary of which they had little understanding….

None of them noticed the man lying face down on the sand bar hidden in the shadows of the Little Blue. The channel of water, just inches deep, trickled over the man's back. Having rinsed away the bloody evidence, the river ran clear and true.

———•———

Years later, Captain Henry E. Palmer wrote The Powder River Expedition, 1865. He attended the Nebraska Commandry of the Military Order of the Loyal Legion of the United States on February 2, 1887, and read the following paper:

> I had known Mrs. Eubank before the Indian trouble–met her at her home in the spring of 1861, just after she had moved from Ohio to brave the dangers of a pioneer life and do the cooking for stagecoach passengers on the old Ben Holliday line. She was a fine-looking woman, full of youth, beauty, and strength, but a short time married, with bright prospects for the future. I remember, too, that her log cabin was unlike anything else I had seen on the road west. The dirt roof, supported by heavy timbers, was hid by cotton cloth, which gave to the interior of the cabin a clean, tidy look; the rough board floor was covered with a plain carpet; real china dishes, not greasy tin pans and cups, appeared upon the table. That, with a fine dinner, made an indelible impression upon my mind. As I stood at the smoking ruins of her home in August, 1864, knowing that her body could not be found, and wondering if she were a captive among the Indians, I thought then: would I ever see her again alive?

chapter twelve

Healer

12 August 1864
Solomon River, Kansas Territory

Mr. Bent called on me again and how delighted I was to see him as
he was so very kind to me. But he didn't stop very long as he said
Mrs. Eubank's babe was quite ill and he was going over to see if it
had proper care. He called on Mrs. Eubanks and found that the child
was improving.

Nancy Morton

Beneath the straggly branches of a choke-cherry bush lounged a
scruffy, brown dog. Among the litter of leaves and rotting
berries, he calmly crunched the bone of a small animal. His eyes
were suspended in a state of contentment—neither asleep nor awake.
The hunger pangs gnawing at my innards were unrelenting, and I
contemplated my chances of grabbing his meal.

The day was lapsing into late afternoon, and the angle of the sun
promised wider patches of shade. The pale skin of my face, neck, and
shoulders was red, blistered, and peeling due to our unsheltered advance
southwest into Indian territory. Feverish and sun-stroked, my skin stung
with such ferocity I wondered if it would ever recover.

After days of travel in the blinding sun, my sunburned shoulders
chafed under the deerskin and produced bloody, broken, oozing sores;
but they were reminders of the first kindness received since forced from
my home. Willie sustained burns as well, despite my efforts to shield
him. He could not remain covered for lengthy periods of time in this
prairie furnace.

I sought the teepee's falling shadow to escape the August heat and
noticed a stenciled crate:

PROPERTY OF GEORGE TRITCH & CO.
CANNED PEACHES.

Dear Dora had an affinity for canned peaches....

My eyes squinted as I looked at a torn piece of blue-colored fabric on the edge of the box flapping in the hot wind. Recognition slowly pierced my thoughts as I pulled an apron from the crate. It belonged to my mother-in-law Ruth. The last time I saw the apron, I had carefully placed it in her trunk. The incongruence of this perfect piece of civilization amid my current squalid environment jarred my emotions. Angry tears spurted from my eyes.

"Mother Ruth?" I asked. "Shall I put this apron in your trunk?"
I gently removed it from Belle's grasp.
"No, Lucy. I have packed one in my satchel. Wear this while I am away," replied the matriarch of the family.
Ruth still called Illinois "home." She was not adjusted to living in her rough cabin on the frontier. She and daughter Sarah were returning to Quincy to visit family. Of course, their first stop would be at Hannah's place in Ellington. Grandchildren, Minnie and Joe, were never far from Ruth's thoughts. Hannah Eubank married my brother, Daniel Walton, eight years earlier. Family bonds held fast with the Eubank clan.
Ruth decided to winter in civilization to salve the wounds inflicted by our primitive life. She was a refined and educated woman whose family encountered challenging times. The war between the states almost brought financial ruin to the family. Living in Missouri during the last few years placed them square in the path of a violence that spilled onto the gentle population. Grandfather Joseph and Ruth were burned out of their homes and businesses twice by the Jayhawkers, who roamed the communities distributing their own form of justice.
"I shall bring you bolts of fabric, Lucinda. Your dresses are fading and thinning to nothing in this Nebraska sun. What colors would you like? I think green for you and blue for little Belle," she interjected without waiting for my reply. Ruth was a strong woman of firm opinions. She knew what was best for us and that was that!
Belle's tiny hand touched the apron again as she gazed shyly at her grandmother. Ruth knelt in front of her granddaughter and was rewarded with a hug. Wispy, blonde curls framed Belle's face and spilled down her back. Her mere presence melted the grandmother's heart like butter.
I anticipated the lovely things Ruth would bestow upon little Isabelle when she returned in the spring. I also knew the unsettling worry Grandmother hid under her calm demeanor. The frontier was a difficult

and dangerous place for her entire family, but especially for her grandchildren. Oh, would she ever adjust to this wild land?

Five months earlier, Will and his brother Joe enticed their parents, along with their two daughters, three sons, and a beloved grandson, to join us in our new venture. Joe used his earnings as a stage driver to buy a home and store building. The ranche was established along the Overland Trail near Kiowa Station.

After marrying in Missouri, Will and I started our new life in this "land of opportunity." Plans were in the works for his father to acquire the parcel adjoining our ranch to expand the future of the Eubank family. Grandfather's portion added huge grassy meadows to the southern reaches of the "empire." A government contract plus hay sales to freighters and travelers boosted our income.

Full of youthful optimism, I embraced this new life with little trepidation. Will's enthusiasm easily squashed my qualms and reservations. His gentle reassurance and confidence infused me with energy to pursue our future together. The Eubank Ranche was a common stopping place for weary settlers, soldiers, and freighters. I cooked meals each day and collected two dollars from each hungry traveler.

The proximity of family members in joint effort provided a sense of security. The long hours spent carving our own life into the history of this new place fueled our motivation. We stashed away gold coins and paper dollars paid by the government for their feed contracts. There were no banks in this land, so we did our best to carefully secure our newfound fortune.

Summer passed with cheerful discussion of the family's progress. Will's brother Fred worked in the lush meadows situated on the south side of the Little Blue. Cattle and horses, acquired in trade from passing travelers, grew fat and sleek on this previously untouched land's bounty.

Will, Joe, and Fred enjoyed a brotherly bond that grew stronger with each passing day. Grandfather's long, gray whiskers bobbed up and down as he laughed with his sons at minor misfortunes or funny incidents. Youngest brother Henry, age eleven, and James, thirteen, were a constant source of amusement. They threw themselves whole-heartedly into this bright world of wide prairie expanses and cool swims in the river's pools. Six-year-old cousin Conrad was encouraged to tag along with the adolescents but usually was found by the side of his beloved grandfather.

Medora was Ruth's doted upon seventeen-year-old daughter affectionately nicknamed Dora. Born with a cheerful countenance that more than compensated for limited mental capacity, her industrious and tireless spirit was most endearing. Ruth was disconsolate that Dora would not return with her to Illinois, but her skills in the kitchen and garden were needed. Belle and Willie adored Dora. She cared for them with immeasurable love and tenderness.

I expected it to last forever....

Interrupting my ruminations, three unfamiliar women approached—their soft deerskin shifts adorned with beads and fringe. Scooting back against the lodge, I expected blows and flinched when one reached out her hand. The inviting gesture produced a spontaneous response from my arm. I reached up and grasped her fingers. Helping me stand, she urged me to follow. We walked through the camp to a strange lodge. Buffalo meat and fried bread with coffee was gratefully devoured.

After the meal, a pretty, young squaw led me to another lodge. Holding the entrance flap open, the woman tilted her head and prompted me to enter alone. As my eyes adjusted to the dim light in the lodge, a deep voice with an unusual inflection said, "How do you do? Come in."

My eyes focused on the figure of a man sitting to my left.

"Don't be afraid. I won't hurt you," he said.

I peered intently at the shadowy face.

"You speak English so well!" I gasped in relief. He nodded and motioned for me to sit. I looked around the lodge and settled nervously onto a folded blanket.

"This is the lodge of my wife Magpie and her mother," he explained. "Magpie is the daughter of Chief Black Kettle."

The dark skin of the man's face contrasted with his white shirt—worn with sleeves rolled up. Moccasins stuck out from his gray trousers. His medium-length hair, gathered into a small top knot, was adorned with a feather. He introduced himself as George Bent and explained his father was the white trader William Bent. His Cheyenne mother was Owl Woman. Once the formal introductions finished, he told me he was educated back East. Now he lived most of the time with his mother's family.

"What will the Indians do with me?" My voice wavered.

"I believe they will keep you until peace is made, then give you up." He paused hesitantly and stirred the fire. "What's your name and where are you from?"

Without warning, my eyes filled with tears.

"Did you lose someone?" Mr. Bent inquired.

Did I detect compassion or victory in his question? My mind jumped to the events of the day when everything changed.

Lucy! Is that Dora screaming?" William asked in alarm.

My neighbor, Laura, the children, and I looked up the path toward the house. We saw Medora running for her life with two Indians in pursuit.

"Run! Hide!" Will yelled.

Frozen in stunned disbelief, we hesitated until Will pushed us toward a buffalo wallow. He pressed us down out of sight in the shade of an oak tree. Stuffing a handkerchief into Belle's little mouth, he rasped, "She must not scream!"

Panting, he kissed the top of Belle's head, stared hard into my face, then launched himself in the direction of the oncoming attack. I pressed Willie's head protectively to my chest. Laura scooped up Belle. The child's face was turning blue from lack of air. She struggled to free herself from Laura's embrace. Stretching her arms toward her brave father, a muffled choked scream rose from her throat. Laura kept her hand clamped against the child's mouth.

I rose slightly over the edge of our hiding place and saw Will running near the riverbank. He was the object of pursuit by six warriors. Dora's voice went silent....

"You will have to excuse me," I mumbled. "I don't feel well, Mr. Bent, and my baby is sick."

I slumped sideways before my haunting world of memories mercifully went black.

I awoke to the sweet scent of burning sage. Feverish, I watched as a squaw dipped a cloth in water and squeezed it. She laid it on my throbbing forehead. Concerned eyes stared down at me.

I squinted at Mr. Bent's face.

"Will, Dora, Belle...."

I tried to lift my head. A shaft of pain flashed white through my brain. I tried to rise. Another bolt slammed my head to the blanket beneath me. My body was heavy and drifting. Behind closed lids, I saw dark smoke rising from charred bones. Dreams of black painted faces harassed me with incomprehensible words. I moaned.

"Shush..." Mr. Bent said as he put a finger to his lips. "I have brought the medicine man. He will help you and the child."

The healer, tall, lean, and older, leaned over me. My eyes shifted to a silver dollar hammered flat; it dangled from his loose, black hair. A necklace of bones, claws, and beads swayed over me. He swept a smoking brand of sweet grass over my body. Downward strokes started at my head and ended with a soft flick off my toes. The medicine man chanted and repeated his ministrations. A warm liquid was poured down my throat from a buffalo horn. Willie lay limply upon my chest. His breathing was shallow and rapid. Turning my head to the side, I noticed a small fire. I tensed and tried to rise.

Mr. Bent quietly pressed me down firmly.

"You must rest. I will come by to see you and the babe in the morning."

He spread a thin saddle blanket over us.

Willie and I slept.

chapter thirteen

Buffalo Feathers

13 August 1864
Solomon River, Kansas Territory

Mr. Eubanks was stationed in a draw near Bierstadt, in order to protect him from the charges of the buffalo, if necessary.

Clarendon E. Adams

F eathers floated above me. Lying in my yard, I smiled as they lifted and spun in the soft breeze. Their whispers of indifference swept gently across my face. The sensation of floating filled me with peace. My body was light as air....

Awareness flickered as I oriented myself. No! I was far from my feather bed. Torn open and emptied by the renegades, my sanctuary was no more.

Opening my eyes, I watched the shrouded shapes painted on the sides of the teepee. This is the village of my captors!

Crashing sounds! Fear and the impulse to flee demanded my body to respond! Recalling dishes smashed and thrown out of my house, the memory pinned itself uninvited into my brain.

Then I saw her. A Cheyenne girl turned and looked at me sheepishly. Quickly she picked up the clattering pots. I was in Big Crow's lodge, which included Heap of Birds and his sister Mochi. The chief treated me cruelly. Fearful of another assault, I lay still breathless, deciding my next move. I must find Isabelle! Lifting Willie, he touched my face, and I drew him in. Revived, his strength and vitality were returning. But my attempt to stand on wobbly legs induced a vapid dizziness. I spun down, down, down.

Lying stiffly, I drifted between this world and the dream world. During a conscious moment, I noticed the afternoon quiet descend over the camp. My eyes opened to the sound of an unidentifiable snort outside the lodge. The sun filtered through the white skin of the enclosure and lit the interior with the shadowy image of a buffalo charging back and forth in the flapping breeze. My vision wavered then drew me into a familiar scene....

"Uncle Joe, tell us the story of the buffalo again!" pleaded young Conrad—his expectant face lit by the dying embers in the fireplace. Grandfather's family settled down within the cramped confines of their log dwelling.

Drowsy, James piped up, "Yes, Uncle Joe, please tell it again!"

Henry quickly sat up on his pallet ready for a detailed rendition of the exciting tale.

Joe stood by the door, ready to leave for his ranch near Kiowa Station. He glanced at his gray-whiskered father, who nodded approvingly. Pulling off his hat, Joe squatted in front of the fire.

"You boys never seem to tire of this story."

Sizing up the boys' anticipation, his grin grew wide across his tanned face.

"Well, it all started back in '63. A painter by the name of Albert Bierstadt made a visit to the Little Blue Valley. Returning on the Overland Stage from a journey to the great Pacific Ocean, he stopped to inquire of Eustis Comstock about a buffalo hunt. Mr. Comstock and his son George asked me to join them."

The boys looked at each other and nodded. They were familiar with the cast of characters.

"We camped in a grove near the Republican River, up at Lost Creek. The next morning, we followed signs to one of the largest herds I have ever come upon. Mr. Bierstadt took one look and exclaimed, 'Time for fun, boys! A wounded, enraged buffalo bellowing and tearing up the ground is the purpose of this day!'

"With that, Bierstadt trotted to a small knoll east of the herd and dismounted. He lifted his easel, canvas, and charcoal bits from the satchel tethered to his saddle. He started with a sketch of the scenery and the gently roaming buffalo."

Joe eased himself into the telling of the story.

"In the meantime, Mr. Comstock selected a bull and with one shot wounded it. Running his horse back and forth, he enticed the enraged beast closer and closer to the artist."

Conrad interrupted. "It was his best horse, the gray, wasn't it Uncle Joe?" He had heard the story enough times to know when a detail was missing.

Joe chuckled and agreed, "Yep, it was his best horse."

Moving his arms in demonstration, Joe continued. "The charging animal became confused as Mr. Comstock swiftly rode in and out of its line of sight. The buffalo's angry eyes, rimmed in red, sought its victim. Spinning furiously, shaking dust from its body, the animal found its mark. Massive head swaying, he saw only Mr. Bierstadt."

Joe paused and shook his head in sweeping arcs, mimicking the menacing buffalo. Stopping with head lowered, he glared at the boys and let out a deep convincing bellow. Conrad and Henry jumped as one and nearly tumbled into one another's laps. The adolescent, James, rolled his eyes. He idolized Joe whose keen wit, confident abilities, and innate frontier instinct made Joe the natural leader of the family. James tried to imitate his older brother's calm in tense situations.

"Well, boys," said Joe, as he reemerged from the imaginary beast. "As you know, a buffalo cannot see to the front very well, so the bull never noticed Mr. Comstock's expert riding skills. Instead, the beast set its sights on the artist, Mr. Bierstadt."

Joe slowly demonstrated the motions of the infuriated buffalo.

"Steam rose from the buffalo's nostrils as it snorted. It pawed the ground with slow, powerful, angry strokes."

The boys waited breathlessly.

"I was fixed with my rifle in hand atop a rise near Mr. Bierstadt to protect him should the beast charge. My heart stopped as the buffalo tossed its head high in the air. I lifted my rifle and aimed, finger on the trigger. Bierstadt took notice of the intended victim— himself! He stood motionless a moment, shocked that his next move might be his last."

Conrad and Henry leaned forward and in unison exclaimed, "Run, Mr. Bierstadt, run!"

"That is just what he did, boys! But being of rotund and heavy countenance, Mr. Bierstadt's efforts seemed in slow motion. I sighted down my rifle as the bellowing buffalo charged at the one thing he saw moving. Bierstadt was hollering for help and running as fast as his heels could go—his coattails sticking straight out."

"The bellowing beast bore down on him and struck the easel splintering it in all directions. I kept aim on the buffalo. It was gaining on Bierstadt with every leap. Mr. Comstock yelled, "Shoot! Shoot!" The enormous horns stroked the fleeing man's haunches. Its lolling tongue dripped as it spewed froth onto the slowing easterner."

"CRACK!" went my rifle. In a single moment both the buffalo and Bierstadt fell. The beast skidded headfirst, plowing into the prairie sod, instantly dead. Well, Mr. Bierstadt lay at its feet, overcome by his brush with death. Suffering from cracked ribs, scratches, and bruises, Mr. Bierstadt limped away from the scene, thankful to be alive!"

Henry whispered, "It would have been a fearful end, for sure."

"For sure…" breathed Conrad, eyes wide with horror.

"Poor Mr. Bierstadt! It took him days to recover. But he assured me he would indeed paint that picture someday. His voice softened as he reflected on the experience. He even gave it a name, The Last of the Buffalo."

James, Henry, and Conrad sighed with satisfaction at another successful telling of the tale. They looked up at their amused grandfather's face and settled down to sleep.

Fondly, I held onto the family scene in my mind.

I noticed the buffalo image, now confined to its painted space on the exterior of the teepee. As the memory receded, my head throbbed in the heat of the evening. I worried about the fate of Joe and his pretty wife Hattie—the young couple who epitomized frontier pioneers.

Willie was insistent I feed him, and I pulled him close.

I longed for a day when the past would be cleanly consumed by the flames of God's mercy—only then would the memories trouble me no more.

chapter fourteen

Ambrose

Mid-August 1864
Solomon River, Kansas Territory

It is His wings that heal our pains,
And soothe the serpent's poisoned stings;
Close to His bosom we must press
To feel His healing wings.

Mrs. Chas. E. Cowman

The unfamiliar sounds of normal camp life added to the burning sensation in my squirming gut. Willie was fussy inside the lodge. On my feet again, I dared to step out for a little fresh air. It was time, but I could not quell the fear. With great trepidation, I looked at our surroundings.

The camp was enormous—its circular groupings of lodges spread beyond my sight. Thousands of Indians occupied both sides of the large river, their herds of horses expanding far onto the plains. By my reckoning, several thousand warriors lived in the great camp.

Cheyenne Dog Men were still out on the warpath. I was relieved by Big Crow's absence. Imprisoned in the chief's lodge, he violently claimed me as his property. His beatings and brutality were frightening. Murder and mayhem controlled the man whose lodge I occupied. Constantly under the watchful eye of the Old Woman, I wondered if she was his mother. Others lived in the lodge, including Heap of Birds and his sister Mochi—a malevolent force in her own right.

Mr. Bent claimed to have no knowledge of Belle's or Conrad's whereabouts. I searched endlessly whenever allowed to leave the lodge, but I was expected to perform chores. Compelled to join the women, who were in continuous motion throughout the day, I hauled wood and water, cooked, sewed, and tanned huge buffalo hides. Beaten often, I never knew when to expect a ferocious battering. I ached from the repeated whippings, kicks, and slaps.

Meanwhile, local men gathered in groups to talk during the heat of the day. As I passed by, their malevolent, dark-eyed stares followed my every move. I trembled in fear for my life. The potential for another violation, even in broad daylight, left me helpless and vulnerable.

The days were oppressively hot. I was parched by the wind which blew ceaselessly across the prairie. Nighttime brought new dangers. I hid in the shadows of the camp as the warriors performed war dances. Then…Big Crow would come looking for me. I knew the torment would increase and wondered if my trembling would ever cease. I regained some strength, but resistance only served to make Big Crow angrier and more abusive. The attacks left me cowering.

I reached for a buffalo bladder, which held a dribble of putrid water. It was impossible to drink enough to quench my thirst and relieve my raw tongue and throat. I threw my head back and pulled on the bag, trying to swallow the liquid. The last of it spilled down my torn bodice.

In contrast to my troubled mind, stillness permeated the camp as the sun set behind distant hills. The air was clear here, and it was possible to see the horizon. A golden orb hung near the tip of a distant bluff just beyond the river. The rays spilled across harmless, pink and red clouds that seemed to tarry in their journeys eastward.

I heard muted voices and the distant barks of dogs, which signaled a calm night. Willie reached into my bodice. I knew my milk was thin, and he was drying up, too. The movement of Indian children caught my eye. I glimpsed them running past the lodge followed by an assortment of yipping pups.

One of them seemed familiar, yet, I was unsure of what I had seen in the lengthening shadows. A small, tentative form stood out among assorted dark heads. He wore trousers and a dingy shirt. I wondered if I was so desperate for family that I imagined the boy.

Quickly following the sounds of the chattering children, I eased past the camp's main fire and rounded the last teepee to the east. I noticed the children trotting toward the creek that fed into the larger river. I lifted my skirt to free my ankles and broke into a run. It was a boy! A boy I knew!

"Hey!" I called out. They did not hear my croakings. "Hey, wait!"

A straggler in the bunch turned around and stopped in his tracks. He shaded his eyes to get a better look at me.

"Aunt Lucy?" he blurted out.

A hand grasped his shoulder from behind him as one of his companions tried to turn him back. He jerked away and stumbled toward me.

"Aunt Lucy!" he cried and began to run.

I charged forward, Willie clinging to my hip. My chapped and bleeding lips parted as I squawked, "Connie! Dear Connie! Come to me child! Hurry!"

He flew into my arms with great sobs.

Slowing his momentum, I twirled the three of us around before we crashed to the dirt. "Oh, Connie, my dear, dear boy! It is you!"

Upon our arrival, the children and I were separated. I had not seen the others since the fierce Dog Soldiers made their victorious camp entry. Now Conrad was back in my arms. I held him and stroked his dirty curls. I squeezed both boys to meld us into a family once again.

Finally gaining my voice, I pleaded, "Have you seen Belle, Connie? Have you seen her here?"

I scanned the vicinity.

His sobs subsided as he turned a tear-streaked face up to mine. I held his face with my free hand and leaned down until our foreheads touched.

"Have you seen her, Conrad? My Belle?"

"No," said Connie. "No little Belle."

Suddenly, we were bowled over by a stocky black and white dog yelping and licking us. It was Butch! Grandfather's constant companion! How did the little fellow keep up with the marauders as we swept into Indian country?

Of course, he had! He would never let the little boy out of his sight! Conrad released me long enough to wrap his arms around the neck of the little bull terrier.

"He never leaves me, Aunt Lucy!" He kissed the dog's snout and repeated, "He never leaves me."

I took the exhausted, sunburned, and hungry little boy with me to Big Crow's tent. I was afraid my absence might provoke another beating by the ever-watchful squaws. When we arrived, they refused Conrad entrance into the lodge. I pushed them away with bearlike strength.

"NO!" I shook my head sternly.

I would protect this boy with my life and was not about to lose him again. The contentious women sensed my resolve as I fought to stay on the edge of reason. They stepped away cautiously and reached a consensus —it might be best to allow me to pass. I glared at them as we claimed our spot in the teepee. No one dared approach.

Conrad was dazed and confused. He barely took notice of where we sat. Slipping into my lap with Willie, he rested his head on my chest. Within moments, the boy was asleep. I promised myself the women would not take him away! Not this child, this night. Butch remained steadfast just outside the teepee and kept watch through the evening.

Later, I moved us to the far side of the lodge, and we settled on a rough woolen blanket.

Conrad, Willie, and I slept in a tight knot that night. The ordeal had taken its toll. For the first time since our capture, determination fought to the forefront of my exhaustion and starvation. These boys were reason enough to keep fighting. We had to find a way to stay alive!

The magnitude of trauma experienced by Conrad burdened me. It seemed more than any young boy could survive. I wondered how he would recover. How would we all recover? I held the children tightly and pushed the nagging voice back into the lockbox which held my most dangerous thoughts. We will survive. I promise.

———⊷———

The new morning brought a sharp sense of foreboding. Conrad was someone's possession and would be missed. I caressed his face as he slowly blinked and winced, then rolled over. The lines between his eyebrows and the jut of his lower lip accented the face of a very worried boy. He began to stretch, then suddenly sat bolt upright. Alarm spread across his tense body. He locked eyes with mine then slowly relaxed.

The similarities between him and my husband were unnerving. Even their hair stood on end in the same manner when first waking in the morning. The family resemblance was distinct, yet, oh so troubling. Pushing the vision down, I cheerfully said, "Good morning, young man!"

Connie smiled meekly and said, "I am happy you are here, Aunt Lucy."

———⊷———

Will's father was especially fond of his oldest daughter, Mary Eliza. Her son, Ambrose Asher, the little boy sitting in my lap, was called Conrad by the family. He was the apple of Grandfather's eye. Ambrose's father was killed at the beginning of the war. Consequently, I never met him.

Grandfather Eubank offered to take Ambrose to Nebraska. Mary Eliza stayed in the states that spring. It was arranged. Mary Eliza planned to travel to Kentucky. She kissed her son farewell and promised to see him again soon. She was confident it was best for the boy.

When her father suggested Ambrose's name be changed to Conrad Eubank, she accepted the idea. It would be easier, he reasoned. Immediately, the family started using the nickname "Connie" for the boy. He enjoyed his pampered place–loved and doted upon by all.

Connie embraced his new life as one who belonged to a large clan of Eubank men. They afforded the guidance and protection a young lad needed to prepare him for manhood.

Connie sat up and asked, "Aunt Lucy, where is Butch? Do you have any food? I'm terribly hungry."

Just then the teepee flap swooshed open. In popped the wrinkled, old woman followed by Butch who slunk in behind her unnoticed. She frowned at us, growled something unintelligible, then plopped a pan of cold bones onto the floor. I guessed it was antelope although the bones were stripped of flesh. We picked off tiny shreds of meat with our fingers. Then I cracked open each bone and used a twig to dig out the nutritious marrow. I fed Willie and Conrad small and tender pieces. My inability to provide more for the hungry children pained me. I thought of my little Belle. She must be suffering terribly.

Butch gnawed on a hip joint next to Conrad. The boy had a dull, far-away look in his eyes and sat silently looking at his hands. I reached out and took one into my grasp squeezing it gently. Eyes filled with an ocean of sadness; the child looked at me imploringly.

"Aunt Lucy," he said quietly. "Uncle James is killed. And Henry, too, I think." He swallowed then began. "Papa spoke to the Indians. He told them not to point their arrows at the oxen. Then they pointed the arrows at him. He took out his tobacco pouch and gave them all he had." Conrad began to cry, and his tiny frame shuddered.

"Shhh," I said and gathered my arms around him. "I know it is very hard, Connie."

"But, Aunt Lucy," gulped the boy, "James jumped off the wagon and ran. Another Indian came out of the tall grass and rode after him. I heard, I heard…." Conrad sobbed harder.

"Yes, I'm sorry," I soothed.

Unsure if I should stop the memories, I hoped comforting words would bring relief to his tortured mind.

"They are dead," concluded Conrad with disturbing finality. "They killed Papa in the wagon and jerked him out by his hands and took his clothes off and...they shot arrows into Buddy and Poke…." His voice trailed off as he recalled the team of oxen with painful affection. Behind a deep, rattling breath, he whispered, "The wagon is burned."

I grieved for my father-in-law. His twinkly blue eyes and long white whiskers floated across my mind. He was the respected patriarch, and I loved him. I sank into the gaping wound opened by the horrific details. I could hear Grandfather's soothing voice and the happy chatter of his children and grandchildren.

Holding Conrad's thin body, I stroked his forearms and noticed the rope burns on his wrists. I checked his ankles. More of the same. His body was healing, but his heart was suffering.

"Where do think Belle is, Aunt Lucy?" he asked urgently with a hopeful raise of his eyebrows.

"I don't know, Connie, but I think Laura is taking good care of her."

He settled into processing this new information.

Swallowing hard, I prayed he would not inquire about the other members of the family. I knew he would soon ask about his uncles, but I had no knowledge of their fates. Questions about his beloved Aunt Dora were sure to follow. I contemplated how to encase the facts in a protective cover of vagueness. The child's whole life was overturned. Facts about the massacre would cause further trauma and grief.

I recalled leaving Dora at the house while Will and I walked Laura home that afternoon. She was anxious to cook the grapes down into jam. Sparkling new jars were set out on the table ready to be filled. I remembered seeing their shattered pieces in the yard as the raiders tied Connie onto one of their ponies. I hoped he did not see Dora's body lying in the yard.

Conrad frowned. He had more to say.

"They lifted me on a horse and tied my arms around its neck…like this." He leaned forward with outstretched arms.

"Umm, hmm."

"Then they tied my legs with a rope that went under the horse's tummy." Conrad paused. "I stayed there and didn't move for all night and all day until the next night."

"I know," I said softly. How had the child managed the long arduous journey in that position?

"I wet my pants, Aunt Lucy. I'm sorry."

"Oh, Conrad. I did, too. And Willie did, too. It's okay."

"Then…I came here…to this camp. Everything is so strange, and I don't know anyone. Except now I do. Now that you found me." The boy smiled weakly. "I stayed with the other Indian children because I didn't know where else to go. I can't understand their talk, Aunt Lucy."

The frightened child reached his arms around my neck and shifted deeper into my lap.

"Papa, Henry, and James are dead…."

"Now, I am only Ambrose."

I held him and rocked him but could find no words.

"Don't leave me, Aunt Lucy! Don't leave me!"

Dear Ambrose….

chapter fifteen

Heroes

13 August 1864
Solomon River, Kansas Territory

In the eyes of the station keeper and the hostler, the stage driver was a hero—a great and shining dignitary, the world's favorite son, the envy of the people, the observed of the nations. The hostlers and station keepers treated the really powerful conductor of the coach merely with the best of what was their idea of civility, but the driver was the only being they bowed down to and worshiped. How admiringly they would gaze up at him in his high seat as he gloved himself with lingering deliberation, while some happy hostler held the bunch of reins aloft, and waited patiently for him to take it! And how they would bombard him with glorifying ejaculations as he cracked his long whip and went careering away.

Mark Twain

Ambrose rested his head on my lap and appeared to be sleeping. We were alone in the quiet of the lodge. Stirring from his slumber, the little boy asked plaintively, "Aunt Lucy? Can you tell me a story?"

"Of course, Ambrose. Would you like to hear the tale of Bierstadt and the Buffalo?" I suggested.

"Naw...Uncle Joe tells that story best," he replied. "How about the Overland Boys? I love the Overland Boys, Aunt Lucy!"

"You bet, Ambrose!" I said, happy for the distraction. "As you know, your Uncle Will and I came to Nebraska after we were married. Do you remember why we moved?"

"Because Uncle Joe was already there, and he said it was the land of opportunity!"

"That's right. And what was he doing when we arrived at Rock Creek Station?"

"He was looking for his oxen."

"What happened to them?"

With downcast eyes and a shake of his head, Ambrose said, "They was stolen, Aunt Lucy. Those dirty rascals only gave them up because Uncle Joe traded his pony for them!"

"Sure enough! Then he had to get back to work. What was Uncle Joe's very important job?"

"Driving the stagecoach!" Ambrose answered brightly. "The coaches run every day from Atchison to Denver, 'course he didn't drive the whole way. There was other drivers, too! Like Mr. Emery, Mr. Gilbert, and Mr. Hickok."

Ambrose was warming to the topic. "Uncle Joe had a very favorite whip, the one with the real silver bands! He was so expert, he could flick a fly off the back of the lead horse while it was runnin'! All them Overland Boys had whips, didn't they, Aunt Lucy?"

"Yes, they were very proud of them," I replied. "And the Concord coaches are the most beautiful in the territory. Red with gold trim and even the drivers wear fancy clothes! The most handsome gray team of horses pulled Uncle Joe's coach! Mr. Holladay wants his business, the Overland Stage Company, to shine! His passengers stop at the Little Blue Station to eat dinner."

"Umm, hmm!" agreed the boy. "And the drivers are my friends, aren't they, Aunt Lucy?"

"That's right, Ambrose. What else did the stagecoaches do besides carry the passengers?" I asked probing his brain to keep him from sinking back inside himself.

"The mail, of course!" He slumped a little and added, "Grandmother Ruth sent me a letter. I showed it to Grandpa...." The boy quieted and bowed his head. A tear trickled slowly down his cheek.

I decided the story should turn to his favorite part. "Ambrose! Remember the story about James Butler Hickok?

He perked up at this. "You mean 'Wild Bill and the Bear'?"

"Yes, but it is too scary to tell right now," I teased.

"No! Aunt Lucy! I am big enough. I don't hardly get skairt when I hear that story anymore. Will you tell it? Please?" he pleaded. "And remember to say that Mr. Hickok is the second best shot in the country. Uncle Joe being the sharpest shooter, of course."

I grinned a little at this. The Eubank boys were partial to their Uncle Joe, who reigned supreme in their minds. I began the bear story hoping it would not frighten the child, but he was clearly pleased to hear it for the hundredth time.

"Well, Ambrose...back in '58, Mr. Hickok was driving freight wagons to Santa Fe. He was a teamster for the great freighting company,

Russell, Majors, and Waddell."

"Yes, yes, I know. They have the general store at Oak Grove now," interrupted the youngster. "Grandpa was gonna buy me a peppermint stick...." He trailed off as he remembered the day of the attack.

Clearly, I needed to move along. "It was at that time Mr. Hickok met...." I paused.

Ambrose eagerly interrupted, "A bear standing in the road. A big bear! It stood up and roared loud. Grrr!!! The oxen was scared and tried to run, but Mr. Hickok pulled out his rifle and shot it!"

"Yes! But he only made it mad," I prompted.

"Tsk! Aunt Lucy! You know what that means. The mad bear attacked Mr. Hickok, didn't it?"

"It did," I agreed.

"And Mr. Hickok struggled and fought as the bear bit and scratched and mauled him. With its big claws!" added the wide-eyed boy.

I decided to sum it up quickly, skipping over the usual gore. "Before Mr. Hickok was crushed by the bear, he killed it."

"Yup. Cut its throat with his big knife! I've seen it! He showed me his big knife," said Ambrose, eyes glowing. "Phew! He is brave!"

"Indeed. But Hickok was very hurt. It took him months to heal up. Then he went to work at the Pony Express Station over at Rock Creek and that is how we met."

"And you've been friends ever since! With Mr. Bill Cody, too! Mr. Hickok told me he saved Mr. Cody's life when he was General Lane's bodyguard."

The boy had a memory like a vice.

"Uncle Joe said some of the Overland Boys called Mr. Hickok 'Wild Bill.'"

I recalled the last evening we spent together with the boy's heroes. Will, Joe, and Mr. Hickok sat amiably together, legs extended toward the fire at the hearth. The men spoke of simple things. They were all perfect frontier specimens who could ride, track, and shoot; but they would never unnecessarily harm or maliciously take the life of man or beast. Tall, lean, and daring, all three sported mustaches. I witnessed them on occasion absent-mindedly twirl their handlebars while deep in thought.

Wild Bill arrived clad in a green shirt and buckskin leggings with two pistols tucked in his belt. His long, red curls were neatly groomed and fell across his shoulders. Upon entering our home, he set his rifle by the door, laid his pistols and Bowie knife on the mantle, and hung his hat on the peg.

Sitting near the fire, Will held our sleeping son casually against his shoulder. Belle climbed onto Mr. Hickok's lap and languidly worked her rosebud lips around her thumb. Slight sucking sounds complemented the friendly crackling of the fire.

I set their drinks on the small stool between them. Mr. Hickok once described the drink to me and called it the "Hailstorm." His journeys took him past the infamous Bent's Fort where he first tasted the drink. News of the new Colorado Territory delectable traveled fast, its recipe shared again and again across the endless plains. Ever since, I kept supplies on hand to stir it up for special frontier guests. With great pleasure, I collected hailstones and stored them in straw in my cellar. If they were still icy when Mr. Hickok visited, I would pour a shot of our best whiskey over the hailstones, add a touch of the sugary simple syrup, and top it with a crushed sprig of mint. The herb was easy to grow and spread prolifically around our home. James Hickok and Will found the drink irresistible and were content to share the toddy whenever the occasion was warranted.

Mr. Hickok looked forward to a respite with our family. Our home afforded a quiet and familiar comfort. Always courteous and humble, I enjoyed his easy manner. He was a striking figure with gentle, gray eyes, but what I remembered most were his soft-spoken ways and shy smile.

The ashes of reminiscence drifted together into a pure summation of our heroes.

chapter sixteen

Big Crow

19 August 1864
Big Crow's Lodge
Solomon River, Kansas Territory

He forced me, by the most terrible threats and menaces, to yield my person to him. He treated me as his wife.

Lucinda Eubank

A streak of glimmering green caught my eye. A tiny lizard stopped to eyeball me before darting into the rocks. The sun was setting between tall cottonwood trees. Glowering with stick in hand, the old squaw hobbled toward me. She yanked Willie from my arms. Pointing at the opening of the teepee, she stood staring at me with sinister, black eyes.

I backed away in horror and refused to comply with her order. She shouted at me then swung Willie by his legs. I rushed to pull him from her grip when a warrior grabbed me from behind. Violently, he shoved me through the flaps of the teepee. Inside, a wrinkled chieftain sat carving a small piece of wood with a long knife. He drew a breath through his beaked nose and slowly scanned my body. I was mortified. He snickered in amusement as his mouth turned up at the corners.

I turned, desperate to leave. The menacing chief grabbed my leg and pulled me to the ground. Screaming and flailing, I fought as he jerked me toward him. Standing over me, he flared his chest and sneered then tilted his strong head back. His breechcloth fell and he pinned me down with his knees on my arms. I shook my head back and forth as he smothered my squeals with his filthy hands. I would not give in to this disgusting savage! I resisted him with all my might.

I bit down hard on his hand.

He reached over me and grabbed his knife. Held to my neck, the blade sliced through my skin. In a deep voice, he said, "Stop, or I kill you and kill papoose."

Crouching over my body, he let out a boisterous laugh. He slapped my face with the front and back of his leathered hands until they were slick with blood. Blow after blow struck my face. Blood spurted from my nose and mouth.

I thought this demon savage from the fiery depths of hell was going to kill me!

"Dear Heavenly Father, please save me, save me, save me!"

———•———

I lay awake all night listening only to my heartbeat. In the dim light of dawn, my breath was shallow under his crushing weight. His hair lay matted and stretched over my bruised body. Smudges of white from his painted face glistened in patches on my chest. My nostrils flared from disgust and his stench, but I dared not move. Petrified he would wake and violate me again, I lay still.

In the twilight of the morning, my mind drifted off. My beautiful Belle. Where in God's name is she? What have they done with her? I longed to hold her close and stroke her soft, honey-kissed hair.

Back at the ranch, I rocked Belle and hummed in her ear. She saw her father coming from the field. Springing from my lap, she ran toward him, her dress floating in the air. She jumped into his outstretched arms. He twirled her around and around until she giggled with delight. I heard him say, "Belle, my Belle." He smiled, as did I, with profound contentment.

Streams of tears pooled inside the caverns of my ears. Dried blood caked my face and neck. My body was riddled with pain. Nights staked to the barren ground left my ankles and wrists stinging and burning from the thongs. May their merciless treatment of me bring them only damnation.

My eyes darted frantically searching the sides of the faintly-lit lodge until I found him. Willie! I caught sight of my son's tiny stomach rising and falling gently as he slept. He was tied on a small flat board, wrapped in vivid blue and red linen. His lemon-yellow hair sprouted in all directions, reflecting a contrast of crimson-red cheeks. Willie awoke and let out a hoarse cry.

The chief stirred at the sound. A slow moan escaped the lips of my gruesome attacker. Half of his sweaty body pressed against mine and his arm draped over my chest. Panicked by the thought of him waking, fear raced through me like blazing fire.

The despicable warrior rolled off me and looked into my blurred eyes. His eyes were cold, empty of emotion. He pulled his loin cloth over his genitals then motioned for me to stand and dress. I pulled my dress over my head. The torn, blood-stained material careened down my calves.

The loathsome defiler crossed the lodge and stopped at the fold of the teepee. He turned and held his gaze on me. Repulsed, I stared back at him with hate. He threw the sandy-colored flap back as sun rays burst into the lodge.

Willie squeezed his eyes shut and fought to pull himself free from the cradleboard. I walked over and sat next to him on the buffalo hide. Looking intently at his sweet face, I untied and lifted him close to me. He drew his tiny arms around my neck. Feeling my wet face, his grip drew tight. "Are you hungry, Willie?" I pulled my dress down and cradled him to my bosom.

Dew still covered the ground. I could hear the river rushing by, jumping and darting between rocks. Sounds of children running outside the teepee and horses snorting stirred the morning. I moved over to the flap and stood slightly to the side to peek out. Eight braves were riding through camp. Young bucks yelling in excitement ran alongside. They stopped at the edge of the village and watched as their brothers and fathers rode off.

Two squaws entered the teepee and motioned for me to go outside. Returning Willie to the board, I pulled the deer hide tight around him. Lifting it, I pushed my arms through the side straps until he was positioned securely on my back. Brushing the hair from the sides of my face with my hands, I secured it with my last pin.

Malicious eyes peered at me as I stepped out of the lodge. Quickly, I ducked back in. Busy voices hushed as the old woman darted inside the teepee and spat in my face. Another squaw joined her. They tugged at my dress and the threads popped as seams gave way.

I felt a hot sting on the back of my arm. The old squaw drew back her branch to strike me again. Repeatedly, she hit me. Hot welts popped up on my arms and neck. Her blind, white eye oozed. Crusty dirt matted the rim of the other eye. Her gaping mouth bared only three yellow teeth.

Finally, the squaws shoved us outside. They surrounded us and threw pots at me. Frowning, they motioned for me to pick berries from nearby bushes. I pulled the fruit and as one pot filled, another was thrown at me. I slid one of the berries in my mouth, and it squirted down my chin. I glanced around and saw several squaws coming toward me with their sticks. I cried as my body throbbed from their beatings. "Help me, dear Lord. Please help me," I whispered.

My heart ached for my husband. Thoughts turned to him, my dear, gentle Will....

"Come on, Lucy. There won't be any cake left if you don't hurry." Placing his hands on my waist, he lifted me into the wagon. Will sat next to me and took my hand in his. Looking at me most intently, he said, "I love you, Lucy. I loved you the moment I saw you. You are the most giving, thoughtful person I have ever met. I want you to be mine forever." He took my face in his hands and said gently, "Lucy, marry me. We will make a wonderful life together. I am a hard worker and a good and decent man. I promise you I will always take care of you."

I did not say anything for what seemed an eternity.

Will cocked his head to the side, his hair falling across his forehead. "Lucy?"

I looked into his questioning eyes and said, "Will, I love you, too! Yes, I will marry you!" He pulled me into his arms and flooded my face with quick kisses, covering my cheeks, forehead, and chin.

Later in the day, I walked by the river. The water appeared translucent as it skipped over glistening rocks. I gazed deeper into the velvety blue and lost consciousness of the why. A sheath of calm wrapped its arms around me. A warm breeze stirred through the tall reeds, then lifted tiny strands of my hair. A white wisp of cottonwood seed danced down my arm then flicked into the cyan sky, carried away.

A reflection formed in the water next to me. The image of the rough-looking half-breed George Bent appeared. I grimaced and he stepped back.

"Mrs. Eubank, I have come to check on you and the babe."

I sat silently.

Seconds passed, then he said, "You are in the lodge of a Cheyenne Dog Solder, Chief Big Crow. Big Crow owns you now. You are his property." He paused for a response.

I put my head in my hands and gave no reply.

He turned and walked away. Dry leaves crackled under his moccasins. I repeated his words in my mind.

We are in the camp of Cheyenne Dog Soldiers!

I am the property of Big Crow, a Cheyenne Dog Man!

"No, merciful Lord, no."

chapter seventeen

ℳrs. ℳorton

Mid-August 1864
Solomon River, Kansas Territory

With naturally sensitive nature, tenderly and affectionately reared,
shuddering at the very thot of cruelty, you can my dear reader,
imagine but only imagine the agony I endured. But neither the gloom
of the forest nor the blackness of night, nor both combined could
begin to symbolize the darkness of my terror stricken heart.

Nancy Morton

C heyenne Dog Soldiers rampaged along the river highways in Kansas and Nebraska Territories. To my relief, Big Crow left with a war party; and I had not seen Two Face since our arrival in camp. I was glad for it. My anger against him was set to a slow burn.

Ambrose was allowed to visit. We were hungry, and I stayed close to the children. A rustling at the teepee flap startled me. I protectively drew Willie and Ambrose closer. A Cheyenne woman I had not seen before stepped in leading a tall, dark-haired white woman by the hand. The woman's face was painted red and blue; feathers adorned her hair. Ambrose scrambled to hide under my arm. The newcomer limped forward, and I thought I heard her groan slightly.

I noticed George Bent standing outside the teepee and surmised the meeting was his doing. Gasping in surprise, the young woman fell to her knees and cried out in English, "Oh, Lord above! Another white woman in this dreadful place!"

Stunned, I threw myself at the visitor and wrapped my arms around her. Crying, we held each other tightly. Pulling away, I found my voice and asked in wonder, "Who are you, poor girl?"

"I am Mrs. Nancy Morton. Who are you?"

I sat back to get a good look at her and answered, "I am Mrs. Lucinda Eubank.

Huddled together, we held one another's hands in a vice-like grip.

She was close to my age. I searched for signs of injury and noticed fresh blood seeping along the left side of her bodice and down her soiled and bloodied skirt. Her gaze fell upon the two lads with me, and she reached to pat the sleeping baby.

"Are these boys yours?"

"This is my son Willie," I replied. "And this young fellow is my nephew Ambrose."

Concerned for the children, a frown creased Mrs. Morton's forehead. She urged me to continue with a nod of her head.

"We were taken days ago from our home on the Little Blue. My young daughter was also captured. Have you seen her in this camp? I am very worried about the poor little thing and terrified something has happened to her."

"Oh dear! I've not seen her, but I think I can help you. I live in Medicine Arrows' lodge. They are kind to me. Perhaps they will help." Then she added, "I met the young woman captured with you. Laura Roper?"

"Oh, yes!" I replied. "Surely Laura knows where Belle is! She cared for Isabelle during the journey. The Indians are convinced Belle is Laura's daughter."

"Oh, I see," said Mrs. Morton, shaking her head. Then she brightened. "Perhaps I can find Laura and your child. The chief's daughter Mitimoni will know what to do. She stays with me day and night. I will tell her and the chief about your girl."

Her hazel eyes lingered compassionately on mine. "I lost a child in this ordeal as well," she said softly. "After the slaughter of my people near Plum Creek."

My eyes widened at this news. "What happened, Mrs. Morton?"

The young woman stared at the flap as though contemplating an escape from her memories. "The Indians tossed me on a vicious horse. Unable to control it, I was thrown violently. The chief, Bull Bear, kicked me repeatedly as I lay in the dirt."

My head popped up at the mention of her attacker. His lodge stood nearby. He frightened me, and I avoided the hulking, formidable chief.

"Several of my ribs were fractured," she said. Lines of grief creased her mouth. "Later that night, I lost the child I was carrying." Tears welled up in her red, swollen eyes. She had been crying. I knew her grief, illness, and losses were unbearable. "I was extremely sick and so sad to lose the wee thing. Mr. Morton and I were pleased to be with child again. You see, we buried two children lost to illness two years ago." Grimacing, she tried to dislodge the painful memory with a shake of her head.

"I was afraid I would perish also," she continued, "especially because the chief was so intent on harming me. He shot at me twice while we traveled to this village. By the grace of God, Mitimoni's brothers traded two horses for me. My treatment improved after that. Their youngest sister died recently; they adopted me into their family—a replacement, I guess. Now I am obliged to call the Indians Father and Mother."

Wincing, she said, "My ribs are broken. Breathing is difficult and the pain…."

The remains of old, peeling blisters were still evident under the paint on her face. A tiny smile formed on her cracked lips as she admired the sleeping baby in my lap. She tipped her head toward the lodge's exit. "Mr. Bent has been kind. He brought a medicine man to heal me. I remember little, but I think days passed. When I was finally well enough to sit up, they brought Miss Roper to see me. She told me you and the children were captured on the Little Blue River." Noticing my reaction, she whispered, "Miss Roper told me about the attack. Horrible, just horrible."

We sat silently contemplating the murders of so many innocents.

"Have you been able to sleep?" she inquired delicately.

I recoiled as I remembered Dora weltering in her own blood. Mrs. Morton squeezed my hand. We sat in the stillness of the warm teepee for a long while. I needed to speak, but my mouth was a desert. My tongue slipped out to the large split in my lower lip. It was salty with a slight metal taste. Still bleeding, I supposed.

"Whose lodge is this?" Mrs. Morton ventured hesitantly.

"Big Crow." I shuddered at the mention of his name.

"Mrs. Eubank!" my visitor whispered as she quickly glanced toward the flap. "Big Crow threw my brother's scalp in my face after the attack. My brother's blood soaked my bodice!" Mrs. Morton spat, "That young Cheyenne is dangerous! We must get you away from him!" She seemed ready to bolt.

"He is an evil savage and most vicious in his treatment of me." Shamed, I dropped my head. "I am terribly afraid of him. Fortunately, he is not in the village just now." Wiping my eyes, I added, "He has taken his cruelty elsewhere."

"Indeed," replied Mrs. Morton. "He forced me to witness his murderous rage as he killed several people in front of me."

Alone in our thoughts, yet, comforted by one another's presence, I was curious.

"Mrs. Morton, what happened to you, to your family? Can you tell me?"

She sighed, and looked down at her hands. Searching for the fortitude to continue, she inhaled deeply. "My husband, brother, cousin, and I were traveling west out of Sidney, Iowa, with three wagon loads of goods. It was our third trip to Denver City. We joined another train of nine wagons at Fort Kearny. There were eleven men and one boy named Danny Marble. He is here with me now. Thank God." Exhaling laboriously, Nancy winced, as her hand lightly touched her ribs.

"During our journey, poor Danny sobbed and whimpered. Bull Bear beat the crying lad to within an inch of his life. The Cheyenne do not tolerate such displays. They consider it weakness." She tsked disapprovingly of the chastening Danny received.

"My husband, Tom Morton, was warned, along with all the other westbound trains, that the Indians were hostile," she continued. "We camped at the Plum Creek Station. My brother and Mr. Marble stood guard during the first part of the night and my husband, and another gentleman took their turn for the second watch. We left early and Tom asked me to drive the team to allow him to sleep. Soon after, I reported seeing men on horseback running in our direction. He replied they must be ranch hands hunting buffalo. He lay back down in the wagon. I was uneasy and continued to watch. Suddenly, to my left, I saw another band of Indians coming. I hollered at Tom. He raised up quickly, and we agreed the Indians were looking to attack!" She furrowed her brow, and her eyes grew more troubled.

"Tom assured me they would not kill me as he reached for his rifle. In moments, warriors surrounded our wagons. They shook their weapons and filled the air with hideous war whoops. It was a frightful commotion! Our mules stampeded, so Tom quickly handed me his gun and grabbed the reins." Nancy shook her head in despair.

"He shouted, 'You can't manage this team, Nan!' Braced against the footrest, he slapped the reins hard! Without thinking, I jumped off the wagon. Now, though, I truly regret my actions.

"Tom hollered after me, 'Oh, my dear! Where are you going?' Those were the last words he ever spoke to me." Sorrow melted into the thick stifling air.

"After I fell, another wagon ran over me," she said quietly. "Strange, but after that, I had no regard to injuries. Driven by fear, I plunged through the grass toward my cousin and brother, both of whom were out of their wagons and seeking safety as well. As I neared my cousin, an arrow struck his side. He struggled to help me but fell to his knees at my feet. Blood flowed profusely from him. As he collapsed, he said, 'Nan, if you get away, take care of my little children.' I could hear the life blood draining from him like water flowing down a stream." Mrs. Morton paused, swallowed hard, and blinked back her tears.

"Next, I saw my dear brother running at top speed yelling, 'Nan! Run to the wagon!' As he reached to put his arm around my waist, three arrows struck him with small thumping sounds. He fell against me and spun to the ground. 'Tell Susan, I am killed,' he pleaded. His last words were, 'Goodbye, my dear sister.' I lost my beloved brother that day." Her voice was soft with emotion. "I witnessed all that mattered most to me perish on the empty prairie. I no longer felt fear for my own life," she continued quietly. "I sank to my knees and lifted my brother's head...."

Nancy's tears ran in rivulets down her painted cheeks. Wiping them away, her hands displayed a mixture of paint and grief. "Thinking of his wife, I spoke in his ear, 'I love you, dear brother.' Then out of nowhere, rough hands jerked me up and a strange voice commanded, 'Get on pony!' A whip lashed my shoulder. Deranged, I screamed like a wild beast. 'I would rather die than go with you! Kill me if you want to!' I did not care about what they could do to me."

Defiance darkened Mrs. Morton's face. Torment and anger pushed to the surface of her rage-filled expression. I held my breath as the gruesome details pulsed in my head like a grist mill, grinding over and over, crushing all we held so dear. She slumped a little.

"Another Indian stopped, threw me on a pony, and led me back to our wagon. My trunk, foodstuffs, and bedding were scavenged and scattered across the prairie. Amid the chaos, I searched for Tom. I never found him. Later I saw a warrior wearing his coat. I demanded he take it off—and he did. I fear Mr. Morton met the same fate as the other men in our group."

I waited as the distraught woman plucked at her sleeve and dabbed her eyes.

"At one point, I saw two dozen soldiers approach across the Platte River. The hideous murderers were most abusive to me. I was stripped and indignities were forced upon me in plain view of the soldiers. Separated by the surging river and badly outnumbered, the troops were helpless. Wrists tied with my own dress; I was forcibly pulled behind a horse for miles." She smoothed the remains of her tattered dress. Gulping hard, she winced again. "When I arrived in this camp, squaws got hold of me and nearly tore me apart. I was beaten, slapped, and punched, then pushed between them until I staggered out of the lineup. Finally, they stopped."

I nodded in remembrance of my own initiation. Staring at her torn and bloody appearance, I ventured to ask about her injuries. I watched her scabby hand slide to her ribs, her waist, then her left thigh. She sighed. "A Frenchman joined the group of warriors I was with. He noticed two arrows sticking out of me. I rode ten miles and took no thought to the source of the sharp pains. I was so distraught about my Tom, brother, and cousin. The man pulled one from my side, just here." Her hand gently rested on the bloody hole in her bodice. "Then he used a small penknife to cut out the arrow lodged in my thigh. The Frenchman looked and dressed like an Indian."

She sat like a statue. Looking up, she added a new wrinkle to the story. "Mrs. Eubank, I suspect white men have joined the Indians to incite them. I met another French half-breed here. John Brown. He was a scoundrel! He noticed my money belt, which I had sewn into my dress. Reaching through a tear at my waist, he grabbed the belt and demanded I give it to him, all the money I had in the world. Five hundred dollars!" Her face showed indignation at the violation.

"When I told him the Indians killed my family, he said he was mighty glad of it. Then he took a large saber, demolished my belt, and stole the money. Mitimoni told her father of his terrible conduct. Medicine Arrows ordered Mr. Brown to return the money. The villain refused. The chief was angry and threatened an end to him if he did not leave the camp at once. Before the thief stomped away, he told me there were two white women in the village. You and Miss Roper. Cursing as he left, he said, 'I hope they chop you into pieces.'"

Distressed, I pulled the children closer, my stomach heaving at the thought. The robbery was upsetting, but his final words speared my heart. The injustice and terror of it all occupied my thoughts. To distract both of us, I questioned, "Did I see George Bent accompany you here?"

"Yes, he made my acquaintance and was helpful during my illness. He told me not to cry, that I would not be hurt. Then he told me Chief Bull Bear, leader of the Cheyenne Dog Soldiers, was my captor. I now live with Medicine Arrows—the man with the most powerful medicine in the tribe. The chief said the Indians will give us up once peace is made."

Hunger gnawed at my innards. "Mrs. Morton," I implored, "have you any food? I have not eaten a single bite for two days. I am very feeble." Nausea and light headedness threatened to topple me.

"Three squaws live in Medicine Arrows' lodge," she answered. "They cook suppers for me. I am so sorry I have nothing to give you now. I will ask for food as soon as I return to them." Her concern for me was clear as she scowled at the severity of my condition.

"Do you think your chief would trade for me?" I begged. "I am sure to starve if I remain in Big Crow's lodge. And my little girl; I am desperate for her." My thoughts raced in apprehension. "Please try to find her."

The Cheyenne woman who brought my new ally opened the flap and motioned for Mrs. Morton to leave. She stood heavily as we embraced. Oh, to keep her! Our shared plight knit us together in a single moment and we were afraid to let go. I had a lifeline in this terrible, new place.

Mrs. Morton's presence was a gift, but our shared trauma was unbearable. I remembered her parting words: "I lie down until they sleep, then sit up and cry until daylight."

chapter eighteen

Friends and Loyalty

Mid-August 1864
Solomon River, Kansas Territory

Mrs. Eubanks was very sad that evening as she couldn't find her little girl. She didn't know what had become of her....

Nancy Morton

aura Roper! She sat near the fire as I entered the lodge. Mrs. Morton held the flap to Medicine Arrows' teepee and followed me inside. Filled with joy, I rushed to our reunion and dropped to my knees. Embracing Laura, my search for Belle turned frantic. Scanning the interior of the lodge, I realized she did not have my child.

"Laura! Where is Belle? Isn't she with you?" Frantically, I searched for any sign of my precious daughter. My confused gaze landed on Laura's face. It was then I noticed her wary expression. I sensed something was amiss.

Laura was aloof and replied, "Belle is not with me, Mrs. Eubank. I don't know where she is, but she is alive. I saw her. She follows the children like a puppy, scuffling behind them in shoes that are too large." Shamefacedly, she attempted a weak smile.

Puzzlement mixed with emotion as I sat back, incredulous. Belle! Lost! The surreal image of the tiny girl wandering alone in the camps was shocking.

I found my voice, its steely edge ready to strike. "Why is she not with you, Laura? You left her to wander *here*? *Alone*?" The idea of Belle soothed by familiar arms all these days was a farce!

Laura cast me a sideways glance as I grappled with her unfathomable reaction. "They took her from me," defended Laura. "I am in the Arapaho camp with Chief Left Hand. Maybe she is with Black Kettle's band." Laura fidgeted with her hands, clasping and unclasping them.

It dawned on me Laura did not fight the Arapaho to keep the child. The toddler was left with strangers—at this moment wandering the

91

sprawling, dangerous camp alone. Dear God! The immensity of the tragedy unfolded in my brain. She left my frail daughter to fend for herself. In this unworldly place, Belle could not communicate her basic needs! Despondent and unable to breathe, I wept bitterly. Shocked by Laura's revelation, I overlooked a figure standing in the shadows. It was a white man who heard the entire exchange. Slowly, he sat down in front of me.

"Mrs. Eubank, may I introduce myself? I am John Smith. I trade with the Indians and have a family in the camp. My wife's father is chief of the Red Willow band. I might be able to help you." His eyes bore intently into mine. The turmoil behind my distraught face gave him pause. He hurriedly suggested, "The Arapaho are preparing to split from the Cheyenne and move out soon. The grazing this late in the season is not sufficient to sustain all the herds. If I move quickly, there might be time to find your daughter."

I lifted my trembling chin and stared fiercely into his face. "I want to take my children home. I am so afraid to lose them. So many members of my family are dead. I cannot bear it. When will they let us go, Mr. Smith?"

My words cut through him as he eyed me sympathetically. "I don't know what the plans are for you. I hear rumors of ransoms and releases, but the situation is volatile. The Arapaho and Cheyenne seek peace, but the Dog Soldiers continue to make war."

He touched my hand tentatively and whispered, "You must stay strong. Think of your children…."

I lowered my head and watched tears spread like dark raindrops onto my thin skirt. Mrs. Morton reached for my hand and squeezed hard. It did little to infuse me with hope or courage.

"Mrs. Eubank." Nancy leaned close to my ear. "Medicine Arrows and this man will find your little Belle. We will bring her to you. I shall ask again. Please do not give up hope. The child is nearby. We just need to find her."

I took a deep breath and looked at Laura, who now stood staring at the sky through the smoke hole. Her lackluster eyes watched an invisible scene above my head. Her thoughts were far away, and I knew she was worried for her family. She was but a girl unsure of the fates of her loved ones; and I knew the abuses she suffered.

The evening was warm, and the lodge stuffy. Laura's matted hair clung in damp tendrils on the sides of her young face. She turned and spoke forlornly. "Mrs. Eubank, do you have any news of my family?"

I remembered her mother's green velvet bonnet on the head of one of the renegades in the camp. Despite the sting of my friend's betrayal, I understood she was a traumatized girl facing the unknown.

"Laura," I said consolingly, "your family may be fine and waiting for your return. Stay hopeful." I pursed my lips, wishing the words were true.

Laura fixed her stare at the flap and said, "Left Hand said he and Black Kettle were at my parents' home. Everything was destroyed. He said Black Kettle wanted to kill my little brother." Sniffling, Laura continued. "I have seen Indians wearing clothing—stolen from our home. Pa's vest and coat, my white and brown checked dress. One of my dresses was ripped apart, the skirt stretched over poles. A papoose sat in its shade—wearing my bodice." Her voice dropped to a whisper. "I begged Left Hand to tell me if they were killed. He said my family was gone when they burned the ranche."

Somberly, I absorbed the enormity of her loss.

Suddenly, Willie rolled out of my lap and onto his hands and knees. Rocking back and forth, he crawled forward. With his new-found mobility, he paused, stopped, and reversed course, then sat on his bottom. Drooling, he gnawed his fist then popped his thumb in his mouth with satisfaction. He wrapped his other hand in the hem of my skirt. I lifted my gaze from the baby to look at Mr. Smith. Tears glistened from the corners of his eyes. Then I understood.

The camp would divide! Its separation was imminent, and our small group of captives would find ourselves alone, each in a distant land with strange people. It was a terrifying revelation.

In my heart, I knew if Belle did not return to me soon…there would be no hope of seeing her again in this world.

chapter nineteen

Five Ponies

Mid-August 1864
Solomon River, Kansas Territory

The chief's son spoke up and said he would marry Mrs. Eubanks if she would have him.

Nancy Morton

The Cheyenne Keeper of the Arrows was coming! Big Crow's mother and sister were told Medicine Arrows and his family would visit today. To make my appearance more presentable, a soft leather shift with leggings replaced my ragged dress. My hair was combed and adorned with curious objects, my face painted red and blue.

Later that afternoon, Medicine Arrows entered the lodge followed by his wife, daughter Mitimoni, and Mrs. Morton. My appearance was obviously startling to Nancy, who did not recognize me at first.

After polite introductions, we conversed about Belle. I was distraught with worry, and Mitimoni said her father understood I was very sad. Nodding while listening, he seemed genuinely concerned. As Mitimoni interpreted his words, I was hopeful yet, cautious. The chief agreed to help find the child. I smiled at Medicine Arrows, eyes brimming with grateful tears.

Soon the old woman of the lodge set a generous pan of meat and bread before the chief. As she backed away, he accepted her offering graciously, and she was pleased. More pans of food appeared for the other guests, even me. This was the first substantial serving of food I had eaten in Big Crow's lodge. I tried not to gulp.

After the meal, the honored tribal leader and his family rose to leave. Before stepping out of the lodge, Mrs. Morton stopped and grasped my hand. She whispered, "Mitimoni and I are working on a plan. You must come live with us. It might be possible to pay Big Crow. I will return soon with news." Smiling, she hugged me.

Relief washed over me. I prayed I might leave the harsh treatment of Big Crow behind.

The next morning, Mrs. Morton arrived with news. Speaking with Medicine Arrows, she explained my plight and asked if a trade might be arranged. He responded that the formidable Chief Bull Bear must grant permission. Nancy was terribly afraid of Bull Bear. Medicine Arrows noticed the hesitation and suggested Mitimoni aid in the negotiations. Her presence, as daughter of the Keeper of the Sacred Arrows, afforded status and protection. Her father's respected position would allow her to safely approach the leader of the Cheyenne Dog Soldiers.

Once in the presence of Bull Bear, Mrs. Morton sat down respectfully at the fire and pulled the torn edges of her dress together. She questioned her sanity and sat uneasily. Consumed by fear, Nancy tried to remember why she decided to put herself in harm's way. Seeking reassurance, her glance sought Mitimoni's eyes where she found strength in the young woman's placid face.

The stern leader's expression was grim, and he stared at her with indifference. His appearance embodied his name, for he was built like a bull. He crossed his arms with the ferocious stubbornness of a bear.

Clearing her throat, Mitimoni began. "Will you allow a trade between Big Crow and Medicine Arrows for the white woman?"

Bull Bear contemplated the request. Annoyed by these troublesome women, he ignored the white woman. A disgruntled exchange followed, then he spoke a final word of disdain, stood abruptly and strode away.

Mitimoni turned and grinned. "He has agreed."

She and Nancy raced to Medicine Arrows' lodge. The price was four ponies. Medicine Arrows told the women to get them from the herd. Crossing the stream, Nancy watched Mitimoni catch two ponies. She motioned for her to hold their lead ropes. The animals were fidgety, and Nancy had trouble controlling them. The other two horses were soon caught, and they were on their way.

In the shade of Big Crow's lodge, I watched my friends approach. Surprised, I quickly stood to greet them. "What are you doing with those ponies, Nancy?"

"We will trade them for you!" she announced triumphantly.

Thrilled, I clapped my hands at the news. Mitimoni's slight giggle put me at ease. Apparently, negotiations were going well.

Big Crow suddenly appeared at the lodge as the women approached. I hung back, holding my breath. Nancy bravely led the horses forward as Mitimoni spoke words of trade. "Medicine Arrows desires to trade for the white woman."

Big Crow held up four fingers and scoffed. "Four ponies? No!"

I detected a bit of pleasure at the game he was about to play.

"The ponies are good," Big Crow explained. "But the white woman no work. She has papoose." He thought for a moment, then held up five fingers. "Five ponies!"

I looked at Mitimoni for a sign the offer would be accepted. Her expression was unreadable.

"You stay here," said Nancy. "I will ask Medicine Arrows if he will pay another pony."

Mitimoni and I wandered a short way from Big Crow's lodge to let the horses graze. The young woman smiled at me. Her English skills were good and quickly improving with Nancy's help. Her parents encouraged their friendship. The young Cheyenne maiden was graceful and lovely. I admired her white doeskin dress trimmed with ivory elk teeth. The intricate beading and ornamentation were exquisite in design and detail.

Mitimoni noticed my focus. "My mother. She make dress for woman ceremony. Mine," explained the pleased young woman.

Our conversation was pleasant as we became acquainted. Soon Nancy returned. Leading the fifth pony, it was clear Medicine Arrows agreed to the purchase price. Unified in purpose, we walked expectantly to Big Crow's lodge again. My ruthless nemesis reached to take the fifth pony. Watching his expression, we froze. His eyes squinted at me, then at the chief's daughter.

"No! Not trade!" he spouted. Unexpectedly, he threw the rope at Mrs. Morton and waved us away before stalking off.

We stood in stunned disbelief—our hopes dashed as suddenly as they had arisen. Nancy held me as I bowed my head and cried. Her tears joined mine, and she brushed my cheek with a kiss. "I will speak again to Medicine Arrows. He is a good man and will know what to do," she consoled.

I tried to calm myself. Hope for our deliverance from this rude and danger-filled existence was smashed. Dejected, we approached Medicine Arrows and saw his dismay at the sight of the five refused ponies. Anger flaring, he and his daughter discussed the refused transaction. Mitimoni turned to Nancy inviting her to explain the trade gone wrong.

"He is a bad man. Mrs. Eubank has nothing to eat," Mrs. Morton said.

Medicine Arrows spat, "He is damn liar! No good! I kill him." There was no love lost between the chief and Big Crow.

Amid the commotion, Mitimoni's brother approached unnoticed. Curious as to the source of his father's ire, he listened to Mitimoni's troubled story. Quietly, her brother suggested he marry Mrs. Eubank. A great discussion followed, and he left for Big Crow's camp.

The next morning, Nancy questioned Mitimoni about the Cheyenne customs for marriage.

"Marriage for Cheyenne important matter," said Mitimoni. "Cheyenne strict rules. Conduct must be proper. Courtship happen under blanket. Other members of tribe see. They say union good or no."

Then she added the unwelcome news. "My brother return from Big Crow. Mrs. Eubank no marry. Brother shamed in front of tribe. He ask you talk with white woman."

Nancy slipped into Big Crow's camp and found me sitting in front of a pile of bones. Earlier, I pleaded with Big Crow for food. He threw buffalo bones at my feet. Hoping to gain nourishment from the broth, I tossed the dirty bones into a boiling pot with trembling hands. I was weak and dizzy.

"Why did you not marry Medicine Arrows' son?" Mrs. Morton cried in exasperation.

Startled by her sudden appearance and confused by her question, I blinked uncomprehendingly.

"We could have brought you to our lodge," she continued.

My eyes widened in horror, for I realized how close I had come to relief.

"Who? What? I did not know," I sputtered. "I, I thought…." In my heart, I knew I would have agreed to almost anything in exchange for protection and food for the children.

"Medicine Arrows' son says he never would have traded you to the whites. He likes you and wants you as a wife. Your refusal has caused a misunderstanding, I'm afraid." Nancy sighed, then said, "There is no help for it now."

Repulsed by the marriage discussion, I sat stunned and perplexed by the turn of events. The phrase "never would have traded me to the whites" sunk in with a finality that left me reeling. What would have become of me had I known who he was and accepted his proposal?

I left the bones to boil and followed Mrs. Morton to Medicine Arrows' lodge. We were taken directly into the teepee where Mitimoni and her mother started to fuss over the puzzled Mrs. Morton. They dressed her in a beautiful, beaded, and fringed shift. Her face was painted in delicate patterns and feathers adorned her carefully braided hair. Admiring their handiwork, they led us out and asked Mrs. Morton to wait beside the teepee.

Exchanging worried glances, Nancy and I were unsure whether the preparations were a positive development or part of an ominous ritual.

The chief's son appeared from behind the lodge dressed in his best finery, a folded blanket draped across his shoulder. He approached Nancy and requested permission to sit with her. In a moment of shyness, he nodded appreciatively at her changed appearance. Fidgeting and uncomfortable, he sent for George Bent to function as translator. A misunderstanding must be avoided at this important moment. We waited in silence. I feared another marriage proposal was forthcoming.

Once Mr. Bent arrived, he entered into discussion with the young brave. Assessing the situation, he directed the question to Mrs. Morton. "Will you marry this brave?"

Aghast at the proposal, Nancy and I looked at each other in disbelief. The mere suggestion she become another man's wife caused her to lose all propriety.

"No, I will not! I will die first!" Nancy stood abruptly and pushed the brave away.

Mr. Bent stepped back to avoid the angry woman.

Medicine Arrows' son clenched his fists at this second refusal of marriage, and his expression darkened. Two companions stepped to either side of Mrs. Morton, bows drawn, arrows nocked—pointed directly at her heart. Disturbed that her well-placed intentions were backfiring, Mrs. Morton realized she was lost in the cultural divide.

At that moment, a group of fifty more painted warriors, bows drawn, slipped into view and circled the panicky woman. Clearly, they intended to save the medicine man's offspring from humiliation—one way or the other.

Mr. Bent stepped beside Mrs. Morton with a warning: insulting behavior would get her killed. She responded they could murder her right now if so desired because she would never consent!

"Nancy!" I pleaded. The thought of joining in matrimony with a heathen was unthinkable, yet, the situation was dire. "Please! Marry him, or they will kill us both! We do not want to be buried here!"

"I don't care! They can't hurt me if I am dead!"

Meanwhile, the surrounding group of agitated warriors closed in. Things were going horribly wrong. I closed my eyes and prayed our deaths would be swift.

Moments later, Medicine Arrows joined the gathering. He moved gracefully into the center of the advancing warriors. Standing tall amid the young bucks, he silenced the milling crowd.

"Mrs. Morton is good woman," Medicine Arrows said in English. "We kill her husband." Turning to Nancy, he added, "You not marry son if no want him."

Shocked, his son responded with determination. "My father! Whe-Ho is pretty and good. I want her."

"No, my son. You not have her. I send her home when peace made. Now go! Whe-Ho very brave."

Those gathered whispered among themselves. The medicine man spoke to his son in the white woman's tongue. What was the interpretation of Mrs. Morton's declaration? Menacingly, they closed in. Shame not only stung their companion but humiliated him as well.

Medicine Arrows stepped in front of Nancy, spread his stance, and crossed his arms. The warriors lowered their bows and looked anxiously from one to another. The Keeper of the Arrows was to be respected and never challenged.

One by one, the young braves shuffled away. Whe-Ho won this battle. Finally, just the son and his two friends were standing defiantly near us. The spurned brave threw down his blanket. Glaring at Nancy, he and his friends brushed past his staunchly positioned father and disappeared. Relieved, Nancy looked to the chief. Placing his hand upon her elbow, he led her into the lodge.

I quietly walked around the edge of a nearby teepee—decidedly choosing a course in the opposite direction of the angry, defiant braves.

Nearly out of ear shot, I heard Nancy calling to me.

"Lucinda! She is here! Lucinda, come quickly!"

I spun around to see Nancy waving urgently for me to come. Heaving Willie onto my hip, I picked up my skirts and ran. Then I saw her, my child, in Nancy's arms!

Nancy cried out, "A squaw found her!"

Belle!

"They think she is my papoose!" Nancy's face was alight with excitement at the reunion.

"Mama! Mama!" Belle shrieked as she threw herself out of Nancy's embrace. Willie, Belle, and I came together in a single movement—the three of us, the family I treasured. Dissolving into tears, I buried my face in Belle's tiny shoulder.

"Oh! Isabelle!"

Crying, my little daughter clung to my neck while trying to climb higher into my arms. Squeezed between us, Willie patted me, then his sister. Nancy tugged him out of my arms to prevent my total collapse.

We were gently guided to a blanket near the entrance of Medicine Arrows' lodge, Mitimoni and her mother joined us. They fawned over the new arrival, and Belle buried her face in my chest. Wrapping my arms around her, it felt as though I held a little bag of bones.

As the child calmed, I inspected Belle from head to toe. I lifted the dress over her head for a closer look. We all gasped in alarm. In the waning light, many wounds were visible. With the help of Medicine Arrows' wife, I washed her injuries and applied a salve. The more severe wounds appeared to be deep arrow punctures. Rattled by Belle's condition, I agonized over what the future would bring. Our destiny hinged upon decisions made in the moment. I shuddered at its magnitude. I could not fathom how she had managed thus far.

Thankfully, Mitimoni and her mother generously shared food and welcomed us into the family teepee. I slept with my children—temporarily free from the threats of Big Crow. I rocked and cuddled Belle for the rest of the night. Tomorrow I would face whatever might come, but for now the relief was excruciating. The pleasure divine. No reunion was sweeter than mine. Tonight, our family was together. So precious to me, to Will. I drifted off to sleep missing my man and holding our offspring close.

Today one captive dared her tormentors to put her to death. The other survived a premarital misunderstanding.

Meanwhile…five ponies grazed peacefully across the river.

chapter twenty

Scout Report

19 August 1864
Tritch Mercantile
Denver City, Colorado Territory

THE INDIAN TROUBLES
THOMPSON'S RANCH, AUG. 9, 1864

*Mr. Sam. Jerome—Sir: The Station keepers as well as all families
have fled from their homes on the Little Blue. The Indians on Sunday
commenced an indiscriminate murder of the inhabitants along the
Blue. Up to this time we know of fifteen families and individuals
being murdered and scalped. Eight of Mr. Eubanks, Mr. Kelly,
Mr. Butler, Mr. Burk, (shot and scalped not yet dead,) Mr. Enley and
Mr. Buoy. All from Comstocks are now here coming down into the
settlement for safety. Your stock is all leaving. Stage Stop. Mr. Smith
will hand you this, and can tell you all the news in relation to our
situation. Can we have any help or protection?*

E. L. Comstock.
G.B. Thompson.

Clerk Ernest Wittemore read the list of goods in a monotone voice. "Stoves, pocket cutlery, table cutlery, plated ware, silver-plated spoons, knives, and forks; scissors, desk and drawer locks, hinges made of brass, iron, and nickel; quite a stock of carpenter tools, planes, saws, squares, and things of that kind. Monkey wrenches...."

George Tritch and Oliver P. Wiggins stood a short distance from the table, examining the open ledger. The stock items and purchase prices were neatly compiled in columns.

Tritch interrupted, "I bought dozens of Coe wrenches." The Denver merchant recalled the fortune he planned to make on that shipment of monkey wrenches alone. "They are quite the newest invention," he added regrettably.

The Denver businessman's entire wagon shipment never arrived from St. Joseph, Missouri. It was his largest supply purchase since starting the Denver establishment on the corner of Wazee and Fifteenth Street. Rumors among the infant city's residents regarding an attack on all manner of freighters produced great speculation and fear. But it did not equal the devastation he was learning about now. Tritch's fists clenched open and closed, and the face of the usually mild-mannered merchant bulged with frustration.

Wiggins was a scout and guide in the service of the U.S. Government. His main duty was to keep the stage road open for travel and commerce alike. He arrived in Denver with outrageous details of a coordinated Indian attack along the Overland Stage route in Nebraska Territory. He was a tall, medium-built man in his early forties. Loose, dark hair spilled from under his broad-brimmed hat. His cool, gray eyes complemented his quiet demeanor. However, troublemakers often mistook Wiggins for a passive, beholden man; but after the first swing thrown by a swaggering fool, the scout would easily gain the upper hand. His buckskin attire spoke to years spent as a trapper, trader, and Indian fighter with Kit Carson. He had lived out West for over two decades and developed the skills needed to survive.

The scout's reputation among the regulars in the frontier was that of an honest, soft-spoken man whose combat skills and logic created a force to be reckoned with. Known for his accuracy and lightning speed, Wiggins' Henry lever-action rifle was always tucked in its scabbard. The new repeating gun was propped against the wall just steps away from the frontiersman.

Tritch stopped pacing the room to admire the rifle but made no move to touch Wiggins' most prized possession. "Breach-loading .44 caliber, sixteen shots," the merchant said nodding appreciatively. "That Confederate rascal Colonel Mosby claims this damned Yankee rifle can be loaded on a Sunday and fired all week."

The nervous clerk looked up from the ledger, looked at his boss, then suspiciously glanced at the rifle. Someone would need to keep an eye on the scout.

A slight grin creased Wiggins' face as he wistfully reminded himself the country was filling with obvious greenhorns. Wittemore was just one of many to come. He turned to Tritch and continued the discussion of current events.

The scout's report began with a description of the wagon train belonging to Simonton and Smith. Encamped near the Eubank Ranche, it was heavily loaded with lead pipe, crockery, and hardware, all bound for Tritch's mercantile. The company was contracted for this specific haul based on their reputation for getting the job done.

Asa Middaugh, a freighter and personal witness to the raid, stood by the open door, watching the passersby. He was a young, enterprising farmer and rancher in his mid-twenties with a small cattle train outfit. As a freighter, he hoped to benefit financially from the boom of merchandise hauled across the plains into Denver.

Recent Indian raids slowed travel to a crawl. Commerce was threatened by the restriction of supplies to the needy influx of settlers as the population rapidly expanded. Asa coughed lightly, hoping to insert his side of the story.

"The oxen were put out on grass a half mile south of the Little Blue River with nine or so herders from the S&S train," said Wiggins. "That night, Indians killed the herders and drove off all the stock. Unfortunately, Horace Smith, the wagon master, and all the teamsters were killed. Not a man is left. Every wagon was partially or completely burned. I am sorry, Mr. Tritch. The entire contents of your load were destroyed or stolen. It is a total loss."

"Where were you when all this happened?" inquired the merchant accusingly.

"On my way up the Platte. I was ordered to hurry down to the Little Blue," replied Wiggins. "When I got to Fort Kearny, the stagecoach company's paymaster, Dave Street, come by. He was paying off. He reported the S&S train captured and burned between the Eubank Ranche and Muddy Station, thirty miles east of Fort Kearney. Took me a day and a half to get to the site. Street said the Indians killed ten drivers, including Smith, and seven of the Eubank family was dead." Wiggins coughed into his fist to control the emotion rising in his voice. "Mrs. Eubank and her children are missing...captives."

Tritch's mind soared past the implication of the poor woman's plight. He could hardly contain his words as he sputtered, "That load was worth $22,000! Are you sure it was mine?"

"I was acquainted with Mr. Simonton for years, so I recognized his outfit. The crates and boxes were labeled TRITCH & CO., DENVER, COLO. S&S was still visible on a couple of the wagons."

"Wiggins, there was a horse-power thrashing machine, very valuable. Patented. Red. Did you see it?" inquired the increasingly desperate Tritch.

"Yes, I did a couple of days after it all happened. It appeared the horses stampeded, and the machinery was driven off the road a ways.

The tugs were cut. That is the way Indians unhitch a team. White men undo the tugs, but Indians cut them. Also, I saw a separator left up where the other wagons were destroyed—riddled with bullets. They set fire to the horsepower and burned it up. Completely ruined. And the separator was demolished too."

Tritch sat down wearily at his desk and nervously tapped his fingers on top of an open book. "Are you telling me no one suspected what the Indians were up to?" He quickly looked up at the scout questioningly. "Do you know which Indians did this?"

"They were Cheyenne Dog Soldiers, Arapaho, and Sioux," answered Wiggins.

"Dammit," groused Tritch under his breath. The enormity of the raid hit hard.

"They did this together? This does not bode well," he trailed off, thinking. "A woman, you say? Taken?" George Tritch soberly contemplated the disaster with new eyes.

Wiggins nodded and continued, "When we finally caught up to them, I saw the Arapaho, Roaring Wind, and the Sioux Chief, Two Face—both Dog Soldiers. It seems the Cheyenne made an alliance with other tribes to stop movement on the trail. George Bent is now raiding with the Cheyenne."

"Whew!" whistled Tritch. "George Bent? The trader's half-breed son? Didn't he go to school back east in St. Louis? I heard he was fighting for the rebels." Tritch paused as the ramifications to this news dawned. "Riding with the Dog Soldiers. With his military experience... the fiercest fighters on the plains...." Tritch groaned and slumped further into his chair as he realized the impact on his thriving Denver business.

"Most recently, Bent was still back east fighting under General Price," said Wiggins. "I heard he was taken prisoner in Missouri but signed an oath of allegiance to the U.S. Then an old family friend got him released from the Union prison. His brother Robert, a staunch Yankee, brought him home to his father's fort."

Simultaneously struck by the same enlightened thought, the two men looked into one another's concerned faces. Alarmed, Tritch was the first to speak what both were thinking.

"Do you suppose Bent is the mastermind behind this Indian trouble?"

"With his trading connections, it would be easy for the rebels to keep the Indians well-armed and supplied for war," Wiggins suggested.

"I need to share this information with Governor Evans and the preacher," responded Tritch. With a decisive nod, he added, "These are troublesome developments."

The two men were silent for a moment until George Tritch picked up his former line of questioning. "You say you know which tribes did this? Did you encounter them?"

"No, they were too far ahead of us. We trailed them out of the Little Blue Valley straight west to their second camp. About forty miles west of where the raid was made, we spotted their rearguard. They were lagging behind to watch us. We got to within three hundred yards of them. Mrs. Eubank was behind Two Face on his horse."

Noticing the puzzled look on Tritch's face, the scout added an explanation. "I have been acquainted with Will and Lucinda Eubank for several years."

"You *saw* Mrs. Eubank?" asked Tritch. "*With* the raiders?"

Wiggins nodded and blinked hard. "Her long hair had come loose from its knot. It is reddish-blonde and shone in the sun. Kinda hard to miss, ya know?" A frown creased his tanned face.

Tritch took note of the scout's worried expression and decided to change the subject. "You've been on the frontier for a long time, haven't you, O.P.?"

"I came out to the plains as a boy in '38, before Denver was even thought of," replied the weathered scout.

Tritch nodded, then walked to stand behind Wittemore, who was still analyzing figures in the books. The bookkeeper asked distractedly, "You know Indians by their signs, I suppose?"

The scout thought for a moment and replied, "The men found dead at the scene were shot with arrows made with steel points. The tip of Arapaho arrows are small and instead of cut down with a brad on each side, they are cut up the other way, so it will pull out."

Wittemore looked up from his books and froze with pencil in hand, intent on this newest subject.

"The Cheyenne arrow is cut with a little bit of a beard. You can't pull a Cheyenne arrow out. Sioux often use arrows with a beard an inch and a quarter long, running on each side," said Wiggins as he used his fingers to show the length. "We saw a good many arrows around. My men picked up sixty or seventy."

The merchant's bushy eyebrows knitted together as he paced the room, hands clasped behind him. He warily appraised the scout, whose calm exterior concealed a man of knowledge and experience.

"What were the Indians armed with?" queried Tritch. "Did you exchange shots?"

"Yes, we did. They were armed, all right! Bows, arrows, and good rifles. We chased the raiders for three or four miles. Lieutenant Williams and I had a company of thirty-two men—mostly Omaha and Winnebago Indians. We could see the band pick up the pace once they spotted us. I counted eighty or so. If we could have got them spread out, we would have given them a fight. However, our horses were too give out to put up much of a chase."

Wiggins tugged on his mustache. "Word has it the Indians have plenty of firearms and ammunition. All the stations and ranches were attacked from Julesburg east to Kiowa Station. Up at Plum Creek, there were ten wagons camped, including Tom Morton's out of Iowa. I heard all the men, including Tom, was killed." Then Wiggins added softly, "Tom's wife was taken captive as well."

Tritch stopped mid-stride with a stricken look of disbelief. He was acquainted with the Mortons and visited with them during the previous two freighting seasons. Could the report get any worse?

"Damnit, O.P.!" sputtered Tritch. "Tell me how the Arapaho and Cheyenne orchestrated this widespread raid. They must have covered hundreds of miles!" His once handsome, pock-marked face drooped with fatigue and grief over the news of lost friends and competitors.

"Man needs an army to look after his prop'ty right now," interjected Asa. He was glad for the opportunity to describe his account. "Them Injuns sneaked eastward in small groups, ten or twenty or so. We seen 'em all along the Little Blue for weeks. Why, when asked where they was a travelin,' them tricky Injuns lied. Sayin' they was goin' to St. Joe!" He spat for emphasis. "Them innocent settlers gave no thought to the idea of an attack."

Tritch's face bulged purple at the enormity of the outrage visited upon so many innocent people.

"What is being done about this, Wiggins?" he thundered.

The scout ignored the explosion and replied, "Two companies of civilians were put together at Marysville. Five companies come out of Nemaha County. They were out on the Little Blue within eight days of the attack. Captains Stoner and Gilbert buried the members of the Eubank family just before they found Captain Murphy's company at Pawnee Ranche. They joined up with cavalry from Fort Kearny and headed south along the Republican. I heard one skirmish there lasted two days." His gaze dropped to his boots as he reluctantly reported the death of a highly respected citizen of Denver City. "The wagon boss, George Constable, and a soldier were killed, their bodies burned near the mouth of Elk Creek."

Tritch's eyes went wide as he sucked in a quick breath. Constable was one of the toughest wagon bosses out there, and Tritch utilized his services in prior years. His success as a freighter had made the merchant prosperous.

"Asa," directed Tritch, "what do you know about this fiasco? You must have seen something!"

"Well, sir," Asa quickly jumped into the conversation. "It was on 'bout Friday night if'n I don't misremember. It was a hot one when me and my brudder started from Kearny. We pitched camp on the Little Blue on Saturdy. That's when we met up with the freighter, Mr. Smith. He and I was acquainted. I know Mr. Simonton, too. Both are, or I should say were, my naybers. I vizted with Mr. Smith fer some time as we summoned up things past. He had six teams and some trail wagons. Among the lot was yer thraishin' machine."

Twisting the hat in his hand, Asa fidgeted and gulped, then hurried on. "Sundy we laid over at the dutch woman's ranche to warsh our shirts. They wuz a little stale," he added earnestly. "The cattle wuz grazin' on t'other side of the river. 'Bout four o'clock, my pony and me gathered 'em up. We hitched 'em to the wagons as the evenin' cooled. The moon was bright. It made fer a good night to travel. I seen the Smith and Simonton train. Tinware and hardware was strewn about fer four or five miles each away. It put me to mind that it was the handiwork of Injuns. When I seen Mr. Smith was kilt, it nearly stopped my ticker. His body shot fulla arrows; and just like O.P. said, everythin' was torn up and burnt."

Asa paused at the magnitude of his own description. Sensing his account was exhausting the merchant's patience, Asa hurried up his tale.

"Well...I tell you," drawled Asa conspiratorially. "We hurrit on and passed through the Narrows quiet as mice. A good place for an Injun ambush on unsuspectin' souls, ya know! I was plumb parched from worrit, so being compelled to fill my canteen, I trotted down to the river in a hurry case we had to make a run fer it. I came across the body of a man."

Asa paled at the memory. "The mute-lation was horrible. Bones disjointed and body parts where they shouldn't be—if you know what I mean...." He sighed and continued, "When the devil made those Injuns, he forgot to put in the quit and added an extra dose of meanness. The poor fella had more than a few arrows in him. I guessed it 'twas) the bullet in his head finished him off though."

Tritch settled back in his chair, arms crossed, scowling.

"I skeedaddled outta thar to find my brudder. He, he, he was up at the Eubank place, just standin' there lookin'round. Even in the scant moonlit, you could see disaster struck! Yup! Like a cyclone churned through their place! I hollered up, 'Holy shit, Ezra! We got a dead body here!' My b-brudder, he got to runnin', tripped over a body and yelt, 'What the hell, Asa! We gotta git outta here! And watch yer noggin! Injuns might knock it off!'"

Asa's voice cracked as he summed up the massacre. "Them folks Mr. Wiggins told of—the Eubank family—well, there was bodies scattered, terrible condition. Smell o' death and blood, I tell ya. And the flies was thick. Terrible sight, most terrible." Asa shook his head slowly, jaw clenched.

George Tritch dropped his head and coughed hard.

Asa shifted his feet scraping the wood floor. "We thot best to hurry on outta thar. Them red devils could be anywhere! We whipped them poor oxen all that night, makin' it to Big Sandy the next mornin'…over twenty-six miles. It was durn providential we arrived in one piece!"

Relieved to report such a narrow escape, he added, "Fortunate me and my brudder stopped to warsh our shirts on Sundy evenin', or I'd be angel by now, I s'pose." He reverently gazed up at the ceiling and said, "Why, yessir! An angel." Then added with a flourish, "With big wings."

Wiggins squinted at Asa and spoke up. "I received a report when I stopped at Liberty Farm for provisions. Five hundred warriors were sighted between the Little Blue and the Republican. They probably would have attacked us if it were not for the local militia's arrival. Their scouts must have spotted the ten companies from Marshall and Nemaha counties. We figured they decided to break camp, take their loot, and head for the hills."

The scout cleared his throat. "Also, more bad news. Joe Roper was with one of the companies, part of an effort to rescue his daughter Laura. She was taken with Mrs. Eubank at the Narrows."

The solemn mood was heightened by the tension created as Tritch commenced pacing the room. The floorboards creaked under each step. As a result of his destroyed trainload of merchandise and the other losses incurred by his competitor's wagon trains, Denver City would be short on supplies during the coming winter.

This unprovoked attack must not go unanswered. The alarmed and vulnerable citizens needed to pressure Governor Evans to organize a force to seek restitution for these outrages.

"You are under the employ of the U.S. government, Wiggins. What are they going to do about this?" Tritch demanded.

"There had only been skirmishes up to this point," said the scout. "But after this big raid, the army's regulations have changed. No wagon train is allowed to pass along the route unless there are at least one hundred men to accompany it. It is considered so dangerous the post commander has expanded his orders from Fort Morgan to Big Sandy."

"Thank you," replied Tritch as he sat down heavily into his leather chair. "You have made a thorough report."

The lanky scout picked up his rifle and stepped out of the office into the busy street followed by Asa. George Tritch silently wished for a thousand just like him. The current situation placed an entire city in peril. Something must be done quickly.

The merchant was a man of action and determination. It was time to check in with the governor. The boisterous preacher, Colonel Chivington, was appointed to lead the Colorado Second Cavalry and the Hundred Day Volunteers. He had the authority to recruit armed men from the clamoring local citizenry. With more manpower and the cunning of Chivington, the operation would cast a wide net. Now there was extra reason to serve up a history-making military action from which the Plains Indians would never recover.

Friendly or hostile, George Tritch knew there would be no distinction made between the members of the tribes, for they had sealed their own collective fate. His business suffered a serious set-back because of the raid. Denver City must ready itself. To prevail, drastic action must be implemented.

As far as he was concerned, the sooner the better.

chapter twenty-one

Keyless Prison

Mid-August 1864
Eastern Kansas Territory

SONG OF THE OVERLAND STAGE DRIVER

You ask me for our leader; I'll soon inform you then;
It's Holladay they call him, and often only Ben.
If you can read the papers, it's easy work to scan;
He beats the world at staging now, "or any other man."

Nat Stein

Big Crow! He will notice I am gone! Unable to savor my first morning with both children, Mitimoni and I hurried to Big Crow's lodge. He demanded my return. I feared for my children but complied. We found his women breaking camp. Upon seeing me, they expressed disgust to Mitimoni and complained bitterly about my limited ability to understand the order of things. Mitimoni conversed with the women briefly until, finally, I was shoved into the far corner of the lodge where Big Crow's belongings lay scattered.

I was to pack the contents of the interior into large baskets and canvas bags. Motioning to a large bear claw necklace hanging from the cross timber of the teepee, Mitimoni said, "Very important. Careful."

Lifting it, I felt its heft. Upon closer examination, I counted twenty-nine honey-colored grizzly claws connected by hide thongs to otter fur. Each four-inch-long nail was separated by bits of red and tan trade cloth. A long, thin fringe of sinew fell at the back of the necklace, and the whole thing was adorned by quillwork. I looked at Mitimoni, who handed me a piece of cloth to use as wrapping.

"Big Crow great warrior," she said. "Much respect. He strong leader with big power. Big Crow hold spirit of bear. Here. Inside," she said as she tapped her breastbone.

I nodded and cautiously placed the item in the basket. The sooner it was out of sight, the better! Mitimoni smiled at me encouragingly and stepped out of the lodge. I was on my own and continued to pack busily in the hopes of avoiding the contentious faction of the lodge, especially Old Woman.

I spotted a decorative wooden framed mirror in the bottom of a basket. My heart plunged as I reached in and pulled out the precious item. It once belonged to my late mother! God rest her soul! Somehow, it was mixed with Big Crow's portion of the plunder. I lovingly caressed the keepsake crafted by our people. The Pennsylvania Dutch were known for their use of ornately carved wooden strips secured by pegs.

Holding up the mirror, I caught the reflection of a wrinkled, haggard, blotchy face. Startled, I nearly dropped it. The face was mine. I examined the image more closely and touched the peeled burned spots on my nose and forehead. Gaunt cheeks sagged beneath haunted eyes. Quickly, I wrapped the mirror and packed it away. My mother would have been mortified by our horrid situation, yet, I wished to keep the memory of her near.... Big Crow would kill me, though! It was best to leave it for now.

Providence intervened again as I lifted a red piece of cloth. A gold watch dropped into my lap. Unbelievable! I picked the item up reverently and read the engraving on the front. "Overland Stage Line." I clicked open the case and there it was! On the left side—a photo of my sister-in-law Hattie. Oh, my word! This is Joe's watch! I stared at the familiar face longingly, then clicked it shut. Turning the time piece over, I read the words, "With appreciation, Ben Holladay."

The new owner of the stage company had given it to Joe for his dedication as Mr. Holladay's personal Nebraska Territory driver. The stage line magnate bankrolled the line's improvements and often rode the entire mail and passenger route inspecting his investments.

Will and Joe were especially excited when new equipment arrived, and the old mules were replaced by Kentucky-bred horses. It was said that the re-routing of the line through Colorado and Wyoming, just two years prior, cost Holladay two million dollars. The federal mail contract was lucrative, so the Eubank hay operation profited as well.

I remembered the day a bugle loudly announced Mr. Holladay's arrival with great fanfare. Joe, the honored driver, and his outriders all wore their Sunday best! The "palace car," pulled by a beautiful, matched gray team, stopped in front of the Little Blue Station. The exterior was painted in the traditional red with gold embellishments. A lovely red and white silk flag fluttered from a pole mounted on the box. A closer look revealed the letters "B.H." embroidered on the pennant. Ben Holladay enjoyed the creature comforts in a most flamboyant way.

As the royal "Stagecoach King" stepped out of his palace on wheels, he tossed twenty-dollar gold pieces to the station master, hostler, and others fortunate enough to work at the station that day. Moments later, his entourage arrived in a separate coach. I was permitted a peek inside at the soft leather upholstery and brass fixtures. The side lamps and door handles were all made of Comstock silver. The seats folded into cozy beds, and side lockers were stocked with food and drink. The inside of the coach was an opulent sight to behold!

One of Mr. Holladay's policies was to reward employees who performed their company duties beyond what was expected. On that visit, I prepared a meal "fit for a king" and was kindly handed a twenty-dollar gold piece of my own. His compliments of my cuisine poured profusely throughout his robust conversations with all in attendance.

The watch I now held in my hand was given to Joe by the "Stage King" himself. It was at that moment my fears for Joe and his family were confirmed. I pressed the watch to my heart, and tears joined the keepsake. Is he really gone? The handsome and capable Joe? No! It cannot be. The teepee spun, and I staggered to stand upright. I must flee! Return to our family!

Without warning, Old Woman entered the lodge and began to bark orders in gibberish. I nearly jumped out of my skin, but it was enough to restart my dying heart. The village was on the move, and I was holding it up. I tucked the watch in the basket with a loving pat. I would find a way to secure that watch, to keep it safe! To return it to…. No, I cannot think of that now!

The uprooting of four hundred and fifty lodges representing over three thousand occupants was an enormous undertaking, yet, it was carried out with practiced efficiency. Big Crow was among six hundred warriors that departed the enormous village at dawn. They headed south to Big Timbers and took their fight against the white invasion onto the Smoky Hill Trail. We were part of the contingent which followed.

The safety of the children was paramount as I prepared for the journey. The women did not notice Belle, except Old Woman who offered her a few dried plums. I watched as the squaw reached out and stroked Belle's golden head. She seemed to marvel at the child's angelic resemblance. I breathed a sigh of relief, for I expected Belle's arrival to cause a stir.

The cradleboard, which the squaws demanded I use, was confining and hot for Willie. He would ride in the sling on my back for now, but the boy was heavy, and I would soon need the board. As for Belle, I would not let her out of my sight. A soft bed on the travois was prepared for her tiny frame and once she was secured in place, I looked down into her face. She wore the haunted look of one traumatized beyond belief. It was going to take time. I planned to walk next to the conveyance with her hand in mine. She was content and smiled weakly at me. I wished for the hundredth time for a cup of sweet milk from Betsy, our cow. The starving child needed nourishment and rest. But it was time to go.

Concern for Belle's health and injuries threatened to overwhelm me, and anxiety showed on my face. Noticing it, Nancy pulled me aside and said, "I see what you see, Lucinda. But you are the only thread holding Belle to this earth. You must remain strong. Your baby girl is frail and weak. She will pull strength from you."

With those words of wisdom, I determined to guard my children from all threats, including those which overwhelmed their mother.

As the day wore on, I was glad to have Nancy's reminder fresh in my head, for the journey was difficult. At the time, little did I realize I would be continuously traveling in this same manner throughout the fall, winter, and into the spring. Sometimes, it is good the future is concealed behind today's curtain, for I could not have endured had I known what was to come. For now, the tribe dictated the cadence of our lives.

We traveled twenty-two miles south with no food and little water. An approaching rain cloud split the sunlight into golden rays encompassed by colorful rainbows. There was a grandeur in the high desert, and I was awed by its beauty and silence. In moments like these, the women would join together in song like musical poems of praise.

Late in the evening, we stopped. Squaws set up the lodges and soon thereafter, fires were built, and pots of food bubbled. I gazed out across the newly established camp. Our circle of teepees opened to the east as the ancient order of things was at work. The small camps formed a giant ring and reminded me of the stars spinning in the Milky Way. Full of mystery and beauty, the people must have observed the night sky and over the eons created their own earthly constellations. However, the darkness held no assurance of safety or security for any of us. It left me feeling alone with a sense of how truly isolated we were. I turned my head away from its black expanse, for it coldly spoke to our insignificance.

Once again, little food was offered after a long day of travel. I was exhausted by the process and speed with which the Cheyenne community lived and moved. Two strips of dry, dirty buffalo were tossed my way.

I was grateful for the little bits of food that kept Willie busy as he tried to drain every bit of flavor from the tiny morsels. The women within our circle of lodges were hostile and aggressive. While they resented my presence, I loathed their crude existence and uncivilized mode of living.

Gathering the children, we made our way down to the edge of the nearby creek. Belle was filthy and needed to be bathed. So thin. I reinspected her back and was shaken to my core by its inflamed condition. Holding her close, I forced my expression into motherly calm, for I could not let her see the impact of her injuries on my face. I did not want to frighten her.

Afterwards Belle sat with Willie on the blanket near me. She delighted in kissing him. No longer satisfied with staying in one place, the baby crawled to his sister, reaching for anything he could put in his mouth. The boy was constantly in motion when relieved of the confines of his sling or cradle- board. I must remain diligent to protect him from the campfires, dogs, knives, and other humans. Most of all, I needed to shield him from the threatening hands of savages.

Our journey continued for days before the Indians stopped for an extended rest. The heat had not abated, but I noticed the air was drier and the sky bluer as we journeyed across the short-grassed plains. Nothing broke the horizon outside our camp.

I considered our chances of survival. Could we slip away during the night? Tempting as it might be, I could not walk away. Belle and Willie would surely perish. I realized my prison was open to all the edges of the earth. I was confined in an immense cell, its boundaries lit by billions of stars. Yet, here I stayed.

Locked within my keyless prison.

chapter twenty-two

Competition

Late August 1864
Big Timbers Camp
Hackberry Creek, Kansas Territory

Fortune seemed to present itself and I observed an antelope on the hillside and taking true aim I killed it the first shot. The whole valley seemed to echo and re-echo with their shouts and screams from one section of the village to the other. I could hear them shouting Brave Whe Ho The White Squaw.

Nancy Morton

N ancy did not seem like herself. Her eyes were swollen and red from crying. When I inquired after her health, she replied that sometimes the hardships we faced nearly rendered her hopeless. She told me she was so heartbroken over the loss of her family that the whole world was dark. Not a single ray of hope could soothe her grief-stricken heart. Only my little children lifted her sagging spirits.

One morning, Nancy joined us at the creek where we bathed the children in a small pool of water. Insects with long legs skated on the surface water, and a fly buzzed my hair. We relished the companionship, and I was glad Nancy shared what moments she could with me. She was free to come and go but was always under the watchful eyes of those with whom she shared a lodge. She took Willie from me, and he happily splashed his fair cheeks with water. He was sunburned and hot at this early hour but was gradually growing stronger.

Above us, a woman from Medicine Arrows' band appeared. She motioned for us to climb up the embankment. As we scrambled to the top, we noticed a man standing near a fire. Approaching, we recognized the visitor as John Smith, the trader and interpreter.

"The soldiers have sent me with word. Negotiations are in process to secure your releases—if peace is kept."

"Where are we, Mr. Smith? Where will they take us for our release?" asked Nancy.

"They will probably take you north of the Arkansas River to Fort Lyon."

Seeing our eyes alight, he added, "One hundred forty miles or so from here."

Mrs. Morton and I exhaled in unison at the thought of such a long journey.

A deep rumbling sound like distant thunder interrupted the conversation. Finding its source among the hills to the south, a ghostly mass of riders, like a swarm of blackbirds, appeared through the heat waves and dust. Hundreds of mounted, screaming warriors charged into camp with a large remuda of dozens of stolen horses and mules in their possession.

The sudden arrival of so many warriors was frightening and unnerving. I grabbed Willie and Belle. Nancy and I wrapped our arms around the children in a protective hold. The warriors dismounted and proudly held up spears with fresh scalps flapping in the wind for others to admire.

"Dog Soldiers!" shouted Mr. Smith over the din. "Raiding again."

One warrior raised his lance high to display three scalps, and the surrounding Indians hollered and shrieked. A second marauder raised his three scalps to the whooping crowd. As the third Indian raised his lance, I felt a tightening in my stomach. The response was an uproar of stomping feet and high-pitched trilling.

I turned my head from the gruesome sight. Nancy covered her mouth and gasped, "There are six scalps from men! But, but…that one looks like woman's hair. Oh, no!"

Nancy was unable to turn away from the long, silky, hair floating in the breeze. She quickly looked at the interpreter and croaked, "You, sir, must find this barbarous! You are white, yet, so familiar with the Indians. How can you stand this?"

Mr. Smith stared at the swinging bits of human skin and hair, then inhaled sharply. He did not answer and was so quiet we turned to investigate. His face was pale and strained. Suddenly, he dropped to his knees and covered his face with his hands.

"That is my sister's hair. I, I don't understand why they would attack her." Tears filled his eyes.

Both Nancy and I looked away, unsure what to do to help the distraught man.

Finally, Mr. Smith gathered his composure and before striding away said, "We must pray to God for peace. We must find a way to return you to your people."

Mrs. Morton and I were stunned by the scene. It held such frightening implications. We were unaware of Mitimoni's presence next to us. Neither of us heard her approach.

The medicine man's daughter said, "Soldiers kill twenty braves. You never go home." She looked at us compassionately and beckoned Willie to come into her arms.

Unaware of the solemnity of what we were witnessing, the baby grinned at the familiar face of the young woman whom he knew and trusted. Once in her arms, he snuggled against her shoulder. The child knew who his friends were among these fearsome people.

Holding Belle in my arms, I cringed again at the bloody scalps dangling in front of the lodges. I reached for Willie, though I knew my thin, weak arms would be no match against a frenzied crowd should they decide to take him. I knew the warrior deaths would be avenged. Seeking safety, I focused on the open prairie and watched as a small dust devil spun wildly across the landscape.

The families of twenty dead warriors would soon come for us! Jarred into action, I whirled past Nancy and screamed, "Run! Hide! Go to your lodge now!"

Running past large stacks of plunder recently taken from captured wagon trains, I heard the drums. Warriors strutted proudly in lady's silk cloaks and bonnets, then launched the ominous scalp dance. Warriors appeared from all edges of the village to perform brutal gyrations within its circling orbit.

Petrified, I charged through the opening of Big Crow's lodge and dove under the buffalo robe. Motionless, we hid, listened, and waited. The children slumbered and I...I willed my heart to beat and my lungs to breathe. We were forgotten as the tribes mourned through the night.

The next morning, Nancy and I fed little bits of corn meal to the children. Big Crow's son, Little Hawk, grabbed Mrs. Morton's arm and lifted her unexpectedly to her feet.

"Come," he said grinning mischievously. Alarmed, I followed as they strode out of camp toward a dry ravine. Nancy was reluctant and hesitated as he pulled her along.

"You no go home today. You buffalo hunter for tribe," he teased.

Pointing to a board set up against a large cottonwood tree, he instructed Nancy in the use of the weapon. But she cut him short and pulled the rifle from his hands.

Looking at him with a challenging stare, she slowly raised the stock to her shoulder. As she took aim, the brave explained menacingly,

"Chief say soldiers kill twenty warriors. Now you shoot mark. You no hit, you die."

Instantly, Nancy swung the barrel in the direction of the tree and fired. In that moment, an antelope appeared on a nearby hillside. She could not pass on this fortunate opportunity. Nancy aimed true and killed it with the first shot.

Now it was the brave's turn to be worried. She lowered the rifle and with one raised eyebrow, tipped her head in the direction of the target.

Never taking his eyes off her, the young warrior, mouth hanging open, slowly reached for the gun. Once he secured the firearm, he raced to the target. Upon his return, he held up the slab of wood which revealed what I already knew. The bullet pierced through its very center.

"Whe-Ho big hunter! No go home. You stay!" he scoffed.

Nancy stared at him and said emphatically, "No! I won't stay!" As she stomped away, I noticed a slight upturn of the corner of her mouth.

I returned to our lodge, careful to avoid the continuing scene of chaos as mourners for the dead chanted, moaned, keened, and slashed themselves. It would last all night.

The next five days and nights were spent in constant travel. Finally, we stopped next to a large stream. The Indians called the place "Big Timbers." It seemed the Indians used this popular spot for eons. The grass was thick and fed the hungry herds.

While gathering wood in the warm evening light, I was surprised to see two horses racing full speed toward me. Alarmed, I stepped behind a nearby tree. As the riders pulled to an abrupt stop a short distance from me, I recognized the winner of the race.

Nancy! She jumped off the sweating animal and ran toward me out of breath. Her face was painted in a most garish manner, the patterns resembling the fierce war paint of Dog Soldiers.

"They are making sport of me, Lucinda," she said shakily. "I'm afraid my shooting and riding skills are a source of great entertainment this afternoon."

Nancy gulped for air, then explained. "The chief ordered me to ride one of the swiftest horses in the village. I was to race this little savage. It was a run for my life, but my animal outdistanced his by a mile."

She breathed a sigh of relief.

I stared at the other racer and recognized Old Woman's grandson. I frowned at the loser. The enemy's torment of the young woman could not be justified.

The excited, young brave announced, "You! Come! Dog feast!"

He grinned at us; but my heart stopped as I contemplated the possibility of finding Ambrose's beloved pet served as our next meal.

Dog feasts were a frequent custom among the Cheyenne. The squaws wrapped a rope around the animal's neck, choked it to death then spread its body across hot coals to singe the fur off. Food. I needed to eat, but the thought of dog meat worsened my illness. I had eaten nothing since the prior morning when offered a bit of unidentified boiled meat. My stomach churned and I was nauseous. Thinking of roasting dogs on the village campfires, I knelt on the ground and vomited.

The thought of Butch reminded me of Ambrose and Dora. The grief of Dora's murder always shadowed me. I sat for a long time, breathing deeply and scanning the nearby cottonwoods for Ambrose and Butch.

"Come!" ordered our unwelcome companion.

We acquiesced and soon trudged back into camp. Nancy rides confidently like a man, I thought, but it is a dangerous competition. As if reading my thoughts, Nancy said, "Lucy, I am so afraid of these games. If I refuse to take part, I think they will kill me. If I join them, it only encourages more attention, and I want to be left alone."

My friend pensively continued alone in her thoughts as we walked. "I never told you this," she said softly. "On my second day in camp, I was forced to run the gauntlet." She stopped, staring directly at me. "Do you know what that is?"

I noticed her hands shake as she tucked her hair back up into its braid. "I have heard of such a thing. What happened?" I asked, fearing the answer.

"The Indians received a report. Soldiers captured their women, and they decided to exact revenge on me. They formed a gauntlet about four to five hundred feet long, which is a path lined on either side by men standing eight to ten feet apart. They put me on a horse and forced me to ride between the two lines as they struck me with whips, clubs, and sticks. They threw stones, lances, and anything else they could get their hands on."

I was dumbfounded. Little could have prepared me for the details she shared. "You must have been injured!"

"I was terribly bruised with cuts and scrapes from the waist down. The worst was the pain where stones struck my broken ribs and head."

I stared at the most courageous person I had ever met. "Nancy, you are alive! It is a miracle that you are still alive!"

We walked on silently digesting the challenges to survival. Upon returning to camp, I was relieved to see the dog laid out on the fire was not our friend Butch. I decided never to call our dog into camp again. I hoped he would run away! Run and never look back, Butch!

Mrs. Morton's reluctant agreement to join the Indians in games of skill had won both of us a meal, for which I was uneasily grateful. Handed a hot chunk of meat, I barely kept it down. The means to survival often altered the staunchest of protests from my innards. I ate slowly. My body needed strength, but illness left me tired and wasted. I concentrated on feeding the children.

Constant travel and hunger were coexistent parts of the tribal tempo. Wild swings from the mundane to the highest challenges left me unbalanced, constantly dreading the next corner.

It was the rhythm of our new life.

chapter twenty-three

Ruth's Ruin

August 1864
Quincy, Illinois

The Indian Atrocities.

We have received a copy of the St. Joseph Herald with an account of the late massacres on the plains by the Indians, from which we learn that Joseph Eubanks, who is probably known to many in the city, had been one of the victims having been killed on the 7th inst. near Uhleg's ranche between Atchison and Fort Kearney. At Oak Grove two men were killed and two wounded and At Eubanks' four miles from this place, three men, three women and one child was killed and a woman carried off prisoner. Murders had also been committed at several other places, making in all some thirty or forty who have been murdered on that route by these brutal red skins. Troops are now on their track and there is doubt but they will exterminate these devils incarnate before they are done with them.

The Quincy Whig, Quincy, Illinois
August 27, 1864

D enver City was dusty and arid hot. The sun sent its blaze down on the city's dirt roads. Horses kicked up red dust, and oxen moaned under the whip. Those who made their home along the front range of this new territory were preparing. Preparing for survival.

The wagon master was looking for George Eubank. He sprang up the stairs in front of the hotel two at a time. He had to find him. He knew George was still in Denver City and so was Bill Walton. They were getting ready to head back east along the trail to pick up a fresh load of supplies. Moving through the lobby and scanning the rooms, he entered the eating area and spotted them. Both of them.

George took a long drink out of his coffee cup as another swallow of eggs slid down Bill's throat. The look on the wagon master's face stopped everyone in his path. Folks were antsy as the threat of Indian attacks bore down on the city. His look of alarm concerned them, and their gazes followed him.

"Eubank!" His urgent tone cut as he moved toward their table. "Have you heard?"

"Heard what?"

"About your family and the ranche."

"No! What about them? Tell me!"

"Jeezus, Eubank! The Indians! It was a massacre. Your family is dead! They killed them all except Will's wife and kids. They took them and burned the ranche down. The bloody savages have killed and rampaged all along the trail!"

George and Bill looked at each other in stunned shock. The cup George held dropped from his hand and crashed on the hotel's china, shattering the plate. Both George and Bill jumped from the table, their chairs falling backwards to the floor.

The wagon master, with his head shaking slowly, looked at Bill Walton and said, "I am sorry about your sister, Bill. I pray she is rescued. Soon. George, we can take the trains back past your ranche as soon as the road opens."

"We have got to get to the ranche now, Bill!" George bellowed.

The wagon master shook his head and hollered, "Eubank, the trail is closed!"

"Like hell it is!" Walton yelled.

———·———

Quincy, Illinois, was a refuge for Ruth. The matriarch of the Eubank family preferred life in a city instead of the rugged pioneer west. Her persistence to visit their daughter Hannah and her family paid off. Joseph, Sr., finally agreed that a trip back east would improve her disposition.

Joe, Jr. drove his mother and sister Sarah as far as Atchison, Kansas. From there, they continued on to Quincy where Ruth's brother-in-law and wife were waiting to greet them. Ruth and Sarah were invited to stay at their home. Both were exhausted from the trip and the toil. They relished the opportunity to rest and socialize with family and friends.

As Ruth caught up on the War of the Rebellion, Sarah was busy reconnecting with old friends, her older sister Hannah, and Hannah's husband, Dan Walton.

Close to three weeks had passed since Ruth and Sarah arrived in Quincy. Joseph Sr.'s brother William put a hand to his forehead and leaned against the house. Dear Lord, he wondered, how am I to tell Ruth? His head shaking, he walked slowly into the house.

"Ruth, Sarah, would you both come into the parlor?" William asked as calmly as he possibly could.

"What is it, dear?" Sarah asked in a smiling tone.

"I need you to both sit down. Please."

"Ruth," William continued, taking hold of her hand. "Something terrible has happened. I picked up a telegram for you. It is from George."

Ruth's brows creased as concern prevailed over her small facial features. Hesitantly, she read the following:

> Mother STOP Indian attack on ranche STOP Father, Dora, boys all dead STOP Lucy and children, kidnapped STOP Headed to Quincy STOP Your loving son, George STOP

Ruth Eubank screamed as if a thousand blood-soaked arrows struck her heart—and fainted. Hopes and dreams of a new life were now full of horror and tragedy.

Later a neighbor arrived with the latest paper out of Kansas. Serpents on newspaper print continued their strikes as Ruth read from the *Marysville* (Kansas) *Enterprise,* August 10, 1864:

Indian Depredations at the West

> This morning our citizens were informed of the sad intelligence that the Indians of the Sioux tribes were committing depredations and murdering ranchmen and white settlers west of us, which greatly excited our people. This excitement has since increased every hour during the day by fresh statements from the west by eye-witnesses of the heinous crimes that these red devils have been committing. These Indians are supposed to be hovering around by the thousand, small portions of which make their appearance at sundry times. Some sixteen whites have been massacred and scalped as far as can be heard from. About dusk this evening teams with wagons loaded down with settlers and station keepers commenced flooding into our city, until it is literally crammed with excited beings, some of whom were personal witnesses of the horrible transactions. People in wagons, hacks, buggies, on foot, on horseback, and every way came in, and found accommodations wherever our friendly citizens could provide for them, and at this hour they are still arriving. Nearly the whole population of Washington county are either in this city or encamped near it.

The following is a list of the unfortunates:

At Eubank Station, near Oak Grove, ten of the Eubank family were massacred and scalped, the wife of Joseph Eubank only remaining, she being absent at the time. Patrick Burke and a Mr. Butler were killed at Pawnee Station. One was killed at Liberty Farm—name unknown. At Oak Grove Station a Mr. Kelly was shot while holding a conversation with an Indian standing in his door, and three or four others were wounded. At this station, some resistance was made by the whites, and one Indian was killed. Three miles east of Oak Grove a Mr. Ulick and another man—name unknown—were massacred. Mr. Burke was shot, scalped, and left by the Indians for dead, but was afterwards found, and when last heard from was breathing.

The principal scene of action was at the Eubank Station, some seventy-five miles west of us. There has been no communication of any source west of the scenes of disaster, and no overland mail and passenger coaches have arrived from above for four days, which gives us good reason to believe that similar outrages have been committed further up the road.

chapter twenty-four

Denver Panic

4 September 1864
Fort Lyon, Colorado Territory

*The outbreak of the Sheyennes (sic) and allied tribes at the present
time is a most unfortunate affair in more ways than one. It interferes
with travel to and from the mountains. It creates wide-spread alarm
even at points where there is no danger, and will doubtless very much
check emigration to Nebraska as well as to other Territories. But
worst of all, it will require so many soldiers to quell it that are needed
to put down the rebels. This Indian war is a God-send to the rebels.*

Nebraska Advertiser
Aug. 18, 1864

Major Edward Wynkoop sipped the tepid coffee in his tin cup and
noted the date on the calendar: September 4, 1864. The morning
sun blazing through his office windows promised another
overheated day on the eastern plains of Colorado Territory. He was the
commander of Fort Lyon. Surrounded by five hundred increasingly
hostile tribes, it was a tiny outpost located in the heart of Indian country.
Small parties of Cheyenne, Apache, Kiowa, Arapaho, or Comanche
Indians appeared occasionally on the horizon, startling the fort's
inhabitants. Their aggressive charges and vocal threats challenged
the soldiers to give chase, only to find their quarry gone without a trace.
Major Wynkoop's superiors issued "kill on sight" orders for all Indians
encountered by his troops; however, up to this point, no serious engagement had occurred.

Often at the start of a new day, his thoughts turned to his beloved
wife Louise. She and their toddler sons joined him without complaint at
this remote assignment. Louise's family lived over two hundred miles
away in Denver. The war between the states, and now the Indian war,
often separated the couple, but Louise never hesitated to follow him
across the frontier whenever possible. He wondered if she was pouring

herself a cup of coffee and thinking of him. He imagined her smile when she fondly called him Ned. He was thankful knowing she was nearby.

Ned thrust himself into the never-ending chores of reports, budgets, inspections, and the fortification of the ever-crumbling fort. He remembered his acute loneliness during years as an unmarried officer. His new family and their safety were foremost in his mind.

Unfortunately, relations between the whites and Indians began to splinter during the prior winter. The safety of those living in the Colorado Territory was the focus of Governor Evans. The strengthening of small forts dispersed over huge swatches of open plains was only a starting point. Established as defensive structures, the initial purpose was to maintain a union presence in the region, to deter the rebellion, and to secure the roads across which commerce and human traffic flowed. But now a war with the surrounding tribes appeared imminent, and the forts' uses were expanded.

In the springtime, the Cheyenne and Arapaho, who set up their traditional hunting camps along the Platte River, did not appear. Tensions between the soldiers of Camp Weld, the citizens of Denver, and the tribes had reached its breaking point. Within months, several violent and destructive events led to distrust between all factions. Negotiations broke down over lost or stolen livestock, and military attacks on Indian camps alarmed the natives, who found the actions to be unprovoked. Those responsible for the actual losses were almost never named. Sensational-ized newspaper articles and editorials inflamed the citizenry of Denver with fright and outrage. The consensus was the native population must be removed from the territory. They represented an obstruction to civilized progress.

Wynkoop sorted through the scattered papers on his desk and reflected on events which precipitated this Indian war. The first report he dug out and placed on top described the actions of a detachment of the Colorado Volunteers on April 9. Recent cattle thefts pointed to the Cheyenne; when a band was found, soldiers attacked. Though devoid of evidence of guilt, retaliation was justified. Three days later, troops fired on a group of Cheyenne Dog Soldiers. Again, no evidence of wrongdoing applied to the individual band. The next week, Indian raiders killed a Denver rancher, and the fight was on. Governor Evans and Colonel Chivington formulated a campaign to punish offenders.

Ned paused and gazed through his smudged office window at a group of soldiers repairing the old adobe walls surrounding the fort. An order by Colonel Chivington dated May 2 assigned Ned to Fort Lyon, formerly known as Fort Wise. His friend, Silas Soule, was promoted to captain and appointed second in command.

Chivington was their commander two years earlier when their union detachment squelched a Confederate invasion into New Mexico Territory. The victory at Glorietta Pass resulted in promotions for both Ned and Silas. Because of growing concerns that an Indian uprising was imminent, Chivington now turned to those he trusted. He assessed the upper Arkansas garrisons to be inadequate in manpower and preparation should they need to repel a rebel invasion or Indian attack. Rebel movements reported by southern scouts, plus the Indian threats, cemented Chivington's resolve to take a more offensive approach to the hostile Indian problem. He planned to increase attacks on the Southern Cheyenne so would need his best men in place.

Wynkoop was familiar with Fort Lyon, conveniently built near the Arkansas River. During his travels along the Smoky Hill Road, he passed the sandstone and adobe garrison. A newly built trading post on the nearby hill was aptly named Bent's New Fort. He read the order again, which included strict instructions to arrest George Bent, the son of the trader William Bent. He was suspected of holding rebel sympathies. Undoubtedly, his famous father had connections.

A sudden gust of wind blew dust through the open door and windows, causing the papers to flutter under their paper weights. Dirt devils were common in this dry country, but an open office was preferable in this heat. After taking a moment to straighten things, the major lifted a stack of newspaper articles. Governor Evans purposely published multiple correspondences in the Denver papers to prove he was protecting Coloradans. As Ned perused them, he read Evans' warning to the Commissioner of Indian Affairs:

> The largest Indian war this country ever had. Get me authority to
> raise a regiment of One Hundred Days mounted men.

Ned thought about the scarcity of horses and ordinance and wondered if an undisciplined ragtag group of citizens and frontiersmen would do more harm than good. He refolded the newspaper and set it aside. Reaching for the next article, his gaze turned once again to the activity in the parade grounds. The troops spent a great deal of time repairing the fort. It seemed impossible to avoid war with the natives. Wynkoop pondered the fort's vulnerability but determined to be ready. The young major opened another newspaper and read the communique from Governor Evans to General Curtis dated June 3:

It will be destruction and death for Colorado if our lines of communication are cut. We are now short of provisions and but few trains are on the way.

Ned shook his head in dismay. The escalation of hostilities and depredations certainly put pressure on the governor. However, his public communications were alarming the population. Wynkoop questioned the governor's motives and approach. The next article highlighted Evans' frustration as he urgently stressed their plight to the Secretary of War, Edward Stanton:

Our lines of communication are cut, and our crops...cannot be gathered by our scattered population. Large bodies of Indians are undoubtedly near to Denver, and we are in danger of destruction both from attacks of Indians and starvation.... It is impossible to exaggerate our danger.

From Ned's point of view, the citizenry must be terrified by now. He thought of Louise's parents living in Denver City. They must be fearful of the current situation with their daughter and her family marooned deep in Indian country. He made a mental note to send them a reassuring telegram, although he doubted it would override the enormity of the governor's words. Ned shifted in his seat and read Evan's final plea to General Curtis:

We look to you to keep the Platte Line open; otherwise our condition is hopeless.

Hopeless. That seemed rather strong language, but Ned doubted the government would heed Evans' sensationalized pleas for help. Military reinforcements in Colorado would deplete the forces of the Union Army. The Confederates were widening their swaths of death and destruction throughout Kansas and Missouri. The concentrated efforts of Union forces to quash the bloody rebellion were consuming resources and manpower. Assistance for the Indian troubles would not be forthcoming.

As Ned tidied up his desk, he noticed the most disturbing item dated June 11. The report of the Hungate family's murder stunned the public. They were farmers living near Fort Lyon. Wynkoop shivered slightly at the memory of the mutilated bodies purposely placed on display in Denver to the horror of its residents. The remaining farmers and ranchers in the area abandoned their homes and crops and fled to the safety of the city.

Wynkoop's thoughts returned to his own family, which gave him pause. Recent rumors of three captive white women held by the Cheyenne reached the fort. They were the victims of the attacks on the Little Blue Valley and Plum Creek one month earlier. He shuddered and absently stared out the window toward the commander's quarters where Louise and his child were safe. He knew captive women were subjected to a hellish existence. Every seasoned Indian fighter considered such a nightmare to be a fate worse than death.

chapter twenty-five

True News

4 September 1864
Fort Lyon, Eastern Colorado Territory

I was bewildered with an exhibition of such patriotism on the part of two savages, and felt myself in the presence of superior beings; and these were the representatives of a race that I had heretofore looked upon without exception as being cruel, treacherous, and blood-thirsty, without feeling or affection for friend or kindred.

Major Edward W. Wynkoop

Ned sat quietly in the stifling heat, mulling the plight of the kidnapped women. A knock on the door interrupted his pensive misgivings. Captain Silas Soule and Lieutenants Harden, Cramer, and Phillips stepped in followed by the Indian agent's son, Dexter Colley. Wynkoop's eyes narrowed as he studied the young trader for a moment. He decided to add an unpleasant item to the morning's agenda.

Samuel Colley and his son traded with the tribes, but Wynkoop was hearing disturbing reports of their activities. William Bent, the area's longest standing and most respected trader, recently recounted having seen boxes of goods marked U.S. UPPER ARKANSAS AGENCY among the traders' wares. Bent tactfully suggested the Indians were buying their own annuities. John Smith, the post interpreter and an active trader himself, might provide information to confirm the rumors. The matter required further investigation.

Major Wynkoop stood and acknowledged the men gathered around his small wooden desk. Moving stacks of reports, he brushed away the newly deposited coating of dirt. Today's meeting, he explained, would address dwindling post supplies and the ever-tightening budget by which the U.S. government required them to abide. In this time of war, the union responded to requests for increased finances with vague acknowledgments and more paperwork. The problems faced by fort occupants were batted away like annoying gnats as the giant war machine ground on in the southern states. Resources and manpower were scarce. Therefore, the furthest outposts were advised to make do—with a lick and a promise of improving conditions sometime in the ever-increasingly distant future.

Just as Wynkoop returned to his chair to address his officers, a familiar face appeared unexpectedly in the doorway. Sergeant Forbes of Company D, the oldest soldier at the fort, was assigned the task of delivering two soldiers to Denver. They were scheduled to muster out of the garrison. What brought him back to Fort Lyon in such short order?

"Sergeant? Can I help you?" asked a slightly perturbed Wynkoop.

"Major Wynkoop, Sir!" announced Forbes adding a crisp salute. "Dobbs, McCarthy, and I are back. Sir!" He seemed flushed and agitated.

Wynkoop stood and returned the salute. "What has happened, Sergeant?"

"On our way to Denver, we came upon them not too far from the fort and proceeded to capture these two Indians and this here squaw. I figured I ought to bring 'em back to the fort, as you'd know how to deal with 'em. Sir!" Forbes straightened his backbone and lifted his stubbly chin while staring, tight-lipped, at the ceiling.

The major felt his hackles rise as he processed the news. Wynkoop relied on Sarge as a capable and attentive assistant. Stationed together in more than one remote outpost during the past few years, the short, stocky, grizzled older man was a trusted and wise confidante. The major's reprimand was uncharacteristically harsh.

"Sergeant! You have disobeyed district orders. There are to be no prisoners. You are to kill all Indians!"

"Sir! We fired on 'em for sure! But during the engagement, I noticed one of 'em holdin' up a paper and making the sign of peace, like they was wantin' to talk to us. I decided the best thing was to bring 'em to you. Sir!" defended Sarge. He thrust a hand forward, which held a sturdy single sheet of rumpled paper. Puzzled, Wynkoop reached for it just as the sergeant added one last bit of critical information.

"The Injuns is waitin' outside yer office. Sir!"

The startled officers drew their weapons and swept past the flustered sergeant. As they dashed out the door, Dexter Colley quickly followed Major Wynkoop. All stopped in unison upon meeting the mounted enemy placidly sitting on their ponies at the bottom of the steps.

"You, there!" commanded Wynkoop. "Dismount from those horses immediately! Secure these prisoners, Sergeant!"

Dexter Colley reached out and placed a hand on the commander's forearm in a surprising action that stopped Wynkoop in his tracks.

His frowning expression silently challenged Dexter to remove his hand, or he would do it for him.

Colley slowly lowered his hand and said, "Major, I know these Indians. They are Southern Cheyenne friendlies who supply valuable services to my father." The young trader lowered his voice and added, "Major, he relies on them for information."

Samuel Colley, his father, had served as the Cheyenne Arapaho agent for years. His reports of tribal movements and intentions aided the military in keeping tabs on the surrounding bands.

Wynkoop nodded, then cleared his throat. "Bring the prisoners in, Sergeant."

The stoic faces of the Indians did little to betray their understanding of the danger faced. The officers quickly surrounded them and roughly shoved them up onto the landing and into Wynkoop's office. Their bound hands made it difficult for them to maintain balance.

The strong odors of the sweating soldiers and the newly arrived Indians permeated the small, stuffy office. The major stepped back and took inventory of the visitors. An older Cheyenne missing an eye seemed to be the leader. He was accompanied by a woman with gray-streaked hair and a tall, younger brave. The old Cheyenne started to speak but was silenced. It would be impossible to continue the conversation until the interpreter arrived.

In the meantime, Wynkoop picked up the missive delivered by Sergeant Forbes. Those in the room waited as he read the letter to himself. After a moment, he shared its contents with the group.

"It appears the Cheyenne Chief Black Kettle has dictated this rudimentary letter dated August 29, 1864, to an Edmund Guerrier and George Bent. It is intended for Agent Samuel Colley and me, as the military commander of Fort Lyon," related Wynkoop, glancing at those assembled.

"It communicates the wishes of Black Kettle and the Arapaho chief Left Hand. They admit to past hostilities but seek peace with the whites. They mention seven white captives in their possession."

Audible grunts escaped from the group of officers. Wynkoop continued to stare at the word "captives." He lifted his eyes to examine the surprised faces of those gathered.

"They wish to give them up—in exchange for our Indian prisoners."

The next sentence gave him pause.

"There are three Cheyenne Dog Soldier war parties out yet and two parties of Arapahos. They have been out some time and are expected back soon."

Major Wynkoop looked up as the shadow of John Smith crossed into the room through the open doorway. The trader, whose wife was Cheyenne, was fluent in the language.

"Do you know these Indians?" asked Wynkoop.

"Yes, I do," replied Smith, smiling at the visitors.

"The old man is Chief Ochinee, known as One Eye. His companion is Min-im-mic. Means Eagle's Head."

The woman, left out of the introductions, stared unabashedly at Wynkoop who was distracted by her boldness. Her stature was tall and erect. Her long braids draped down past her neck, falling to her waist. The ornamentation on her doeskin dress was attractively arranged along the yoke and hem. Wynkoop had never been in such close proximity with an Indian woman of her obvious rank. He concluded she must be the Chief's wife, so similar was their bearing and presence in the room.

Wynkoop returned his attention to One Eye.

"Did you not know that an Indian coming within range of this post was certain to be killed?"

"I knew it."

"How was it you dared to approach as you did?" queried the astonished major.

One Eye pulled his blanket around his shoulders. The major noticed a muscled, lean arm emerge from the folds and the long, sinewy fingers that grasped it, knuckles bulging with age. The chief stood with head high and paused before he addressed the officers. Wynkoop listened intently as John Smith delivered One Eye's words:

> There was a time when the young men of my nation could leave their Lodges containing wives and children, and go off to hunt the Buffaloe and the Antelope, when returning from the chase would find their families safe, happy, and contented; that time has passed, our white Brothers have made war upon us, have struck us, and we have struck them in return; they are many and we are few, they have arms and ammunition and cannon, while we have but Bows, Arrows and Spears. When we fight we have also to provide food for our women and children and protect them from the whites, if we leave our tepees to hunt the Buffalo to procure food for our families we return to find the places where our Lodges stood, desolate, our Camp has been alarmed our families fled; at all hours of the day or night, in bitter cold weather, and in the storm, our women and children are scattered over the Prairie, fearing the approach of your troops; they fall down and die, there is wailing and mourning throughout our whole nation. We have tried to make peace, thinking that our white brothers would take pity on us, and that our Great Father when he knew that his Red

Children were suffering and that they did not desire or wish to be at war with their white brothers would stretch forth his hand and say to his Soldiers—Stop; but whenever we have tried to let the white man know that we wanted peace, our young men have been fired upon and sometimes killed—I am young no longer, I have been a Warrior, I have not been afraid to die when I was young, why should I be when I am old, therefore the Great Spirit whispered to me and said: 'You must try and save your people' and I said to the Council of our head chiefs; give me true news, such as is written to carry to the Chief at the Fort, and I am here.

The Indian's single eye gazed intently at Wynkoop. Discomfited, the major asked again, "But did you not fear being killed when you advanced upon the fort?"

"I think I be killed, but know paper be found on dead body, you see it, maybe give peace my people again."

Wynkoop examined the chief's face closely, then asked, "Are your people sincere about relinquishing the white prisoners?"

"For risk of my life, I promise true words," was the solemn reply.

The major inclined his head to the younger man. "What about him?"

"Min-im-mic not let old One Eye go alone. If we die, he go with to Happy Hunting Grounds. Look down, see people happy again." Min-im-mic stepped forward to stand shoulder to shoulder with his elder companion.

It was in that moment Wynkoop felt a shift in his perception of these men. Such loyalty on the part of two natives was incongruent with what he thought he knew of their race. He painted them without exception as a brutal, sullen, and coldblooded people—void of sentiment for their fellow beings.

Now, however, a new thought crossed his mind. He was in the company of noble men—envoys of a people who baffled his logic and rocked the foundation of all he knew. He stood as a commander in the United States Army, yet the foe was eloquent and dignified. Wynkoop paused at this revelation, and his facial muscles relaxed.

One Eye saw the major's softening demeanor and took the opportunity to lay out the next part of his plan. "Come to camp," he invited. "We deliver you white captives—three women, four children."

Noticing the startled and concerned change on the major's face, One Eye held up his fingers and repeated, "Three women, four children."

Captives. Alive! To be delivered! It was an astounding new development and would not have come to light if Sergeant Forbes had obeyed orders and sent these men to the "Happy Hunting Grounds."

chapter twenty-six

Ocean of Doubt and Trust

Early September 1864
East of Fort Lyon, Colorado Territory

*...only the officers endeavoured to dissuade me from what they con-
sidered a rash enterprise, they not having the same confidence I had
in the good faith of the two Indians; but how could I doubt them after
the exhibition of their willingness to sacrifice themselves for the good
of their people.*

Major Edward W. Wynkoop

One Eye described the Grand Council to Major Wynkoop. Thousands of Indians from the far reaches of the Colorado and Kansas Territories lived in the village. Chiefs from various tribes and bands would assemble for the meeting. Despite the Indian emissary's assurances, Wynkoop and his officers were uneasy as they prepared to leave the relative safety of the fort.

Major Wynkoop had not issued a direct order, choosing to request soldier volunteers for this rescue expedition. Of course, his friend, Captain Silas Soule, stood steadfastly by his decision and committed to go, as did Lieutenant Cramer.

Wynkoop was confident in the good faith motives of the visiting Indians, but One Eye warned war parties still roamed the plains. The soldiers could expect trouble if they ran into Dog Soldiers. The recent arrival of infantry from New Mexico supplied reinforcement of fort security. The safety of Louise, his children, and the other families within the fort was secure.

Wynkoop and One Eye looked over crude maps in his office to decipher the details of the upcoming journey. The old chief finally placed his finger down on a tributary of the Smoky Hill River just inside the Kansas line and proclaimed it "Big Timbers." He described it as a favorite home of the Southern Cheyenne and Arapaho. The large cotton-woods and scarce underbrush made it a pleasant stop in their nomadic wanderings. By Wynkoop's calculations, the massive village was located one hundred forty miles northeast of Fort Lyon.

By One Eye's estimation, four thousand people populated the village. Fascinated by the map, he traced the pending movements of the tribes with his finger. He spoke with urgency. "We go! Camp move to other hunting grounds soon."

As the occupants of Fort Lyon learned of the women and children held captive in the large Indian encampment, the hearts of the soldiers ached with sympathy and remembrances of their own families and loved ones. These fond attachments were compounded by unpleasant reports of Indian depredations. The war parties were especially cruel in their dealings with women and children.

The whole garrison, including its officers, considered the expedition a foolish and risky endeavor. The reluctant soldiers predicted treacheries at every turn; yet, one hundred and twenty-seven men set aside their misgivings and accepted the mission. Under the leadership of the major, freeing the captives seemed a viable and honorable endeavor.

The next day, Major Wynkoop's column of cavalry soldiers and officers rode out of the fort. The small force of rescuers rode into the empty and desolate ocean of prairie. No banter was heard among the men. Behind them, three Cheyenne prisoners followed on their ponies with John Smith. Soldiers dragged along two howitzers to get the attention of marauders who might be watching.

The second day of travel was pleasant with cooler temperatures and a slight breeze. Silas whistled a tune as the column covered mile after mile without a single sighting of man nor beast. Toward the end of the day, the terrain became hilly. The dry grasses grew taller here, and the horses were glad of it. They foraged through the night on their lines as the restless men tried to sleep. The approaching autumn chilled the evenings, and temperatures dropped near freezing on the arid plains.

Late on the third day, the contingent dropped into a wide cut in the landscape through which a stream shimmered. The torrid air emanating from the floor of the gorge baked the riders. To the east, blue curtains of rain fell beneath billowy clouds rising vertically. Yet, not a drop relieved the dusty troops.

Early September was a contradiction of itself—stifling days followed by chilly dry nights. Pointing to brilliant yellow-leaved cottonwood trees in the distance, Sergeant Forbes described it as "Indian Summer."

"Silas," said Wynkoop as he leaned close to his friend. "We must try to secure all the captives. They will not survive a winter in this country. And it is coming soon, I'm afraid."

Silas Soule nodded somberly. "Think of it, Ned. Women and children suffering from hunger and cold as the tribes try to subsist on limited government annuities. With much of the game gone in this region, the hunting will be slim pickings. It's been a long drought. I haven't seen enough game to keep a coyote alive."

The two friends pondered the plight of the captives privately as they trotted through powdery, rust-colored dust in a parched creek bed. Wynkoop urged his mount to quicken its pace, hoping to alleviate the urgency in his heart.

"We must be getting close to the Big Timbers," said Silas. His dirt-caked face rimmed two bright blue eyes. He smiled warmly at Ned, who returned a nervous grin.

"I think so, Silas. The real dance begins now, eh?"

Silas looked over his shoulder.

"The men are getting jumpy. I'm surprised they haven't bolted for the fort at this point. Let's stop for water and give them a rest. It should calm them."

The thirsty and tired men dismounted. Horses bent their necks and waded into the water, splashing and tossing their heads. The shade thrown by large cottonwood trees offered a cool retreat as the soldiers talked quietly among themselves. Their eyes constantly roamed the landscape for any hint of movement.

Wynkoop offered water from his canteen to One Eye who held up a hand in polite refusal and patted his fully replenished buffalo bladder. For the first time since leaving, the major spoke with the old one about the upcoming council. He tried to hide the fact he was second-guessing himself. Wynkoop genuinely respected the man and tried to appear confident in their joint effort for peace. However, Ned was adrift in an ocean of doubt versus trust.

Without acknowledging the obvious, Wynkoop knew his soldiers would be overwhelmed should an engagement ensue. He asked One Eye if the chiefs were willing to "bury the hatchet."

The Indian showed his appreciation of the expression by responding to the interpreter with a grin, but the major's nerves were rattled. He wished he had chosen his words better.

"When you arrive, chiefs desire to meet you, take you by hand, and smoke peace pipe. We close now. It be good to make camp soon and send word."

The warrior's good eye stared north.

Wynkoop nodded, then stood and gathered the reins of his horse's bridle. Swinging into the saddle with one fluid motion, he signaled it was time to mount up. He motioned for Min-im-mic and John Smith to ride next to him.

"Mr. Smith," Wynkoop opened the conversation. "How is it that One Eye came by his name? He obviously has lost it under duress, but I wonder about the circumstances."

John Smith, who was a quiet man, warmed to the story as a means of alleviating the growing tension. "There was an attack by Kiowa Indians upon a wagon train led by William Bent. He was returning to his fort from Santa Fe with wagons loaded with trade supplies. The Kiowa ambushed them in a canyon. Fortunately for Mr. Bent, a Cheyenne hunting party was in the vicinity watching the Kiowa. When it appeared they would be routed, the Cheyenne charged down the rim of the canyon and drove the Kiowa off. In the skirmish, One Eye was injured. He stopped a club from crushing Mr. Bent's head and was clobbered instead. The eye socket smashed."

Wynkoop digested this information as they rode along, then turned back and motioned to Min-im-mic. The young Indian smiled widely and trotted to join them.

"Mr. Smith, please tell Min-im-mic I want him to ride ahead to the village. Tell the chiefs I have come because I read their letter. We will ride west one mile and halt for the night. Return to us as soon as possible."

Wynkoop watched carefully as Smith translated the message. The young brave nodded vigorously and charged off in the direction of the still unseen Indian camp.

Later, after those under his command settled in for the night, Min-im-mic returned with news the Indians were aware of their presence. Wynkoop doubled his original order of five lookouts to ten per shift through the night. He slept little. Tomorrow would bring him, and those who put their trust in him, face-to-face with the enemy.

In the enveloping darkness, his restless dreams revealed the enemy: a benign, old Indian with one eye transformed into a horde of young, strong, adept warriors complete with war paint, weapons, and a singular aggrieved spirit. The Indians multiplied in his dreams until thousands of angry aggressive braves rode at him thrusting their lances over and over…each strike more painful than the last.

Wynkoop sat bolt upright in a cold sweat panting. Calming his pounding heart, he stared into the darkness. He could hear nothing but the muted stampings of the horses and muffled snoring of those blessed enough to sleep.

Ned forced his mind to replay the events of the past few days as he logically came to the same conclusion. This mission was noble. But had his emotions overruled his head? Certainly, they had.

As a soldier, he submitted to a higher authority. Yet he had disregarded the chain of command by making a snap decision and placing his men in imminent danger. On the other hand, he could not pass up the opportunity to secure the captives. And sooner was certainly better than later. If he missed this chance to save the women and children, he would regret it. He could hardly imagine their current plight.

In the end, logic overcame doubt. He remembered One Eye's astonishing bravery and eloquent speech. A bemused Wynkoop humbly noted his thought processes coming full circle with a surprisingly profound glimpse into the Cheyenne way.

A man's rash and determined willingness to sacrifice himself for the good of his people seemed a prevalent characteristic among members of *both* races.

However, this would be a matter of life or death.

chapter twenty-seven

Emissary

10 September 1864
Eastern Plains, Colorado Territory

That tough but a small Chief, he had a band of Warriors who would obey him, and if any attempt was made to injure me or those who accompanied me, he with his band would defend us against his own people.

Major Edward W. Wynkoop

M ajor Ned Wynkoop stood naked near a concealing clump of salt cedars. A faint glow spread across the eastern horizon. The hairs on his body stood on end as the morning freshness washed over him. He splashed a little of the remaining water in his canteen over his face and neck after shaving. The drips and drabbles slid down his legs, and he wished for a more thorough cleansing.

Standing at over six feet, three inches, his broad shoulders and athletic build combined to create a figure which towered over most. A tanned face revealed blue eyes set wide within creases that come from a life spent outdoors. The major's stoic demeanor held no guile. His men found him to be fair, reasonable, and trustworthy. Possessing a military bearing which belied his twenty-seven years, his maturity was molded and pressed by years of frontier life.

The entire camp was uneasy and restless the night before. Small cook fires warmed their meals and were extinguished before dark as a precaution. The land's inhabitants were aware of their presence, but there was no need to advertise.

No one slept. Warm and silent, stars delivered only a meager light from the moonless sky. Sensing the nearness of the large Indian camp, he wandered the perimeter of the compactly organized bivouac—watching, listening, and watching some more. The village was invisible from this position, and a good thing, too, for his small band of brave and hearty volunteers might run for the hills at first sight. There was close and then there was too close.

Now, with the dawn of a new day, he involuntarily swiveled his head to the north for a quick look. The landscape was unchanged since the last one hundred times he checked.

A dusty pile of travel garments lay folded on a stone next to a sizeable sage bush. Wynkoop reached into his bag and was rewarded with an armful of fresh military garb. His best dark blue uniform, complete with gold buttons and braids, made the journey intact. With a solemnity due his rank, the major ceremonially straightened each piece of clothing as his persona filled its shell. He struggled to pull on the worn boots as he leaned against the stone. The jingle of his spurs joined the songs of the morning birds.

Once completely vested, the full dress of an army commander strengthened his belief in its granted authority. He straightened to his full height, forced his shoulders into the seams of the jacket, and listened. Nature performed its symphony with simple efficiency unconcerned by unfolding events.

Major Wynkoop waited in the peace of the morning, then swore under his breath. It was a gamble and his men trusted him. But did he trust himself?

Reaching into his saddle bag, he retrieved Black Kettle's letter.

Cheyenne Village Aug. 29th/64
Maj. Colley

Sir
We received a letter from Bent wishing us to make peace We held a cousel in regard to it all came to the conclusion to make peace with you providing you make peace with the Kiowas Commenches Arapahoes Apaches and Siouxs. We are going to send a messenger to the Kiowas and to the other nations about our going to make with you. We heard that you some prisoners in Denver. We have seven prisoners of you which we are willing to give up providing you give up yours. There are three war parties out yet and two of Arapahoes. They have been out some time and exspect now soon. When we held this counsel there were few Arapahoes and Siouxs present. we want true news from you. in return, that is a letter

Black Kettle
& other Chieves
Brought to Ft Lyon Sunday sept 4th 1864 by One Eye—

To represent the United States military and the Great White Father in Washington is a soldier's mission; but to do so without the approval of one's superiors limited the gallant endeavor to an implausibility. Wynkoop reasoned for the thousandth time—the essence of his actions might save the lives of women and children. The remoteness of the operation coupled with the urgency of the situation demanded a rational decision.

What was it Silas Soule always said? It is easier to ask forgiveness than to wait for permission.

The mustache covering the corner of his mouth twitched at the thought of his humorous comrade and friend. Silas tackled danger with a quip or a saying which bolstered those around him and lightened any mood. Silas was indeed a man of quiet integrity and dry wit—the perfect combination for a soldier.

Contemplating the task ahead, Wynkoop wondered...would this day be his last? He might accomplish the dubious mission of stepping into a tangle of volatile, angry Cheyenne and Arapaho warriors, but would his men live to tell about it?

The Indians' numbers and skills vastly overshadowed those of his small but able team. The Fort Lyon's troops had volunteered in the heat of emotion, but the consequences were only now coming to fruition. He understood their doubts and felt the weight of their trust in his abilities.

Wynkoop hefted the saber in his hand, testing its balanced weight. The sword completed his military vestments but would not go with him today. Words were his chosen weapons—to be used carefully and persuasively.

Finished with preparations, Wynkoop heaved the pack onto his back with a heavy sigh. He adjusted his hat forward and relief washed over him. The anticipation was over. Now the challenge would truly begin. The undertaking was fraught with contradictions, but the sameness of the morning ritual settled his nerves. He was ready.

Before turning to camp, Ned stood motionless and watched the sun's appearance on the horizon. A growing wall of strength connected him with the light of goodness some said abided in all men. He closed his eyes briefly and felt his dear wife beside him. Her last kiss lingered on his cheek. A light breeze whispered promises.

The sinister thoughts that hounded him through the night evaporated. A barrier of prayerful protection propelled him forward. Women and children were in peril and waiting for him. This day would be about them. He refolded the letter and placed it inside his breast coat pocket. With a renewed mind, he focused on the day's single purpose.

The bright orb rose higher and colored the tinted hills, then quickly washed the plains in a shimmering glare. Major Edward W. Wynkoop inhaled deeply and stepped into his future.

———— • ————

Eight hundred warriors screaming in unison threw the column of soldiers into confusion. Horses bolted, spun, and reared as their startled riders tried to exert control over the melee. Wynkoop's detachment had trotted a mere four miles when an intimidating battle line of Cheyenne and Arapaho warriors emerged over a rise. The mounted, painted, armed, and intimidating welcome party appeared as one enormous, crawling organism—bows raised, arrows nocked, rifles cocked.

Wynkoop ordered his troops to fan out across the flat expanse of prairie. Like a zipper opening, alternate riders turned left, then right. Artillery was hauled to positions along the ridge for effect, but all knew the heavy cannonballs were useless against a swift and savvy rival.

Regaining a semblance of order, the one hundred and twenty-seven soldiers responded to the call to advance upon the agitated line of an overpowering enemy. They marched forward boldly until the major called a halt. He motioned for One Eye to proceed forward with instructions: It was understood the tribes wanted to end the war and give up their white prisoners. The old chief nodded, then winked his good eye as a token of sincerity and rode off at a gallop. As the tiny man on the thin pony reached the battle-ready horde, he disappeared into the milling throng.

Exposed and vulnerable, Wynkoop remained steady, but his troops exchanged looks of distress—their anxiety caused the horses to toss their heads and side-step; the hardware on their bridles chimed in the clear morning air. The adversaries brandished weapons, shouted threats, and screeched obscenities. Reaching a crescendo, the major keenly waited for a sign of his link to the chaos. Were they betrayed? An attack appeared certain.

Major Wynkoop instinctively raised his hand to hold the battle line. Moments passed. Then he detected a lone voice rising from the enemy, one tongue expressing words above the howling din. The high-pitched foe stilled as the confrontation was swept into a tense pause.

"What soldiers want?" the voice demanded. A chief with a colossal eagle feather headdress appeared between the lines of mounted braves astride an equally massive white horse. Its mane and tail were adorned with ornaments and feathers which spun in the breeze.

Wynkoop inhaled sharply at the sight. The large man was almost royal in his presentation.

The chief rode forward.

Min-im-mic urged his mount closer to the major. "Black Kettle, chief of Cheyenne," he announced.

Wynkoop nodded an acknowledgement and looked to John Smith. The interpreter declared loudly in Cheyenne, "The white chief comes to talk."

With snorts of derision from those surrounding him, the voice asked loudly, "Why bring soldiers and cannon? You ready to fight!"

Wynkoop did not wait for Smith to translate but answered boldly, "I come prepared to defend myself in case of treachery!"

This response caused the Indians to shout and wave their weapons menacingly. The inferior numbers of soldiers settled their horses, grasped their weapons, and prepared for the massacre sure to come.

Inexplicably, shouts turned inward as the Indians argued among themselves. The energy and tension eased within the throngs of warriors. As they quieted, Chief Black Kettle announced he would lead the soldiers to a place where they must wait. Ostensibly, it was far enough to keep his people safe and near enough for the soldiers to remain under supervision.

Wynkoop ordered his troops to fall back at the direction of the chief. Forming a column, the detachment was immediately surrounded by hundreds of warriors. By their sheer numbers, the Indians controlled the flow of riders and wagons. As animals and men churned through the turn, the helpless soldiers realized they were captive and at the mercy of these commanders of the plains.

One Eye, the emissary who assured their protection, was nowhere to be seen.

Having no choice, Wynkoop ordered his men to comply as the Indians escorted his entire command back two miles. He established a defensible posture by circling the supply wagons. As the troops worked, they noted with alarm a large group of braves dismounting. The antagonists were settling in and planning to stay. Chief Black Kettle disappeared with a sizable portion of the warriors, who rode back from whence they came.

John Cramer soon arrived with news it was time to hold council. Major Wynkoop, Captains Soule and Cramer, Lieutenant Phillips, and the interpreter Smith prepared to leave. A contingent of warriors guided them to the south fork of the Smoky Hill River. The Indian village appeared in the distance on Hackberry Creek. Wynkoop indicated to his companions they were likely in Kansas Territory now.

Approaching a large grove of trees near the river, Wynkoop noticed Indians finishing preparations in a businesslike manner.

As natives converged on the spot, news of the officers' arrival spread quickly. Wynkoop's men were neither greeted nor acknowledged but told to dismount, sit, and wait. The small group of officers strained to maintain composure. It was imperative they show no sign of weakness.

Wynkoop watched as chiefs in large headdresses assembled in a circle, lesser-ranked braves sitting behind them. Interestingly, he noticed a buckskin-clad George Bent walking with the chiefs. The eyes of the two men met as Bent nodded at the major, but the half-breed remained silent. Wynkoop carefully surveyed the faces in the council circle but found no other visage he recognized. Where were Black Kettle and One Eye?

The heat of the day, the demands of the morning, and the uncertainty of the occasion were taking a toll on Wynkoop. Sweating, he opened his canteen, and placed it to his parched lips. After draining its contents, he settled to formulate thoughts into words.

It was time to speak peace.

It was time to secure captives.

It was time to stand in the gap.

Finally, the emissary One Eye appeared through the trees followed by four chiefs whose honored presence quieted the council. They took their places within the primary circle and One Eye walked to the military representatives.

"Come," he said. "It is time."

The major stood up confidently, straightened his hat with both hands, and walked toward the assemblage. Silas stood to follow until a dismissive wave by One Eye stopped him. Silas was not invited.

Smiling at his friend, Ned said, "Thanks, Silas. I will go."

chapter twenty-eight

Until the Sun Has Kissed the Prairie

10 September 1864
Big Timbers Indian Camp
Hackberry Creek, Kansas Territory

Return upon the trail on which you came with your soldiers, until the sun has kissed the prairie, there camp and remain until another sun has gone. Before that time passes you will have news from Make-tava-tah.

Cheyenne Chief Black Kettle

A flurry of activity rippled through the village. Mitimoni said soldiers were coming to meet with the chiefs. Fearing troops would take us by force, Nancy, Laura, and I were forced to crawl under buffalo robes in Left Hand's teepee. Willie was carried away by Mitimoni despite my protests. She left with assurances he would be cared for.

Before stepping out of his lodge, Chief Left Hand motioned to his wife by slashing a finger under his throat in demonstration. She was to kill us if we made a sound. Not daring to move, we waited. Soon English syllables and words floated past us in jumbled confusion. Was it possible the soldiers were negotiating for us?

Sweat dripped into my eyes. To relieve a leg cramp, I shifted under the stifling buffalo hide. A quick kick and guttural growl reminded me to make no sound. Frozen in place, I fantasized about freedom and an end to the nightmare.

The embers of the small fire glowed in a shallow pit ringed by rocks. Major Wynkoop and John Smith sat on rugs within the council circle. This defenseless position was even more precarious by the absence of their weapons.

An entourage of chiefs approached through the trees and took their places of honor. As each man entered the circle, John Smith identified him by name. The major sat motionless, focused on committing each name to memory.

"Bull Bear, White Antelope, Big Wolf, Sitting Bear. These are chiefs of the Cheyenne people." He continued as another group of Indians entered the circle. "Chiefs Left Hand, Little Raven, Neva, Big Mouth—leaders of the Arapaho people." Wynkoop noticed medallions on ribbons hanging around the necks of several chiefs.

Lastly, Black Kettle stepped into the circle and sat near the major, who noted the chief's chiseled stone-like face. The man was strong but older. He reminded Wynkoop of a bull elk reaching the end of his prime. A bronze medallion dangled on his chest—a gift from the Great Father in Washington, D.C. The engraved image was not visible in the leaf-speckled shadows afforded by the cottonwood trees overhead. Wynkoop wondered how the visit to a modern city affected the dominant leader's perspective on the lives of his people in a changing world.

The council waited in silence, and a pipe was prepared. Lit by a fire brand, the Indians passed it around the main circle. Wynkoop pulled gently on the pipe and was pleasantly surprised by the sweet flavor of its contents. All eyes watched as he nodded appreciatively and handed the pipe to the next man. Noticing the ease with which each man blew the contents of his lungs into the air, Wynkoop controlled his exhalation to prevent a coughing spasm.

Finally, White Antelope spoke to Wynkoop. "What words does Tall Chief speak?"

John Smith noticed a look of confusion on the major's face.

"Major, the Cheyenne have given you the name Tall Chief because you tower over most others."

Wynkoop remained seated and looked around at the glaring, unfriendly eyes. He reached into his chest pocket which caused a stir. Distrust permeated the grove in the trees. Slowly and carefully, he pulled the contents from his coat and held up Black Kettle's letter for all attendees to view.

"Is this message intended for me by your authority?" the major asked in a direct manner.

Black Kettle nodded an affirmative response.

Shaking out the paper, Wynkoop began. "My objective for meeting with you is to talk relative to the proposition you have stated herein." Grunts of acknowledgement circled the council. "You state a desire for peace and to deliver up the white captives in your possession. I do not wish to deceive you. I am not a big enough chief to settle terms of peace, but I wish you to deliver into my hands the white captives. This would be the strongest guarantee my people could have. It would show your sincerity to live in amity with your white brothers."

Wynkoop summoned his most authoritative tone. This was no time to show weakness. "Should you respond to my demands, I assure you I will use my utmost endeavors to establish amicable relations. I will take with me such chiefs as you select to represent you, and we will proceed to a higher chief than myself in Denver City. I have no doubt that after the proper representations, this big chief, Governor Evans, will grant you the boon you desire."

Instantly, he regretted his less than diplomatic tone, for the ferocious faces of those assembled caused the hair to stand on the back of his neck. Dusky eyes flashed, and the angry exchanges between those seated seemed akin to badgers snarling over a kill. It was obvious he had said something wrong; they were incensed. He glanced at his uniformed companions, who shifted into more alert positions. Fear outlined each soldier's strained face.

A soldier riding into the grove at a dead run interrupted the council. He threw himself out of the saddle before bringing his mount to a complete stop. The man's complexion appeared slightly green. It was Lieutenant George Hardin, the man left to oversee camp set-up.

"Sir!" he stammered breathlessly. "I need to speak to you immediately!"

Wynkoop's concern increased as he stepped outside the circle to meet this latest crisis. The officer listened quietly to the agitated messenger and his face flushed. Blood pumped loudly through the arteries in his neck.

"The warriors have invaded and taken control of the camp!" exclaimed Hardin hoarsely. "They are verbally assaulting the men, threatening us with their weapons, and raiding the provision wagon. They surrounded the howitzers, filled them with stones, and ordered us to stay away." He gulped, then added, "There must be five hundred of them and the situation is spiraling out of control. We will have a disaster on our hands before you return."

Major Wynkoop directed his fury at this new turn of events. Despite his controlled demeanor up to this point, he now angrily interrupted the proceedings and demanded the interlopers be forced to leave the military camp at once. As John Smith interpreted the exchange, Black Kettle slowly stood. He spoke directly to the interpreter. Without explanation or acknowledgement of the major's concerns, the chief left the council.

"Make-tava-tah will ride to the white camp with the Lieutenant," explained Smith. All watched the chief ride away in a cloud of dust.

Wynkoop later learned Black Kettle chastised the braves and forced the marauders out of the camp. As a parting gift, the raiders set fire to the prairie. Amid the smoke and flames, the soldiers hitched up the wagons and made a hasty retreat. Riding hard twelve miles to the west, they halted and uneasily fortified a new camp. They reluctantly agreed to wait until the officers returned from the council, though they were unsure it was prudent to be sitting ducks should relations sour.

Wynkoop rejoined the council and waited as it settled after the disturbing disruption to proceedings. The tension within the council members was unmistakable, but the unflappable major spoke again and reiterated his hopes that trouble could be avoided. He suggested they should try to understand each other and strongly emphasized his desire to secure the white prisoners, so he might return them to their homes.

Suddenly, out of the corner of his eye, Wynkoop noticed an enormous Indian spring to his feet. Bull Bear, O-go-ah-nac-co, chief of the Dog Men, was on him within two steps and motioned emphatically for the soldier to stand. Wynkoop rose to his feet and placed himself directly in front of the stocky, barrel-chested warrior whose nose and hooded eyes were inches from his face. Neither man backed away.

The two silently surveyed one another until Bull Bear placed a finger on Wynkoop's chest and pushed. The major firmly stood his ground, solid as a statue. The Indian pointed his finger accusingly again at Wynkoop's nose and shouted angrily, "This white man thinks we are children, but I tell him we are not papoose or squaw. We are men, warriors, chiefs. We say to him we want to trade. We have given many horses and many buffalo robes to other tribes for these white prisoners. We now say we will trade them for "peace?" And this white soldier chief says, 'Give me the white prisoners, and I will give you nothing in return.' Does he think we are fools that he comes to laugh at us?"

A rattled John Smith translated. "I am talking for our lives now, major," he whispered. "Big Bear's brother, Lean Bear, was murdered last May while trying to stop a military attack upon his village."

Other chiefs echoed Bull Bear's sentiments as their ire rose to a fevered pitch. All pointed and gestured at Wynkoop suggesting his death could not come soon enough.

Wynkoop called out to George Bent to verify the accuracy of Smith's translation and asked him to translate should it become necessary. Bent agreed as the uproar subsided.

Bull Bear drilled the major with dagger-like eyes before sauntering to his place in the circle. He sat down and swept a hand across the gathering as a signal for talks to proceed.

The Arapaho chief, Left Hand, was the next man to stand and face Tall Chief. Wynkoop recognized him as taking part in the amateur theater group he and Louise formed in Denver three years earlier. Left Hand was fluent in English and performed his lines perfectly during the production of *Lady of Lyons*. Afterwards, he gave an impassioned speech asking the whites and the Indians to find common ground. He eloquently appealed to the crowd and asked there be no more talk of fighting Indians. His message was well received during peaceful times. Wynkoop suppressed a grin at the memory.

Left Hand spat, "I have been peaceful and have tried to learn the white man's ways. This summer I tried to return stolen stock to Fort Larned but was fired upon as I approached. After that, I have followed the war path with the Dog Men and Kiowas. How can peace be found where there is no good faith?" Without waiting for a reply, the Arapaho chief returned to his seat.

Next, Nah-ka-he-se, Little Raven, declared he agreed with Bull Bear, and no peace could be found.

This set off another round of shouting as the disgruntled council members unified in their anger toward Tall Chief. The agitated Bull Bear sprang to his feet, his agility belying his size. He hollered, "We do not trust the whites. The time has come to fight!"

Smith's eyes shifted anxiously from face to face. He ceased to translate, and Wynkoop drew his own conclusions. Glancing around, Tall Chief was unsure which warrior would deliver the initial blow. His guts twisted as the tension reached new heights. His doubts and misgivings were founded in truth. He questioned his judgment once again.

Wynkoop drew in a deep breath to steady his nerves. Through the clamor, he noticed One Eye approach from a seat outside the council circle. As the old chief advanced, sunlight glinted off the tomahawk in his hand. Wynkoop raised a hand to shield his eyes from the glare and realized One Eye was passionately shouting above the melee. Though not entitled to a seat at council, the lesser chief insisted he be heard.

One Eye stepped into the circle and stolidly held his ground. Voice raised, he said, "I am the one who carried the message to Tall Chief. I offered my life for the welfare of our people. I am the same who pledged my faith to this white man that he may come and go unharmed—whatsoever might be the result of the council's decision. I will offer to divide my own horses if any of you who are so offended will be quiet. I am a small chief, but I have a band of warriors who will obey me if any one of you tries to injure Tall Chief or his companions. We will defend them against our own people!"

A collective uproar ensued as warriors leapt to their feet while reaching for hidden weapons.

Black Kettle stuck out a hand from within his blanket and silenced the council with a single swipe. He spoke quiet words to One Eye, who returned to his place in the outer ring.

Bull Bear stood his ground, then to save face, he declared, "I go take two One Eye's finest horses. Then I quiet." He stomped off toward the herds satisfied with having his say and profiting from it as well.

Black Kettle slowly stood, gathered his blanket around him, and walked to Tall Chief. Reaching out, he tightly grasped the soldier's hand. Turning a complete circle as if dancing, the great leader positioned himself shoulder to shoulder with the representative of the United States military. Then Black Kettle embraced Tall Chief twice and led him into the center of the council ring. Black Kettle addressed the assemblage as John Smith spoke the following words for the chief:

> This white man is not here to laugh at us, nor does he regard us as children, but on the contrary unlike the balance of his race, he comes with confidence in the pledges given by the Red man. He has been told by one of our bravest warriors, that he should come and go unharmed. He did not close his ears, but with his eyes shut followed on the trail of him whom we had sent as our messenger. It was like coming through the fire, for a white man to follow and believe in the words of one of our race, whom they have always branded as unworthy of confidence or belief. He has not come with a forked tongue or with two hearts, but his words are straight and his heart single. Had he told us that he would give us peace, on the condition of our delivering to him the white prisoners, he would have told us a lie. For I know that he cannot give us peace, there is a greater Chief in the far off camp of the White Soldiers who must talk to one even still mightier, to our Great Father in Washington, who must tell his Soldiers to bury the hatchet, before we can again roam over the prairies in safety and hunt the Buffaloe. Had this white soldier come to us with crooked words, I myself would have despised him; and would have asked whether he thought we were fools, that he could sing sweet words into our ears, and laugh at us when we believed them. But he has come with words of truth; and confidence, in the pledges of his red brothers, and whatever be the result of these deliberations; he shall return unharmed to his lodge from whence he came. It is I, Make-ta-va-tah, who says it. Return upon the trail on which you came with your soldiers, until the sun has kissed the Prairie, there camp and remain until another sun has gone; before

that time passes you will have news from Make-tava-tah; our Chiefs will spend the night in Council.

Black Kettle turned to Major Wynkoop and clasped his hand firmly, then walked to Silas Soule and shook his hand in a gesture that diffused the general animosity. This proved to be the turning point in negotiations. Suspicious and angry expressions tempered as sanity returned to the council grove. Following Black Kettle's example, the chiefs stood and approached Wynkoop. Kindly faces surfaced as each extended his hand to Tall Chief and said, "How! How!" It seemed a resolution had been reached.

Major Wynkoop and his relieved escort mounted their horses and quickly galloped onto the prairie with increasing concern over the fates of the men left behind. As the council ground faded from view, the soldiers picked up the pace along the burned-out trail to their original bivouac only to find it deserted. The tracks of the horses and wagons were plain. Major Wynkoop discerned his brave volunteers wasted no time in marching miles to put distance between them and their agitated foe.

Meanwhile, unnoticed by the soldiers, three captive women stood among the trees and watched their departure....

—————————

The heavy buffalo robes were thrown off our prone bodies, and fresh air rushed over us in cooling waves. Nancy, Laura, and I stood, blinked, and wiped the sweat from our faces. Sharing confused looks, we realized the soldiers were nowhere to be seen. Nothing was said as Mitimoni handed a content Willie to me and urged us to follow her. We obediently trailed her through the fallen timber, heads down to watch our steps. Leading us to the edge of the trees, Mitimoni stopped and pointed.

The distant scene enveloped us in a dazed and desolate despair. The United States army officers were leaving the village. Groaning, we clapped our hands over our mouths, for to cry out would have meant instant death. Dejectedly, we watched our means of freedom grow smaller and smaller in the haze. Sneering braves passed us in the trees, deliberately bumping us. The evidence of pain on our faces only served to feed their cruelty.

Mitimoni stood with us a long time until only a whisper of dust settled on the distant path of our dashed hopes. She gathered our hands and squeezed them. We gazed sorrowfully at each other but said nothing. Then she led us back to our respective captor's lodges.

I sank slowly onto the hide inside the teepee with Willie asleep in my arms. I was alone. It seemed as if time stopped. My brain tried to conjure sorrow, but I was left cold, numb, and tearless.

The weeks of captivity and mistreatment challenged every bone in my body, but now the fight within me physically collapsed. I thought of Will. Which one of us would have prevailed in this wilderness of strange faces? Perhaps, I should have been the one left on the sand bar. The will to go on drained quietly out of my soul.

———•———

The day's events unnerved Wynkoop. The tired officer understood why his men abandoned him and the escort. He, Silas, and the other officers swiftly covered twelve miles to find his spooked company hunkered down. They were discussing their next move. Should they leave the major and his cohorts to their fate? Or return to collect their mutilated bodies?

As the small entourage of officers approached the circled wagons, Sergeant Forbes walked out to meet them. Anxiously awaiting their return, he expressed elation at their unscathed condition—half expecting them to have been dismembered along the way.

"Major Wynkoop! Sir!" he hailed.

Approaching his dismounted commander, he summed up the crisis in his usual brief analysis. "I am afraid we have a situation in the camp. I thought I would warn you before you found yourself in the middle of a mutiny." He turned and coughed, causing a stream of spittle mixed with chewed tobacco to splat on the ground near his boot.

"The men wish to return to Fort Lyon at once. And, uh-sir, they ain't askin,' they are demandin'. If you know what I mean."

The exhausted officers exchanged worried glances.

"I don't mean to tell you what to do," continued the smoke smudged sergeant deferentially as he plowed ahead. "I recommend you give them a fervent speech. After what they just been through, them antsy nerves are giving the men twitchy fingers."

Ned looked at Silas as they jointly marshalled a show of authority. They shook off their fatigue and entered camp.

After attending to the complaints of the distraught soldiers, the major spoke meaningfully about the council's proceedings, leaving out the dramatic details. He reminded the men of the white captives whose lives hung in the balance.

Silas featured the bravery of their commander and emphasized the reassurances extended to them by Black Kettle. The detachment would not be attacked on their return to the fort.

The crisis was averted as the mentally and physically exhausted men of Company D settled in for another night in enemy territory. Dreams of rampaging Cheyenne warriors appeared through the smoky curtains of their nightmares.

———•———

A dog cowered at the far edge of the herd. Shading my eyes with a hand, I squinted to get a better look. Its black and white coat contrasted with the dry golden field, and as the dog leapt through the tall grass, I realized it was Butch. Ambrose must be nearby! Willie, Belle, and I waited in a shaded grassy area where the horses and mules grazed.

"Butch!" I called. The frightened animal was too far away to hear. Nose to the ground, he slinked away. Then, Ambrose appeared in the clearing. Noticing me, he raced toward me followed by his exuberant dog Butch.

Sliding to his knees next to us, the dear boy exclaimed excitedly, "Look, Aunt Lucy! Look what I have!" He held a ledger book tied on the left side with a leather thong. I reached for the book, opened it, and was astonished by the artwork inside.

"Where did you find this?"

"He gave it to me!" Ambrose replied happily as he pointed to a tall Indian standing in the trees, holding the reins of a saddled horse. "Alights on the Cloud. He is my friend. He drew these pictures. See all the Indians, soldiers, and horses? He draws pictures of battles."

Ambrose reached for his book and held it open admiringly. I kissed his forehead. He smiled and quickly bussed my cheek. "I love you, Aunt Lucy!"

Suddenly, out of the corner of my eye, I saw Alights on the Cloud behind me, lifting Belle onto his horse. How had the man approached without my noticing? Alarmed and confused, I stood and rushed to my daughter. He shoved me roughly, and I skidded backward onto the ground. A confused Ambrose ran to my defense. Quickly hoisted by the collar and seat of his pants, he was tossed onto the horse with Belle.

Alights on the Cloud towered over me for a moment, our eyes welded. I grabbed at his ankles.

"No! No!" I shrieked.

The Indian stumbled backward and jerked his leg from my grip. I struggled to rise, but a swift kick to my stomach knocked the wind out of me, and I doubled over.

Alights on the Cloud mounted his horse behind the children. Then, he did the unthinkable. He rode away with my family!

chapter twenty-nine

Laura's Tears

12 September 1864
Eastern Plains, Colorado Territory

*An Indian by the name of Left Hand, a Cheyenne or Arapahoe,
bought her from the other Indians and gave seven ponies for her, and
afterward turned her over to Major Winecoop.*

Paulina Roper

T he night's mission was semi-successful as the officers set up a
doubly reinforced night guard. Its dual purposes were to watch for
Indians and to prevent deserters from slipping away. Wynkoop
needed each man for the day ahead.

Major Wynkoop rose tired but alert. "Well, Silas," said the gaunt-
faced major, "the mutiny seems to be quelled for now, my friend.
Desperate times called for desperate measures." The two chuckled
companionably. "I think we can remove the guard now, don't you?"

The gritty and unwavering Silas grunted in agreement as he hoisted
a saddle onto his horse.

Ned continued his commentary. "It was a sleepless night. My mind
locked onto the thousands of Indians whose intentions, hostile or not,
are an open question. A little daylight will pull the men together. God
willing, we leave peaceably for the fort with all the captives."

The soft light of morning lit Silas' face as he said, "Yep. The concerns
expressed last night about Indian treachery were justified. Our men
withstood an army of five to one yesterday. Fortunately, they escaped
without a shot fired. It stands to reason the troops are pretty shaken up."

"They will settle down once the captives are released. Now it's time
to hurry up and wait, eh?" winked Ned. "Although you look like you
could use a bit of shut-eye."

Silas waved him off and strode purposefully to his post. Ned admired
his stalwart friend. He watched Silas settle into a comfortable position

on a nearby wagon tongue. He was ready to scan the eastern horizon for as long as it took.

As the blazing sun crept higher, the day dawned brightly with no sign of Indians. The exhausted officers found individual solace in the unusual stillness of the camp and waited for Black Kettle's response. The troops gathered in small groups within the confines of their circle of wagons. Ever vigilant, each man peered across the vast, flat emptiness around him.

Major Wynkoop rested near the creek. Reclining in the shade, he reflected on the happenings of the prior days. He dwelt on the man he had come to know as Black Kettle. Personal acknowledged prejudices against the Indians were shifting again. First by his encounter with One Eye, and now upon meeting Black Kettle. Ned picked up his journal and wrote:

> Make-tava-tah, a Cheyenne chief of the Crooked Lance Society, is a man of dignity and lofty bearing, combined with his sagacity and intelligence, has the moral effect which places him in the position of a potentate. The whole force of his nature is concentrated in the one idea of how best to act for the good of the Tsisitsistas, his race; he knows the power of the white man, and is aware that from thence might spring most of the evils that could befall his people. I have come through the fire to meet with the Southern Cheyenne. Now to obtain the white prisoners and transport the chiefs to Denver. I do not have the power to ensure peace for your people, Black Kettle, but we will journey towards it together.

Ned squinted into the sky above the golden cottonwood trees and noted the sun was nearly overhead. Just as he began to fret about the sincerity of Black Kettle's instructions, Sergeant Forbes called out from his standing position atop one of the supply wagons.

"Indians approaching!"

Each soldier grabbed his weapon and hurried to peer in the direction of Forbes' pointed finger. Wynkoop was beside his assistant in an instant. Using his spyglass, he counted the silhouettes rising in the distance. Relief spilled across the camp as he identified the riders.

"I see one horse with two riders joined by five others. Silas, do you see them? Does it look like a woman?" asked Ned quietly.

Silas nodded, then momentarily added, "I think a woman is behind one of the warriors."

The camp buzzed as the news passed from one soldier to the next. "A woman, a woman! Thanks be to God; it is a woman!"

Wynkoop and Silas rode out to meet the party and soon recognized

Neva and Left Hand. Behind Chief Left Hand rode a young woman. Ned steered his mount between Left Hand and the main group of Arapaho warriors. They did nothing to intercede.

"Chief Left Hand, you have come. Are you releasing this captive into my custody?"

Left Hand smiled broadly and spoke in perfect English. "We are here to present our first gesture toward peace for our people. This woman is a gift and has been bought at great cost to me but requires no gift in return. Chiefs will attend the proposed council with the governor."

The chief slipped his arm around the waist of the young woman and eased her to the ground. She was crying hard and could not form a word. Shielding her eyes in the stark light, she gazed up at the major and took a timorous step toward his horse. Wynkoop pointed to Silas, who kicked one boot out of its stirrup to make it easier for the girl to mount up. Reaching down, Silas offered the girl his hand. She spryly slipped a moccasin foot into the stirrup and hauled up behind the captain in one swift movement. The young woman did not return the smile offered by Silas but continued to sob loudly.

Neva spoke sharply in English. "Indian no like woman cry. Stop!"

Major Wynkoop reached across Silas to the young woman and gently rested his hand on her shoulder. "It is all going to be okay. You are all right now."

Comforted by his gentle touch, a slight smile crossed her lips.

"I have been charged with a message for you from Make-tava-tah," Left Hand said. "He will come tomorrow and will bring the remaining prisoners."

Wynkoop nodded, thanked Left Hand for delivering the captive, then nudged his horse closer to the chief. They clasped hands with crossed arms, then reversed their grip in the customary gesture of respect. The men looked intently into each other's eyes as their handhold lingered.

Moments later, Left Hand motioned for Wynkoop to look up. Fluffy, white clouds parted, and a beam of light touched each man's face with a fresh glow. It was a good day.

Wynkoop watched the Indians disappear in the distance. Chief Left Hand turned his horse and raised his hand in farewell. The major responded in kind.

Ned introduced himself to the lovely, young woman. "I am Major Wynkoop, commander of Fort Lyon. Are you well, young lady?"

She nodded as tears erupted again. Blubbering and wheezing, she finally gathered herself together. "Laura. Roper." She wiped her damp face with the tattered edge of her sleeve but seemed unable to speak further. It was going to take time, Ned thought.

"Are you ready to ride now, Miss Roper? I would like very much to move you to the safety of our camp."

Laura blinked hard as comprehension dawned. Others were waiting to protect her, to carry her to civilization, to reunite her with her people. She nodded and between deep inhalations and trembling heaves, managed to pant, "Yes." Resting her head on Silas' back between his shoulders, she wrapped her arms around his waist, nearly crushing the captain.

Sympathetically, both men nodded in acknowledgement of her distress. Feeling helpless, they urged their horses into a lope. A woman just released from Indian captivity would encounter suspicion and gossip from all sides, and Miss Roper would need protection from the scrutiny to come. Wynkoop pondered her response to rescue and rode next to Silas with much to think about.

Knowing Chief Left Hand as he did, Wynkoop was conflicted. His recent experience at the council was still fresh in his mind. He tried to reconcile the integrity of the man with the certainty of captive abuse. In his heart, he imagined her treatment during captivity was brutal. To protect her honor, he would clamp down on the speculation she would face once the fort full of soldiers spun stories of recent events. He was simply glad to have one young woman in his custody and, ultimately, on her way home. The days to come would prove challenging enough, but after all she endured, he knew she was strong.

Ned's thoughts turned to potential female allies at the fort. His own wife Louise would console the young woman; and Mrs. Lambert, the stage station operator's wife, would ease Laura Roper's tears.

Major Wynkoop expected a victorious thrill after the release of a captive, but his brow furrowed with concern for the silent girl in his care. He pulled the brim of his hat firmly onto his forehead and pressed his horse into a run. She was in safe hands now, and Wynkoop resolved to save the other captives.

chapter thirty

Wynkoop's Reward

13 September 1864
Eastern Plains, Colorado Territory

The feelings I then experienced I would be powerless to fully describe. Here was the realization of my most sanguine hopes; the balance of the poor captives of my race within reach and soon to be under our protection. Such happiness I never experienced before, never since, and do not expect to in this world.

Major Edward W. Wynkoop

The day dawned with expectation as the soldiers tended to their morning chores. Major Wynkoop noticed an increased alertness and vigor, as each man could not resist the compulsive urge to glance toward the horizon for a sign of things to come. The air was still and cool as the smoldering campfires sent smoke up in soft, gray billows that belied the tense undercurrent of the camp.

The troops made ready for an imminent departure—not dependent on the results of coming events. With or without further captives, the nervous men were ready to head for the safety of the distant fort. Tints of gold tinged the nearby cottonwood trees, but their cheerfulness was lost on the troops. Pleased to have secured one hostage, the prospects of additional captives did not diminish their desire to see Miss Roper to safety. Ned's horse War Eagle and Silas' mount were saddled and standing at the ready along with ten others.

Near noon, a messenger approached from the east, and all activity ceased. Wynkoop and Soule rode out side-by-side in cautious expectation. The rest of the party followed in column. The threat of annihilation was still a possibility, and cool heads needed to prevail.

The men recognized the lead Indian, who spoke rudimentary English, and were relieved when he halted some distance from them to wait. After exchanging polite greetings, the man relayed his message that

Make-tava-tah was coming with captives. He was only a few miles away. The messenger offered to guide the soldiers to meet the procession.

The major tried to calm his rising emotions. An hour's gallop did much to settle him. His thoughts focused on securing the balance of the captives. He knew not to revel in yesterday's personal triumph. His hopes for this day still needed to overcome unseen obstacles. In silent prayer, the humble and somewhat hapless instrument asked Divine Providence to save the remaining unfortunates.

The guide slowed his mount to a trot, then stopped. Wynkoop raised his hand and halted the column. He watched as a large group of twenty to thirty Indians approached. He sensed the soldiers should keep their distance to assure the coming assemblage of their peaceful intentions. The safety of the captives was not guaranteed, and any spark could result in less than a favorable outcome.

Soon the approaching Cheyenne stopped and waited. A new wind lifted the feathers in their hair. Major Wynkoop squeezed his horse forward into a trot across the expanse separating the two parties. Advancing, he saw Chief Black Kettle do the same. Tall Chief and Black Kettle halted side by side and extended their arms, clasping hands at the elbows. Friendly greetings followed, and Wynkoop indicated the chief and his people should follow him to camp for food and talk. John Smith, the interpreter, arrived to complete the invitation as Wynkoop and Black Kettle discussed the transaction.

The chief explained he bought the white captives in exchange for ponies. Three other prisoners were located days away on the Republican River. They would be delivered as soon as the whites made peace.

Wynkoop emphasized his desire to escort a delegation of Indian leaders to Denver for a council with the territorial governor. Black Kettle agreed and shook the hand of Tall Chief again.

The discussion was interrupted by a fine-looking lad on an Indian pony riding toward them. He was about nine years old. The boy stopped next to Wynkoop and extended his hand, offering a firm handshake.

"Well, my boy, who are you?" the astonished major asked.

"My name is Dan," he replied. "I have been a prisoner with the Indians. Are you the soldier man who has come to get me?"

The major smiled. "I am."

Dan grinned and said, "Well, bully for you!"

"Are you glad to get away from these Indians?" Wynkoop asked.

"Oh, you bet! But, say, will they let me keep this pony?" queried Dan. The thought struck the boy that his fortunes were changing, and he might shoot for the moon.

Wynkoop chuckled and replied with a promise, "No, but you shall have a better one."

"All right," agreed Dan as if concluding negotiations. "My friend Ambrose is behind me. He's kinda quiet, but you'll get used to him." Danny picked up the leather rein, kicked the horse, and rode toward the soldiers spread across a nearby rise.

Wynkoop watched the boy ride off. Once assured of his safety, the major turned and greeted a reticent young boy about seven years of age. He appeared forlorn and sad. Ambrose followed his fast, young friend, passing Wynkoop without a word.

At the same time, a mounted Cheyenne woman, whom Wynkoop had scarcely noticed, rode forward with a bundle on her back. The soldier's pulse quickened, for peeping out from the folds of the blanket was a little head covered with golden ringlets.

The major nudged his horse nearer when suddenly, two little arms popped out of the folds and stretched toward him. In an instant, he reached forward and drew the little girl into his arms. He seated her on the saddle in front of him. The tiny child put her arms around his neck and laid her head upon his breast. With gulping sobs, she whimpered, "I want to see my mama." Her flaxen hair lifted in the breeze as she stared up at the soldier with tear-streaked cheeks and repeated, "I want my mama."

The vision of her beautiful, pale blue eyes, imploring yet infinitely sad, stopped his heart and something cracked in Wynkoop's core. The steely resolve of a soldier who suppressed all trace of softness was dispelled in an instant. The chasm widened and from its depths sprang a cry. The protective casing around his heart could no longer shield him from emotion. The intensity of his feelings echoed in the vast, empty space, and he hoped those around him could not hear it. The warmth of her little body lingered as she desperately clung to him. He looked at the damp tendrils that clung to her neck as she burrowed deeper into his arms.

Ned tried to control the schism that rendered him helpless. The child shivered despite the warmth of the day, and the tiny action brought him out of his paralyzed trance. He swallowed hard, spun War Eagle around, and urged the horse into a run. He clung to his prize while gaining distance from his feelings and the inquisitive eyes of the Indians and his comrades on the hill.

The major galloped past the column of soldiers with his golden-headed charge, clearly headed back to camp. The young boys' Indian ponies squealed and kicked up their heels, almost unseating their young riders. The soldiers quickly settled the two boys into a protective formation and followed Tall Chief at a brisk trot. Black Kettle returned to his band of warriors, and soon the entire group was confidently following the troops.

Major Wynkoop ran his horse straight into the alarmed camp and was promptly encircled by droves of cheering and excited men. The tiny girl held her grip around the major's neck and looked out fearfully at their gritty, happy faces. Recognition dawned on the men, and their celebration turned to somber silence.

Heads bowed, those who doubted the nobleness of their mission removed their hats in contrition. The hardest of hearts melted in absolution mingled with awe and admiration for the young leader whose bravery and courage outshined them all.

"Corporal Alexander, please care for the child and deliver her to my wife as soon as we return to Fort Lyon. Mrs. Wynkoop will know what to do," said the major. His cheeks bore the ruddy appearance of one flushed with sentiment.

----•----

Later that night, Major Edward W. Wynkoop wrote in his journal these words about his men:

> With great concern they cast pitying looks at the poor desolate motherless child while down the bronzed cheek of many a battle-scarred rough soldier coursed a tear. Finally, bursting from the throng rushed an old soldier who reached up and took the child. With a choking voice, he asked forgiveness for his former conduct. He had been the leader of the mutineers.

chapter thirty-one

Fort Lyon

13 September 1864
Fort Lyon, Eastern Colorado Territory

Seven leading Chiefs of the Cheyenne and Arapahoe Indians accompanied us by my desire for the purpose of holding a consultation with our authorities to endeavor to arrange terms of peace, Black Kettle being at the head of the Delegation.

Major Edward W. Wynkoop

Wagon wheels ground through the dusty tracks of the trail to Fort Lyon. Soldiers, freed captives, and an entourage of Indian chiefs and their families wound their way across the one hundred forty miles of desert. The soldiers directed to care for the two boys doted on the youngsters. The entire company collected $76.50 for Danny and Ambrose to buy necessaries upon arrival at the fort. Major Wynkoop placed Private William Smith of Company D in charge of the boys' welfare, and he took Ambrose and Danny under his wing. Good will and celebration surrounded the boys, who seemed to physically have weathered their experience, but little Ambrose was still reserved and troubled.

As the returning soldiers neared the fort, its massive, wooden gates opened. The entire garrison turned out to meet the brave heroes with enthusiastic congratulations and cheers. All were incredulous such a dangerous and feckless mission was conducted without a fight.

Corporal Si Alexander noticed the arrival of Captain Soule. A young woman rode behind him and peeked cautiously at the soldiers, who were noisily pointing and grinning at her. Alexander stepped in to clear the way. With the efficiency of an old school marm, the soldier took charge and shouted for the animated troops to give the lady space. He barked orders demanding quarters, food, and a hot cup of coffee be prepared while all the time preening over his new charge.

Miss Roper appeared bewildered and in shock. She was, no doubt, overcome with relief and overwhelmed at the reception. She took in the friendly faces and the civilized trappings of the camp. The primitive military environment, so different from the Indian camps, was reassuring. Yet, her shaken demeanor was cloaked in a cloud, and she spoke not a word.

"Excuse us," responded Silas as he urged his horse through the crowd. "Miss Roper needs to be attended to by someone besides you bunch of rapscallions." He smiled and pressed on through the murmuring crowd of curious fort dwellers.

Laura, eyes swollen from crying, rode silently behind Silas, who guided his horse through the crowd to the home of the Lamberts. The operator of the fort's stage station stepped forward and reached for the horse's bridle. He stared into the face of the captain. Silas smiled and gave a slight nod that summed up that the mission had gone well.

"The others?" inquired Lambert.

"Coming with the major," responded Captain Soule quietly. "Two boys and a little girl."

Lambert's face lit up in joyous disbelief. Emotions tangled with duty as he swallowed hard and turned his face abruptly to the matter at hand.

"Julia!" he called. "We have a visitor!"

Wiping her hands on an apron, his tiny, yet sturdy wife stepped from the house. She stopped abruptly and stared open-mouthed at the disheveled, young woman behind the captain. Summing up the situation, she flew into action.

"Captain! Give the poor thing to me!"

Silas helped Miss Roper as she slowly dismounted from the horse. Julia rushed to the girl and threw her arms around her. Just as quickly, she released the stunned girl, then tenderly held her in her arms again. "Everything is going to be fine now," Mrs. Lambert muttered consolingly. "Come inside with me, you dear girl."

Leading Laura up the steps, she turned to look over her shoulder at Silas. Julia's wide-eyed expression of horror and concern was bolstered by Silas' encouraging smile.

"She is in good hands now. Thank you, Mrs. Lambert," said Silas.

Within hours, the garrison was diverted by reports of the arrival of a large group of Indians camped ten miles up Ash Creek. The delegation of Cheyenne and Arapaho chiefs would prepare for their journey to Denver. With this news, life at Fort Lyon settled into its usual rhythm.

Days later, Major Wynkoop sat at his desk recalling recent events. He chuckled to himself as he remembered Louise's exuberant reaction to his safe return. The woman was a saint, and the worry of the past weeks were etched around her tired eyes. He knew she spent sleepless nights begging God to protect him and his men.

While staring in front of him at the blank page, Ned reached for his ink bottle and pen. The dual thrills of conducting the captive rescue mission and arranging a meeting to secure peace on the plains were replaced by the task ahead. He contemplated his next move. He must make a full report. Ned knew he acted under his own authority. His superiors knew nothing of those decisions. Prompt action was required as the opportunity presented itself, he reasoned, yet it was sure to ruffle feathers.

Most importantly, however, the Arapaho and Cheyenne chiefs agreed to meet with the governor—who by all measures would be a cool participant. Evans did not have the benefit of parlaying with individual Indian leaders face to face. Ned earned a truer understanding of the peaceful intentions of the Indians. It was clear; however, the motives of the military did not swing both ways. Pondering where to begin, he heard footsteps outside his door, then a knock.

"Enter," he called as he set down his pen, relieved from the difficult job at hand.

Indian Agent, Samuel Colley, stepped inside, removed his dark, broad-brimmed hat, and swept his long hair back into place along his forehead.

"Congratulations, Major," he said with a genuine smile. "You surprised a lot of betting men by bringing in those captives and returning in one piece."

"Thank you," replied Wynkoop. "We have matters to deal with regarding the Indians who have accompanied us to the fort. We can expect large numbers of Cheyenne and Arapaho to come in and camp near this post. I want you to distribute annuities to the bands and supplement those supplies with army rations. They will transport the goods back to their villages on Hackberry Creek," he instructed. "Take Edmond Guerrier with you."

He did not trust Agent Colley to fully abide by his instructions. He suspected Colley and his wife were profiting from government annuities intended for the tribes. Rumor was his wife was making pies from the dried apples and flour in the native's rations. She was selling the pies to the troops and pocketing the profit. He made a mental note to clean up that corruption at the next opportunity.

Noting the surprised look on Colley's face, Wynkoop shifted the direction of their conversation to his next purpose. "I am taking a delegation to Denver for an audience with the governor. I want to make a good faith effort to assure the friendlies of their leaders' safety. Also, I want you to communicate to the various bands they are protected from attack by the army."

"Yes, sir. But which chiefs are going with you?" inquired Colley.

"Besides Black Kettle, I have asked several others to go with me. White Antelope, Lone Bear, Little Robe, and Bull Bear."

"And they agreed to this?" Colley sputtered incredulously. "Bull Bear is one dangerous Indian. I would be careful if I were you, Major."

"I agree, Mr. Colley. But I am impressed by Black Kettle's skills as a leader, and he has guaranteed a peaceful meeting." Wynkoop paused, then continued. "The Arapaho are sending Left Hand, Neva, Heap of Buffalo, and Bosse. Please explain to their bands that the chiefs are going to Denver for a peace council and will return safely. We want to avoid any skirmishes until a truce has been confirmed. Remind them it would be prudent to avoid the army."

"The Indians already told me about their change of plans in that regard," said Colley. "They decided not to winter at Fort Larned but instead will camp at the mouth of Running Creek in the Smoky Hill River country. There they will wait for word from Black Kettle and the other chiefs."

"Thank you for your help, Mr. Colley," said the major. "Now we keep our fingers crossed regarding what kind of reception awaits the chiefs in Denver." Unconsciously, he looked down at the blank piece of paper on his desk.

Samuel Colley took his leave as Major Wynkoop dipped his pen in the ink. The major straightened his aching back and steeled himself for the daunting compositions. He intended to send reports to General Curtis and his immediate commander of the District of the Upper Arkansas, Colonel Ford. But first, he would inform Governor Evans of his plans for what he termed the Camp Weld Council. He hoped beyond hope the man would be amenable.

Major Ned Wynkoop wrote the following:

September 18, 1864
Fort Lyon, Colorado Territory

To: His Excellency John Evans
        Governor of Colorado

        District of Upper Arkansas
        Fort Lyon, Colorado Territory

Sir

I have the honor to state that on the 3rd inst three Cheyenne Indians were met a few miles outside of this Post by some of my men en-route for Denver and were brought in.

They came as stated, bearing with them a proposition for peace from Black Kettle and other chiefs of the Cheyenne nation. Their propositions were to this effect: that they, the Cheyennes and Arapahoes, had in their possession seven white prisoners, whom they offered to deliver up in case we should come to terms of peace with them. They told me that the Arapahoes, Cheyennes, and Sioux were congregated for mutual protection at what is called the bunch of timbers, on the head waters of the Smoky Hill, at a distance of one hundred and forty miles north-east of this post, numbering altogether about three thousand warriors, and were anxious and desirous to make peace with the whites.

Feeling extremely anxious at all odds, to effect the release of these white prisoners, and my command just having been reinforced by a detachment of Infantry sent from New Mexico I found I would be enabled to leave sufficient garrison for this post by taking one hundred and thirty men with me, (including one section of the battery) and concluded to march to this Indian rendezvous for the purpose of procuring the white prisoners afore mentioned, and to be governed by circumstances as in what manner I should proceed to accomplish that object.

Taking with me under a strict guard, the Indians who had come in, I reached my destination, and was confronted by from six to eight hundred Indian warriors drawn up in line of battle and prepared to fight.

Putting on as bold a front as I could under the circumstances, I formed my command in good order, for the purpose of acting on the defensive if necessary and advanced toward them, at the same time sending forward one of the Indians I had with me, as emissary to state that I have come for the purpose of holding a consultation with the chiefs of the Arapahoes and Cheyennes to come to an understanding which might result in mutual benefit; that I had not come desiring strife, but was prepared for it, if necessary, and advised them to listen to what I had to say previous to making any more warlike demonstrations.

They consented to meet me in council, and I then proposed to them that, if they desired peace, to give me palpable evidence of their sincerity by delivering into my hands their white prisoners. I told them I was not authorized to conclude terms of peace with them, but if they acceded to my proposition, I would take what chiefs they might choose to select to the Governor of Colorado Territory; state the circumstances to him, and that I believed it would result in what it was their desire to accomplish—"peace with their white brothers." I had reference particularly to the Arapahoe and Cheyenne tribes.

The council was divided, and could not come to an understanding among themselves. Finding this to be the case I told them that I would march to a certain locality, distant twelve miles, and await a given time for their action in the matter. I took a strong position in the locality named, and remained three days.

In the interval they brought and turned over four white prisoners, all that was possible for them at the time the balance of the seven being (as they stated) with another band far to the northward.

The released captives that I have now with me at this post consist of one female named Laura Roper, aged sixteen, and three children (two boys and one girl) named Isabel Ubanks, Ambrose Usher, and Daniel Marble; the three first mentioned being taken on Blue River, in the neighborhood of what is known as Liberty Farm and the last captured at some place on the South Platte with a train of which all the men belonging to were murdered. I have the principal chiefs of the two tribes with me, and propose starting immediately to Denver to put into effect the proposition made by me to them.

They agree to deliver up the balance of the prisoners as soon as it is possible to procure them, which can be done better from Denver City than from this point.

I have the honor, governor, to be your obedient servant,

E. W. Wynkoop
Maj. 1st Colorado Cavalry
Commanding Fort-Lyon

chapter thirty-two

Unspoken

17 September 1864
Home of Julia Lambert
Fort Lyon, Colorado Territory

The loathsome manner of living and the indignities I was subjected to almost drove me mad.

Laura Roper

Julia Lambert tipped the pitcher slowly over the young woman in the wash tub. Laura groaned as the warm water trickled through her scalp and down her back. The Lambert children were sent to the Colley's home for the night so the newcomer could bathe and rest in peace.

Laura sighed. For the first time in over a month, she felt the tension in her neck and shoulders release. Julia used a comb to work out the tangles and pull the occasional nit from the girl's hair. Laura appreciated the woman's gentle touch. She knew her companion was full of questions, as were all the inhabitants of Fort Lyon.

Laura leaned back and offered a positive tidbit of information. "My hair," she said. "The chief's young daughters took pleasure in combing it, sometimes for hours at a time. They were fascinated by my long, blonde hair."

"Oh? What was it like in the camp?" queried Julia cautiously.

"Loathsome!" snapped Laura with conviction. Immediately, she pursed her lips together, regretting the rude response. She was reluctant to expound on the subject.

Julia could see the girl was tortured and needed relief. She would allow things to proceed at Laura's pace. The older woman gathered up her skirts, tucked them around her legs, and sat down on the stool next to the tub. Laura's eyes closed tightly as if to shut out all she had seen. Her jaw muscles clenched together.

Almost inaudibly, Laura asked, "Do you know what happened to Mrs. Eubank?" Her haunted voice trembled as if the dam of emotion might burst into a million pieces at any moment.

Julia swallowed hard and answered, "Black Kettle told Major Wynkoop she and her baby are now prisoners of the Sioux. He was unable to secure their release because they are two hundred miles away. It was an impossibility. I am sorry, Laura."

Sitting upright, Laura's eyes popped open as she exclaimed, "No, Julia, it is not right! I know it is not! Mrs. Morton, Mrs. Eubank, and her baby were in camp the day I left!" Laura covered her face with her hands and wept softly.

Julia sat stunned at the news. She must tell Major Wynkoop of this development.

"I am so frightened for her. She lives in the lodge of a terrible, terrible savage. I saw him wrap ropes of grass around the baby's ankles. Then he would...." Laura gagged at the memory. "He would...."

Julia froze, dreading what was coming.

"He would light them. Just to torture the helpless babe in front of Mrs. Eubank," the girl whispered hoarsely.

Julia gasped and covered her mouth, unable to bear the cruel images damaging her sensibilities. The two women embraced, their foreheads touching, but no sound escaped their lips as the shocking admission ticked through their horrified connection.

Recovering somewhat, Laura finally said, "Just knowing the danger poor Mrs. Eubank must be facing...." Her voice trailed off. Fiercely grasping Julia's hand, she stared at their entwined fists. "The indignities to which we were subjected almost drove us mad."

The young woman struggled to regain mastery of her face as she explicitly told the shameful abuses heaped upon her person and that of Mrs. Eubank.

Nearly spent, Laura turned to look at the ragged remains of her dress lying in a pile on the floor.

"The Indians completely ransacked the Eubank's homes." Her vacant eyes suddenly saw what clearly was not there. "And one savage held the scalp of Dora, Mr. Eubank's sister. He swung the long dark hair directly at me. It slapped blood and gore all over my bodice."

Julia gasped as the traumatized girl continued.

"The blow flies. They laid their eggs on that dress, my face, and chest. The maggots...."

Suddenly, Laura rose from the tub as the shaken Julia hastily reached for the linen towel on the back of a chair. Before she could wrap it around

Laura, the girl screamed, "The maggots! They hatched and crawled all over my body!" Shivering, she vehemently slapped her naked torso again and again. "No! No!" she cried as she tried to sweep away the imaginary offenders.

Julia gripped the girl's wrists and panted, "Laura, stop! It is all over now. They are gone. Gone!"

Laura's eyes cleared as she struggled for sanity. Hanging her head in shame, she murmured, "I'm sorry. So sorry…."

Staring once again at the ragged dress on the floor, she wrinkled her nose and shook her damp head violently. Julia ran to the dress, which reeked of smoke, blood, urine, and decay. Deftly picking up the garment with two fingers, she threw the stinking mass out the door.

Wrapping the towel around the young woman, Julia noticed the ribs and spine protruding through her skin. She made note to fortify the steaming milk on the stove with a bit more cream, sugar, and a medicinal dose of whisky. Recovery must be taken slowly, in steps. Clearly, the girl lost flesh during her weeks of captivity.

"I lived in the lodge of Chief Black Kettle when I first arrived in the camp," said Laura pensively.

Julia was tempted to stop the stricken young woman from going too far down the road of raw recollections. She needed time. But Laura continued, "His woman allowed me to go to the stream to wash my dress, which was covered in blood. Not much left of it now, I am afraid," she added looking at the door.

Laura gently touched the arc of the ugly scab on her cheek and tapped the perimeter of her slightly discolored and swollen nose. "I was kicked in the face by a mule," she explained. "It was a mass of blisters after days of travel in the blazing sun and heat. I did my best to rinse off."

"Umm, it is bruised, but healing," acknowledged Julia. "Perhaps you should get ready for bed now."

Pointing to the girl's moccasins on the floor, Julia tried a new tact to distract Laura's mind of her private horrors. "The women of the fort will be around tomorrow with whatever they can share. Hopefully, someone has a pair of shoes." She filled a mug with the healing brew and handed it to Laura, who sipped it gratefully.

"I have a spare dress to give you, Laura," she said with a twinge of guilt. How she wished she had more to offer, but weeks away from Denver had turned into months. Supply deliveries slowed because of the Indian troubles. After remaking one skirt into clothing for the children, she was down to her last two dresses.

"We will visit the sutler's store and find things you can use. We will get you fixed up in a hurry so you can arrive in Denver like the civilized young woman you are."

Mrs. Lambert was beautiful with fine features and a tiny stature that belied her strength. Laura looked closely at her before she pulled the sleeping gown over her head. She shook her hair to loosen its wet strands, then began vigorously rubbing sections between the folds of a clean linen. Her mind would not be quiet, though, and continued to lead her back. She froze as if held hostage to a thought. Her eyes were remote as though envisioning something else. She whispered with an undertone of desolation.

"I was the property of Black Kettle."

Julia paused with aprehension. Her heart was heavy with Laura's words. She held her breath.

"I was his property," repeated Laura slowly, "to do with as he saw fit."

Her eyes met Julia's. "Submit or be killed," she said as if confessing. "A girl of seventeen among beasts. They can hardly be called human." Laura trembled. "There was no respect or regard for me."

Laura seemed desperate to purge the details. Spitting the words that were poisoning her soul, she spoke rapidly. "My arms and legs were tied to stakes driven into the ground at night to prevent my escape. There was little food. We ate dog! Each time a war party returned to camp, the screeching and drumming was frightfully unbearable. The things I have seen.... I was terrified."

Grabbing a small towel to staunch the flow of tears and snot, Laura collapsed onto the stool next to the wash tub and held her head in her hands. Julia placed a hand on her shoulder. Careful not to probe with invasive questions, she waited. Then dropping to her knees, Julia wrapped her arms tightly around the distraught girl's shoulders.

Finally, Laura leaned into the embrace and said, "I had no idea what part of the country we were in, so there was no possibility of escape." Her eyes darted around the room as if seeking deliverance from the memory.

Julia shuddered, then replied, "I am so glad you are safe with us now. Safe!" She emphasized the word as a reminder—the ordeal was over. The older woman was deeply affected by the story. She rubbed her nose and blinked back tears that threatened to malign her feigned composure.

"It is indeed a relief," wheezed Laura.

Exhaustion was evident in her face. Smudged by dark circles, hollow eyes stared vacantly past Julia. Her pupils dilated into pools of suffocating black. The effects of fatigue and whisky were slowing her churning mind.

"I was captured by a Cheyenne. He traded me for five ponies to an Arapaho named Neva. He and his brother Niwot spoke English and treated me better. They said it was wrong for me to be held and thought I would be released soon. Neva told me his chief sent two Indians here to Fort Lyon. Neva said if they got into the fort alive, they would tell the commanding officer they had white prisoners to give up. He said if the Indians returned safely in three days, they would send up a smoke signal to let the Indians know the soldiers were coming after their prisoners." Laura plucked at a scab on her wrist.

"One day, the entire village was in an uproar. Word spread that soldiers were nearby. Neva showed me the signal smoke. I was overjoyed when I saw them coming. But the Indians were afraid the soldiers would try to take me by force. The chief quickly hid me in his lodge and threatened to kill me if I made a sound. The other women and I were forced to lie hidden under a buffalo robe, afraid to move until the soldiers left. It was horrid to step out of the teepee later and watch our rescuers ride over the hill."

Laura choked on these words. Revealed by the light of the flickering fire, lines of grief creased her mouth and eyes. She willed herself to sort through the hodgepodge of confusion to finish the story.

"Days later, Neva and Niwot took me out of camp and turned me over to the soldiers who rode out to meet us," Laura said. "I was so overcome with relief that I was unable to speak—could barely make a sound. It was numbing. I did not dare to imagine my release for fear my hopes would be dashed." She quietly added, "I was careful to stay close to Major Wynkoop and Captain Soule on the trip here to the fort. I was so afraid to lose them, to be captured again." A tremor ran through her body.

Julia waited.

Finally, the girl said softly, "Everyone here has showered me with kindness and sympathy. I am so thankful for the wonderful food. Wild game was scarce, so there was little to eat. But I am so humiliated because of...." She struggled through her delirium to put words together.

Julia rested a hand on the girl's feverish forehead.

At last, Laura whispered, "I am so ashamed...because of the things I have endured." Swallowing hard, she looked imploringly at Julia. "I do not wish to meet people or talk to anyone."

Julia realized the prospect of inquiries and attention were overwhelming Laura. Words could not supply the reassurance she needed at this moment.

Julia processed Laura's tale and made a decision.

Laura's story would stoke the furnaces of revenge in the hearts of Denver's citizens. The Indian war was taking a toll on commerce and security, not to mention the lives lost. Major Wynkoop hoped to foster peace between the Indians and the territorial governor. The unhindered broadcast of young Laura's suffering would shatter any hope of reaching an amicable solution. The tales would be sensationalized in the newspapers, and salacious details would render her already sullied reputation to a point of no remedy. Future harm was simply unnecessary.

"Laura," she said, taking the tender hands in hers. "You must never share the things you have told me. Ever. To anyone." She bent her head nearer to coax Laura's eyes to hers. "It is for the best."

Laura sniffed and nodded in agreement, her wet cheeks gleaming.

"The people here at the fort are good folks and have taken up a collection to give you money to return to your family."

Laura began to cry again. "Mrs. Lambert, I don't know where they are. Are they alive?"

Julia stopped to think, but Laura was ready to share her doubts.

"When I was in camp, I saw an Indian wearing my father's coat and vest. Another was wearing my mother's green velvet hat! Left Hand told me he did not want to kill my brother. But Black Kettle said he should die." She looked pitifully into Julia's eyes. "Do you think they are dead?"

Julia reached for the distraught girl and pulled her close. "We shall try to contact them. Have you any idea where they might have gone after the attack?"

Laura paused to inspect the linens, then brightened. "They may have gone to Kansas. Fairbury. We have family and friends there."

Julia nodded and said reassuringly, "We will send a telegram. You will find them, my dear." She was not confident in her words.

"I asked No-Ta-Nee if they killed my people. He said no. The people were gone. But he also admitted they burned our home and everything in it. I just do not know if he is telling the truth. Maybe the Indians killed them. Killed them all. Like the Eubanks!" Tears spurted from the distraught girl's eyes as she fumbled with the mug, nearly dropping it.

There was something else bothering her. "Marshall," she whispered. "Mrs. Lambert, I am engaged. Engaged to Mr. Marshall Kelley." She glanced down at her empty ring finger and said softly, "I wore his signet ring. The Indians took it."

They both stared at the empty finger as the fire crackled nearby.

"My Marshall left the day of the raid," continued Laura. "He was going to Atchison for supplies…and our marriage certificate. My father asked Marshall and his partner, Mr. Butler, to go with me to our neighbors' home. The Eubanks. Father was concerned for my safety. Indians stole three of his horses right out of our yard the week before."

The crying, which had ebbed, now began again in earnest. "Do you think Marshall could be alive?"

"We will find your family. It will be all right," said Julia in as calming a voice as she could muster.

Suddenly, there was a knock on the door. Julia rose to open it. Captain Soule stood uneasily on the step outside.

"Silas!" exclaimed Julia. "What can I do for you?"

"How is Miss Roper? I have come to check on her," said the soldier quietly. "I have been thinking about my fiancé. The two are so similar. I wish I could do something to help her."

"Perhaps later," suggested Julia. "She is ready to retire."

"Of course," replied Silas. "Um, Mrs. Lambert. I want her to have this." He held out a tiny signet ring.

"She has lost so much. Tell her it is from me and my betrothed. We hope it will cheer her a little."

"Thank you, Captain Soule," Julia said as she looked at the shy gentleman at her door. He appeared stricken by events as well, and she realized just how young the brave captain was.

Closing the door, she leaned her forehead on it momentarily. Such tenderness in the rough frontier. Chills coursed up and down her spine. The ring. How? Shaking her head, she looked up to the ceiling, expecting to see an angel smiling down from above. The circumstances were so incongruent and awful, yet the prevailing kindness of others so timely.

Julia eased the girl towards the bed. As Laura sat down, she placed the ring in the girl's palm and closed her fingers around it. "From Captain Soule," was all she said as she guided Laura's head gently onto the pillow.

The crying ebbed as Laura inspected the gift. "Oh…he is so kind to me, even though I am ruined." Laura sighed heavily, rubbed her swollen eyes, and lay still.

Julia pulled the bed sheet over her prone body and smoothed the hair away from her brow. "You are okay, Laura," she soothed. "But you must never talk about the indignities you have endured. In our world, it is important to maintain the illusion of virtue, or you will be shunned."

Julia envisioned the tattered spirit dwelling within the young woman. Laura's body and emotions had reached their end. The tiny form in the bed sank from sight as the pretty girl woman succumbed to the dreamy comfort of clean, soft bedding. Moments later, Laura was fast asleep.

Julia sank into the rocking chair by the fire. Thinking. Praying. Rocking. Arms wound tightly around her chest. The tough frontier woman's composure was rattled to its core. This was a rough country for such tender spirits. It is a great burden to care for those who cannot be fixed.

Rocking slowly, she thought of her own loved ones and replayed the images described by Laura. The motherly instinct to protect her charge grew stronger. She would do her best to shield the girl from the sensationalism surrounding her arrival in the fort.

Fatigue settled into Julia's bones as she begged the divine to protect all whom she held so dear.

Emotions roiling, she rocked, then rocked some more.

Julia felt vulnerable in this remote outpost. Could the fort and its soldiers shield her family from the threats just outside the gates? She thought of Laura, of the imagery her words created.

And Julia imagined.

She conjured up all the things left unspoken.

chapter thirty-three

War Dance

Mid-September 1864
Southwestern Kansas Territory

Nearly all the old men are opposed to war, but the young men could not be controlled; they were determined to sweep the Platte and the country as far as they could; they know that if the white men follow up the war for two or three years they would get rubbed out, but meanwhile they would kill plenty of whites.

Elbridge Gerry

Forcing air into my lungs was impossible; all I could manage was to cough and choke. I lifted a desperate hand grasping, clawing after the kidnapped children as Alights on a Cloud rode quickly out of sight with Belle and Ambrose. Gripping my abdomen, I crawled toward Willie. He sat, thumb in his mouth, watching the horse gallop away. He screwed up his face, reached his hands toward his sister and cousin, and began to scream. I barely reached him before I collapsed.

The world spun through a cloudless sky. Lights sparked and flashed, then turned to flowers and floated away. My foggy brain turned on, then off, then stopped on the memory of dear Dora. Her face always lit up at the sight of the dog.

Dora...I fought to remain conscious but could not breathe. If only I could have reached her, comforted her. I remembered her last words to me. "Don't leave me...."

Belle. Belle, what are you saying?

"Don't leave me...."

But there was no choice. I did leave her.

Dora.

I was forced to leave her. And Butch left her as well.

Belle. You must not leave me!

"Butch! Follow Ambrose! Now! Please Butch, follow my Belle."

Willie! Holding the child against my chest, I rolled onto my back

177

and tapped on the celestial gate. The sky turned black as darkness descended. A gate key dropped into my hand. But I did not need it anymore....

———•———

Death did not come for me that day. I was destined to tread the farthest reaches of the planet without the children. The familiar love for those who were gone robbed courage from my heart and stole strength from my fragile mind. I understood what Nancy was lacking and why she often fell into pits of darkness and worry for all the children's safety overwhelmed us. Were Ambrose and Belle taken to live with Laura in Black Kettle's band? Were they taken to be killed? Ransomed? The children were absent from my watchful eye and surely in danger. The murderous bents of some in the camps were unpredictable. I was anxious and continuously fretful. The unknown presented opportunities for my imagination to take me down dark paths and I fell into an endless cycle of numbness and constant apprehension.

Day and night, Nancy and I stumbled like the walking dead. Two weeks had passed since Laura disappeared and the children were taken. The tribe continued its relentless trek across treeless landscapes. I was inconsolable and in a stupor. Nancy was unwell and tormented by the loss of Belle and Ambrose. We endeavored to keep baby Willie alive but gave little thought to ourselves. With little sustenance and no rest, we were wasting away.

The Indians made camp on the Cimarron River. That evening, a warrior victoriously drove a wagon filled with guns and ammo into the center of the village. I surmised from the excited conversations around the cargo that southern white men were supplying weapons to the tribes.

Was it possible the rebels were subverting the native population? Two wars were being waged. The Union and the Confederacy battled it out over slavery, while the tribes' war against the whites was meant to stop westward expansion. Nancy and I discussed the recent event as a welcome diversion from our deep depression. We decided the rebels were creeping up from the South and were actively pursuing a policy to spread the union thin.

The next morning, as the camp prepared to move out, the wagon load of munitions went with us. I remembered the five hundred dollars stolen from Nancy by John Brown. I recalled Nancy's words about the rogue weeks before.

"My family was killed, and he said he was glad of it."

I considered it, and my anger burned against the man—John Brown. His ilk were the fostering agents of our troubles on the plains! Peace seemed an impossibility.

I remembered the chief's words: when peace is made, you will be released.

Increasingly desperate for information about the children, my requests were met with vague explanations or annoyed silence. Mitimoni shared rumors that tied their disappearance to the departure of several Cheyenne and Arapaho chiefs.

The world was big and our lives so insignificant. Belle alone in that world was irreconcilable. The need to act, to protect her, to shield her began to override all logic. Where was she taken? The elusive outcome of this mystery would remain unknown forever.

The following morning, I shared a small portion of boiled buffalo meat with Willie and cried bitterly for Belle. Nancy and I could no longer bear up under the loss and hardship. It was now or never. It was time to escape.

I peered at a dust cloud in the distance. A war party was rapidly approaching camp. Their arrival spawned the ceremonial thrumming of drums. Men dismounted from lathered ponies and joined a circle of the camp's male occupants. Five dead warriors lashed to their ponies arrived to the collective outrage of the entire camp.

"War dance!" squawked Old Woman from her stance outside the lodge. Frightened, I stepped toward the teepee flap. Nancy joined me. Our apprehension increased as Big Crow attired himself in his war shirt, long strands of scalp hair dangling.

The customs and structure of the tribal community were constantly unfolding, Nancy and I learned from our interactions with Mr. Smith and the English-speaking Indians such as Mitimoni. Theirs was a complex society. Mitimoni explained Bull Bear was the leader of the Dog Soldiers. Described as fierce fighters and suicide soldiers, they functioned as rear guards or sacrificial decoys. Staked to the ground with rope during battle, they considered it an honor to die in defense of the tribe.

Nancy and I knew their ruthless methods firsthand. We were astounded to have survived the raids which killed our families. Open and exposed once again, we worried. The mood of the village was ominous.

Without warning, Big Crow lunged toward Nancy and yanked her by the arm into the center of the drummers. He threw the scalp, hands, and feet of a white woman at her face. Her screams fed his desire to torture her with more revolting, bloody pieces of war. Big Crow's ability to conjure up the most grotesque treatment was unrelenting. We cringed as the ceremonial fervor increased. Nancy vomited on the ground. Clinging to Willie, I did my best to hold her upright.

Witnessing Nancy's distress, Mitimoni stepped forward and pulled the sickened young woman from Big Crow's grasp. Mitimoni demanded he leave her alone. The daughter of Medicine Arrows held influence within the tribe, but Big Crow simply scoffed and spat in her face. Nancy was led away as I searched for a hiding place.

My heart nearly stopped as the personification of malice and mayhem entered his teepee. Surely, Big Crow was contemplating new methods of torment. He quickly returned with a tomahawk and shook it in my face as he passed. Reflexively, I jumped back with the agility of a frightened rabbit. He jubilantly joined the revelers as they reenacted the dismembering of their enemies.

A pole was erected in the center of the circle and decked with human scalps. The numbers of warriors increased as they circled the pole, then thrust their heads to the ground and moaned. The next second, they arose and threw their lances into the air along with a war whoop, which rang through the village.

The debauchery of their performance elicited terror. The war regalia and finery were opulent, yet disturbing. Feathered war bonnets swung and bounced lithely; long strings of eagle feathers brushed the ground. Silver half dollars pounded thin were sewn onto leather thongs, then fastened to their long hair. From their scalps, braids swayed and twisted with the rhythm of the drums.

Hundreds of mounted braves poured in on the scene, creating one large, flowing circle of horseflesh. Highly decorated ponies streamed past. Half broke away to form a clockwise movement within the main circle. The incensed warriors rode with speed and precision, narrowly passing each other.

War whoops and drums thundered through the dust-filled air. I hid behind a lodge and watched as mock battles were performed by thousands of painted, decorated warriors. Bodies contorted as they brandished weapons while jumping and stomping in unison. With sharp yelps and threatening gestures, they slashed and carved at their imaginary enemies—eyes bulging and mouths frothing. The final act was the frenzied taking of imaginary scalps, exultantly held high as proof of their valor. I could not escape my dark imaginings of a dead-eyed Big Crow stalking me from the edges of the shadows. My skin prickled a terrifying warning. Menace surrounded us.

The bodies of the dead warriors, now wrapped in buffalo robes, were raised on tall platforms constructed of willow branches and four strong poles. Keening and moaning, five squaws sat near the platforms, slashing their arms with knives.

I held the baby with a steely grip, ears buzzing, and sweat pouring down my neck and back.

It was then I saw Two Face. Recognition dawned as I watched him ride out of the ceremony. Absent from the camp for weeks, I assumed he was on the warpath in distant places.

On cue, Two Face halted his war horse, and both rings of riders stopped. Chief Bull Bear dismounted. His powerful, white horse reared in response as if ready to charge into battle. A dozen braves pushed a woman through the crowd. Bull Bear reached through the hideously howling throng and grabbed her. It was Nancy!

Covering my mouth with a hand, I squelched a shriek. Her face was painted red, yellow, and green; her hands and feet a blood red. Bull Bear jerked her into the center. She seemed to comprehend. She faced a new challenge—a life-or-death demand.

The warriors on the ground formed a small ring, enclosing my friend with bows and arrows drawn, ready to murder her should she fail. The wildest, most savage horse was pulled rearing and squealing into the circle. It was colorfully painted across every inch of its body. Six braves held the animal as Nancy was thrown upon its back.

One of the warriors violently struck the horse's rear end with a large whip. It bolted and ran madly about the scene. After the third time around, Nancy was wide-eyed and terrified. Bravely, she gave a war whoop so loud it rivaled the shout of the stoutest renegade.

The crowd screamed in appreciation. "Brave Whe Ho!" Arrows intended for her murder now arced into the darkening sky.

When intimidated, Nancy threw caution to the wind and directed her aggression at her attackers. They seemed slightly in awe of the young woman. Forcing her into male Cheyenne activities, the seriousness of the tests escalated. Could she hold up? It frightened me.

Sliding off the spinning, raging horse, Nancy staggered through the crowd toward me. Our eyes locked in mutual distress. Nodding my head, I reached my free arm toward her. Seeking safety, we stumbled into an embrace and wept on each other's shoulders. For once, I was the anchor. My dear Nancy was adrift and completely spent. I began to cautiously back away from the scene, holding both my baby and friend.

The perfectly formed circles spun again, then disintegrated as riders charged in and out of mock battles. Abruptly, seven hundred warriors peeled out of camp, running in a northerly direction—intent on their next raid on the whites. Whoops and hollers followed them down the dusty trail and over a distant hill.

Mitimoni appeared. Wrapping an arm around Nancy's waist, she cradled her and walked to Medicine Arrows' lodge. Away from Big Crow, away from the distracted crowd.

I inched into safety at the camp's edge and backed into a large, powerfully built figure. Startled, I heard the words "Fire Hair Squaw" whispered into the hair above my temple. Two Face! He leaned against me and grinned toothily. His nearness incited me to rail against him.

"Those warriors are going to kill more white people! I want it to stop!" I yelled.

He dismissed my flaring anger with a sharp twist of my arm. I quieted and he instantly let go.

"I want my daughter, Two Face!" I hissed.

He shrugged and said, "She gone. Black Kettle take children to soldiers."

The news struck my addled brain with the force of a hammer. I lurched away from the message as a veil of darkness smothered me in its embrace. The staggering heat of the day did nothing to thwart the clamminess that crawled up my spine. My child was truly gone. I paled at the realization that a chasm opened and swallowed what I held most dear. How could I ever find my girl? The distance between us was no small thing. Miles and miles of emptiness was as effective as a wall of stone.

Two Face viewed my face with unconcealed interest, although I detected a faint note of sympathy in the creases of his eyes. He reverted back to the day's events.

"Mrs. Morton, Brave Whe-Ho. No die today." He gestured toward Medicine Arrows' lodge. "Cheyenne people honor. She no be killed. She no cry, so no die."

Tears blurred my vision; I did not acknowledge his presence. Belle was gone. My knees buckled, yet I would not let him see me fall. My feet scrabbled to find balance. Inhaling deeply, I planted myself on the foundation of defiance. I thought of how Big Crow forced himself upon me with threats and physical violence—how I detested him!

Mrs. Morton was accepted as a daughter within the Arrow Keeper's family. Her captivity demanded cooperation, while mine was defined by the sheer will to endure. Yet, both of us remained defiant. Our mutual goal—survival. Now, I must find my daughter. It was time to go.

Two Face lingered a moment longer. "You same brave, Fire Hair. But you fight different. You quiet strong Whe-Ho." His hand lightly touched the tangled golden red braid that draped over my shoulder. I jerked violently away from his touch and swore under my breath. Two Face grunted, then strode off.

Adrenaline coursed through my body. I was left icy by the encounter. The Sioux angered me, but today I would not crumble under his mocking gaze. I would never forget what was done to my family. Soon he would fight again with the rest of the Dog Soldiers.

I hoped he would meet his end.

chapter thirty-four

Escape

Mid-September 1864
Southeastern Colorado Territory

You all got a mighty fine head of hair for the Injuns to git, honey.
This frightened and made her nervous and she replied,
Oh, don't say that, for I have heard such terrible stories of how they
abuse their prisoners.

Aunt Eliza's and Mrs. Anna Snyder

T he camp was alive, lit like candles flickering against the mountains. Standing in the opening of the lodge, I watched the sun melt into the prairie. Lights glowed and shadows danced inside the golden, cone-shaped teepees. I heard the creek running and jumping as it gutted down the sides of its rocky banks.

As I closed the flap on the teepee, my hair was viciously yanked. Big Crow grabbed my head and slammed it in the dirt. My screams were stilled by his rough, dirt-caked hand as he ripped my dress from my body. My stomach turned at his familiar stench. My body heaved as I kicked and fought against his relentless abuse. My mind raced and swirled into a black abyss.

A tall man with a top hat and black suit extended his hand. His manner was most respectful as he explained that my chest would ride well on the back of the stagecoach. I gathered my skirt and petticoat with one hand, then reached for the shiny bar on the side of the coach and stepped aboard. The doors inside the coach gleamed with ornate, gold accents and the drapes covering the window openings were a plush purple velvet.

Positioning myself, I smoothed my skirt and settled into the soft seat. My eyes lifted to find another woman sitting across from me. She nodded and told me she admired my hat. I caught a glimpse of its emerald-

colored feathers dancing and curling around the side of my face. I smiled slightly through twinkling eyes and thanked her.

The stage rocked as we travelled, and I heard our driver talk to the horses. Looking through the window, I caught glimpses of black men digging in a rose garden. The overseer, adorned with a long sword, watched over them from his horse. We continued through the beautiful park with lush trees and a large blue lake in the middle. Graceful, white swans floated so close I could almost touch them. Birds of the brightest colors of blue, yellow, and red chirped and swooped across the sky.

A large, black buggy with red fringe jiggling along the top turned onto the brick road running along the lake. The horse's shoes clipped as they moved across the bricks. I quickly turned my head to look at the passing buggy. Familiar sounds of a child's laughter rang out. I focused my eyes seeking to put a face to this music. Then a small figure with long, blonde hair poked her face up from the back window. Waving, she smiled wide then her lips formed the words, "I love you, Mama!" I lunged my torso through the window and caught my skirt on the golden scrolls surrounding the door handle. The wind whipped my hair and sent my hat spiraling through the air.

The clip, clip, clip of the horse's hooves intensified against my screams! "Belle, stop! Where are you going? Will, are you in there? Will! Stop, please stop! You must stop!"

Heads sprang around from the end of the buggy, looking back at me. I could see Will's family! His father, brothers, and sister were smiling and waving at me. "Papa? Fred? Dora? James? Henry? Stop!" My body shook uncontrollably as I watched them roll down the brick road. The driver turned and looked straight at me. It was Joe! "Joe! My God! Joe Stop!" I stared in disbelief as the rolling buggy shrunk from sight.

I screamed at the coachman to help me. I pleaded for him to stop the horses. No response! Could he not hear my screams? Why couldn't anyone hear me? Desperate, I looked in horror at the woman sitting across the seat from me. She tilted her head and smiled sweetly. I sat stunned, staring at her. What was this insanity?

Jerked awake by the sounds of a crying baby, I whispered, "Willie?" There was an outline of a squaw across the teepee. She was holding my baby while another squaw placed a cold compress on my forehead. Blood oozed from my temple. I tried to sit up, but the limbs of my naked body were tied and staked to the ground. "Please untie me!" I shook my head back and forth begging and crying. "Please, please, let me go!"

Later, starved and exhausted, I sat in Big Crow's lodge for what I hoped was the final time. A tiny morsel of jack rabbit was divided by seven people and my innards gnawed upon themselves. I gave my portion of meat to Willie. After setting up camp that evening, I ventured to Nancy's lodge to beg for food. There was none to give, but I returned with our escape plan carefully outlined in my mind.

Whispering, Nancy and I agreed it was time to leave the Cheyenne camp. Two Face confirmed the children's release, and I was determined to follow Belle. As the tribe trekked southward, I knew each step separated us further.

An ally agreed to join us. Mrs. Snyder. Having seen the newest captive woman but twice, I knew little of her situation. However, Nancy found opportunities to speak with her and learned the poor woman's story. She shared that Anna Snyder was traveling with a party of only three men in a wagon that left Booneville for the day's ride to Fort Lyon. Attacked en route, all were killed, including her husband. Mrs. Snyder survived, and Little Raven's son brought her to his lodge in the Arapaho village. Terrified and mistreated, she resolved to escape or die trying. I conceded that Willie and I might perish during the escape attempt, but we were certain to die from starvation or the knife if we stayed. Besides, Belle was out there somewhere, possibly headed for Denver City.

After the camp settled for the night, I feigned sleep next to Old Woman. Her heavy breathing and loud snoring were a benefit for once. I hoped it would conceal my passage. The meager warmth of the fire's embers did little to hinder ripples of fear, which scattered in all directions. Soon all the people within the lodge were asleep, and I was ready to follow the North Star. I slowly rose from my blanket. Willie stirred a little as I stood. Before we went to bed, I purposely placed him in the deer-hide sling. He made small smacking noises as I crouched near the flap.

Slowly, without stopping, I lifted the flap and stuck my foot onto the side of freedom. I dared not leave it open enough for the cool night air to slide in and awaken the others. With one movement, I slipped into the fresh, dry air and drew a deep quivering breath. It was a moonless night, but the starlit sky welcomed me. I tried to get my bearings to find the distant ravine where we planned to meet.

I stepped lightly around the first lodge, then the second and soon was beyond the first circle of teepees. I quickened my progress, stopping occasionally to listen for following footsteps. It was a calm, quiet night, and I wished for a slight breeze to cause the skins on the teepees to flap. The noise would cover the beat of my departing heart.

Gaining confident passage around the next circle of lodges, two Indians appeared out of the shadows.

"Uhn!" grunted the shorter one as he grabbed my arm.

I nearly fainted.

"I am going to relieve myself," I replied in broken Cheyenne, hoping to convince him.

"No! You try leave," said the taller one. "You far from lodge." His eyes narrowed as he grabbed the arm I had thrown protectively around the babe.

I glanced down at Willie and realized he was wide-eyed, gauging my response to the strangers. I patted him reassuringly and said, "Shhh, it's okay, Willie." Thankfully, he remained quiet. I did not want his cries to alert the camp and interfere with my fleeing companions' escapes. Hopefully, they made it past these two unsavory brutes.

The camp guards promptly marched me back to the lodge where the sleeping, unsuspecting chief was roused and appraised of the situation. I waited outside, body trembling, tears streaming. I feared his response to my escape attempt and worried that Mrs. Morton's cleverness at avoiding detection had been foiled. They were surely checking all the captives, yet I hoped I would not see her in the morning. We agreed we would not leave without the other, but now I realized her only chance at freedom was ruined. For all that Mrs. Morton endured, her willingness to join her captors in dangerous games of challenge and skill won headway in her treatment. Yet daily, I fought a life-or-death battle against a conniving fiend. She was the one who tried to blend in with these frightening and barbarous people to gain their confidence, while I resisted stubbornly and suffered from my captor's indifference. I hoped she was running for her life!

Discouraged and fearful, I questioned my reason for hope. Who could prevail in this place? Had I just sealed our fate? I knew I could never stop fighting my captors, but if we survived this latest transgression, I needed to quell my defiance. I would do anything to ensure Willie's survival. What was I thinking?

Within moments, I was shoved into the lodge. My guardians loudly proclaimed my crimes. Big Crow stood and cuffed me hard on my ear, then beat me with his fists about the head and shoulders. Throwing me onto my sleeping robe, he grabbed my foot. He yanked and pulled on the moccasin, twisting my ankle back and forth. I flopped painfully side to side, using my other leg to kick and fight. The moccasin finally released, and he threw it at Old Woman. I crab-walked backward toward the edge of the teepee to protect my other foot from attack, but it was futile. Strict instructions were given to Old Woman. She was responsible to ensure my feet never wore shoes again.

Thrust between Old Woman and her daughter, my head pounded and ears rang. Before his hulking frame stomped through the teepee flap, he turned once again to face me. In the firelight, his visage was ferocious and threatening. He growled something I did not understand, then drew his forefinger across his throat. Gripped by the knowledge I had nearly drawn my last breath; the message was clear— any more escape attempts and my fate would be torturous and final.

Old Woman, her daughter, and I lay in a tight bundle until the sun rose hours later. None of us slept, unsure of Big Crow's return. The women were quiet, their assignment paramount in their minds; and my dreams of freedom retreated into an inky pool of resignation. I must not surrender...I must hold on...if I survive until dawn.

Before the sun could warm the frost off the grass, the camp was filled with loud voices and shouts. Willie and I joined our sleepless companions and ran toward the sound. Native voices echoed a death chant, for the spirits must be appeased. Running through the village, I followed the sounds and came upon a large group of Indians callously observing the scene. I nearly slid to the ground at the sight before me.

The sides of a teepee were dismantled. A woman hung from the apex of the lodge poles, a rope around her neck. It was the lithe, golden-haired Anna Snyder. Her feet dangled beneath her swinging skirts, one shoe missing from a delicate foot. Her beautiful face now bulged, bloated by her gruesome death. Tears and snot streamed through my clenched fist covering my mouth. Shuddering, I could not turn away.

Shocked and obviously still captive, Mrs. Morton was brought to examine the body. As we tried to move toward one another, the crowd shoved us to the ground. Passersby kicked dust into our faces and relished our humiliation. Struggling to stand, we pressed in closer. Linking arms, we pulled a blanket over our heads to create a haven against accusing eyes.

Nancy leaned in and whispered the news about Mrs. Snyder. "The woman escaped, was tracked down, and returned to the village. The Indians said she hanged herself, but Mitimoni is convinced Anna was strung up—as punishment. This is a warning. Mitimoni insists we not try to escape again, or we will be killed."

Pondering the folly of our plans, we grew silent. Then realization sank in.

"Nancy!" I whispered wide-eyed. "The poor woman could not have secured the hanging rope at the top of the poles by herself. They are almost twelve feet above the ground!"

We stared at each other and without a word, shakily contemplated the murder.

"Big Crow," we whispered simultaneously.

How had we escaped a similar fate? Medicine Arrows silently stepped next to Nancy and pulled her away. Then she was gone.

Fear engulfed me as I turned and flailed desperately through the throngs of onlookers, trying in vain to find safety. There was no place to hide, no place to run. I kept my head down and hoped no one would notice another troublesome white woman.

In time the village was on the move again. Walking tenderly next to Old Woman, I watched Big Crow march to Nancy's horse and tie a woman's scalp to her saddle. It was Anna's. He threatened Nancy—if she dared remove the sorrowful and sinister reminder, he would replace the scalp with her own.

Leaving the place of murder and gore, I grimly accepted the fact Mrs. Snyder succeeded in her final escape. Despair and defeat would shadow us in the nightmares to come.

I wondered what would become of the poor woman's body.

chapter thirty-five

Shortest Road to the People's Hearts

25 September 1864
Office of the Colorado Territorial Governor
Denver City, Colorado Territory

On the frontier this was the shortest road to the people's hearts: give the Indians a whipping and the voters would give you any office you asked of them.

George Bent

Colonel George H. Shoup read the telegram again. A Hundred Days Regiment was to be organized for the purpose of operating in Colorado Territory against the Indians. Sounded simple enough, but here he was, still in limbo as to when they would be ready to move. Captain Robbins interrupted his thoughts as he entered the room.

"Sir, you called for me?" asked the lanky, young man.

"Yes, Robbins. I want a readiness update on the First Colorado Volunteers and the Hundred Days Regiment. We need to see action before they muster out. The Secretary sent the order two months ago," replied the Colonel, "and nothing has happened. This is not going to look good back in Washington. What have you to report?"

"Sir, we have had great difficulty in procuring horses and the ordinance stores necessary to mount and equip the regiment."

Because of the disruption in the flow of animals and goods into Denver, it was a frustrating feat to obtain the supplies and stock necessary to outfit the entire force. The Indians prevented not only the freight trains from passing through, but also communication with suppliers had been haphazard.

"Captain Robbins. We must move now. The Colorado Volunteers have less than thirty days left on their commission! The governor wants

190

to see results; and politically, Washington only hears our complaints and excuses. This is rubbing our supporters in D.C. the wrong way. Tell me, how many mounted men can we have ready by the first of November?" demanded Shoup.

"My most recent inventory shows a total of seven hundred men ready to move out, which is only part of the six companies of the First Regiment. Plus, we must contend with the Hundred Days men."

"No matter," interrupted Shoup. "Chivington said he will join the volunteers on the fifteenth of November. It is imperative you make sure he has what he needs. The preacher is anxious to bring the fight to the Cheyenne!"

<hr />

Governor John Evans and Colonel John Milton Chivington sat comfortably in one another's presence smoking cigars. The colonel's outstretched legs extended far beyond the confines of the overstuffed horsehair chair. He was an imposing man: six-foot, five-inches tall, weighing in at two hundred sixty pounds.

Due to Chivington's self-professed talents as a Methodist minister, his initial commission with the First Colorado Regiment was as chaplain. That assignment was short-lived, for he requested a fighting rather than praying assignment—which was tendered with a promotion.

Possessing a confident military bearing, Chivington proved his heroism by defeating the Confederate invasion at Glorietta Pass in New Mexico Territory. This garnered him recognition on a national stage as Colorado's "Fighting Parson." His ambitions leaned toward becoming the first Colorado congressman once statehood was achieved. He planned to increase his notoriety for such political purposes.

In contrast, the governor was of smaller stature, yet robust, with the authority of a man who understood his duty. He hoped to link his future designs on prosperity with the growing economy of the territory. The two men found companionship based on their common goals. Although neither man considered the other a friend, they were content to work as a team in their pursuit of power and recognition in the fledgling territory.

"Let me offer you congratulations on your recent selection as candidate for Congress," said Evans. He nipped the tip off a fresh cigar which dangled from his fingers, then spat the nib into the bowl of the smoking stand next to his chair. "Teller and I are campaigning for you right along with Colorado statehood."

Lifting his cigar in salute, Evans twirled it between his lips. Spittle soaked the rolled tobacco end. Stretching his neck forward with stogie aimed at the burning candle on the table, he puffed sufficiently until the lit end flared. Blue smoke swirled around his head as he leaned back confidently.

"Now that the Secretary of War has authorized the enlistment of a cavalry to fight Indians, we can work together to remove this obstacle to statehood." The governor held no qualms in discussing matters of a political nature. "Since Congress authorized the Union Pacific to meet the Central, it is possible for Denver to secure a connecting route with the transcontinental railroad. That boost to Colorado's economy is beyond measure!"

Evans took another drag on his cigar and concluded, "It is urgent this Indian trouble be resolved, so we can clear the way for the future of the territory."

"Indeed," replied Chivington, tapping ash from the end of his fuming cigar. "With Colorado's superior resources, the state's pathway to progress must not be impeded by the natives. Now that I no longer must accept an assignment back in the states, I hope to represent Colorado from a position of victory over the current problem." The corners of his mouth twisted up in anticipation. "It is the only way forward."

"Umm hmm," nodded Evans distractedly.

Now that pleasantries were set aside, their amiable conversation turned to more serious matters. Each man planned to exchange intelligences regarding the Indian problem.

"You know, of course, the road into Denver has been completely closed. No mail in nor out since August fifteenth," snorted the governor.

"Sending mail by way of Panama and San Francisco is a hindrance to progress. Completely ridiculous!" retorted Chivington.

"That is one of the reasons I invited you here. I would like to share with you a report I received from Robert North," said Evans.

"You mean the white man married to the Arapaho squaw?" interjected Chivington.

"One and the same. He is my main source of information regarding the activities of the various bands which affect the security of Coloradans. He met with the Indians last spring."

Clearing his throat, the governor rested his cigar in the stand and picked up a paper from the tabletop. He coughed to clear his throat, then began to read Robert North's report.

> I saw the principal chiefs pledge to each other that they would be
> friendly and shake hands with the whites until they procured ammu-
> nition and guns, so as to be ready when they strike. Plundering to get

means has already commenced, and the plan is to begin the war at several points in the sparse settlements.

"They certainly have the local citizenry worried," said Chivington.

"Well, they should be! Elbridge Gerry stopped in recently at my request and confirmed this report." Evans spit out a small piece of stogie and waved the letter in the air. "Before this Indian war began, Gerry met with Black Kettle. He expressed a willingness to discuss matters. However, the chiefs unilaterally denounced the Fort Wise Treaty. When Gerry explained I wanted them to live like white men, the Dog Soldier Bull Bear said, 'You tell white chief, Indian maybe not so low yet.'" Evans scoffed derisively and threw the report back onto the table.

"Since the recent escalation of conflicts, Gerry has informed me he will no longer offer guidance on the Indians' movements, and I should not expect further information regarding their intentions. Pretty clear which side he is on!" snapped the governor.

Chivington grunted and added, "He is a nit, not worth a nickel! The tribes are intent on disrupting travel and commerce. Now the cost of flour is forty-five dollars a sack! I suspect rebel emissaries have been inserted among the tribes to incite this violence."

Chivington and Evans paused to pull on their cigars and contemplate the unholy alliance between the Indians and the southern rebels.

"George Bent," stated Chivington, eyes narrowing. "The educated half-breed son of William Bent. You know of him?"

"Yes, I am familiar with him. Go on," said Evans.

"He is a rebel and served under General Price in Missouri. He was taken prisoner, then paroled. Swore an oath of allegiance to the United States but then joined up with the Cheyenne, his mother's people. I suspect he is the strategist behind the Indian raids. And from whom are they buying their weapons?" Chivington grumbled as he squinted suspiciously at the end of his cigar.

"Hmm..." replied Evans deep in thought. "Based on our suspicions, it would behoove us to issue a warrant for his immediate arrest. He is trouble, that man!" said Evans as he cleared his throat and continued. "Along those lines, the main reason I invited you here tonight is to discuss Major Wynkoop." Evans leaned forward in confidence and lowered his voice, "He has gone rogue on us, I fear. I received this report from him regarding events at Hackberry Creek out on the southern branch of the Smoky Hill River." He handed the letter to Chivington.

"It seems he secured the release of a young white woman and three children from the Cheyenne camp," said Evans as a frown creased his plump face.

Chivington's expression of surprise went unnoticed.

Evans continued, "One small child, Isabelle Eubank, is in poor condition, I am afraid." The governor shook his head at the thought of what the captives had endured. "Wynkoop parlayed with the chiefs, without permission, I might add, and endangered an entire detachment by his reckless actions. Now he informs me the chiefs will arrive in Denver soon for a council."

The anger in his voice was palpable. "I want nothing to do with these tribes! The fact that Wynkoop committed me to this meeting in the first place is contemptible!"

"Umph!" grunted Chivington as he continued to review the report while absently parking his cigar on the stand next to his chair. The report was the usual orderly and well-written composition Chivington knew to expect from the young major. Setting it aside, he looked into the face of his exasperated companion and said, "Governor, now that we are at war with the Indians, I believe this to be a matter for the military."

Formalizing a plan, the colonel deliberately and carefully chose his words. "Now that the 3rd Regiment is filled, we must utilize the might of the United States Army or risk accusations of pandering to the Indian. We need to be perceived as finding a more permanent solution."

He reached for the glass of brandy offered by Evans and nodded his thanks. The governor served himself and resumed his position opposite his confidant. "Perhaps we can look at this as an opportunity," Chivington continued. He twirled the amber liquid slowly before taking a sip. "I imagine the girl's injuries are unfortunate. The Denver citizenry should be informed...in detail. Your office can certainly sympathize with the victims publicly. It is important to communicate all evil deeds perpetrated by the Indians. It is the shortest road to people's hearts."

The colonel shifted in his chair, then crossed his legs. "Meet with the enemy, Governor."

Evans nearly spit out his cigar. Confounded by this concession, one thick brow raised in query. He prepared to state his opposition to the proposal, but Chivington plowed forward.

"Find no common ground with the Cheyenne and Arapaho. We can justify the use of force based on the Indians' refusal to concede to our demands."

The governor leaned back in his chair and considered the mind of the man before him. Politics, often devious and dark, are ingrained in the natures of ambitious men. With a nod of his head, Evans raised his glass of brandy in acknowledgment and drained its contents.

Chivington smiled and said, "Let me do my job, Governor, so you can do yours."

———•———

Summoned to the Planter's Hotel the next morning, Major Wynkoop entered the lobby. He found Dexter Colley and the governor amiably chatting in one of the comfortable seating areas set apart from the busy front desk.

Wynkoop was surprised to see Evans. Upon his arrival the night before, he presented himself at Governor Evans' home and was promptly turned away. The governor was ill and not available to see him. Yet, here he sat and by all appearances, was in the best of health.

After exchanging polite greetings, Wynkoop asked if the governor received his report on the events at Hackberry Creek. The governor replied he read the letter but had misgivings about what the major was trying to accomplish by his actions.

Major Wynkoop pressed on. "Will you meet with the chiefs, sir? They will arrive in Denver in a few days. I have arranged for a council to discuss peace."

"I want nothing to do with these Indian chiefs, Major Wynkoop," growled the governor. "Besides, I have plans to start in the morning for the Ute Agency. These Cheyenne and Arapaho have declared war against the United States; therefore, they are the responsibility of the military authorities." The governor stopped himself as he looked around the busy lobby, reminding himself to control the volume of his voice. There were always ears on the hunt for juicy local information. "You must go through the proper channels, Major," he hissed. "I suggest you contact General Curtis, who I might add, is at this moment preparing a course of action. He intends for the Indians to pay full restitution for all losses, then go to their reservations and stay there!"

His voice dropped to a whisper. "May I also remind you that Colonel Chivington has recruited the One Hundred Days Regiment? How will I explain their purpose and associated expenses to Washington if they muster out before firing a shot?"

"Governor, if I could persuade you to meet with the chiefs. A way forward can lead to peace, not war. They acted in good faith by releasing the prisoners and are now ready to discuss…."

"These Indians have not been sufficiently punished!" sputtered the angry governor.

Wynkoop decided to take a different tact. "As this territory moves toward statehood, would it not be beneficial to the citizenry that a solution be reached without further bloodshed? The residents of Denver certainly look to your office for assurances of safety and the restoration of normalcy. This meeting would go far to calm their fears. Also..." he added softly, "I promised the Indians an interview with you, sir. May I respectfully request you honor the commitment?"

The governor pondered the underlying tone of Wynkoop's suggestion. The passion behind the young officer's eyes reminded him of the undulating dance of a trout just beneath the water. It was time to cast the line. He knew the newspapers would report on his willingness or reluctance to meet with the Indians. He also knew his presence at a council would be more favorable than running from the problem to visit the Utes.

Evans set his jaw and feigned defeat. He would appear to relent as Colonel Chivington had proposed. He looked again into the eyes of his prey and said simply, "Major Wynkoop, I will postpone my trip to preside over the meeting at Camp Weld. Of course, the proper military authorities should be in attendance." As an afterthought, he added, "Please ask Colonel Shoup, the new commander of the 3rd Regiment, and Colonel Chivington to be in attendance. Make the arrangements, but let it be known I am merely supplying the venue for this military conference."

Standing abruptly, the governor said, "Good day, gentlemen."

Watching the politician walk out the door, a relieved Wynkoop thought he detected victory in the man's demeanor. Yet, Wynkoop wondered...had he won the battle but not the war? Evans was not a man to be underestimated. Political aspirations tempered his decisions, and the fall-out could go either way.

No matter. There was much to do before the council convened in a couple of days' time. Wynkoop looked at Dexter Colley, who was grinning at him. Ned tried to quell the smile forming on his own face... but contained his enthusiasm to adopt a businesslike demeanor. "I require the interpretation services of John Smith and Sam Ashcraft. Please ask them to meet me at Camp Weld this afternoon." Wynkoop turned to leave but could no longer suppress the grin on his face. Perhaps a way to peace could be forged.

Little did he know—the hook was set.

chapter thirty-six

Like Coming Through the Fire

28 September 1864
Camp Weld, Colorado Territory

*The Cheyennes and Arapahoes, we learn, have asked for peace, and
that General Blunt has protested against peace overtures. The devils
are starved down, but if Uncle Sam feeds them through the winter,
they will be fresh and ready for blood again when spring opens.*

The Smoky Hill and Republican Union, Junction City, Kansas
October 08, 1864

Ned's thoughts drifted to the tiny, golden-haired girl. He arranged
for his friends, the Sanfords, to take Isabelle Eubank into their
home. Belle was pale, thin, and very frail. She needed a tender
mother figure, and Mollie Sanford was pleased to help.

Steadying their mounts, Wynkoop and Captain Soule watched the
military wagon escort enter Denver City on the main thoroughfare. Ned's
family, seven Cheyenne and Arapaho leaders, and the surrey with
the former captives rambled past in good order. Their arrival created
considerable excitement among the citizens. They halted in front of the
governor's residence where Ned's father-in-law, George Wakely, took
a photo.

The chiefs were directed to a location south of the city where their
families erected lodges. Of course, the Cheyenne and Arapaho Indians
knew the area well. It had been their summer camping grounds for
generations. The released captives were tucked away in the Planter's
Hotel. After the initial uproar died down, Ned and Silas finished
preparations for the great council.

The morning dawned bright and cold without a cloud in the sky. The
young officers rode two miles southwest of Denver to Camp Weld. Ned

reflected on how little things had changed at the camp since he was commander the prior spring.

Upon riding through the main eastern entrance, he noticed the central square filled with a volunteer militia, also known as the One Hundred Days Regiment. The rag tag bunch were not mounted or supplied, yet they spent days practicing military drills. Their current detail was to prepare to fight Indians. Wynkoop wondered what impression the novice soldiers would make on the arriving dignitaries.

The two men dismounted and tied their horses in front of the officers' headquarters. Ned surveyed the soldiers' quarters, mess hall, hospital, and guard house. Smoke floated up from huge fireplaces at the ends of the buildings. The warm September days were tempered by cold nights and the air floating up from the river was brisk.

Entering the large meeting hall, the Indian Agent, Simeon Whiteley, greeted the men. "Good morning, officers!" he said cheerfully as he finished moving the ink well into position on the long polished pine table. Whiteley would officially document the meeting on its gleaming, knotty-ringed surface.

Captain Soule directed the interpreters, John Smith and Sam Ashcraft, to their places, and everyone fidgeted nervously. It was a momentous occasion, and each man held a notion as to what would constitute success or failure.

Moments later, Governor Evans appeared, followed by the imposing Colonel Chivington. "Gentlemen," he said briskly as he took off his coat and headed toward the fireplace. He wasted no time in declaring, "I am still unyielding in my opinion that the Indians have declared war. This telegram, which Colonel Chivington received from General Curtis this morning, supports that opinion. I do not wish to linger at this council any longer than necessary. I intend to glean information regarding Indian locations and culpability in recent raids. I will follow the General's directives explicitly."

Evans handed the missive to Wynkoop. Ned read the message in his hands, then looked at Silas, whose face had gone pale.

Dispatch from Major General Curtis to Colonel Chivington
Fort Leavenworth, September 28, 1864

> I shall require the bad Indians delivered up; restoration of equal numbers of stock—also hostages, to secure. I want no peace till the Indians suffer more. "Left Hand" is said to be a good chief of the Arapahoes; but "Big Mouth" is a rascal. I fear agent of Interior Department will be ready to make presents too soon. It is better to chastise before giving anything but a little tobacco to talk over. No peace must be made without my directions. Furthermore, the idea that Indians should seek safety at military posts directly contradicts my plan to keep the Indians starving and on the run throughout the winter months.

"No peace until the Indians suffer more," repeated Wynkoop glancing at the governor. Silas and Ned looked at each other in astonishment. Negotiations were about to begin, and hostility was on full view.

"I gave you my word I would grant them an audience, but that is the extent of my involvement," stated the governor firmly.

Evans and Chivington took their places at the table near the fireplace at the front of the room. The other military representatives, including Colonel George Shoup, Commander of the 3rd Regiment; and Lieutenant Cramer, along with local officials, took their places in the seats behind the council.

The presence of seven robed chiefs darkened the double doors. Wynkoop greeted Make-tava-tah and extended his hand. "Welcome, Chief Black Kettle! Please, come in."

The chief's long, black braids rested against the shoulders of his white shirt. A blue scarf was tied about his neck and tucked within the collar. His buckskin leggings and moccasins were tastefully decorated with tiny red, blue, and yellow beads—the patterns arranged along fringed edges. He was draped in a finely spun wool blanket, its creamy background striped in red and black.

Black Kettle's stature was that of a wise and pleasant elder. Wynkoop thought once again of the contrast between the man and the general opinion he once held of an Indian chief. Black Kettle's presence personalized his position, and Wynkoop was drawn to him. A friendship had grown from their recent interactions out on the endless prairie, where pretense and pride withered in the sun.

Attired in a fresh pressed uniform, Silas escorted each leader into the room. They shook hands with all present before taking their seats around the tables.

Wynkoop introduced each man to Agent Whitely who recorded the names of the attendees. The Cheyenne leaders included Bull Bear, White Antelope, and Lone Bear. The Arapaho delegation included Neva, Heap of Buffalo, No-ta-nee, and Bosse.

Chief Black Kettle offered the pipe to the officers and governor, explaining it was a symbol of truth to be spoken at the council. He passed the pipe among those gathered.

Once formalities were finished, Governor Evans instructed the interpreter to ask the Indians why they had come.

Black Kettle, the presumed leader of the Indian delegation, stood to speak first. John Smith interpreted Black Kettle's words:

> On sight of your circular of June 27, 1864, I took hold of the matter, and have now come to talk to you about it. I told Mr. Bent, who brought it, that I accepted it, but it would take some time to get all my people together—many of my young men being absent—and I have done everything in my power, since then, to keep peace with the whites. As soon as I could get my people together, we held a council, and got a half-breed who was with them to write a letter to inform Major Wynkoop, or other military officer nearest to them, of their intention to comply with the terms of the circular. Major Wynkoop was kind enough to receive the letter, and visited them in camp, to whom they delivered four white prisoners—one other (Mrs. Snyder,) having killed herself; that there are two women and one child yet in their camp, whom they will deliver up as soon as we can get them in: Laura Roper 16 or 17 years; Ambrose Asher, 7 or 8 years; Daniel Marble, 7 or 8 years, Isabel Ubanks, 4 or 5 years. The prisoners still with them [are] Mrs. Ubanks and babe, and a Mrs. Morton, who was taken on the Platte. Mrs. Snyder is the name of the woman who hung herself. The boys were taken between Fort Kearney and the Blue. I followed Maj. Wynkoop to Fort Lyon, and Major Wynkoop proposed that we come up to see you. We have come with our eyes shut, following his handful of men, like coming through the fire. All we ask is that we may have peace with the whites. We want to hold you by the hand. You are our father. We have been travelling through a cloud. The sky has been dark ever since the war began. These braves who are with me are all willing to do what I say. We want to take good tidings home to our people, that they may sleep in peace. I want you to give all these chiefs of the soldiers here to understand that we are for peace, and that we have made peace, that we may not be mistaken by them for enemies. I have not come here with a little wolf's bark, but have come to talk plain with you. We must live near the buffalo, or starve. When we came here we came free, without any apprehension, to see you, and when I go home and tell my people that I have taken your hand, and

200

the hands of all the chiefs here in Denver, they will feel well, and so will all the different tribes of Indians on the plains, after we have eaten and drank with them.

The chief sat down. Governor Evans made it obvious he was not impressed by the speech. He sat back in his chair, which squeaked in protest. After a long pause, Evans boldly replied. He had gone to significant effort to arrange a peace conference in July 1863. The governor spoke words of criticism:

> I am sorry you did not respond to my appeal at once. You have gone into an alliance with the Sioux, who were at war with us. You have done a great deal of damage—have stolen stock, and now have possession of it. However much a few individuals may have tried to keep the peace, as a nation you have gone to war. While we have been spending thousands of dollars in opening farms for you, and making preparations to feed, protect, and make you comfortable, you have joined our enemies and gone to war…I had presents, and would make you a feast, but you sent word to me that you did not want to have anything to do with me…Bull Bear wanted to come in to see me, at the head of the Republican, but his people held a council and would not let him come…Your people went away and smoked the war pipe with our enemies.

"This is a mistake," replied Black Kettle. The chiefs shifted in their seats and murmured protests. "We have made no alliance with the Sioux or anyone else."

Neva, who was following the dispute, rose and spoke in English. "We acknowledge that our actions have given you reason to believe this."

"Indeed!" concurred Evans.

> So far as making a treaty now, is concerned, we are in no condition to do it. Your young men are on the warpath. My soldiers are preparing for the fight. You so far, have had the advantage; but the time is near at hand when the plains will swarm with United States soldiers. I understand that these men who have come to see me now, have been opposed to the war all the time, but that their people have controlled them and they could not help themselves. Is that so?

"It has been so," agreed White Antelope.

The governor was surprised at the honesty of the men before him. The power of the pipe certainly was in evidence. Anger rising, Evans continued his litany of grievances and reprimanded the chiefs.

> The fact that they have not been able to prevent their people from going to war in the past spring, when there was plenty of grass and game, makes me believe that they will not be able to make a peace which will last longer than until winter is past…The time when you can make war best is in the summertime; when I can make war best is in the winter. You, so far, have had the advantage; my time is just coming. I have learned that you understand that as the whites are at war among themselves, you think you can now drive the whites from this country. But this reliance is false. The Great Father at Washington has men enough to drive all the Indians off the plains; and whip the rebels at the same time. Now, the war with the whites is nearly through, and the Great Father will not know what to do with all his soldiers, except to send them after the Indians on the plains.

The eyes of the chiefs widened at this information, except for Bull Bear. His eyes narrowed at Evans who cast him a wary glance, then quickly looked away. Chivington crossed his arms and stared defiantly at the Indian chiefs.

Evans finished his statement:

> My proposition to the friendly Indians has gone out; I shall be glad to have them all come in, under it. I have no new propositions to make. Another reason that I am not in a condition to make a treaty, is, that war is begun, and the power to make a treaty of peace has passed from me to the great War Chief. My advice to you, is, to turn on the side of the government and show, by your acts, that friendly disposition you profess to me. It is utterly out of the question for you to be at peace with us, while living with our enemies, and being on friendly terms with them…The only way you can show this friendship is by making some arrangement with the soldiers to help them.

Governor Evans sat down and clasped his hands across his midsection, fully satisfied with his message. The only sounds heard were the scratchings of Simeon Whitely's pen on the long paper which held evidence of things spoken.

Black Kettle looked at the paper, then at the governor, and said,

> We will return with Major Wynkoop to Fort Lyon; we will then proceed to our village, and take back word to my young men, every word you say. I cannot answer for all of them, but think there will be but little difficulty in getting them to assent to help the soldiers.

Major Wynkoop, who had been silently taking in every word of the exchange, asked hopefully, "Did not the Dog Soldiers agree, when I had my council with you, to do whatever you said after you had been here?"

Black Kettle looked into the eyes of his friend and his mouth turned up slightly at the bravery of Tall Chief. Even the Dog Soldiers would be held accountable by the irascible young officer. "Yes," he replied, satisfied with the progress made thus far.

Black Kettle listened as the governor reiterated his position and issued a stern warning. Without an arrangement with the soldiers, the tribes would be treated as enemies. Then the white chief stepped away slightly from his original stance of no concession given. Perhaps an arrangement was possible with the soldiers. Tall Chief would help.

Ever perceptive, White Antelope rose slowly to speak. He wore the medal he received on a trip to Washington two years earlier. It was clear to him the governor would be true to his threat. White Antelope knew the power and numbers of the whites first-hand. His gaze shifted to the big colonel whose mood matched the governor's words. John Smith continued to interpret for the Indian chief.

White Antelope said:

> I understand every word you have said, and will hold on to it. I will give you an answer directly. The Cheyennes, all of them, have their eyes open this way, and they will hear what you say. He is proud to have seen the chief of all whites in this country. He will tell his people. Ever since he went to Washington and received this medal, I have called all white men as my brothers. But other Indians have since been to Washington, and got medals, and now the soldiers do not shake hands, but seek to kill me. What do you mean by us fighting your enemies? Who are they?

"All Indians who are fighting us," replied the governor with a grand gesture to the plains outside the windows.

White Antelope's concern grew. "How can we be protected from the soldiers on the plains?"

"You must make that arrangement with the military chief."

White Antelope replied tentatively, "I fear these new soldiers who have gone out may kill some of my people while I am here."

"Yes," agreed Evans unsympathetically. "There is a great danger of it."

White Antelope pressed on:

> When we sent our letter to Major Wynkoop, it was like going through a strong fire or blast, for Major Wynkoop's men to come to our camp; it was the same for us to come to see you…When Major Wynkoop came, we proposed to make peace. He said he had no power to make peace, except to bring them here and return them safe.

Governor Evans was tiring of the persistent chief and said slowly as though speaking to a child, "Whatever peace you make must be with soldiers, and not with me."

White Antelope wanted to explain the causes of the current conflict, and other chiefs offered their views as well. But Governor Evans stopped them short with a wave of his hand.

"I have heard enough. Now I would like you and the others to answer questions we have," he said with a nod to the foreboding figure of Chivington next to him.

For the next several hours, the governor demanded to know which tribes were responsible for certain attacks, raids, thefts, and killings. Where was each of these offending bands located? Repeatedly, Evans asked questions, and each was answered by the chiefs.

Major Wynkoop's ears rang as the interrogation droned on into the afternoon. At one point, Bull Bear expressed a desire to prove his peaceful intentions by fighting the enemies of the whites. His offer was dismissed without acknowledgement. As questions about depredations continued, the conference dissolved into disputes and accusations.

The Arapaho Chief, Little Raven, mentioned tribal grievances, including the loss of timber which the whites used for fuel and buildings. The constant stream of traffic on the major trails crossed their ancestral hunting grounds and disrupted ancient migration buffalo paths.

The frequent interruptions by interpreters and Simeon Whitely for clarification slowed the proceedings. Whiteley recorded the testimony in long hand, and he was tiring. Tempers were running short.

Staying silent throughout the proceedings, Colonel Chivington was losing patience. He was uninterested in learning the identities of the perpetrators or listening to the chiefs excuse their roles in the current hostilities. He knew where the United States Army stood on the handling of the Indian War, and he regarded their pledges of peace as mere platitudes. He carefully observed young Major Wynkoop's newfound friendship with the Indians and concluded it would not work to his advantage. He was sure General Curtis was aware of the major's misplaced intentions. It was time to adjourn this meeting, and Chivington would say what was necessary to keep the enemy's focus off the forthcoming attacks. Indeed, these Indians were the enemy and did not require further attention from the honorable governor.

Colonel Chivington rose slowly from his seat.

The council quieted as he drew himself up to tower over the wary chiefs. His display of dominance and displeasure brought everyone to attention. Then John Chivington spoke:

> I am not a big war chief, but all the soldiers in this country are at my command. My rule of fighting white men or Indians is to fight them until they lay down their arms and submit to military authority. They are nearer Major Wynkoop than any one else, and they can go to him when they get ready to do that.

With this, he declared the Camp Weld Council ended.

Samuel Ashcraft looked at John Smith and deferred to him to translate the confusing message. The chiefs listened to the interpretation of the colonel's words and felt perplexed and unsettled. They questioned his meaning.

Major Wynkoop hesitated a moment, discerned that Chivington was finished, and moved to dismiss the Indians. Approaching Black Kettle, the chief embraced Ned heartily. He then moved to embrace a surprised Governor Evans. The chief continued around the room shaking hands with all those in attendance.

As Governor Evans moved to leave the room, he slowed his gait as he passed Agent Colley. Leaning in, he said in a hushed tone, "The chiefs brought in by Major Wynkoop have been heard. I have declined to make treaty with them. Make it known."

Meanwhile, Major Wynkoop led the chiefs to the far corner of the room where the photographer waited in front of his curtained set. The chiefs were fascinated by the large, boxy camera with the large lens.

After posing for photographs, Black Kettle shook hands with John Smith and expressed his satisfaction with the council. The peace he sought for his people was within their grasp. Smith encouraged the chief to return with Major Wynkoop to their camp in the vicinity of Fort Lyon and await the decision of the military authorities. The chiefs assured themselves that eventually everything would be all right, and they pledged to wait in good faith.

White Antelope, however, stood alone. He stared at the large soldier chief, Chivington, as though seeing something in the beyond—in another realm. The vision left him empty, his face expressionless. He had seen the future and knew the end was near.

chapter thirty-seven

Go With God

5 October 1864
Denver City, Colorado Territory

She was to be adopted by someone, so I thought I would take her. I
did but I could not stand it. She would arouse from sleep at night
with piercing screams, shrieking, "Don't kill my papa, don't kill my
brother, don't kill me!

Mollie E. Sanford

Mollie Sanford gathered the feverish, whimpering child onto her
lap. Pressing Belle's limp body tightly against her chest,
she gently rocked. Mollie stared into the candlelight—another
midnight vigil. She smoothed Belle's wispy, blonde hair and sighed. The
child was gently bathed and given warm milk each night, but it did little
to soothe her torment.

The journey across the eastern plains was long and arduous. Belle's
physical condition seemed only slightly improved since her arrival in
Denver from Fort Lyon. It was her state of mind that troubled Mollie the
most.

The inconsolable three-year-old girl's experiences involved so much
tragedy. Isabelle Eubank awakened each night—screaming and terrified,
asking, imploring, pleading for "mama" and "papa." Her cries for her
father reached a crescendo that dissolved into uncontrollable hiccups
which caused her frail body to tremble. Too many frightening memories
for one so young.

Belle settled as Mollie hummed softly. Belle's quiet weeping was
accented by hoarse gulps of air and halting spits of exhalation. Losing
strength, Mollie found her efforts to heal the child unsatisfactory.

For months, Mollie feared an attack by renegade Indians, and she
was exhausted. Ready to flee at a moment's warning, she slept fully
clothed. The eyes and ears of the Denver population were riveted on

the crisis—the impending war could extend onto their doorsteps at any moment.

Then there was Mr. Woods. Mollie's husband Byron tasked the soldier with protecting his family while he worked in the mountains at Gold Hill. Rumors and hurried preparations for defense fueled Mr. Wood's fervor. He took his assignment seriously and cautioned Mollie to sleep with one eye open. She wondered if he relished the descriptions of depredations and danger a bit too excessively. After months of near hysteria among the citizens of Denver, no attack materialized.

A week earlier, Denver was abuzz with news of the release of white captives to Major Wynkoop. Seventeen-year-old Laura Roper and two boys, Ambrose Asher and Danny Marble, were released along with the child in her arms. Initially, they stayed at the hotel then moved in with Mollie until other quarters could be arranged.

Mollie possessed a young mother's heart and set her sights on adopting little Belle. Ned Wynkoop was a close friend and had approached Mollie with the idea. He had a personal stake in the child's outcome.

The children shared harrowing tales of attack and captivity. It was surmised Miss Roper suffered unimaginable violations, though she never spoke of them. Danny was more forthcoming, six-year-old Ambrose Asher rarely spoke at all.

Belle quieted and fell asleep. Mollie's two-year-old son Bertie was restless and cried in his sleep. Mollie gently placed Belle on her bed, and after a quick check of Bertie's soaked nappy, she quickly changed him, and he settled back into slumber.

Bertie accepted the newcomers; the older boys held an endless fascination to him. But Mollie was having doubts about the adoption and longed for the days when Bertie was her only concern. The anguish caused by Belle's distress was taxing, and young Bertie seemed disturbed as well.

Mollie hesitated as her thoughts turned to the delightful memories of early motherhood. The shine of a new baby in his mother's eyes knows no bounds. What light had Belle's mother reflected onto this beautiful child? Oh, the sorrow that must seep from Belle's mother's wounded heart. Mollie contemplated the loss—to be robbed of the happy sounds of her toddler, to have no knowledge of her well-being. It was unfathomable.

On those rare occasions when Belle relaxed in her arms, the girl often gazed into Mollie's face with a quiet intensity as if searching for the familiar. Once, she reached tiny fingers to touch Mollie's eyes and mouth. The tiny act of tenderness brought tears to her eyes. During those times, Mollie wondered about the mother's features and appearance. Was she fair and diminutive like the child? Did the mother and child share the small chin, rosebud lips, and pale blue eyes?

It was unthinkable Mollie would abandon this poor woman's babe. Mollie and her husband wanted to keep Belle, to raise her as their daughter, as a sister to sweet Bertie.

But...oh, the screams.... They woke the household each night, and those eyes staring off into the dark! In vivid detail, little Belle recounted the events which destroyed her family. Her limited toddler language did nothing to sanitize the whole bloody event. The episodes continued to play havoc with Mollie's hopes for a normal family life.

The pitiful child had physical scars as well—her delicate skin marred by the squaws. It was said the Indians did not allow their children to cry. Arrowheads pressed into the skin left oozing imprints on her back. Was it punishment? Or did the Indian women seek to release harassing evil spirits from the child suffering nightmares? Most concerning were the puffy, infected puncture wounds. Was Belle shot with arrows? Dr. Burdsal examined them but could not determine how deeply the injuries penetrated the child's torso. His instructions for her care were followed carefully, yet Mollie worried about the girl's lackluster appetite and lethargy.

Belle's beautiful eyes were always sad. She held her tightly and imagined the hurt, forlorn child wandering the Indian camp, searching for her mother. Mollie doubted her ability to cope with such an injured soul. As tiredness invaded her mind, Mollie felt despair rob her of rest.

She must decide.

Belle's mother, the only healing balm which would truly relieve the child's pain, was taken away by a distant band of Indians—probably never to return.

Rocking and thinking, she finally resigned herself to the bitter conclusion. The nagging question in her mind was resolved—she and her husband would not adopt tiny Isabelle. The child was sick, weak, and so traumatized. She would ask Dr. Burdsal to care for her. He and his wife were childless, and Mollie was sure the competent couple would love Belle and provide the necessary medical care. Possibly, the good man and his wife were the answer.

Mollie snuggled Belle and caressed her face.

No, little one, I am unable to heal you.

Go with God....

Weeks later, Mollie sat in her parlor, holding the newest copy of the Rocky Mountains Daily News. She leaned in closer to the window. Daylight illuminated the bold headline:

IDENTIFIED AT LAST!

The chairman of our Relief Association, Major Fillmore, informs us that the parents of the little boy who was captured from the Indians last summer on the Arkansas have been found and heard from. It appears that the little girl, captured at that time also, when Mrs. Eubanks was carried off or killed, is the daughter of Mrs. Eubanks. The boy's mother lives in Kentucky, and is coming to Atchison to meet him, as soon as the Committee gets an opportunity to send him comfortably on there. The little girl will be kept here, raised and educated by some family.

Rocky Mountain Daily News
November 24, 1864

chapter thirty-eight

Death Sentence

Early October 1864
Near Fort Union, New Mexico Territory

At one time the fire was kindled for her cremation and only the admiration of the savages for the coolness and courage with which she witnessed these preparations saved her from this terrible fate. She affected great joy that she was about to relieve them of the burden of her maintenance and that she would soon pass to the happy hunting grounds beyond.

Truth Stranger Than Fiction
Fremont County Herald, Sidney, Iowa
December 28, 1899

S tarvation clawed incessantly, demanding, tugging, persistent. Ravenously, Nancy and I braved the spines of prickly pear cactus and rose hips along the trail. Using our fingernails, we tore out the pulp and chewed the tough fibers, sucking out every bit of pulp and moisture. Enormous spiders covered in black and orange fur roamed the countryside in solitary migration. Mitimoni called them tar-an-tu-las. Intent on following some internal compass, they appeared anywhere, anytime.

The morning began with one such encounter. Upon waking, I swept my hand across my chest in response to a crawling sensation. The light thunk of a heavy spider against the side of the teepee shocked me into dumbfounded terror. Old Woman merely scooped up the offender and tossed it through the flap. Grinning her crooked smile, she chuckled and said something unintelligible—funny only to herself. The lodges were dismantled, and household items stowed before daybreak. No food was offered, and I wondered about the edibility of tarantulas.

Mitimoni told Nancy soldiers were in hot pursuit. The camp separated to divide the troops. Two hundred and fifty lodges moved directly south and two hundred headed southeast. The constant travel was grueling, and the village was hungry. The tribes moved quickly, keeping to the lowlands. Within the hour, we prepared for another water crossing.

The Pawnee River, a broad stretch of clear running water, flowed smoothly past shelved banks of clay, gravel, and silt. The ponies were accustomed to swimming rivers, but this waterway caused more than one animal to shy away. I watched as Nancy coaxed her anxious horse to the water's edge. The spooky animal lowered its head to sniff, then spun away in panic. Mrs. Morton's riding abilities far surpassed mine and I envied her stickiness in the saddle. Just as she was about to win the trust of the pony, it reared violently shaking its head. The girth on the saddle broke as the animal jerked left and Nancy came off directly into the fast-moving water. Entangled within the ropes and straps of the saddle, the horse struggled to stop its slide into the river hind end first. Its front leg caught in the tie rope—holding its head down to its knee. The horse was swept away. Unable to raise its head, the poor animal quickly vanished under the rushing water. I did not see it again.

Moments later, I noticed chaotic activity on the shore as three other horses succumbed to the pull of the deceptively docile river. Indian women clung to their babies and any bit of mane, tail, or parcel they could grab. Braves quickly leapt from their mounts and dove in to save the drowning women and papooses. A strong swimmer quickly caught Nancy.

Dragged from the flooding river onto the shallow bank, the mothers stood stunned. Swimmers launched themselves back into the river, searching in vain for the children—so precious to the continuance of their tribe. Three papooses were gone. Distraught women were left to their grief as men heaved others onto ponies. Grasping bridles, the braves swam beside each horse to guide it across the pulsing water.

I watched horrified. Spinning my head back and forth, I searched for another way across. A young man with somber eyes startled me. Grasping my horse's bridle, he jerked us down the bank into the icy water. Shouting, he signaled for me to lean over the horse's neck and wrap my arms and legs around its body. The bags and baskets tied around me floated as the pony lost its footing on the bottom of the river. Swimming, the animal snorted, grunted, and strained against the current. Eventually, we reached the far side and jolted up the slippery bank. I sputtered and coughed as air rushed out of my lungs.

Our guide turned to pull others from the river. Relieved, I felt the squirm of my little one as he entwined his fingers in my hair. Encouraged by the strength of his yank, I heard him grunt as the pony trotted to join the others on the trail.

I turned to face the river. Death and chaos did not to stop the flow of people. The women who lost babies were absorbed into the dripping, stumbling, and determined multitude. The oppressive, hollow feeling in my abdomen crept up to my heart with a strangling hold. I contemplated their losses and wondered at their ability to grieve, yet continue on. Women had done it for millennium. I realized it was the only guarantee for the tribe's survival. Yet the emptiness of their arms and milky fullness in their breasts would pain them as the scent of their children lingered.

Vast expanses of rolling hills and swaying grasses lay ahead. The sun rose high in the autumn sky, and the chill in my bones eased as my leather shift dried. By noon we ascended into the foothills, mountains, and mesas. I had never seen such landscape! We joined a camp of another two hundred and fifty lodges by a beautiful stream of water spilling out of a sparkling lake. It was here the tribe stopped to rest.

———•———

A small falcon hovered over the grassy meadow, then plunged out of the sky to snatch its meal. A dozen women approached and told Nancy and me to follow them out of camp. Carrying baskets and bags, we found a plum thicket brimming with ripe fruit. The heavily laden branches gave way as we pulled the treats from spindly twigs. Nancy and I ate our fill. Willie enjoyed every bite and begged for more.

Nancy and I carefully maneuvered our picking toward Mitimoni, and soon we had her to ourselves. Eventually, our talk turned to serious matters.

"Mitimoni, please. Mrs. Eubank wants to know what has happened to her children," began Nancy. "Have you learned anything more? Have they returned to the white people?"

"Yes," replied Mitimoni. "Father speak same true words. Chiefs travel with children to council. Talk of peace."

"Why do warriors continue to bring more horses and fresh scalps into camp?" Nancy asked.

"Black Kettle, White Antelope, Little Raven, go to Denver," Mitimoni replied. "While gone, young men make war."

Upon returning to camp, Old Woman pointed out three chiefs recently arrived from Fort Union. They came with news. The fort soldiers wanted to make peace. One chief took notice of us and approached with long strides. His large imposing appearance and ornamentation caused both of us to look for a way of escape. He held up his hand, stopping us. His eyes were friendly, and the feather attached to his long hair fluttered in the breeze. He held out a small piece of paper.

"Soldier letter," he said proudly.

Nancy cautiously took it from his hand. By the look on his face, she realized he could not read the English words. Reading the neatly written script, her face did not betray the intent of the letter. Slowly, she passed the flapping paper into my hand. Staring directly into my eyes, she paused long enough to put me on notice. I was to guard my reaction.

> We will kill the chiefs if you can convince them to release you. You must be starving.

The note was a death sentence. The chief smiled, pointed to the paper, and asked what was written. Nancy told him he was to bring us to the fort, in exchange for sugar and coffee. The offer excited the Indian, who sent a Sioux and a Cheyenne to Fort Union to parlay our release. Hours later, two braves rode hard into camp with news. The soldiers hanged the two chiefs. There was a battle against the white soldier chief Blunt, and nine more Indians were killed.

The anger in the camp was tangible. Drums began a slow ominous thump, thump, thump. Alarmed, Nancy grabbed my arm as we sought a hiding place.

Without warning, Old Woman approached and despite our protests, pulled Willie from my arms. Another squaw latched onto us and dragged us to a large stake driven into the ground. Four women were splitting kindling. An immense amount of wood was piled around the post. Nancy demanded to know what they were doing, but the women did not respond or even look at us. Looking at one another's panicky faces, recognition dawned simultaneously in our minds. Execution!

The pounding of drums grew louder, more insistent. Calling. Calling for revenge.

Livid warriors gathered around the post, headdresses bobbing, feet stomping, dust rising. Circling, circling, circling. Four braves stepped out of the ceremony's shadowy reaches and approached us menacingly. As lions hunting their prey, they leapt, throwing us to the ground. Fresh scalps were thrust into our faces, smearing us with human remains. The scent of blood filled my nostrils. I spit and wretched as a scalp was shoved between my lips and rubbed against my clenched teeth. The ground spun beneath me, and I curled my knees to my chin, trying to protect myself from striking blows and kicks.

"Move!" snarled a brave, who grabbed each of us by the arm, forcing us to our feet. Nancy and I stumbled forward, weak, and frozen with fear. The blood drained from Nancy's face. We struggled and fought as strong hands clamped down hard—to the point of snapping our bones. Scrabbling squaws hurried into the fray to strip us of our clothing. The warriors continued their threats, angrily having their way with us while dragging us to the stake.

Shoved against the post, our wrists and ankles were bound, cutting off the blood supply to our extremities. I leaned my head back, breathing heavily. Smoke and heat from the nearby bonfire scorched my lungs. I could not catch a full breath. Flames of hair whipped my face, driven by the fire's hot wind. I squeezed my eyes shut, blocking the moment when the tinder at our feet was lit. Holding my breath, I knew a gulp of air might be my last. The heat of the flames would incinerate my lungs.

Naked. Poised at destiny's door. The fragile, woven veil between this world and the next was about to shred. Light poured in. Suspended in the duality of time and space, I tugged against the tethers holding me. It was time. Time to walk through the veil.... I waited for the moment of release.

Next to me, Nancy cried out at the top of her lungs. "Go ahead! Burn me! I want to die! Now!"

The drums beat faster. Feet stomped. Haunting voices chanted, "Hi-Ohhh, Hi-Oh, Aya! Aya! Aya! Hi-Ohhh." Fire crackled beneath us.

Lunacy had a stranglehold on Nancy as she bellowed with the force of raging bull. "I want to die! Do it! Send me to the happy hunting grounds! I want to go, then you will be free of me! Burn me!"

Snapped back into awareness by her crazed words, I loudly issued a warning, hoping to halt her mania. "Woman! Stop talking that way! Stop taunting them!"

She could not hear. Her demands and screams filled the air.

"Light the fire! Do it, you spittle-faced snakes!"

The shouts of the crowd echoed through the village. "Brave Whe-Ho! Brave Squaw!"

My feet tingled as the heat crept closer. I tried a different tact. "Nancy! Do not leave our smoking remains here!" I begged. "Abandoned on this heartless hillside! Eaten by ravens! Think of Willie!"

Nancy turned her head slightly toward me. Her bulging eyes were wild, unseeing. She parted her foam-covered lips in a grimace and pulled against the bands which held her wrists to the stake. The fire flared under our bare feet. The pain was intense. Nancy and I shrieked in unison.

Without warning, Medicine Arrows appeared from behind a lodge, followed by Mitimoni. He strode deliberately towards us, eyes ablaze, and stopped near the brave who squatted at our feet to ogle our dying burning bodies. The chief yanked him to a standing position—nose to nose. The great leader was a head taller than the young Cheyenne. He spoke harshly, expressing deep-throated commands. The young man glared angrily at Medicine Arrows, but a slight shift of the elder's head caused our assailant to step back and drop his eyes. Wisely relenting, he submitted to the Keeper of the Arrows and quickly reached through the fire with a knife to slice the leather thongs around our wrists and ankles. Then he slipped away.

Nancy's frantic voice echoed after him. "Run! You filthy bastard! May the crows pluck out your eyes! I hope you all rot in hell!"

The old chief paused and waited for Nancy's dramatic pronouncements to fade away. "You brave. We no kill you. You want die. Brave Whe-Ho. You come."

Mitimoni arrived with a parfleche of water. She splashed it onto the smoking soles of our feet. Then she wrapped an arm around the overwrought, limping Mrs. Morton and led her away. Nancy continued to holler in defiance. Mitimoni hustled her out of sight before her words changed the minds of the fire builders.

Danger always surrounded us, but this brush with death left me wilted and rubber legged. The burns on my feet needed tending and the pain was beyond control. Consumed by the urge to flee, I searched for Willie. Where was my baby? Desperate to find him, I pivoted to face the stake. Something was burning!

"Willie!" I screamed, running toward the towering flames.

Expecting to see my baby engulfed in a blaze, I arrived to find buffalo heads tossed into the fire and consumed by its fury. One head exploded from the heat sending bits of fiery bone into the air.

I stood unsteadily on two feet, fighting the urge to fling my body into oblivion. The need to find my baby grounded me as my bleary eyes cleared. The fire flared, consuming the wood and igniting the posts. Drumbeats echoed and reverberated through the air.

The angry brave returned and stood by my side. He whispered menacingly, "Now we war dance!"

Instantly dragged into the ring, I struggled against the hold of the revenge-filled Dog Soldier. I spotted Old Woman as she stood to the side with Willie in her arms. He was in danger!

"No! Run! Hide the baby!" I screeched.

Without warning, a large, black-faced warrior jerked the child from the old squaw's arms. Willie's shriek was instantly quelled as the demon lifted him by his ankles—like a trophy. His beautiful, blonde curls bounced below his bobbing head. The crazed dancer stomped along the shadows of the firelit circle. He spun around and around. Willie dangled helplessly. Deliberately taking aim at the intense conflagration, the warrior was set to launch the baby into the fire. A final, forceful spin, and Willie was airborne. I could not free myself from clutching hands, forcing me to watch.

Instantly, a large shadowy figure appeared through the smoke and caught the babe. Two Face! Entering the fray, he held the child against his shoulder and ran toward me. A host of revelers dragged me from the scene, but he intercepted them. Wrapping his free arm about my waist, he pulled me away from the attackers. I collapsed to my knees. Stunned by his painted appearance and surprised by his intervention, I allowed him to help me to my feet. I had not seen Two Face in weeks, yet he appeared in time to rescue Willie. Panting, he placed the terrorized child into my arms. The concern on his face was short-lived.

A large group of mounted braves dashed into the village. Their war whoops ignited a new fervor among the dancers. Women trilled louder. Drums beat faster. Dust combined with smoke and filled the camp with a menacing gloom.

Then it happened.

A mystical figure appeared as a vision through the dissonance. A white woman. Long blonde hair flowing. Astride a large rearing horse, the whites of its rolling eyes displayed its wrath.

Dog Soldiers broke the trance as they pulled the new arrival into the center of the ring and whipped the horse with the reins. Clinging desperately to the animal, the young woman struggled to stay on its back. Alarmed, she watched dozens of Dog Soldiers press in, surround her, and try to unseat her. To the shock of the crowd, she reached into the pocket of her skirt and pulled out a pistol.

Immediately, the melee froze and went silent. Warriors stepped back as a strange light revealed the woman who was about to take matters into her own hands. Taking careful aim at the closest shock-faced Indian, she fired—killing him instantly with a bullet through the brain. Staring vacantly at her handiwork, she placed the muzzle of the pistol to her temple…and pulled the trigger.

The gun clicked.

Her eyes flew wide.

It clicked again.

Misfire!

Chaos erupted as the woman disappeared, swallowed whole into the revenge-filled mob. Her fate was sealed. Condemned from the moment she arrived, it was now a matter of deciding the manner of death. Fiends leaped upon her, knocking her to the ground. Stretched with limbs staked, knives glinted and flashed, gashing her arms and legs. Gunpowder was poured into the lacerated skin. Suffering defiantly, she remained silent— until the executioners approached with hot irons.

"Nooo!" she howled.

The woman ignited. Her dreadful shrieks split the ether. Reflexively, her body jerked and writhed on the ground. Then with the voice of a fallen angel, a single thin wail filled the village. Drawing no breath, the endless keening lanced the soul and pierced the heart.

Drained and shuddering from exertion, I was caught in a trap. The tangled thread held me suspended in a state of horror, revulsion, and pity. I watched the woman's tissue explode as a labyrinth of flesh muddled the exterior of her form. The smoke from the gun powder burned the back of my nose and throat. I could not turn away. A moist, webby netting held us together, its clammy white tendrils silky soft. Escape was impossible. Watching her mouth gaping and groping, I no longer heard her cry through deaf ears.

Old Woman, unable to stand it any longer, ran to the poor soul. Crouched beside her, she yelled at the nearest braves. Scanning the crowd for help, Old Woman begged one warrior after another to end the woman's suffering. None responded. There was nothing she could do!

Without warning, Big Crow stepped out of the crowd and marched toward his mother. Grabbing her upper arms, he stopped her in her tracks.

Old Woman's eyes pleaded with him.

A simple nod of his head completed their silent communication.

Big Crow turned to the woman agonizing on the ground.

The arcing tomahawk's swing was swift and final.

chapter thirty-nine

Shattered

Mid October 1864
Arkansas River, Colorado Territory

...the demons would whip us and throw stones and scalps in our faces and threatened to take our lives.

Nancy Morton

Food filled my dreams—most recently they centered around my kitchen at the Little Blue Station. I usually offered two spreads daily, charging two dollars per meal. Breakfast included biscuits, ham, fresh eggs, milk, and coffee. Mmmm...I could almost smell it! The most enticing images included dinners of pork chops, beef steaks, rice pudding, and fresh bread with jam. Fantasies like these can lead to madness when the new day dawns and reality sets in.

I had not consumed a bite of food for days. This morning, however, Nancy and I were offered part of a raw antelope liver. Our primitive circumstances and starved condition summoned primal urges. Ladylike facades were disemboweled and laid bare. Growling, I ripped and tore at the bloody organ. My eyes met those of my alarmed dining partner. After assessing my sanity, she let out a slow chuckle and growled deeply.

"I am so hungry I could eat anything that didn't crawl, run, or jump away from me," I said with a gulp.

I thought of the family dog Butch. He voraciously devoured succulent tidbits with gusto. I made note to be more generous with our next dog.... That is, if there ever was a dog again. Or a home. Or a pot with extra bites of food.

"My William would remind me to never throw out food but be thankful for every bite."

I tried to assume a more dainty-like posture with the moist, slippery liver. No doubt about it! Will would be mortified by my living conditions.

I would never share this shameful part of my plight with anyone. The baby reached for the bloody organ and smeared his mouth before I could intervene.

"Our dog back home is probably eating better this morning than we are," Nancy said. For effect, she growled deeply again and tore at the meat.

I offered a flimsy smile at the depths to which we had descended. I thought of my Belle and worried. The children had been gone for nearly a month. Tears stung my sunburned cheeks.

A long day's journey lay ahead, and I was thankful for the sustenance given by the antelope. However, nausea ensued and left my gut stirring and head reeling. I promptly vomited, ribs grinding with each retching spasm. The day passed with a foggy numbness as I trudged mile after mile, summoning strength for each step.

The entire contingent of young and old walked through the day and into the night. The tribe's silent flight was pushed onward by reports of soldiers scouting the area. I made my way barefooted through the sagebrush, cactus, and stones. My feet were scratched, bleeding, and bruised. Each step brought new injury to the battered soles and scraped toes. I struggled to walk as we pressed on through the night.

Finally, Old Woman, riding a tired, gray mare next to me, stopped. She hoiked us behind her with a strength I did not expect. Willie and I were exhausted and wobbled on its back. The monotonous cadence lulled me to sleep. I fought to stay awake. Old Woman was ever vigilant, though, and pinched my thigh when she felt me upsetting the balance.

A new morning peaked over the horizon as rain began a steady beat. Cold droplets were soon running down the back of my thin shift as we rode along the damp trail. I opened the soft leather of Willie's sling and wrapped it around my neck. I tried to pull it up around my cold, wet ears. One ear pained me, and I felt feverish despite the falling temperatures. I peeked between the folds at Willie. He was heavy and subdued this morning. I shifted his weight farther toward my hip and continued to drag the two of us across the rocky flatness.

We reached a river about midday.

"Arkansas," said an old man trudging near me.

I noticed the stream of humanity slow perceptively, then plunge into the water without hesitation. The depth in the middle required another swim, and I regarded their methods with life-preserving interest. Fear surged, overriding my fatigue.

Depleted and feeble-minded, I grasped the need to formulate a plan for the river crossing. I had only to grab onto a leather strap or bundle of lodge poles. No, that was not sufficient. Though adrenaline scrambled my thoughts, I realized Willie and I were in danger.

Frantically I searched for Nancy, hoping to find an aide with which to ford the river. She might have an idea of how to get Willie safely to the other side. Our prior crossings had been difficult, but once done, we dried at once in the autumn sunshine. Now, however, the weather had turned. Facing the perilous crossing, dread combined with the chill, and my skin rippled.

Standing on the bank, I eyed the roiling waters with little comprehension. Nancy approached me leading a pony. Her presence lifted me from a cold stupor. Noticing my weariness, she took over operations. She tied Willie into a cradleboard with trembling hands and strapped him high onto the saddle horn of her horse. Pushed up behind him, I slumped into the worn saddle. The wind whipped the steady rain against me, and I wrapped the empty sling around my shoulders to block its icy invasion.

My touchstone with reality said in a muffled, far-away voice, "Lucinda, you are fading, dying."

I replied with another spurt of vomit, then wiped my mouth with the back of my hand.

The pony stepped cautiously down the rocky bank, and I shivered. It snorted then stopped to paw and splash the cold water. A firm slap from behind caused us to lurch forward, and I clung to cantle and saddle horn. Looking over my shoulder to check on Nancy, my stupor was broken by screaming and a loud commotion.

A papoose inside a cradleboard slipped off its pony into the water face down. The mother was swept downstream, struggling to stay afloat. Several braves rushed into the water and passed the mother with strong strokes. The current swept the crisis around a bend. Soon all could be seen standing on the opposite gravelly shore. The papoose dangled from a soaked brave's arm. He lifted it toward the woman and shook his head. Her piercing cries unnerved me.

Distracted by the Indian mother's ordeal, I lost focus on my own progress. The horse heaved and surged into the river, then began to swim. I leaned to reach Willie just as my horse's head went under. I fell forward onto its neck. The desperate animal threw its head up hitting my chin hard stunning me. As the drenched animal regained its footing the current diminished. We clambered laboriously up the slippery slope to the ledge above.

A bone-chilling gust of wind blew my wet skirt against the dripping sides of the horse. Teeth chattering, a pronounced weakness threatened to overwhelm me. I glanced back at the procession, but the young mother who lost her papoose to the impassionate river was gone. I leaned to touch Willie and felt my body slide. I blinked, slid, lurched, then thudded against the muddy ground. Sound muffled around me then faded away. I made my grave by the side of the road, then lifted out of my body in blissful escape—into the lulling darkness. Away....

Darling Belle reaches for me. I touch her sweet, smiling face, and we sink together into a soft white feather bed.

"Lucinda, wake up! Come on, sweetheart, it is time to go!"

I open sleepy eyes and meet the freshly shaven face of Will, smiling and ready for the day. The early light of dawn illuminates my new lace curtains, and the room holds a light as soft as my little girl's cottony crown. She snores softly next to me.

"Today we plant the garden! Let's start early," he coaxes. "You and my son will benefit from fresh air!" Will caresses my blooming belly. He is sure our second child is a boy.

I ease away from Belle without waking her and heave myself upright to plant my feet upon the rag rug. The morning sickness, which plagued me through the spring, is gone. Now is the perfect time in my pregnancy to work, work, work. There is much to do to prepare for the baby, raise food for the family, and cook for passing travelers. I brush the hair from my eyes and untie my long braid. The act causes my husband to cup my face with his rough palm.

"You are beautiful in the morning," he whispers.

It is a morning to remember.

Later we find ourselves working side by side in the large, fenced garden. The soil is rich and brown. Vegetables grow to enormous size here in the fertile Little Blue Valley. I look over at Will who has stopped digging. He kneels beside the fresh row. His hand grasps a large chunk of soil which he holds up for me to see.

"It is like black gold, Lucy!" he exclaims. His hat tips back to reveal a wide-toothed grin. "Almost good enough to eat!"

He chuckles and playfully lifts the handful of dirt to his mouth.

I laugh hysterically and lift a chunk to my mouth.

I chew.

Bits of soil drop onto my blouse.

Still, I eat more, and we laugh.

I chew and swallow...giggling.

Then we dig... laughing, laughing madly.

My arm hurts!

I hold Belle. But the comforting embrace stinks. The bed is brown and muddy. Isabelle slides into the mud. It covers her up. I dig and dig trying to find her. Crying, I fall on my face and bite the ground.

Arms reach around me and pull me into a sitting position. I bite one of the arms so severely it begins to bleed.

I am bleeding. It is my arm....

"Lucinda! Stop it!" a voice shouted in my ear.

Shaken violently, the voice coaxed, "Please, Lucinda, stop. Do not eat the mud. Stop biting your arm. The chief is watching!"

The voice was desperate. An alarm bell sounded in my head, and I looked around to find the source of the voice.

Big Crow?

He is watching?

I saw Nancy on her knees, begging, pleading with me. "They think you are crazy! They will kill you! Please come back to me, Lucinda!" She held me, rocked me, and stroked my soaked hair.

Slowly, recognition dawned. I was no longer in the place of safety with my husband. A captive. We are all captives.

I sat backward onto the slippery mire and looked at my arms and hands covered in mud and blood. Nancy busily wiped my mouth with the corner of her dress.

"There, there now," she said with false bravado. "You are coming back to me. Thank you, God in heaven! Look at me!"

I stared at her, then blinked. "Oh, my friend. I love you."

The stricken look on Nancy's face cleared my head. I glanced around. Mounted warriors in full war regalia rushed past in a hooting mob.

"Oh, they are going to kill more whites!" I sobbed.

Tears mixed with rain.

Nancy called to Big Crow as he mounted his war horse. Turning, he stared at me, then scowled, his eyes narrowed with suspicion. "Food!" Nancy demanded, pointing to her mouth. "She is sick! She needs food!"

"I take papoose," he commanded.

A squaw lifted Willie out of the mud.

"No!" I yelled, panicked at the sight of my son in the arms of Big Crow. Thrashing wildly, I tried to stand, to take back my child from the devil incarnate.

"You help Fire-Hair," commanded the chief, pointing at Nancy.

He rode away with Willie. I charged forward on hands and knees, then ran to grab his ankle. A swift kick hit me solidly in the ribs. I slammed to the ground and curled into a ball as flashes of pain stroked my back through the hollowness of my stomach.

Minutes, perhaps hours, passed before Nancy and Old Woman dragged me onto a travois. My wrists were tied to its wooden frame. I kicked at the buffalo robe covering me and begged repeatedly for my baby. He must be under it. I twisted, I cried, I screamed, but Willie was lost!

Nancy pressed her cool hand to my forehead, then held my cheeks. Her words calmed me temporarily. In my derangement, all I could see was a threatening stranger. I was inconsolable.

Hours later, my mind began to clear. I noticed the moon. No longer restrained, Willie was in my arms. How long had I been like this?

I heard a creek nearby, then water splashing. Looking over my shoulder, I recognized Nancy on the horse strapped to my travois. She kicked the animal repeatedly. It was floundering. Water washed over us. In my confusion, I knew not what to do. Why was Willie's face under water?

"Quicksand!" screamed Mrs. Morton. "Lucinda, get up! We are stuck in quicksand!"

I strained to free us. The robes and baggage were piled on the soaked buffalo hide between the poles of the travois. I flipped onto my knees and began throwing items clear of the trap holding us.

"Jump!" Nancy yelled as she flung herself off the flailing horse.

I picked up Willie and threw the babe into the water, then leapt into the hostile current. The horse rolled trying to free its feet from the pull of the sucking sand. With the extra weight gone, the animal made one final heave and liberated itself. It plunged and jumped to the opposite bank.

I was tangled, wrapped in the mess. The water dragged me through rocks and boulders. The contents of the travois trapped me like the legs of a giant spider. I slapped and tugged until finally free of its web. I groped in the dark, swift water for Willie.

Nancy was soon by my side, pulling me, carrying a limp Willie over her shoulder. With super-human strength, she yanked us both onto the soggy grass. We stumbled and fell. I rolled my head to one side and watched indifferently as she placed Willie face down on her lap. She pushed between his shoulders with the palms of her hands. Water poured from his mouth, and he choked. Cradling his head, she pulled him tightly against her chest. Sobbing, Nancy buried his head in her neck, then turned him face down on her lap again.

"Oh, my dear boy! You are alive. Now breathe! Again, Willie! Breathe!" She continued to press water out of him. Willie sputtered and coughed. I felt no emotion. It meant nothing to me.

Staring up at the stars, I spoke to them. They blinked and twinkled. I was mesmerized. I did not see who carried me and lifted me back onto the travois. Those stars....

Drifting away for another eternity, I woke to the warm sun's glow through the walls of a lodge. Nancy was spooning watery broth into my mouth. We did not speak. I gawked at her face as recognition and fragments of our story mingled gel-like in my mind. She looked distraught.

"Lucinda," she pleaded. "Come back! Jesus, help her!"

"I am," a voice croaked near me. The words were mine, emerging from my rough, dry throat. I nodded, then repeated, "I am here, Nancy."

"Hurry, dear. They are coming soon!" She urged my full attention.

At that moment, Medicine Arrows entered the teepee. "Crazy woman come with me," he commanded.

"No, no!" exclaimed Nancy as she clung to me. "She is getting better. See? Better! If you kill her, the babe will have nothing to nurse."

The chief paused and considered the new information. Looking at the blonde, curly head of the baby in Nancy's lap, he nodded and turned away.

———•———

The village rested for a week along the river. I tried to swallow small morsels of food, but it usually heaved upward, coating me with a sticky, yellow fluid. I did not possess the strength to rise from my sleeping pallet. Finally, the fever broke, and the bone broth stayed down.

The next afternoon, Old Woman decided it was time for me to get back to work. I suspected I should make myself useful. She roused me and sent me in search of wood.

Walking through the cottonwood trees with an armload of kindling, a crackling sound caught my attention. Something was there.

It was a group of young braves to my left. Another group matched our pace to the right. They were stalking me! I broke into a run, but the pack kept up stride for stride. Closing in on me....

Panicked, I dropped the wood and sprinted. It was futile. The wolves jumped. Young and old, the rapacious creatures took turns violently abusing me in every way imaginable. The men of the village continued to ravish me until I lost consciousness. Lacking strength, I was too weak to fight against their attacks. I slipped through the cloak of consciousness, but the onslaught was never-ending. Mercifully, my essence refused to emerge, and I stayed in the grave.

Later one of my assailants carried me—naked, battered, and bleeding—slumped over his shoulder through the dark. Dumped onto the stones along the riverbank, the lower part of my body was submerged in the shallows. The evidence of torturous indignities floated to the surface. Cool, quiet ripples flowed through the channel. The river's sparkling water song cleansed me in the light of the moon.

chapter forty

Forked Lightning

End of October 1864
Beaver Creek, Northern Kansas Territory

The Cheyennes and Sioux held a conference as to whether they should sue for peace or continue the war. They failed to agree and parted. One side was for peace and the other for war. They divided their plunder and prisoners, and in the division of prisoners, Mrs. Eubanks and babe fell to the side of war.

George H. Smith

After the attack on the Arkansas and my bout with madness, I was reluctant to venture far from the lodge. The tribe spent days trekking northward. I lost track of time and eventually performed tasks as one in a trance. Old Woman did not ask me to gather water or wood alone again. A young woman, Happy, was assigned to be my constant companion. I was comforted by her presence, for she was indeed of a pleasant and kindly disposition.

Mrs. Morton and I often sat together scraping hides which were constantly curing. Permitted to construct bags for our personal use, we hoped for another opportunity to escape. The ability to carry water and food parfleches would help our chances of survival.

After soaking buffalo hides, we pegged pieces to the ground, then removed the hair. Folding the hide into an envelope, we added holes for ties. Used as saddle bags, the women became accustomed to seeing our meager possessions packed and secured to horses or travois. They suspected nothing.

Nancy and I spent days making a dried meat mixture called pemmican. Bull berries were harvested from their silvery shrubs and mixed with plums, nuts, and meat, then pounded flat and dried. Cut into strips, we gradually squirreled away bits of pemmican in our parfleches. Using buffalo flank skins, we sewed water bags and carried them with us. When the time came, we would not arouse suspicion. We were ready.

One afternoon, the squaws set out to a patch of grape vines in a nearby ravine. Nancy and I were handed baskets and instructed to follow. We exchanged knowing glances. This was just the opportunity we needed. Walking along, Nancy and I slowly slipped to the rear of the group. Once sufficiently distanced from listening ears, Nancy whispered, "Are your parfleche and satchel ready?"

"Yes. Are you feeling well enough?" I asked, for Nancy had been quite ill.

"Lucy, I am well enough! We must try!"

Soon the group of women worked their way down into a ravine, and I took notice of the surrounding terrain.

"Nancy! This is perfect!" I said in a hushed tone. "See how the boulders hide the turn in the ravine? There! Just beyond the grapes nestled along its bottom."

She nodded.

"If we can ease ourselves past the turn, our escape route might be concealed...."

"We can do it," whispered Nancy.

Two hours later, we slipped around the turn in the ravine and ran through its channel. After charging through its twists and turns, we scrambled up over the edge. Keeping our profiles low, we sprinted, following the dips and washes in terrain. After the first couple of miles, we slowed for a breather and to check for pursuers.

Sure enough, two women on ponies were quickly approaching. They each led a spare horse.

"Oh!" exhaled Nancy. She threw her arms around me and Willie. "I am so sorry, Lucy, so sorry."

Crying, we held each other tightly not knowing what to expect. As the squaws drew near, I recognized Happy. She was smiling as she pulled up in front of us.

"You no go," she said simply.

Expecting a lashing, we obediently mounted and returned to camp. No punishment followed, which was puzzling but also a great relief. However, consequences of a different sort were forthcoming.

The next morning, the village criers announced the large camp was to split. One group would go north, the other south. Nancy came running from her lodge in a panic.

"I think they will separate us!"

"Surely not. We will go together as we always have!" I said a little too confidently.

The squaws were tight-lipped in response to our pleading inquiries. Watching the camp pack, it became clear that it would split into two factions—a well-orchestrated and practiced move. The travois were fastened to the horses and large dogs. The peoples' earthly belongings were strapped, tied, and carefully balanced on every possible conveyance— human backs included. Nancy and I knew the routine. We gathered up the precious few things we owned and packed our tattered bags.

Expecting to be forced apart, we steeled ourselves for the imminent and final separation. Despite our protests, the tribe would not allow us to stay together.

Nancy and I were thin, gaunt, sunburned, and disheveled; but I admired her stamina and courage. Holding her at arm's length, I stared into her lovely, young face. We embraced and tearfully choked our goodbyes. Willie sensed the difference in the day's farewell and leaned from my arms, crying, reaching for Nancy. Hugging him tightly, she caressed his head, then his cheeks, then smothered him with tearful kisses. Willie would not be consoled. We both feared separation from the familiar friend whose gentle care provided fleeting moments of security and ease. We relied on one another for comfort and companionship, for a bite of food, for rescue from danger, for the grip of a friend's hand when derangement and lunacy threatened to drive one over the edge.

For the first time since our captivity began, Willie and I would walk alone in our enveloping sea of strangers.

Worry for Nancy's future clutched at my chest with a panicky pressure—nearly stopping my heart. What would happen to my sweet friend? Who would offer the nibbles of food she generously shared with Willie? How would we survive without her?

Nancy was my motivation to live. Now my tether to this world was trudging off in the opposite direction. Recalling my hopeful words, "I know we will go together," the echoing words haunted me.

Little did I know we would never see each other again in this world.

———◆———

I watched the glow of sunrise move far along the horizon and enfold the high plains. A sense of foreboding left me stark and vulnerable in its light. Plodding slowly along the edge of the boundless landscape, our trail took us southeast to Big Sandy. A meadowlark sang in the distance. The Cheyenne herds trotted and flowed in unison as a rolling wave, pushing its singular will to a new destination. The animals knew this trail, but I faced the unknown.

The day's fresh sun slipped quietly into wind-swept clouds, lending a flat light to the morning chill. Fatigued to the core, I forced each foot forward, stumbling blindly. Discouragement rose like venom from my empty stomach. I lacked the means to ground myself to this world. The fragrant sagebrush and short grass dotted an endless, treeless desert.

Numbly, I watched the trail pass beneath my feet, noting the tracks of those who sucked me along in the stream of sojourners. So many moccasin, dog, and horse prints. The drag marks of loaded travois....

I scuffed at the tiny rocks in the dust of this ancient path. These tracks did not belong to my people or my animals. These prints did not lead to my home.

I reached the top of the rise and hesitated. Searching the weaving line of humanity in the distance, I squinted for a final glimpse of Nancy. Where was she?

A gleaming, sun-bleached bonnet bobbed up in the middle of the crawling thread of dark-haired peoples. A swift jolt of realization nearly knocked me off my feet. I took a step toward her, my hand impulsively raised. Old Woman pulled my arm down, frowned and shook her head. Gray strands of hair blew about her face which showed concern and annoyance. Insistently, she tugged me away from the northern view. A shivering sensation rattled my body. Two magnets suddenly lost all power to connect. Deep sobs welled up out of the gap.

Pointing to the winding, northbound tribe, I could only croak, "Where?"

Happy replied, "Denver—to give Mrs. Morton up." Her features softened as the message was reiterated. Nancy would be traded up north and sent home....

The assurances, meant to placate me, were hollowly received by my captive heart. I simply nodded, dropped my shoulders in resignation, and shuffled up the trail.

Turning for a final look, I saw the storm approach. Thunder rumbled in the distance. Sheets of rain swept the prairie. The wind picked up and blew dust into my eyes.

Without warning, lightning cracked in the sky above. It struck two places—one hit the ground to the north and the other struck to the south. I jumped as an explosive clap of thunder boomed overhead. A cry of alarm escaped my lips! Squeezing my eyes closed, the image of red-forked lightning burned brightly on my retinas.

I was alone; and the truth of it impaled my soul.

chapter forty-one

Surgeon Stitches

Early November 1864
Northeastern Plains, Colorado Territory

Beautiful hands are they that do
Deeds that are noble good and true;
Beautiful feet are they that go
Swiftly to lighten another's woe.

McGuffey Reader 1830

T he nudge in my ribs was insistent. I rolled over and opened my eyes, instinctively reaching for Willie. He slumbered on his stomach next to me, arms and legs splayed out. His appearance attested to the fact the crawling baby was indeed growing despite my starved condition. Happy often carried him as she went about her chores, offering him tidbits of food. I pulled his warm body to me and gathered him in to nurse.

The pre-dawn light in the teepee smudged the outlines of those around me. The men were already gone, settled into their saddles before daylight. The older camp guards barked orders urging the people to hurry along with their duties. During our travels, these men protected the rear. Warriors to life's end.

The presence of white soldiers was monitored by native scouts scattered across the vast plains. As the village advanced, the scouts covered the country, surrounding its progress, hoping to avoid confrontations. The tribespeople operated under a general state of apprehension, for the danger of attack was ever present.

Day after day, I scanned the horizon, wondering if my deliverers were in close proximity. But the camp was a moving target. Each arduous day brought only disappointment.

The prior evening, the village criers walked through the camp as usual. They shouted unexpected news, giving formal notice to the camp's inhabitants. Black Kettle and other chiefs met with the white chief in Denver. The tribe was to move to Sand Creek on the border of their reservation. Recently, the Arapahos under Left Hand set up their winter village at Sand Creek. The chief returned plunder taken in the summer raids to Fort Lyon and was given provisions. The tribes were promised safety. Flavored by assurances, the village criers' deep, strong voices repeated the specific destination.

I focused on Old Woman, now my constant companion. Accustomed to the rhythm of tribal movement, I simply followed instructions. However, this morning Old Woman was not performing her normal activities. In fact, she seemed to hurry as she placed items in baskets and rolled up garments and robes. She spoke to me in a hushed voice with commands I still did not understand. I stood quickly as she handed me a basket of dried venison. Not yet healed from the severe injuries inflicted on me at the Arkansas camp, I was dizzy when I bent over. Mentally, I was sliding off my rails in slow motion.

"We go," Old Woman stated plainly.

I quickly stood and stepped through the flap into fresh, cool air. I breathed deeply, then headed toward the trees to relieve myself. Happy followed, chattering and playing with Willie. The entire camp rustled with expediency in the calm morning air. Barking dogs added to the commotion. The village residents were quiet in their activities as women struck their teepees and loaded the pack animals with household goods. The village was coming down with amazing speed and efficiency. Families were already moving off. The women mounted ponies and pulled travois filled with the old, the young, and the contents of their lives.

The sun appeared between the horizon and a layer of clouds, its brilliant rays lighting the front of the Cheyenne column already a mile out. It was time to clean up Willie. I removed the absorbent, soft grass and milk weed puffs from his nappy. The women had taught me this technique, but by now he was soaked. I rinsed a rag each evening and retrieved the dry one tied to my waist. I quickly wrapped him and tied him in his cradleboard.

The beauty of the morning was disturbed by memories of the evening before. Six hundred warriors returned from their days-long absence, bringing with them the rewards of their raids. Horses and mules loaded with all manner of items were led into camp. Some dragged lead pipes to be melted into bullets. Mr. Bent told me the Dog Soldiers continued to make war on the whites. Their dramatic and celebrated arrival caused a great uproar. The excited war whoops of the braves chilled me to the bone. Feathered headdresses swept the ground. Colorful strips of cloth flapped on the glinting spears thrust skyward. Their victory cries were answered by animated trills and yips.

I noticed scalps hanging from saddles. I cringed at the sight of one in particular—a woman's! Its shiny, dark hair was nearly three feet in length. The Indian women, who followed the warriors, arrived later. In their possession was a three-month-old white baby. The renegades murdered her ma and pa. The squaws passed around the mother's pocketbook. Wrapped within a silk handkerchief was a gold ring stamped inside with the initials MC. Also found was a tintype likeness of the baby's parents. The father wore a captain's uniform and the mother a lovely, high-necked gown. Who were these people—their lives snuffed out in a bloody instant? I grieved over the child's mother. The thought of her body left unburied on the open plain for wolves to tear apart sickened me.

I named the baby Nancy Jane.

Were soldiers on the move to answer for the recent killing? Would they find me before I met a similar fate?

That evening, I hid in the teepee with two small items of contraband discovered in a parcel of loot. A little bag held a lead pencil and a small, leather-covered book. Leaving the Scalp Dance as the drums began, I hid the prize in Willie's sling and slipped into the lodge unnoticed. Ears tuned to the approach of a lodge occupant; my eyes riveted on this precious piece of civilization. Sitting near the lit embers of the fire, I held the book open. Beautiful script filled a quarter of the pages. Medical treatment notes and illustrations covered the stained pages. I flipped to the front flap and upon closer examination learned the prior owner's identity:

Dr. Lowell Little, Esq.
Surgeon, 11th Ohio Cavalry
Fort Collins, Colorado Territory

The first entry described "Camp Collins" on October 14, 1864. It detailed the newly built company and officer's quarters as well as the kitchen, guardhouse, and company stables. The hospital was located between the laundress' quarters and the sutler's store. Another smudged entry described bands of "friendly" Indians from Chief Friday's band, who visited the fort seeking protection per the governor's proclamation. I looked about the interior of the teepee as if searching for direction. How far was Fort Collins?

Curiosity compelled me to read a bit of the man's life, and I wondered as to his fate. Heart pounding, I quickly scanned entries dated January 1864. Dr. Little treated a soldier injured in a skirmish with the Arapaho. It occurred on the Cherokee Trail between Laporte, the headquarters of the Overland Mail and Express Company and Virginia Dale. The victim, Private William Alvin Parker, was part of an Overland stage escort on the route when he received an arrow through the thigh. Removed and stitched, the diagram illustrated treatment details.

Fear of discovery prompted me to focus on the task at hand. I turned to a blank page and began to hastily scribble:

I am a captive of the Cheyenne.
Tribe headed to Sand Creek.
Please rescue me and my son.
Mrs. Lucinda Eubank

I folded the note into the shape of an envelope and admired the sturdy square of hope. I placed it in my satchel and planned to drop it at a crossing of a well-traveled road. If soldiers knew I was alive, they would find me. I remembered seeing mounted soldiers on the third or fourth day of captivity. They spotted me but did not pursue. Perhaps their horses were too worn out to make chase. I planned to drop messages to remind rescuers of my existence, to guide them to me. It seemed foolish, but the expression crossed my mind: Hope springs eternal.

The next morning, as the camp prepared to leave, I picked up my satchel and slid the strap across my body. Patting its contents, I was comforted and buoyed by the prospect of doing something that might bring freedom. My fingers lingered on the small circle of my wedding band sewn into the lining. I had so few things, but what I owned was precious and useful—never to be taken for granted.

A heavy, ashen snow shower hung over the prairie as far as I could see. Walking against wind gusts, I coughed and hastily pulled a fold of blanket across my nose and mouth. The Indians traveled over twenty miles along a windblown trail that day. It was very cold. Navigating unmarked routes by an inner tribal compass, we crossed dry streambeds and rock shelves and circled buttes, mesas, and shallow canyons. The location of water directed our path. A spring, stream, or puddle was valuable in this dry, arid land.

The speed at which a huge mass of humans and their belongings could travel was a sight to see. Throughout the summer before my captivity, I remembered watching massive wagons slowly trundle past our ranche. The pace at which a yoke of oxen could travel barely reached ten miles a day. The lumbering animals of the white man pulled sturdily built wagons loaded with people and freight. The Indians traveled with few wagons. They moved at an even pace as a singular unit. The young and old rode ponies while the strong walked purposefully—each one a link in a mighty, undulating chain.

The camp's dogs and pups trotted along the edges of the trail. Occasionally, they raced off as a pack in pursuit of a rabbit. Noses deep in the ground, they dug vigorously—dirt flying, hind ends and curled tails raised. Attempts to dig out one of the thousands of prairie dogs were usually unsuccessful. Mocking the hapless intruders, the tunnel dwellers barked and chirped from the safety of distant mounds.

The front of the procession topped a rise in the terrain, and excitement spread through the people.

"Buffalo!" exclaimed Big Crow's daughter as she pointed at a distant cloud of dust.

The men quickly organized a hunting party and rode off on their strongest and best horses. I wound my way across the rocky sagebrush-covered ridge and crawled to the top to survey the valley below. Willie stood on stout little legs, clinging to my skirt for balance. Looking out across the wide-open expanse, I pushed my bonnet onto my shoulders and gaped at the scene below.

The vista revealed an enormous sea of brown, hunched buffalo grazing on the northern slopes. I had never seen a herd so large! Dark forms dotted the golden hills extending beyond my range of vision. Within moments, the animals spotted mounted hunters moving toward them. Trotting then running, they tossed their massive heads, signaling the direction the herd would surge. With great speed and precision, the galloping hunters brought down two large buffalo and one calf. The delayed reports of rifle action dropped the animals before we heard shots. Hunters used spears to dispatch the fallen buffalo while others launched arrows into the beasts. A direct hit behind the shoulder would penetrate the heart or, at the very least, the lung and bring it down. Animal after animal fell. The herd stampeded out of sight although their thundering hooves still echoed across the landscape.

The next phase of the hunt began in earnest. Small groups of women turned their conveyances toward the fallen animals, their sole purpose to quickly butcher the dead and dying. Serving as walking pantries, government mules were led by children to the scene. Long, narrow strips of bountiful meat were sliced thinly to be carried back to camp. The strips would be hung to dry in the cool air.

Life in the Nebraska frontier had altered my food options in unusual ways. I loved the taste of buffalo! Growls erupted from my empty stomach as I quickened my step in anticipation of the evening meal. Reaching the nearest animal, I knelt near its head and was handed a severed tongue.

My ears caught cries of distress blown in on the wind.

Old Woman!

Raising my head, I searched, then spotted her running and waving both arms in alarm. I snatched up Willie and sprinted. She grabbed my hands and pulled me along while rapidly recounting a crisis which I could not decipher.

Reaching the side of the largest bull lying on its arrow-filled side, I noticed it was alive, heaving, grunting, and lifting its head. A young buck lay sprawled on his back, just feet from the massive buffalo. He was writhing and moaning, gripping his side. The tang of mingled blood assaulted my nose. It poured out onto the ground and seemed to belong to both the dying animal and the injured Indian.

Two women arrived ahead of us and knelt near the victim. Plunging a blade between the ribs into its heart, a third squaw killed the beast with her skinning knife. A final jerk of its head and slash of its horns were directed at the squaw. She was ready and jumped back, narrowly escaping the deadly swipe. Then I knew exactly what happened. The boy's reflexes were not so quick. Blood and snot bubbled from the bull's nose as it exhaled its final breath.

With a wary eye on the huge creature, I carefully laid my hands on the youngster's flushed cheeks. His eyes bulged in fear and pain. I recognized him as Little Hawk, Big Crow's grandson. Speaking Cheyenne words to comfort him, I looked into the face of Old Woman, who stood frozen with fear. This was her favored grandchild.

Years on the frontier presented me with plenty of opportunities to gain medical skill. I treated my share of smashed fingers, burnt skin, stomach ills, infections, and jaws swollen with abscessed teeth. But I certainly was unprepared for prairie surgery and its consequences. Big Crow would blame me for the outcome.

Regardless, I pulled my satchel around to the front of my hip and pulled out a fresh, sun-dried nappy. Applying it to the rib wound with steady pressure, I motioned for the woman kneeling next to me to press on it as I dug into my sparse sewing kit. The bleeding slowed, and I lifted the cloth to inspect the gash in the boy's side. A flicker of white rib bone appeared when the wound expanded as Little Hawk gulped for air. He cried out in pain. I guessed he was suffering from a cracked rib or two.

Watching the opening, I saw no bubbles escape from a puncture in his lung. Hopefully, it was still intact.

The spool of fine thread was gone from my satchel. No matter for it now. I plucked a hair from the tail of the old sorrel pony standing nearby—hindfoot cocked, glad for the rest. I was thankful to have salvaged a needle from the discarded camp loot. I quickly stuck the end of the tail hair in my mouth to moisten it, then threaded the needle. Although I repaired clothing for Nancy, Willie, and myself, I did not expect to use my skills on human flesh. Gripping my hands together to calm the shaking, I bowed my head and quickly prayed asking for help. Amen!

Opening my eyes, Old Woman nodded and removed a leather strap from her personal bag to set between her grandson's teeth. He clamped down; terrified eyes focused on his grandmother. With a swift tilt of her chin, she grimly encouraged me to begin.

Chaos continued in the distance as thundering hooves and human shouts dimmed. Blotting out the mayhem of the hunt, I focused on the body lying in front of me. I startled as one last buffalo cow and calf trampled past followed by a mounted hunter. The shaking ground pitched beneath me.

Wiping clammy hands on my skirt, I carefully pinched the skin together at the narrowest part of the wound. Fortunately, it was a clean slice with no obvious debris or jagged edges. I recalled the good Dr. Little's illustration and tried to copy the stitch pattern. I looked at my patient, noting his sallow skin and beads of sweat glistening on his forehead and upper lip. He managed a tense smile, then his smooth face contorted as a spasm of pain clamped down on his abdomen. The boy pushed aside any qualms he held that I might harm him and bravely submitted to my ministering. As insurance, he reached into the sheath on his belt and gently pulled out a substantial-looking knife. He held it tightly to his chest and glared at me. Not reassured in the slightest, I paused until Little Hawk murmured through clenched teeth, "Go!"

Quickly stabbing the needle through each piece of skin, I pulled the thread, closing the tiny stitches. The rigid patient let out an occasional strangled cry as I pressed the needle repeatedly into his side. Soon the wound was closed and his ribs held in place by a strip of cloth from Old Woman's bag. As I knotted the final stitch, the boy twitched slightly but held onto his pride.

I sat back to inspect my handywork. Tiny drops of blood welled from the punctures, but the wound was neatly stitched. I rinsed the area with water from my parfleche.

Stroking the boy's head, Grandmother spoke to him softly. After a gulp of water, he laid his head back—clearly relieved the ordeal was over. Within minutes, he sat up. Lean, dark arms cradled his head between his knees. Relieved, Old Woman looked at me with what could be construed as appreciation.

Startled by a huge shadow looming over my shoulder, I turned to find Big Crow inspecting the scene. With a satisfied grunt, he turned, mounted his large silver horse, and galloped away. Inhaling sharply, I sat back on my heels and watched the threat disappear, thinking of the grave consequences had my first surgery failed. The women around me hunched their backs and returned to their butchering tasks.

Willie, left unattended during the crisis, crawled through the slime and gore surrounding the carcass. Grasping the curly shoulder of the dead bull, he stood on wobbly legs with a victorious grin revealing four, beautiful new teeth. Old Woman pulled a piece of dried buffalo from her bag and put it into Willie's hand. He stuffed the end in his mouth and gnawed. She patted his back and nodded at me.

"Thank you, Whe-Ho," she said.

I looked into her good eye now brimming with tears, and for the first time in the months spent living in her lodge, we connected woman to woman. My status as slave labor did not change, but the rod wielded so harshly by her hand never struck me again.

chapter forty-two

Tall Chief

26 November 1864
Smoky Hill Trail, Kansas Territory

The settlers of the Arkansas Valley had returned to their ranches from which they fled, had taken in their crops and had been resting in perfect security under assurances from myself that they were in no danger for the present thus saving the country from what must inevitably become almost a famine were they to lose their crops; the lines of communication were opened and travel across the plains rendered perfectly safe through the Cheyenne and Arapahoe country.

Major Edward W. Wynkoop

T he stout horse and rider stood on the summit of a rocky knoll. The animal held its head erect; nostrils flared, inhaling the chilly morning air. Ears pricked forward; the alert gelding appraised his surroundings. Sufficiently satisfied, he cropped the feathery grasses at his feet. The panoramic view of the Smoky Hill Trail was familiar territory.

Major Ned Wynkoop gazed east. The horizon held a fuzzy distinction between land and sky as the frosty air obscured the road below. To the west, the rim of snow-covered mountains trimmed the horizon like a foaming ocean wave. They appeared deceptively close through the thin, high-altitude air.

Ned removed the spotting glass from his pocket and examined the road. With a twenty-eight-man escort, a dozen immense wagons left Fort Lyon at dawn. Six yokes of oxen strained under each heavy load of commerce and goods. The carriage transporting Louise and his two young sons followed the wagon carrying their possessions to a new assignment.

The twenty-eight-year-old major of the 1st Colorado Cavalry was unexpectedly dismissed from his command at Fort Lyon and ordered to report to district headquarters at Fort Riley, Kansas. Punishment was swift.

The Wynkoops expected to winter in Colorado, so the prospect of another move was daunting—even for his unflappable partner. Ever resilient, Louise accepted their new commission in Kansas and repacked their belongings without complaint. Ned hoped the weather would hold for the entire journey. The blizzard-whipped drifts of early November storms were sober reminders of the freezing danger on the trail.

The captives' release weeks earlier earned him a moment in the spotlight. Lured by the opportunity to free white prisoners, he acted decisively…and alone. His position as commander of the remote outpost seemed like that of a ship's captain. One had only to stand on the deck, view the oceanic expanse, and dare to venture forth.

The Indians' desire for peace strengthened his resolve to prevent future depredations on the frontier. The major acknowledged he made crucial decisions without consulting those in authority. Army personnel were placed in harm's way by venturing into Indian country at risk of annihilation. His superiors criticized his methods and chastised him for arranging the meeting between the chiefs and Governor Evans.

Once he secured the captives and placated the tribal elders' concerns for the safety of their families, Wynkoop's broader understanding produced a profound shift in his commander's role. At the time, it seemed positive results would override the voices of dissent. Now he understood his own self-flattery and ambition doomed the outcome of an otherwise successful mission.

Sitting quietly on his mount, Wynkoop inhaled the pungent scent of sagebrush mixed with damp earth. He exhaled fully to calm his restless and disjointed soul. The sweep of recent events collided with his own march toward a destiny he could not have imagined months ago.

Ned reflected on his arrival in Kansas eight years earlier. He worked as a clerk in the General Land Office. As government sales of native lands reached its zenith, Ned turned his sights to the Rocky Mountains. Together with James W. Denver, he organized a party to journey west into Pike's Peak country. The party traversed a tall grass plain which boasted an abundance of game—buffalo being the most prolific and picturesque. The prairie grasses grew shorter as the elevation rose. The expedition ended at Cherry Creek.

Ned witnessed the birth of a small townsite on the sparse, open range at the base of the mountains. As one of the original incorporators of the newly appointed community, his friend's name was applied to the new Denver City.

The settlement of land held limitless possibilities for his entrepreneurial companions. Their enthusiasm for commercial interests grew robust. The land appeared pristine and clean, the air pure and thin, the resources unlimited and unexplored. Was it avarice they experienced in those early days? Yes, Ned was one of them.

Denver's growth exploded. Substantial buildings were built where tents and cabins once squatted. Masses of humanity engaged in commerce within the boundaries of the boom town. Rude huts along the outskirts were inhabited by those stranded with their unrealized dreams of gold. Unimaginable wealth was elusive, and soon optimistic sojourners became the impoverished dregs of society. Unsavory characters, bandits, and brutes often terrorized the fledgling town...and the nearby Indian villages.

The land so eagerly allocated to the whites meant something to its beleaguered original occupants. The concept of people owning the land was offensive to the Indians. The earth itself was the possessor and nurturer of their tribes. Now it was stripped away, divided into pieces, and sold to the highest bidder. His prior actions brought a sense of accomplishment when assessed by his contemporaries but brought disaster to those deserving a life of their own choosing.

For thousands of years, the Indian coexisted with the environment. Within mere months, the influx of hundreds of thousands of his own people assaulted and subdued it. Generations of Arapaho and Cheyenne wintered in solitude. Now they were relegated to the status of annoying "vermin" or threatening menaces. Their teepee-filled camps west of Denver inflamed and terrified the white population. Ned marveled at the speed with which the native peoples were pushed to the limits of their benevolence.

During earlier visits to the region, Wynkoop was fascinated by, yet wary of, the Indians and their culture. Now he considered many to be his friends. They were proud, confident men dealing with new challenges. Their integrity and wisdom impressed him. But the elders faced an altered future which endangered their people's entire way of life.

In the past three months, Ned had turned circumspect. The struggles of the tribal elders had become his struggles, their priorities his priorities, their frustrations now his as well. His youthful boldness tempered as he witnessed tragic and cruel events play out between the races. Against the backdrop of time and progress, the unpredictability of the human condition was frightening.

The Indians honored him with the name Tall Chief based on his physical stature. More importantly, however, he hoped to stand tall in his newfound relationship with the elders. How would he bring honor to the United States, obtain respect from the Denver citizenry, and be true to his self-imposed duty to principle? Ned's regrets were darkly woven threads through the tapestry of his inner conflict. He had matured from military man to Indian advocate.

War Eagle shook his long mane, snorted, and stepped forward to nibble another sprig of gramma grass. Ned gazed upward and stroked his long moustache, then rubbed the stubble along his prominent chin. He stretched his back. It was injured the prior year when War Eagle, still wild and untested, reared and dumped Ned unceremoniously on Larimer Street. He never truly recovered from the fall.

Remembering the engagement with the Confederate army two years earlier at Glorietta Pass, he looked to the south. His commander, John Chivington, had skillfully and successfully engaged the enemy. Wynkoop was one of thirty sharpshooters who subdued a camp of rebels and took them as prisoners. The victory solidified his relationship with Chivington and led to a promotion. The citizens of Denver expounded freely about the success of the New Mexico campaign. They supplemented their accolades by presenting him with a gift: War Eagle. Ned remembered every word of his theatrical response to their gift:

> I desire no nobler grave than the spot on which I render up my spirit
> to the God who gave it, no better epitaph than "he was a Coloradan."

Ned regretted his grandiose words and hoped for a contrite and repentant man to emerge from the sifting of recent events.

Concerned by Chivington's perception of the "Indian Problem," doubt crept perniciously into the recesses of Ned's mind. His opinion of his former commander was corrupted. Recent atrocities and violence perpetrated by the Indians instilled hatred in Chivington and poisoned any peaceful purpose within the man. A true Coloradan would defend the newborn territory with his life. But Chivington and Evans' Indian war held a nefarious and sinister purpose.

Ned knew his loyalty to Colorado would be challenged. He would face the ire of his superiors and the disdain of his equals. Living in the nearly defenseless town, his adopted frontier kinsmen were strained beyond reason by fear and isolation. Depredations by renegade warriors were concerning, but Wynkoop leaned to a renewed hope of peace lasting through the winter. Not a single overt act by the Indians occurred on the

Denver Road since the Weld Council between Governor Evans and the chiefs. The Rocky Mountain News touted his achievement:

> The people of the Arkansas valley desire to further express our appreciation of your bravery, as well as your sense of right, and earnestly express the hope that the merit (sic) which is justly your due may not go unrewarded, in official preferment, as well as the gratitude of private citizens.

Rocky Mountain News
October 20, 1864

Wynkoop followed the governor's suggestion to bring the bands closer to Fort Lyon and distribute the promised rations. The Arapaho and Cheyenne decided to bring their families to live peaceably forty miles north on Sand Creek. He contacted General Curtis's headquarters at Fort Leavenworth, seeking permission to make peace with the Indians and procure supplies.

Not only was the approval for peace terms rejected, but the unthinkable also occurred. The tribes were considered prisoners of war and placed under the direct control of the military. Wynkoop was relieved of his post.

Ned could not shake his uneasiness. He worried the United States Army might not honor his personal commitment to protect the Cheyenne and Arapaho. Would the strained relationship sustain itself under new military leadership? His replacement, Major Anthony, was transferred out of Fort Larned and arrived at Fort Lyon on the second of November. His tarnished mindset was the same Wynkoop held when first commanding the post. But Anthony had never looked into Black Kettle's face and shaken his hand. He had never been in the presence of the calm elder, nor seen the wink of his eye as Ned faced down angry warriors during the council on Hackberry Creek. The trust between Wynkoop and Black Kettle was the only fragile strand holding together tenuous peace.

It was a mistake for Wynkoop to leave now. He must follow orders, but Major Anthony's smug dismissal of Ned's concerns was disheartening and offensive. Wynkoop made a serious mistake in thinking he would play a role in the tribes' future.

Before Wynkoop left the fort, he and Anthony met with the chiefs. Supplies were dwindling, and the shared vision of the tribes was disintegrating. Black Kettle and Left Hand agreed to control or expel the warring factions within their tribes. Instructed to fly the United States flag along with a white banner, the chiefs could signal their village as peaceful. Ned wondered what more could be done.

Anthony agreed to uphold the pledge of protection and to continue the prisoner rations. However, he insisted the Indians make restitution for stolen stock and explained General Curtis demanded they relinquish their arms. As the snows arrived and the distributions dried up, Wynkoop worried about the tribes' abilities to survive the winter. After heated discussion, Anthony returned weapons to the braves with an admonishment to leave Sand Creek only to hunt buffalo.

Black Kettle and Left Hand needed to be wary. There was reason to believe the tensions in Denver would spread, and the soldiers would be ordered to do what they had always done in times of war....

Ned strained to see the wagon train, almost expecting Louise's face to appear through the curtained window of the coach. His wife of three years was the vessel through which he made sense of his transformation. He credited her with softening his stance toward the tribes. His beloved spouse easily peeled away his masculine military bearing to reveal its true humanity. Louise and his closest friend, Silas Soule, were the only ones who understood his dilemma. He wished to alleviate the plight of the natives, who sought peace while dually serving at the behest of the United States Army.

Prior to recent events, his popularity and reputation in the Denver community was attributed to his military feats. He had to admit, it was tempting to fabricate achievements to perpetuate his renown as the brave Union soldier and Indian fighter. But no, he was a different man now. Ned had become a dreaded Indian sympathizer. Louise knew it and loved him for it. The citizenry of Denver, however, would never understand.

Ned shifted in the saddle. The muscles in his stiff back reminded him of the hundreds of miles ridden that autumn. But even more annoying, his pride was smarting.

Major Edward W. Wynkoop entered Fort Lyon as a combatant. Now he was leaving as a hapless arbiter of peace. Justice for the native and peace for the white gave him purpose. Trying to discern the future, Ned sensed his imminent ruin, but the outcome was not in his hands. He held the vision of a humbled man. He would toil to that end.

With a deep inhalation, Wynkoop straightened his form, pulled down the brim of his hat, and put his heel to the side of his companion. War Eagle felt the nudge and stepped into a quick trot down the trail leading to Fort Riley.

———•———

Unknown to Wynkoop, Colorado's leadership was on the move as well. Conveniently, Governor Evans left the territory on a coach headed for Washington, D.C. He planned to discuss a confidential matter with the War Department on behalf of General Curtis. Additional support was necessary for the upcoming Indian campaign. A successful "battle" of valor just might convince the powerful to get behind a full-blown military action. The governor's departure could not have been more perfectly timed.

Colonel John Chivington knew where the main body of Cheyenne was wintering. He was ready. The arrival of his five hundred man regiment surprised the occupants of Bent's Old Fort. Their approach was covered in secrecy; an advance squad of troops detained travelers and mail to ensure silence. Chivington ordered the arrest of all traders and ranchers with ties to Indians through family and business relations.

Now "Tall Chief" was out of the way. Chivington marched into Fort Lyon, secured the perimeter, and allowed no one to slip through to alert the Indian camp. An attack was looming, and the colonel was confident his actions would lift him to the top of Colorado's legacy.

chapter forty-three

The Trade

28 November 1864
Sand Creek Indian Camp
Eastern Colorado Territory

He traded me to Two Face, a Sioux,who did not treat me as a wife,
but forced me to do all menial labor done by squaws.

Lucinda Eubank

The roar of the wind, accentuated by the popping of tree limbs, slammed into the Indian camp without warning. The setting sun disappeared behind a dingy cloud of dust creating a thick, murky sky. The wind increased its fury. Blowing sand mixed with hard snow crept into every fold and crevice. Days earlier, a storm dumped deep snow onto the village. The wind spun drifts around each lodge.

Big Thunder, Doc Billy, and Two Face headed toward the outskirts of the Indian camp. I followed. Two Face's lodge was situated amid other Sioux lodges on the northeastern reaches of the village. Ten Arapaho lodges were situated southeast of the main Cheyenne village. All camps created one large community spread along the edges of Sand Creek.

Seeking immediate shelter from the frigid wind, we diverted to a cut-out bank of the creek. The gale was persistent and nearly ripped the buffalo robe off my shoulders. Its wild flapping sent icy blasts up my shift and set my teeth rattling. I ducked my head, leaned against its pummeling force, and stumbled blindly—occasionally shoved by my newest captors. The heavy covering wrapped around us muffled Willie's cries of discomfort.

Through grit-encrusted lids, I squinted at my feet, forcing them forward. Streams and waves of sand mixed with tiny balls of snow swirled at my feet. Mesmerized by the patterns, they reminded me of a flowing river. The sand beat against my moccasins, and I was glad soft leather covered my ankles. Climbing the protective bank, my Sioux captors found relief from the relentless howling wind, although the noise was still deafening. Hair whipped across my eyes as I shook my head to free my sight from its webby net. The dim light of evening followed as we entered a shallow enclave and sat down to wait.

Cautiously looking at my new captors' faces, I recognized Big Thunder and Doc Billy as two who took part in the massacre at our ranche. They stared at me through large, black eyes deeply set within smooth faces and striking features. I dared not allow my gaze to linger and quickly looked at Two Face. I felt betrayal. Pulling the robe to hide my face, I tried to control my emotions. Willie was fast asleep in the warmth of our cocoon.

By my reckoning, it was late November. My captivity of almost four months seemed like a lifetime. Now I was leaving the Cheyenne. Bull Bear arranged the trade. From what I understood of the negotiations, he expounded upon the great benefits the Sioux would receive by returning me to the soldiers in the spring. Big Crow was not present when I left his lodge. Since the attack on the Arkansas, he used me exclusively. His mother carefully protected me from all others.

I sat huddled with my newest captors and realized the promises of my pending release held no true meaning. My circumstances had progressed from unbearable treatment by Big Crow to an abrupt and frightening new change. I was now the property of the Sioux. The fierce appearances of the chiefs magnified my apprehension. I had no assurance of protection from mistreatment or starvation, and I was not sure if Willie was part of their plan. I hoped to be home before winter, but the night brought more than a physical chill to my bones. The uncertainty I faced paired with the threat of frigid winter misery.

Occasionally, a shift in the gale caused an explosion of debris to drift into our sandy shelter deep in the bank of the creek. I stayed alert and tense in the darkness with the tough skin of the buffalo pulled tightly under my chin. Two Face traded for me with plans to join the Oglala and Brulé Sioux bands living near Fort Laramie in the spring. He told me the price of my ransom was sure to impress the fort's commanders. I feared more travel, though, for the life of a nomad in the more temperate months was tiring and difficult. I could hardly master my thoughts as I imagined a ruinous end to both our lives from exposure, starvation, and abuse.

The past few weeks in the camp along Sand Creek were peaceful. I noticed a large United States flag flying above Black Kettle's lodge. Traders and soldiers were frequent visitors. Of course, I remained out of sight, but it was comforting to hear a familiar word float my way, and I found myself straining now as I listened to the wind. My access to freedom was near, yet I was closely guarded. In the large camp of eight hundred lodges, my countrymen never discovered my presence.

Darkness overtook the storm and when the wind abated briefly, Two Face and I trudged to his lodge. Stepping through the flap on the east side of the teepee, I welcomed the warmth. Two Face, although not particularly kind, showed favoritism by settling us onto a sleeping pallet, the one closest to the fire. The women of Two Face's lodge were not subtle in their displeasure at my presence. One of them kicked me in passing and I batted her leg then watched her fall. Her words were unintelligible, but it was clear—jealousy prevailed in his lodge. Two Face spoke harshly to his women, and the evening settled into a tense standoff. Relieved to be away from Big Crow, I knew trouble was brewing in my new circumstances.

Little did I know how fortuitous it was to no longer be a prisoner among the Cheyenne.

The force of the wind picked up again; dirt and snow scraped the outer skins of the teepee.

I dreamed of stones in a stream, shining brightly as water flowed over them.

Alarmingly, horses' feet plunged and tramped through the water.

Bodies lay strewn in rivers of blood.

I awoke with a gasp and sat up trying to calm my disturbed heart.

The sleeping village was unaware of the true storm approaching from the south. Its dark cell brought thundering hooves, fire, and death.

It was near.

chapter forty-four

Sand Creek
(Po-eneo-o'hee)

29 November 1864
Eastern Colorado Territory

Massacre at Sand Creek

Mr. Wiggins once told the Record correspondent that the testimony of Mrs. Eubank was to the effect that she as the captive of Two Face, was at Sand Creek. With characteristic cunning Two Face had his teepee some distance from the camp, and when the attack was made Mrs. Eubank had no chance to escape or make herself known.

The Anaconda Standard, Anaconda, Montana
August 13, 1897

The regiment's forty-mile trek from Fort Lyon to Sand Creek through the night was treacherous. The temperature dropped drastically, and frigid wind gusts intensified the cold Colorado dawn.

Young Captain Silas Soule replayed the events of the prior evening as he and seven hundred soldiers comprised of the 1st and 3rd Regiments streamed toward the quiet Indian camp. Soule's abhorrent disgust over the upcoming dastardly attack was ever apparent. Except for Major Scott Anthony, the officers and soldiers at Fort Lyon supported his disapproval. Holding no compassion for the Indians, Anthony eagerly followed Colonel Chivington's orders and prepared his men at the fort for battle.

Captain Soule's appeals to Chivington to abort his plan the night before launched into a thundering dispute. Chivington declared, "Damn any man in sympathy with the Indians!" Through his browbeating and threats, the soldiers at the fort were convinced any resistance would ultimately end their lives. The Methodist preacher, who carefully wove his plan for political stature, would allow nothing to interfere with his highly sought acclaim.

Silas continued his ride in silence as they approached the Sand Creek village. Drawing nearer, he reflected on the events of recent months and the Indians' desire for peace. He was aware Black Kettle agreed to submit to military authority and move his people to Sand Creek for protection. Silas Soule also knew Black Kettle trusted Wynkoop's words. Repulsed, Silas shook his head, wrapped the collar of his coat tighter around his neck, and spit on the cold, hard ground.

Lifting my head, I quickly scanned the inside of the lodge. The fire continued its slow, orange glow. Willie slept close to me under a thick buffalo robe. His little legs moved the robe up and down, producing scant puffs of air to cross over us.

The camp was peaceful. I could hear children playing and the quiet morning voices of their mothers. The crackle of kindling and the movement of pots set up the harmony of the day.

The serenity of the tranquil morning split when one of the women screamed into the frosted air, "Soldiers! Soldiers!"

Indians rushed frantically about. Alarmed women and children gathered in the middle of camp. Dogs ran wild and barked anxiously. Braves bolted from their lodges to find the pony herd gone, then rushed back inside the teepees for their weapons. While trying to calm his people, Black Kettle stood in front of his teepee, holding the American flag and a white flag as they waved in the dawn's light.

Two Face barreled into his lodge. He threw a buffalo robe toward me and hollered, "Go! Now!"

I grabbed the cradleboard and with shaking hands secured Willie inside. Spinning around the teepee, I spotted my satchel. Clutching my precious belongings, I sprang through the flap.

Doc Billy and Blackfoot were mounted and waiting at the teepee with two ponies in tow. Two Face hoisted me on the back of one and fastened the cradleboard to the other. He jumped on the back of his horse with Willie attached and looked at me with blazing eyes. He shouted, "Go fast, Fire-Hair Woman!" With complete havoc bearing down on us, we dug our heels into the alarmed ponies' sides and raced away from the once placid village with the others in Two Face's band.

Chivington sat rigid on his great black steed. The knoll where he stopped provided an ample view of the sprawling Indian village below.

He squinted his beady eyes and peered toward the camp with a sense of great satisfaction.

A petrified Robert Bent sat mounted next to him with his head down. Robert watched the neck of his horse twitch as its hoof pawed the frozen ground. On his way to Fort Lyon, Chivington arrested the half-breed son of William Bent and told him, "I haven't had an Indian to eat in a long time. If you fool with me and don't lead us to that camp, I'll have you for breakfast." Knowing his native brothers and sisters would soon lie dead on the ground, Bent's gut wrenched.

Wasting no time, Chivington shouted orders to the officers of the Colorado 1st Company, "Ride between the herd and the village. Cut off the herd and take your positions!" To the incensed volunteers of the Hundred Days men, Chivington yelled, "Remember the slain women and children on the Platte!"

In opposition to the attack and with full defiance to Chivington's orders, Soule ordered his squadron not to fire. He kept his soldiers together as they rode down the side of the south creek, witnessing the brutal massacre unfold.

The soldiers' advance continued as shots flew across the village, and Indians fled in all directions. Many ran across the snow-covered ground to the creek bottoms where they feverishly dug sand pits with their hands for cover. Black Kettle and his wife, Medicine Woman Later, continued their stance in front of their lodge joined by White Antelope. Black Kettle believed there must be a misunderstanding. They were friendly Indians…advised to camp at Sand Creek.

Complete chaos encompassed the village. Realizing there was no stopping the attack, Black Kettle and his wife ran up the creek bed. White Antelope waved his arms and shouted to the soldiers to stop fire. The troops continued their attack, but the brave Cheyenne held his ground. He stood with his arms crossed, the medal he received in Washington draped around his neck.

Bullets riddled White Antelope's body.

Stealing a glance over my shoulder, I saw the horrible scene. Red fire showered the camp as Indians fled up the creek bed, and others fell to the ground. Screams permeated the air. Black ash floated. I couldn't breathe, I couldn't think. More death.

Two Face ran his pony next to mine, forcing it to keep pace as we galloped through the icy air toward the Dog Soldier camp at Big Timbers.

Attempting to flee, Black Kettle and Medicine Woman Later followed their people. Medicine Woman Later was shot several times and fell to the ground. Thinking she was dead, Black Kettle fled through the melee.

The Cheyenne and Arapaho fought bravely. Many escaped, but multitudes were cut down. Some women and children made it to the sand pits only to die by vicious barbarity.

———— • ————

Racing into the Big Timbers camp, Two Face, Doc Billy, and Blackfoot roared news of the attack. Braves immediately grabbed their weapons and ran to the pony herd. In haste, they dashed in the direction of Sand Creek to search for survivors. Squaws screamed and slashed themselves. Blood stained the snow.

With a guarded eye, I watched Two Face's every move. He entered a nearby teepee, and I followed, stopping just outside the entrance. As I sat down beside the fire, an old squaw flew at me in a rage. Her hands slapped me in a flurry until I fell backwards on the ground. Four more squaws began to beat and kick me. Horrified, I screamed and scrambled across the icy ground on my hands and knees away from the abuse.

Clutching my stomach, I searched the area for Willie. Pools of water filled my eyes. Oh, my God! Panic-stricken, I shrieked his name from the pit of my stomach! Frantically, I ran around the nearby lodges until I heard a faint cry. Following the familiar sound, I found him inside one of the teepees, still strapped inside his cradleboard. My hands trembled as I freed him from its latches and pulled him tight to my breast.

Despairing thoughts raced through my mind. I am certain these deaths will be avenged. I prepared for an attack in the only way I knew how. I prayed. Heavenly Father, please protect us. Please, Lord, help us! I fear they will kill us!

Wrapping my robe tightly around Willie, I moved to a different fire. Elders began beating their drums. Blood continued to trickle down the legs and arms of the squaws. I felt their horror and lowered my head in the crease of my robe as the drums thumped.

Survivors began their agonizing procession into the gray-tinged Dog Soldier camp. Hurt. Cold. Starving. I had to help them and began administering to their wounds, one with the enemy. The ridicule and scornful looks from the squaws subsided as I moved from one injury to the next.

As night approached, Black Kettle returned to Sand Creek to retrieve his wife's body. He found her still alive. He rode slowly into the Big Timbers camp with Medicine Woman Later draped over his horse.

Penetrated by nine bullets, her blood-soaked body was carefully lifted into a lodge.

Trying to remain calm on the outside, my insides were raw and petrified. Sensing danger approach, I cast my eyes toward a figure erratically searching about the camp. In an instant, Mochi grasped my hair. As my head flung back, the blade of her knife lay at my neck. Her anguished, blood-curdling shrieks filled my ears. Writhing, twisting, and turning, I fought against my woman assailant as she dragged my body toward the fire. Flames singed the bottoms of my feet as the smell of my burning flesh and painful screams filled the gloomy, damp air.

Two Face grabbed my shoulders and broke Mochi's forceful grip. Rabid rancor flew from Mochi's enraged eyes. Two Face swiftly carried me into the lodge and laid me on a pallet. He wrapped my feet, then abruptly left without speaking.

The wailing continued throughout the next day. Although I wanted to help, I lived in fear of revenge and knew I must only protect myself and Willie now. Hidden away in the lodge, I heard pitiful cries announce the dead. One Eye was killed. One Eye was killed. The warrior Min-im-mic escaped but his wife and two daughters were brutally killed. Chief Left Hand's family was dead, and he was critically injured.

The weary, heartbroken survivors repeated the stories of their men, women, and children brutally killed and mutilated. I could not understand this meaningless loss of life. This war. What purpose did it hold?

War drums echoed throughout the camp....

> As we rode into that camp…everyone was crying, even the warriors and the women and children screaming and wailing. Nearly everyone present had lost some relations or friends, many of them in their grief were gashing themselves with their knives until the blood flowed in streams.
>
> George Bent

William (Will) Eubank, Sr.
Authors' Collection

Lucinda Walton Eubank
Courtesy National Park Service
Fort Laramie NHS

Willie Joseph (Willie) Eubank, Jr.
History Nebraska

Joseph Eubank, Sr.
Authors' Collection

Ruth Adamson Eubank
Authors' Collection

Joseph (Joe) Eubank, Jr
Overland stagecoach driver
*Courtesy National Park Service,
Fort Laramie NHS*

Harriet (Hattie) Palmer Eubank
and Josephine Eubank
Authors' Collection

Medora (Dora) and Sarah Eubank
Authors' Collection

Captives Released in Denver
(from L-R) Ambrose Asher, Laura Roper,
Isabelle Eubank, Danny Marble
History Nebraska

Lucinda Walton Eubank
Authors' Collection

Unidentified woman
Believed to be a Eubank or Walton
Authors' Collection

Beatrice, Lucy and Blanche Eubank
Daughters of William Eubank, Jr.
Authors' Collection

Beatrice Eubank Ellis
Authors' Grandmother
Daughter of William Eubank, Jr.
Authors' Collection

Daniel Walton
Husband of Hannah Eubank
Brother of Lucinda Eubank
Authors' Collection

Hannah EubankWalton
Wife of Daniel Walton
Sister of William Eubank, Sr.
Authors' Collection

Camp Weld Council

(Front row L-R)
Major Wynkoop, Captain Silas Soule

(Seated L-R)
White Antelope, Bull Bear, Black Kettle,
Neva and No-Ta-Nee

(Back row L-R)
unknown, Dexter Coley, interpreter John
Smith, Heap-of-Buffalo, Bosse, Samuel
Elbert and unknown soldier.

History Colorado

Edward (Ned) Wynkoop
History Colorado

Willie Eubank and family

(Front row seated L-R) Lucy, William, Jr. (Willie), Sarah Jane (Jennie) Frogge, Art
(Back row standing L-R) Beatrice, Kenneth, Ollie, Loren, Virgil, Blanche

Lucinda Eubank

chapter forty-five

Winter's War

Early January 1865
The Moon of Frost in the Lodge
Cherry Creek, Northeastern Colorado Territory

The plains, from Julesburg west, for more than one hundred miles, are red with the blood of murdered men, women, and children —ranches are in ashes—stock all driven off—the country utterly desolate...The truth is a gigantic Indian war is upon us.

Omaha Nebraska Republican
February 3, 1865

Two Face's wife, daughter of Calfskin, nudged me with her foot. It was time. I knew to rise at once before she lashed me with the whipping stick kept around for that purpose. Her jealousy and resentment had reached a tipping point. She was either going to kill me or order me out of her lodge permanently. A dangerous situation. Two Face avoided the contentious women by spending time in his mother's teepee

I left Willie asleep on the robes and ventured into the frigid predawn light. Setting up the pot for the meal of the day, I looked for Two Face. I heard him slip under his wife's buffalo robe during the night. Piling wood onto the fire and filling the cooking pot with water, I saw him stride through the morning fog, leading his favorite war horse. Something was different about this day, and I was uneasy.

The hazy dawn's light increased, then I noticed the men. They were in preparation mode—for war. Boys were returning from the outskirts of camp with horses. So many horses. Hundreds of men were painting themselves and their mounts, all the while adorning themselves— headdresses, shields, medicine bags, and weapons. Voices were quiet, and the people's breath hung in the icy air.

Everywhere I looked, it was the same. A thousand warriors were about to leave camp! But it was unheard of during the Month of Frost in the Lodge! It was common knowledge: the Indians went into winter camps to lay up while the weather was cold. With nothing but snowdrifts and windswept plains sprinkled with bits of dried grasses, little feed was available for their horse herds. The animals grew weak during the winter. Yet today they were leaving to battle an unsuspecting foe. I was aware of skirmishes—white and Indian, but not on this scale. Something big was about to happen.

Shrieking wildly, the warriors streamed out of the village and headed north along a ridge of bluffs that framed the South Platte River. Where were they going? What was their target?

George Bent, dressed in warrior raiment, rode by with a group of whites and Mexicans. A large man with reddish hair and whiskers rode past on a bob-tailed sorrel. The secesh flag of Texas planted upright in a leather sheath near the stirrup was supported by his right hand. His horse danced through the center of camp as the lone star flapped wildly. The white warrior careened by—his rebel yell joined the war whoops as the last of the braves galloped out of camp. With a final shot from his pistol, he yelled, 'To Julesburg!' His fleet horse swept out of camp as if on the wind. With incredible speed, it quickly overtook the leaders of the party. The powerful Cheyenne, with the help of the rebels, were bent on destruction.

Julesburg! Comprehension dawned, and foreboding swept through my mind. I was familiar with the place. We must be near the most important trail in the area. From the frequent travels of family members who worked for the freight companies, I knew Julesburg was at the junction of two main roads which separated from the Overland Trail. One ran south to Denver, the other west to Salt Lake City and beyond.

Julesburg had grown into a town and enveloped such necessities as a stage station, saloon, boarding house, blacksmith shop, and most importantly, a telegraph office. The survey of the railroad, which would run west to the ocean, would put Julesburg on the map as a hub to Denver. The Eubank boys excitedly told of the military post nearby. Camp Rankin was now officially Fort Sedgwick. A garrison of soldiers must be housed there now. Greatly concerned, I stood facing north toward Julesburg. I worried about the surprise attack and prayed for the protection of the unsuspecting folks who lived and worked there.

I also wondered…how close was I to salvation? Could I make it to the settlement? The military post? Would there be anything left after today? Was it possible my family members might be there? Were they in danger? It was all unsettling, and I spent the rest of the day scraping a buffalo hide, ruminating, tending to Willie, and trying to stay out of the way of the women in Two Face's band.

Three days later, the warriors rode into camp with great fanfare. The plunder they carried was so burdensome it slowed their return. The entire village turned out to sort through the clothing, hardware, and food items. Along with herds of horses and mules, fresh beef on the hoof appeared over the horizon. The meat was sorely needed for all were hungry. Two Face's daughter offered Willie a piece of citron candy, which he relished with slobbery glee.

The avengers of Sand Creek made their first strike and, to my dismay, were very successful. Drums pounded throughout the night. Dancers performed, and the entire village of eight hundred lodges feasted. Over one hundred beeves were butchered. Canned goods by the crate were opened and consumed—the tins scattered along the banks of Cherry Creek. The Cheyenne, whose time of sorrow was hidden under the mourning blanket for weeks, were finally able to join the celebration.

Repeatedly, the victors reenacted deeds of heroism and prowess as they told of the astuteness of their great leaders who proved cunning in the defeat of the whites. Big Crow led the first wave of decoys into luring the soldiers out of the post. The Cheyenne trilled with excitement as Starving Elk, Old Crow, and two Sioux were drawn into the theatrical telling of the story. My stomach turned at the thought of so few white men against such a motivated and ferocious enemy. Scalps of the victims were few. I hoped something remained of Julesburg and its people.

Throughout the next few weeks, I noticed war parties leave camp in smaller groups headed in different directions. Even though travel along the emigrant trails was nearly non-existent in the winter, the Dog Soldiers focused on lonely travelers, undefended outposts, and ranches along the South Platte River. With an eye to the coming spring migration, the Indians determined to wipe out all supportive resources.

About mid-January, the camp moved to a new location. To cross the frozen Platte, squaws threw sand on the ice to prevent the feet of the ponies and people from slipping. It was bitter cold.

Two Face drew a crude map in the sand to explain our travels. I concealed my motives and hid the notes in my satchel to drop along the way. He happily accommodated my "interest" in the rhythm of tribal life and regularly shared information. The camp was now situated halfway between the southern forks of the Republican and South Platte Rivers on a stream called White Butte Creek.

The raiders continued to leave camp, returning with fresh scalps, livestock, and plunder. One day, their haul included a woman. The warriors dropped her off in the center of camp. A large group of village squaws administered the initiation beating Nancy and I endured upon our arrival. The attack ended abruptly, and with unintelligible instructions, Two Face's squaw pushed me toward the bleeding woman crumpled on the ground. She was now my problem.

I gathered her up as best I could and half-carried her into the lodge of Two Face's mother. The woman was nearly frozen to the point of no return. I covered her with blankets and a buffalo robe and gave her a ladle full of bone broth, which dribbled from blue lips. I tried to mend her clothing and wounds as best I could and continued my efforts to warm and revive her. She lay incoherent for a day and a half until finally regaining consciousness.

The woman spoke hoarsely but urgently to me. "My child. Have you seen my child?"

A rock landed in the pit of my stomach. Reluctantly, I replied I had not seen a child. Grief and trauma overwhelmed her again as she lapsed into a catatonic state. Hours later, I offered food and she responded with eye contact and a quick nod of her head but no words. As she ate, I waited. The woman perhaps my elder by a decade, had long, brown hair ripped out in patches. Her face spoke of time in the sun and the elements, and her hands showed hard labor. Her clothing was faded and worn.

As she improved, a brief conversation confirmed that Mrs. Morrison was of pioneer stock and, like me, managed a road ranch known as the American. I remembered it from the now defunct Pony Express map which hung on the wall at the Little Blue Station. She told haltingly of the American's burned-out ruins and the murders of eight people including family members. She and her youngest child were taken during an especially severe cold spell, and now the child was gone. I suspected it lay frozen on the empty plains.

Understanding her wretched, emotional condition, I knew she faced grave danger. No white woman was safe. The recent massacre of so many at Sand Creek was not easily avenged. Many whites would die before the scales were even—if ever they would be.

My fears were confirmed two days later while sitting outside shivering in the sunshine. The temperature was certainly below zero. Big Crow appeared without warning. Lifting Mrs. Morrison off her feet and throwing her over his shoulder, he stomped away with the squirming, screaming woman.

I scrambled to my feet and followed. His intentions were clear. I pleaded with him to stop though, in my heart, I knew mercy did not abide in Big Crow. The large hulk carried her to his lodge, threw her violently through the flap, then entered. Shakily, I remained outside listening. The struggle was great, and Mrs. Morrison fought him with all she had, for I heard him bellow in pain. In turn she cried out in agony. I remembered the strength of Big Crow and the futility of resisting such a malicious attacker.

Suddenly, the flap was thrown open and Mrs. Morrison was heaved like a sack of flour onto the ground. Big Crow appeared, yelling at two warriors in the vicinity. At once, they left on a mission and Big Crow began to tie leather straps around each wrist and ankle of the woman. His slaps and a knee on her neck succeeded in quieting her, but I knew what was coming.

"Big Crow! Stop! Don't do this!"

Noticing me for the first time, he narrowed his eyes, stood up, and backhanded me. I was quick enough to dodge the full force of the strike but ended up sprawled in the snow. Within moments, the young warriors returned with two horses. Leaping to my feet, I shouted, "No! No! Nooo!!"

Two braves instantly pinned me down.

Mrs. Morrison's limbs were tethered to the excited horses. Held facing opposite directions, they crabbed and bolted, jerking the woman's form in a tug of war, which was just a prelude of things to come.

"Big Crow!" I screamed. "Don't do this, Big Crow! I will do anything you want!"

He scowled and sized up my proposition.

I cowered and quickly stepped back.

His voice boomed across the camp as he announced the death of this woman was in exchange for the murders at Sand Creek. With a hideous yell while howling at the sky, he raised his arm to signal the release of the horses then brought it down with a vengeance.

The horses were turned loose. Bolting forward, they hit the ends of the ropes. Continuously whipped, each strained against the pull of the other. Mrs. Morrison shrieked in pain. Minutes later, the popping of her limbs resounded through the camp. Then she was quiet, head hanging limply askew. The braves beat the horses viciously until two of her limbs tore from her body.

Then she was free. Lying still, she was breathing but clearly in the last moments of life. A warrior stepped forward and finished her with the thrust of his spear.

Drums began at the moment of Mrs. Morrison's death and thrummed dully in my ears. I must hide! In shock, I stumbled blindly, face buried in my hands, crying out. I must return to the circle of Two Face's band! The mood in the camp was ominous, and fear coursed through my being. The hair on my entire body stood on end. I knew I was in danger. The warriors chanted and stomped the ground around her body. Big Crow stood near her, bellowing with blood vengeance. His eyes met mine. Images of torture and death fueled his rage. Pointing, he lunged toward me. I slipped beyond his reach and ran for my life.

Two Face! I must find Two Face!

Twisting and turning through the maze of teepees, I ran headlong into the young Cheyenne woman, Mochi. She and her husband, Medicine Water, grabbed at me, barely catching my sleeve. Jerking away, I sprinted past them. Malice-filled eyes followed as I clambered and stumbled into Two Face's lodge.

I stood breathlessly, mind racing. Picking up Willie, I squeezed him tightly enough to elicit a squeak from the child. Mochi! Danger! Heart pounding, I remembered....

The families of Mochi and her husband were killed at Sand Creek. While camped at Smoky Hill after our escape from the massacre, I witnessed Mochi's transformation. Parading past, she would confront me and spout obscenities.

Wary of the violence she might be planning, I did not doubt her capabilities. Now she was a full-fledged warrior and rode with the raiders—herself a colorful display of war paint and weaponry. In fact, her entire persona hid the fact she was a woman. Mochi proved herself to be a fierce Cheyenne warrior. Lauded as a merciless fighter during scalp dances...I feared her.

I had become prey to her predatory tendencies.

Was I to be the next sacrifice in their vengeful dance of death?

Terrified, I pulled the buffalo robe over us. Unmolested for the rest of the night, I was grateful for this obscure place of refuge.

———•———

Days passed as more attacks were carried out. The tenor of the camp was no longer a victory celebration but intensified to sheer blood lust. Success fed the desire to eliminate whites completely in the area, then move on to new targets.

I could not sleep, for nightmares of Mrs. Morrison haunted my dreams. I forced myself to stay alert, awake, aware. I knew we were not safe, but from which direction would our attackers materialize?

The answer came the next evening as the bonfires and war drums grew in intensity. It was to be another night of vanquishing foes. Mochi, her husband, and three other Cheyenne appeared at the lodge. Two Face stepped out to greet them. Hoping to avoid detection, I hid quietly in the lodge. The conversation grew tense as they demanded I be given over to them. Two Face stepped solidly in front of the teepee entrance. Shaking his head, he firmly and loudly expelled the entire group from his band's circle of lodges.

Afterwards, he entered the teepee and sat down.

Wrapped in a blanket, my teeth chattered as I tried to warm up from the bone-chilling fear.

Two Face stirred the fire. Without looking at me directly, he said, "Cheyenne come to buy you, Fire-Hair."

"No! Two Face!"

He continued solemnly, "They want burn you at stake…tonight."

My heart stopped. Did he? Had he? Was I condemned?

Two Face looked up from the embers and said, "I tell them no. Fire-Hair not for trade."

Abruptly, I stood and stepped outside. I needed air and to ponder my fate. The Sioux and the Cheyenne were formidable. I detested living with them, but at this moment, I cautiously breathed a sigh of relief. My desire to live another day spoke to the life force within me. But I wondered if I would spend the rest of my life as a foreigner among the Sioux people. I shook my head no, for it was only a matter of time. My life was balanced on a thread.

Yet…how had Willie and I been preserved? Yes, we had been harmed in ways that brought us near the brink of death, but we were still alive. It occurred to me…Two Face! He had saved our lives more than once.

I thought of our children, the only links Will and I had to the future. If new generations were ever to come, it would be through our children. Alas, Belle…I thought painfully of the last day we spent together. Such a tender life and sweet spirit. Her memory always brought tears and remorse. The women in Two Face's band constantly punished me for nursing Willie. They demanded I wean the child; if I did, I would never see him again. Our connection extended beyond mother and child. We might be all that remained of our immediate family, and I loved him fiercely and forever.

Now, for the first time in our captivity, I wondered how Willie, such a young child, survived among the ruthless savages? They were not known to accommodate a captive so young. As the violence of the war path continued unabated, we were dragged along. Yes, sometimes close to death, sometimes wishing for death. Yet, we prevailed.

Staring into the large shining eyes of the child in my arms, I deliberated....

Truly, how could it be? We were not disemboweled, murdered, mutilated, ripped limb from limb. We still breathed, though we were fodder for the pent-up vengeance of others. From threat to threat, we narrowly escaped as if directed by an unseen hand. Victims, yes. But not yet victims forever bound in a grave on the vast and lonely plains.

I looked up at the darkening winter sky. The lights from inside the glowing lodges and scattered campfires did not account for the unusual glow. Seeking its source, I spun to the north and gasped. The emptiness of space was filled with an unusual green and purple light that wavered, moved, and changed as though alive. Others noticed the phenomenon, and the village quieted to stare at the lights in the northern sky. The otherworldly, luminous waves performed their own dance above our heads. After they faded and disappeared, the inhabitants left the frigid fires of revenge and retreated to the warmth of their lodges to speculate on the omen.

Usually, I refused to reflect upon our travails and suffering since becoming prisoners; but now it was clear. There was a means of protection afforded to us. How had we been shielded thus far?

The revelation prompted prayer. "Thank you, Lord...."

Two Face stepped out of his teepee, which glowed from the fire within.

Staring at him, I mouthed, "And...*thank you*."

With those words, the light inside me steadied and grew strong.

chapter forty-six

Blood of the Innocent

January 1865
Eastern Dakotah Territory

*Men and horses must be had immediately, or else we must yield
ourselves living sacrifices to inhuman savages; and who of us all
are prepared to do this?*

Colonel Thomas Moonlight

C razy Horse. The newcomer arrived in the village, and his presence
bolstered the warriors. His name was spoken with admiration. It
was said the tribes of the north received word of the massacred
Cheyenne at Sand Creek, and Sitting Bull sent the young chief south to
help survivors. He was to guide the people to the great camp along the
Powder River, Dakotah Territory. I saw him from a distance, his long,
light-colored hair such a contrast to his swarthy companions. He was hard
to miss.

The war camp moved to the bank of the South Platte River
across from Harlow's Ranch. After its destruction, the warrior Cut
Belly brought in another woman prisoner. I never learned her fate. Two
Face was gone much of the time. I knew he was part of the attack on a
group of freighters near Julesburg and the burning of Gillette's Ranch.
Plunder continued to fill the camp and was a beneficial support to its
inhabitants. Food was no longer scarce.

Before leaving Colorado Territory, the raiders turned their sights once
again on Julesburg. Freshly equipped with superior arms including
Enfield rifles and carbines, the Indians were intent on finishing the job.
Crazy Horse would ride with them. The entire force of fifteen hundred
warriors left as eight hundred lodges began to come down. The people
were on the move again.

The trail opened to the view of ballooning black smoke rising like thunder clouds of summer. Buildings and haystacks burned in the distance, attesting to the parting gift of a successful campaign against the Denver road's inhabitants and their resources. Those who attacked Julesburg loaded an enormous quantity of goods onto pack horses and into wagons, then rejoined the village.

The warriors swept north and continued their excursions of total ruin. They attacked telegraph stations at Lodgepole Creek and Mud Springs. Talking wires were pulled to the ground and dismantled. The tribe abandoned wagon loads of goods as they bogged down in the sandhills.

At one point, a thousand raiders discovered a small company of soldiers. The resistance was admirable, but the warriors were swift and tactical. The overwhelming numbers of Indian braves left fifteen defenders dead. It was best to strike with the lethal efficiency of the wolf, killing more than necessary. Rather than finishing off the prey, the wolf pack slipped out of danger, their numbers still intact.

Catching them was an easy enough matter, but we had a terribly hard time letting them go.

Private George Nelson

One young Cheyenne brave, however, was not fortunate enough to escape unscathed. He took a bullet in the chest yet made an amazing escape while riding flat on his fleet pony into camp. Yellow Nose struggled to breathe as blood and bubbles spurted from his nose. They laid him at my feet, his eyes wide with pain and fright. I quickly found the entry wound and after staunching the blood flow, I inserted my finger into the wound far enough to touch a flattened piece of lead lodged against a rib. I guessed the bone broke and punctured his lung. After cutting and digging, I removed the bullet and sewed up the wound. Yellow Nose survived to fight again, but I also won a token of tolerance from my captives. I was beginning to be known as a healer. Still hated— but of value, nonetheless.

Shortly thereafter, a scouting party spotted soldiers with four companies of cavalry escorting wagons fifteen miles distant. The village moved quickly from its camp along Rush Creek. It was a pleasant valley protected by rocky bluffs along the North Platte River. The clear water of the nearby springs was not completely frozen, so water was readily available. Grass peeked out of patches of snow, supplying nourishment for the herds. The women grumbled as they packed to move from one of their favored camps. The war parties upset the natural balance of things, but the leaders encouraged the families to push on, for soon the bands would settle in for the winter. Our nomadic days culminated in scalp dances at night. The Winter War was unstoppable.

Finally, the people reached the high country at the head of Brown's Creek where we rested for three days. Then the tribes marched through the sand hills to their most cherished home, the Black Hills. At its base, the Sioux and Cheyenne peoples danced under the light of the full moon with an unmatched exuberance of spirit.

Around this time, the leaders of the Sioux, Cheyenne, and Arapaho held a council. Spotted Tail suggested the bands separate into three great spears. The Lakota would head north into the Black Hills. The Cheyenne, including the Sand Creek survivors, would turn northwest into the Powder River country. The Blue Clouds planned to winter in a region somewhere between them. Black Kettle made the decision to head south with his eighty lodges. He hoped to find peace and safety for his band among Little Raven's Arapaho clan.

The chiefs considered the sweep across the Holy Road a success. The Indians acquired herds of cattle and horses, keeping only the best. The warriors planned to continue to fight all whites as they moved their people into winter camps. Cold gripped the village, and it was time to protect the young and old—human and beast alike.

———•———

The soldiers returned to their forts, and Colonel Moonlight accepted a new post at Fort Laramie. The reports of Indian depredations were concerning. It was time to open a line of communication with the governor. It was time to plan the winter campaign. There would be a day of reckoning.

HEADQUARTERS DISTRICT OF COLORADO
Denver, January 17, 1865.
Hon. S. H. Elbert
Acting Governor, Colorado Territory

Sir:

By reason of the scarcity of troops in this district, our natural enemies the Indians, have possessed themselves of our lines of communication. They have burned ranches, killed innocent women and children, destroyed government property wherever it was found, driven off the stage stock, killed the drivers and passengers traveling on the coaches; in short, they are making it a war of extermination.

We may look in vain for such timely military assistance as will protect the lives and property of settlers; nor can we hope for an eastern communication this winter, unless the citizens of the Territory band themselves together in a military organization, and spring to arms at your call as chief executive. The blood of the innocent and unoffending martyrs cries aloud for vengeance, and starvation stares in the face of the living. You nor I cannot longer remain inactive, and be considered guiltless. It devolves upon the militia, as matters now stand to open the overland route, and keep it open until troops can be had from the east to make war on these savages of the plains, until there remains not a vestige of their originality. On behalf of the general government, and on my own responsibility, (trusting to the justice of the cause for my own protection,) I will furnish carbines to the first mounted and accepted company, and rifled weapons of improved pattern to all the balance; also, rations for the same as United States troops, and forage for the animals, with the proper allowance of transportation, and also horse equipments. My scouts inform me that the Indian spies are now prowling around the very skirts of this place, so that, in addition to your call for militia for field service, the city companies should at once be placed on a war footing, having daily drills, with appointed places of rendezvous, that we may not be caught napping.

I am very respectfully, your obedient servant,

T. MOONLIGHT,
Colonel 11th Kansas Cavalry, Commanding.

chapter forty-seven

Bear Butte
(Mato Paha)

Mid-February 1865
Black Hills, Dakotah Territory

We shall have hundreds of thousands of disbanded soldiers… I am going to try to attract them to the hidden wealth of our mountain ranges, where there is room for all. Tell the miners for me that I shall promote their interests to the utmost of my ability because their prosperity is the prosperity of the nation and we shall prove in a very few years that we are the treasury of the world.

Abraham Lincoln

Two Face's mother rolled out from under the large buffalo robe we shared. The frigid air rushed into our cocoon, and the baby stirred. As she stepped through the teepee flap, I noticed four inches of fresh, powdery snow covered the outside world. The deep cold from the night before hung in wispy whiteness over the half-frozen creek—its gurgling sound a pleasant change from the noise of the wind that slammed into us during the night. I flipped onto my back and poked my face above the edge of our covering. The hair from the robe's former occupant tickled my neck, and I breathed deeply to rid my lungs of the sour air in the lodge. The bed of cottonwood leaves rustled under the rude muslin pallet we placed on the ground each night. I wiggled my toes to get the blood flowing and was relieved when sensation returned to my extremities. Gazing up through the smoke hole of the lodge, I spotted a huge cottonwood branch. It held tenaciously to a few dried brown leaves. An empty bird nest sat perched on its limb. Nothing stirred.

The day before we traveled under an overcast blanket heavy with the promise of snow. Foothills in the distance were barely discernable, and I saw nothing beyond them. By my calculations, we were more than three hundred miles north of Sand Creek. I shivered. The memory of the attack chilled my soul.

Willie's head rested in the crook of my numb arm. He began to rouse. The toddler swatted at the heavy covering with open hands. I had bartered for a bonnet when the weather turned colder, and his long, blonde curls peeked out beneath. It had spun round during the night and now covered one of his eyes. He grabbed at the peach calico ties and tugged mightily to remove the head wear. A constant, biting wind reigned in this barren country, and I coveted warm head coverings. Scraps of random animal furs reinforced the inside of his cap, adding extra warmth.

Willie kicked his tiny moccasins ferociously at the covering. Rolling onto his hands and knees, he emerged from his hidey-hole. I was thankful for the tiny deerskin leggings and fringed coat, which were sufficiently warm but very dirty from the rigors of travel.

He smiled at me and said, "Mama?" Then he threw himself onto my chest and raised up to inspect my face. The child always took his cues from me to figure out our current relative safety. He seemed happy as I pronounced it a good morning with a smile.

The journey with Two Face and the large band of Cheyenne worried me. I would never trust them. Their demeanor was one of indifference— as though I was one of their horses. Valuable…somewhat. To be fed and watered, roughly pushed to continue. That was the sum of it. I was property.

Occasionally, I caught glimpses of anger from small groups talking quietly among themselves. The trauma of recent events showed in their grim, sorrow-filled faces. I imagined their thoughts often leaned toward justice for the deaths of their loved ones, and I was the perfect target. It must have been on Two Face's mind as well, for we always slept in the same lodge now. His watchfulness was ever vigilant. His usual casual and taunting demeanor was replaced by seriousness often punctuated by physical roughness. I supposed he must show no leniency to the white woman captive who was a constant reminder of the enemy in their midst. I considered myself most vulnerable when he rode off on a raid.

Basic humanity bound me to the tribes. We shared the need to survive in a bleak and inhospitable land during the dead of winter. The occupants of Two Face's lodges spoke among themselves, not in Cheyenne, to which I had become familiar, but in a different language which Two Face identified as Lakota. The words he used to describe his mother's people were "Teton Sioux," their homeland situated far to the north. I learned Two Face was, indeed, of double heritage. His father was Cheyenne and his mother Sioux. Although he spoke in broken English, we conversed on a range of subjects. To hear my language spoken comforted me in unexpected ways. Also, I noticed he had money and recalled his trade dealings between the Sioux and the whites before the current conflict.

Lifting the flap, the sun was a frozen glass orb sparkling boldly along the eastern horizon. Brilliant hues of violet, pink, orange, gold, and rose formed pastel layers of sky. The crisp air lay muted behind a silvery veil. As was my practice, I scanned the area. My skin rippled in goose flesh as I spotted a group of younger braves down the creek—a safe enough distance. I decided to take this moment for a little privacy. I stood, stretched, and cranked my spine into alignment, then picked up my toddler. Once relieved, I pulled my long red blanket around the both of us.

Turning away from the sunrise, I stood stunned. The scenery behind me was beyond imagination. The gloomy weather of the past couple of days had obscured the view beyond the foothills. But now....

The scene left me breathless. Before me, a gleaming mountain stood firmly in the flatness of the terrain. The blowing snow had scoured its sides clean. White drifts accented hollows and gullies. The treeless ridge lines gleamed with pure granite—like exposed teeth. After weeks of traversing an endlessly wild and trackless country, I stood transfixed by the glory before me.

Two Face approached from the edge of the creek where the hobbled horses shuffled through the snow in search of dried grasses. I pointed to the mountain standing starkly in the clear air. A rare smile cracked the face of my companion.

"Black Hills," he said sweeping his arm across the range of mountains. Then pointing to the imposing mound, he added, "Mato Paha, Bear Butte. Sacred Mountain." He stepped slightly behind my shoulder and pointed out the image on the mountain's northern side. "See head down, hump on shoulder? Like giant bear climbing down from sky."

"Hmm.... Yes, I can see it," I replied.

"You like color, I think. I climb today. Good place to scout."

"I'm going with you," I responded.

He raised his eyebrows. "Mmfph! We go soon. Coffee and meat first."

My interest was personal. Could there be a settlement nearby?

Turning toward the lodge, I noticed circles of snow-covered, round stones around a cold campfire. The concentric shapes were arranged in a large arc. I was surprised I did not see them when we arrived last evening. I recognized the remnants of a previously occupied Indian camp.

"Whose lodges stood here?" I asked Two Face.

Without looking up from the fire's crackling warmth, he replied, "Chiefs Niwot and Neva. Left Hand's people come here. Visit northern brothers in Moon of Good Red Berries." He shook his head as he remembered there were few Arapaho alive to return in the summer.

As we were packing later, I decided a climb today would do me good. After a short ride up the steep incline, we dismounted at the foot of the lofty mountain. The youth named Calico stayed with the horses as we hiked up the steep sides. Loose gravel near the top plus the weight of the baby on my back nearly caused a long and painful tumble to the bottom. Two Face reached a hand to pull me up the final steps of hard scrabble.

The flat area of this unusual pinnacle was larger than it appeared from the valley below. I put Willie down and spun around to take in the panoramic view. Free of my grasp, he stood firmly on his pins. I smiled as he tested his newfound ability. Moments later, Willie tottered, grabbed my leggings, but did not fall.

The exploration of this new country left me amazed. It was beyond description. Was I the first white woman to stand atop Bear Butte? It was a beautiful place, but my growing appreciation of the Indian's holy mountain left me conflicted. What would become of this prized home-land once the massive influx of settlers discovered it? Blood was sure to soak this holy ground.

As if reading my thoughts, Two Face spoke. "Mato Paha, Bear Butte. Creator give breath to mountain and mountain give breath to me," he said touching his lungs. "Sun, wind, earth—all gifts to man."

I ventured a look at his face.

He stared east across the distant plains devoid of man's touch. Purity in its simplest form. Did he see the throngs of people to come? It was inevitable, and he understood it.

The frigid air invigorated me, and the infinite scenery spurred a rare and precious lift to my spirit. Two Face squatted near Willie, helping him place stones in a circular pattern in the dirt. Intent on the business at hand, Willie handed the man one stone after another until the circle was complete. Then Willie, with Two Face's help, placed two sticks in the center. Two Face stood to soak in the place where the earth meets the sky.

Looking north, I questioned no one in particular. " There we go?"

Jabbing a finger to the northeast, Two Face said, "No. I go.... And you..." he added, the levity gone from his voice. "You go to Powder River."

Alarm bells were deafening. Pulling my child defensively to my chest, I shouted, "No, Two Face! I will not go!"

"You go," he said firmly, pointing to the sticks. "Your path take you northwest to village on Powder."

I stared hard at my stick.

Bending to touch it, Two Face sighed and said, "My women no like you. Much fighting. True words say man plant his moccasin hard on warpath when no peace in lodge. Winter comes and my moccasins stay by fire. Two Face need peace. I go to Niobrara."

Oh, my Lord! I panicked, digesting his words. I was to be cast out of Two Face's band. It was true. The ferocity of the whippings increased whenever he was present, but I withstood them. I knew it would be a long winter. One I might not survive. His women were making their point.

But what would happen to us now? Powder River? I was terrified of what lay out there near the end of the earth. Before I could voice a protest, I noticed a flash of movement beside me.

Willie!

My son was walking, arms outspread, toward Two Face. The chief squatted down and caught the boy as his forward motion propelled him into the man's arms. Lifting the boy, Two Face grinned and said something manly to him in Lakota. Then he quickly turned Willie back to toddle my way.

Straightening up, Two Face said, "When man takes first walk on holy ground, he need important name. Now boy is…." He paused. Looking directly into my eyes, Two Face declared, "Cikala-Mato-Mani."

The pleased expression on his face mollified to something like sorrow. "Little Bear Walks grow strong." Then he said softly, "Your eyes… blue…like winter sky."

"What?"

Two Face turned his back to me and said, "I will see winter eyes again. I find you."

Confused, I was taken aback by his sudden sentimentality. Soon Two Face would push us in a different direction. I stared at the point of my stick and followed its forecast to the horizon of my exile. Find me? Willie and I were to be sent into the unknown. Away from our tenuous but constant source of protection.

It was all so unsettling. I gathered up the boy, bent my head to the trail and started down—unsure of where the endless sojourn would take us. Would we ever find our place in the world?

Life.

Its force manifests in tiny ways. My son was growing and now walking. The milestone excited and saddened me. I thought of his father, wishing we could have proudly shared this moment. Ever thankful for our little one, I said to my husband, "Today, Will, your boy walked. This treasured moment I will take with me. The first steps of our boy! The one we christened William Joseph Eubank, Jr."

I smiled wistfully at the pronouncement, for it gave rise to thoughts of grandchildren, great-grandchildren, and their families. Perhaps the Eubank name would continue into the next century—if I could just get this boy home.

And now he carried an Indian name as well.

———— • ————

The next day, three spears launched in different directions. I listened for their thunder but heard only the scritching, crunching sounds which rolled out from under the hooves and feet of those I followed. Two Face and his band were gone.

Head down, shoulders hunched, I followed the moccasins of Old Woman once again. As we trudged along the crusty, frozen path, I envisioned Little Mato Walks on the mountaintop.

I remembered his gift to me—the freshest of first steps.

chapter forty-eight

Shining Mountains

First of March 1865
The Moon of Snow Blindness
Powder River, Dakotah Territory

Up there is one of the strangest mountains that I ever did see. It is a diamond mountain, shaped something like a cone. I saw it in the sun for two days before I got to it, and then at night I camped right near it. I hadn't more than got my horse lariated out—it was a little dusky—when I saw a camp-fire and some Injuns right through the mountain on the other side. So I didn't build any fire, but I could see them just as plain as if there hadn't been anything but air. In the morning I noticed the Injuns were gone, and I thought I would like to see the other side of the mountain. So, I rode around to the other side and it took me half a day. In the morning I went up and knocked off a corner of it, a piece of rock as big as my arm, a big long piece of diamond, and brought it out, and afterwards gave it to a man, and he said it was a diamond all right.

Jim Bridger

S itting Bull sat in council with the elders of the tribes at the base of the Shining Mountains. With a voice deep and resonant, he spoke: "The truth-bearers have come with word of our southern brothers. Two moons ago, soldiers attack their village in place called Sand Creek. Many people killed, lodges burned."

Those gathered grumbled angrily among themselves. Yes, they had heard the rumors. Sitting Bull swiped his hand across the council teepee; all the voices quieted.

"The great white chief promised safety for the People near the soldier's fort. The soldier chief spoke with two tongues."

Discussions grew loud and angry. What was to be expected? The lies and treachery of the whites were costing the People their way of life.

"The Southern Cheyenne, Lakota, Bear Oglala, and Spotted Tail's Brulés...they come. Their journey brings them north to us here on Powder River. They walk with Blue Clouds, who lead nine hundred lodges." He held up nine fingers which elicited an impressed response. "It is a hard walk—like climbing through arms of great tree."

Sitting Bull paused, then added, "The longtime peace chief, Black Kettle, turned back to the south with those who remain in his band. He goes to Arkansas River country to join Little Raven and the Arapaho."

The men in attendance looked at one another but did not speak against Black Kettle.

"The people will reach our village in three days. They do not come as whipped dogs. They have been fighting the whites, killing along the way. They bring plunder to share."

Murmurs of assent filled the council lodge.

"Cheyenne bring a white woman and child." Those nearest him covered their faces with blankets and grunted disapprovingly.

Red Cloud spoke up. "They will die. The fire in our hearts burns with those of our southern brothers. Vengeance will come, but it is important for Cheyenne to exact their revenge. The woman is theirs. It is better if captives stay in Cheyenne lodge—away from others."

"Ahh, Ho," agreed the council. The need for vengeance was strong, but all understood the unwritten protocol for such things.

"The Lakota shall be honored guests," said Sitting Bull. "They were first to accept the pipe moons ago. Their vision is clear. Together we must repel the white man's advances. We must drive them off Holy Road and out of Black Hills." Sitting Bull gestured with a broad arc of his hand for emphasis. "It is reported the heart of Spotted Tail has changed. He frees his people from white man's handouts. His warriors are powerful and ready to follow the fringe on his heels. He joins us as strong leader once again!"

The news was good, and the chiefs felt big.

"There have been many small battles," said Red Cloud, "but the time for war has come! The whites increase in number and trespass in the home of the Sioux." He paused for effect. "The southern warriors will unite with us. They have laid waste a dark trail of bloody steps across the white man's road—like a prairie fire consuming all in its path."

Raised fists and shouts of agreement exploded in the teepee. "Ahh, Ho! Ahh, Ho!"

Red Cloud continued, "The raids will bring trouble. The soldiers will come. Let it be so!"

"We are ready!" shouted a voice from the rear.

Sitting Bull nodded and said, "The Hunkpatilas sent listening ears to Fort Laramie. Big Mouth and Loafers now wear soldier coats over their breechcloths. They carry knife guns to pursue and control their own people."

As those in attendance expressed shock at this latest information, the great chief added, "The spies sent runners who carry the straight word. The big war between the whites in the south will end soon. It is said big soldier chief Connor prepares to bring warpath north this spring—to fight the People."

The council erupted in renewed anger, but Sitting Bull continued the list of grievances.

"The white man's iron horse will soon make tracks across the ancient game paths. The soldiers build army posts through middle of Sioux buffalo hunting grounds. Powder River country will soon see soldiers and their buffalo hunters!"

"They take the hides and leave the buffalo to rot. It must stop!" yelled a warrior.

Loud, indignant voices filled the air.

Red Cloud raised his voice and hollered, "Now it is war against every white! Already warriors shoot soldiers at La Prelle Creek!"

The tent full of braves stood to their feet, brandished their weapons, filling the council tent with war cries.

Sitting Bull looked around the great circle as the meeting settled into discontented conversation. The attendees resumed their seats. Then he brought forth the most surprising news. "The spies tell of plan spoken in quiet circles by Laramie commanders. There is talk of moving fort Indians to Missouri country."

A clamoring roar shook the great teepee.

One young warrior shouted, "They go to Pawnee country!"

Several attendees pulled knives from their sheaths. Others shot to their feet ready for instant battle against their hated enemies. The chiefs waited patiently as the warriors discussed this new development among themselves. Many words were spoken until all were ready to listen again.

Sitting Bull looked around the council, eyes searching each man's face. Somberly, he summarized the situation. "Indian time finished if no action taken. Lakota leaders carry war pipe. We must smoke with our brothers."

All present loudly expressed agreement.

Sitting Bull continued, "Just like Old Smoke, the one wrapped in his blanket on his death platform. The old ways of friendship and trade with the whites are gone. No more molasses and crackers to appease and fatten us. The vision is clear! The time for war has come! A war to the end!"

The council members understood. There was no need to wait for a sign. All hearts knew what needed to be done.

Crazy Horse listened and allowed the words of his leaders to settle deep in his heart. For centuries, young Sioux braves waged war to count coups or to steal horses. Now, however, Crazy Horse understood his life held a new and different purpose—a final reckoning for his people. He would stand tall in the forest of warriors to fight for the right of his people to live. Danger to his people and their way of life towered over them. There was no other way. All were in accord. It was time to fight or die. The great leaders would follow the steps of Sitting Bull's moccasins.

Crazy Horse would pray for victory. The future existence of his people depended on the combined strength of the Sioux and Cheyenne tribes. The prior spring, he had seen it in a vision. He was meant for this time. The Great Spirit called him to this fight. Yet, the ending was cloudy and blurred.

Perhaps his quest revealed only the purpose—not the outcome.

Crazy Horse would listen to the stirring in his breast calling him to rise.

To stand, to lead, to fight.

———•———

The winter was extremely cold, snowy, and often windy. Days spent inside the lodge of Old Woman and the rest of the clan were unbearable. The open hostility of the younger women, and certainly the braves, led to inhumane cruelty. There was no place to hide, to slip away, to be invisible.

Old Woman explained with signs and the few words we shared that Big Crow was arrested one moon ago. I was overjoyed to learn soldiers sent two traders to ransom Mrs. Morton. Her return to Fort Laramie included a stop at the Deer Creek garrison. Big Crow rode with the traders to the post, hoping to beg supplies. Old Woman venomously blamed Mrs. Morton for naming Big Crow as one of our abusive captors. Soldiers arrested and manacled him at once and escorted him to Fort Laramie. Now he sat in the guardhouse.

Trying to warm ourselves, Willie and I sat out of the wind. By my figuring, it was March or April, and we were north—extremely far north. I had no way to get my bearings, but Two Face told me I would go to Powder River country and the Shining Mountains. My best guess was we were in northern Dakotah Territory. I breathed deeply of the frigid air, thankful to escape the confines and dangers inside the lodge. The sun reflected off the snow and brightened the side of the teepee. A wandering breeze shook the nearby pines scattering crystalline flakes from their branches. Magically, they floated through the air with the sound of winter's whisper.

After the arrival of the Sand Creek survivors, the great village spread out in camps along the river's edge. Thousands of inhabitants rested inside their fire-lit lodges at night. It presented a scene like none other in my experience. Resembling stars in the galaxy, the glow of the teepees reflected off the snow-covered valley each evening. The large gathering spoke to their strength and resolve. They would hold on to what was given by the Creator to sustain and protect them since the beginning of time.

Willie crawled to a flat, dry spot scoured clean by the wind. Though we sat in sunshine, another storm was dropping in from the north. The toddler played with pinecones near stacked firewood. I closed my eyes and turned my face toward the warmth.

Sensing a presence block the sun, I opened my eyes and squinted up at a most startling face. Gaining focus, the day's light revealed a young warrior staring down at us. He did not wear the garb so common among the young men in camp, who liked to sport American coats, hats, and other accoutrements. This Indian was different. Nothing of the white man adorned his clothing. He wore only beautiful buckskins with thick rabbit skin trim and elaborately decorated moccasins. A single feather attached to a piece of loose hair fluttered in the breeze. He was stunning! I remembered seeing him from afar during the final push of our northward path to Sitting Bull's camp.

Pale gray eyes set in a light-complexioned face calmly looked down at me. His astonishing light brown hair hung in loose waves across his shoulders and down his back to his waist. He neither smiled nor scowled as his curious gaze shifted from me to Willie.

Alarmed, I jumped between him and Willie as he squatted in front of the child. He looked at me, and I saw no malice. Stepping aside, I watched as the warrior touched one of Willie's golden curls. The little boy eyed the stranger with an expression of no particular interest. The stranger smiled, then lifted a sun-lightened tip of his own hair to compare with the child's locks. A perfect match. He inspected my son in such a deliberate and meditative way that my apprehension faded. His was a calm and peaceful presence.

After a few moments, the warrior stood and untied a snow-white rabbit from his belt. He removed the leather thong from its neck and dropped it in front of Willie, then walked away.

With heart thrumming, I picked up the fresh kill. I looked again toward the stranger, who strode away. Old Woman appeared from between the lodges and pointed. She smiled her toothless grin.

"Tashunka Witco."

I looked across the circle of lodges for our benefactor, but he was gone.

Old Woman pointed a crooked finger at the rabbit and smiled again broadly as she gazed in his general direction. "Crazy Horse. He bring gifts to others. Keep none for self. He carry good Spirit. Inside. Here," she explained tapping her heart.

Lifting the gift, I gathered my tools for skinning small animals and with a swift practiced swipe of my scraping stone, gutted the rabbit and removed its skin. "I will make you a soft, furry hat, Willie." The small act of kindness from the strange Oglala matched the sun-kissed smile on my son's face. It lifted my spirits out of the depths of hunger. He was different, this Crazy Horse. His glowing countenance left behind the misty presence of someone from beyond the veil.

I pondered this for a moment, then turned to the task at hand.

Later in the day, the members of the lodge consumed the rabbit and rested. I stood outside hunched over a kettle of boiling bones. A blanket draped over my head created a hood to hide behind. Performing the duties of the old ones in the tribe left me unnoticeable. As I stirred, I stared absentmindedly into the pot.

Then it happened. A slight flutter. My hand instinctively covered the spot. Then it happened again! The fleeting touch of a butterfly inside my womb. I dropped the spoon and covered my abdomen with both hands. The sensation was familiar.

I looked down and stretched the loose doeskin shift across my middle. Hunger had been my constant companion for months, yet there it was! A bulging, firming, ripening about my waist. Willie was a year old, and I still nursed him. The absence of monthly courses could be accounted for by starvation and exhaustion. I was thin, sure enough, yet my breasts seemed more engorged than normal. Biting my lower lip, I recalled the nausea and fatigue washing over me for months.

Caressing my abdomen once again, I was sure of it. A heaviness in the womb!

"No!" I blurted.

Glancing around, I hoped no one else noticed this revelation. Panicked eyes met those of Old Woman. With recognition on her face, she stepped forward and grabbed me around the waist. With practiced hands, she pressed and kneaded my womb. While stroking my belly, she looked up questioningly into my face as if to ask the identity of its sire. We had been together for many weeks off and on during my captivity. I quickly counted back through the moons. I saw her mind doing the same. To feel the movement, the pregnancy must be five months along by now.

"Big Crow!" I hissed.

Old Woman grinned from ear to ear.

"Big Crow!" she exclaimed.

The progeny of her son was the new life inside my body.

Uncountable numbers of warriors attacked me throughout my ordeal yet months ago, I was the sole property of the man I detested most—and Old Woman knew it better than anyone. The insane brutality of the man who planted the seed, the man whom I most feared, now dwelt inside me. The one whose embodiment of the devil had come close to destroying me! Big Crow's grip on me would be complete through this half-breed foundling. I would never be free of him!

Lightheaded, my knees crumbled beneath me, and I folded to the ground. The instinct to flee was strong, but I slumped face down on my hands and knees in the dirty snow. Curtains of tangled hair hid frozen tears.

Gulping wildly, I swallowed hard, then promptly ejected the contents of my stomach.

chapter forty-nine

Conscience and Courage

26 April 1865
Fort Riley, Kansas Territory

Captain Silas S. Soule belonging to my command at Fort Lyon when ordered by Col Chivington to accompany him with his troop and obeyed but when the attack was made upon the Indian village refused positively to go into action and when threatened by Chivington of being placed in irons openly and to his teeth defied him and his men when ordered to fire refused to do so but sat like statues upon their horses without taking any part in the engagement although directly under the fire of the Indians who were doing their best to defend themselves.... Col. Chivington never dared to place Capt. Soule in arrest but some months subsequently had him murdered at night in the streets of Denver by an assassin whom he had hired for that purpose.

Major E.W. Wynkoop

Silas Soule assassinated! Ned held the telegram in his hand, which shook as he poured another shot of whiskey into his glass. The memorial service had been held today in Denver—without him. He regretted not having time to make the trip. It was probably for the better. The escaped assassins were on the lam. Ned struggled to control the urge to hunt them down and finish them off. Details of the murder were limited, but he reflected on what he knew.

Denver was a hotbed of controversy over Sand Creek and Silas was at ground zero. Wynkoop recalled his conversation with General Curtis at Fort Leavenworth in late December to discuss the massacre. Ned could not bring himself to call it a battle. He brought with him letters written by Silas and Cramer. In addition to this evidence, he included the endorsements of the Fort Lyon officers and the citizens of the Arkansas Valley. He insisted the cold-blooded dastardly murderers be punished.

The general listened to the details and agreed. Chivington and his comrades should be held responsible. Wynkoop was ordered to investigate the acts perpetrated against the tribes and to provide a complete detailed report—without delay. He rode to the site for a first-hand look at man's cruelty to man. He remembered his rage as he viewed the gruesome, prone remains of people he knew. The evidence of atrocities committed was unimaginable—not just words in reports.

After receiving Wynkoop's report, the top brass exonerated him from blame and officially praised his actions. Colonel Ford placed him in charge of Fort Lyon in January and by February the military commission investigating Sand Creek convened. Silas was the first witness. After his testimony, he returned to Denver as commander of the provost guard, which functioned as a police force for the city and its neighborhoods.

Ned buried both hands in his hair as he stared down at the report. The lines of murderous details swirled below him like the flicking tongues of writhing snakes. He swallowed hard, closed his eyes, and dropped his forehead onto his arms. A good and innocent man was dead as evil continued to grind on into Denver from Sand Creek. Lighting his pipe, he sighed and continued reading.

Three nights earlier, Silas was drawn to a Denver building while investigating shots fired. He encountered Charles Squiers of the Colorado Second and a man named Morrow seated in a doorway. They were waiting for him. Standing, Squiers pointed a gun at Silas, who fired injuring the man's hand. His cohort Morrow fired a single head shot and Silas was dead.

Ned was convinced the assassination was a result of Silas' testimony which condemned Chivington and all culpable parties. The killing was deliberately intended to intimidate other witnesses from coming forward. The inquiry continued to proceed at Fort Lyon, but things were at work in Washington, D.C. A Congressional commission was established, and a larger investigation was now underway. The political ramifications put witnesses in danger, but Ned hoped the truth would be documented and preserved.

Unable to attend the funeral service, Ned was compelled to share a personal eulogy. Not only did Ned admire Silas, but he also considered Silas a faithful friend. Now that friend was gone. He picked up his pen to finish the letter to Hersa Coberly, Silas's new bride of three weeks:

> Born to abolitionist parents, Silas Soule grew up helping people escape bondage. He spent time with his father as a conductor on the Underground Railroad and was involved with the Jay Hawker Ten in rescuing imprisoned slaves.

Struck by gold fever, Silas moved from Lawrence, Kansas, to Colorado Territory in 1860. Soon dismayed by the unproductive search for the shiny mineral, he enlisted in the Army. Under the command of Major John Chivington, Soule fought in New Mexico with the Colorado First Regiment to overturn a Confederate invasion at the Battle of Glorietta Pass. For his bravery in this battle, Chivington promoted the young soldier to the rank of Captain, and he was stationed at Fort Lyon. Silas was a man of conscience and a portrait of courage.

Ned picked up the last letter he would ever receive from Silas and read it again. He had distributed it to his commanding officers. As a result of Soule's testimony, Chivington's political aspirations were demolished. Looking at the letter written in good conscience, Ned stopped at Silas' signature.

The consummate soldier had signed his own death warrant.

Fort Lyon, C.T.
December 14, 1864

Dear Ned:

Two days after you left here the 3rd Reg't with a Battalion of the 1st arrived here, having moved so secretly that we were not aware of their approach until they had Pickets around the post, allowing no one to pass out! They arrested Capt. Bent and John Vogle and placed guards around their houses. They then declared their intention to massacre the friendly Indians camped on Sand Creek. Major Anthony gave all information, and eagerly Joined in with Chivington and Co. and ordered Lieut. Cramer with his whole Co. to Join the command. As soon as I knew of their movement I was indignant as you would have been were you here and went to Cannon's room, where a number officers of the 1st and 3rd were congregated and told them that any man who would take part in the murders, knowing the circumstances as we did, was a low lived cowardly son of a bitch. Capt. Y. J. Johnson and Lieut. Harding went to camp and reported to Chiv, Downing and the whole outfit what I had said, and you can bet hell was to pay in camp.

Chiv and all hands swore they would hang me before they moved camp, but I stuck it out, and all the officers at the Post, except Anthony backed me. I was then ordered with my whole company to Major A— with 20 days rations. I told him I would not take part in their intended murder, but if they were going after the Sioux, Kiowa's or any fighting Indians, I would go as far as any of them. They said that was what they were going for and I joined them. We arrived at Black Kettles and Left Hand's Camp at daylight. Lieut. Wilson with

Co. s "C", "E" & "G" were ordered to in advance to cut off their herd. He made a circle to the rear and formed a line 200 yds from the village, and opened fire.

Poor Old John Smith and Louderbeck ran out with white flags but they paid no attention to them, and they ran back into the tents. Anthony then rushed up with Co's "D" "K" & "G" to within one hundred yards and commenced firing. I refused to fire and swore that none but a coward would for by this time hundreds of women and children were coming toward us and getting on their knees for mercy. Anthony shouted, "kill the sons of bitches" Smith and Louderbeck came to our command, although I am confident there were 200 shots fired at them, for I heard an officer say that Old Smith and anyone who sympathized with the Indians, ought to be killed and now was a good time to do it. The Battery then came up in our rear, and opened on them. I took my Comp'y across the Creek, and by this time the whole of the 3rd and the Batteries were firing into them and you can form some idea of the slaughter.

When the Indians found there was no hope for them they went for the Creek and got under the banks and some of the bucks got their Bows and a few rifles and defended themselves as well as they could. By this time there was no organization among our troops, they were a perfect mob–every man on his own hook. My Co. was the only one that kept their formation and we did not fire a shot.

The massacre lasted six or eight hours, and a good many Indians escaped. I tell you Ned it was hard to see little children on their knees have their brains beat out by men professing to be civilized. One squaw was wounded and a fellow took a hatchet to finish her, and he cut one arm off, and held the other with one hand and dashed the hatchet through her brain. One squaw with her two children, were on their knees, begging for their lives of a dozen soldiers, within ten feet of them all firing-when one succeeded in hitting the squaw in the thigh, when she took a knife and cut the throats of both children and then killed herself. One Old Squaw hung herself in the lodge-there was not enough room for her to hang and she held up her knees and choked herself to death. Some tried to escape on the Prairie, but most of them were run down by horsemen. I saw two Indians hold one of anothers hands, chased until they were exhausted, when they kneeled down, and clasped each other around the neck and both were shot together. They were all scalped, and as high as half a dozen taken from one head. They were horribly mutilated. One woman was cut open and a child taken out of her, and scalped.

White Antelope, War Bonnet and a number of others had Ears and Privates cut off. Squaws snatches were cut out for trophies. You would think it impossible for white men to butcher and mutilate human beings as they did there, but every word I have told you is the truth, which they do not deny. It was almost impossible to save any of them. Charly Autobee save John Smith and Winsers squaw. I saved little Charlie Bent. Geo. Bent was killed.

287

Jack Smith was taken prisoner, and murdered the next day in his tent by one of Dunn's Co. "E". I understand the man received a horse for doing the job. They were going to murder Charlie Bent, but I run him into the Fort. They were going to kill Old Uncle John Smith, but Lt. Cannon and the boys of Ft. Lyon, interfered, and saved him. They would have murdered Old Bents family, if Col. Tappan had not taken the matter in hand. Cramer went up with twenty (20) men, and they did not like to buck against so many of the 1st. Chivington has gone to Washington to be made General, I suppose, and get authority to raise a nine months Reg't to hunt Indians. He said Downing will have me cashiered if possible. If they do I want you to help me. I think they will try the same for Cramer for he has shot his mouth off a good deal, and did not shoot his pistol off in the Massacre. Joe has behaved first rate during this whole affair. Chivington reports five or six hundred killed, but there were not more than two hundred, about 140 women and children and 60 Bucks. A good many were out hunting buffalo. Our best Indians were killed. Black Kettle, One Eye, Minnemic and Left Hand. Geo. Pierce of Co. "F" was killed trying to save John Smith. There was one other of the 1st killed and nine of the 3rd all through their own fault. They would get up to the edge of the bank and look over, to get a shot at an Indian under them. When the women were killed the Bucks did not seem to try and get away, but fought desperately. Charly Autobee wished me to write all about it to you. He says he would have given anything if you could have been there.

I suppose Cramer has written to you, all the particulars, so I will write half. Your family is well. Billy Wilker, Col. Tappen, Wilson (who was wounded in the arm) start for Denver in the morning. There is no news I can think of. I expect we will have a hell of a time with Indians this winter. We have (200) men at the Post-Anthony in command. I think he will dismissed when the facts are known in Washington. Give my regards to any friends you come across, and write as soon as possible.

Yours, SS
(signed) S.S. Soule

chapter fifty

Forty Warriors

Early May 1865
The Moon of Shedding Ponies
Niobrara River, Nebraska Territory

During the winter she and her little son had been brought north by
the Cheyennes and sold to Two Face and Black Foot. These Indian
chiefs had compelled her to labor as their squaw. She was in a
wretched condition....

Leroy W. Hagerty

B lood is a mystery. Its thick liquid holds genuine truths of the flesh which echo through the ages. My daughter and son, nieces, and nephews matured with similar physical features linking them to family. But what about the gesture, the expression, the tone of voice?

Willie was shedding his charming baby traits to become an extension of his father. Shadows of my husband appeared fleetingly, bringing soft memories to my recollection. I watched fascinated as Willie changed and grew, for he was the picture of his father. Glimpses into their connection were more frequent now, and I savored the little face which took me back to family. The Waltons, the Eubanks—all rolled into one perfect package, binding the child to generations past and those to come.

My heart sang and broke simultaneously.

What did blood carry as it pulsed between mother and the new form growing inside?

I took no delight from the imagining.

I saw only the face of evil and its mark upon my soul. Would the face of the innocent share my face, my mannerisms, my legacy, or those of its sire? I angrily turned from the thought.

Life's links run deep, and I preferred to think of those to come. Willie's children and his children's children....

I hoped to know them—someday.

Horses trudged and slipped their way wearily through the melting slush along the narrow trail. Food was scarce. Occasionally, we camped near a spring where dry grasses were clear of snow, and green shoots sprouted. A week earlier, the tribes moved onto the Tongue River and the chiefs held council to finish details of the upcoming war path. The southern Cheyenne enthusiastically performed the shield dance nightly. Tiny metal bells on their ankles jingled with each collective stomp of their feet. War whoops still chilled my blood and raised the hair on my neck; I would always be fearful during such ceremonies. Buffalo was plentiful, and feasts strengthened the tribes for what was to come.

Runners arrived in the village with news. The soldier man Moonlight was on the march. Scouts watched as the long column left Fort Laramie under the dark of night. Five hundred cavalry troops with wagon guns crept along the road guided by the old mountain man, Jim Bridger. His presence disturbed the Indians. Their families would stay in the north where it was considered safer.

The chiefs surmised Moonlight was trying to hide his advance into the Wind River country. The fort spies said he planned a surprise attack. Unknown to him, the Indian scouts watched, and the village was clear of his intended destination. The People chuckled at the thought of big American horses worn down and turning back—only snow would be found on Moonlight's trail.

Crazy Horse organized a scouting party of forty warriors to prepare the way for the larger force to come. Lodges and women would go with them. The bulk of the warriors would depart as soon as the grass was high enough to support the pony herds.

Old Woman arose early one morning and began to gather the few things belonging to me. She tied them to a travois strapped to a stout mare. Full of questions, I followed her as she hurried about her business. No explanation was forthcoming, but I understood I was to leave with the warriors. The raiders would move south to scout the area and fight all they encountered—like the tip of the spear.

With a gleam in her one eye, Old Woman watched as I mounted the mare in the flat light of the overcast morning. She delivered Willie into my arms, patted my abdomen, and turned away.

Joining the departing group, I assessed my new companions. What new dangers did they pose to me and my child? The only familiar faces were those of Big Crow's brother and his young wife, Red Woman. And, of course, Crazy Horse. As leader of the war party, the best and strongest warriors followed him. They formed an elite group ready to launch the Sioux war against the whites.

With great trepidation and an uneasy sense of forthcoming events, I turned my horse away from the great camp to follow the forty warriors south and east. We were returning to the scene of last winter's raids—this time with a huge gathering storm of Indians behind us.

I turned one last time to look at the village. Old Woman stood and watched—a tiny survivor whose harsh ways tempered over the months of travel together. Next to her stood Happy, crying.

I set my face southward and did not look back....

———•———

After a week of travel, I recognized the sandhills and tall, chimney-like stone features we passed months earlier. Puffy and bleary-eyed, Willie was sick and taking a turn for the worse. Suffering from fever and a swelling of his cheeks, the child refused to eat and constantly rubbed his left ear. I tried to shield his unhappiness from the eyes and ears of the warriors. They would not consider the child's life worth slowing their progress.

Riding down the side of a high bluff, the boy would not stop crying. His insistent screams echoed through the valley below us. A scowling warrior pulled his horse next to mine and hollered threats before galloping off. I pulled Willie's sling under the blanket covering my shoulders, but the cross child kicked and cried pushing the blanket away from his scarlet face.

My apprehension only exasperated the situation, and I looked to the other women riding nearby. Red Woman signaled we stop. She reached for Willie, who struggled against my shoulder, screeching at the top of his lungs. Digging through a small bag hanging from her waist, she dipped her finger into an old tobacco tin. Rubbing salve on Willie's neck and chest, she dabbed a little in his mouth. His expression changed from pain and indignation to shock and disgust. He screwed up his face, gagged, and worked his tongue to rid it of the bitter taste.

The woman placed a small piece of buffalo jerky in his mouth to distract him while tying him into the cradleboard. This distressed him, for he had grown larger during our time on the Powder. The squaw fastened the contraption to the travois, and we jogged our horses to rejoin the others. However, Willie could not be consoled. He was ill and uncomfortable, and his cries ruffled the feathers of the warriors. They were counting on a silent advance into enemy territory.

The line of travelers dipped down into the trees along the bluff. The Indian who was annoyed earlier suddenly raced back to me. Reaching down, he grabbed my rein and stopped the mare, then leaped off his horse. With one swift movement, he cut the thong of the cradleboard and tossed my baby off the cliff into the trees below. I watched horrified as the board spun and dropped into the abyss.

Screaming, I sprang from the horse and ran straight into the young warrior. He decided now would be a suitable time to rid the group of two troubles. His strong arms clamped down across my chest, and we tousled in the scrabble rock of the trail. I pulled against the brave as he strained to throw me off the nearest precipice. I flung myself to the ground as the warrior grappled with the full weight of my body.

From the corner of my eye, I noticed another commotion taking place at the front of the line. Drawn by the cries of the baby, two newcomers rode into our group. One of the riders raced toward me. He jumped upon the warrior as he dragged me to the edge. In the tussle, my attacker released his grip. The two men regained their footing, and, as recognition dawned, stepped apart.

The dust began to clear, and I found myself pulled upright by Two Face!

Blackfoot sat astride his pony in the shadows of the trees, as stiff and indifferent as ever. Not distracted by this surprising turn of events, I screamed Willie's name and lunged toward the edge of the bluff. Dashing back and forth, I tried to scramble down the cliff.

"Willie!"

Two Face grabbed my arm and led me back up the trail to a cut in the bluff. Sliding and slipping, we made our way into the pine trees below. Rocks bounced and rattled past us following the fall line. We landed on a trail crossing the steep incline. Stopping, listening, we heard nothing. No sound.

Running along the trail, we looked up into the trees, turning, spinning, hoping to catch a glimpse of the cradleboard. Moments later, there it was—dangling upside down. Its strap caught on a branch about ten feet above the path. Two Face joined me under it, and we both twisted and turned our necks to spy the boy's face. Was he alive?

A small whimper, then a cough stopped us in our tracks.

The breeze spun the board and there he was, red faced and frightened, his eyes huge with terror and surprise. The branch popped, and the precariously balanced cradleboard dropped a couple of inches. Two Face pulled me to the base of the tree, then hoisted me up. With each of my feet braced on his hands, I gained traction on the pine's massive trunk and scratched my way up to sit on a supporting branch. Stretching forward, I slowly crept on my stomach toward Willie.

Two Face positioned himself below the toddler, hands upraised ready to make the final catch.

Pressing my body across the branch, I carefully scooted closer to the strap holding Willie. It was just beyond my reach. My shaky progress caused the cradleboard to spin. One more reach, and I grasped the strap with one hand while wrapping my other arm around the branch. I held my breath as I pulled on the strap. Once, then again. Finally, it released. I gripped the strap but it slipped through my fingers. Willie fell into the waiting hands of Two Face, who caught him with a satisfied grunt.

A huge sigh escaped my throat as I lay my head on the rough bark. I breathed in its vanilla pine scent—relishing the sweet aroma, thanking the Lord, and thanking the great tree. Huffing, I backed down the trunk, dropped to the trail, and ran to Willie.

"Thank you, Two Face, thank you!"

Willie was out of his restraint and Two Face stood holding the boy face to face. He was saying something in Lakota. Turning to me, Two Face said with a grin, "Little Mato Walks. He grow some today."

———•———

After the chance encounter on the bluff, Two Face and Blackfoot joined the Sioux warriors, and we rode on. Crazy Horse found a campsite in an aspen grove near a stream. Still rattled by the attempt on my child's life, I shakily stacked wood on the cooking fire and watched the men with a wary eye. The horses grazed, nipping at any green sprig brave enough to stick its head above ground. We had traveled quickly for days, sleeping on the ground, meeting no one. That is, until today.

I looked forward to a brief rest, for the weather had warmed and the snow was gone. A cool, clean brook gurgled nearby. Willie needed to recover as well, for he was cranky and feverish. I worried about his health.

The respite was short-lived, however, as the next morning, I awoke to the alarming sound of horses charging into the midst of camp. It was Crazy Horse and the forty warriors! While scouting along the North Platte, they spotted a large group of freight wagons parked on the opposite bank. The frightened freighters instantly sent a rider in the direction of a small military outpost eight miles away. Soldiers would soon cross the river and find us.

Women were urgently dismantling teepees and loading supplies. The warriors helped by haphazardly throwing lodges onto travois. One by one, the women left when their load was ready. The situation called for a quick escape.

Two Face noticed I was hurrying, but the child slowed me down. The lodge I oversaw was the last one standing. As we threw items about, he quickly explained he and Blackfoot were taking us to their band one day's ride away. He grumbled under his breath: he had exchanged one of his mules for me, and Blackfoot had thrown in a horse. I was now common property. But there was no time to dwell on this new development.

Impatiently, Two Face urged me on. "Egalakapo, we go!" he said as he grabbed my arm and pulled me toward Blackfoot, who held the reins of Two Face's great war horse.

"No! Wait!" I exclaimed.

An idea dawned in my scattered brain. I pulled away and rushed into the lone lodge standing among leafless aspen trees. Pulling Will's photo and my ring from the satchel, I placed the beloved bag on top of stacked bedding pallets. Jumping back through the partially dismantled side of the teepee, I turned for a final look. The morning sun lit the exposed interior of the lodge and highlighted the bag. Ruth had embroidered my initials onto the front of the satchel.

$$\mathscr{R}.\mathscr{L}.\mathscr{E}$$

Ruby Lucinda Eubank. I hesitated, changed my mind, turned to retrieve my only possession, then stopped. I must leave it. Perhaps the soldiers will find it. A fresh letter waited inside to reveal my existence. Reluctantly, I left my worldly possession with a wing and a prayer.

Rushing away from the teepee, I positioned Willie tightly in his sling, then reached up both my arms as Two Face raced his horse past me. Grasping my forearms, he swept us up behind him and we loped away.

Away to the Niobrara.

Away from the forty warriors.

Away from the North Platte.

Away from my satchel.

We had come full circle, Two Face and I.

Yet, I was still nowhere to be found.

chapter fifty-one

The Satchel

Early May 1865
Ash Hollow, Nebraska Territory

*In the lodge was a satchel that had been carried by Mrs. Eubanks,
and in it were several letters written, to the effect that she was a prisoner among Indians and would like to be rescued.*

Antoine Bordeaux

ntoine Bordeaux sat on his haunches and stirred the embers of the
fire to life. He added dried brush and sticks to encourage a flame.
Too restless to sleep, he stretched and located the night watchmen.
The wagon train would not start for a couple of hours. James Bordeaux's
wagons, laden with skins and Indian trade goods, were part of a train
encompassing one hundred freight wagons. Moving slowly eastward
along the south side of the North Platte River, it stopped to camp at Ash
Hollow. Travel was slow and laborious as six yokes of oxen pulled each
wagon. Twelve hundred cattle required a sizable number of bullwhackers
to care for them.

Now that Antoine had worked on the trail for three seasons, his father
was ready to send him back East to purchase bulls and wagons so the
family might expand their freighting business. The young Bordeaux took
the responsibility very seriously.

The family's ties to the whites and the location of their trading post
put them directly in the path of commerce...as well as raiders and
bandits. He was watchful day and night. Two of his sisters slept in
the wagon which their father fashioned to make the long journey
comfortable. The older Bordeaux assigned the girls into Antoine's care
with a stern warning. His father predicted the recent Indian troubles
would turn into a full-blown war, and he feared for their safety. It was
time to send them East to school.

Depredations and violence were sure to come with the spring. Even though Antoine's mother was a full-blooded Sioux, known as Red Cormorant Woman, his father reminded him their heritage might not be ascertained quickly enough in the heat of battle to save their skins.

Antoine rubbed his chin and felt short, bristly sprouts. He was nineteen years old and was yet to shave a full-grown beard. He wondered if he might grow facial hair thick and wild like his French father's or if he would sport the smooth skin of his mother's people. Probably he would take a little from both, and it would not be a respectable combination. He gloomily assented to the possibility he was destined to the sparce, coarse hairs around the mouth and chin his older brothers wore. Ach! Well, it did not matter, for there was no razor in his bag anyway.

The nicker of a horse from across the river interrupted Antoine's musings. The moonlight behind him cast beams on mounted Indians watching him from the trees. He slowly lowered the small branch in his hand to the ground. Any movement might draw their attention, and he imagined the sharp twang of an arrow piercing his pounding heart. Unsure of his next move, he strained to get a good look at the group of forty braves or more. The rushing water concealed the sounds of their movements.

Slowly emerging from the trees, they halted their horses on the river's sandy edge. The attire and face paint seemed unfamiliar to him. Focusing, he quickly noted the tell-tale marks of Cheyenne Dog Soldiers among the more familiar Sioux. He froze. The situation had gone from serious to critical. From this point on, every move counted.

Old Ben, the seasoned freighter with whom his father entrusted his wagons for years, spoke slowly behind him. "Don't move, boy. Let's give them an opportunity to ride on."

Antoine stopped breathing as he thought of his younger sisters tucked away in their beds. Without moving his head, he swiveled his eyes towards their wagon, which seemed quiet and unmolested for the moment. He and Ben watched as the party turned their horses to the west and passed by without a sound. They remained in place for what seemed an eternity. Once Ben believed the coast was clear, he grabbed the arm of his companion and pulled him behind a wagon out of arrow range.

The entire freighting party gathered near Antoine's wagon as alarm spread through the camp. The cattle, brought into the corral for safety the night before, milled about bellowing softly. The men discussed their next course of action and decided it was best to send for troops. A fort was located ten miles distant—inside the confluence of the North and

South Platte Rivers. Young Bordeaux's horse was the swiftest, so the group chose him to lead the mission. Old Ben promised to personally look after his sisters.

Antoine left camp at a gallop with a small entourage of seven men mounted on the precious few horses in their remuda. The dimly lit trail presented fearsome shadows resembling threats all around. He hoped they would return before his sisters became aware of the danger. Forty prepared warriors against eighteen men caught off guard would be a short but lethal engagement.

Reaching the fort in record time, a column of armed soldiers was mounted and on its way within the hour. As the sun began to rise, the early light and increased manpower raised the spirits of those who feared an attack. The entire column raced up the Platte, feeling the warm sun on their shoulders. It was imperative they reach the wagon train before the war party returned.

Splashing their horses across Ree Creek, the freighters and soldiers saw Indians moving at a rapid pace through distant sandhills. Having passed their hidden camp in the night unmolested, they gave a short chase of the rearguard. Fearing a trap, the soldiers and freighters turned back.

Antoine noticed a lone teepee standing in a grove of trees. The morning light reflected off its white sides. Though partially dismantled, the Indians were unable to pack the final lodge before making their escape.

The commander shouted to Antoine to check the contents of the lodge as others rode over to join him. Antoine cautiously approached the teepee and was relieved to find it unoccupied. Upon further inspection, he noticed items strewn about the interior. To his surprise, a bright ray of sunlight hit an item perched on top of abandoned bedding. It shined like a beacon and appeared to be a woman's embroidered satchel.

Antoine stepped between the poles and reached for the bag's strap. It was warm in his hands. Respectfully, he opened the bag and reached inside. Small letters placed delicately at the opening suggested the owner planned for their discovery.

The commander of the detachment stepped into the lodge. The eyes of both men met over the curious contents. In wonderment, they pondered the existence of these small items so incongruent to their surroundings. The officer directed Antoine to open and read the letter.

A large group of soldiers now gathered near the teepee and one asked Antoine to speak up, for they all wanted to hear. He stared at the neat writing and read:

To soldiers of the United States Army:
I am prisoner of Sioux chiefs Two Face and Blackfoot.
Please rescue me and my baby.
They head east along the bluffs north of the river.
Please come.
Please.

Mrs. Lucinda Eubank

chapter fifty-two

Month of the Black Choke Cherries

Early May 1865
Sioux Camp, Niobrara River Country

This spring, the Sioux, in great numbers, made their appearance on a hunting trip. They continued to come at intervals until August, paying for their goods in pelts or cash. Their camp at this time was down, or in, the Indian Territory. About the first of August, I began to notice a change in their demeanor. They seemed sulky and ill-natured, so that I became uneasy.

James Bainter

T*he shimmering, gold moon looked so near it seemed to beg me to touch it. Its brilliant light lit up the sky, causing the cottonwoods along the river to dance. Fireflies dove between the trees, creating their own sparkling refection off the water. Patches of white daisies sprung from the warm ground, enhancing shifts of light across the prairie.*

I picked up the last of the dishes on the table. Stagecoach passengers and drivers traveling through our blue valley enjoyed my cooking and were always appreciative. I picked up part of a roll and brushed crumbs from my white linen tablecloth into my hand. As I glanced around once more making sure everything looked tidy, Dora flew in the door almost knocking me over. "Let's hurry!" she shouted. "Everyone is going to beat us to the dance! The music started already. You can hear it outside!"

The Fourth of July celebration at the Oak Grove Station was the subject of conversation for the past month. The excitement had us all abuzz. Even mother Ruth took part in the banter with me and her daughters, Sarah and Dora.

"What dress do you think I should I wear, Lucy?" Sarah asked.

"I think you should wear the pink one your Ma just finished embroidering," I said.

Mother Ruth quipped, "Sarah, you would look lovely in any of your dresses."

Dora piped in, "I do hope George makes it back from his freight run to Denver in time! Do you think there will be anyone new at the dance for us to meet? Do you think the cherry pies we baked will be enjoyed? I am so excited, Ma! I cannot wait to get there!"

We were happy when Sarah told us she didn't have to report to her job at Liberty Farm today. The farm was recently purchased by Charles Emery from the James Lemmon family. This was a bustling stage station and former Pony Express stop. Charles' Irish wife Mary cooked for the endless droves of people stopping on their way west. Charles had the best reputation around the valley for his excellent stage-handling skills and Mary was as good a cook as you could get.

Will told everyone to climb in the wagon, and he would drive us over to Oak Grove Ranche. James, Henry, and our nephew Conrad jumped in the back. Will lifted Dora, Sarah, and me in behind them. Ruth handed me Willie, and Will sat Belle on Sarah's lap. Pa loaded up the pies and breads then lifted Ruth onto the driver's seat. Will climbed up on one side of his mother, and his Pa sat on the other. Grabbing the reins, Will gave the horses a slap, and we were on our way to the gala event.

Erastus Comstock owned Oak Grove Ranche. It was one of the largest in the valley with certainly the best barn to hold the dance. As we approached, we could hear the music getting louder and louder. Dora was smiling and swaying back and forth. The boys were pretending they were playing instruments, and we were all laughing excitedly.

Finally, we arrived. Upon entering the Comstock barn, we stopped in awe over the beautiful red, white, and blue decorations tumbling from the walls and jumping out in every direction. We stared at the grandeur of our nation's flag draped in the most elegant form from the barn's rafters. The Comstock sons, James and George, welcomed us eagerly and asked us how we liked the barn's new look? Proudly, they told us how they helped decorate. James, manager of the Little Blue mail station, told us he brought some extra tables to hold all the food. George added he hauled the hay bales in from his ranch, Thirty-Two Mile Station, where his wife Hannah and their four children live. They were both very proud they could help their father with this star-spangled event.

Joe and Hattie saw us. Smiling, they quickly moved toward our direction. They both commented on how spectacular the barn looked, and we all could not agree more. Hattie was just glowing with her first *pregnancy. Her dark brown hair was pulled back and held by a shimmering beautiful ivory clip. I was happy to see her relaxed, knowing how the heat sometimes bothered her. All of us were eager to welcome the new Eubank baby, and we shared in their excitement. Joe was in his usual jovial mood. He playfully acted like he was roughing up his brothers; James and Henry did the same back to him. Excitedly, Joe twirled around and started telling his father and Will about the horses he traded earlier in the day.*

Will's brother Fred and Hattie's brother, John Palmer, walked toward Joe with plates heaped high with roast beef and potatoes. Both brothers worked at Joe and Hattie's ranche, and John was in partnership with Joe. You could tell they all got along well by the way they constantly laughed and teased each other.

Standing near the lemonade, John Gilbert, an Overland Stage driver living at Kiowa Station, was talking with Libby Artist, who worked at Thirty-Two Mile Station. Libby looked radiant in her new pink calico dress. John was quite smitten by her. It was fun to watch their flirtations.

Ruth placed two of our pies on the dessert table. The widow, Mrs. Joanna Uhlig, joined her in conversation. The woman's sons Edmund, Otto, and Theodore accompanied her to the celebration. They were known around the valley as "The Germans" and settled in a nice cabin not too far from our ranche.

The music stopped, and the band set their instruments down before stepping from the stage. William and Elizabeth Mudge were from England, and Joe and Sally Milligan hailed from Ireland. Both families ran Buffalo Ranche, and their cold storage business kept them busy slaughtering buffalo for sale. Before Sally needed to pick up her fiddle to play again, Mary Emery made her way over to talk to her about their shared Irish roots.

Over on the right side of the barn, Joseph and Paulina Roper sat at a table with their two, young daughters, Francis and Kate. Joseph bounced his gleeful son Marsh on his knee. Their two older daughters, Laura and Clarissa, were talking to Marshall and Albert Kelly. Marshal was in partnership with Mr. Roper. He and the young Laura were engaged to be married.

Will was holding Willie when the music started up again. He placed our baby in Joe's arms and steered Belle to Hattie, who grasped our daughter's tiny hand. Smiling, he turned to me and asked if he could please have a dance. I saw a twinkle in his eyes and slipped my hand in his. He twirled me out on the dance floor, then pulled me close. I felt my face blush and squinted my eyes at him to create a decent dancing distance. He laughed and spun me around the floor.

After our dance, we walked over to get some lemonade for Belle. Lining up for the Virginia Reel, Mr. and Mrs. Newton Metcalf from Pawnee Ranche joined James Bainter and his wife from Spring Ranche. We watched as our amused neighbors do-si-doed.

As everyone was enjoying the music and slapping their knees, I quietly stepped back from the crowd. Standing alone, I felt something was wrong. Something just felt off, and then I sensed dread. My eyes transfixed and held their stare. In my trance, I felt someone was watching us. Something looming, closing in like a pack of wolves. Hovering, then moving closer in the darkness of the night. Staring, sniffing, snarling, hair standing straight on their backs....

My eyes flew open. I was dreaming! Dreaming of a time gone by and of loved ones gone forever. Thank God Ruth and Sarah were spared, but what must have happened to our beloved neighbors? Unexpected horror pulverized our once vibrant and joyful existence. The lush beauty of our valley could only be held in memory now. Our Nebraska home was ruins and ash. The water in the Little Blue River now stained a deep red.

The wind howled around Blackfoot's teepee, and its flap beat the side. It was a chilly morning, and the firewood pile dwindled. I lay in fear the warrior sleeping next to me would wake at any moment and jerk my body toward him. Staring at him, my chin quivered and my skin crawled. I felt nothing more than disgust and a deep hatred. Blackfoot believed when he and Two Face traded for me, I was his property. He owned me to ravage and molest. My body was pummeled, covered with welts...but my spirit would prevail.

chapter fifty-three

The Brink

12 May 1865
Sioux Camp on the Snake Fork of the White River
Northwestern Nebraska Territory

This hill, though high, I covet to ascend;
The difficulty will not me offend.
For I perceive the way to life lies here.
Come, pluck up, heart; let's neither faint nor fear.

John Bunyan
Pilgrim's Progress

I died last August; still, I walked. Hope was quenched a little by every step. Still, I walked. Now it was spring, though I had no way to calculate the date. The attack on the Eubank Ranche marked the delineation between the beginning and the end for me. I trudged from one plight to the next with monotonous resignation broken only by moments of sheer pain and terror.

The last memory of Belle left me with unbearable sadness, for I knew nothing of her fate. The growing child within my womb used all my reserves, leaving me tired and weak through the darkness of winter. I felt no affection for it.

Since the separation from Mrs. Morton, I suffered alone. I constantly struggled with the Lakota and Cheyenne languages. It was isolating and often plunged me into a nightmarish circle of misunderstandings and harsh consequences. The constant travel combined with living among a remote people, who themselves struggled for survival, produced a constant strain. I was numb.

But as green life pushed its tendrils up through a dead land, a flicker appeared in my being, begging me to live, to grow strong, to push on.

I now lived in Blackfoot's lodge as one of his wives. I continued to fight his advances. He took pleasure in beating me and when finished would leave me in the capable hands of his women. They lashed me often while scolding me for not yielding to their chief. Blackfoot was possessive with a malicious intent. Soon Swift Bear and the members of his Brulé Corn Band joined us. Rumors reached my ears: the whites were offering a ransom for any white woman captive. It was with great interest that I perceived the truth of the matter. Blackfoot would not kill the goose who would lay his next golden egg. With this knowledge, I no longer cowered but withstood the punishments with a small but painful degree of satisfaction. Forced to accept the daily labor and mistreatment, I no longer walked as one dead in her soul like a worn-down dog, tail dragging, near death. It had been a long winter, but as vigor returned to my body, my mind crawled slowly up out of the depths of despair.

Just as the earth moves through its own cycle of birth and growth in the new season, the breezes of spring blew softly on my weary soul. A new pulse began its faint cadence deep within me. Hope was being reborn. Is it April...or could it be May? My awareness of the change began perceptibly. Then the thinness in my brain started to expand as I saw tender shoots push up through rocks, ice, and snow. The wind was still harsh and frigid, but my young body could not deny the surge of the life force within.

Two days earlier, Two Face approached me as I hauled water in a large cast iron kettle. It was out of character for him to initiate communication, so I was surprised when he spoke quickly and quietly in English. He explained he was preparing for our departure.

Our departure? I perked up. My raised eyebrows caused him to caution me.

"Shhh...others maybe watch. Listen only," he said.

Then he described his plan to release me to the soldiers at Fort Laramie. He had my interest now. Pointing to a rocky outcrop near the edge of the grazing pony herd, he commanded, "Remember that!" His motives were unclear, but he insisted we keep his plans a secret. He would tell me more soon.

Fort Laramie! He said Fort Laramie! A tangible connection to my world! I had considered it distant and unattainable. But now...release. Was freedom truly possible? It consumed my thoughts as I waited hopefully, wondering if each night would bring escape.

Two days later, Two Face sat with me near the small fire in Blackfoot's lodge. Short flames flickered and threw shadows against the white deerskins hanging inside the lodge from the center horizontal poles. The skins extended to the hide-covered ground, providing extra protection from the winter cold and wind still holding us in an unrelenting grip.

I sat quietly with hands clenched in my lap and let out a slow, fatigued sigh. I did not know what to expect from this man who brought so much pain and salvation into my life. His treatment of me had evolved into a history of contradictions. As his name indicated, Two Face was a contrary man.

At times, when I spurned his advances, his anger threatened violence. Other times, he acted like a wounded pup and avoided me altogether. Eventually, he would return to me, and the familiarity supplied an incongruous relief. I remained steadfast in my position to never submit to his advances but had come to realize that if he intended to harm me, it would have happened long ago.

My life was often in danger by the hands of others, but the determination to go on never allowed me to completely acquiesce to their demands. They could injure my body, but they would never bend my will.

Two Face's quiet presence unnerved me. I relaxed my tense jaw and waited. And here we sat. The warrior's middle-aged face was etched with deep lines. His shiny, long, black braids lay flat against his broad shoulders. His lips were grim and restrained upon the stony face. His large, obsidian eyes, which usually mocked me, held my gaze intently. Then Two Face whispered his plan.

"We meet at edge of pony herd across small creek. Remember rock I show you?"

I nodded.

"I bring fast horses. Leave tonight before moon rises. Make sure boy make no sound. I take you out of camp. Blackfoot not know. He argue talk with me. He say he kill you if he want. You not safe here. Our people need ammunition, guns, food. I trade you."

I looked up in surprise.

"Fire-Hair," Two Face said low and deep enough for me to hold his gaze. "You mine from beginning." He reached up and softly touched the long tangles of matted hair on my shoulder. I leaned slightly away from his fingers. He sighed and laid his clenched fist back onto his knee. "I leave you with Cheyenne when I fight with Dog Soldiers, but I not forget you. I trade for you at Sand Creek. I want you for wife, but you and my women say no to me."

His eyes narrowed. "You not know…I want you. But I not born right person for you."

My entire body resisted his words as indignation ascended from the deep.

He continued, "My anger burn against you, Fire-Hair. I tell squaws to work you, to make you grateful for life with the People. I want squaws break you, but you not be broken." He paused, then asked plaintively, "Why so stubborn…like mule?"

He seemed to genuinely want to get to the source of my rejection.

I stared hard into his eyes, while at the same time seeing the heart's blood of each loved one lost. It spilled and seeped into the earth. "You have taken everything from me, Two Face. Everything—except this boy." I pointed to the sleeping toddler whose small fist stuck out from under the blanket.

"And I thank you for saving us when death threatened." My chin trembled as fragile emotions surfaced. "But, never, Two Face, never! Your people are not my people!"

Then the crack appeared. "I want to go home, Two Face. I…want… to…go…home."

Two Face sat up abruptly as if slapped across the face. His eyes went cold as he said, "I trade you for ammunition and weapons. Indians make more war against whites! Against your people. We drive you from our lands. Lakota and Cheyenne have big power ready for spring war." He lifted his chin defiantly as if his bravado would make it so.

I had lived with the People for ten months and knew their ways were changing. Some were resigned to the new world as it evolved, but Two Face was one who would never be inclined to accept the white man's ways. He knew both worlds. At one time, he thrived in alliance with the businessmen along the trail. But the future of his people was now threatened, and I knew he would fight to preserve what he could of their way of life.

I looked at his determined face. At that moment, I realized his end would be a hard one. I had seen depravity on both sides of the change. I survived two massacres. I would never forget the destruction of all those I loved at my home on the Little Blue, and yet the horror of Sand Creek was unimaginable. The innocents caught up in the slaughter caused by these cataclysmic events would never return. I blinked back tears.

In contrast to his prior mood, Two Face said softly, "Remember, we leave quiet tonight. Blackfoot not sleep hard. Tie boy tight against your body. We ride fast."

He rose to leave. Pulling on his leggings to stop him, I pleaded, "I want one thing." Looking him square in the eye, I plowed on. "I want my dress—the one I wore when you took me from my home. Your squaws took it."

Two Face threw me a puzzled glance and, in typical fashion, remained tight-lipped. Opening the flap, he stepped out with cat-like ease. He was huge by Indian standards, yet his movements were as graceful and stealthy as a panther's.

———◆———

Late that night, I made my escape. The Lakota were tired and slept soundly. The winter was a long and hungry one. They usually slept late into the morning, saving their energy for the next day's toils. Complacent, they no longer watched my every move.

As I approached the murky rock outcropping, Two Face stepped forward from the shadows of the trees. The snow, still on the ground from the storm three days prior, crunched under the hooves of two horses. Quickly adjusting the sleeping toddler on my chest, Two Face spun him to rest against my back. He lifted both of us with one smooth toss onto the back of the horse. I was grateful for a saddle and quickly set my moccasins into the stirrups, adjusted to fit me. I noticed Two Face glide effortlessly onto the blanketed back of his large paint horse.

With a silent jerk of his head, Two Face indicated it was time to go. He kicked his animal into a run as we leapt forward and charged into the night. With ears pinned back, my mare snorted as we raced behind the panther. I ventured a glance back at the sleeping village. No one stirred. Listening to the pounding hooves, I settled into the rhythm of an even gallop. My resolve lay only forward.

Minutes later, our silhouettes were lit by the rising moon. I held tightly to the reins and mane of the black horse as it leaned into its running pace. The distance between us and the Indian village increased. The mare stretched out, nose forward, tail streaming. Mile after mile, we ran as the small camp receded into history. Racing across the open plains, kicking up snow, gravel, and ice, we peeled along the faint trail seen only by Two Face. Occasionally, I turned my head to search for pursuers, but my sight was blurred by the freezing wind. I resigned myself to let Two Face manage the chase—if there was one.

The terrain flattened out, and I imagined watching us from the surface of the moon. Two tiny souls fleeing from our joint past with reluctant urgency. Charging into the unknown, our mutual distrust of one another contradicted the need to form a union. Hair streamed across my face and with a flip of my head, it flowed like the fiery mane of an archangel headed into battle. A leather bag tied to the saddle horn flapped against my thigh and copied the rhythm of the running animal beneath me.

The horses were breathing hard when we finally slowed to a trot, then a walk as the terrain led up an incline. Two Face pulled up next to me and we rode silently. Stopping in a grove of aspen at the top of a ridge, we stared at the snow-covered plains just traversed. I tried to steady my ragged breath, but the cold was numbing. I reflected on how silently we left camp in the chilled pre-dawn—quite different from our arrival in the overheated camps so many months before.

Two Face and I sat watching the sky as light crept above the earth's eastern edge. Flat, yellow, heart-shaped aspen leaves tumbled and swirled around us, joining their companions on the rocky ground. One spiraled past me and settled on a large boulder near my horse's foot. I stared at the moss-covered granite and admired the perfection of the leaf, its midrib and veins a shadow of the lacy skeleton within. A sudden puff of wind blew the leaf to freedom as it glinted happily in the brilliant rays of a new sun. I shaded my eyes against the morning and gazed east toward home.

Reaching behind me, I touched the toddler. His little kick reassured me he was awake and okay. The muted colors of the terrain blazed with each ray of light; and the fresh, damp, smoke-free fragrance of this first morning away from Indian camps stirred up memories. As we turned, I thought of events in my life tucked away since before my captivity....

The United States was divided. War fever infected the men. Awkward and coarse in their boisterous expectancy of battle, many a young man adopted an air of naïve invincibility. The tilt of a chin portrayed a desire for the baseness of the warrior, but the look in the eye betrayed the fear of untested abilities. Glory seemed just within reach, yet I knew many would die. The loved ones left behind would long for their sweet presence—never to taste it again in this generation.

The war held little interest for me. Prior to its beginning, Will, Joe, and I set our sights on a new frontier. It was within this tumultuous time that a new American holiday was declared. Thanksgiving. I wondered about the merit of being thankful for a broken nation. But gratitude won the day within the warm embrace of our own family that first Thanksgiving. Oh...the sweet smells of feast and murmurs of pleasant conversation. There was that hope swelling within me again. Yet, I knew all had changed. My Will and Belle and so many others would be forever absent. I was anxious to return. To become a member of a family again.

Willie squirmed in the bundle on my back. His discomfort and need for food required attention. The baby's spindly, thin arms and legs were no longer contained in the wrappings, and I was concerned he might be cold. I tucked scraps of animal skins about his appendages as best I could and continued down the trail behind Two Face. Despite the hardships, my baby had grown into a fair-haired and quiet toddler. As inhabitants of Indian camps, Willie and I were involuntary participants in the destinies of others. I was disturbed by the fact that the strangers with whom we lived were familiar to Willie; and the people to whom we were returning would be strangers.

Thrust unexpectedly into a desperate situation that August day, and limited by my own untested abilities, I held something in common with the soldiers of the blue and gray. So many battles. The most personal ones often forced the taste of blood to my tongue with every slap of a hand.

There was regret in my mood. I should have stayed stronger, not given up. I remembered the dress...something so benign fostered my own survivor instinct. It served as a simple reminder of my past life. I asked for it, but it was gone. Shredded and pulled apart by the wind on an empty plain. Still, I was glad Willie and I had managed to reach the end of every day alive.

As morning turned to midafternoon, I longed to dismount. Two Face pressed on with an urgency driven by the knowledge of what it means to be the hunted. Hunger and weakness permeated my bones. I wobbled a little as the pony stepped wearily along the path. It, too, had endured a long, cold winter and known hunger—evident by its protruding ribs.

As I rode, my gaze barely had time to absorb the changing landscape. The People shared a spiritual yearning for existence in a world defined by expanse. Horizons, rivers, mountain ranges. Not cities, states, territories, or political persuasions. My home was defined by measured sections of the planet.

Wandering directionless for months, my footsteps stroked the solid ground and molded me to the earth. The days of endless sky and galaxy-filled nights fixed my position in the universe. My person connected to this magnificent planet. Its natural characteristics were but mere tokens of another world, a metaphysical world where indifference and hatred held no sway. I wondered about the Indians' final downfall into a pen of boundaries and fences—all of the white man's making. They would no longer move with the rhythm of water and seasons.

The sun disappeared behind a bank of clouds, and the landscape turned bleak. The wind picked up—my body shivered to warm its vitals. Moving alone through the vast emptiness, I saw no fort or signs of civilization. The immense force of raw isolation caused my future to seem uninhabitable. Hopelessness followed me between gleams of sunshine. My plight often cemented dreams of a full and happy life into the prison of fear and derangement. The weight of my ponderings bore down on me as we traveled hunched, our heads to the wind.

I was transformed. The revelation alone created a new woman who longed for her old life. I searched but could not see....I bargained and begged the Almighty for the common life. The simple motions of making biscuits, frying bacon, rocking babies—all tied me to the thin thread of reason. My body was weary and battered, but a defiant heart thumped its steady rhythm. From this remote perspective, a sharp pang reminded me that Isabelle's tiny heart was forever tied to mine.

A familiar hymn came to mind, and my humming soon changed to quiet singing:

> Lord, I would clasp Thy hand in mine,
> Nor ever murmur nor repine,
> Content, whatever lot I see,
> Since 'tis my God that leadeth me.

God leads me?

At times, He seemed distant in this lost place, but I sensed my continual longing for Him was the force which kept me going. The connection to my Maker was a lifeline. His doing. I recalled each time I relinquished myself to doom. He pulled me back and stayed in step with me, holding my hand.

God continued to reel me in....

Yes, God Almighty would always bring his child back....

Back from the brink.

chapter fifty-four

Running Waters

15 May 1865
Indian Village of Spotted Tail and Little Thunder
North Platte River, Dakotah Territory

In seasons of high water this river assumes a beautiful appearance; its broad bosom is dotted with islands of richest verdure, and adorned with gorgeous hued flowers & delicate vining vegetation. These islands are of the height of adjacent shores, having been formed by the action of the changing currents that have forced their way around them. Some are miles in length, while other are mere dots of verdure on the breast of the broad water.

Sarah Larimer

Blackfoot must have been furious to find me gone three mornings ago. Two Face and I traveled swiftly, carrying few provisions. Starting early this morning, we loped the final miles to the river's edge. The journey to the combined villages of Spotted Tail and Little Thunder was formidable. The camp was immense, and I grew frightened. Smoke swirled above hundreds of teepees scattered through the valley. What was to become of me? I knew enough to expect any number of outcomes. I looked at Two Face as we slowed to a walk. He reached over and grabbed the rein of my horse's bridle as if claiming me.

Riding silently through the village, Two Face acknowledged no one. We rode to the front of an oversized lodge. Dismounting, he lifted us off our horse. Willie was hungry and let it be known. His cries filled the camp. Two Face instructed a woman to get food. She nodded and backed away before hustling into the teepee. Willie's hunger was soon slated as he smacked on a hunk of flatbread. I was given nothing.

Within moments, a huge Indian stepped out of the highly decorated teepee. He was the largest man I had ever seen. His lined face spoke to many years, and he was slightly infirmed.

Two Face leaned toward me and said in English, "Chief Little Thunder, Brulé Sioux."

His name did not equate to his appearance. I dared one astonished look at the man whose height I estimated at six and a half feet tall. His build was remarkably proportioned and stout. He exuded strength in every muscle. A giant in our midst. He was middle-aged with clear eyes and mannerisms which spoke to a superior intelligence.

Afraid, I stepped behind Two Face in hopes my presence would go unnoticed. The imposing chief spoke briefly with Two Face who explained his mission. They discussed a plan for crossing to the south side of the Platte which was running dangerously high. Little Thunder pointed to the remnants of a raft. If lashed together properly it might float.

Soon Two Face and the chief were served boiled meat as they conversed near the fire. I understood little of what was said and received no part of the meal. Kneeling quietly behind Two Face, I occasionally ventured a glance at the big tribal chief. Several times Little Thunder looked directly at me with a dark-eyed stare communicating it would be good to be rid of me.

Curious village inhabitants silently gathered around. All eyes were fixed on the strange white woman clad with only the sparest of Indian garments. Willie and I were covered in what skins and wrappings I had stitched together through the winter. A dirty deerskin shift hung loosely on my body, and the leggings were worn through in places. I pulled my filthy, ragged blanket tighter about my shoulders and kept my head down, hiding behind my matted hair.

Fortunately, Willie slept peacefully in my lap, content to be off the horse. The miles of travel and exposure to the elements had taken a toll on the boy. The wounds on my back pained me, and gaunt skin stretched across my sunken cheeks. It all spoke to my wretched condition. I was exhausted from ten moons of travel and continual privation. The horrors experienced during my captivity robbed me of sleep and rest. The unrelenting cold was my most formidable foe. It threatened to leach the last bit of life from my body. I must appear as a pale ghost to those who stared at the shell of a woman in their midst.

With eyes downcast, my agitation increased. Unable to calm myself, I unconsciously tapped my temples with shaking flicks of my fingers. The Indians closest to me murmured suspiciously—which unnerved me more. I remembered what they did to crazy people and instantly stopped. Fleetingly, I looked around for a means of escape. My stomach reached up through my throat and threatened to choke me. I needed to run, to hide.

Sensing my growing panic, Two Face turned and grabbed my wrist, which yielded to his commanding touch. We stood and walked toward the river's edge. He reached into his bag and handed me a strip of dried buffalo jerk.

"Eat!" he said firmly.

As I gobbled the offering with both hands, he explained he would take me to Fort Laramie to release me to my people. My people? Still frightened, I was not processing his words. Two Face repeated the plan, but I was breathing fast and looking in every direction. Indians! They were everywhere! Fear of ambush would not release its grip. Two Face grasped my upper arms and shook me. I stared at the familiar face. I listened. Deranged, my mind was convinced the only chance to find release from this morbid life was to leave it. To journey to the next life. To die. Finally, his words penetrated the fog. I was close to freedom, to my people.

Little Thunder interrupted my thoughts as his great shadow fell over me. He beckoned Two Face to follow, and the two men turned back to the village with even strides. Sensing danger, I quickly looked around; seeing no movement, I eased Willie and myself into the brush. I quickly placed the boy into his cradleboard and laced him firmly. He was drowsy and protested weakly with tiny bleats and grunts. I stood him against a tree in the shade and sat with my back against it, arms curled protectively about my knees.

A war cry from behind brought me scrambling to my feet. I whirled to face the sound and was surrounded by a group of ten or twelve shrieking, young braves. Startled by their blood-curdling yells, I lost my balance and fell face down in the dirt. Immediately, they were on me—jeering, laughing, and shoving one another. One yanked the buckskin shift over my head, and another pulled the leggings off as I tried to crawl away. A sharp blow landed on the back of my head as a howling attacker gripped me from behind. War cries intensified as he ravished his conquest. Finished, another pulled me slipping and sliding into the shallows of the river. Gravel ground into my shredded knees and forearms mixing with blood. The assailant jumped onto my back and my knees buckled. Using both hands, he held my head under water. The savage took intense pleasure in violating me and daring others to drown me.

Floundering, I gasped for air. Buckets of inhaled water left no room for a life-sustaining breath. Coughing and choking, I was helpless as wave after wave of human flesh knocked me off my feet and altered my direction. I no longer faced the shore, and the pull of the river's swift channel sought to sweep me away. Clenched in a bruising grip, one warrior pulled me back through the surging, muddy waters. I staggered and slipped on the stones in the river.

Without warning, lightning struck a nearby tree. The impact sent projectiles of smoking wood into the air. Ears ringing, eyes sightless, I stood waist deep in the waters of a small inlet. Alone. Abruptly releasing me, the young warriors scurried away. The storm unleashed its fury upon the scene, and I watched as they ran up the bank through the pouring rain. The scream of the wind was deafening as the tempest rolled over me. Rain-driven sand and grit scoured my chilled skin. Thunder exploded directly overhead and knocked me backward into the boiling water. Stretching my arms toward any solid form of salvation, I fought for control. The retinas of my eyes registered the next bolt of lightning in vivid, red detail.

Blinking, my vision cleared. Then I saw him. Two Face, striding down to the water's edge, his long loose hair blowing behind him. His face oblivious to the chaos of the storm, his eyes fixed on mine. He picked up the pace. Without pausing, he walked into the river, lifted me like a child, and carried me to shore. He lay my body in the shelter of a massive rock. The squall was quickly passing, and darkness surrounded us. The pouring rain ran in rivulets around me. Unable to move, I lay passively and stared at the rolling, black and gray clouds. I flinched from the onslaught of huge raindrops splattering my face and body. I shuddered, then violently began to shake, limbs flopping uncontrollably. Mercifully, my system succumbed to shock, and blackness slowly enveloped me.

I awoke to a vigorous massaging of my extremities and face. Opening my eyes, I stared into the frightened, dark visage of Two Face. I was covered in a soaked blanket. Staring into my eyes, he leaned toward me and cupped my face with his hands. Alarmed, I summoned the strength to wrench my head away and croak, "No!" He stopped. Frowning, his features hardened, contemplating the conflict between his desire and my unwillingness. I closed my eyes once again and slipped away.

Not sure how much time passed, I gradually became aware of a rustling sound. I sat up abruptly, expecting more attackers. It was Two Face holding my shift and motioning for me to put it on. I tried to slip it over my soaked head but simply could not manage to thrust my limbs through the arm holes. Two Face hoisted me to my feet and held me upright. He adjusted the soaked leather down past my waist and pulled my arms through the openings. My knees knocked, and I noticed blood streaming between my legs. My whole body was scraped and throbbing.

A tangled mass of hair clung to my face. The ribs on my right side hurt terribly.

"Willie," I gasped, trying not to breathe too deeply. "Where is Willie?" Innate dread welled up from the source of a mother's instinct.

Holding one of my arms, Two Face reached for the cradleboard propped near us, then lost his grip. I fell again. Crawling to my child, I wrapped my arms around the cradleboard, clutching it to my chest. Two Face tried to lift the board and child from my arms, but I jerked away and held on with fierce determination. Unhinged, I was ready to withstand the ire of a thousand roused braves.

Two Face squatted in front of me and spoke soothingly. I did not hear him but relaxed at his tone. Finally, I allowed him to raise me up by the elbow and half carry, half drag us to the river's edge. The repaired make-shift raft was waiting. Watching my face for possible backlash, Two Face slowly slipped my arms through the straps of the cradleboard and positioned it firmly on my back. He gestured for me to sit.

Little Thunder stood squarely on the bank and lifted a massive hand in farewell to Two Face. As we pushed off, I stared into the black depths of current next to me. The placid surface of the deep river hid the force beneath. It shimmered, eddied, and swirled in the midday light. Indians using crudely crafted paddles and sticks steered our tiny craft across the broad expanse of the North Platte. Running Waters, as the Sioux called it, flooded past the rims of the banks. Spring rains caused it to ripple and swell as it raced to join its sister river, the South Platte. The last time I crossed it, huge slabs of ice floated along as I was dragged through the icy waters on a rope behind a horse.

Now I knelt quietly on the unstable log and branch, watching debris float past. Careful not to tip the balance, I adjusted the knot on the sling which pressed Willie to my back. A breeze lifted off the frigid waters and swirled the air around us. The baby shivered slightly. The horses, which had carried us over the last one hundred miles, swam near the raft. They strained against the pull of the formidable current. With out-stretched arms, Two Face and a companion tightly gripped ropes attached to the horses' bridles, straining to support their heads above the water.

Squinting to the east, I searched the horizon and imagined the river flowing to the edge of a flat earth—rushing, pounding, draining off a massive waterfall into oblivion. The weight of the child pushed me toward its shining surface. Though kneeling on wood, I felt nothing solid. Peace beckoned from the soft nebulous water. No more pain. The river was a living, breathing thing. Running Waters called me forward into its embrace.

Will! Belle! Just below the surface—beckoning, calling to me. Come! Come to Running Waters! I felt the gentle touch of my husband's fingers on my cheek. I reached out my hand. Placing one foot under me, I pushed off into the waiting arms of my family. A gentle wave washed over me, and I held my breath.

"No!" Two Face's muffled voice commanded. I heard a commotion behind me.

Hurry! I must hurry. I tipped further into the water where relief awaited, and this time I did not hold my breath. Water filled my lungs. Nothing else mattered. I was free. Free of my body, free of the nightmare. Just filled with quiet joy at our reunion.

Before succumbing to the blazing white, flickering light, I swatted aimlessly at a pain in my leg. It hurt—a lot. Twisted at the hip. A shot of physical agony jolted me. Away from the peace. My family. My leg. It was caught. I kicked. Wait. No, my body was yanked. Pulled up out of the shining water's solace. Body writhing, my head was hauled from its watery pillow and bounced across the wet surface of the raft. Darkness became my mantle. Once again, I drifted away.

"Fire-Hair!" shouted the muted voice. "Come back, damn you!"

Moaning, my body uncoiled, rotated. Water spouted from my mouth as Two Face pounded on my chest. Willie coughed and choked between strangled cries and gasps for air. Water gurgled up from my stomach and lungs. More shot out of my mouth. I gulped air, sputtered, and retched. My sinuses filled with an unpleasant, fishy sludge, and I coughed. Water streamed from my nose.

Two Face jerked me to a standing position. He gripped my shoulders and shook me until the vacant look in my eyes was replaced with fear. Noticing my surroundings for the first time, I whipped my head from side to side. Where was the next molestation coming from?

"Ten miles to fort!" Two Face hissed. His face was drawn, and I noticed his hands were shaking. "You be strong, Fire-Hair! Whe-Ho! Be strong!"

He called to one of his companions, who wrestled me ashore and roughly pushed me up the muddy slope. The harsh handling of my body by yet another stranger startled me. I flinched, waiting for the next act of violence, but it did not come. I continued to labor for air and fell to my knees. I coughed and gagged until air filled my lungs. I fell face down on the soil, hands clawing the mud. I exhaled and lay still.

Two Face hauled me upright to inspect my drenched remains. Satisfied I would live, he boosted me onto a dripping pony. "We go trading post," he said. "Make plan. We hurry. Go safe to fort."

He stopped talking and looked deeply into my eyes.

"Fire-Hair," he whispered.

I took no notice.

"Lucinda."

My eyes widened upon hearing my given name. He had never spoken it.

"Lucinda Eubank. We close. Be strong. You go home."

I focused on his mouth and processed his words, then nodded. He let out a sigh of relief, patted my foot, then reached for the rein of my horse. Mounted, we turned west.

chapter fifty-five

Bordeaux's Trading Post

16 May 1865
Ten Miles East of Fort Laramie, Dakotah Territory

If you lose your sky, you will soon lose your earth.

Mrs. Chas. E. Cowan

A low-slung roof appeared, the structure hidden behind a grassy knoll. Smoke drifted from its rock chimney. It was the first substantial building I had seen in almost a year. I stood in my stirrups and stared at the scene before me. Dozens of teepees dotted the hay meadows along the river. Corrals filled with horses, mules, and oxen spoke to the prosperity of the owner. Wagons were scattered about the premises—some loaded, others empty. Stout buildings nestled amid the village. Tears filled my eyes, and my heart hammered in my chest. Each step closed the distance between me and the Bordeaux Trading Post, a small piece of civilization wrapped in a recognizable Indian presence.

Dare I allow sweet relief to overwhelm me? Was it possible this was a place of safety? My train of thought prickled with prospect and cleared away the fog. Was this liberty's door? Fears of abuse, pain, and injury were just beneath the surface. I hesitated. Feelings of misgivings filled me with a need to run through the door and latch onto freedom—never to let go.

Two Face and I stood alone in the yard. Two horses were tied to the hitching post. I watched as he paused to inspect a large robe press stationed outside the log building. The machine compressed and bundled cured buffalo robes. Dozens were piled to the eaves of the building. Two Face touched the robes and sighed, his confidence subdued. He shook it off, however, as we entered the building.

Clinging to the tattered remains of my shift, I followed him. I was weak and chilled to the bone. Willie was asleep in the sling on my back.

I carried no possessions. I thought of my worn and threadbare satchel which once held the most prized links to my old life—the tintype likeness of William and my wedding ring. But the bag was gone, too.

The neatly stacked bolts of fabric, implements, shiny pans, bags of flour, and cornmeal were familiar, yet so foreign to me. The warmth of the stove eased into my consciousness with a reassurance—the world of such things still existed. Three Indians stood at the counter and halted their conversation to scrutinize the newcomers. They wore blue U.S. military jackets and caps. Their native leggings and footwear spoke to dual identities. They stepped forward with loud, welcoming shouts and handshakes.

Two Face relaxed, smiled, then spotted the man he had come to see. "Big Mouth!" he hailed.

A heavy-set Indian wearing a badge stepped away from the fireplace. "Now you head of agency police, eh?"

"Ah Ho!" replied the large man in the tight uniform. He adjusted his cap and added in English, "I sergeant now." Smiling, he pointed to the stripes on his sleeve. "Twenty soldiers in my band. Brulé and Oglala."

Shifting his focus to me, he said, "Who white woman and papoose? She no look so good."

Two Face looked over at me as if noticing my wretched condition for the first time. I stood with my head down and shoulders slumped, hair damp and stringy. Scant remnants of clothing did little to cover my bruises. One eye was swollen. Baby Willie rested his head on my shoulder. He was reticent and thin.

Two Face lowered his voice and said, "I want take woman and papoose to fort. Surrender them. Prove I friendly. Get reward. I bought her. My own expense. Bring her to white soldiers. Show I good Indian."

"Ahh…" grunted Big Mouth. His jovial expression changed to concern.

Two Face picked up the shift in mood and asked, "How I go to fort safely?"

Big Mouth thought for a moment, then declared, "I go with you. Also, be wise. Take white men with us."

Two Face nodded agreement with the able sergeant's perceptiveness.

Big Mouth, brows drawn together in thought, continued to voice a plan. "We ask agent Gereau and trader Beauvais go with us. Fort dangerous. Frenchmen talk to white officers, explain you come as friend. Be careful, Chief Moonlight."

The two men walked outside to continue their conversation.

A short, stout man, whom I assumed to be Bordeaux, the owner of the post, stepped from behind the counter. He paused mid-step and gawked at me. Hesitantly, a look of decision passed over his face. Smiling kindly, he spoke not a word but left to join the men outside. It was clear the popular trader kept abreast of all goings on.

The arrival of a white captive woman was creating quite a stir.

Unsure of what to do, I inched toward the fire. Two Indian women stepped out of a side room and greeted me. Sharing knowing looks, they hustled the rest of the curious outside. The younger woman turned her attentions to me, concern creasing her placid face.

"Hello. I am Mrs. John Farnham, Win Pelim, Woman's Hair. I am daughter of Big Mouth," she said politely. Gently grasping my shoulders, she turned me toward the window to appraise me. I flinched at her touch, but as her words washed over me, I promptly fell to pieces. Sobs burst forth from my deepest scars, and I covered my face.

"Shhh..." she whispered. "You are safe now."

Leading me to a rocking chair next to the fire, she draped a blanket about my shoulders. The crying would not stop. The other woman gathered the children behind the counter, uncertain about the unhinged bedraggled visitor. The world was melting around me as my disoriented mind stopped functioning. Mrs. Farnham spoke to me in English asking questions, but it was all a jumble. My trembling lips prevented coherent speech.

The older, shorter Indian woman shuffled up to me and quietly said, "I am Mrs. Marie Bordeaux, Huntkalutawin, Red Cormorant Woman." She sat down on a stool near me and rested her hand on mine.

Embarrassed, I jumped at her tender gesture. A small girl crept up cautiously and stood next to us. She watched her mother's face for clues as to whether I was friend or foe. My tears subsided as I looked into the child's soft, brown eyes, her face framed by sleek dark braids. I felt bathed in the light of her shy smile. She seemed an old soul in a child's body. Wisdom and compassion wavered about her as if a special touch from God graced her tiny frame.

"This is my daughter Susan," said Marie by way of introduction. Then she motioned for a thin, dark-haired youth to join us. "And this is my son Louis." He was taller than the girl with bright blue eyes shining through a smooth, brown face.

"Very nice to meet you, mademoiselle," he said in French-accented English.

I searched the faces of the family surrounding me, and a sense of relief tapped my brain. The curtain surrounding my stupor began to lift. But only briefly. For I thought of my little Belle and without warning, wracking sobs welled up threatening to burst through my chest. Willie squirmed in my arms, concerned by the condition of his mother. He looked around anxiously as though trying to perceive our nearest threat, then began to cry. Marie patted my hand, then reached for Willie, who slipped into her arms and quieted. Indian women had become a daily part of his life.

Minutes later, Mrs. Farnham placed a warm meal in my hands. Willie was cleaned up and fed— but never taken more than a few steps from me. Mrs. Bordeaux noticed I was bleeding and helped me out of the chair. Blood streamed down my leg and puddled on the floor. Cramps tightened, then released, then began again. I doubled over. The children were sent out, and Mrs. Farnham went to work.

Pulling the damp shift over my head, she stared at my pale form. I stood before her, battered, naked, bleeding, and…obviously pregnant. Her eyes met mine, and I noticed a flicker of panic cross her face. Without delay, she began to minister to me, supplying me with what I needed to staunch the flow.

Mrs. Bordeaux poured hot water over herbs in a lovely teacup. I accepted the brew gratefully but could barely lift it to my lips. The delicate china felt warm and welcoming in my hand. I sipped, then drained the contents. My vision began to waver, and I felt faint. I stumbled toward the chair. Both women reached me before I slid to the floor. Placing me on a cot behind a curtain, they slipped an extra blanket over my shuddering body. The cramps continued. My legs shook uncontrollably, and my teeth chattered.

Was my body reacting to the cold, the agony, or the trauma? Was my body finally going to dispel the fetus within? Or was this reaction induced by something else?

Freedom's possibilities overwhelmed my system. I could not control my emotions. Crying, moaning, I tossed my head back and forth. Mrs. Bordeaux placed a cool hand on my forehead and began to pray in French. Crossing herself, she finished and settled herself on a chair next to me, her hand in mine. Finally, I slept fitfully.

Waking later, I was unsure how long I slept, but it was dark in the room except for the light from an oil lamp. Mrs. Bordeaux offered another spoonful of warm broth, though I could not remember the first. The salty taste of it lingered on my tongue and settled my stomach. I noticed the cramps were gone.

"Marie. Mrs. Farnham," I said weakly. "Thank you."

"You bear marks of great suffering," said Marie as she leaned into the firelight. Tossing another chunk of wood, she added with a tiny smile,

"But you are with friends."

The balm of spoken English refreshed my soul, and I allowed hope's touch just the slightest caress.

"What has happened to you?" Mrs. Farnham asked gently.

I eased myself upright, but she would not allow me to rise. Placing a soft bundle beneath my head, she leaned me back gently and waited.

I started slowly, telling of my family, our home, the raid, my captivity. She listened and nodded as my story unfolded. I finished with the telling of the repeated violations at the hands of the men of Little Thunder's band. She clicked her tongue, snapped her eyes, and said something disapproving in Lakota. She tamped down her anger, sensing it would cause more strain. We sat companionably for a while as the women digested my words.

Finished, I closed my eyes exhausted.

Mrs. Farnham ventured to speak what was on her mind. "The babe… in your womb," she said pointing at my abdomen. "Whose is it? Do you know?"

"Yes," I whispered hesitantly. "After I was taken to the Cheyenne camp, I became the property of a chief. He acted terribly towards me and …." I drifted off.

"The chief. He is the one who made this child?" asked Marie.

I shuddered at the memory of his cruelty and treachery.

"Who was it?" prodded Mrs. Farnham.

"Big Crow," I said in the tiniest whisper, my voice a mere reflection of itself.

Both women exclaimed in unison, "No! Big Crow?"

I quickly deserted my haunted memories of the fiend to focus on their reaction.

"He was hung at the fort just days ago!"

I was stunned. My greatest menace gone! All the evil malice he embodied no longer held power over anyone. Justice washed over me. The women urged me for more details of the story, but I was cautious. My mind raced as it tracked from Big Crow to Old Woman to my friend Nancy.

"He was accused of stealing horses from the emigrants," explained Mrs. Bordeaux. "A white woman was ransomed, brought to the fort during the month when trees crack with cold. She told of white people he killed and bad ways he treated captive women. The anger of the white soldier chiefs burned against him."

"Yes. I know the woman," I replied. "She is my friend, Mrs. Morton." Memories of Nancy bathed my hurting soul.

"I not know her name," replied Red Cormorant Woman. Her deep-set eyes drew together as she thought. "She young like you. Taken on Plum Creek on Holy Road."

"Now she is free?" I asked.

Both women nodded, and I sighed with relief. I missed my companion. During my darkest hours, I always imagined that Nancy Morton would prevail.

"Later. You talk to sutler's wife at fort. She tell you more," said Marie.

I sighed, closed my eyes and for the first time in months, fell into a deep sleep.

———•———

The next morning, Two Face, Big Mouth, Agent Charles Gereau, Mr. James Beauvais, and I traveled by horse along the river toward the fort. The words of Two Face surfaced in my thoughts. My people. I was going to my people. The hidden prospect of ending my ordeal mingled with doubt and a dash of hope. Was it possible? Yes, here I was in the company of white men. The promise of freedom had been elusive for so long. I dared not speak the word aloud, but I touched my lips and mouthed, "Home."

The men stopped along the water's edge for the night. I wondered... was this my final sleep on the run? Would I no longer live with those who hate me? Visions of what tomorrow would bring overwhelmed the shattered pieces of my being.

Willie and I settled onto the damp ground under our blanket near the campfire. Two Face approached. "I take you to fort tomorrow. You tell officers I good Indian?" He seemed uncharacteristically concerned.

I nodded and replied quietly, "Yes, Two Face, I will tell them."

The cold and dank crept into my bones. With a shuddering sigh, I curled my body around Willie and determined to get through one more night....

I dreamed of giving birth.

Pains. Contractions. Tumbling visions of childbirth, a watery explosion.

The naked babe, slick with blood. Squatting, I catch the girl child.

"Beautiful, like her mother," says Will.

I stare at the babe's coal black eyes. The tender baby's face is lovely.

I caress the straight, black hair and inhale her sweet ancient earthiness. My heart is full.

Then unbidden, a threat—stark, black, emerging from a cave in a broad stone mountain.

I look again at the babe in my arms.

The human face loses its mortal essence. Shrunken flesh withers against the bones.

The evil features of dead Big Crow grin at me with disturbingly grim malevolence.

I shriek, "You brute! I rebuke you! I hate you!"

Delivering a crushing blow, I stab again and again.

Waking, I held a knife in my hand. The faces encircling me were male, dusky, concerned. A hand removed the stick from my grip. Pressed to the ground, my eyes darted about deliriously hunting for shelter. Soft rain pattered my face. The blanket hid me. I drifted back into the nightmare....

I am lost. I fight my way between boulders and gnarly trees.

A crevice opens in the churned earth. I hide in its cavity.

I sleep. I wake. I seek...but she is gone.

chapter fifty-six

Two Cages

17 May 1865
South Bank, North Platte River
Captivity Ends—Day 212

We have caught Mr. Two Face and his five lodges. He and his warriors
are now sweeping the parade ground with a ball and chain to their heels.
And I think ere long will be dancing between heaven and earth.

William Bullock

D eprived of hope for so long, I fought to shed the gray shroud cast around my bony shoulders, angular and thin under the skin. Clouds of despair clung to the dissolving mantle. Was I truly to return from the dead? Was today the day? I sensed light coming, warm, blinding, life-giving. I gathered my courage and wrapped myself in its flimsy veil. The feel of the day was changing. Cradling Willie fiercely against my bosom, I turned in the direction of my people. Fort Laramie stood beyond the river as a shining, white beacon on the green plains. I was ready but not prepared.

The rushing waters of the North Platte were the final obstacle to my release. I was deeply afraid of river crossings, but this one was especially daunting. The frigid night and rains to the west filled the water with thin floating slabs of ice. The steady, fresh wind hastened their movement across the water's surface.

Two Face knew the ponies were weak. We might not be able to cross on their backs. He commanded me to tie Willie in his cradleboard, which was the usual method of crossing with papooses. The screaming protests of my son heightened my trepidation. Two Face instructed me to take off my shift, and we tied it into a bundle around the horn of my saddle. He removed and secured his clothing to the saddle as well. Wearing soaked, heavy leather during a river crossing was dangerous. I knew from experience my legs would tangle and become useless in the river.

Heaving me into the saddle, Two Face reminded me, "If pony sink, slide off here." He swept his hand down the rump of the horse. "Hold tail. He pull you." With a bold gaze into my face, he added, "Swim for your life, Fire-Hair."

Straddling the pony, I looked at the water, then back at Two Face. He fastened a rope across his shoulder, then attached it to his horse. My mount was tied behind. Dry mouthed, I watched him wade into the water leading the train. He promptly lost his footing and began to swim with powerful strokes. The horses struggled against the current and within minutes, my pony slipped beneath the surface with barely a ripple. It was drowning.

"Off!" shouted Two Face.

Reluctant to leave Willie, I hesitated. The horse lifted its head once again, snorting and puffing, eyes wild. We were going down. Inching off its pumping haunches, I slid into the icy water. Immediately, the river swept me away. The tips of my fingers reached out as I kicked with all my strength. At the final moment, I felt the light touch of tail hairs flowing over my hand. Grasping desperately, I managed to twist both hands in the tail. A floating slab of ice slammed into my arm, its sharp edges grinding as it tipped up, then over my arm. After my slippery dismount, the pony lurched forward and thrust its head and neck high above the water. Its pumping legs gained direction against the current. Soon I was hauled sputtering and drenched from the foreboding, frigid waters. I quickly dressed and wrapped myself into a worn, stale, soaked blanket.

The others followed in the same manner. Miraculously, we each arrived safely on the opposite shore. It was decided to send Mr. Gereau and Big Mouth to the fort. Two Face and I would keep a cautious distance under the watchful eye of Mr. Beauvais.

Within the hour, we spotted four riders returning. I noticed the approaching newcomers wore military jackets. One pulled his horse up within speaking distance and eyed me curiously. "I am Lieutenant Colonel Baumer, commander of Fort Laramie, and this is my orderly, Mr. Lingelbach," he said loudly. "I am told that you, madame, are Mrs. Eubank. Is that correct?"

"Y-Yes," I stammered. His accent was distinctly German and reminded me of my mother's people in Pennsylvania. Switching to German, I replied, "Sir, may we speak in your native language?"

His eyebrows shot up. "How do you come to speak German?"

After a quick explanation, I suggested we continue in our common language. "Two Face has a good understanding of English," I said. The colonel understood that our conversation would benefit from privacy.

"Are you well, Mrs. Eubank? How have you been treated?" His questions were genuine, and I could see concern behind his stiff façade. His mahogany-tanned face spoke of months in the western sun. He was broad in the shoulder and narrow at the waist, which his trim uniform outlined neatly. His chiseled face was fresh-shaven and wore a friendly expression tinged with wariness.

Continuing our private conversation, I told of my ten-month captivity. Noting his concern at my appearance, I realized I must resemble a demented vagabond. Mud-caked and waterlogged, my hair was a jumbled mass of snarls. By the look on his face, I could tell my appearance was shocking. Compulsively, I smoothed my ragged, deer-skin shift and told him my child and I were not entirely well. Beyond this obvious description, I described the beastly treatment received at the hands of the Cheyenne and Sioux. Adrenaline-charged, my mind raced. Jumbled words and convoluted details fell out of my mouth. Hanging by a thread, how could I summarize my lengthy ordeal? From the edge of insanity, I pleaded for help.

"Please forgive me, sir. My son and I have been traveling for so long...."

Colonel Baumer's stern expression switched to a look of surprise as he noticed little Willie. "Mrs. Eubank, I am astounded to see your young companion." He watched as I carefully removed Willie from the cradleboard and held him in my arms. The thin, pale child was soaked, shivering, and alarmingly silent. He had not fully recovered from his bout with the fever.

"How?" stammered Baumer. "How?" he repeated. Pulling himself together, he said, "It is quite unusual for a child so young to survive such a harrowing experience." He swallowed hard and quickly wiped an eye with the gauntlet on his left wrist.

Emotions plagued us all. Slurring my words, I struggled to introduce my son. Slowly, my brain remembered. William...Joseph...Eubank, Jr. The little boy was busy examining the white faces and uniforms of the strangers. Empty of any memory of his father and our family members, he was fascinated by these odd beings in a new world. He was quiet, as usual, and unsure of our new circumstances. Seeking reassurance, he looked first into my eyes, then focused on Two Face. His little hands stretched out from their wrappings toward the chief as the child grunted, "Uh, uh." He sought comfort from the only other person within his circle of protection.

The colonel was taken aback. He looked at me, then at Two Face, then regarded me quizzically. A small reflexive twitch bounced at the corner of his eye. His expression seemed to ask, "What is going on here?" He started to speak but abandoned the idea to remain professional. Colonel Baumer quickly assessed the situation. The good soldier tried to disguise his rising anger. I was sure our desperate condition was obvious to anyone with eyes. I watched as his expression changed from interested to incensed. As he aimed to control his wrath, he reminded himself aloud in German that it would be wise to feign a friendly disposition. Then he said, "Mrs. Eubank, you are not yet free."

He turned to his orderly with a stiff smile and addressed him in German as well. "Private Lingelbach, slip off to the fort. Once out of sight, run with all your might and bring enough soldiers to capture this Indian. Remember, act as if you are not party to our discussions. I will try to distract the Indian with mention of rewards."

At these instructions, the young orderly strolled away to walk along the river in the opposite direction of the fort. He whistled and threw sticks and rocks into the water as if he had not a care in the world. Soon he was out of sight; and I hoped he was running toward the fort with all the energy he could muster.

Meanwhile, Colonel Baumer dismounted and tried to appear as non-threatening as possible. It was imperative Two Face not be spooked. The colonel began negotiating for the return of the white woman. What would Two Face consider a fair price for bringing the woman to the fort? Guns and ammo? Horses?

Suddenly, a detachment of soldiers riding hard and fast appeared to our left, another to the right. In moments, we were surrounded by soldiers wielding weapons at all angles. Mr. Beauvais was just as startled as Two Face, for he had bought the ruse as well.

Lt. Colonel Baumer remounted his horse and slowly eased himself into his saddle. "We will return to the fort and meet with Colonel Moonlight, the Plains District Commander."

Two Face reined his horse to the south ready to flee but stopped at the sight of a group of soldiers behind him. Our eyes met with a shared expression of regret. The wild man who had known only freedom braced against the coming doom. In the game, his final move involved a woman, and he had lost. His dark eyes reflected an image—it was me.

Baumer diffused the situation by politely inviting Two Face to the fort to discuss the terms of ransom. Two Face's body language was like that of a mountain lion sensing a trap, alert and suspicious. He looked at me as we urged our horses forward. I nodded to him in reassurance that I would honor our agreement and portray him as a "good Indian."

"Be careful, watch words, Fire-Hair," Two Face warned in Lakota. His voice hid an odd note, half menacing and half mournful.

Fearing my physical condition might betray me at any moment, I mustered what dignity I could and sat tall, chin thrust forward. Adrenaline coursed through my exhausted body in anticipation of freedom. Venturing into the unknown, I feigned bravery, but inside I was falling apart.

Escaping the shroud, I hurled myself through the crack as my cage door swung open.

Two Face's cage door closed—with a click of its lock.

chapter fifty-seven

Disjointed

18 May 1865
Fort Laramie, Dakotah Territory

A few weeks after her rescue from the Indians I met her again at Fort Laramie. The bright-eyed woman appeared to me to be twenty years older. Her hair was streaked with gray, her face gave evidence of painful suffering, and her back, as shown to General Conner and myself, was a mass of raw sores from her neck to her waist, where she had been whipped and beaten by Two Face's squaws. The sores had not been permitted to heal, and were a sight most sickening to behold. The poor woman was crushed in spirit and almost a maniac.

Captain Henry E. Palmer

T he silence in the room was broken by curses. "What the hell!" "Damn savages!" Apologizing for their outbursts, the fort officers stared at the mass of oozing, open sores on my back. I clutched the neck of the dress to my throat with one hand and held it around my bulging waist with the other. It did little to hide the evidence of my shame. Mrs. Bullock, the sutler's wife, gave the simple calico dress to me when I arrived at the fort, and I was grateful. The saggy doeskin shift I had worn for months was filthy and ragged. Its short length revealed bare legs and covered little else. The leggings were lost in the attack at Little Thunder's camp.

Upon my arrival, Moonlight introduced his clerk, Thomas Dewey. The diligent young man recorded the interview as the colonel dispensed with such formalities as my identity and background. Upon hearing my story and the description of the massacre, Dewey was nothing short of stunned. He held his pen suspended mid-air while gaping at me as though seeing me with new light.

"Oh, my God! This is the woman? The Eubank woman!" he exclaimed

330

looking at the others. "The whole family was killed by Indians on the Little Blue last fall!"

Even the most seasoned soldier was shaken to the core by my tale. It was daunting to coherently describe the events, for the trauma was still fresh. I was exhausted. Noting my faltering condition, Mrs. Bullock insisted the debriefing be hastened.

I stood with flushed faced as Colonel Moonlight and Lieutenant Colonel Baumer inspected the damage. The post doctor was in attendance as well. Mrs. Bullock held the dress open in as modest a fashion as possible. "I thought you should see this," she said. "I have cleaned the area, but infection appears to have been present for a long time. I thought she should be seen by the surgeon."

"I agree, Mrs. Bullock. I appreciate you bringing the matter to my attention," replied Colonel Moonlight wryly. He was tall, handsome, and impeccably dressed in his officer's uniform.

The post surgeon, Dr. John Bell, inspected me carefully. He pressed on various ribs checking for broken bones. I winced and cried out in pain as he found a spot on my left side which had bothered me for weeks. "A fractured rib, I am afraid, and a lot of bruising about her arms and thighs as well." One green and yellow bruised cheekbone was still tender to the touch. The doctor closely inspected my back. "She needs treatment for these infected wounds. They have not been allowed to heal, and she is obviously suffering from severe malnutrition."

Mrs. Bullock gingerly placed a hand on my shoulder to steady me. "She is feverish, Doctor Bell."

Obviously distressed, Moonlight demanded, "Who did this to you, Mrs. Eubank? Two Face? Others? Who?"

"Y-Yes," I stammered. My eyes, blurred by fever, did not focus on the source of the voice. "Ah…yes. His squaws." *The stick came down hard on my bare back.* I flinched. "Many squaws." *Strike after strike. Blow after blow.* "And warriors. And horrid Cheyenne Dog Soldiers." I trembled and tried to gather my disjointed memories. *Attackers pushing me under water. Grabbing, shoving, pushing. Hands like vices. Probing, slapping, violating.* My eyes searched the room for an exit. I was chilled and shivered even though the room was overheated with fetid air.

The good doctor interrupted. "Mentally, she is what we would describe as manic. Poor woman. With treatment, rest, and attention to these physical sores, I expect she will recover. Mentally, however? Well…." he sighed as he stepped away from me. I heard him whisper, "She is young, but maybe never."

"Big Crow, the Cheyenne, so many," I mumbled. My muddled words became a mishmash of the guilty.

"Yes, yes, Mrs. Eubank. Indians," said Colonel Baumer. "But we need more names. Did Two Face hurt you? Blackfoot?"

"Yes. Yes. Blackfoot. Ummm....Blackfoot."

"Where is this Blackfoot now?" inquired the incensed colonel.

"Where? Waiting. He is...far. Far from the fort. He wants supplies. Food, blankets, guns...." I fumbled with the fabric of the dress.

Colonel Moonlight interrupted the medical examination to update the others on matters at hand. "I held a hearing earlier and, despite his assurances of friendliness, Two Face is now confined to the guardhouse. Mrs. Eubank gave Baumer the location of Blackfoot's village—approximately one hundred miles northeast near the White River. I sent Charley Elliston with Big Mouth and twenty of his Indian police to the camp. They will lure Blackfoot here under the pretense of receiving renumeration. I have given instructions to bring in the entire band, dead or alive." Murmurs of satisfaction circled the room. Someone was going to pay for this!

Dr. Bell gently palpated my neck, skull, and collar bone as he continued his assessment with a clinical, monotone voice. "Her physical system has been greatly taxed. I suggest we clean these wounds at once with a solution of carbolic acid. Her diet is to be gradually increased. I am afraid she will carry the scars of these lash marks on her back for the rest of her life."

"Please remove your, ahem, footwear, Mrs. Eubank. I would like to inspect your feet."

I looked down at the moccasins given to me by Mitimoni, which peeked out below the hem of the unfamiliar dress. How did I get this dress?

Mrs. Bullock gently pulled the bodice together at the back and fastened the buttons. The fabric clung to the bloody, sticky mass of wounds. I sat on the wooden bench and painfully took off each of the moccasins. The surgeon lifted one foot and pressed on the red scars from the burns I suffered at the hands of the Cheyenne. The seared, scorched flesh and blisters were healed to a point, but I was left with a queer, cushiony numbness. The area surrounding one of the deepest burns was filled with pus and blazed angrily with infection. The weeks of shoeless travel across the Great Plains desert last fall had inflicted an abundance of injuries. After inspecting both feet, Dr. Bell finally looked into my eyes and kindly asked, "Mrs. Eubank, can you explain these injuries to your feet?"

I tried to describe the ill treatment: the punishment for my escape attempt, the fires that singed me more than once, the stomps and kicks. As the words poured out, the faces of the officers grew increasingly stiff with rage. Dr. Bell looked at them and offered his assessment. "I have examined her child as well. He also shows burn scars, pitiful thing, around his wrists and ankles."

A purple-faced Moonlight chewed his lip and asked, "Who did this, Mrs. Eubank? Think. Who burned you and the child? I want a name."

"A woman. Dog Soldier Woman."

The commander looked at those gathered with raised eyebrows. Woman warriors ventured into the myth category. Perhaps this poor lady was completely crazy after all.

"Her name. Mochi. Her husband. Medicine Water. But others, too. So many others." I struggled to disassemble the tangled weeds in my brain. *Dragged to the stake. Wood piled around. Fire lit. Burning sensation at my feet. Searing pain.*

"Stop! No More!" I shouted.

There was a great intake of breath by those in the room.

"The whole village ravished me. They beat me unconscious."

"Captain Palmer. You say you know the woman. Perhaps you can help," suggested a very pale Moonlight.

The young man raised an eyebrow, rose from his chair, and politely asked, "May I, Mrs. Eubank?"

I nodded, still lost.

"Shhh, now. It's okay. You are safe." A familiar voice pulled me back. "Look at me. Remember me? I am your friend. Henry Palmer."

I stared vacantly into compassionate eyes. Back into the light, I searched the room, then focused. A friend stood in front of me, holding my shoulders. "Oh. Captain Palmer. It is you. Thank you," I whispered. I laid my head on his shoulder. "Thank you."

Wrapping his arms around me, he whispered hoarsely, "It will be okay, Mrs. Eubank. You are safe now. I will make sure of it." It was warm in his gentle embrace. He stroked the back of my head. Afraid to move lest he cause further pain, the captain lingered, then stepped back. True compassion exuded from his eyes.

Looking down at the floor, I nodded. "Henry. Will's gone."

Fleeting thoughts of pleasant times sprang out of the deepest recesses of my mind. Just as quickly, shame descended, and I looked away. I heard him inhale sharply to control his increasing fury. I wondered what he must think of my appearance now compared to our visits over dinner in my home on the Little Blue. I quickly tucked a strand of hair back into its twisted braid. My fingers trembled and I felt faint, feverish, and nauseous. The light coming through the window dimmed as the sun slipped behind a cloud.

Moonlight interrupted and said, "That will be enough, Mrs. Bullock. Thank you. Now if you will allow us to speak privately with Mrs. Eubank regarding her ordeal...." He trailed off.

"Of course, colonel," she replied shakily. "I will see to the babe."

Willie and I had been in her care since our arrival at the fort the evening before. She quickly stepped out the door and onto the step, grateful for air.

"Captain Palmer, please bring Mrs. Eubank a blanket. She is chilled." Then turning to me he spoke softly. "Mrs. Eubank, are you feeling well enough to talk with us for a few more minutes?"

I nodded.

"We need to know who did this to you? Specifically, I mean. Who has beaten you?"

I tried to compose myself. "Many in the camp beat me. Big Crow. Blackfoot. Their women. Most of the time I did not know why. I worked like a slave and was beaten for the smallest infraction. Sometimes, for larger acts of defiance, too." My mind shot back to Mrs. Morrison, and I gulped as tears spilled in streams down my cheeks.

Colonel Moonlight noticed and pressed gently. "Can you share with us any specific instances?"

Alarmed, I quickly glanced into his eyes. Did he see the horrible scene playing out in my head? The lives of other captives snuffed out, ended in horrific torturous deaths?

"Please, Mrs. Eubank. We want to hold to account all those who have harmed you...and the others."

I dabbed at my eyes with my sleeve and took a deep breath. Quietly, without intonation, I began.

"I traveled with the survivors of Sand Creek. The Cheyenne...they attacked every ranch and stage stop in their path. They targeted anything that moved—wagons, stagecoaches, drovers. I recall one ranch. It was attacked a couple of months ago. All the men were killed, and a woman...a woman...." I gulped. "She was brought into camp....Mrs. Morrison" I whispered haltingly.

The men stayed silent but glanced at one another knowingly.

Words were not sufficient. Haunted by the images, I struggled to speak.

"Begin slowly, Mrs. Eubank, and tell us what happened to Mrs. Morrison. It is important for us to know," Moonlight explained.

Facing him, I stared hard into his eyes and labored in my explanation. "She resisted. She tried to fight them off. She refused to submit...." I squeezed my eyes shut in a feeble attempt to block the memory. "She is gone."

"Perhaps if you tell us, you will relieve yourself of this burden, Mrs. Eubank," Captain Baumer said in German.

I looked up at him, reassured by his quick nod of encouragement. I continued, "They, they tied her limbs...." I wretched. "And they stretched her between two horses." Dry heaves brought an immediate response as hankies were yanked from pockets and placed in my hands. Collectively, the men in the room lowered their heads and tried to count the knots in the wood floor. They waited.

Colonel Moonlight said delicately, "Go on."

"She was torn apart...."

As soon as the words slipped from my lips, the details poured out. "I tried! I tried to stop him! I offered myself in return for her life. Take me instead! Big Crow! Just let her live! He laughed as the poor woman screamed and struggled."

I watched soldiers mouth the name to others. Big Crow? *The* Big Crow? They all knew where *he* was hanging.

My head jerked up, and I frantically looked around the room. It was as if the scene was replaying itself in real time. "Noooo!" I shouted maniacally. "Stop!"

Then a stone-cold statue stood slack in the middle of the room, head down, arms dangling.

It was me.

Where was I? Looking about, I saw the room. I was at the fort. Covering my eyes with my hands, I sank into a chair. The austere, whitewashed room grew dark. Moments passed. I collected my deranged thoughts and added, "She lived...after...for a while," I whispered. "I could do nothing...."

Nothing....

chapter fifty-eight

Fate Absolute

24 May 1865
Fort Laramie, Dakotah Territory

Fort Laramie, May 17, 1865 – General Moonlight has just captured the Indians, Two Face and band, who had Mrs. Ewbanks prisoner. She was captured by the Cheyennes last August on the Little Blue. Her little girl was taken to Denver with Miss Roper. The mother is very anxious to know if she is still there; please enquire and answer. Any person having knowledge of the little girl in question will please leave word at this office:

Rocky Mountain Daily News
May 19, 1865

E liza Bullock guided me to her lovely, cottage-style home nestled twenty yards northeast of the store. Its lace curtains and welcoming porch seemed so incongruent with the austere buildings scattered within the confines of the fort. A yellow rose grew to the side of the step, its soft petals scattered along the path. Entering the parlor, I noticed everything was orderly. A small fire crackled on the hearth; its glow reflected on the polished floor. The faint aroma of fresh-baked bread welcomed and comforted me. A walnut secretary lay open on a table revealing the accessories of a woman who knew her business, wrote letters, and took her leisure in books.

"Come, come, Mrs. Eubank. Let us sit a while, get to know one another. I am always pleased to meet a new friend in this remote outpost." She smiled warmly and tickled Willie under the chin.

We were both apprehensive, and I felt my cheeks flush at her kind reception. I was embarrassed to speak to her since the meeting with the officers. My mental state had been abysmal.

Today, though, our conversation passed amiably, but I struggled with the mundane subjects of butter, biscuits, and button-topped shoes. I was ill at ease among the friendly people of the fort, for I knew my mind was injured. Reason simply appeared on the edges of my façade, but my face wore the expression of a wild animal—leery, wary, and expectant of danger. When Nancy left, my life among the Cheyenne and the Sioux became a lonely existence filled with silence and despair. No cheerful voices, no one to care if I lived or died. Often, I wondered what would become of me if my spirit left its mortal ties. Would my sun-bleached bones lie alone on the stark plains—half-eaten by the wolf, the bear, the raven?

I was thankful to the Lord above for the end of those long days of privation, hunger, and thirst. Yet, the gratitude had not developed roots; it applied no salve to the deeper wounds. It would come with time. I knew it would. However, I was reluctant to share the details of my life before the massacre of my family. I knew Mrs. Bullock was curious. Respectfully, she did not pry and directed the conversation to light-hearted topics, which included her history and that of her husband and how they had come to live at Fort Laramie.

As the conversation stalled, I looked down at my hands, which were fidgeting and plucking at the skirt of my dress. I stopped at once. So many oddities accompanied me from the Indian camps—a result of the trauma I carried within. But I had to ask. I so wanted to know the details. I looked into the older woman's pleasant face and felt safe.

"Mrs. Bullock, I have heard rumors, but ah…I am wondering…can you tell me about my friend, Mrs. Morton? I am so relieved she was released. Did you have a chance to speak to her? Was she well?" I had so many questions. I tried to steady myself against the tide of memories washing over me. I clammed up, waiting for her response.

"Indeed!" replied Mrs. Bullock. "I have happy news to report." She smiled and took a sip from her little, blue floral teacup. Like my own china set. At home. No more. "From the beginning," she said, clearing her throat. "Well, Mrs. Sarah Larimer lived here with her husband until last month when they moved to Denver. She herself had been a captive. She was friendly with the Indians living around the fort you know." I stared blankly at Mrs. Bullock as she plowed ahead. "The loafer squaws mentioned a white woman living in an Arapaho village up north. The Indians got word of a ransom connected to the release of the woman and decided to start their inquiries with Mrs. Larimer."

Mrs. Bullock rose from the table and rustled through the papers on her desk. "Here it is!" she exclaimed, lifting a wrinkled fort newspaper. She handed it to me and directed me to the item she wanted me to read.

Garrison-Deer Creek
Dec 26' 1864

    Jules Ecoffey is hereby authorized to proceed in the capacity of a messenger of the Military Authority Commanding in this Section to the Cheyenne Village North of this station eighty miles more or less a view to in order to procure by trade or purchase a white woman said to be held by the Cheyenne Indians as a prisoner and he shall be treated while acting upon the duty herein assigned him with the respect due to his mission.

Signed,
G Marshall
Capt. 11th Ohio Vol. Cav.
Commissioned

"Mrs. Larimer communicated this information with the commander and an immediate plan for Mrs. Morton's rescue was set in motion. Mr. Reshaw, the old mountain man in these parts, offered to send his half-breed son with gifts of sugar, coffee, blankets, and horses. Surprisingly, he returned without the woman. Apparently, he was rudely inappropriate to her." Mrs. Bullock lowered her voice and added confidentially, "I could have told them he was not to be trusted—that one!"

I found my eyes wandering back to the Deer Creek order. Were Nancy and I held captive in Sitting Bull's village at the same time?

Mrs. Bullock interrupted my thoughts. "Mrs. Morton refused his offer of rescue and begged her chief to provide a different escort. The chief was angry and ordered the half-breed out of the village saying, 'a man of honor shall come for her, or I will wait until the snows have left the ground and then carry her to the fort myself.' Two weeks later, the French trader, Mr. Jules Ecoffey, accompanied by a Sioux named Suisnett and an Arapaho called Black Eyes, was sent after her. Loaded with even more gifts, plus money totaling $1,700, the chief was not satisfied. He asked for two of the commander's prized horses. They were a handsome and swift pair! After the trade, the Indians reneged on the agreement and desired the return of Mrs. Morton; and the chase was on. Her harrowing escape proved difficult, for it occurred during a terrible cold snap last January." Mrs. Bullock shivered in remembrance.

"Several Indians accompanied the traders out of the village—one being the Sioux Chief Big Foot and the other a Cheyenne Chief by the name of Big Crow." She focused intently on my reaction. "Ah, yes," she said gently. "Mrs. Morton shared many things about the fiend." She paused, "You know he is the one hanging now just outside the fort?"

I nodded and looked down at my belly, which I stroked subconsciously. The motion had not gone undetected by Mrs. Bullock. She set her cup carefully into its saucer and stared out the window. Moments later, she sighed and picked up the story.

"Mrs. Morton suffered greatly on the journey here, but the entire fort welcomed her and celebrated her arrival." Mrs. Bullock blinked at me, then checked herself as she realized my reception had taken a different turn. My wretched and shamefully obvious condition tempered any jubilation.

"It was during supper on the eve of Mrs. Morton's arrival that the conversation turned to her experiences, which she freely shared being caught up in the fanfare of the moment. She somberly told of Big Crow's abhorrent conduct, the massacre of the wagon train, and his constant torture of her. The perpetrator parted ways with the rescuers before nearing Laramie. I suspect Big Crow had designs on ending her life before she reached us but never had the opportunity. The Provost Marshall, Lieutenant Triggs, sat at our table that night and ordered troops to arrest the offender at once. He was taken at Deer Creek Station and put in irons, then brought here where he spent three months in the guardhouse."

It was confirmed! The Indian swinging from the gallows on the hill west of the fort was Big Crow! My most dangerous nemesis was truly dead! I tried to calm the hammering in my head.

Mrs. Bullock quietly sipped her lukewarm tea, contemplating. "That Cheyenne was a demon, Mrs. Eubank!" she uttered in disgust. "A woman's scalp was fastened to his belt when he was brought in."

I looked up at this observation. Little did she know....

Mrs. Bullock warmed to the more gruesome aspects of the story. With a shake of her head as if incredulous of the details, she launched into a description of the hanging.

"As it happens, in the middle of February, the 11th Ohio returned from battles at Rush Creek and Mud Springs, feeling a little stung by the Indians' cunning. These soldiers broke into the guardhouse and dragged Big Crow out with a rope—ball and chain still affixed to his leg. A mob joined in, and soon they were pulling him apart in a tug of war. Colonel Collins heard the hoopla, pushed through the men, and with a swing of his sword, cut the rope. The soldiers collapsed into heaps on either end. Mr. Bullock says these new companies of soldiers are very undisciplined."

I swallowed hard. Sweat dripped down the back of my neck.

"Big Crow sat in his cell until just last month when General Connor sent a telegram ordering him hung in chains. His body was to remain suspended as a grisly warning to the tribes."

I watched the trembling in my right leg. Discretely, I pressed on it to stop the twitching. What was wrong with me? I developed nervous tics at the oddest moments.

"On April twenty-fourth, that insolent Cheyenne was taken to the gallows while singing his death song. Secured by chains around his neck, hands tied in front of him, he stood defiantly inside the wagon box. As it rolled forward, he grabbed the chain and with the strength of a bear, climbed to the top of the gallows."

I was feeling a bit faint. The man was not human. Big Crow, the Chief of the Crooked Lance Society, would fight the whites to the bitter end. "Did they shoot him?" I asked tremulously.

"Not exactly. The order for the hanging stood. The soldiers pushed a strong, Swedish comrade forward, and he scaled the scaffold. A struggle ensued, and both the Swede and the chief fell to the ground. A thoroughly distasteful event."

She coughed quietly behind her hand. "There was to be no reprieve. Big Crow was successfully hanged the second time. A squad fired bullets twice into his body to finish him off. He often threatened to kill more white people, starting with Mrs. Morton. He claimed he would take her scalp, and she would never return home."

Yes indeed, I thought. He would follow through on a threat and was never to be underestimated. I truly hoped it was his body swinging from the gallows.

"Tsk, the poor woman never felt safe here and to tell you the truth, the entire fort was relieved when a proper escort was arranged for her departure east. She left on February twenty-sixth, and I have since received a letter. She is reunited with her parents. Thank the Lord," sighed Mrs. Bullock.

Willie played on the floor near us. He was a silent observer of the new sights around him. Mrs. Bullock had given him a spoon to play with, but he preferred to stare at the white woman's face as she talked. Her language, her appearance, her home were all strangeness to the child. In his memory, he held only visions of Indians, their lodges, their things.

I marveled at the strength, stamina, and bravery of the women who followed their men into such dangerous and remote outposts as Fort Laramie. I had done the same. Looking back, however, I now understood the risks. I excused myself amid Mrs. Bullock's prolific and loving ministrations. Lifting Willie into my arms, I headed for the door.

She stopped me and pleaded, "Please visit again before you leave. Take heart, Mrs. Eubank. You will be home soon." She kissed me on the cheek, then focused on the child and wiggled his hand playfully. "Master Willie, you have been such a good boy! He is a perfect little gentleman!" Looking at me, she asked, "Does he ever cry?"

The question stabbed my heart. I shook my head and mumbled something polite. Mrs. Bullock did not see his scars and knew nothing of his suffering. Of course, she would not understand the reason for his reticence. My baby learned not to cry from the squaws, who harshly discouraged it. Tears brimmed along my lashes, and I began to tremble.

"Oh dear," frowned Mrs. Bullock. "I have upset you. Now you must go home and rest." Her tender sympathies lay like a salve on my soul.

I smiled weakly at the ever-hospitable sutler's wife and bid her farewell. I was nauseous and shaken. The grisly and brutal details of life on the frontier continued to pile up in the crevices of my emotions. I was overwhelmed, to say the least.

Quickly crossing the parade grounds, I hurried toward the commander's office. Thankful for our safe spot inside the white man's fortress, I knew the journey ahead would be fraught with danger. Would the worry ever subside? The entwined fates of Nancy, Big Crow, and myself ended with the execution of our tormentor. His was a brutal path from which he could not escape the foregone conclusion. He lived by violence and died by it. Big Crow was dead; yet, Nancy, Willie, and I were still alive— our fates no longer controlled by the wicked. We were free of his threats, and I was glad he would never hurt another. But the pity and fear I felt for all those lost simmered in my soul. Why does evil attach itself so absolutely to the human condition?

I looked at Willie's face. The child was engrossed by the constant motion of the fort and things never seen before. Buildings, soldiers, the snapping flag atop the pole at the center of the parade grounds—all new and sometimes scary. Yet, he was adaptable. Children are such miracles!

I kept an eye on the lookout for Colonel Moonlight and, fortunately, intercepted him as he stepped out the door of his office. "Excuse me, sir," I called as I approached him. The brilliant prairie sun blinded me momentarily as I stepped closer to look at the man who turned to face me. "I have a request to make, if you please."

His eyebrows shot up, but he kindly replied, "How may I assist you, Mrs. Eubank?"

"I would like to send a telegram. To Denver," I added, then hurried on with my explanation. "Would it be possible to contact the newspaper there in the hopes of getting word to my family who work as teamsters? They may still reside in the city. Also, I hope to obtain word of my daughter," I concluded, carefully tucking back the rising emotions. I wished to appear dignified in his presence.

"I think the sutler, Mr. Bullock, will be pleased to assist you with the telegram," he said, then quickly added, "Please step into my office. I have several items for you."

Colonel Moonlight held the door open as I stepped into the room. I was more lucid than I was a week ago. Our recovery was slow, but Willie and I were gaining ground. I nearly fainted when I spotted my satchel on his desk.

"Oh! Colonel Moonlight! My satchel! How did you come by it?"

"A few weeks ago, soldiers found it with your note. We were certainly surprised to learn of your existence." The colonel smiled generously. "I also have this pouch. It was found on the saddle of one of Two Face's horses. Might it belong to you?"

I recognized the deerskin bag which Two Face tied to my saddle horn the morning we left Blackfoot's band. Looking at the officer, I paused, then opened the bag. It was my dress! Or what was left of it. I examined the thin, faded calico I had worn on the day of my capture. Its tattered, blue fabric stirred memories of Will. He loved the dress. I clung to it— a precious reminder of our final day together. What would Will think of me today? Was I a woman of fortitude, a fire-haired warrior? Or just a deranged soul never to be redeemed. It did not matter, for I met each new sunrise with duty clear in my mind. Protect his son. Redeem our family. Raise a Eubank man.

Colonel Moonlight pensively interrupted my thoughts by clearing his throat. "Excuse me, ma'am. There is something else. Surprised, I waited as he opened his desk drawer to retrieve an envelope. "Two Face requested I give you this."

Confused, I reached for the packet and opened it.

"Two hundred and seventy dollars," said the colonel, answering my questioning expression. "Two hundred and twenty were in Two Face's possession, and we found another fifty dollars among the others arrested. He said it might as well be yours. He would not need it where he was going."

Flabbergasted, I froze, looked at the bills, then at the officer.

"It is yours," he reassured. "It will help you purchase things for your journey. In a week's time, you are leaving with a military escort to head east."

Pleased by the news, my cheeks flushed with a warm tingle.

"And, may I say," he added delicately. "You are looking well, Mrs. Eubank."

"Thank you, sir," I replied, as the blushing of my cheeks grew to full bloom. "I am much improved." I turned to leave, and then it dawned on me. "Colonel Moonlight, you said Two Face would not need this money where he was going. Where might that be?"

"The Happy Hunting Grounds. I suspect he will be executed once proceedings are completed."

"Wait! Sir! Two Face…he…." I tried to formulate my plea. "He should be spared!" I said emphatically.

The colonel stopped in his tracks and stared hard into my face. "Madam, I do not understand. The mistreatment you endured. He must be held accountable!"

"No! Others. Yes, Blackfoot. But I must object. Not Two Face! Please! He helped me—he saved us from certain death many times! I beg you, please. Not Two Face!"

Moonlight interrupted, "This is quite unusual, Mrs. Eubank. The victim speaking on behalf of the wrong doer." He stared at me through new eyes as though any decent woman would not boldly plead for an Indian's life.

Staying quiet, I noticed his stern demeanor thaw a little. "Mr. Bullock pleads for the life of Two Face as well." Lifting a paper from his desk, the colonel added, "We found this letter from Colonel Fleming in your satchel. Mr. Two Face claimed to be a good Indian. To protect his band, he asked for a letter to present should they encounter soldiers. Mrs. Eubank, is he a "good" Indian as he professes?"

Remembering my promise to Two Face, I looked in Moonlight's eyes and nodded yes. "It would be a great injustice. You must not do this!"

Colonel Moonlight sighed and summed up the discussion. "Perhaps I will investigate things further. Although, the outcome will not be up to me. General Connor will be apprised of the matter. I will take your personal views into consideration."

"Thank you, sir," I sputtered. I felt no reassurance.

"Yes," he replied. "We must prepare for a trial once General Connor arrives."

Concerned and dismayed, I left the man's office and decided to find Mr. Bullock.

———•———

Now that sanity was returning in spurts and starts, I set my course to communicate with our family. They needed to hear from me. Telegrams must be composed and sent. Perhaps it was possible to find Belle. My heart skipped a beat. Then my thoughts turned to my mother-in-law Ruth. I must tell of her granddaughter's disappearance and her grandson's survival. After nearly a year in captivity, we must have been given up as dead. As I bounced Willie along in my arms, I rejoiced. The little man had endured. He had a life in front of him.

"Grandmother Ruth will be so very pleased to see you!" I exclaimed. "You look more like your father every day," I whispered as I kissed his rosy cheek.

Then I checked myself. The future ahead of us would be without William. I was a widow and Willie was fatherless. I stopped and stared hard at my son. He would live, become a man, and grow old.

But for now, he was…fresh and fragile as a seedling in spring.

chapter fifty-nine

Verdict

25 May 1865
Fort Laramie, Dakotah Territory

My father, First Lieut. James G. Smith, Co. A, 7th Iowa Cav. was on duty as Officer of the Day, and saw that the Indians were all put under guard, and the four chiefs were taken to the blacksmith shop and irons riveted on them by his orders. Mrs. Eubanks did intercede all she could for one of the young chiefs who saved her babe....

George H. Smith

Fury was palpable around the fort. The sun had set twenty minutes earlier, yet the soldiers of the California and Colorado regiments continued to ride a rising tide of indignation. Tales of the brutal outrages suffered by Mrs. Eubank were repeated with unrestrained fervor. The unspoken story behind the details enflamed the men's imaginations— fueling threats on their lips and revenge in their hearts. William Bullock stood behind the counter of his store and watched the angry crowd of customers. He knew the Indians locked in the post guardhouse would not be safe for long.

Earlier that morning, Charley Elliston, Big Mouth, and Blackfoot's band arrived at the boat crossing near the fort. The clan's women and children were miles behind pulling lodges and supplies. The tribe was expectant of the good will and gifts to be given. Charlie Gereau and a small group of Big Mouth's Indian scouts met them at the ferry.

"Two Face is in the guardhouse. You should not have come. You have been deceived," said Gereau.

Blackfoot's son, Thunder Bear, looked at his father in surprise. His father was equally perplexed. Gereau continued, "The white woman told of the bad things you have done. The commanders have tricked you into coming. There is no ransom. They intend to hold you responsible."

"We buy Whe-Ho with own ponies," insisted Blackfoot.

The six, young warriors with Blackfoot grew uneasy and looked from Big Mouth to Gereau, then back to Blackfoot. What was happening? They had come to help carry the rewards for their band's good intentions back to camp.

Without warning, the soldiers drew their weapons. A second group of troops charged over the rise. Instantly, Blackfoot and his stepsons, Standing Cloud and Red Dog, were restrained. His son refused to go down willingly. As Thunder Bear struggled to free himself, Blackfoot spoke, "Son, you do no wrong. Now not time to fight. They free you soon."

Two adolescent braves, Long Legged Wolf and Yellow Bear, took their cue from Blackfoot and surrendered. All were confident they would be freed. After all, the chief was friendly to the whites and Two Face had the "good paper."

A remuda of stolen government horses and mules was confiscated as proof of the serious crime of livestock theft. Upon the Indians' arrival, the fort's occupants reveled in their arrest. Rumors swirled. These were the Indians responsible for stealing women and children. The reports of murder and mayhem throughout the winter fed a deep desire to punish the Sioux. Now the fort's occupants celebrated the capture of the guilty. The officer of the day chained Blackfoot and his braves in irons, then secured them in the guardhouse with Two Face.

Big Mouth and Charles Elliston reported to the commander's office. Looking up from the papers on his desk, Colonel Moonlight motioned for the men to sit with the bevy of officers in attendance. He needed details for the Indians' trial preliminaries. Evidence presented would aid in the determination of guilt or innocence. Foregoing all pleasantries, the commander said, "I expect a full report of the mission. Charley, you may begin."

Elliston cleared his throat and nodded. "Big Mouth and I, along with ten Indian police, rode to the Snake Fork. We entered Blackfoot's village after dark. I instructed the men to keep an eye on the chief in case he suspected something amiss and tried to escape. Big Mouth implied the soldiers would welcome his entire band to the fort. They would receive gifts. Lured by promises, Blackfoot left with us early the next morning. The women and children followed with their lodges. They await word now."

"Good. Tell them all is well, and their men will be free soon. They are to make camp downriver at Bordeaux's with the Brulés," replied Moonlight. "It is important not to alarm them."

Charles Gereau, clearly unsettled by the turn of events, spoke what was on his mind. "Colonel Moonlight," he began, "there are two adolescents taken prisoner. I suggest they be released."

Moonlight considered this latest information. He was not totally convinced of their youth but did not want a scandal to arise for the condemnation of children. "Have them weighed on the platform in the quarter master's supply building. If they are truly youths, provide them with rations and send them to their mothers. Please assure the tribe the remaining prisoners will return. We do not want an uprising."

The colonel stood, clasped his hands behind his back, and began a formal accounting of the crimes for which the chiefs were accused. "Mrs. Eubank has testified of her capture and removal from her home on the Little Blue. Cheyenne Dog Soldiers killed members of her family in a widespread massacre last August. Sioux and Arapaho tribes are implicated as well. She shared details of her harrowing journey. The Indians took her to the Arkansas River camp where the whole village ravished her and almost killed her. Kept naked, she was forced to perform hard labor as their slave."

The officers sat in silence as they digested the case presented before them. All thoughts were on their mothers, sisters, and wives.

Moonlight continued, "Mrs. Eubank identifies the Sioux chiefs, Two Face and Blackfoot, as among those who perpetrated the raid on the Eubank Ranche. They also traded with the Cheyenne at Sand Creek to regain possession of her back in November."

"Sand Creek?" interrupted Colonel Baumer. "Was the poor woman at Sand Creek during the battle?"

"It appears so," replied Moonlight. "Then she was kept by roving bands of warriors who sought to avenge those killed. She suffered while in their hands." He shook his head. "She is a ruined woman now. Her treatment was beastly, and she arrived here in a wretched condition. She has seen much and sufficiently supplied the grim details of offenses against herself and others. It is my desire to make an example of these chiefs. Indians of like character must be made aware retaliation will be swift for any who commit outrages upon the white race."

The officers murmured in agreement. Big Mouth and Elliston looked questioningly at one another. Were the Indians in the guardhouse truly responsible?

Moonlight continued, "Now I have met with Mr. Two Face and Mr. Blackfoot. They claim to have rescued her from the hostiles. Despite their so-called honorable intentions, I suggest we believe the victim's testimony, although it is rather disjointed given its atrocious nature and her mental condition."

The commander sat down to peruse the notes taken from his interview with Two Face and Blackfoot. "I interrogated the prisoners, and as the interview deteriorated, the chiefs came to realize I mean business. They changed their tune and admitted to their crimes. They confessed to killing many whites and threatened to kill more if free. Defiant buggers!"

Lt. Colonel Baumer spoke up. "What is the verdict? Mrs. Eubank has suggested Two Face was not especially cruel to her. Should that be a consideration?"

"No. The evidence is sufficient and compelling enough that Two Face and Blackfoot should be executed. Who concurs?"

The officers responded with a unified verdict. "Aye, aye, aye."

"Good. I will telegraph General Connor for specific orders. You are dismissed!"

———————

News of the verdict reached the sutler's store. Bullock noticed a shift in the crowd's mood. The concerned fort inhabitants were quickly becoming an unruly mob. The officers should be notified of this turn of events. Before he could act, a veteran Indian fighter leapt upon a barrel near the counter and spewed curses upon all Indians and their actions. He loudly challenged the manhood of the spectators and called upon all frontiersmen to avenge the violations of decency. Furthering the incitement, he added details of other women and children whose captivity and murders were still fresh on the minds of the throng. It was savage! The response must be quick and decisive! It was time to teach those responsible a lesson!

The crowd roared in agreement, and the entire stomping roomful of men spilled out the doors into the street. "To the guardhouse!" they yelled.

Four soldiers took it upon themselves to force the steel bars open. They hacked at the grating with axes, and it fell with a loud clatter. The guardhouse was breached. Sentries posted at the door knew better than to interfere with the vigilantes. The chiefs and four young braves were jerked through the door. They emerged to find themselves surrounded by a kicking, pushing, mauling, screaming crowd of soldiers and civilians.

Targeting Blackfoot's son, two grizzled trappers dragged the terrified Thunder Bear to the flagpole at the center of the parade grounds. The leader of the mob yelled, "Tie him! Tie his big red hands to the flagpole, and cut his dirty scalp from him!"

Hearing the commotion, I watched from between the curtains of my quarters facing the parade grounds. The blunt end of a rifle butt thwarted the young brave's effort to escape. Just as a knife was produced, another voice echoed from the crowd. "Bring the woman! She shall have her own revenge!" The yelling increased as the crowd shifted its flow in my direction.

Loud scraping feet tramped to my door, and a persistent knocking startled me. Before I could turn the mob away, the door was kicked open. I was hauled out by the not so gentle hands of my "benefactors." Willie was left standing and squalling in the middle of the floor. Within moments, I was scooped up and deposited in front of Thunder Bear with a long skinning knife in my hand. Shoved toward the young brave, shouts of "Finish him!" "Kill the savage!" filled the air.

During the tussle, my hair had fallen from its bun and blew wildly about my face. Shaken and panting, I shook its matted mop from my eyes. Vision was difficult in the gathering dusk. I tried to make sense of the high-pitched clamor around me.

Then familiar dark eyes met mine. Two Face was bleeding from his nose and mouth. Silently, he tipped his head toward the flagpole and shook his head no. The mob cursed him, and he disappeared from sight into a mass of swinging arms and kicking boots.

Those holding the captive stepped aside to grant me access to the victim. Fright was evident on Thunder Bear's face. Instantly, I remembered that look. It was the same expression he wore when he swam the Arkansas River after Willie's cradleboard months earlier. Thunder Bear and I had a lengthy and troubled history. He could not have been more than twenty, but was, in my mind, an extension of his father, whom I detested with every bone in my body. Yet, his death would supply no comfort to me. No! I would not take his life.

I stared into the resolute face of the buckskin clad trapper who held the knife in my hand. His face blazed with triumph at the prospect of retaliation, and he thrust my hand forward. Pressed against him, I summoned all the strength I could. With feet planted firmly, I threw myself backward against the crowd. The movement caught them by surprise. Suddenly, released from the raging crush of bodies behind me, I stood solidly in front of Thunder Bear. Lowering my free arm, the knife clattered to the ground.

"No! I cannot!" I shouted. "Stop this bloodshed! I will not take the life of another!"

The mob went silent.

Holding my arm, a young frontiersman coaxed me away from the scene. "Come, Mrs. Eubank. I will see you safely away...."

Rumbling voices directed threats at me. They grew louder. "Indian lover!" one shouted. "Dishonorable woman!" spat another.

Led onto the porch, my rescuer tipped his hat and said, "Finn Burnett at your service, ma'am. With your permission, I think I will abide awhile. Just in case...."

Frightened by the mob's intensity and their accusations against me, I gathered Willie into my arms and blockaded the door. Watching from the window, I saw the rabble rousers tie a rope around Thunder Bear's neck. His tormentors pulled him off his feet and dragged him through the dirt. He regained his footing and stood only to be tripped again. Lugged through the dust, the rope tightened around his neck. The incensed crowd would not be denied, and their ire rose against the bundle of humanity struggling on the ground.

Mr. Burnett stood, arms crossed, on the step, but the unruly bunch was focused on the guilty. Passing us, they steered the victims toward the commander's office. At that moment, Colonel Baumer stepped onto the landing. The mob stalled in front of him, unsure of the consequences for disrespecting military authority. Civilians were curious where his sympathies rested.

"Men!" he called firmly. "Listen to me!"

The beatings and jeering descended into mumbling and cursing.

"I understand your hatred for the actions of these savages, and I respect your manhood in desiring to make an example of them so other Indians will remember. But there is something beyond our present feelings to consider...."

Dangling this tempting bit of information before the mob, Baumer cleverly allied himself to his subordinates. "The result we desire tonight can be accomplished properly and officially if we proceed through military channels."

Boos and heckles were thrown at the colonel, but he pushed on louder.

"If we continue as we have started, none of you will be allowed to join General Connor's expedition! All will be confined to quarters; some of you most assuredly will be severely dealt with." Baumer paused for effect, then adopted a conciliatory tone. "Let me urge you to put these Indians back into the guardhouse while I telegraph the general at Fort Sedgwick for instructions. I know him to be fair and as much of a man as any one of us. I am sure he will tell us to go ahead with what we all desire."

The outraged mob wavered. Then a voice from the rear of the conflagration shouted, "But what if the general says to let them go?"

Hoarse from the evening's ferocity, gravelly voices demanded an answer to the fresh scenario.

Baumer paused as if searching for wisdom to settle this matter before he lost control of the entire fort. "In that case, I will wash my hands of all responsibility," he replied. "You can do as you wish—if that happens."

Arguments briefly broke out, but the wind had picked up and cooled the tempers of the avengers. It was true. The general was known to be a man of his word. He should be trusted with the dispensing of justice. The crowd parted as Baumer instructed a dozen soldiers to return the Indians to the guardhouse.

The horde was not finished. They drifted to the tiny telegraph office and were joined by the operator pulled from his supper. A telegram to General Connor must be sent at once! Would the killing be a "by the book" military affair, or would a lynching be the order of the night? I overheard discussion of what the hoped-for answer would entail.

To the milling throng's satisfaction, three soldiers were allowed to stand inside the small office. In the failing light, I could see the pale faces and red-rimmed eyes of the tense participants as lantern light shone through the window and door. Tobacco smoke soon obscured the happenings inside the office. All leaned over the operator's shoulder in anticipation of the instrument's fateful decision.

Minutes passed, and it seemed that resolution would have to wait until morning. I noticed the telegraph operator lean forward followed by the crowd inside and outside of the office. Moments later, a loud voice relayed General Connor's response:

> ...hang Two Face and Black Foot with fifth chains. After hanging twenty minutes, fire a volley of twenty pieces at them, and leave them hanging until further order.

I shivered, stepped inside my room, and closed the door, which did nothing to smother the cheers of the throng outside.

I realized I could do nothing to stop the execution of Two Face!

Headquarters, North Sub District of the Plains
Fort Laramie, Dakotah Territory
May 25, 1865

Special Orders No. 4

The Indian Chiefs Two Face and Black Foot of the Sioux nation, Oglala Tribe now in confinement at this post. Will be hung tomorrow at 2 p.m. as an example to all Indians of like character and in retaliation for the many wrongs and outrages they have committed on the white race. Abundant and satisfactory proof of which has been furnished at these head quarters, viz murdering white men, women and children, keeping white women prisoners and treating them like brutes, stealing govt property and inciting the Sioux and Cheyennes to make war on the whites.

The Commanding Officer of Fort Laramie is charged with the execution of this order and will see it properly and promptly carried out. The execution will be conducted in a sober soldierly manner and the bodies will be left hanging as a warning to others. No citizen or soldiers, nor Indian will be permitted to visit or touch the dead bodies without permission from these headquarters or that of the post.

By order of Colonel T. Moonlight
11th Kansas Cavalry

chapter sixty

A Little Hasty

26 May 1865
Fort Laramie, Dakotah Territory

It matters not how strait the gate,
How charged with punishments the scroll,
I am the master of my fate: I am the captain of my soul.

William Ernest Henley

Two Face and Blackfoot sit manacled in the wagon box, wrists bleeding, hands tied in front, elbows chained behind. Ropes encircle their knees and ankles. Pain shoots through their shoulders with each bounce of the wheels in the ruts of the road. The wagon meanders past the limp flags atop the pole and out through the gates of Fort Laramie. In a drizzling rain, the prisoners turn north. Below, smoke-like clouds billow and boil between the ridges. Low-slung clouds and a drifting chill fill the depressions of nearby rolling hills.

Standing rain-streaked and forlorn atop the plateau, newly erected gallows consist of upright posts and a cross beam. One lone, decayed body sways from a nearby scaffold. The chains creak and rattle, disturbing the morning's silence. Stolid mules lean into their harnesses as they haul their human cargo up the sloping hill. A mounted column of soldiers follows as the fort band plays the "Dead March in Saul."

The white-walled fort grows smaller in the distance. Two Face looks into the eyes of Blackfoot. He sees no fear. They have known each other their entire lives. A low vibration emanates from Blackfoot's chest. He hums his death song. Its intensity increases with every breath. His eyes close…remembering. The two chiefs ride on, empty faces upturned, asking the rain to freshen the reservoirs of their spirits.

"Hold your cup, and I will fill it. Drink of solitude. Taste its mortal chill," replies the Creator. "Remain still. Your earthly walk ends. A sacred journey lies ahead."

Every warrior knows his steps on the earth will grow short, someday to stop. The death chant begins….

Nothing stays the same except the earth and mountains.
Man is like the prairie grass.
Today it flourishes, tomorrow it withers and is cast into the fire.
Nothing lives forever, nothing lives for long,
Except the earth and the mountains.

The jingle of the traces joins the chimes of chains which dangle from the scaffold. Muffled voices mingle as soldiers instruct the driver to pull under the cross beam. The wagon halts. The sheen of the new wood and droplets of rain reflect the overcast clouds in varying shades of gray. Rough hands lift each of the chiefs. Now standing, the song is strong.

A soldier climbs the scaffold to check the iron bolts on the chains. No mistakes this time. No rope nooses to snap the neck. Too quick. Wide manacles attach to fifth chains and drop beside each head. The iron is bolted about each neck. Braids of hair are pulled out and draped on the shoulders. Nothing must pad the bare neck. More bolts.

It will not be an easy death. It will not be a quick death. It will not be an honorable death.

The chant rises higher, rings pure through the air. Two Face looks to the hills. The clouds open and a lone shaft of sunlight finds him. Astride their war horses, his people wait proudly. Spotted Tail, Thunder Bear, others. They hear his voice—a comfort to the spirit of the Oglala. His death chant is loud and splits the sky, melding with Blackfoot's song.

Blood thrums through his ears, leaving him deaf. Soldier chief is talking. Words mean nothing. No crime. No wrong. The paper is folded and returned to the pocket. The bugle's strain announces their fate. So many strange faces, so many eyes. Watching, waiting. It is time to die. To his ears, his voice sounds raspy, choked, distant.

I am Ite Nunjpa, of the Tapisleca band.
I am Two Face of the Spleen band.
Oglala Mother! Cheyenne Father!
Meah washts!
I am brave!

Lungs bursting, the song of Two Face carries his respect to those watching a leader's departure. Spotted Tail raises his lance in farewell. The feathers along its length flutter in the breeze. Two Face breathes deeply. He sees his people. It is good they have come. He is not alone among so many spirits.

The driver holds the reins, reaches down, and releases the wheel brake. The soldier chief holds his saber high. The silent crowd waits. A flash of metal, and the saber drops. Reins snap. Mules lurch forward, and the wagon drags away. Moccasin feet scrabble the box, paw the wood. Slowly at first, then a burst—the platform is gone.

The plunge, the jerk. A shuddering impact shocks the body. Bones pop. Chanting stops. Exhale. Cannot breathe. Back arched. Eyes bulging. Crossbeam creaking.

Now kicking. Spinning. Bucking. Choking. Muscles clench and fight. Fingers grasp the waist chain. Lightning flashes. Sparks fly at the edges of his orbs. Searing pain at the neck. Hands cannot reach. Feet cannot stand.

Breaths. Futile. Blackness. Warm wetness streams down the legs. Life drains through the toes. Minutes pass. Floundering. Strength unknown urges the warrior to battle. Death does not come.

Behind the darkness, he sees her eyes like winter sky. Fire-Hair.

The soldier chief shouts. Rifles. Shots. Stabbing assault. Muscles loosen, relax, stretch. He longs to touch the earth. Toes extend searching. A cool breeze caresses his face. Another volley…and his heart bursts, shatters into shreds of fluttering flesh. Pumps no more.

Spirit vanishes like a flame extinguished—

He listens….
A whinny.
Unbound, his mind summons across the distance.
No time, no space, no natural law.
The sky opens. Light pours like a waterfall filling a golden cup.
It envelops him.
The death mask shatters, his earthly garb is cast aside.

A shining warrior appears. The sun's benediction warms him.
The stallion flies to him, whickering at the sight of its master.
He drops astride its back.
They are free to roam the world unfettered.
A squeeze and they race away—up the hill and through the clouds.
A flash of mane and tail, then *Toksa. Good-bye.*
Two Face is gone.

———•———

Overlooking the plateau, Spotted Tail and Thunder Bear sat on their ponies and soberly watched the scene below. Thunder Bear narrowly escaped the vigilante mob before his release from the fort. The scene below was like a descending storm. They had a bird's eye view of the white man's justice.

News of the pending execution reached the Indian villages on the outskirts of Bordeaux's trading post early that morning. Racing into camp on a lathered pony, the Oglala rider announced the soldiers would soon hang Two Face and Blackfoot! Hoping to stop the execution Spotted Tail and several others rode fast to the fort. Determined to rescue his father, Thunder Bear concealed a revolver beneath his shirt. But it was too late. The hanging was underway.

The wise Spotted Tail noticed the weapon but knew there was nothing the youth could do. The concerned elder spoke instead. "Big wrong done to us, Thunder Bear. We go to war soon; then we avenge the deaths of our leaders. The whites will pay for this injustice. But we cannot stop it now."

The seething youth sat stonily upon his pony. His jaws flexed and his expression was grim. The Sioux chiefs should have intervened, but he knew to heed the counsel of the respected ones. Thunder Bear's heart burned black, and he scowled. "Why do they kill them? They brought the white woman in as the soldiers said," reasoned the boy. "Now they use chains to hang the innocent."

"Ah, ho," agreed Spotted Tail quietly. "Yes. It is a strange way to kill your enemy. To die in this way—with feet raised from earth, leaves the tortured spirit to hover, to never find the sacred trail."

"Spotted Tail, soldier chief has done bad thing," said the youth.

"Ung," grunted the chief. "Loafers say trader whiskey on his tongue. Turns good men to bad."

"What about the good paper? The one given to Two Face by fort chief moons ago," pleaded Thunder Bear.

"Some say Two Face gave to white woman to keep in her bag. Blue coats found bag in lodge. Soldier chief see it. But woman speak of many hard things done to her."

Two Face and Blackfoot struggled below…. Alone in their thoughts, each man beckoned the great spirit, asking for their safe passage to the land of the ancestors. The Land of Many Lodges. Rich in the good things of the earth. A lush and abundant place where all things live forever.

"We return? Give proper burial?"

"No, soldiers with spear guns will walk as they do for Big Crow. The Cheyenne's leg lies on the ground chained to big iron ball. It is a great offense," explained Spotted Tail. "All Indians on the Holy Road will see this."

The drizzling rain and low clouds matched the drab scene. It was a hard thing to watch men die in such a way. Thunder Bear would never forget. A volley of gunshots echoed sharply among the hills. Then another. He flinched and swore under his breath.

Spotted Tail declared, "Now the white men will say: They truly good Indians."

I did not want to see. I did not want to hear. I would not witness the deaths. I sat on a chair in the darkened room of my quarters. Why did Moonlight not honor my request and spare Two Face? Am I such a ruined woman that he would not listen?

I heard the wagons cross the parade grounds and roll through the heavy gates. I sat, eyes closed, head down, hands folded on my lap. Conflicted. I heard his voice. I covered my ears to stop the death chant. The wagon turned away.

Wait! One more look! I must see him! I ran to the gate and stopped. My knees faltered, and I leaned against the gate's great wooden post. Begging it to hold me up, I wrapped my arms around its solid foundation. Hold me up. Just long enough....

Back straight, Two Face left his past to face his future. His body was marked by struggle and fight.

I had lived as a slave dropped into a void. He had carried me through the fire more than once. Then we climbed one painful step at a time to reach this day. Would I be here if not for him?

Two Face. Quickly find the spirit trail.

I rested my head on the wet wood. Steady. Alone.

Gun shots in the distance.

I fell to my knees.

Heart on the ground.

I was a little hasty.
Bring them to Julesburg and give the wretches a trial.

General Connor

Dear General,
I obeyed your first order before I received the second.

Colonel Moonlight

357

chapter sixty-one

The Sutler

9 June 1865
Fort Laramie, Dakotah Territory

We have now the Indians hanging in sight of the post. This barbarity is only calculated to make them more vicious and determined....

William Bullock

The sutler, William Bullock, tripped going up the porch step. He repositioned his beaver skin top hat and smoothed his long sideburns and the whiskers on his chin. He took out a handkerchief and wiped his clean-shaven upper lip. No mustache for him. Based on an illustration of President Lincoln, he decided to adopt the same distinguished facial hair.

The view from the officer's post revealed a mass of wagons, tents, and paraphernalia on the plains outside the fort. Three thousand emigrants were camped across the valley. Waiting. In contrast, a thousand white cavalry tents were neatly positioned in preparation for a push into Indian country. Desperate to stop the ever-growing depredations along this expanse of the western plains, the army employed volunteer enlistees with no experience in fighting Indians. A warm body was the only requirement. The resentment Bullock harbored against the ill-prepared and incompetent 2nd California Cavalry festered. Their boastings and shenanigans were insufferable. He looked forward to the day their enlistments expired, and they returned to Fort Bridger. He would be glad when the volunteers were gone!

In comparison, battle-tested and military-hardened U.S. soldiers were a different breed. He admired these brave men stationed sparingly along the transcontinental routes—especially between Fort Kearny and South Pass. Colonel Moonlight positioned the 11th Kansas battalions between Fort Laramie and Platte Bridge. Bullock's warnings of the lack of natural grass, coupled with the dwindling supply of corn, left the horses and mules in poor condition. This fact was evident to the Indians as well. Any show of weakness left the army at a disadvantage. They were vulnerable without adequate resources to guard a train, let alone the posts. He knew munition stores were also low. The removal of all cavalries from the road was imminent if supplies did not arrive soon.

The telegraph station at Deer Creek was recently attacked, and sixteen miles of lines between Horseshoe Station and Bonte Creek were torn down. St. Mary's Station was burned to the ground, and scuffles occurred as Sioux and Cheyenne warriors brazenly attacked any contingent in sight, including the government supply train just nine miles below Platte Bridge. An entire company of soldiers guarding those wagons had not been enough to discourage the harassing waves of raiders.

The sutler spat on the porch, adding emphasis to his discontentment. The war against the Indians was picking up, and requests for reinforcements plus requisitions for horses and supplies were backlogged. Supplies were slow in coming! To sustain a lengthy campaign against the hostile tribes, he would need the miraculous ability of Jesus to multiply loaves and fishes!

Bullock stomped through the door, only to realize he had forgotten to knock. As a former colonel and longstanding merchant at the fort, he usually adopted a respectful demeanor with his most valuable customer—the United States Army and War Department. Colonel Moonlight looked up from his desk at the intruder, and upon spotting Bullock, managed a thin-lipped smile.

"Come in, Bill," he said setting aside his pen. "Just the man I need to talk to. General Connor has ordered an expedition. We are to conduct an Indian cleanup mission around here to prevent the hostiles from receiving supplies and sanctuary from those bands more peaceably inclined. The bands living around the fort are to be removed to Fort Kearny as soon as possible. Nebraska Territory will hold them until they can be pushed on to the Missouri River. This should make it easier for the military to find the evasive warriors who continue to raid between here and there."

"Sir? Which Indians are you vacating?" asked Bullock as he tried to disguise his anxiety. He quickly deduced the destruction of lucrative trade provided by the friendlies. Many had lived in the vicinity of the fort for thirty years. This was bad news indeed.

"Spotted Tail and Little Thunder's Brulé lodges and all the Sioux living near the fort, including Blackfoot's Oglala band. All half-breeds and whites with Indian families are ordered to leave as well. It is important to discourage the aiding and abetting of hostiles by relatives," explained Moonlight. "We have promised they will receive their treaty annuities upon arrival at the reservation, thereby reducing military expenses to freight the goods here. The plan is to confine them on the Pawnee Reservation on the Missouri River indefinitely."

Bullock's eyes widened at the news. "The Pawnee!" he exclaimed. "The Sioux and Pawnee are mortal enemies!"

"An Indian is an Indian according to the government bureaucrats who decide these things," replied Moonlight as he thumbed through the papers on his desk.

Bullock found it surprising that the colonel was unconcerned. Surely the tribes would not cooperate with this carrot and stick gambit! He thought of the French American fur trader, James Bordeaux, and his Brulé wife, Red Cormorant Woman. She had been a fixture in the area for almost twenty-five years. As the sacred banner carrier and pipe bearer in the White Buffalo ceremony, she was an honored member of the tribe. Together they had eight children. The family would be reluctant to leave—despite the offering of annuities. Bordeaux was a savvy merchant, and Bullock surmised any plans to leave his trading post would be temporary.

As if reading the sutler's mind, Moonlight said, "I am appointing Bordeaux Assistant Indian Agent. He plans to take his family to pick up their annuities. He should be gone several weeks."

"Who the hell is General Connor planning on putting in charge?" demanded the sutler, lowering his voice. "Sorry for my impertinence, sir. It is just…I do not think the General understands he is preparing to send fifteen hundred western plains Indians to live in Pawnee country. They won't like it…and, let me mention, they are in a foul mood. Two Face and Blackfoot have been left hanging for nearly two weeks now." Bullock added the final dig as he remembered the injustice of not allowing the Indians to bury their dead.

"Yes, yes," responded Moonlight as he burrowed through missives on his desk. Picking up one, he summarized its contents. "General Connor is moving his district headquarters to this fort on June 10th. He plans a campaign to strike at the heart of Indian country. He wants them subdued before another winter. He will supervise the plans and preparations of the exodus. That is where you come in, Bullock. I want your supply lists as soon as you can get them to me. It is imperative this expedition be conducted successfully."

"If I may throw in my two cents worth," suggested Bill. Without waiting for the Colonel's response, he explained, "The Sioux are going to be reluctant to leave. Some have lived hereabouts for a long time."

Moonlight stared at him as a man annoyed by details.

"Who is going to provide the escort?" continued Bullock as the enormity of this news took hold. This information was a crucial part of the task at hand.

"Captain Fouts, three officers from the 7th Iowa Cavalry, and one hundred and thirty-five enlisted men. Twenty Indian scouts headed by Charley Elliston and Sergeant Big Mouth will assist in maintaining order along the way."

"Captain Fouts is a good choice," conceded Bullock. He recalled the captain's involvement in repelling the attack on Muddy Creek two years earlier. He was a local hero. "Umm, will the captain's wife and children be traveling with him?" The wheels in his head were already spinning regarding special considerations.

"Yes. Mrs. Eubank and child are going also. It is a suitable time to return her safely to her family in Illinois," said Moonlight absent-mindedly. Returning his attentions to his desk, he picked up his pen and dipped it in the ink. "You are dismissed."

Bullock turned to leave. The words "return her safely" conflicted with the vision of fifteen hundred reluctant and grudging Sioux heading east from their secure and dependent fort home life. They were unofficially considered prisoners of war at this point. Since the executions of the chiefs, the undercurrent at the fort had changed from peaceful to suspicious on all sides. The Indians were not pleased with Moonlight's blunder. It had cost them strong leaders. Most of the Indians possessed guns and ammunition, which they often purchased from his store. Their status as "friendlies" could change at the drop of a hat.

The sutler paused. He decided to voice this nagging concern. "Colonel Moonlight."

Aggravated by another interruption, the exasperated commander barked, "What is it, Bullock?"

"The hangings, sir," he began. "The tribes are provoked. As word of the chiefs' deaths reaches the hostiles, it is possible they might amass a strike against this garrison. They have the forces to massacre everyone. Believe me, such a barbarous action could destroy the fort."

"Oh, really?" replied Moonlight. "A massacre? Ha! I know two Indians who will not take part in it! Dismissed!!"

The chastised sutler carefully stepped off the offending porch, shook his head in disbelief, then sighed in resignation. The machinations of the U. S. Army were huge and, at times, incomprehensible. As just one cog in the wheel, Bullock set his mind to the job at hand. When would the supplies he ordered arrive? The telegraph line repairs were underway. If the well-guarded crews were unmolested, the lines of communication could link him with suppliers once again. That would require another miracle, he mused.

The sutler stood in the parade grounds and looked around. Fort Laramie would look different soon. He swallowed hard. Yup, very different without the natives. He surveyed the mundane activity around the fort and made note of the old men, women, and children languishing in the shade of its buildings and porches—their colorful garb and blankets setting them apart from the soldiers. He could not shake off his misgivings about the possible outcome of such a foolhardy venture. The hangings would not be forgotten. Two Face's death in particular. The army's credibility had suffered a fatal wound. Bullock cautioned Moonlight and Baumer to reconsider the executions. From what he could discern, it was unjust. The Sioux would avenge their deaths. They would deem it an honorable killing—to be exacted at the time of their choosing. And upon the people of their choosing. He thought of Lucinda Eubank.

<hr>

Pensively, I entered the store. It was my first foray into the world of merchandise since my arrival at the fort. I had come out of hiding. With Two Face's money, I decided to gather clothing and provisions for the next leg of the journey commencing in a few days. I gratefully accepted the offerings of clothing and items from Mrs. Fouts and others whose generous efforts met my immediate needs. However, there was one purchase I needed to dispense with. I still felt unsafe. Nightmares were frequent. The effects of my ordeal, and most recently the gruesome hangings, haunted my dreams.

Upon entering the log building, I noticed all manner of people clustered amid the hustle and bustle of commerce. Indian men, women with papooses tied to their backs, and children mingled with soldiers, emigrants, teamsters, interpreters, and traders. The furs, dark blue uniforms, leather buckskins, blankets, and shawls contrasted with skirts, bonnets, bags, and colorful shirts. Clothing was optional for toddlers and some of the Indians. The odor inside the building was an odd mixture of human sweat, tobacco, cheese, and fish as well as a hint of peppermint from the child near me who was enjoying a stick.

Attracted by the sight of ribbons, beads, buttons, and bolts of fabrics, I stepped toward the long counter. My eyes wandered over the tempting stack when I noticed a silent pause to the commotion. All eyes were on me. Acknowledging the curious with a polite nod of my head, the shoppers cleared their throats, shuffled their feet, and turned away.

Mr. Bullock broke the silence by welcoming me with a loud, friendly voice. I noticed several side-eyed glances and knew my story was a topic of fort gossip. Many folks genuinely seemed pleased about my release, but the obvious bulge under the empire waist of my dress increased their suspicion. Perhaps I was not such a virtuous woman—having given in to the passions of my captors. Ah, how little they understood!

Confidence waning, I stared at the moccasins on my feet. Despite my efforts to stop the ghosts of footsteps past, the memories flooded back. I clenched my teeth, clasped my hands to stop the trembling, and focused on the mission. I still had a small sewing kit in my fringed leather pouch but needed to replenish it. I planned to sew a little jacket and breeches for Willie, who was no longer a baby. He needed proper clothing, for he was walking and running about the store dressed in buck-skin breeches and a cotton child's dress cut off to shirt length. I needed to sew up underclothing, including bloomers and a petticoat. The muslin was on the top shelf. Shoes and boots were needed by both of us though none were on the shelves. I still used the worn blanket given to me by Mrs. Bordeaux at the trading post.

Contemplating my widowhood, I considered it the proper time to start the formal grieving process. Our family's customs included a lengthy period of mourning when black was worn by the bereaved. However, I knew there was no time to stitch together suitable clothing to signal my grief and hide my growing waistline. I patted the limited finances in my satchel and decided one item was far more important than my appearance. It was time to prepare for a future of normalcy, but reaching it would be perilous. Stepping from one disjointed world into another would require courage…and an equalizer.

Lost in my thoughts, I barely noticed the busy proprietor, Mr. Bullock, step up to attend to my requests. "How may I assist you, Mrs. Eubank?" he asked kindly.

I stared into his face. It was time. A turning point. Lucinda Eubank would protect herself and her child on the return trip to the states. She would not rely on the whims of fate. This second chance at life was hers and she would defend it.

Glancing about at the others in the store, I was relieved to see they were distracted with matters at hand. I leaned forward slightly at the counter and lowered my voice, "Mr. Bullock. I shall like to purchase a pistol." The surprised expression on his face was met by my own direct stare indicating I would appreciate his confidence in the matter.

"Mmm, hmm," he muttered, reaching below the counter. "I believe I have exactly what you are looking for. Are you familiar with the use of…" he paused, looking around, "such an item?"

"Yes, sir," I replied.

Will, Joe, and I had lived several years on the frontier. During the rare occasions when they were away, I was alone. Travelers passed our place daily, and it was wise to assume some might be rather notorious. Recently, Will replaced our heavy dragoon with a new Colt army revolver. It was a cap and ball percussion weapon, and Will kept it primed at all times. We practiced often, and I was comfortable with its action. It was easy to handle and packed plenty of power. The hog leg was not only sleek and handsome but also heavy. Too weighty for my purposes.

Mr. Bullock slipped a box across the counter to me.

I looked soberly into his face.

"Open it," he said.

Inside the velvet-lined box, two engraved pocket pistols gleamed.

"Philadelphia Deringers, sold as a set," said the sutler.

I leaned down and admired their smooth, dark wood handles and short barrels.

"It is the exact make and model of the gun which killed President Lincoln," he whispered. My eyes locked onto his. "A woman might carry it in her pocket, don't you think?"

Indeed. I planned to keep this weapon in my skirt pocket, concealed by an apron.

"Looks like they could do the job," I murmured.

"Mrs. Eubank, these are forty-four caliber pistols. Think cannons, ma'am." He smiled a bit grimly.

"Mr. Bullock, are you willing to sell just one?"

He eyed me for a moment, but I knew he had already decided. "Six dollars. For one."

I nodded, then reached into my satchel.

The sutler cleared his throat, causing me to pause. "It might be best if I bring it to you, Mrs. Eubank. I will load and place the percussion caps on it for you. You will need the powder horn tin, balls, caps, etc."

Willie and I faced one final, lengthy sojourn into the risky environs of the Great Plains. The Overland Road was now famous for Indian attacks, ruffians, bandits, and marauders. I intended to be ready for what might come and was adamant to never be captured by Indians again. Never! A strong statement, but I planned to reserve one little bullet should I ever face recapture and a return to hell.

Grateful for his discretion in the matter, I said, "Thank you, Mr. Bullock. I appreciate your help. Regarding another matter...." I paused waiting for him to shift to the new subject. "Colonel Moonlight suggested you might help me send a telegram to the Denver newspaper. I wish to post a notice in the hopes of contacting relatives."

Minutes later, the message was composed, and the kind sutler was on his way to the fort's telegraph office.

Relieved, we stepped outside into the fresh air and stood on the stoop. It had been a tense experience, but I resolved to press on, accept whatever kindnesses were extended, and ignore the rest.

Fort Laramie was an impressive structure placed like a lodestar on a large plateau. Looking around with fresh eyes, I estimated its thick walls to be thirty feet high. It was built of mud bricks with four cannons mounted in the corners. Dozens of alert soldiers stood on the wide catwalk built high inside the walls. Six men could march abreast along its perimeter. Shining, white houses dotted the grounds, and I assumed they were the officers' family residences. It all spoke to the allure of civilization for those who had been away too long. Within its main grounds, I identified various buildings besides the sutler's store: a grocery, the lengthy soldiers' quarters, the stable, and a magazine house—its munitions under guard day and night. I did not allow my eyes to linger long on the guardhouse.

After my absence from civilization, the fort revealed itself as a fine-looking settlement. I felt constrained, yet secure within its confines. Scanning the grounds past the walls, I wistfully stared eastward at the road which led home. A frightening proposition, but it was time to go.

Mrs. Ewbanks, the woman that was captured by the Indians last fall, on the Little Blue, and lately rescued by Col. Moonlight's command, desires information concerning the whereabouts of George Ewbanks, Wm Walton, and Ambrose Ewbanks who she states came to this city about the time of her capture. Should this matter meet the eye of either of the persons named, or any one that can give the desired information, they will please report to this office or to Dr. Burdsal, in East Denver.

Rocky Mountain Daily News, June 13, 1865

chapter sixty-two

Signal Smokes

11 June 1865
Eastern Dakotah Territory

Nothing of interest transpired during the first three days of the march, except signal smokes by Indians north of the Platte by day, and reputed conferences by night between them…

Captain John Wilcox

The cavalcade's departure from Fort Laramie shall always remain etched into my memory. Thousands of emigrants camped on the Laramie Plains awaiting an escort west. I gave the hopefuls one last glance before turning my face eastward. I wished them well but, in my heart, desired for them to turn back. The perils were real, and many families would not arrive intact in the land of promise.

Once, I ventured forth as a pioneer to Nebraska Territory, and my heart ached for innocence lost. I could not have imagined this outcome when the Eubank families set out to build a better life together. My view was now jaded by the harsh reality of what the sojourners would face. Hundreds of souls were buried along the trails, and countless others suffered in their efforts to arrive in the beautiful Laramie Valley.

My thoughts turned to Nancy Morton, and I was fortified knowing she had survived. My friend's innate strength and courage had served her well. I lifted my eyes to the eastern horizon, filled my lungs with freedom, and was grateful.

In the three weeks since my release into the care of the United States military, I anticipated the day when I would leave Indian country for good. As I climbed aboard the coach which would carry me east, the fort band assembled near the sutler's store and began to play. I hesitated before sitting down and realized all eyes were riveted on me. The song was familiar to all. Voices melded in unison as soldiers heartily sang words which eased my soul.

Home Sweet Home

Joy to thee happy friend,
Thy bark has passed the rough sea's foam.
Now the long yearnings of the soul are stirred.
Home! Home!
Thy peace is won,
Thy heart is filled,
Thou art going home.

I lifted a hand in salute to all those gathered and sat down shakily. I dabbed at tears with a tiny, embroidered hanky given to me by Mrs. Bullock as a farewell gift. Her kindness had carried me from a state of near lunacy to a private resignation that I would heal. It would take time she said. Yes, it would take time....

Lieutenant James G. Smith, officer of the day, approached me. Colonel Moonlight had assigned him to assist me during my stay at the fort. He stepped smartly to the side of the coach, performed a snappy salute, and handed me a small, leather drawstring bag. Curly, dark hair peeked out from under the brim of his hat. He had the youthful look of vitality and strength. Tugging his uniform jacket down neatly, he announced in a loud, formal voice, "Mrs. Eubank, as a token of our friendship, we present you with three hundred dollars. You are going home! Godspeed!"

I clutched the bag to my chest and waved a final time as the coach pulled out of Fort Laramie. The prospect of joining my loved ones brought a flood of tears to my eyes and a fresh stitch to my wounded heart. Belle would not return home with us, and I suffered terribly not knowing what had become of my beautiful three-year-old. Her precious face followed me daily, sometimes with the strained visage of duress contorting her image; other times, she held the peaceful smile of a safe and happy child. I closed my eyes and prayed as I always did that she was with a good family and, Lord willing, we would be reunited someday.

Captain William Fouts, along with the 7th Iowa Cavalry, rode at the head of the column followed by a mile-long train of loaded wagons. Ten army wagons lumbered along followed by fur traders with their Indian families. By my count, the fifteen traders each had two or three wagons. Combined with their large herds of horses, beeves, and milk cows, it all created quite a spectacle. Four commissioned officers and one hundred and thirty-five enlisted men were entrusted with special orders to transport the Fort Laramie Indians to Fort Kearny. I recognized

Mr. Charles Elliston, who led the company of Indian police uniformed by the government to supervise the relocation. He and his second in command, Big Mouth, were also responsible for the seventy thousand pounds of government rations which would supply the passage.

Two officers' families, Willie, and I were passengers in a large coach called an ambulance. The mules pulling it were fresh from the post corral and had not yet shed their winter's coat. I marveled at the wildflowers covering the green, treeless swells and valleys around us. Freedom brought release, and I was at liberty now to admire my surroundings. I breathed in the scene as a herd of antelope with young ones turned tail and ran into the distance. I was awakening—cautiously, tentatively, tenderly.

An enormous Indian contingent flowed behind us; their travois loaded with tightly bound skins, baskets, cargo, children, and the elderly were strapped to ponies and large dogs. The women carted the rest on their backs while carrying papooses. It was strange to be in my world now, separated from the ones who had brought me through their home-lands. The relief I felt was indescribable, yet my skin rippled as a familiar trepidation gnawed at my tattered emotions. Two thousand free-roaming Indians traveled in an orderly manner which only one closely associated with their habits could understand. The people were surrounded by their livestock, remudas of loose ponies, and dogs, always dogs. Human voices, the barking of assorted canines, and the rumble of wagons raised a cacophony at the beginning of this new day but settled into an indistinct and robust reverberation that shook the ground.

I spotted the twenty-one ox-drawn freight wagons of James Beauvais, from the Upper Platte Agency headquarters, followed by a couple of drovers slowly driving his fifty head of beeves. He had decided to leave his ranch at the old American Fur Company post with everything he owned. The rich merchant drove a nice team and seemed quite comfortable in his light buckboard.

As the wagon train wound its way around the first, gentle curve along the crest of a hill, I could see the bodies of Big Crow, Two Face, and Blackfoot. Their gruesome forms twisted slightly in the soft breeze. My past was hanging off those scaffolds, and my innards churned. I feared I would vomit.

Turning away from the white man's justice one last time, I leaned in my seat to catch a glimpse of the procession's end. Far to the rear, I spotted remnants of Two Face and Blackfoot's band followed by the army's rearguard, which included twenty Sioux scouts. Three young pris-oners trailed the wagon that held a fourth Oglala prisoner. I knew them.

On ponies, Thunder Bear, Black War Bonnet, and Calico followed with heavy ankle chains and iron balls balanced in their laps. Osape, or Standing Cloud as he was called, rode in the wagon. The manacle fastened about his ankle had caused his foot to swell, and he was unable to ride with the others. I pondered their fates.

The death of Two Face weighed heavily on my mind, and I wondered again what I might have done to prevent it; but, oh, what a state I was in when rescued. I could not intelligently put two words together, let alone summarize the events of the past ten months of my captivity. I was glad Blackfoot was gone, but Two Face....

I focused on my present circumstances and the odd mixture of mankind rolling eastward. I wondered at this extraordinary event which, to my mind, would never be repeated in the history of the continent. I reflected on the sight of friend and foe, captives and captors, U.S. soldiers and Sioux Indian warriors, merchants, and traders—strung out along a singular path.

I began to relax. The dust-filled air sifted back onto us by the ever-prevalent wind. I pulled the scarf around my neck up over my nose in anticipation of the pesky dirt and flies that were common elements of the trail. I squinted out from under my new sun bonnet at the open land-scape and delighted in the eastward direction of our journey. Willie and I were finally on our way home. I held the child tightly as we swayed and lurched in the slow-moving coach.

After months of wandering endlessly and hopelessly across vast wild regions belonging to no one, I was overcome by this momentous new direction. I had nearly given up the idea of ever stepping foot upon a trail that would lead me home. However, where was my home now? Home had always been wherever my dear William smiled, worked, loved, and laid his head. Home was not a structure. I knew our ranche along the Narrows of the Little Blue River was gone, but I longed for the treasured connection of family.

I hoped to see Grandma Ruth, but what would I tell her about the apple of her eye, my dear Isabelle? I wondered about those who had lived at Kiowa Station. What had become of Joe, Hattie, and their new wee bairn? What about Will's younger brother Fred and Hattie's brother John? Would I find a happy reunion or dusty, sunken graves?

The terrible memory of the attack on my loved ones had been forced into the recesses of my jumbled mind as a survival mechanism during my captivity. But now with each step closing the gap between me and our beautiful ranche in the fertile valley, the morose hand of gloom clutched at my heart. I knew lovely Medora did not survive that terrible day. Was she buried? Was there a sweet stone marking her resting place with a carving of a lamb and ivy adorning her name? Quite possibly, her unmarked grave was indistinguishable from the fertile soil of our land. The fact that one with such sweet disposition could be bloodied and damaged beyond repair, cut down at the apex of her beauty and youth, was unfathomable. Dreading what lay ahead, I was filled with unbearable confusion: the needs to see, to avoid, to linger, to run. The vision of lovely Dora dissolved into thoughts of graves.

I remembered the final day I spent with young Ambrose in the Indian camp. His descriptions of the deaths of Grandpa Joseph, Henry, and James were still crushing. Where were their final resting places? My separation from Ambrose had been abrupt and unanticipated. I hoped with all my heart he was nestled in the bosom of our loved ones. His heart had been broken, and I fully understood their love would be key to his healing. What a sweet, dear boy!

Just before dark, I noticed signal smokes from the hills to our left and pointed them out to Mrs. Fouts. She brushed off the sighting, but others saw the signals as well. I spent months traveling with the Sioux, and this new development presented a looming threat. Our movements were being tracked. We were being watched. What could it mean?

The huge caravan made its first night's camp near the Bordeaux Ranche. As darkness fell, the smoke signals continued to nag at me. It seemed as if a lifetime had passed since Two Face delivered me to the trading post here. I remembered what a luxury it was to stand inside the building and look upon the wares of civilization! The memory of it was fresh, and I looked at their ranche house hoping Marie would venture out to find me. I wanted to see her. In the past weeks, I had stepped out of the musty shell of existence back into a semblance of life. I was alive again, and she had been a small part of the gift.

Since my first visit to the Bordeaux's, fear and misery had been soothed by safety and the generosity of others. Yet, the signal smokes tainted the precious peace I treasured. Uneasiness permeated my tenuous calm. Instinctively, I recognized the hazard posed by the presence of wild Indians following our progress. Alarm bells would not be quelled, and I found myself pushing away my half-eaten plate of dinner.

Two young soldiers leaned against a wagon wheel nearby, and I found myself eavesdropping on their conversation.

"It's hard to believe that old Fouts would give them Injuns ammunition straight out of our wagons when we haven't got a single bullet in our rifles," complained one as he blew tobacco smoke out through his nose.

"Hunting birds, they said," griped his dusty companion, who spat his wad of chewed up tobacco onto the ground at his feet. "Let them eat rations, I say. It don't make no sense that we have five hundred armed warriors following us. Damn! If it was up to me, I'd make 'em surrender their bows as well!"

"Well, we don't have a pot to piss in. Our opinions don't amount to a hill of beans, if I say so myself," concluded his companion as he slapped his hat against his leg and sauntered off.

I continued to the military tent pitched for me next to the large one belonging to Captain Fouts. His wife and two daughters were settled in for the night. I laid the sleeping babe on the cot, unbuttoned my skirt, and shook it out. The dust billowed in the candlelight up into the shadowy crevices of the tent's pinnacle.

Apprehension filled my thoughts. It was true. We could all be in danger, for we were clearly outnumbered and virtually unarmed. Concern mingled with my overwhelming need to get home.

Home to those who remained. Those who were waiting.

As I drifted off into a fitful, exhausted sleep, I heard myself whisper, "Hurry."

chapter sixty-three

Snake Bite Treachery

12 June 1865
Thick Ears, Cold Springs Camp
Fifteen Miles East of Fort Laramie

Behold, I send you forth as sheep in the midst of wolves:
Be ye therefore wise as serpents and harmless as doves.

Matthew 10:16

T houghts of Belle filled the monotonous spaces of my day. Each trill of a bird and glistening blade of new grass reminded me of the gentle child who brought so much joy into our lives. With each turn of the wagon's wheels, my passage out of darkness rolled into light. Earlier, another mother and daughter pair stirred my thoughts. The Bordeaux family joined our procession with wagons, drivers, and live-stock. Mrs. Bordeaux and her daughter Susan approached me, and we engaged in friendly conversation. They seemed genuinely relieved by my improved condition. The diminutive Marie was congenial and accustomed to life among the whites. She expressed her wish that Willie and I join them later for dinner at the Cold Springs Camp. I accepted the invitation gladly and looked forward to joining her family again under better circumstances.

I pulled the little square of folded paper out of my pocket and read it again. Had my telegram to the Denver newspaper been published today? Was a family member's response awaiting me at the next fort? My spirits lifted as I imagined my little girl safe in Denver. It was as though redemption from the clutches of despair was spilling out along the trail as we crossed the lush prairie.

I read the telegram again and remembered the telegraph operator. His eyes misted a little as he sought words of encouragement. "Let us pray that one of your teaghlach will be found, my dear," he said in

Scottish brogue.

Teaghlach. My clan. My kin. One might have thought he had given me a gift. A reminder of my Scottish father. I turned the folded item over and over. The comment made my heart sing unexpectedly—an unfamiliar sensation, silent for so long.

I returned the telegram to my pocket, its presence reassuring and full of possibilities. Its unspoken message of love and bonds created a mysterious light in my soul, forsaken no more. My imagination sent roots down into what might be revealed. Was it a glimpse of a future regained and a hope renewed? If our minds could speak across the span of miles and experience, I should like to catch a glimpse of the faces of my waiting loved ones just as they are now. I had roamed the world without them; now my mind was unfettered. I allowed it to wander to love. Please, Lord, allow us the pleasure of a warm embrace at our journey's end.

A large bug flew into my face and clouted me hard across the bridge of my nose. I quickly wiped away the interruption and looked around at our current position. The wagon train was shifting. The straight plodding across the flat landscape changed into the dusty, well-rehearsed corralling of wagons for the night.

The day was warm, and Willie's flushed face could use a dousing with cool water. He squirmed in my lap, and I reached into my other pocket for a hard cracker to keep him occupied as we set up camp. He smiled shyly, then pointed to several mounted Indian military scouts as they raced past the wagons. Was it my imagination, or were they pointing at us? Automatically, my eyes searched the horizon and, sure enough, signal smokes puffed slowly behind a nearby hill.

Willie and I later walked to the Bordeaux camp. Marie and Susan looked up as we approached their campfire. "Hello, Red Cormorant Woman," I said. The use of her Indian name was natural, and I caught myself. Their social norms were ingrained in my habits.

A large cast iron pot on a tripod was bubbling with meat and onions. I never ceased to be thankful for the delicious food I had eaten while at the fort and now on the road as well. I handed biscuits wrapped in a cloth and a jar of jam to Mrs. Bordeaux. She smiled and offered a seat on a crate next to her.

"Welcome, Mrs. Eubank! We are pleased you are looking well."

"Yes," I smiled. "I am grateful for all you have done to help me." Lowering my eyes, I added, "I apologize for my behavior when I arrived.

I was…not in my right mind."

"I remember," she replied, gazing kindly into my face. "I am pleased you are recovering. We go with the Indians to where annuities will be issued."

"Oh? Is your whole family here?"

"Yes. My Indian family also. My brother is Swift Bear. His lodges travel with us." She gestured back to the large Indian encampment.

The conversation stalled for a moment, then Mrs. Bordeaux asked delicately, "You go to your family? Your husband?"

"I go to my family in Illinois. My husband…William…was killed."

She nodded gravely.

I reached into my satchel and pulled out the small, hinged metal box which held the photograph of Will. I unwrapped the hankie, cradled it gently, and wiped the surface—for it was beginning to look a little spotted. I handed the small tintype to her, and she murmured approvingly while holding it delicately up in the evening light. She grimaced slightly as she handed it back. She understood his fate.

Returning his likeness to my bag, I added, "My little girl was taken. She is missing. I hope to find her soon." Mrs. Bordeaux and Susan exchanged somber glances and reflexively grasped one another by the hand. I quickly interjected, a little too cheerfully, "I think she is in Denver." My thoughts trailed off.

Looking at our surroundings, I searched for a reason to change the subject. I was drawn to movement across the circle of wagons. Lieutenant Triggs, Mrs. Fouts, and three soldiers urgently marched across the corral in our direction. I was astonished to see two familiar figures following them. It was Old Woman and Happy. I stepped forward to greet them. Happy ran and threw her arms around me. "Help!" she cried. Worry creased her face. Old Woman hobbled up and reached for both my hands. Holding them in her iron grip, both women spoke rapidly. I shook my head in confusion. Old Woman tugged and pulled me away from the group. "We go. Little Hawk hurt! We go!"

"Hold on there," interrupted James Bordeaux. He stepped around the wagon with a young son in tow. Calmly speaking to the hunched squaw, he soothed the distraught elder enough to find the cause for alarm. I picked up the word "snake" from the conversation and listened sympathetically as she explained. Mr. Bordeaux interpreted for those gathered.

"This afternoon, a group of young men from the Indian camp went out to shoot birds. Her grandson, Little Hawk, was bitten by a rattlesnake. Mrs. Eubank," he said turning to me. "She is begging you to tend to his injury. She is convinced you can relieve his suffering."

"Of course," I replied. I picked up my satchel and slung it across my body, quickly turning to go with Old Woman and Happy.

"Come!" said Mr. Bordeaux's son as he grabbed my hand. "I will go with you," he offered.

"Louis, that may not be…" began his father.

"Wait!" interrupted Mrs. Fouts loudly. "Surely there is some treachery involved! You cannot intend to go into that Indian camp and risk capture again!"

I stopped in my tracks. Instinctively, I realized my connection to the people with whom I lived for months on end was not broken. I looked into the pleading eyes of Old Woman with whom I had slept, cooked, and eaten….

Confused, I looked around at those witnessing the exchange.

"I must caution you, Mrs. Eubank," said Lieutenant Triggs. "It is possibly a trap. Their ire is up due to the recent hangings; and if I know Indians, they are looking for a revenge killing. You did testify against the chiefs."

I noticed an undercurrent among the whites gathered around. My immediate reaction to help an Indian was met with disapproval. It confirmed their suspicions about me. I blinked hard and looked at Mrs. Bordeaux. She straddled the gulf between two cultures, and I knew in that moment my familiarity with her people left me vulnerable around my own. Her stoic face offered no answer either way. It was her husband who stepped forward and spoke definitively regarding my current quandary.

"You must desist from following your heart in this matter and use your head. It is possible you are taking a grave chance of never returning to your people if you continue to yolk yourself with the tribe." He added soberly, "It is true that your life may be at risk."

I watched the faces of those who held their collective breath, anticipating my response.

"Thank you," I replied, then pulled my hands from the old woman's grasp. I looked into her dark, pleading eyes, shook my head "no" and stepped back.

I heard Mrs. Fouts sigh with relief and mutter, "Thank God above!"

Stunned by my refusal, Old Woman and Happy were led away, looking at me over their shoulders. I never saw them again.

Later that evening as we finished our meal, Marie walked with me to my tent.

"If I may…" she trailed off. "If I may be so bold," she continued. "I fear the Cheyenne seek to avenge the deaths of those who hang at the fort. But I think there may be another reason…why they want you to return to the tribe."

I stopped abruptly, towering over her in the darkness, my form shading her face from the moonlight.

Our eyes met, and she spoke words that shook me to my core.

"The child you carry. It is theirs—it belongs to the tribe…."

chapter sixty-four

Saplings and Secrets

13 June 1865
Confluence of Horse Creek and the North Platte River
Dakotah Territory

One does not sell the land upon which people walk.

Tashanka Witko (Crazy Horse), Oglala

The blazing summer sun hung low in the sky as the evening light gilded the scene below. Captain Fouts rested his mount on the rise above the confluence of Horse Creek and the pulsing Platte River, just forty miles downstream from Fort Laramie. Observing the activity in the Indian village on the west side of the creek, he contemplated the task ahead. To establish order and routine during the journey, he maintained an easy march the first two days. But even that was difficult. Untying the kerchief from his neck, he removed his hat and wiped the sweat from his face and bald head. The horse grunted under the soldier's substantial weight. Fouts was tiring of these Indians already.

The warm, sunny, and virtually cloudless sky offered perfect conditions, but today's progress was slow compared to standard military movements. The soldiers, civilians, wagons, livestock, and multitudes of Sioux Indians followed the North Platte River to Horse Creek. A rocky crossing was located, and each wagon successfully forded the swollen stream. The water was high and nearly submerged the swimming horses as they struggled to pull the weight of each floating wagon. The military escort and civilian contingent accomplished the task of crossing to the east side by late afternoon. They settled on a peaceful, flat area a mile further along the trail. The large Indian village did not cross but pitched their teepees on the western shore. The military rearguard set up camp behind them. Fouts permitted it more out of exasperation than strategy.

To hasten each morning's departure, the captain collected his orderlies and rode to the rear of the Indian camp. The Sioux were undoubtedly adept at breaking camp but seemed determined to slow things down in defiance of his orders. Fouts circled their camp at a brisk trot and issued sharp commands accompanied by considerable loud swearing. But this action only produced a slower response. It was futile to prod these loafers into making up lost time. Even promises of annuity gifts at the Missouri River did nothing to motivate this reluctant group. To his relief, his orders only required him to push two thousand Sioux as far as Fort Kearny.

The bothersome "agency" Indians, made up of the mixed remnants of Oglala and Brulé bands, would not be missed around Fort Laramie. The removal of the supposed friendly groups would be another nail in the coffin of the wild bands living to the north. He resolved to uphold his severe demeanor; and if needed, he would demonstrate the full authority of the United States Army.

With plenty of daylight left, the folks of the wagon train had time to get chores done, prepare a meal, and relax in the heat of late afternoon. The Sioux appeared to be doing the same. He squinted at the dark-skinned children playing in the shallows along the shoreline. The water gleamed off their jet-black hair and their backs as they splashed, laughed, and played. The boys who had ridden pell-mell on their ponies through the caravan during the day's march could be seen racing again just beyond the lodges.

Early that morning, Fouts confronted a row of headmen sitting in the center of the Indian camp. He spoke directly to Chiefs Spotted Tail and Little Thunder through his interpreter, Charley Elliston. He issued a lengthy diatribe regarding the pernicious behavior of the Indian boys who raced their ponies between the wagons and infantry. They were disrupting the peaceful flow of travel. He personally ordered them to stop and threatened to have the offenders tied to a wagon wheel with twenty-five lashes applied to the backs of the upstarts. He snorted at the thought of teaching the youngsters a lesson or two.

As Charley repeated the order, Fouts noticed the chiefs pass looks among themselves as if plotting new ways to show disrespect. However, the friendly response by Spotted Tail made light of the situation. He explained it was customary for boys to race when the tribe moved from place to place. Fouts caught a wink from Little Thunder toward the men sitting next to him. The captain did not appreciate the chiefs' enjoyment of his verbal threats. Severe chastisement and intimidation on his part were intended to temper the youth, not amuse the chiefs. Fouts glared at these thorns in his side.

The Sioux were settling in for the evening, and all appeared peaceful. Just before turning his horse away, he noticed soldiers from the rearguard tossing sacks into the creek. Their cheers and yells required closer inspection. He removed his spotting glass from its leather sheath on his saddle horn to get a closer look. Startled, he realized the bundles were babies and toddlers. The soldiers were making a game of betting on which ones could swim back to shore. A group of women frantically tried to retrieve their children from the rushing river, and he noticed several swept downstream. The angry and terrified mothers shielded their children from the reach of the soldiers as they carried their little ones back to camp.

Captain Fouts sat motionless watching the action unfold. So...it was true. Even the youngest of the heathens could swim. He doubted any of the offending troops would fare so well in the river, for he knew few could swim. Maybe he would speak to Lieutenant Haywood about the behavior of the soldiers, but maybe not. If the men wanted to amuse themselves by throwing papooses into the river to cheer their dexterity in swimming out...well, there were much bigger things to worry about.

Captain Fouts fixed his eyes westward, contemplating the long, shining strands of both rivers which cut the open prairie. Tonight's sunset was on full display. Oh well, the task of taking so many across this vast, open wilderness did not allow for sentimentality. He sighed wearily. He was tired of the West and hoped his next assignment would take him back to Ohio. He was sending his family home now, for he considered it unsafe to remain in Indian country another moment.

The overheated captain recalled his decision to permit the Indians to keep their weapons. Out of generosity, he had rescinded his decision to withhold ammunition. The chiefs pleaded with him for lead and powder to hunt and shoot birds to feed the vast camp. A few concessions might speed up the process, so the munitions were delivered; but the concession was infuriating.

Replacing his hat, he noticed several Indians on horseback in the Platte River. They were driving cut saplings into the ground at the water's edge and across the channel. The late afternoon shadows of the saplings created slanted, black stripes on the sparkling water. He lifted his spotting glass and focused on the man astride the horse in the middle of the river. He recognized Black Wolf, one of the prominent braves in the band. He shook his head. The trail to Scottsbluff would follow the great river but not cross it. He pondered their actions, then turned his horse back toward his tent where his wife Charity was waiting with his supper. He focused on putting some distance between himself and the Indian camp for a brief evening's respite.

As he kicked his horse into a trot, Captain Fouts shook his head and said to no one in particular, "I will never understand the nature of the Indian people." The truth of his statement would soon become apparent.

———•———

Returning to camp, Fouts greeted me curtly and stepped inside his tent. I overheard his conversation with Charity in which he described the soldiers' behavior with the papooses. The next moment, he was standing outside his tent surveying the camp, a lit cigar in his mouth.

"Sir," I said as I approached. "I could not help overhearing your story of papooses thrown into the river for the entertainment of your men. What have you done to stop it?"

Glaring down his nose at me, he responded glibly, "Boys will be boys."

Hackles raised, I touched his sleeve and whispered vehemently, "Sir! I demand they be stopped! It is unconscionable for civilized men to treat babies in such a manner! You must agree!"

The captain shook off my offending hand and stared at me with unconcealed interest. I could see his face quite clearly in the evening light. The man snorted and turned to walk away. Under his breath, he issued a threat. "Mrs. Eubank, your affection for the brutes is disturbing. I suggest you control these unreasonable emotions. Your actions are rather damning, don't you think?"

Suspicion and gossip were rampant among the soldiers. And now, it seemed, even the officers were infected with the vileness.

———•———

Darkness closed in around the wide circle of Indian lodges standing along the edge of Running Waters. The moon hid behind the smooth hills along the horizon. In an open rocky area on the bank, the sounds of rushing water covered voices. They gathered in hunched shadows around the fire—its light reflecting on their faces. The group of three hundred and eighty warriors sat quietly with blankets draped loosely about their shoulders. They waited. The peace chiefs Red Leaf, Iron Shell, and Bad Wound were not invited to the council this night. Despite the tension, the evening's dog feast left them satisfied. Cool air rising from the river enveloped them.

Mysteriously out of the darkness appeared a warrior. He quietly slipped into the group and sat in the spot prepared for him near the embers. His short, fine-boned stature, light-complexioned features, and long, wavy, light brown hair belied the respect with which he was received. The full-blooded Lakota modestly sat next to his cousin, Touch the Clouds. Grunts and nods of those seated around the council fire welcomed him. Tashanka Witko had arrived. Finally, the secret council was ready to begin.

"Welcome, Crazy Horse," whispered Touch the Clouds. The men grinned at each other, then settled into the solemnity of the gathering.

Crazy Horse had been recently appointed leader of the Oglala. The young chief proved his bravery in battles and developed alliances with both the Cheyenne and Arapahos. He was Red Cloud's representative and a member of the northern wild bands who shunned the white man's ways.

The exclusive meeting of Brulé and Oglala picked up where it left off two nights before when the bands prepared to leave Fort Laramie. Young boys in small groups took up casual positions along the perimeter —a warning system should others come too close.

Spotted Tail was an intelligent and dignified leader respected by Indians and whites alike. The great leader began to detail recent events which contributed to the current situation. The prior winter had been a difficult one. More Sioux moved near the fort to receive food allotments and supplies. Winter's wrath, endless snow drifts, and bitter cold stopped the sustaining wagon trains necessary to support the ever-growing bands living near the fort. Feed for the stock that hauled freight such great distances across snowy plains was not available. Did not the United States government understand this? Hunger and discontentment grew in proportion to the demand. Relatives of those at the fort would often arrive, receive their rations, then leave for the wilds, further depleting the fort's ability to feed the Indian families. He reminded those in the circle about the Great Sioux Reserve Treaty. The rich and bountiful country promised to them was enfolded within the geographic boundaries of the Platte River, the Bighorn Mountains, Yellowstone to the north, and the plains to the east.

These latest orders forced the removal of their people to the Missouri River. The plan was not for the benefit of the Indian. It would solve the costly problem of hauling enormous quantities of annuities across the plains. To receive supplies directly from boats, the Sioux would be required to move onto the reservation of the hated Pawnee. Confrontation was inevitable. The Sioux would surely be disarmed, then killed by their ancient and mortal enemies. Spotted Tail suspected this mass relocation was a scheme to separate them from their homeland—perhaps never to return.

"I wish to guide our people toward peace. Chief Little Thunder and I try to restrain the younger warriors, but their hearts follow the old ways. They have not seen the might of the whites. Two years ago, the Cheyennes Black Kettle and Lean Bear went to Washington to speak with the Great Father. They saw the white man's villages—as numerous as the stars." He waved broadly toward the night sky.

Chief Little Thunder spoke hoarsely and summarized their grievances. "Waves of whites occupy the plains. They wait to go west. More will come. The spring grasses are eaten to a nub before sprouts can grow. The trespasses will not stop without war. The coming season will be like swarms of locusts eating all in their path. We must keep the hordes away from the Black Hills. Gold gleams in the eyes of the whites, so they do not abide by treaty."

Spotted Tail looked at Little Thunder and said, "Great Spirit has given much to his children of the prairie. We have everything we need, but the whites covet our land. If we do nothing to stop them, they will take it all. We will not give up the Powder River or the Blacks Hills. We can live without annuities for years to come—if we keep the whites out. The removal of our people to the land of the Pawnee will leave us defenseless when it is time to return. We do not need the white man's goods. We approve of the plan to return now to the summer hunting grounds."

"Ah, ho!" agreed the council.

Once those in the circle quieted, Swift Bear mentioned the newest wrinkle in the blanket. "True reports are the big soldier chief Connor will come against us and make war in Powder River country to punish the Cheyenne and the Sioux because we have smoked the war pipe together."

The council stirred up again. As the commotion increased, Black Wolf spoke loudly. "The Cheyenne Chief, Young Man Afraid of His Horses, is raiding this spring on both the North and South Platte Rivers. Red Cloud raided much this winter below the Laramie. Many braves wish to join them!" The warrior Hump joined the chorus. "The Oglala and Brulé Sioux are prairie people! We do not want big river country to the east. We do not obey soldier chief Fouts. We are many, and they are few! Tomorrow, we fight!"

Packs His Drums growled with disgust at the soldiers taking young Sioux women into their tents at night. Scowls of disapproval showed on the men's faces. Swift Bear described the unbelievable actions of soldiers who spent the evening throwing papooses into the river. And the idea their boys would be tied to wagon wheels and whipped for racing was infuriating. With these reminders, the warriors wrapped their anger inside their blankets, and the young men whispered behind the hand, "We must kill all the white soldiers."

Black Wolf was not finished. His anger energized the meeting. "The loud talking soldier chief Fouts forces our young men to be driven along by horse soldiers—with chains still on their feet. We step closer and closer to Pawnee land where chains are ready for all of us! Our enemy waits as we hurry to join them far from our country. Ugly captain speaks rudely until his face turns red. He stinks even when not on the whiskey cup. Foolish to follow him! Now time to lead our people away! No good will come if we leave this land and our freedom."

Black Wolf pressed his point. Now was the time to wipe out the soldiers completely. The Sioux camp held hundreds of battle-ready braves, while the soldiers numbered few. Crazy Horse's wild Indian warriors tucked away in the nearby hills numbered five hundred. It would be easy to annihilate the troops. The Indian scouts said the soldiers had no bullets, just empty guns and one wagon of ammunition. "We destroy the bullet wagon, kill troops while our families cross Running Waters, and disappear into the hills."

Many voices approved this strategy. However, Swift Bear warned their appetite for elimination of the soldiers clouded their short-sighted vision.

The young braves were unhappy with this comment and nudged their companions. Black Wolf shouted vehemently, "Some chiefs have lived with the whites so long, they do nothing. They tell us to hold back, to wait. We will not! What does Crazy Horse say? He is a true warrior like us! Let him speak!"

Swift Bear waited for Black Wolf to conclude his words, then said, "We are of two minds. Red Cloud wants war and Spotted Tail talks peace. If we pursue the path of peace, it is true…we will pay a terrible price—death of the Indian way. What does Crazy Horse say?"

The council grew silent as all eyes rested on the quiet figure sitting cross-legged by the fire. Crazy Horse's grey eyes looked around at their dark expressions. "Your hearts have seen the white man's ways and now desire to fight on the Indian path," he stated. "It is good."

All sat silently waiting, for each warrior understood that wildness lived in Crazy Horse. He never took part in the placations of the whites. He refused to grow fat eating their crackers and molasses. He did not join talk of appeasing the interlopers. He spoke little but always held to his convictions. Crazy Horse was chosen as leader because he insisted on preserving the People's Way. He helped the most vulnerable of his tribe. Rather than receive handouts from the Great White Father, he chose to hunt and give meat to the old and hungry. Outside of respect for his generosity, those gathered remained quiet, listening, reflecting. They remembered his courage and bravery in battle. He was a young man, but all acknowledged his unusual spiritual powers.

"A foolish heart will lead its possessor to destruction," said Crazy Horse softly. "If you go where the sky is big and there is solitude for an angry man, you will find the long sight. Wisdom can find its way into the strongest brave's heart."

Ahhh, yes. They nodded and continued to listen.

"We will fight tomorrow. The soldiers will try to ride down and kill our women and children, but the crossing is bad for them. The soldiers and their horses are not trained to swim such a strong current. With many braves, we will form a shield while others taunt the enemy. If we are cunning like the wolf," he said tapping his temple, "we will save the killing of soldiers for another day. Our role as protectors gives power."

All agreed and cast glances down to their feet. They were humbled to receive such simple counsel. The difficulty for those meeting this night had been to reach an agreement. An escape plan was devised for their families to leave the whites safely. For this reason, those gathered were pleased to hear the words of Crazy Horse.

Revenge for the killings would come, but this was not the time. It was best not to provoke the cub of a giant mother bear, for the chiefs were increasingly aware of the size and scope of the white invasion. Kill the cub, and the sow would never stop hunting them. Take the fight to the sow, and destroy her by the might of the Indian nations.

After the men settled into their own thoughts, Black Wolf looked to Crazy Horse for guidance and details. Politely, he suggested the young leader speak what was in his mind.

Crazy Horse sat quietly a moment, then explained: the warriors should charge the soldiers, threaten them, then pull back to charge again. The troops will be distracted until all the Indian families are safely away. If the military pursues them, the Platte River will be the warriors' secret ally. The entire village knows how to cross the swollen waters, but the soldiers will drown in their efforts to chase the fleeing families. The young chief persuasively added that five hundred warriors from the north were tucked into the hills to ensure the People's escape.

Then Crazy Horse spoke the words that each man held in his heart from that time forward: "The Great Spirit gave us this country as home.

He gave us plenty of land to live on. The buffalo, deer, antelope. We want to live as our fathers did and their fathers before them. We want peace and to be left alone. We did not ask the white men to come here. They draw boundaries around our home and promise to sell us a piece of earth in trade for trinkets. One does not sell the land upon which people walk. We do not want their civilization. Once the white invasion is stopped, the Sioux bands will live without their goods and poisonous ways for years to come."

Nods of agreement and affirming grunts followed his words. They encouraged the young chief to say more, but his tongue was finished.

Finally, Touch the Clouds spoke. "The People will not forget the death songs of Two Face, Blackfoot, and the Cheyenne Big Crow."

Spotted Tail agreed. Gesturing to the west, he remembered. "Thunder Bear and I sat together on our horses on the hill. We watched them die. Big Mouth told the officers that Two Face rescued the woman. But their ears did not hear. The Sioux scouts who ride with the soldiers on this trail have agreed to recapture the woman who caused all this trouble. Now the Sioux join the Cheyenne and seek to avenge the killings through her death."

One of the Cheyenne chiefs in attendance spoke up. "The white woman is with us too long. The wheel dust of the soldiers, the traders, chokes our women and children—all who must carry heavy packs on their backs. Worn-out mares pull travois filled with little ones, the sick, and the old. They cough as the white woman's wagon races past."

"And she carries the child of Big Crow," said Little Thunder.

Eyebrows raised as those in attendance murmured among themselves.

"The child belongs to the Southern Cheyenne," he continued. "Many children were lost to the soldiers at Sand Creek. For the Cheyenne to continue to walk together on the land, they must hold their children. They must seize her child...."

Nods and grunts of agreement spread through the council.

"How is this to be accomplished?" Swift Bear asked.

Two plans were discussed that night. The first, involving snake bite trickery, had failed. The second would apply force. It would be done.

The white woman would not escape.

chapter sixty-five

Horse Creek Avalanche

14 June 1865
Horse Creek, Dakotah Territory

From the hills to our left, they were bearing down like an avalanche upon us. Seeing that we were assailed by more than five hundred warriors, (they had evidently been largely reinforced during the previous night,) equally armed and better mounted than my little squad, I thought that to stand, be surrounded, and cut off from our defenses and ammunition, would involve the entire command in indiscriminate massacre, as well as the capture of the train and animals. Deeming "prudence the better part of valor," I remounted my men and fell back to our defenses…

Captain John Wilcox

C razy Horse and Touch the Clouds crept up the rise of the hill over-looking the Indian village on the bank of the river. Lying flat on their bellies, they used the far-seeing glasses to watch. Soon it would be time to signal the five hundred mounted Oglala Sioux warriors waiting on the other side. As the first light of dawn crept up around them, the waterways below shimmered in mercurial ribbons that stretched to the earth's distant edges. The soldier horns played reveille on the east side of Horse Creek, and the sounds of animals and people carried on the breeze up to their position.

Crazy Horse was tempted. It would be easy to wipe out the soldiers, but what of the Indian families mixed in with the white traders? Even if the battle was successful, some Indian relations might fall to the ground before the day was finished.

He had seen it before. The bodies of helpless ones scattered about a camp. Their bodies torn to bits by the wagon guns and knife guns used by the soldiers. He remembered Yellow Woman. The Cheyenne moccasins she made for him still covered his feet. Her lifeless eyes stared at the cold sky above, her young son lying next to her—a bullet through

386

his newborn breast. She had been left behind, hidden on the trail of fleeing, because her time was upon her. Now she was gone, and a fire burned within his heart.

The cries of the Sand Creek dead reached the Oglalas. They covered their faces with the mourning blankets when they heard the names of friends and relatives—names which were never to be spoken again. Shameful things were done to those whose journey had taken them from this world—their private parts and scalps shown at the whiskey houses in the white man's town, Denver. Mothers cut open and their babies lying butchered beside them. Yellow Woman was one of these.

The warpath pulled at him—unrelenting. Avenging the deaths of so many innocents could begin now. But the young warriors must learn wisdom—when to fight, when to protect. He would follow the plan decided upon at council. No one was to risk shooting the family members who were part of the wagon train. The soldiers would be allowed to live; the people of the caravan would leave unmolested. Except one. Fire-Hair Woman would be picked up by the scouts and returned to the Cheyenne, for their vengeance was hot. Meanwhile, the warriors would ensure the people moved fast across the river to scatter northward like black ants. Their footprints would be hard to follow once they reached the sandhills.

The occupants of the one hundred and eighty-five lodges below were strangely quiet—not sleeping, he knew. Two thousand Sioux were preparing to make their escape. All were aware of his position behind the hills above the river bottoms where nothing would betray the presence of his mounted resistance. The young runner from the Indian camp arrived with news that all was ready. Wait. Listen. Rifles. Prepare. Crazy Horse left his watching spot, mounted up, and turned his golden palomino to the approaching sun. He closed his eyes and offered up his morning prayer. Today he was Lakota. A warrior. One in a forest of warriors whose hearts were strong and numbers mighty. Today held victory. Today would free his people. Today was not a day to exact revenge upon the whites. That day would come....

Reveille sounded at three o'clock on the fourth morning of our journey. Captain Fouts instructed us to be ready, for he planned to traverse the eighteen miles to Camp Mitchell by nightfall. We must pick up the pace. After a brief farewell, the captain mounted his horse and with three orderlies loped off in the direction of the Indian camp. Per his instructions, the wagons were hitched, the horses saddled, and the whole caravan fell into line before dawn. Captain John Wilcox led the advance guard. At the two-mile mark, we halted awaiting word from the rear that all was in order before proceeding.

I nursed Willie, who was tucked securely in the soft leather sling that had served me so well. I watched the early morning light illuminate the prairie around us. The birds were in full-throated song as they greeted the new day. The occasional stamping of an ox hoof or snort of a mule, plus the jingling of tracings, signaled the pause before the march. Charity Fouts was seated next to me, for she enjoyed my company. We exchanged pleasantries when suddenly we heard the sharp reports of gunfire from the direction of the Indian camp. I jerked my head toward the creek and scanned the trail behind us. I was startled to see a messenger race past the wagons, then pull to a sliding stop beside Captain Wilcox.

"Captain Fouts has been killed! Captain Fouts is dead!" he shouted. "The Indians killed the captain, sir! And all three of his men!"

"Lieutenant Triggs! Are you sure?"

"Yes, sir! I saw him take a bullet to the head and one through his heart!" shouted the young officer.

Charity Fouts and I swiveled our heads in unison, staring wild-eyed into each other's faces. Her hand flew up and covered her mouth as she began to shriek. Willie stopped his suckling, looked at our horrified faces, and started to squall. "No! Oh, no! No!" screamed Mrs. Fouts while trying to jump from the wagon seat. I caught her by the arm and yanked her body toward me. I threw my arms around her and Willie as I tried to calm them both by force. The more I squeezed, the more hysterical they became.

"Shhh…" I adjured them. "Shhh…."

I pressed her head down on my chest. This time she did not struggle but buried her head to hide her face from the nightmare. Sobbing loudly, her tears soaked my bodice.

I looked around frantically to assess the best course of action. Immediately, Captain Wilcox signaled us to run for an open area a quarter mile ahead. There we would form a barricade-like corral. The entire wagon train bolted at the commander's direction. Our driver whipped the mules into a dead run as our coach bounced through the ruts. The trader Beauvais clattered past in his light buckboard, a rifle balanced between his knees. He furiously struck the plodding oxen of his wagons into gallops with his long bull whip urgently forcing them forward. The bullwhackers scrambled behind, trying to navigate the wagon wheels and hooves pounding the dirt around them.

Within moments, our coach was set upon by the military's own Sioux scouts. Two riding in front reached for the reins of the lead mules while others began shooting into the window openings. I pressed the women down onto the floor, then fumbled for the pistol in my pocket. The Deringer's cold steel fueled my adrenaline. I raised my head to the window and found myself face to face with an Indian scout turned warrior. Threatening, he pointed his rifle at me. A bullet whizzed past my head but struck no one. I raised my pistol and pointed at his heart, my trigger finger twitching. The air splintered into piercing yelps. Our eyes met; with snarling lips, the pursuer and his cohorts peeled away, breaking off the chase. Confused, I watched them race back to the rear of the train. Was I their intended target?

The teamsters expertly turned the overly excited animals to the inside of a circle, creating an enclosure from which to prepare our defense. Our coach slowed and began a wide swing. The army wagons did the same. A protective corral was forming with the trader wagons facing west to shield the military wagonloads of ammunition and weapons.

At the same time, I heard Captain Wilcox dispatch a courier to Fort Mitchell. The rider gathered the reins of the fastest horse, leapt into the saddle, and sprinted east on an eighteen-mile run of desperation. His blue cap flew off his head and fluttered momentarily in the air before landing among the prairie flowers. A second courier on a swift horse was sent to Fort Laramie with a distress call for Colonel Moonlight. I noticed an Indian pursuer behind each messenger.

Willie and I, along with the other women and children, were urgently instructed to leave the wagons and take a position in the center of the corral. A barrier was hastily being built to shield us from bullets and arrows. I quickly stepped out of the coach with Willie, then hauled Mrs. Fouts and her adolescent daughters off the wagon seats. They crumpled to the ground at my feet. My head jerked from one scene to the next as the situation was changing rapidly. The panic around us was tangible. Powerless, vertigo threatened to take me down. The sensation of tumbling into a deep dark well was interrupted by the sight of my help-less companions. Reason gained the upper ground.

I shook the oldest girl and commanded her, "Hurry! Take shelter! Over there!" I pointed to a stack of haphazardly stacked crates and barrels. I pulled and pushed each of the women to the dubious shelter, and we hunkered down in the dirt like a flock of frightened doves. I put my arm around Mrs. Fouts as she sat with her back against a barrel, face buried in her hands. She moaned loudly while rocking back and forth.

I noticed her youngest daughter walking aimlessly amid the shouting and running men trying to bring order to chaos.

Leaving Willie, I sprinted a few steps, grabbed her arm, dragged her back to our shelter, and pushed her down between her sister and mother. Both girls looked up at me with dirty, tear-streaked faces, and cried out simultaneously, "Papa!" The cry broke my heart as hysteria began anew for the three Fouts women.

I stood to see where the next threat might materialize. And materialize, it did. Several of Big Mouth's Indian scouts from the rear convoy rode directly into the center of the corralled wagons. One spotted me and with an ear-piercing yell, pointed at me with his rifle. Instantly, I was surrounded.

One scout leapt off his horse, threw his arms around me, and dragged me hither and yon while trying to catch his mount. Others dismounted and ran to the aid of my assailant. I struggled to reach my pistol, but my arms were pinned. Bedlam broke out as I clobbered my attacker in the groin with the rear kick of a mule. He dropped to his knees, and I jerked away only to back into another brave, who threw an elbow around my neck. Hauling me backward, I tilted my head and met the eyes of Thunder Bear. He growled and tightened his grip around my throat. I screamed with all my might.

The raucous commotion attracted the attentions of a dozen soldiers digging feverishly nearby. "Hey! What are they doing?" hollered one young corporal who ran toward us. White faces mixed with those of the swarthy scouts who responded by pointing their rifles directly at the soldiers' heads. Everyone froze.

Holding one rein, Thunder Bear pulled me toward his horse. The rearing, whirling, and crabbing animal continued to sidestep away. I could not breathe and was desperately pulling on his arm as it crushed my windpipe. One hand fumbled for my skirt pocket. My attacker picked me up off the ground and tossed me astride his horse. The movement opened my pocket and there it was! In seconds I had the pistol in hand, cocked and pointed at Thunder Bear, who was preparing to jump up behind me. He stopped instantly, almost mid-stride. Stunned, he lunged to the side.

"No!" I yelled at the top of my voice. Reflexively, my finger squeezed the trigger. The explosion and the kick of the weapon in my hand startled me. The small cloud of black powder smoke blew into my face. My eyes watered. A miss. Without speaking, he drew a large knife from the sheath fastened to his waist. The clarity of the moment froze as the slash of the blade against my forearm glinted in the sun. The elkhorn handle was adorned with a beaded leather strip. I clearly saw the red, yellow, and blue zigzags. Black dots. In slow motion, I glimpsed the stroke of the knife and saw the blood spurt as he raised the knife again and reached for my foot. Kicking wildly, I seized the moment to slide off the spinning horse's rump and run into the arms of the nearby soldiers, who stood shocked, their only weapons being sabers and empty rifles.

Thunder Bear and the other scouts quickly gauged the situation, mounted their horses, and hurriedly fled the scene—taking with them a dozen military horses and mules. The dust from the departing scouts obscured my view but out of the corner of my eye, I spotted Susan Bordeaux's son Louis. He had pulled a rifle out of his father's wagon and was taking aim. The bullet struck Thunder Bear in the foot at the same moment his father reached him. James Bordeaux snatched the rifle out of his son's hands. "You stop!" he shouted. "Your Uncle Swift Bear is among them. We do not want the shooting to start!" Louis's little sister Susan ran to her brother and pulled him to his mother's side.

Moments later, the soldiers of the rearguard arrived on foaming horses. Captain Wilcox had ridden into the scene of my near kidnapping, and his face displayed shock, surprise, and terror. Watching me slide off the pony with pistol in hand, he turned to his men.

"Lieutenant Haywood!" Wilcox shouted. "Why haven't you made your stand at the rear?"

"Sir!" came the breathless reply. "We have no bullets!"

"Damn it all! Explain yourselves!" demanded the captain.

"Captain Fouts allowed us to carry our weapons but did not issue cartridges. The Indians are preparing to attack, sir!" shouted a frightened private.

I ran to Captain Wilcox's horse and grabbed the bridle. The shocked officer looked down at me. "Don't trust the scouts, Captain!" I hollered. He tried to back his mount away from me while distractedly scanning the developing situation outside the corral. "Sir!" I repeated loudly. "They are here to fight you! Do not trust the Indian scouts!" I repeated. With a dreadful and growing apprehension, it took a moment for me to realize how close I had come to being kidnapped. My mouth went dry. A deep, growling sound exploded from my throat. "They want me, Captain!"

Wilcox stared at me as though seeing me for the first time. He hesitated, processing what I said, then gave a quick nod. "Are you all right?" he hollered. Before I could respond, his fidgeting horse backed into an orderly who was scrambling to mount his own animal. The captain's eyes lingered on mine a moment before he shouted, "Morey! Guard this woman! And find a rifle with ammo!"

The quick-thinking Wilcox spun his horse away and shouted orders at his two lieutenants, Smith and Triggs,who came to my defense. "Order the men to use their empty weapons and sabers! Dig a trench and bulwark around the women and children! They must be protected!" Then he commanded those from the rearguard to distribute the ammunition stored in wooden crates. The increasingly desperate soldiers hastily formed a line to pass out boxes of bullets and were soon loading their weapons.

Wilcox set to work at dividing the enlisted men and the civilians. Company A, armed now with loaded rifles, was ordered to form a perimeter line of defense in preparation for the first assault. Along with the sixty-five men of Company B, Lieutenants Smith and Triggs enlisted the efforts of the teamsters, traders, and merchants to dig rifle pits outside of the corral.

Breathing hard, I shoved the hot pistol into my pocket. Skirts billowing, I sat down with a thunk next to Mrs. Fouts and pressed my back hard against the barrel. Clamping my eyes shut, I heard the grinding of my own teeth. I was confused by what had just occurred. How close had I come to being recaptured? Freakishly, my nervous system pulsed with erratic swings between clarity and stupor. Mayhem reigned all about me.

I clutched the frightened Willie to my chest and tried to quiet the hysterical Mrs. Fouts. Her daughters squeezed in on either side of me as their anchor in the storm. Their screams and cries were drowned by the shouts of men, cargo being stacked, animals panicking, and dogs barking. Willie was frightened out of his head. His screeching could be heard above the tumult. He struggled to be released from my grasp, but I was determined not to lose this boy after all we had been through. Wind whipped my hair wildly about, and flying grit scalded my exposed skin. The bleeding wound on my arm welled up and formed a dripping pool. I stared vacantly at it.

Disturbingly, my mind slowed, and sounds muffled as though under water. I allowed the current to carry me safely to the other side. Will's face appeared through a mist. He was smiling and pointing at me. Touching his own heart, he nodded his head and slipped back through the veil. Peace entered my soul. Before our children had arrived, we would often hunt together. Why had I thought of that? It was unrelated to the windstorm of violence I was experiencing. Yet, it was my gun which had turned the course of recent events. Will knows I am strong. He knows I will live!

My hand slipped under the weight of Willie's body draped above my abdomen where the child within rolled and squirmed. I knew at once we would be okay. Will was reminding me to trust my instincts. I knew this foe. I had lived with them. Their war cries and threats still sent my skin rippling, but it was familiar. I had seen their scalp dances and knew firsthand what they were capable of inflicting upon their enemies. They were indeed fearsome. Yet, in the knowing, I found strength.

My senses fully returned and were on high alert. The will to fight coiled in my gut ready to be released upon the next comer. I watched as Captain Wilcox ordered Haywood to signal the bugler. It was time to direct seventy mounted soldiers into a charge on the Indian camp. The sharp report of the bugle pierced the atmosphere. Within moments, the entire detachment followed the leaders down the trail until nothing remained but an enveloping cloud of dust.

"Stop the bleeding," I uttered. Fumbling through my satchel, I pulled out one of Willie's fresh nappies. Pressing it against my arm, I willed myself to stand on trembling legs. Climbing upon the nearest crate, I shaded my eyes and scanned the scene. From my vantage point, I watched the hills to the east of the trail for signs of battle. To my horror, I spotted hundreds of mounted warriors pour down out of the hills like a dark, menacing avalanche. On the crest of a nearby bluff, a lone, mounted Indian sat surveying the scene below. Following the direction of his gaze, I realized the warriors were flanking the unsuspecting soldiers. I whipped my head back to the ridge, but the figure was gone.

I stood on the seat of a freight wagon and strained to see what was happening near the Indian camp. As the soldiers ran headlong toward it, my back stiffened in terror. Hundreds of warriors were riding back and forth across the prairie in anticipation of the battle to come. Women, children, and papooses were swimming the river on their ponies while warriors circled and maneuvered their painted war horses in a hostile display of power and might.

In the distance, I was shocked to see Captain Wilcox slow his command to within six hundred yards of the Indians, then stop. Charley Elliston rode slowly toward the turmoil. As the official interpreter, he communicated they were friends and with hand gestures, he coaxed them to return to the caravan peaceably.

In response, the Indian warriors charged with hostile and hideous yells. I heard the firing of their guns. The troops answered with rapid volleys of gun shots. The smoke rising from the scene shielded my view of the clash. Riding out of the pandemonium, I realized Captain Wilcox finally spotted the warriors racing down out of the hills to his left. The tactic would soon overwhelm his troops. The bugler signaled retreat.

Wilcox and his men were in a vulnerable position on the open plain—vastly outnumbered by their enemies. The soldiers turned and fled while firing their weapons to the rear. Soon flanked by a flood of braves, they shot wildly at the raiders. Streams of warriors enveloped them. Fortunately, a second company raced toward the battle. They were now within range of the engagement. The Indians suddenly broke off, and the skirmish ended. The troops rushed back into the relative protection of the wagons, their ammunition completely spent.

Fast-working men inside the corral dug a doughnut-shaped ditch deep enough to shelter us. Lieutenant Triggs swept past with his young family, coaxing us to follow. Soon women and children were squatting within the dirt works. Suddenly, an officer's wife appeared in the distance, running for the wagons, two Indians in hot pursuit. They launched a shower of arrows at her before turning away. The dust blew up all around her feet as the arrows rained down. Unhurt, she hurled herself over the embankment. Standing up, she dusted off her cherry calico dress, repositioned her red shawl, and gasped for air. I pulled her down beside me. The soldiers stood their ground on the edge of our enclosure while exchanging gunfire with Indians, who continued to circle the corral.

The uproar around our loosely held position intensified. I was terrified by those who had taken so much from me. I fought the paralysis creeping up my spine. Although tortured by memories, I was a different person from the one who was thrust helpless into their midst. It was time to fight for what was mine. I pulled the pistol from my pocket and prepared for a breach in our defenses.

The Sioux pulled back. Continuing to impress us with their threats, they remained at a safe distance. Captain Wilcox took advantage of the opportunity to regroup. He feared an attack upon our limited defenses would be swift and thorough. He set about organizing fifty fresh horses with rearmed men to advance and stall the attackers long enough for reinforcements to arrive from Fort Mitchell.

The charging cavalry followed the retreating Indians about three miles down Horse Creek when I noticed lines of warriors appearing above the rise to the west with others gathering to their rear. The gap was closing. I heard myself yell, "It's a trap!" The Indians were luring the soldiers into a tactical maneuver from which there would be no escape.

Anxiety spread throughout those watching within the circle of wagons. Even the men who were hastily digging defenses stood up and paused to gape in horror at the unfolding events. The warriors' ponies were slightly winded, whereas the cavalry troops were riding their best horses, which proved to their advantage. At the last moment, they slipped the noose and charged back toward us. The Indians followed but pulled up just out of reach of our guns.

Captain Wilcox arrived and quickly used the pause in battle to prepare for the arrival of a detachment out of Camp Mitchell. He understood reinforcements were our only hope of preventing the Sioux from destroying the entire wagon train. As he spoke to the troops around him, an increasingly agitated and angry Mrs. Fouts confronted him.

"My husband is dead!" she shrieked while standing nose to nose with the officer. "I demand you kill every full-blood and half-breed in this wagon train immediately!" Hands shaking, she grabbed his arm. Her coiled bun hung limply on the side of her neck. Loose hairs sprang crazily from her scalp. Captain Wilcox tried to step from her grasp as the mad woman bellowed, "I order you to do it! Now!"

Captain Wilcox stood firm and grasped the woman by her upper arms. "Mrs. Fouts! Calm down! There will be no killings of anyone!" Vengeance-possessed, the deranged new widow turned her attentions upon the soldiers and begged them to do the killing.

It was then we saw him. An old, bent Indian with four children in hand stepped between the soldiers and Mrs. Fouts. "I Green Plum," he said. "Full-blood Sioux. I alone in world. Little papooses same. No father, no mother." He pointed at the astonished woman and continued, "If you want…kill us. Now your chance. We struggle to live. Burden to others. Better—we not live."

A quiet descended upon the scene. I watched as the woman's anger collapsed and was replaced by overwhelming grief. The insanity infecting Mrs. Fouts was mollified, but I knew it would rise again to torment her. Shoulders slumped, she dropped her head and stared into the faces of the somber children at her feet.

"No," she said shaking her head. "No, it would not be right." As if her bones had turned to mush, she slumped down in the dirt and began to sob. Her daughters rushed to her side, and all who looked upon the sight felt great pity in their hearts.

Now mid-morning, preparations for another assault were underway. A soldier standing on a wagon shouted news that the 11th Ohio was storming down the road. A relieved Captain Wilcox was ready with fresh mounts. One detachment would form a skirmish line and the other provide a defense around the perimeter of the wagon corral. He summarized the situation for officer Shuman, whose reaction to the news of the estimated thousand warriors awaiting them was one of incredulity. How had the entire wagon train not been massacred?

Wilcox and Haywood led the men down to the river where they discovered a deserted Indian camp. Upon reaching the Platte, the officers deduced the Sioux had crossed the river and disappeared into the hills. A sergeant pointed to a brave who sat quietly on a large yellow horse on the top of the nearest bluff. "Crazy Horse," said the soldier knowingly. The very name caused most to pause in awe. A quiet murmur spread throughout the detachment as if a mysterious entity had overseen the battle and performed a miracle. In moments, he was gone.

Soldiers scoured the area. All that remained of the two thousand Indians from Fort Laramie was the rearguard of warriors watching from the hill tops across the Platte. They could be heard taunting the soldiers to follow, but Wilcox knew the folly of such a move. He ordered his men to hold up. However, a few rushed their horses into the water and were nearly drowned. Two horses were lost. It was inconceivable that women and children had forded the river. The saplings used to guide the Indians on the rocks across the dangerous current were gone.

Captain Wilcox ordered the Sioux lodges and possessions burned. The three privates killed with Captain Fouts were buried where they had fallen. Mr. Bordeaux and other civilians rolled the dead in their bedrolls and laid each man in a separate grave. Flat rocks were placed on the mounds to prevent animals from disturbing the bodies. Mrs. Fouts was insistent her husband's final resting spot never be in this God-forsaken place. The mutilated and naked body of Captain Fouts was carefully wrapped and loaded into a wagon for burial at Fort Mitchell.

After repairing the telegraph lines broken by the Indians, the greatly diminished caravan resumed their line of march. It was thought safer to leave Horse Creek and travel through the night. The assemblage arrived at Fort Mitchell in the wee hours of the morning.

As for me, my pistol still rested in my pocket as we entered Fort Mitchell at dawn. I refused to go another mile without it, so I stepped onto the ground prepared. In my hands was the first means of defense I had possessed since leaving my home on the Little Blue. My growing resolve was much stronger, wrapped within a valiant heart—not to prey upon the weak, but to defend the innocent.

Ten days later, the remainder of the caravan was advised by the Indian agent to return to Laramie for the winter. It was decided I would wait with the officers' families at Fort Mitchell for another escort. Those under Captain Wilcox's command would return to Fort Laramie after a search for the escapees.

Colonel Thomas Moonlight received news of the attack and commented to Mr. Bullock, "There must have been some unwarranted provocation on the part of Captain Fouts, leading the Indians to believe they were not to be honorably dealt with." He immediately ordered a march from Fort Laramie to perform a severe chastisement of the offenders. I learned later his attempt was but a foolish escapade. As his troops enjoyed their breakfasts, Crazy Horse's wild bunch stole the horses out from under their noses. The soldiers walked in shame over forty miles to the fort, saddles on their backs.

The compromise reached by the Sioux chiefs' secret council produced a victory for the agency tribes—the schemes of the United States government were thwarted.

Meanwhile, hidden in the high place, five strong warriors spoke softly. Much had happened the day of the battle on Horse Creek. It all started with the man Fouts. He had come in the morning with the interpreter Elliston. His severe words to the chiefs had borne no respect, and Elliston was quick to repeat them with equal rudeness. Charging Shield and Foam killed the soldier chief who was so disliked by the Lakota. Elliston was wounded. These acts were considered just.

The braves spoke of the four old Lakota chiefs who died at the hands of the other Indians, careful not to speak their names. The respected leaders stood for peace that morning and refused to leave the white man's path. It cost them their lives. The shooting was never mentioned, but the soft keening of their families was heard as the people followed the chief's sons northward.

The warriors noticed the large herds of horses owned by the traders; they especially admired the different breeds with unusual markings. Touch the Clouds chuckled lightly as he recounted the story of a beautiful stallion. The horse was covered in dark blue marks like a spotted bean. It was said the owner cried like a baby as it was swept along with other captured horses.

Crazy Horse recalled the moments when the escaping squaws cried out. First, when the soldiers tried to cross the river. To encourage them, Black Wolf promised to perform the Sun Dance when all were safe. And the second time, the women watched the burning lodges at Horse Creek. The wailing was joined by frightened old ones; but all felt the protection of strong warriors like Hump, who rode behind them. Just ahead were the northern brothers who waited with many pack horses loaded with robes and teepees. Soon they would be in the sacred hills with plenty of buffalo for all.

The Cheyenne deaths at Sand Creek were mourned, and no one found a reason to laugh for many moons. Now, however, Crazy Horse chuckled aloud at the memory of watching the line of soldiers walk out of Indian country. Like mules, they carried saddles on sore backs. Their horses grazed contentedly in the Indian herds where they belonged.

chapter sixty-six

Isabelle

22 June 1865
Fort Sedgwick, Colorado Territory

Died in this city, on the 18th inst. of inflammation of the brain, Mary Ewbanks, aged 4 years. She was the girl captured from the Indians on the Arkansas last fall. Her death was caused indirectly from three arrow wounds, in different parts of her body.

Rocky Mountain Daily News, Denver, Colorado
March 21, 1865

Fort Sedgwick was located just outside Julesburg and was but another stop along the barren trails. Grateful for the protection of the soldiers, I prayed we would find some peace within the confines of this small fort.

Everyone knew I was the Indian captive traveling home. I still had on the moccasins I wore when I arrived at Fort Laramie. I had no choice but to continue wearing them.

I could not help but wonder what the soldiers thought as they peered at us under their hats. I lifted my dress high, securing it under my bosom to cover my growing stomach. A white woman pregnant by an Indian was considered indecent by all standards.

One of the soldiers introduced me to the only other woman at the fort, Mrs. Wade, the laundress. She and Mr. Wade invited us to stay with them. She was a kind lady who tried her best to accommodate us as we waited for more troops to accompany our stage.

Mrs. Wade recalled when Lucinda reached Fort Sedgwick:

I was washing and doing other work for the officers at the Fort at the time and remember well when Mrs. Ewbanks was brought in by a detachment of soldiers from Fort Laramie. She was a young woman of good looks, although she was roughly clad and showed many signs of the terrible usage to which she had been subjected. I recall especially she had long, red hair, and while I can imagine with proper care it would have added much to her personal appearance, the absence of such toilet articles as comb and brush robbed it of much of its attractiveness. I recall also she wore the garb of the Indian women, blanket supplemented with the furs of such wild animals as she had been able to get hold of.

Feeling exhausted from travel, I explained I was in much need of some rest. Mrs. Wade offered to watch over Willie and showed me to our room. I put my satchel on the bed and closed the door. The fresh smell of newly laundered linens relaxed my aching body. Noticing the wildflowers on the window ledge, I fell asleep at once.

A ray of light sprayed through the window and warmed my face. The short nap was refreshing, but I was still tired. Walking over to the mirror hanging on the wall, I looked at my reflection. There was a different woman looking at me. There was no color in this woman's face. Her hair was dull and streaked with gray, and her eyes were hollow. My hand moved in slow motion as I picked up a comb from the dresser and ran it though my hair. There were a few hairpins, and I pulled my straggled locks back for the first time in almost a year.

There was a light knock on the door. I heard Mrs. Wade say, "Mrs. Eubank, there is a gentleman here to see you. His name is Mr. Davenport. He has travelled from Denver City and says he has some important information for you." I pinched my cheeks, smoothed my dress, and opened the door.

The waiting gentleman was tall and smartly dressed. He tipped his black suede hat at me as I stepped into the room. Was this messenger going to tell me my brother William or maybe Will's brother George were on their way from Denver?

My thoughts vanished as he said the unfathomable. "I have come to offer my condolences regarding your daughter Isabelle."

What was he saying? Condolences? I just stared at him in disbelief. My throat closed.

He continued, "I know this is upsetting news. I was at the Planter's Hotel in Denver City when your daughter arrived."

A sick look etched my face.

"Citizens were crowded up and down the street and watched as four children arrived by coach. First, the young woman, Laura Roper, stepped out followed by two younger boys. Then Major Wynkoop reached into the coach and lifted out your daughter."

"Was it really Belle?" I blurted. "What did she look like?"

He hesitated. Then he told me her face was smudged, her eyes

400

swollen. Mr. Davenport explained, "Major Wynkoop carried her into the hotel."

The blood completely drained from my face.

He asked, "Do you want me to continue, Mrs. Eubank? I know this must be excruciating for you."

I had no words! I could not speak.

"Mrs. Eubank?"

I slowly nodded my head and murmured, "Yes."

Mr. Davenport cleared his throat and said, "I followed them inside the hotel. Major Wynkoop requested refreshments for the children. Later, one of the ladies from the Colorado Relief Society asked for volunteers to take the children. They needed to be bathed and dressed in clean clothes."

"I am sad to tell you, Mrs. Eubank, your daughter would not or just could not speak. Major Wynkoop provided her name and the names of the other children, and their pictures were taken." He reached into his pocket and presented a small photograph. Astonished, I stared at the familiar faces. A forlorn Belle sat on Laura's lap. On the left, I recognized Grandmother Ruth's deep-set eyes in the face of Ambrose. To the right, the young lad Danny's vacant and frightened stare chilled me. I stared at the picture in silence as tears streamed down my cheeks. Mr. Davenport continued, "Molly Sanford, a kind woman in Denver City, offered to keep Belle."

My heart pounded. "Tell me she is waiting for me to take her home!" I shouted. "Tell me, Mr. Davenport!" He hung his head. What was he saying? This cannot be!

The kind stranger looked at me compassionately and said, "I am so sorry, Mrs. Eubank. Mrs. Sanford tried her best to care for Belle, but listening to your distressed child cry for you night after night affected her deeply."

I shook my head back and forth and buried it in my hands. "What happened to her then?" I whispered.

"Isabelle was taken in by Dr. Burdsal, then given up to a Dr. Smith. Neither was able to keep her. During this time, one of the families changed her name to Mary. Finally, my wife and I took her in."

"Mr. Davenport, when I was at Fort Laramie, I read from the Denver newspaper a girl named Mary Ewbanks died. Was she my Isabelle?" I asked.

"Yes, Mrs. Eubank. She suffered greatly from abuse and neglect in the Indian camps. I hope you can find some solace in knowing your daughter was cared for until the time of her death. She had a proper burial in the Prospect Hill Cemetery in Denver City."

My heart froze.

"I brought this for you, too."

Mr. Davenport handed me a small, brown package. I looked down at it and unfolded the paper. Inside was a small, tattered dress. The same gaily flowered dress I slipped over Belle's sweet face the morning of that hot August day.

Mr. Davenport gently took one of my hands and bowed his head. As I stood there silently weeping, he turned slowly on his heel and walked out of the room. I heard him thank Mrs. Wade as he left. She bade him goodbye, stepped in the room, and gently wrapped her arms around me. Inconsolable waves of agony gripped my very soul. This was not happening. Through my sobs I cried out, "No! She is not dead! I will never believe it! My Belle is not dead. No! She is not dead...."

Sitting me in a chair, Mrs. Wade said, "Mrs. Eubank, my dear, what can I do for you? Let me get you some tea and draw you a bath." She filled a kettle with water as I wandered with Willie back to our room. Before I knew it, she led me to a bathtub.

I turned and unbuttoned the front of my dress. As I pulled it down, I heard her gasp. Her voice was faint and rattled. "Oh, my dear! What have they done to you? Lashes cover every inch of your back, and your entire body is bruised!"

Revealing my tortures to Colonel Moonlight and Lieutenant Colonel Baumer was agonizing. Humiliated, I did not tell them everything. To heal, part of me needed to address what my body revealed. I wished to put this horrific experience behind me. But not yet. I did not respond to Mrs. Wade's inquiries and slipped down in the warmth of the water.

Later that night, the kind laundress sat in a large rocking chair with my son on her lap. Reaching into her apron pocket, she pulled out a tiny item and held it in her palm for me to see. A shiny, white pearl button glistened in the fire light. "I tried to think of something to give you to soothe your hurting soul," she said. "Perhaps this keepsake will remind you of the little girl you held most dear."

Tears brimming, I thanked her for the gift and for allowing me some time to myself, then gathered my sleepy boy in my arms. Once he was asleep, I returned to the porch, intent on answering her questions and washing away the sins of my attackers.

Mrs. Wade said Lucinda told her the following:

Not the chief alone of the Cheyenne but the entire band took every possible liberty with her, and she was so tortured by them that she lost consciousness and never knew by how many of them she had been misused; but as the raiding band consisted of about forty men, she did not doubt that she had suffered from that number. Relating the particulars of some of her experiences when in camp she said that on more than one occasion when she had refused to comply with all the brutal demands of Blackfoot, the squaws would bind her to a stake and surround her with pieces of firewood as if they intended to burn her alive. At other times they would scorch the soles of her feet. Again, they would take the baby by the heels, swing him over their heads and bring his little body down as if with the intent of dashing his brains out. For some reason, however, she and he were always spared.

Completely shaken, I whispered, "I am now with child. Big Crow made me his wife." The abhorrent disgust inside me was indescribable. "They robbed me of my beloved husband and my precious daughter, Mrs. Wade! They killed almost everyone in my dear husband's family. How can I give birth to this Indian baby fathered by such a vile and vicious beast? I do not know what I shall do!"

With eyes cast down, I murmured to myself, "We are all alone now."

chapter sixty-seven

Testimony

22 June 1865
Fort Sedgwick, Colorado Territory

They ordered me frequently to wean my baby, but I always refused: for I felt convinced if he was weaned, they should take him from me, and I would never see him again. They took my daughter from me just after we were captured, and I never saw her after that.

Lucinda Eubank

My voice was strong, my hand was raised, but they belonged to someone else. Shakily, I repeated the oath of loyalty to my country.

> I, Lucinda Eubank, do solemnly swear that I have never borne arms against the United States, nor aided and abetted the enemies thereof in the late rebellion; that I will support, protect, and defend the Constitution and Government of the United States against all enemies, whether domestic or foreign, and that I will bear true faith, allegiance, and loyalty to the same, any ordinance, resolution, or law of my State, Convention or Legislature to the contrary notwithstanding; and I further trust I do this with a full determination, pledge, and purpose without any mental reservation or evasion whatever; and further that I will well and faithfully perform all the duties which may be required of me by law, so help me God.

Congress ordered an investigation into the Sand Creek Massacre. The office of the Judge Advocate, District of the Plains, requested my testimony upon arrival at Fort Sedgwick, Colorado Territory. It would be included in the report of the Joint Committee on the Conduct of the War, Massacre of the Cheyenne Indians, 38th Congress, Second Session.

The clerk turned the handwritten page of my oath around on the table to face me and asked for my signature. Months of travel through the wilderness adversely affected my vision. Summer or winter, the brilliant sky produced an intense glare. Now my eyes watered incessantly and were sensitive to light. The glow of a candle or an oil lamp at night were the exceptions. With a slight tremor, I strained to focus and signed my name on the legal document declaring my loyalty to a land far away— in both distance and memory. Two witnesses added their signatures under my own. Their freshly brushed, navy-blue military uniforms were a stark contrast to my own dusty and worn dress. I recognized Lieutenant Triggs of Company D. He and his family accompanied us from Fort Laramie, but the other man was a stranger.

In January, the Cheyenne attacked the town of Julesburg and nearby Fort Sedgwick. Most of it was burned and laid waste. The desolate and blackened remnants only increased the disorienting cloud of purgatory around me. The sight of the recently burned-out buildings added to an overall gray discouragement. To relive those terrifying events and describe the conditions of my captivity in the presence of strangers would require strength and fortitude. My "growing" condition was difficult to hide. I sensed ridicule, judgment, and fascination emanating from the attendees.

I pulled my shawl tightly across my shoulders and braced myself for the task at hand. I determined to stand straight like the soldiers at the council and to speak clearly of matters too horrible to hide in my darkest nightmares. This story must be shared with the representatives of the United States Government, a story for the ages.

"Thank you, Mrs. Eubank," declared a voice from one of the three men seated at the table facing me. Startled, I located the speaker. Our eyes met as he looked up from the papers displayed neatly in front of him. Every person in the room stared at the captive woman in suspense.

"Please have a seat, Mrs. Eubank. I am Captain Zabriskie, Judge Advocate for the Plains District here in Julesburg, Colorado Territory. We are here to record an account of your recent captivity among the Cheyenne, Arapaho, and Sioux Indians. A journalist from the Daily Rocky Mountain News is here and will prepare a report for the newspaper."

I perked up at this news and began to look around the room for the man. Captain Zabriskie followed my lead and waved a hand toward a gentleman standing near the window. He held a pencil and pad of paper in his hand. The reporter tipped his head in acknowledgement.

"Please, tell us a little about yourself," prompted the captain. "Where are you from?"

"I was born in Pennsylvania."

"And what is your age, Mrs. Eubank?"

"I am 24 years old," I replied. The simple answer was oddly reassuring. Still alive.

"Where did you reside just prior to your captivity?"

"I lived with my husband, William Eubank, our two young children, and Will's family on the Little Blue River—near the Narrows," I began. "In 1858, my husband and I were married in Missouri. We settled in Nebraska the next spring after the government opened the land to settlers. My brother-in-law, Joe Eubank, lived in the area for a year prior and drove a stage for the Overland Stage Company. He encouraged us to join him. Our ranch was situated directly on the Overland Trail, and we supplied hay to the freighters and travelers who passed by."

"Please tell us about the events of Sunday, August 7, 1864," said Zabriskie. "When you are ready," he added gently.

I bit my lip and guardedly began my tale. "Our home was attacked, robbed, and burned. I was taken prisoner along with my two children, my nephew, and Miss Laura Roper, a neighbor."

"Who took you prisoner, Mrs. Eubank?" he interrupted.

"Indians. Sioux and Arapaho and…Cheyenne Dog Soldiers."

I heard a collective intake of breath by those assembled about the room.

"About a dozen in all," I added.

"Do you know the identities of any of the Indians who took you?"

"I came to know their names during my captivity. Heap of Birds, Blackfoot, Gall, Left Hand, Black Kettle, and…Two Face." I looked at my hand. There it was again—the anxious plucking of my skirt whenever I thought of…it all.

"How old were your children at the time?"

"My daughter Isabelle was three years. My son Willie was nine months, and my nephew Ambrose was six years."

"Where did the Indians take you?" he asked.

"They took us south across the Republican River, then west to a creek where we camped in their village for a brief time. I was taken to the lodge of an old chief…." I drifted off.

"What was his name?" interrupted the captain.

"I do not remember. I did not understand their language. Later, I ended up in the lodge of the Dog Soldier, Big Crow."

The soldiers murmured amongst themselves. A sharp glance from Captain Zabriskie brought the room to order again.

"How did this chief treat you?"

I swallowed, thought a moment, and plunged ahead to describe the ordeal. "He forced me…" I said, "by the most terrible threats and menaces…to yield my person to him. He treated me as his wife." My chin dropped, and I stared at my feet.

Captain Zabriski paused and moved on. "Tell me about how you arrived at Sand Creek."

Thoughtfully, I set about the task of summarizing the endless days of roaming the plains. Coherence was difficult, but I had rehearsed the facts. I described the persons and events leading up to Sand Creek. I answered personal and somewhat accusing questions regarding my captivity. The actual details of the massacre itself were etched in my memory as images, frozen and appalling. Putting them into words proved impossible. United States soldiers attacked a peaceful village. The blood and gore, horror and tragedy were stories for others to tell. My escape with Two Face, however, seemed of great interest to the curious and macabre within the crowd.

"How is it you came to be with the Sioux Indians, Mrs. Eubank?" asked the captain.

"The chief who had held me for nearly four months last fall traded me to the Sioux Indian, Two Face," I explained.

"What treatment did you receive from Two Face?"

The crowd leaned forward in anticipation of my answer.

"He did not treat me as a wife but forced me to do all menial labor done by squaws." I shrugged my shoulders, feeling the tightness of the healing scars on my back. "Then he traded me to Blackfoot, another chief in his band. Blackfoot treated me as his wife. Because I resisted him, his squaws abused and ill-used me. Blackfoot beat me unmercifully. The Indians treated me like a dog because I detested the chief so much."

I paused in my story and noticed I was clenching my fists. Dragging a breath of air deeply into my lungs, I tried to calm the pounding in my temples. My mouth was dry, and I licked my cracked lips. No water was offered.

"Please continue," said the captain, apologetically.

"The Sioux treated me better than the Cheyenne. That is, the Sioux gave me more to eat." As an afterthought, I added, "When I was with the Cheyenne, I was often hungry."

"Can you tell us anything about the Indians' activities during the winter?" he asked.

I thought a moment, and a frightening memory surfaced. "During the winter, the Cheyenne came to buy me and the child for the purpose of burning us, but Two Face would not let them have me. We were on the North Platte. The Indians were killing the whites all the time and running off their stock. They would bring in the scalps of the whites and show them to me and laugh about it." I winced at the memory....

"Tell me about your children during all of this, Mrs. Eubank." The captain understood I needed a shift to make it through the testimony. My weariness must be apparent, I thought.

"Willie has been with me throughout our entire captivity. The Indians ordered me often to wean my baby, but I always refused. I was convinced if I weaned him, they would take him from me, and I would never see him again."

"And your daughter? Isabelle?"

"We were separated after our capture. I saw her briefly in the camp, but she was given up by the Cheyenne to Major Wynkoop and released in Denver. I never saw her again." Tears welled up and I wiped my eyes repeatedly while regaining my composure.

"Today I met the man who had her. His name is Davenport. He received her from a Dr. Smith. She was quite ill from injuries received while with the Indians. Mr. Davenport told me she died last February." I paused and choked back the grief. Dust particles floated in the sunbeams striking through the windows. The room was quiet except for my own soft weeping. Struggling to regain my voice, I rasped, "My nephew was given up to Major Wynkoop as well. I am told he also died by mistreatment by the Indians."

"I am terribly sorry, Mrs. Eubank. I know this is difficult," Captain Zabriski replied. "How was it you came to be released at Fort Laramie?" He seemed relieved to change the subject.

I shifted in my chair and recalled my escape from Blackfoot's lodge with Two Face. Memories of moccasins stepping through the teepee flap and moving quickly and silently in the early morning hours would not be spoken. They were my own.

"Two Face took me to the fort." I paused, opened my mouth, and shut it again. I had no words, for emotions were overriding self-control. Anger and indignation surged within me. Rankled by the current gossip, I was getting my dander up. "I have heard it stated that a story was told by me to the effect that Two Face's son saved my life."

This latest information caused a stir among the listeners.

"I never made any such statement, as I have no knowledge of any such thing."

The sting in my voice was noticeable to all. I was ready to finish. I sat erect, lifted my head, and said, "I think if my life had been in danger, he would not have troubled himself about it." I heard small coughs and clearing of throats behind me and noticed others suppress their reactions.

The remote and impersonal description of my disturbing story left me shaken and hollow, but now it was official record. I would come to regret the disjointed and sterilized version I had given. Trying to condense my experience was impossible and unreasonable. However, my testimony was sufficient, and I decided I would not speak of it again.

Later that afternoon, I was relieved to learn a stagecoach would leave soon with the required one hundred man escort. The added military supply wagons amply bolstered the growing line of wagons, horses, oxen, mules, freighters, and stagecoaches. All were impatient to continue the journey east. The overstuffed mail bags piled on coaches and wagons were visible reminders of the unscheduled interruptions to the regular mail service.

As we left the devastation of Julesburg caused by the Indian attacks, I wondered if the whole continent had gone up in flames. General Curtis ordered all vegetation along the trail be torched to make it difficult for the tribes to continue waging war. This crucial connection between civilization and Denver City would not feed Indian ponies. The scorched earth along the trail was ashen gray. It summoned a dark mood among the men who likened the surroundings to a lunar landscape.

It was rumored the tactic had not produced the desired results. Nothing could stop those on the path of war—white or native.

STATEMENT OF MRS. EWBANKS.

Of Mrs..Ewbanks,.giving an account of her captivity among the Indians. She was taken by the CHEYENNES, and was one of the prisoners proposed to be given up by Black Kettle, White Antelope and others, in the Council at Denver.

Mrs. Lucinda Ewbanks states she was born in Pennsylvania; is 24 years of age; she resided on the Little Blue, at or near the Narrows. She says that on the 8th day of August, 1864, the house was attacked, robbed, burned, and herself and two children, with her nephew and a Miss Roper, were captured by the Cheyenne Indians. Her eldest child at the time was three years old; her nephew was six years old. When taken from her home was by the Indians taken south across the Republican, and west to a creek, the name of which she does not remember. Here for a short time was their village or camping place. They were traveling all Winter. When first taken by the Cheyennes, she was taken to the lodge of an old Chief, whose name she does not recollect. He forced me, by the most terrible threats and menaces, to yield my person to him. He treated me as his wife. He then traded me to Two Face, a Sioux, who did not treat me as a wife, but forced

409

me to do all menial labor done by squaws, and he beat me terribly. Two Face traded me to Black Foot (Sioux) who treated me as his wife, and because I resisted him his squaws abused and ill used me. Black Foot also beat me unmercifully and the Indians generally, treated me as though I was a dog, on account of my showing so much detestation toward Black Foot. Two Face traded for me again. I then received a little better treatment. I was better treated among the Sioux than the Cheyennes—that is, the Sioux gave me more to eat. When with the Cheyennes I was often hungry. My purchase from the Cheyennes was made early last Fall, and I remained with them until May 1865. During the Winter the Cheyennes came to buy me and the child, for the purpose of burning us, but Two Face would not let them have me. During the Winter we were on the North Platte the Indians were killing the whites all the time and running off their stock. They would bring in the scalps of the whites and show them to me and laugh about it. They ordered me frequently to wean my baby, but I always refused, for I felt convinced if he was weaned they would take him from me and I should never see him again. They took my daughter from me just after we were captured, and I never saw her after. I have seen the man to-day who had her—his name is Davenport, he lives in Denver. He received her from a Dr. Smith. She was given up by the Cheyennes to Major Wynkoop, but from injuries received while with the Indians she died last February. My nephew also was given up to Major Wynkoop, but he too died at Denver. The doctor said it was caused by bad treatment from the Indians. Whilst encamped on the North Platte, Elston came to the village and I went with him and Two Face to Fort Laramie.

I have heard it stated that a story had been told by me, to the effect that Two Face's son had saved my life. I never made any such statement, as I have no knowledge of any such thing, and I think if my life had been in danger, he would not have troubled himself about it.

LUCINDA EWBANKS.

Witness: J. H. Triggs,
First Lieutenant Commanding Company D, Seventh Iowa Cavalry.

E.B. ZABRISKIE, Captain First Cavalry Nevada Volunteers,
Judge Advocate, District of the Plains, Julesburg (C.T.)

Daily Rocky Mountain News, Denver, Co.,
Monday, 13 September 1865

chapter sixty-eight

Trust Reborn

Early July 1865
Alkali Station, Nebraska Territory

Mrs. Eubank was liberated at Fort Laramie by Two Face, who offered her for ransom. When Mrs. Eubank came down to Alkali on her way from Laramie, Wiggins talked with her, and she told him the whole story of her capture and release.

Walter M. Camp

The river's edge was blooming. The pale green of the willows contrasted with the luminous, yellow blossoms of yarrow. The waters shown like flat silver. The trees along the shoreline waved their leafy arms in celebration of warm breezes and clear skies.

The wagon train made a noonday stop at Alkali Station just a mile south of the Platte. My coach left the train and pulled up outside the stockade. Brain-addled and aching from the endless rocking and bouncing motion of the coach, I stepped out to stretch. Alkali had been a Pony Express Station, then a stage stop, and was now converted into a cavalry post for the purpose of guarding the Overland Trail. I peered through the dust and rising heat waves to scan the officer's quarters, barracks, storehouse, and stables.

Overheated, I sat down precariously on a stool in the shade of the coach and began to vigorously fan myself. Eyes closed, I sensed an intrusion into my space. It was a man. He had ridden up and dismounted from an enormously sturdy bay horse. Standing well over six feet tall, the unusual stranger's long hair was tied loosely at the base of his neck. His red shirt and worn leather leggings reminded me of the Indian attire worn by those who lived at Fort Laramie. Several times in the past few days, I noticed him ride past the coach. Through my dust-choked weariness, I wondered at his appearance and overall authority among the troops and teamsters.

The man stopped in front of me and cleared his throat. "I remember meeting you and your husband at the Little Blue Station some time back," he began. "I am Oliver P. Wiggins, U.S. Army scout. General Heath requested I join your escort for the remainder of your trip to Fort Kearny."

Squinting up into his face, I saw pale blue eyes deeply set in a very wrinkled, leathery face. His knowledge of my husband startled me. I did remember meeting him. He frequented my table for a meal at the Little Blue Station. Polite and friendly, I always enjoyed his stories and wealth of knowledge—for he had lived most of his life on the frontier. Usually, I bid a hasty welcome to the men who ate at the station and left them in the company of my husband. Sparks of my old life began to ignite.

"Thank you, Mr. Wiggins. It is good to see a familiar face," I replied.

"I want to apologize to you," he said abruptly. He removed his hat and began to turn its rim slowly between his fingers. "Ma'am, not long after you were taken, I was sent to find you."

Stunned, I gawked at the solemn man standing before me. "That was you?"

"I oversaw a mounted regiment of one hundred Winnebago Indians at the time. The government hired me to keep the road open. We left Fort Kearny and followed the renegades for two or three days." He inhaled sharply, "I saw you riding behind Two Face with your babe."

Noticing my consternation, he continued his explanation. "I was sent to find the Indian raiders' camp. We stopped on a rise to look around. That is when I saw a group of warriors riding fast with Roaring Wind bringing up the rearguard. I recognized you. Your long, red hair."

My shaking hand betrayed a lack of composure as I quickly tucked a strand of hair back under my sun bonnet. It had become tangled and infested during the winter and was still unmanageable. The wisps around my face would not stay in the bun.

"Your hair," he continued. "It was shimmering…in the sun. I knew it was you." Mr. Wiggins blushed an unspoken apology at his forwardness. "I knew Will and Joe well," he continued after he recovered. "Joe Eubank was your brother-in-law, correct?"

My head jerked up to face him as I blinked hard and stammered. "Knew Joe? Was my brother-in-law? What do you mean by that, sir?" I asked. The air instantly sucked out of my lungs in a vacuum. What had happened to him?

Mr. Wiggins' face registered as to the coarse and unintended manner to which he had just brought terrible news. His sober eyes were tinged with sadness. "I guess you are still trying to put the pieces together, aren't you, ma'am? Well...." He paused as if trying to apply himself properly to the delivery of such news. "I regret to tell you Joe and his brother Fred did not survive the attack on Kiowa Station. He was killed out on the road about a mile and a half from his place." He hurried on as my mind began to calculate the others who might have been lost. "His wife Hattie escaped with the help of John Palmer. Her brother, you know."

"Oh...Hattie, Joe, Fred, John," I spoke quietly to myself. So often, thoughts of the two beloved newlyweds, Joe and Hattie, entertained me during the long hours of mind-numbing drudgery in the Indian camps. Handsome Fred was a modest and reserved young man so full of promise —never one to spurn hard work. A pleasant soul who reveled in helping others.

The killing of Joe seemed impossible, though. His strength, ability, and fortitude bespoke a man with super-human abilities. Unlike those who were novices in a primitive and unbroken land, Joe thrived with a remarkable ease and sense of oneness with the wild. His spirit was soft yet tough, never to be dominated or harnessed.

So, Hattie and John survived. Her babe would be several months old by now. I longed to see them again; yet, in the remoteness of my surroundings, it seemed impossible. They must certainly have returned home to Marysville, Kansas, where family would care for and comfort the mourning young widow.

Mr. Wiggins interrupted my thoughts as the memories of loved ones tumbled into focus. "I am truly sorry for your losses, Mrs. Eubank."

Surprisingly, timid little Willie toddled up to the tall stranger and wrapped his arms around the man's knee. The wind fluttered his blond curls as he tilted his head back and squinted at the towering stranger.

"I wondered what happened to you and the young one," Mr. Wiggins continued quietly. He patted Willie on the head and smiled down at the child. "I want you to know the day we saw you, we would have given chase if our horses had not been so worn down. Two Face and I were ac-quainted with each other for a long time before this Indian war. I often think I could have talked him into releasing you sooner." Mr. Wiggin's voice was filled with regret as he reached up to his saddle horn and began to finger the lead rope wrapped around it. "Was sorry to hear about his end at Fort Laramie. My son-in-law is the telegraph operator up there." Wiggins cleared his throat. "He told me about...it. Two Face was a friend of mine...before this...." He hastily looked at me and added, "Not that he wasn't wrong in what he did...." His voice trailed off.

I said nothing. The baby in me turned over with a kick, and I was suffering in the heat. A fly buzzed my face. I remained quiet. The dreadful events of that day were compounded by this terrible news. I had heard enough. I felt sick in my soul.

The commotion of men's voices blended with the whinnies of horses. Iron chains clanked against wooden traces. All were familiar signals that movement of our lengthy train of wagons and coaches was about to begin again. I stood and bade Mr. Wiggins a curt good-bye and lifted Willie into the coach.

Just as I grabbed the strap on the side of the stagecoach and queasily stepped onto the mounting ledge, I felt a pair of gentle hands around my expanded waist. I was lifted into the shady interior. I sat next to my boy and turned to thank Mr. Wiggins for the assistance. What I saw in the scout's concerned face stopped me. Genuine compassion and understanding emanated in silent connection. He gave a nod and latched the door. In that moment, as our eyes met, a mutual respect was defined. A long-forgotten sensation of trust was reborn in my hurting heart; an element missing in all my encounters with people since my capture.

Before reaching Fort Kearny, we passed Plum Creek Station and I thought of my dear and faithful friend, Nancy Morton. The graves along the side of the road were numerous. Most certainly, some held the remains of her husband, brother, and cousin who were killed a year ago. The blackened remnants of the Morton/Pratt wagons still lay strewn about the prairie.

Our weary caravan limped into Fort Kearny twenty-six days after leaving Fort Laramie. The arrival of the civilian convoy was received with a subdued and failure-laden aura that permeated from the top commanders down to the stable hands. The U. S. Army with whom we began our journey returned to Fort Laramie without their Indian charges and prisoners. The renowned Captain Fouts and three soldiers were left in the ground.

My presence created a bit of sensation, but soon I was delivered to the domicile of the scout, Mr. Wiggins. He and his wife Martha arranged for me to stay in their home. They were currently assigned to Alkali Station and would reside there indefinitely. Mr. Wiggins continued to personally monitor the movements of travel up and down the trail.

A three-week delay was anticipated before new preparations could be made for our transport east. Mr. Wiggins' cheerful attention to my comfort, and to the needs of Willie, intersected with my exhaustion and apprehension. I was grateful. He never explained where he had taken up quarters, but I had the impression he was a man accustomed to the rigors of living in sub-par conditions. A hayloft or hard ground were preferable to crowded barracks and seemed to be no trouble to him. He thoughtfully left us to retire in relative peace.

Throughout the days which followed, O.P. always knocked before entering his home to retrieve items or clothing. I was relieved no further attempts at discussion were forthcoming. It was as though his polite avoidance of me was meant to provide relief and escape from the rigors of travel and the ever-enveloping memories. The dark circles under my eyes and my green complexion surely told the story.

Folks around the fort were polite, but when passing, the men barely raised their heads as they tipped their hats. The women subconsciously gathered their blouses together at the neck and lowered their bonnets as if my ravished condition somehow endangered them. Eye contact was avoided. The snapping of the Union flag atop the flagpole in the ever-present wind joined the inaudible sound of their "tsk, tsk" at my unfortunate circumstance.

However, I rejoiced in the fact Willie was beginning to relax a little. The benefits of food, rest, and the ministrations of the attentive scout had done much to aid his recuperation. Friendly interactions and peaceful treatment of his mother contributed to easing Willie's constant and fearful wariness.

I knew I was the subject of great discussion. The horrifying details and imaginings of my captivity were whispered at every opportunity. Shame and embarrassment followed me through each leg of the journey. My loneliness became a cocoon of security as I withdrew from all but the most necessary interactions.

Oliver Wiggins was different, though. His quiet ways and subtle reassurances were comforting. My disjointed person was gathering itself together again, piece by piece. Solitude amid safety afforded me a path to a new patchwork of wholeness.

chapter sixty-nine

Rise Again

30 July 1865
Nebraska Territory

Light of love shined in my cell,
Turned to gold the iron bars,
Opened windows to the stars,
Peace stood there as sentinel.

Mrs. Charles E. Cowman

A *rosy, plump cheek pressed against mine. Wrapped lovingly around my neck, her tiny arms drooped then lost their grip. I squeezed her desperately against my breast, but her form shrank smaller and smaller to the size of a snuggly puppy. A whimpering groan escaped my throat. I clung to her, willing her to stay. Suddenly, my embrace held only the emptiness of her small dress and a hint of her sweet fragrance—like spring grass. She was gone!*

My eyes shot open when I heard a scream, "Isabelle!"

It was *my* voice.

Restless night sweats increased in frequency now that I possessed Belle's dress. I sat up in bed and noticed dawn breaking through the muslin curtains. Fort Kearny was coming alive as the reliable reveille bugle sounded.

The child within the womb had been active all night. With the dawn, it turned over, stretched, twisted, kicked, then lay quiet—undisturbed by my own distress. This pregnancy brought none of the usual joy. Instead, it was a stark reminder of the one I despised. Even though he was hanging from the gallows, I knew no relief. In my dreams, I experienced vivid reenactments of wicked events. Now, however, I was able to calm myself upon awakening. I would repeat, "He is dead. He is dead."

The sun's attempt to bring light into my dark mind was met with the familiar, overwhelming grief that no earthly force could dispel. The limp, torn, and stained dress spoke of Belle's ordeal. I dropped it in a rumpled heap onto my lap. No child filled its shell. Her pleading eyes came to me as I smoothed the garment to fold it once again. I found the repetitive action comforting, but I knew that its compulsive attraction could lead to insanity. Derangement lay just beneath the surface, and I toiled daily to keep a grip on reality.

I folded her frock and said aloud, "I must stop!" Yet, I never let it out of my sight and rarely set it down. As I dressed each morning, I placed it inside my chemise. When I slept, I held it gently against my cheek. The calico fabric, the colors of a sunflower, was meticulously and lovingly sewn by Grandmother Ruth. I tenderly fingered the tiny heart embroidered into its collar—a tiny message of love. The weight of loss clawed mercilessly at me. I could not accept her death. There was a mistake.

The mental push off the cliff was followed by a deep sob as I fell apart yet again. Tears beyond restraint spurted from my eyes. My slumped shoulders quaked as spasms racked my body. I struggled to sit upright on the bed, but my imaginings spurred me on. No hand of comfort reached out to touch me. The strangers of Fort Kearny slipped away as phantoms sliding into the fog of my peripheral vision. Their eyes avoided mine, but my expanding pregnancy and news of Belle's passing generated sympathy mixed with judgment.

How many minutes passed as I drifted away to the familiar safety of the irrational? Only Willie's tug on my wrist brought me back…as he had done so many times before. The marvel of his survival was repeatedly applied to my credit; but, in truth, Willie was the one who saved *me*, pulled *me*, loved *me*—to rise again.

Willie climbed onto my lap, and we sat together. Turning to face me, his shiny, brown eyes stared into mine, imploring me to focus on him. He was an old soul with a wisdom that comes from a life's worth of experiences that exceeded his tender age. Ever so gently, he patted my cheeks with both hands. His serious expression always concerned me. He had seen a lifetime of sadness, fear, and sorrow. What did he see in me now?

Oh, my child…. Will you ever be young again? The sores and scars on his feet, ankles, knees, and head had finally begun to heal, but would his soul ever regain its innocence? Would his grim, downturned little mouth ever relax? His tiny, furrowed brow released as I spoke to him. "It's time to go."

Abruptly, we stood together, his hand in mine. I had one more job to do before returning to the states. I dreaded it. I needed it. Then it would be finished.

Through the window, a soft light encased us in peace.

———•———

The road east of Fort Kearny was wide and well-used by all manner of conveyance. After a troubled and restless three weeks in the home of Mr. and Mrs. Wiggins, our journey resumed. We passed freighters, wagon trains, stagecoaches, buggies, military companies, and every variety of westward-leaning human face. Now entrusted into the care of General Heath and his escort, I was thankful for another layer of safety.

I relaxed a little as we passed souls fresh out of civilization. Their expectant faces caused me to turn my head away. I consciously avoided all conversation with these sojourners. What a troublesome tale I could share, but I had no idea where to begin and where my story would end. My hands still trembled, and I was easily startled by the slightest urgency in a person's or animal's mannerisms. Yet, just the nearness of folks who hailed from Missouri, Illinois, and every other state in the union brought me comfort.

The transcontinental railroad was a popular topic among those in my wagon train. The idea of an iron horse chugging reliably along at ten to fifteen miles per hour across the vast plains seemed incredible. The potential for such a thing to keep the union pinned together by its hard, iron spikes and parallel rails was astonishing. It was easy to see this piece of America was rapidly changing to become a place of blinding transformation and uncharted growth.

The life I had known no longer existed. My surroundings seemed strange and unrecognizable. The news of the war's end and the saving of the union created an air of celebration among my companions. It held no interest for me. Along the road, I saw the destruction the Indians left in their wake. Skirmishes were still occurring, and those who survived the raids were reluctant to return. There was no life to pick up again—for the time being.

Continuing east along the Overland Trail, each upcoming stage station or road ranche was announced by the drivers. The passengers looked forward to each destination with a somewhat unwholesome taste for the macabre. The waste and destruction along this road to ruin held many tales—the embellishment of which eased long hours of boredom. It was a diversion from the heat and dirt, but I offered no story, no tale of woe. I desired peace—which still eluded me.

Approaching the Gilman Ranche, those in the know began their litany of who escaped and who succumbed. While so many were killed in the days following the raid at our ranche, how the Gilman family remained unscathed was a mystery. My ears perked up as the story now included none other than Two Face. Apparently, he warned his friends the Cheyenne were on the warpath early last summer. The Gilmans were somewhat prepared when the Indians suddenly surrounded their ranche. The raiders rode around and around the house in an aggressive manner, then left the scene after burning a couple wagonloads of goods.

The Gilman family fled seventeen miles to Fort McPherson unmolested. A claim was later made that Two Face ensured their safe passage, that he assigned a group of his band's braves to follow the family. Even though nearly a thousand warriors were reported nearby, not a hair on a Gilman head was touched. It was a salacious story and a miracle, too.

Two Face's protection of Willie and me was monumental. In retrospect, I would always remember hearing his death song. I felt true remorse for my hapless involvement in his demise. In fact, it sickened me. Yet, somehow the Gilman story reinforced what I had come to understand about the man. He was strong, steady, and faithful to his people. He was one of the few who explored the benefits of dipping his toe into the lives of another race. His band might have survived intact if the Indians were not provoked into defense of their homeland. Now the bands of Two Face and Blackfoot were scattered, absorbed into larger bands—never to be whole again.

I wondered how history would describe Two Face. They say it is written by the victors. Alas, I heard the exaggerated details of this particular "predatory" Sioux from my fellow travelers but knew his true character would never fully be understood.

The next stop, Midway Stage Station, interrupted the speculative conversation, and I was relieved. I wandered to the privy while looking past my fellow travelers. It was not their faces I saw. My thoughts were consumed by the faces and places I still loved so much. I remembered our home the way it was before the raid, which seemed unusual to me. Inexplicably, my fondest recollections were always interrupted by the memory of my final glance back. My torn and tattered lace curtains flapped in the breeze through the broken windows as if waving their sad goodbyes.

I thought of Will. Where was he resting? Could I find the spot?

The Eubank Ranches, or what remained, would be filled with dreadful recollections. I steeled myself for what lay ahead and wondered how I might disengage from the wagon train.

Stopping to make camp for the night, Mr. Wiggins rode up and greeted me through the stage window at my shoulder. He peered at me hesitantly, then dismounted and stepped nearer. "Are you thinking about your family the closer we get to the Little Blue?" he asked cautiously.

I nodded. The force of my emotions increased mile by mile. I longed to see the ranche again no matter its current condition.

"You want to see your home, don't you?" he asked gently.

I nodded again and said, "I just do not know how it would be possible. I am under the care of General Heath, and he has instructed the wagon master to take me all the way to Fort Atchison."

Mr. Wiggins abruptly mounted his horse and spun away without explanation.

I turned my attention to Willie, who was tall and strong enough to ride on the seat next to me. I wrapped my arm protectively around him. He looked up at me and smiled shyly. My heart took a double beat at the sight of his cherubic face. Willie had borne his trials with admirable stoicism. He was wary of the attentions of the other passengers but had formed a special attachment to Mr. Wiggins.

A short time later, O.P. returned to the coach. "It's all arranged," he announced loudly over the noise of the corralling wagons. "Tomorrow, you will be provided with a borrowed carriage, and I will escort you. With an added security detachment, we can make a stop at your ranche. You will have a couple of hours there before we need to hustle along and catch up to the train before dark."

My heart leapt within my chest. I smiled anemically at Oliver Wiggins and was thankful for his friendship and help. Soon I would face the most difficult moments of my long journey, but I would not be alone.

The next morning, we rolled eastward again. I heard the announce-ment that Liberty Farm lay just ahead. The once successful station was of special interest to me. Will and I often visited his sister Sarah who worked there. The wagons ambled through the yard of Liberty Farm but did not stop. I drew in a ragged breath, saddened to see charred piles of the once thriving business. Nestled among the trees on the rise overlooking the river was the Little Blue Station. It, too, was gone.

Meandering along Nine Mile Ridge, the blackened trees stood tall. We rolled down the slope toward the river, and the coach passed through the Narrows. I spied the buffalo wallow next to the large bur oak tree where Will hid us. Reluctantly, I pulled my eyes from the now peaceful setting and leaned to look at the river where I left my man. Across a small channel of water, my sight froze on the spot where his lifeless body had rested sprawled upon a sand bar. I remembered his sun-lightened hair lift in the breeze as though he was alive, but the back of his bloody head bore evidence of a bullet's mayhem. His torso bristled with the arrows of his murderers.

Drawing closer, I could hear the cries of his sister Dora as she fought the attackers. She died an undeserving death; and her mutilated body was an assault to the memory of one brimming with joy and life. Tears welled up, and I pulled my bonnet down over my brow.

The Eubank Ranche appeared, and I eased forward in my seat in anticipation. The coach slowed to a stop. I stepped out into my yard. Expecting to see our ranche in shambles, nothing prepared me for its utter desolation. Our home was a misshapen mass of collapsed roof and walls. Fire consumed our existence, leaving it lifeless and gloomy on the trail—an ominous warning of abiding evil.

Nothing was left to speak of our presence. We had been erased from the Little Blue Valley. Its rolling, wild hay fields, gardens, and tilled land lay abandoned and untended. The beauty and promise of the place were suspended in carnage. The scene took my breath away. Open mouthed, I soaked in the obliterated surroundings. A place once treasured by a family. A family who lived and loved together.

chapter seventy

Eight Stones

7 August 1865
Eubank Ranche, Nebraska Territory

In this sad world of ours, sorrow comes to all; And, to the young, it comes with bitterest agony, Because it takes them unawares.

Abraham Lincoln

There it was. Will's parents' family home. Though hastily built, it was like a reverie of things to come. A grander, more accommodating structure was planned once roots grew down into the loamy soil of the Little Blue Valley. O. P. Wiggins and I stood looking at what had been the Eubank Ranche. The blackened foundation stones rose like cairns around the charred dwelling. We wandered about the yard and identified two burial sites: sunken, stone-covered mounds of woe.

I gazed at the gently sloping hills. Thick bunches of fine grass sprouted out of the rich soil. All of it a stark reminder of what attracted settlers to the fertile bottom lands. All was quiet...in direct contrast to my last memories of the place.

A horse whinnied at the top of the rise above the river where the soldiers watched and waited. The escort was ordered to stay with us while the main wagon train lumbered ahead. Indian trouble was still possible in the area for those who might stray from the trail.

My hand instinctively touched my pistol. Uncomfortable, I smoothed the dress across my abdomen and lifted the weight off my midriff. The child was nearly full term now. It would not be a Eubank. I pushed the unsettling thoughts into the recesses of my mind and squinted at the family home. The odds and ends of our lives, scattered by the raiders, were gone. Scavenged long ago, the space was now an empty shell.

Mr. Wiggins held Willie's hand. The boy was characteristically quiet and occasionally glanced at his tall friend as if taking cues from him.

The big scout showed me where Henry's body was found and told me Daniel Freeman discovered the body behind the house days after the massacre. I remembered Henry's presence among the shrubs that day. I prayed he did not suffer long. The boy, once so full of life...I turned away from the void. Death's sting would never fade.

Mr. Wiggins helped move several foundation stones into the yard. We worked in the heat for an hour, gathering stones, piling them into smaller and smaller layers as the Eubank Cairn gained height. A flat piece of sandstone was placed on top, and it was done. I wiped my brow and straightened my rumpled clothing. Untying the leather-fringed bag hanging from my waist, I recalled Two Face tying it to my saddle the night of our escape from Blackfoot's village.

"Mr. Wiggins," I said, "Will you join me as I remember our family?" He removed his hat and nodded once.

I cleared my throat, looked at Willie, then closed my eyes. I whispered, "Lord, with your help...." My voice choked. I struggled for composure.

Thankfully, Mr. Wiggins noticed my distress. He began to pray in his deep rich voice. "O God, Creator and Redeemer of all your faithful people, grant to the souls of all these faithful departed your mercy, light, and peace."

I lifted Willie and cradled him in my arms, then bowed my head and wept. The child patted my cheek. Gazing at his somber face, my strength returned, and I resolved to complete the important task at hand. I reached down for the four, biscuit-sized granite stones I selected from the remains of our home's foundation. They served as representations of my husband's father and three of his young sons.

> *Grandfather Joseph, Fred, James, and Henry,*
> *Deep peace of the flowing air to you.*
> *Deep peace of the quiet earth to you.*
> *Deep peace of the Son of Peace to you.*
> *We commit your spirits to the Lord.*

I lovingly placed each rock on the cairn making sure they were touching. Next, I picked up the stone I had chosen at Alkali Station when I learned of Joe's death. It was smooth, round, and black—about the size of a goose egg. I thought of the strength and vitality which exuded from my brother-in-law. I remembered his tenacity and ability, his gentleness and humor. I looked eastward down the road toward Joe and Hattie's ranche.

Joseph Eubank, Jr.,
May the road rise up to meet you.
May the wind be always at your back.
May the sun shine warm upon your face.
We honor your memory.

Mr. Wiggins added an Amen. Next, I pulled out the beautiful, sparkling quartz stone laced with gold.

For you, sweet Medora.
We loved you so!
Deep peace of the shining sky to you.
May your star shine brightest in your heavenly home.

My hand lingered as I placed it on the mound. I patted the glittering piece of purity and smiled. I decided at this moment to always remember her *before....*

With a trembling hand, I reached into my bag and withdrew the heart-shaped stone I grabbed during the assault by the young warrior on this spot one year ago. Holding Willie's hand in mine, together we placed it gently on the cairn.

Dear husband and beloved father,
May the serenity of the tallest mountain
and the peace of the smallest stone be your repose.
May the stillness of the stars watch over you.
May the everlasting music of the breeze lull you to rest.

We rested our hands on Will's stone. The token held our child's attention. The breeze cooled my brow and brought with it the faint scent of honeysuckle. The rustling of tall grasses along the hillside produced a gentle song of eternity, which I found oddly comforting. We stood quietly in the landscape of contrasts. The beauty of our surroundings was marred by the passing of...an entire family, a family taken from this earth too soon.

I blinked back the tears and finally picked out of my bag the pearl that Mrs. Wade gave to me after learning of Isabelle's death. I placed its smooth, pale chubbiness against my lips and remembered the cheek I adored. I thought of Belle's little face that shone like beams on water whenever she saw her father. I thought of her sparkling songs as she sang the family hymns in her baby language. "A mighty horse best is our God." Her child's voice brought joy and laughter to all.

I love you Isabelle, m'annsacha, my blessing,
flesh of my flesh, bone of my bone.
Until we meet again,
May you be held safe in God's eternal love.

Mr. Wiggins rested his hand on my shuddering shoulder as the never-ending grief manifested itself in my physical body—like so many times before. I moaned as grief's power laid waste my body. Gradually, the emotions ebbed, and I looked hard at our memorial. Eight stones nestled neatly atop the cairn. I placed a finger upon each one for a final touch. Willie held the handful of wildflowers we gathered earlier, and together we placed the bouquet on the cairn's shelf.

The scout ventured forward and rested a hand on top of the cairn. He stood several moments with head bowed. Then he gently patted the cairn and turned to me. Replacing his hat upon his head, he said respectfully, "A fine service, Mrs. Eubank." Tipping his hat, he took Willie by the hand and walked up the hill. I was grateful for a few private moments.

I wandered to our nearby home and stood among its ruins. Shoving aside the burned remnant of a roof timber, I swept ashes off the once beautiful rug, then dragged it away. The floorboards at my feet were scorched. I fumbled through the dirt and ash with my fingers seeking the iron D-ring. Within seconds, I lifted the hatch door. Pulling it up on its hinges, I felt a twinge in my belly.

Inhaling deeply, I stared into the cavernous hole below, then descended the ladder. Sunlight poured down through the top of our roof-less cabin and lit the dirt floor. Dusty specks swirled around me, and I felt the familiar coolness of the cellar. As I scanned the shelves, I was shocked to see the contents removed. Shelves that once held canned goods were empty. Sacks of flour and sugar stored in stoneware crocks with lids were gone. Jars of pickled vegetables were absent, leaving only rings of dirt to prove their prior stations.

I eased my way to the far corner of the cellar and began to dig in the sand. The small tintype of Will endured a journey of miles, river crossings, and the elements. But there were other personal items. Where were they? I pawed through the dirt.

A handful of onions turned up but were desperately tossed aside as I sifted through the sand with my fingers. Where was it? Minutes later, I plunked back onto my bottom, elbows on my knees, head in my hands. Our metal cash box wrapped in a flour sack was gone! The gold coins, the paper money, and the deeds were missing. Our photographs! The treasured studio likenesses of Will and me on our wedding day. Everything was gone! Anxiously, I looked around as if the thief stood behind me, breathing down my neck.

I knew the Indians had not discovered the cellar during the ransack of our home. None of the stored goods had shown up in their plunder. Who else would have known to look? It was said many citizens from nearby towns roamed the trail, scooping up the loose stock and any goods which lay strewn for miles. Someone must have passed the ranche after the raid and stolen from the cellar. After all, there was no one left to claim its contents. The Eubank family was extinguished in one mighty blow.

Grandmother Ruth!

The family money was gone. Now we were both financially destitute.

I emerged from the remains of the Eubank Ranche shaken but standing. With the funeral behind me, I needed to do one final thing.

chapter seventy-one

Flag in the Sand

7 August 1865
Little Blue River, Nebraska Territory

And then a voice stills all my soul,
As stilled the waves on Galilee:
"Canst thou not bear the furnace heat,
If 'mid the flames I walk with thee?"

Mrs. Chas. E Cowman

Picking up my skirts with one hand, the other hand supported the weighty roundness of my burden. I ran to the Little Blue. Breathing hard, I reached the embankment and eyed the shallow channel before me. The main part of the river flowed freely just past a smooth, sun-bleached barrier of sand and gravel. I bathed my hot, bare feet in the coolness of the water, then crossed the trickling stream, stopping on the sand bar. Shielding my eyes from the intense sun, I turned to check on Willie. Mr. Wiggins waved, then picked up the child and joined the soldiers on top of the knoll.

Satisfied in solitude, my toes dug into the damp softness of the sand. I recalled our bare feet on the sandy path along the Narrows…exactly one lifetime ago. Children safe in our embrace, we tarried—enjoying one another's presence.

A gripping pain raced across my abdomen, and I breathed deeply. I knew my time was soon to come. I hoped to make it to Daniel and Hannah's home before the baby arrived. Hannah was a shelter in any storm, but she was unaware of the one approaching. I did not mention my condition in my telegram from Fort Kearny. Full of calm and wisdom, she would know what to do. I loved her so. My bulging womb contracted again as it had been doing for days. I tried to quell the urgency to find sanctuary, but I needed Will.

Upon entering a shady enclave on the edge of the sand bar, I closed my eyes and stood—listening to the rustling leaves of the surrounding cottonwood trees. A breeze lifted the damp tendrils that stuck to my neck and face under my bonnet. I reached up and removed its shady brim, turning my face up to the sun. I let the bonnet dangle at my side and felt its ribbon glide through my fingers. It floated to the sand.

"Will," I exhaled.

Fragrant, wild roses grew along the bank and the cooing of a dove joined the song of the late summer cicadas. Grief's explosion tore me to pieces in this place one year ago. The day when I saw my man for the final time. I remembered the terror in his eyes as he pulled his family into the buffalo wallow before running to the house to help Dora. He stuffed his handkerchief into poor Belle's mouth and told her to "Shhh!" The frightened child choked and fought to follow her father. Knowing there was nothing he could do to save any of us, he ran...ran bravely to his death. He fell dead on this spot. His life force drained away.

Belle's face turned blue, then black. She could not breathe. The raiders rode past our place of concealment—the Roper's Ranche their intended target. Upon removal of the handkerchief, Belle's screams pierced the air. Within moments, the black-painted devils whirled around and were upon us...Will's scalp spinning from an Indian pony's bridle.

Loss in its deepest form, sorrow's tug was unrelenting, fresh but heavy, old but new.

"Will!" I cried out. "I lost her. I lost our little Belle."

Wilting to my knees, I bowed my head and pressed my palms deep into my eye sockets. I waited for tears that would not come. "Willie and I have come home," I whispered as I looked at the spot where he fell so violently. The overheated air melded into the rippled sand beneath me. My breaths came in rapid pants. There would never be a stone over this ground. Never an endearment carved by which to honor him. No reminder of that fateful day, Sunday, August 7, 1864. He was never coming back.

"My gentle, kind man," I sighed. "You will always be my touchstone." Kneeling in anguish, time's dimension lost its grip on me. My mind wandered to our loving embrace shared near this spot as we lay in the grass. I remembered the strong beat of his heart under my hand as it rested gently on his chest. The shattered pieces of my soul spilled onto the ground—never to be whole again. I shuddered, forced the air out of my lungs, and willed my heart to beat.

Reaching into my satchel, my fingers gently found the final article. I pulled out the thin, faded shred of flag sewn from the remains of my dress—worn the day we left our yard. Oh, so long ago. So many miles ago....

I looked around and spied a smooth, straight stick. The long piece of wood was weathered gray by wind and water. Near one end of the branch, I carefully fashioned the flag. I held it up and watched it flap in the soft breeze.

"A pretty reminder of our fresh start. I want you to have this dress, Lucy. It matches the color of your eyes."

On this lonely island in the river's bed, I placed the small flag in the sand and watched the colors of the fabric brighten in the sunshine. Yellow flowers danced with blue forget-me-nots, oblivious to the pain. The flag flipped and fluttered, yielding to Will's living essence as it flowed up out of the sand.

A dizzying sensation overcame me. My body leaned sharply left and folded onto itself as grayness closed in. The air lost its voice, enveloping me in a warm earthly cushion. The sand cradled my head. Silence was all that remained.

No longer tethered to the planet, my spirit hovered. As an isolated wanderer, peril and privation followed me through the twin wildernesses of body and truth. There had been pursuers to elude, hunger and thirst to endure. I had seen the quenching of an eye's brightness in death. I had met the venomous strikes of men and serpents. These menacing phantoms faded and were replaced by tiny flowers in the midday sun. The tribulations of this world lifted just as a mighty hand caressed me with unspeakable tenderness. The Creator's touch brought comfort and love.

Opening my eyes, I blinked uncomprehendingly at the blue canopy above. And there it was—unmistakable, unexpected. A moment of peace. Summoning me, showing me the divide between those who fight the unrelenting battle to live and those who surrender. Life! It was the truth behind this most humbling existence. I relaxed and rested in the world's embrace. Light spread from the desperate throws of emptiness across the horizon and encompassed the sky. A warm habitation. Cleansed. Bitterness lifted from my heart as the gift of grace met me. How strange that it would find me here.

Remarkably, I sensed release. Time began to tick again. My eyes strayed from the heaven above to the sight of the little flag standing by my shoulder. My mind sought the familiar, the personal, the reason for being. I recalled my purpose, and the hole in my heart began to fill. When breath ceases within me, my soul will still belong to you. Nothing lost, just changed.

And I was grateful.
Grateful that a cold stone would not mark his spot.
Grateful that the shadow of his smile would grace the face of his son.
Grateful to have been Mrs. William Eubank.
Grateful…for the flag in the sand.

chapter seventy-two

Hattie

Q: Did you afterwards see Lucy?
A: Yes, at Pawnee Station.
Q: How long after she had been taken?
A: Close on one year."

Harriett Eubank Adams

After passing Oak Grove station and seeing the burned remains of the buildings, even the store, I was disconsolate. Consumed by troubling thoughts, the monotonous miles slowly rolled past. My companions on the stagecoach were curious but respected my reticence. I limited my interaction to pleasantries. With great sadness, we passed a large elm tree where Joe was buried. No marker stood on his resting place.

Passing Kiowa Station, I forced myself to see what had become of the place. It grieved me to see Joe and Hattie's lovely home and newly built log store burned to the ground. Her garden was filled with dried and twisted remnants of last year's bounty.

Fifty miles later, the driver hollered, "Pawnee Station!"

Tired travelers quickly exited while the team of horses was exchanged for fresh ones. The driver reached for Willie and extended a hand to help my heavy-laden body onto the step.

An exclamation of joy emanated from the station's interior. A familiar voice among the mulling passengers. "Lucy! Oh, praise be to God! Lucinda! Over here! It's me! Hattie!"

I scanned the crowd and watched as the waving, young woman jumped over the threshold and ran toward me, wiping her hands on a kitchen towel. It was Hattie, Joe's young widow. Following behind her was her lanky, black-haired brother, John Palmer. Falling into one another's arms, Willie and I were possessively encircled, then half-carried into the stage station. Their elation at my surprise arrival turned to sorrow. Even though Willie and I had returned from the vast unknown, one little person did not.

"Belle?" asked Hattie, looking around the yard and the nearest wagons.

Tearing up, I shook my head. "She is gone...."

"Oh!" cried Hattie. "We knew she made it to Denver, Lucinda! Last November, I met Miss Roper on my way to Marysville. We were on the same wagon train! She told all she knew about you and the children. At least, we knew you were still alive!"

"Yes," I replied, "the children were taken from the Indian camp to Denver. I met a man in Julesburg who told me...he told me...of my Belle's passing...."

Stunned, Hattie and John stood as though slapped.

"She was quite ill from the injuries inflicted by the Indians...."

"Poor thing. We loved her so! Oh, you have been through so much!" Hattie said.

"Hattie," I sniffed. "I know Joe and Fred are dead. It is impossible to imagine...." We fiercely held one another in the hopes of surviving the landslide of loss.

The scene created a clamor among my fellow passengers, their curiosity piqued. The word "captive" made whispered rounds by those who had read my story in the newspaper. My notoriety was now on full display. They gathered around me in the stifling room, asking questions and discussing the "facts" of my ordeal between themselves.

Rattled and faint, I sat down on a bench with Hattie's arms wrapped around my shoulders. John appeared with a mug of cool water and a sympathetic smile.

"Move back, please. Give the lady some breathing room," he said firmly.

Mr. Wiggins entered the station and seeing the commotion, rescued Willie from the travelers' renewed interest. He carried the boy outside. Timid around strangers, Willie was happy to go anywhere with his friend, the scout. I noticed him pulling Oliver's large mustache while the man chuckled. He asked if Willie would like to see the puppies on the porch.

Hattie leaned forward to peer into my face. "I have someone to show you," she said, then walked to a small cradle near the window. Carefully lifting its drowsy occupant, she hurried to my side.

"Oh, Hattie! Is this...?" The sight of the precious baby simultaneously thrilled and razed my heart. I was thinking of Joe.

"Yes, Lucy. This is little Miss Josie. Josephine." She added unnecessarily, "She is named after her father."

The young mother preened and stroked her child lovingly. "She is nearly five months old now." Enveloping the baby in my arms, I said admiringly, "She is a beautiful girl! Joe would be so proud!"

With those words, our sadness mingled—the enormity of what was lost, of what should have been, pressed its full weight onto our shoulders. Hattie breathed deeply and squeezed my hand.

"The baby and I are okay, thanks to John," she said smiling up at her brother. He seemed smitten by the babe. I had to agree. She was a lovely child. Dressed in her little, white gown and cap, Josie squirmed, opened her eyes, smacked her rosebud mouth, then promptly fell asleep in my arms. I admired the newest member of the family and said softly, "Very nice to meet you, Josephine…." I imagined Joe's pleasure. Surely, he smiled down from heaven at the newest addition to the Eubank family.

Staring at Hattie, I grieved for all that was lost. She was with child when our lives changed forever. I remembered how she suffered with illness throughout the summer. Her brother John trekked daily to a nearby sulfur spring. The bitter water she craved settled her stomach. I sorrowed anew over the losses of both Joe and Fred, who labored together on that fateful day.

"Come, Lucinda, let's sit under the cottonwood trees." Hattie's tone implied to those around us that they were excluded. The crowd gradually dissipated as they sought relief for their hunger, thirst, and necessaries. They kept an eye on me, however, in the event I might suddenly launch into a detailed, salacious description of my ordeal. A palpable sigh of disappointment coincided with our stepping out the door and turning toward the river.

I wavered under the weight of heat and emotion. Hattie took my hand and led me to the shade of nearby trees. We sat quietly a moment, contemplating. Each survivor, alone in her thoughts. Unified in sorrow, the exhilaration of our reunion gave way to the wiping of tears. We tried to regain composure enough to find words.

Finally, Hattie placed a hand on my bulging midsection and said, "You first, my dove."

With a halting voice, I tried to navigate within the fragments of my story—treading through the horrors while mitigating the cruelest details. Hattie sat frozen—hand covering her mouth.

Finally, I sighed and said, "Hattie, I am sorry to bring you pain. I cannot bear to tell it all right now. Do you mind if we leave off here? Tell me. What happened to you?"

Hattie's eyes blinked back emotion. She nodded, smoothed her skirts, and began to outline the events at Kiowa Station. She motioned for John to join us and asked him to share in the telling.

"About four o'clock," began her brother. "Joe, Fred, and I were putting up hay in a field near the river. Hattie asked me to bring her water from the spring about a half mile away. Joe mentioned he would ride a ways down the road to look for another field to mow. After filling the bottle at the spring, I passed back by the field to check on Fred. That's when I found him. Dead. Shot full of arrows." He looked at me tenderly as if questioning my desire for more details.

"John, I must know. Mother Ruth. She will have questions when I see her. Besides, I am no longer as naive as I may have been once. Tell me. Please," I muttered while quickly looking down at my wringing hands.

John nodded sympathetically and added slowly, "Scalped. His body lay draped across the Buckeye mower." The recollections rattled John, but he continued the story. "I raced to the house and saw Indians riding up the hill about three hundred yards northwest. Fearing what I would find when I entered the house, I was relieved to see Hattie unharmed. The drivers saw the Indians and were fixin' to fight for their lives."

Hattie picked up where he left off.

"The Indians were all around Kiowa Station for about a half an hour before John arrived. I saw them coming and ran into the house, securing all the windows and doors. It was terrifying. They were all painted in their highest colors, and I noticed their weapons." She shivered slightly despite the afternoon heat. "John, finding me in one piece, loaded me up on our old mare. We quickly made our way to the ox train corralled at the station. Preparing for an attack, the men were busy shooting the old loads out of their guns and reloading."

"Right away, we spotted more Indians nearby," said John. "They came down and killed a boy right under the hill below the house, then rode on down the river. They drove off nearly every bit of the stock—even Joe's prized stallion and Mr. Holladay's brood mares. What they didn't drive off, they shot full of arrows—mostly the oxen. There were twenty-five eastbound wagons, and I was thankful for all the drivers at the stage stop who offered some protection. We spent the night together, but I am sure no one slept."

Hattie continued, "Sometime during the night, the Indians crept up to the station and our house. They torched it all, including the hay and outbuildings. The blaze lit up the sky, but there was nothing we could do for fear the Indians were lying in wait."

"How did you get away?" I asked breathlessly.

"It was about four o'clock in the afternoon, and the freighters were ready to move. We climbed into Mr. Wilder's wagon. Everything was lost, but there was no time to despair. After starting out, about twenty-five warriors attacked. We fought them all the way down to Big Sandy. We kept them off, but two freight drivers were wounded. Fortunately, we got away and stayed with the wagon train for the next fifty miles until we made it to our father's house in Marysville."

John picked up my hand and held it in his. "Now we need to talk about the family. Can you do it, Lucy?"

I nodded and braced myself.

"The morning after the attack, we went to look for Joe with four of the drivers. We found him about a mile and half down the road west of the house. He was lying on his face, shot with three arrows in the back and one in the arm. Hattie was inconsolable. I sent her back to the house with a couple of the men and we buried him."

Through tears, Hattie said, "The Indians robbed him of his gold watch and chain. And he had four hundred dollars in gold coins in his pockets when he left the house. The attack was so unexpected. We never feared the Indians before. There was no reason to be armed." Hattie was finding it difficult to continue. She wiped her eyes with a handkerchief before adding, "Poor Grandpa Joe, Dora, and the boys. None of them had a chance."

"The Indians were still roaming the area, but Hattie and I needed to know what had become of your family. Passing Oak Grove, we found the bodies of Marshall Kelly and Mr. Butler. They were left in the smoke house which was torched. After that, we rode to your ranche. That is when we found them…" said John huskily. "Are you sure you want the details?"

I nodded, and he continued, "On the road, just about a half mile from the house, I found Grandfather and James. We moved their bodies to the yard…and found Dora…."

"Yes, I remember her lying injured, still alive, but they would not let me go to her. Was she dead when you arrived?"

John hesitated.

"Tell me, John. I need to know. Everything."

"She was stripped and staked to the ground. A lance empaled her body in the most revolting way." His voice trailed off.

"Go ahead, John. Did you find Will?"

"Yes, he was lying on a sandbar just beyond the shallow turn along the Narrows."

I remembered.

John steadied himself and continued. "Lucinda, he was stripped, scalped, and his body was mutilated. They all were. I am so sorry."

My stomach turned, and sparks flew about the periphery of my vision.

"Henry was tomahawked, then crawled away. It appeared he lived a bit longer. He must have given those Indians a fight trying to protect Dora!"

Between hitching sniffles, Hattie went on. "Lucy, I cannot tell you the anguish we suffered. To not find you or the children!" She wiped her face with her apron. "I was so distraught when John returned and told me you were missing. The more time passed, well…we lost hope. It is such a relief to find you alive and well!"

My face tightened. No, not well, but breathing. I stared up at the pale, drawn sky and remembered. There was nothing left but tumbled chimney stones. The fires of the past year played havoc in my life, leaving me singed and smoking. And, as such, I returned to the United States.

———◆———

There is a proverb in the Bible that warns: bitterness brings rottenness to the bearer's bones.

As the beautiful, red and gold Concord pulled out of Pawnee Station, I reflexively swiveled on the bench seat and turned to look back. I hoped to catch a final glimpse of Hattie. Also, I yearned to look west a final time. To see the actual line where wildness ends, and civilization begins.

Leaving eight loved ones in its forbidden ground, I closed the box on my pioneer life. Dabbing my eyes to staunch the tears, I pivoted forward. Eastward. Toward the only path I could follow. It held no promise. But Willie and I would find our loved ones…and whatever our futures held.

Yes, bitterness is an insidious and dangerous companion. Better to leave it behind.

As the Overland Trail separated itself from the river for the final time, I tasted the unsavory acridness of resentment, and I left it stranded in the eternal shallows of the Little Blue River.

chapter seventy-three

The Long Journey Home

11 August 1865
Nebraska Territory to Quincy, Illinois

*My heart many times has gone out to you pioneer women. While many
are gone, I know there are a number yet living, and I have wondered how
time has dwelt with you and have hoped that their portion has been peace,
plenty and contentment, after all you have endured; that, surrounded by
children and grandchildren, they have enjoyed a well-earned rest and a
peace that the throbbing world around you cannot comprehend. A rich
reward to compensate you for the harrowing scenes upon which you have
been compelled to look, for the noble deeds which you have done and the
example you have set for the youth of our country.*

Julia S. Lambert

The ground under the stage rolled by in a vigilant blur. I was tired
and emotionally depleted. Rest made an occasional visit but only
in small, treasured spurts while Willie slept.

We were suffocating in the stifling August heat. Sweat ran down the
sides of my face as if caught in a rainstorm. Willie's hair was plastered
to his head. The stage rocked constantly from side to side, and my
condition did nothing to ease my discomfort. Our coach held several
travelers, and I wondered if some were pioneers who found the wilderness too harsh so were returning east. I could understand if they were.
They did not converse much but were polite and let us sit near the
window for air.

Anticipation of seeing my family intensified with every hoofbeat. I
sighed and drew a heavy breath, thinking about the train ride to Quincy.
How would I react when we arrived? How would they? My heart was
full of joy imagining our reunion, but I knew joy would be short-lived.
Oh, how I want this trip to end! Light collided with dark as my thoughts
played out the reunion over and over again. I never thought we would

be reunited. Never believed this reunion was possible.

My heart became sentimental as I reminisced about my loved ones. My beloved Daniel and Hannah…we so desperately needed them now. Hannah must have been overjoyed when her mother and sister traveled back to Quincy for a visit. Had Ruth and Sarah forfeited their trip, Ruth would have surely been killed. If not killed, Sarah would have suffered the same indignities and cruelties I had. I swung around in the seat in hopes new scenery would dissolve these memories.

———•———

Arriving in Atchison, Kansas, Willie was wide-eyed and mystified with the bustle of this riverboat town. Walking through the loud and constant commotion, we watched as freight drivers filled their wagons, bullwhackers whipped their oxen, and stages rolled past. Outfitters stood upon their wooden slats, yelling their prices were the best and the cheapest. The hopeful faces of parents and excitement of their children saddened me. I watched as innocent pioneers loaded their covered wagons to embark on their journey west. I knew the hardships they would encounter. Their trip would be harrowing and long. Some would never see their destination. I could only shake my head.

Five cents was the fee to ferry across the Missouri River from Atchison to St. Joe, Missouri. We climbed aboard the rather empty boat and took our place by an inside panel. I recalled my first trip on this same ferry from St. Joe to Atchison on our way to Nebraska. It was thick with oxen, horses, chickens, and anything else the aspiring homesteader could pack. Will and I were married only a short time then, so our material belongings were slim in comparison. I shifted Willie in my lap and watched the hustling shoreline of Atchison disappear.

———•———

After a night's rest at the Patee House Hotel in St. Joe, I sent my last telegram to Daniel. In a prior telegram, I told him Belle and Conrad would not be coming back with me. I explained Belle's death and that I did not know Conrad's whereabouts.

We made our way to the station and boarded the train to Palmyra, Missouri. The great iron horse, the Hannibal/St Joseph Short Line, crossed the entire state of Missouri. It was crammed with travelers and all sorts of baggage. Willie was astonished and fascinated. He squirmed about and squealed as the train chugged along the tracks.

In Palmyra, we switched trains and boarded the Quincy/Palmyra Line for the short ride to Quincy. As the train drew close to our destination, folks prepared to disembark. The life inside me kicked as I gazed at their movement. Then I heard him.

"An incredibly beautiful woman was born in August!"

My heart pounded.

Will's voice resonated in my ear. He said the same, sweet thing to me every year on my birthday. Today I turned twenty-five years old.

I stared off.

As the train whistle acknowledged our arrival in Quincy, Willie stood on the seat, hitting the window with his hands. His stringy drools covered the glass as amused passengers looked on. Smiles spread across their faces as they enjoyed watching my son's excitement.

Shifting my skirts from the seat, I stood and scanned the platform for Daniel's face. He was there! Oh, my dear brother was there! Waiting with him was Hannah and their children, seven-year-old Minnie and four-year-old Joseph. They were on their tiptoes looking from one passenger's face to another until, finally, Daniel's eyes met mine. At that moment, I felt an overwhelming sense of happiness.

Eager to exit the train car, I lifted Willie from our seat and grabbed our worn satchel. My heart felt as if it would leap from my chest as we moved quickly down the aisle.

"Excuse us. Can we get by, please?"

The conductor peered over the top of his silver-rimmed glasses and then looked down the crowded aisle. Noticing my anxiousness and recognizing I had a toddler in tow, he offered his assistance. Relieving me of my satchel, he let us pass quickly. Stepping off the stairs of the train, I turned and smiled at him. He returned a robust smile, handed me our satchel, and tipped his gray cap.

The platform was flooded with people dashing in different directions. I felt someone grab my arm and twirl me around. It was Daniel! Hannah hastily lifted Willie from me, and I flung my arms around his shoulders. I burst into tears in his strong, comforting arms. He let my uncontrollable sobs unleash until the worst of my agony expelled itself. Then he stepped back to gaze at me. Softly, he swept strands of grey hair from around my face. Staring intently, he looked into my hollow, lifeless eyes. He studied the sunken, dark circles underneath them. Then he carefully stroked the wrinkles etched on my face with his thumb. I could see the dismay and concern in his eyes. His lips drew thin and tight.

I waited in apprehension for his reaction to my protruding stomach. Instead, he held me by the shoulders and in a quiet voice said, "You are safe now, Lucy. We will take care of you."

Daniel turned and lifted Willie from the waiting Hannah. She gently placed her arms around me. Fighting to hold back her own tears, we broke down together in our frozen embrace. We cried for her father, brothers and sister, niece and nephew, and the untold suffering.

Standing just beyond Hannah, I spotted the sullen face of my father Robert. He was biting his quivering lip. I stepped toward him, and he put his arms around me. Patting my back and trying to be strong, he affirmed to me everything would be all right, but I knew nothing would be right and buried my head in his chest.

Silently, we walked toward the buggy and situated ourselves for the ride to Daniel and Hannah's farm. They lived in the township of Ellington on the outskirts of Quincy. I gazed at my beautiful niece and nephew and longed for my own sweet daughter. Belle would be the same age as Joseph. Minnie slipped her hand into mine and gave me a reassuring squeeze.

Daniel drove the buggy through the gate and down their lane. Beyond the trees in the clearing, I saw a woman in a black dress, darting from the house. It was Will's mother Ruth.

My eye caught someone running right behind her.

Conrad!

chapter seventy-four

Widow Weeds

13 August 1865
Ellington, Illinois

Sweet are the uses of adversity,
Which, like the toad, ugly and venomous,
Wears but a precious jewel in his head.

Shakespeare

R uth flung her arms around my numb body. Grief's wicked hand etched sharp, deep lines over the landscape of her face. Her frail voice cracked like tiny, trampled twigs.

"Luuucy! Luucy!"

Waves of agony poured from her poor, tormented soul as she shook her head back and forth.

"Oh, Mother Ruth!" Her arms clung to me as her body began a slow descent. Daniel grabbed her and gently guided her into the house. Conrad gingerly took my satchel, and Hannah graciously lifted Willie from the buggy.

As we entered the neatly decorated parlor, I looked around at the loving display of framed pictures that lined the fireplace mantle. Will's entire family was there next to photos of my siblings and parents. Watching for my reaction, Hannah's concerned eyes squinted at me, and I returned a slight smile. She gave me a relieved look and excused herself.

Conrad sat on the floor next to Willie. He frequently shifted his eyes from Willie to his distressed grandmother. Daniel and his children were seated nearby. I slowly sat down next to Ruth on the sofa and took both of her hands in mine. We sat in silence for several minutes.

Finally, Ruth lowered her head and with trembling whispers, slowly named her beloved fallen family. "Joseph, Will, Joe, Dora, Fred, James,

Henry, and Isabelle. Will we ever get past our grief, Lucinda?"

No one spoke, no one moved.

Hannah walked into the parlor and broke the somber silence. "You must be starving, Lucy! Move into the dining room, I have supper on the table. And, Ambrose, I made your favorite pie!"

"Ambrose?" I looked at Daniel in confusion.

"Mary Eliza decided the boy needed to retain his given name, Ambrose Asher, and Ambrose agreed. With a wink, Daniel added, "He also said he wanted to be here when you arrived."

I looked over at Ambrose's sweet face.

"My ma will be here tomorrow with Aunt Sarah. They are gonna be really happy to see you. I told my ma all about them Indians and what they done, Aunt Lucy."

"Sit down at the table, Ambrose," Daniel said. "You and I will talk about it at another time."

I looked over at a shrunken Ruth staring blankly at the plate in front of her. Hannah placed a helping of roast beef and green beans on her mother's plate and passed the bowl around the table.

"Mother, please try to eat something," Hannah begged.

Ruth gave Hannah a nod in acknowledgement and picked up her fork. She tried to be compliant, but her loss of appetite was obvious. Breaking bread around the table with Will's family was bittersweet. I felt their despair. Willie's incessant gibberish was the only thing that brought some light to the supper.

Afterwards, we moved into the drawing room. Ruth took my hands as we sat down next to each other. Tears filled the matriarch's eyes as she uttered, "I'm so sorry, my dear girl. I cannot even begin to imagine what you have been through. No one can." She looked at my protruding stomach and lovingly said, "No matter what, by the grace of God, we will find the strength to go on. That is what our husbands would want us to do, Lucinda." I nodded my head and tried to smile.

Our visit lasted into the night. Exhausted, I excused myself and bid everyone a good evening. Hannah made our room tidy and purposefully bright. I was at once grateful to climb in between crisp, fresh, white sheets. To lie in a real bed and be in a home with my loved ones seemed surreal.

Nestling next to Willie, I closed my eyes. Banishing the stinging flashes from my mind, I reminded myself not to allow evil events to control my thoughts. Remain strong. Force yourself. When I shut my eyes, a future without Will and Belle started to swirl in my head. Stop! Stop! I begged for sleep to come.

The sound of a slow-creaking door woke me in the early morning. I moved slowly not to wake Willie and peered down the hall. Will's sisters, Mary Eliza and Sarah, had arrived and were talking to Ruth and Hannah. I reached for the soft robe Hannah left on a chair and scurried out to Will's sisters. They stretched out their arms and with hearts full of sorrow, we clung to each other.

Hannah brought coffee and cups to us on a tray. I started talking about my trip from Fort Laramie. My voice trailed off. With downcast eyes, I said, "I just cannot talk about it yet. I am so sorry you lost your father and your brothers and sister."

Gently, Hannah said, "It will take all of us an awfully long time to get through this grief, if we ever do."

I left the room to look in on Willie and heard my sisters-in-law whispering to each other with deep concern. "Oh, my God! She doesn't even look like Lucy! Poor thing!" Mary Eliza said.

Sarah replied, "I hardly recognize the beautiful, young woman our brother married. She will, no doubt, need much rest and more. By the looks of it, the baby will be here soon."

The baby....

I slipped into the black widow's weeds hanging on the peg in our room. Hannah knew I would need this dress. It was exactly as I expected it to be. Black and heavy, sad like my heart. I pulled the dress up over my extended stomach and pinched the small black buttons lining the front. My fingers progressively worked down the loops over each button covering my scarred breasts and throat.

How would I provide and care for Willie and...a new baby?

chapter seventy-five

Peace

End of August 1865
McKee, Adams County, Illinois

Made a squaw to two different chiefs, their victim ancestor had confided of such tortures as seeing her baby son encircled by fire she was forced to run through. She was also bound night and day before being freed after several months.

The Nelson (Nebr.) Gazette
Thursday, August 13, 1964

Moonlight shimmered through the small bedroom window. Its beauty brought little solace to my restlessness and the frequency of my contractions. It was time. Rising from the bed, I placed one foot on the floor and steadied myself on the side of the headboard. Pulling myself up, I hunched over in pain. The baby was coming. I had to wake Hannah.

Knocking gently on the door of Daniel and Hannah's bedroom, I choked out, "Hannah, it's time." There was rustling inside the room, and Daniel jerked the door open.

"I'll get some water and clean cloths," he said as he rushed by me.

I bent over with another pulling contraction and doubled in half. Hannah was at my side instantly and helped me to my bed. Willie was stirring but still asleep.

Sitting next to me on the bed, Hannah said, "I'm going to put these pillows behind your head and slide you back. Take some deep breaths, and try to relax."

Daniel appeared in the room with some towels and instruments on a tray that rattled as he walked. "Hannah, let me know if you need anything else or if there is anything I can do," he said before stepping from the room.

Bathed in sweat, I panted intensely as the labor wore on.

"I hope I find peace after this baby is born. It is the final link, Hannah." I groaned. "You and Daniel have done so much for me already. Knowing you will raise this baby for me is overwhelming."

"Do not worry about this, Lucy. This baby will be loved as if it were our own. This I promise."

Another contraction struck, and a scream flew from my throat.

"The baby is coming, it's coming" Hannah said calmly. She shouted for Sarah and Mary Eliza. Both women ran into the room. "Mary Eliza, wet some towels. Sarah, put dry ones next to them. One of you grab a sheet. It is way too hot for a blanket."

My face grimaced, and a long moan escaped my mouth. "Hannah, place a chair near the bed and put a blanket on the floor near it. Help me to the chair," I whispered.

Will's sisters looked at my pained face and shook their heads in bewilderment. "Please, just do as I ask. I helped birth many Indian babies, and this is the best way. Trust me," I groaned.

The sisters helped me over to the chair. Crouching down, I grabbed the back of the chair with both hands and pushed. Bearing down, the baby dispelled into Hannah's hands. She carefully laid it on the blanket beneath me.

It was over. The cord that bound me to my Indian captor was severed. Peacefulness shrouded my being, and a mercy I never felt before spread over me.

———•———

Will's sisters doted over Willie and the new baby girl. They insisted I rest. They brought me the child when it was time to suckle. Holding my newborn, I looked into her deep ebony eyes and stroked her thick black hair. I held her close while she slept. Her innocence bore no evidence to the violence of her conception.

Daniel told me he would make certain the baby would be raised with everything she needed. I knew she would be loved as I loved her. I wanted her to be protected from the knowledge of her beginnings.

My life would be tarnished forever—but this life would not be stained. I wouldn't let it.

chapter seventy-six

Moon of the Snowblind

1866-1886
Illinois and Missouri

She suffered every indignation by said Indians that it was possible for them to inflict....

William Hess, Attorney

W ill's brother George quit his job as a freighter on the Overland Trail and moved to Illinois to help his mother Ruth. He advised both of us to seek an attorney and file Indian Depredation claims. George said he and Joe were acquainted with an attorney who worked at the Virginia Station. George deemed him honorable and felt his knowledge of the Nebraska Territory beneficial. Hannah and Daniel were both in agreement, so Ruth and I asked him to contact Mr. William Hess.

Through George's efforts, Mr. Hess met with the family at the end of 1865. During an agonizing four hours, we described the tragic murders of our family members and the horrors we endured.

The Notary Public in the Nebraska Territory, Kearney County, wrote the following from the affidavit of Attorney William Hess:

> Mrs. Joseph Eubank was at the time the depredation was committed on a visit East and she and Mrs. Wm Eubank and the child that survived her imprisonment is nearly all that is left of the said family and that by the destruction of the said property they are left entirely destitute and upon the mercy of the world helpless and heartbroken.

Ruth provided Mr. Hess with an itemized list of everything lost in the raid. The total amount came to $5,603.00. The attorney included the following:

And as attorney for Mrs. Wm Eubank asks payment for private injuries to her character and person in the sum of Ten Thousand Dollars.

Mr. Hess informed us he obtained affidavits from our ranche neighbors in Nebraska: Erastus and George Comstock, along with Charles Emery, James Douglas, James Bainter, Andrew Hammonds, and Edward Uhlig. All stated our claim was valid and true.

On March 21, 1866, Ruth delivered her affidavit at the courthouse in Quincy, Adams County, Illinois. She continued to live with her brother-in-law William and his wife Sarah. The only items of clothing Ruth owned were those she packed for her visit back to Quincy. She was completely dependent now on her son George and her husband's brother.

I had only a sparce amount of clothing for myself and Willie. The money belonging to Two Face, given to me at Fort Laramie was gone. I had my cherished photo of Will, though. The last photo ever taken of him.

———•———

Not long after the baby was born, Daniel introduced me to an acquaintance of his named James Bartholomew. He met James at the mill where they worked. Daniel knew James was single-handedly raising two young boys and was certain James would welcome a wife into his fold. Hannah frequently invited him and his sons to supper. He and Daniel talked about farming and their livestock. James was attentive and kind. He had good manners, and I was told he was a hard worker.

I had several discussions with Daniel about our future and what he thought was best for us. We talked about how one day I may come into money from the claim. And, yes, it would help provide us with some comforts; but the fact of the matter was, we had nothing.

After supper one evening, James proposed.

"I need someone to help care for my boys, Lucy. If you will have me, I can provide enough for us to get by."

Willie and I needed someone who was willing to care for us. A raped woman was no longer desirable. So, I decided to marry James and become a mother to his two boys.

I was scheduled to give my statement of facts at the courthouse on March 28, 1866. We decided to marry the same day.

My heart was full of sorrow once again as I gave testimony of the events of the raid and my captivity.

I signed my name at the bottom of the affidavit.

Lucinday Eubank—for the last time.

James Bartholomew signed as a witness.

Tear drops spread through the threads of the paper....

Immediately after delivering the affidavit, we moved into another room in the courthouse. I stood vacant in front of the Justice of the Peace.

"Do you, Lucinda Eubank, take James Bartholomew as your lawfully wedded husband?"

Silence.

My body turned cold.

I swallowed hard.

"I do."

I signed my name,

Lucinday Bartholomew....

———————

Shortly after our marriage, Daniel and Hannah moved their family to Benton, Cedar County, Missouri. Arrangements were made for Willie to help Daniel on his farm during the summers.

I tended the house, planted a garden, and cooked for James and our boys. I was grateful for a home, but it was not the home I yearned for. Our relationship lacked affection. My yearning for warmth and enrichment clashed with James' aloofness. There was no romance, only two humans brought together to satisfy the others' hardships.

Our shell of a marriage did bestow a glimmer of happiness. On January 11, 1868, I gave birth to another baby girl in Liberty, Adams County, Illinois. We named her Lottie. She was a beautiful child with reddish-gold hair and beautiful green eyes. She brought me a joy I felt I was incapable of feeling again.

———————

Over the years, I continued to correspond with Oliver Wiggins. At the end of 1868, I received a newspaper clipping from him. I stared at the headline, and my hands trembled as I continued to read from the Chicago Evening Post dated December 5, 1868:

BLACK KETTLE, Death of a Big Indian

From the St. Louis Republican
Black Kettle, head chief of the Cheyenne nation, reported killed by Gen. Custer's command, was a man of more than ordinary natural ability, and has held a distinguished position for years among the

tribes of the West. Black Kettle seemed to be earnest in his desire for peace and appeared anxious to bring into the council the treacherous "dog-soldiers," whose tomahawks were reeking with the blood of many innocent whites.

This was not the Cheyenne Chief Black Kettle I knew. I closed my eyes and saw his leathered face and heard his gravelly voice. Was he not among the chiefs who ordered me and Nancy Morton under buffalo robes when the soldiers came to negotiate? Did he not lie to Governor Evans about not knowing our whereabouts? Why did he celebrate the coups and victories of his warriors, and why did he allow his people to beat, rape, and abuse me and my children?

I understood my questions would never be answered. But with George Bent's experience in the Confederate Army, there is no doubt he described the force of the white people's army to Black Kettle. After realizing the magnitude of their offenses along the Overland Trail and the repercussions to follow, the chief knew seeking peace was the only hope of survival for his people. He may not have always been a *peace* chief.

———•———

Ruth Eubank passed away in 1874 while still residing in Quincy, Illinois. She lived out the rest of her years caring for her grandson Ambrose after the death of his mother, Mary Eliza, in 1869.

We were living in Nevada, Vernon County, Missouri, when tragedy struck again. In 1879, our beloved Lottie died. She was only eleven years old. We buried her in the Deepwood Cemetery in Nevada, Missouri. My heart was full of grief, plunging me further into sorrow.

———•———

Hannah and Daniel welcomed another baby in 1879 and named him Claude. He joined the couple's four other children: a nineteen-year-old son, Joseph, named after her father, and three daughters, ages fourteen, thirteen, and ten.

They still resided in Benton, Missouri.

In 1881, Ambrose married Verina Isabelle (Belle) Harrison in California, Moniteau County, Missouri. We were delighted to hear the news of their marriage. Ambrose was adored as a child and grew to be a kind, gentle man. We looked forward to their new life together.

In 1883, Hattie's brother, John Palmer, was called to deliver his account of events of the raid for the depredation claim. Nineteen years had passed:

Liberty, Neb., Dec 18 1883
Chars & Wm B. King, Attys
Washington DC.
Gentlemen:-

The following as nearly as my memory serves me are the particulars of this massacre: -

In the month of May 1864-the Eubanks family, composed of Joseph Eubank and Ruth Eubank, his wife, their two married sons Joseph and William with their wives; also, three younger sons and two younger daughters the names of whom I do not distinctively remember and myself settled near the line dividing the present counties of Nucholls and Thayer the state of Nebraska. (The present counties did not then exist.) Our settlement was about 50 miles west of the present city of Beatrice Gage Co. Neb then our nearest trading point-From what I can now learn our settlement was about 8 miles nearly due east of the present town of Nelson, Nucholls Co. Neb.

This land had been surveyed by the U.S. Govt-and was open for settlement. The Eubanks & myself had taken claims. The Pawnee Reservation was about 40 miles distant from our settlement and was the nearest Indian settlement to us. The massacre was committed by two bands of Indians one of them Arapahoes and one of them Cheyennes.

The massacre of the Eubanks took place late in the afternoon-(about 4 or 5 o'clock) of the 7th day of August 1864. This was on Sunday evening. The Eubanks were all at their houses excepting one of the younger sons before mentioned who was with me - we were putting up some hay. Young Eubank was raking hay while I was going to a spring about a half mile distant for water. I was absent about half an hour - upon my return I found young Eubank dead and scalped - he had been shot with arrows.

Joseph Eubank Jr. & his wife who was my sister - the young Eubanks just mentioned & myself lived together. About an hour before the massacre I saw Jos. Eubanks Jr & his wife at our house – after the younger Eubanks & myself had gone into the field to rake hay Jos. Eubank Jr. left the house to go to look for some more grass to mow. He was found dead and scalped about 3 days after - about 1 ½ miles from his house.

When I found the younger Eubanks dead in the hay field upon my return with the water from the spring I at once ran to the house to see if my sister - who was Jos E. Jr.s wife was safe. When I got to the house I saw the Indians ride to the top of a hill about 300 yards north-west from the house - A train of freighters was corralled about 600 yds southeast from the house - I found my sister unharmed and we ran with all possible haste to the freighters camp. The Indians then left and I did not see anything more of them.

My sister & I remained with the freighters that night and the next day I went to where the Eubanks lived—about 4 miles northwest from where we lived. When I reached their house I found five dead bodies i.e. those of Joseph E-Sr., William and two younger sons aged about 14 & 16 yrs & a daughter aged 17 all children of Joseph E.-Sr Two children of William's and a boy about 7 yrs old - a grandchild of Joseph E-Sr. were captured. All had been shot with arrows except William - he was shot in the head with a bullet. All were scalped except Jos. Sr. and entirely stripped of their clothing.

I, with some of the freighters before mentioned, buried all of them. The wife of Wm Eubank was taken captive and was with the Indians over a year. At the same time Miss Roper who lived about a mile from the house of the Eubanks was taken captive & kept by the Indians about 6 weeks.

I can only give the names and P.O. of the following witnesses: -
Miss Roper – now Mrs. Soper – Liberty, Neb
James Comstock – Nelson, Neb
Harriet Adams – my sister – Gunnison City, Col
I would further say that the houses were all burned, the furniture destroyed and carried off - all the horses were taken away by the Indians and the oxen and cattle shot with arrows and killed.

These are the facts relating to the massacre as I remember them. Should any questions present themselves to you upon reading this I will at all times be ready to try to answer them.

Trusting this may be satisfactory to you –I am

Yours very truly,
John Palmer

My relationship with James continued to disintegrate after Lottie's death. He grew belligerent as time went on. He saw no depredation compensation in our future, his only interest in me by this time. Once again, we moved, this time to Moundville, Vernon County, Missouri, hoping James could find work. Willie was seventeen years old now and farming with Daniel.

By 1886, we were living in Mountain Grove, Wright County, Missouri. It was then I decided to leave James. His demeanor became unbearable, so I went to live with Willie, Daniel, and Hannah in Missouri. James moved back to Quincy, Illinois, and filed for divorce.

My well-being was most important to me at this stage in my life. Through all the trials and tribulations presented to me, I would overcome this one, too. I would survive. I had survived much worse.

chapter seventy-seven

The Following Years

1891-1913
Illinois and Missouri

Many are the times grandmother cried about her little lost Isabelle, but she said little about the incident except to one very close niece.

Beatrice Eubank Ellis

A long-time friendship forged between the Frogge, Atkinson, and Eubank families dated back to the late eighteenth century. As the new nation expanded west, portions of these families moved from Virginia to Kentucky and into Illinois, Missouri, Kansas, and Colorado.

Several members settled in Crawford County, Kansas, including the widow, Doctor Franklin (Dock) Atkinson. Dock was previously married to Martha Elizabeth Barton, who died early in 1885. Before their marriage, Martha was married to John Frogge, son of the Frogge family from Scotland. One of Martha and John's daughters was Sarah Jane "Jennie" Frogge. After her mother's death, Dock raised Jennie and her three Frogge siblings, along with his two children from his union with Martha.

A decent and compassionate man, Dock was loved and admired by all. Because his name was Doctor, he was often confused as one, but he was a farmer. Dock and I married June 28, 1893.

Thankfully, my nightmares stopped not long after we were married. I felt settled and more content surrounded by family in the nearby towns of Kansas and Missouri.

A romance kindled between Willie and Jennie. Their courtship brought me sweet memories of the one Will and I shared. It was not long before my son and Jennie Frogge were engaged.

In February of 1894, an amendment was filed stating the Indians were chargeable for their depredations by reason of treaty. Our attorney,

William Hess, died, and Daniel took over as administrator of the estate. On April 24, 1894, Ambrose Asher gave his deposition in Pettis County, Missouri:

Ambrose Asher Deposition
THE COURT OF CLAIMS OF THE UNITED STATES.
INDIAN DEPREDATIONS.

Daniel Walton administrator, Number 2733
vs.
United States and The Arapaho, Cheyenne and Sioux Indians.

The deposition of Ambrose Asher, witness for the claimant taken by consent on this 24 day of April 1894, before Joseph D. Donnohue Notary Public in and for Pettis County, Missouri, in the presence of Mr. H. Lamm, Attorney for the claimant, and W.H. Robeson, Attorney for the United States, for the Defendants.

The said witness Ambrose Asher being first sworn to tell truth, the whole truth and nothing but the truth says that his name is Ambrose Asher, his age is about 37 years; his occupation is that of a teamster, and his residence California, Mo. In answer to questions propounded him by claimants said counsel, he says:

Q. 1. State what relation, if any, you bore to Joseph Eubanks, Sr. whose administrator, Daniel Walton is claimant in this case.
ANS. I am his grandson.

Q. 2. Were you present at the time he and some of his children were killed by the Indians, if so state about when it was, and where it was, and all the facts and circumstances of the matter as near as possible, in accordance with your recollection.
ANS. I was present at the time. I cannot state exactly when it was, but it was about the end of the Civil War. It was in Nebraska and I think it was near the Little Blue River. I remember my grandfather very well. He was an old gentleman with long gray whiskers. I was living with him at the time. My mother was his daughter and she was living back with my grandmother where my grandfather had moved from. There was living with my grandfather some of his children, my uncles and aunts. I do not know what month it was in, but it was hay making time. I was on the wagon with my father and two uncles going after hay. One Indian rode up out of the tall grass which is higher than a man on horse back. The Indian asked my grandfather for a chew of tobacco. My grandfather took a twist from his pocket, cut it in two and handed one piece to the Indian. The Indian took a chew and put the remainder of the piece in a sack he had with him. The Indian then got his bow and arrow and made a

453

motion as though he would shoot one of the oxen. My grandfather told him by sign and words not to do that, and the Indian then presented the bow successively at my grandfathers son, then at me, and finally at my grandfather himself. The Indian ended his performance by shooting my grandfather with a number of arrows. My grandfather's two sons started to run back to the ranch when a large number of Indians maybe fifty or seventy five arose from the tall grass with a yell, and killed my two uncles. All this time I was hanging to the wagon, as a boy would, and one of the Indians rode up, dismounted , and threw me on the horse behind him. The Indians taking me with them then went on to the ranch where they killed another one of my uncles, and my Aunt Dora. They took prisoners also my aunt Lucy and her two children, and at a point some distance from the ranch they killed also my Uncle Fred who was in the hay field. The Indians then tied my feet under a horse, and tied my hands under the horse's neck and in this way I rode to where the Indians stopped a few moments—I suppose for water—they then proceeded until some time the next day when we reached their camp. They untied me then from the horse, and when I got off began to kick and cuff me around until a squaw came and took me away from them. I was with the Indians some months, but was finally taken away by some soldiers, and after some delay sent back to Missouri or Illinois to my mother. I was too young to remember now the dates of these occurrences, but I remember the killing of my kin folks, and the incidents of my captivity.

Q. 3.   State if you remember the general character of the property, if any, owned by your grandfather, and what became of it at the time of the murder of your people.

ANS. I remember my grandfather had two wagons. One was an ox wagon and the other a two horse wagon. I remember he had three work horses. The way I came to remember this is because I recollect he had two teams, and one horse got his leg broke in the spokes of a wagon. And we had to kill the horse and that left us only three. I know he had some work oxen, for I remember they had ox teams, and he had some cows and calves, but I do not remember how many and I do not remember how many oxen. I do not remember and I don't know that I ever knew what became of this property, I always understood that the Indians took it, but I do not know that of my own knowledge. I remember when I was in the Indian camp that I saw a dog that belonged to my grandfather, but I have no memory about seeing the property there. I saw the Indians burn my grandfather's house, and I remember they ripped up the feather bed and threw the feathers out, and they burnt the furniture and the stuff that was in the house, what they didn't carry away.

Q. 4. State whether you know the value of the property that was taken or destroyed.

ANS. I was too small to know anything about the value of the property.

Q. 5. When did your mother die? And when did your father die? And have you any brothers and sisters alive? And are you yourself a married man? And when were you married, if at all?

ANS. My mother died as near as I remember about three or four years after I came back from the Indians. I think I was about twelve years old at the time. I have no remembrance whatever of my father, and he must have died when I was very young. I had a half brother, younger than myself, but I have not seen or heard of him for 18 years and I don't know whether he is dead or alive. I am a married man myself and have a wife and five children who reside with me at California, Mo. Where we have resided for 16 or 17 years.

Q. 6. State if you know Hannah Walton and what relation she bore to Joseph Eubanks, Sr., and whether or not she is the only child living of said Eubanks?

ANS. I know Hannah Walton and she is the only child now living, of my grandfather Joseph Eubanks, Sr.

Q. 7. Who were recaptured, or reexchanged at the time you were taken from the Indians by the soldiers?

ANS. Laura Roper, Daniel Marvel, myself and one cousin, a little girl. My Aunt Lucy and her other child were not taken from the Indians at the same time.

Q. 8. Do you know what tribe the Indians belonged to that murdered your people and sacked your grandfathers ranch, and took you into captivity?

ANS. I was too young the to know the difference between the different tribes of Indians. I always understood that it was the Sioux and some other Indians with them—the Arapahos and Cheyennes.

Q. 9. Who was your aunt Lucy spoken of by you?

ANS. She was the wife of my uncle William Eubanks who was killed by the Indians at the time.

CROSS-EXAMINATION
By W.H. Robeson, Assistant United States attorney.

Q. 1. Were your five uncles and aunts who were killed at the time you mention, and your mother the only children of Joseph Eubanks?

ANS. They and my uncle Joseph who was also killed on this same day at a ranch above my grandfathers were his only children.

Q. 2. Do you know whether your uncle Joseph was killed before your grandfather was?

ANS. No, I do not know.

Q.3. State if any other of your uncles and aunts left any children except your Aunt Lucy whose children you have already mentioned.

ANS. At this time none other of my uncles and aunts had any children, though I understand that my Uncle Joseph Eubanks wife subsequently bore a child by that marriage. I do not know whether that child is living, but I have heard that she was. The little boy that my aunt Lucy brought away from the Indians when she was subsequently rescued is alive, as I am informed. The child that was rescued with me died at Denver in a short time afterwards.

Q. 4. Then is the statement correct that the heirs of Joseph Eubanks, Sr. are Hannah Walton, yourself, your half-brother George Dye, the child if any, of your uncle Joseph Eubanks, Jr., and your aunt Lucy's child, William Eubanks?

ANS. In addition to the names mentioned there are the two children of my uncle George Eubanks who was not a victim of this massacre but who afterwards died in Missouri. Their names are William Eubanks, now living I think at Kirksville, Adair County, Missouri, and Dora, whose present name and residence, if living, I do not know.

I do not know anything further of interest or material to the matters in controversy.

Signed Ambrose Asher
Subscribed and sworn to me before me this 24th day of April 1894.

Signed Joe D. Donnohue,
Notary Public of Pettis County, Mo

Six months after giving his deposition, Ambrose died on October 6, 1894, from malaria fever while residing in California, Missouri. He was survived by his wife Verina (Belle) and their five children. I prayed that during his short life he was not haunted by the gruesome deaths of his grandfather, aunt, and uncles. Unfortunately, Ambrose never knew his biological father.

On October 2, 1895, Jennie Frogge and Willie were married in our home in McCune, Crawford County, Kansas. He followed in the path of his father and grandfather as a farmer.

Jennie and Willie started their family a few years later, and Jennie meticulously recorded their children's names and birth dates in the Bible Dock and I gave them as a wedding present. My namesake, Ruby

Lucinda (Lucy), was born in January 1897 in Sheldon, Vernon County, Missouri, and Virgil Frances was born in the same town in November 1898.

Also in November of 1898, Harriet (Hattie) Eubank Adams delivered her deposition for a depredation claim in the amount of $18,443.50. The Indians destroyed the ranche home she shared with Joe—as well as their store, livestock, and all personal belongings at Kiowa Station.

Willie's family moved to Osage Township, Crawford County, Kansas, and by April 1900, Arthur Lowell Eubank was born.

Dock's sons, Sterling and Edgar, lived with us during the time the 1900 census was taken. I acknowledged I had borne four children. Sadly, only two of my children were still living.

Grandson Ollie Max was born in St. Paul, Neosho County, Kansas, in August 1902.

In 1904, Jennie gave birth to a son, Joseph Noel, on March 24. He died the same day and was buried in the Frogge Family Cemetery in McCune, Kansas.

On March 7, 1905, Beatrice Evelyn Eubank was born in McCune, Kansas, and following her in April 1907, Blanche Elizabeth was welcomed to Willie and Jennie's growing family.

My dear Dock passed away on April 7, 1907. He was buried in the family cemetery. I will always remember him as a kind soul who gave me serenity. We were good friends and excellent companions.

In 1909, another grandchild, Daniel Loren, was born in McCune, Kansas. He was named after my brother Daniel but was called Loren.

The following year, Willie and Jennie moved with their children to a new farm in Sheridan, Crawford County, Kansas. I stayed in McCune and shared my home with Dock's son Edgar and Edgar's wife Mittie.

In 1913, Jennie and Willie happily announced they were expecting another baby. This baby was due in August. As always, we were excited and anxious to meet the new Eubank baby.

I longed for Will to see his grandchildren.

He would have loved them as I do.

chapter seventy-eight

Homecoming

4 April 1913
McCune, Crawford County, Kansas

I've never understood how they could torture a year-old baby, but my father's body bore scars from their taunting arrowheads until the day of his death in 1935.

Beatrice Eubank Ellis

The morning dawn caressed the gentle, rolling hills around the Eubank farm. Brilliant prisms of red, green, and yellow danced across the hardwood floor, darting from the stained-glass window in my bedroom. The air smelled fresh from the soft rain during the night. Tiny sprouts of grass peaked from the clutches of the earth. I watched as robins dipped, bobbed, and shook their feathers in the puddles down the lane.

My youngest grandchildren were gleefully playing down the hall. Their voices were like music to me. Willie and Jennie were in the kitchen planning a family picnic on Saturday, hoping the spring weather would grace us with a warm sun.

Feeling somewhat tired, I rested for a while longer, although I slept well throughout the night. I dreamt about Will and our early life together. It was a vivid dream. Serene. I could hear his and Isabelle's voices. Loving words. His gentle laugh. Belle's tiny giggles like golden chimes in the distance. I called those types of dreams "The cherished ones." Dreams you never want to end. I took a deep breath, filled my lungs with satisfaction, and exhaled slowly.

The blanket on the bed was lamb soft. I wanted to linger under it a bit longer but knew the dawning would require me to help with breakfast. I needed to get up if I wanted to be included in the picnic plans.

The smell of Jennie's coffee was coaxing me to rise. I finally sat up and glanced over at my satchel in the corner of the room. It held its steady place on the white wicker chair propped against the wall. After a long stretch, I shuffled over to it. This morning I opened the satchel for some reason and peeked inside. My eyes rested on the pair of moccasins Mitimoni gave me to protect my feet forty-eight years ago. Tranquility exuded as I thought of her and pulled them from the bag. The perfectly placed, hand-sewn, red and blue beads were still intact on the soft leather. They were the only Indian remnant I kept. I thought of Mitimoni and hoped she had lived a life without burden.

Gazing away from the moccasins in my hand, I looked over to the tintype picture of my handsome Will, sitting on the dresser. I remembered the day we married and had our likenesses taken. It was an exhilarating day for us both. Will had on his dark, three-piece suit with his watch tucked in the pocket of his vest. I wore a new, silk dress with a tiny diamond pattern and white buttons from my neck down to my waist. He chose to stand by a tree placed in front of a backdrop in the photographer's studio, and I chose to stand behind a chair. Then we had our likenesses taken together.

Interrupting my reminiscences, granddaughter Blanche ran into the room and jumped on my bed. Smiling at the beautiful, tow-headed child, I told her she nearly took my breath away! We laughed, then she dashed out of the room to find her sister Beatrice.

After tucking the moccasins back into the satchel, I stopped to admire my embroidered initials 𝒜ℒℰ still holding prominence on the front of the bag. I treasured this gift from my mother-in-law Ruth and was relieved when it was returned to me at the fort.

The wooden chest Willie built for me sat at the end of the bed. I gently lifted both Lottie's and Belle's dresses from its depths. Holding them in my hands, I shut my eyes and pressed them to my face. I inhaled deeply, longing for their sweet fragrance. Instead of returning them to the chest, I placed them on the dresser. Once I slipped into the day's attire, I tucked their dresses under my arm and moved toward the kitchen. Feeling rather dizzy, I stepped out on the porch for some air.

The porch wrapped around two sides of their large farmhouse. Willie had just hung the baskets of pansies Jennie planted from the cross posts. The flowers' purple faces and yellow eyes brightened up the morning. I had to smile as I admired Jennie's connection to the earth. She had a way with growing flowers and vegetables—canning the bounty was her forte. The Eubank family never hungered.

As I rocked, eight-year-old Beatrice scrambled onto my lap. A large, white bow held back Bea's light brown curls that twisted down her shoulders. Her dark, gentle doe eyes sparkled as she hummed her favorite song.

Blanche was six years old. She was the blonde child in Willie's family. Her icy-blue eyes shimmered like fairy dust. Four-year-old Loren had olive skin, and his dark hair fell over brown, deep-set eyes.

First-born grandchild Lucy was sixteen years old and had grown into a beautiful girl. The older grandsons, Virgil, Art, and Ollie, were handsome lads like their father.

Seven grandchildren and one due in August. It made my heart sing. I adored them and knew they were here only by the grace of God.

Willie stepped out onto the porch, sat in his rocker, and reached to shift Beatrice to his lap.

"Are you feeling okay, Mother?"

I clung to Bea momentarily and kissed her on the forehead. "Give that kiss to your own granddaughters someday, dear Bea."

I placed my left hand on top of Willie's and squeezed it. He was my Little Mato Walks all grown up now with children of his own.

I rested both hands in my lap. The wedding band given to me by Will glistened in the sun. I had worn it on my right hand every day since my release.

"I am just a little tired this morning, Son."

"Do you hear the turtle doves, Grandma?" Blanche asked.

"Yes, honey, I can hear them."

Lucinda shut her eyes.
Slowly, she rocked.
Her breath was shallow.
Warmth caressed her.

She felt him near.
"Come to me, Will."
Through a thin veil, she saw him.
His radiant, blue eyes pierced hers.

She gazed deeper.
Will held the hand of a little girl.
Rosy cheeks and large, melting-blue eyes held her innocence.
Long, blonde curls flowed as she walked.

On his opposite side, another young girl strode.
A reddish-golden braid tumbled down one shoulder.
Wild, unruly strands framed her delicate face.
Black lashes outlined her emerald-green eyes.

Closer and closer they came.
Lucinda grasped Will's extended hand.
Little dresses floated to the ground as she stood.
Faint voices echoed, "Mama, Mama!"

Will pulled her into his arms.
White mist enfolded them.
She gazed into his face at last....

"Will."

Aftermath

1913-1937
Kansas and Colorado

L ucinda Eubank Atkinson died at the home of her son, William Eubank, Jr., on April 13, 1913, in McCune, Crawford County, Kansas. She was buried along with Willie and Jennie's son, William Joseph Noel, in the Frogge/Frogue Family Cemetery in Crawford County, Kansas.

After almost fifty years of endless affidavits, depositions, investigations, and attorneys working to recover any compensation for their losses, Ruth and Lucinda's depredation claim was denied on December 8, 1913. It was ruled that the Cheyenne and Arapaho Indians were not in amity with the United States during the time of the Eubank family massacre. By this time, both Ruth and Lucinda were dead. Hannah Eubank Walton lost her father, sister, and five brothers in the raid. She and the remaining Eubank heirs received nothing.

On August 23, 1913, Willie and Jennie's last child, Kenneth Charles Eubank, was born in St. Paul, Neosho County, Kansas.

Hannah Walton, the only surviving child of Ruth and Joseph Eubank, died on September 15, 1915, in Sheldon, Vernon County, Missouri, at age 77. Her husband, Daniel Walton (Lucinda's brother), died in Sheldon on September 9, 1918. He was 87 years old. Both Hannah and Daniel were buried in Sheldon, Missouri.

By 1917, the William Eubank, Jr. family had moved to Crow Creek, Weld County, Colorado.

In the 1930 census, William Eubank, Jr. was residing with his wife Jennie and Kenneth, their sixteen-year-old son, in Pierce, Weld County, Colorado.

William Joseph Eubank, Jr. died at his home in Pierce, Colorado, on March 3, 1935. He was buried in the Eaton Cemetery, Weld County, Colorado.

Sarah Jane (Jennie) Frogge Eubank died at the home of her son Kenneth in Corvallis, Oregon, on July 27, 1937. She was buried next to Willie in the Eaton Cemetery, Weld County, Colorado.

Epilogue

In conclusion, Larry Skogen, in his book Indian Depredation Claims, 1796-1920, said:

> *Of all the August victims, the Eubanks family certainly suffered more than most. Ruth Eubanks lost her husband, five sons, and a daughter. Her pregnant daughter-in-law, Harriet, also became a widow, as did Lucinda Eubanks, who as well endured captivity for eleven months. During this time Lucinda also lost a daughter. If compensation was appropriate, the Eubanks family, probably more than anyone else, deserved it for their losses resulting from the August attacks. As we have seen, though, the Indian depredation claims system did not provide indemnity for human suffering or death.*

This is the story of a family—of loved ones lost and precious ones who survived. It represents the authors' mutual perspective and interpretation of events. And so…the tellers of this epic story end with this:

Lucinda's appearance spoke to months of captivity and hardship. The journey through the untamed plains wilderness left her skin wrinkled and scarred. She was thin and her visage was both wary and withdrawn. To those with whom she shared a past, Lucinda was a shadow of her earlier self. It seemed a breeze could parachute her away like a dandelion wisp. Other times she was brittle enough to shatter into pieces as if flung against the rocks along the great Platte River. Yet, the essence of her story exudes strength and resilience. Those who persevere are not always the most attractive, most intelligent, most ruthless, or the luckiest. Sometimes the ordinary are the ones who survive. All of creation, from the greatest to the humblest, will face the inevitable covenant of life just as Lucinda did; and she did it with grace, forgiveness, and love.

As written on the bottom of her tombstone, Lucinda is….

Gone—But Not Forgotten.

Authors' Notes

FIRE-HAIR WOMAN is a novel based on many true events as described by others— captives, natives, scouts, soldiers, pioneers, and settlers. Here are some of the common questions the authors are asked:

Did Lucinda write about her experiences?

Lucinda revealed little of the personal nature of her ordeal. No written account by Lucinda is in existence today. However, a reference to Lucinda's book showed up in a letter to Walter M. Camp, Chicago, Illinois, from George Smith. He stated: "I am unable to tell you the title of the paper back pamphlet or book written by Mrs. Eubanks. The same was sent by her from some place in Illinois to my father, Lieut. James G. Smith, who was officer of the day at the time Mrs. Eubanks was brought in by Two Face's tribe and the four Indian chiefs. My father has been dead more than twenty years and I do not know what ever become of the book written and sent him by Mrs. Eubanks."

George Smith's father, First Lieutenant James G. Smith, Co. A, 7th Iowa Cav., Kansas City, Missouri, was quoted in the National Tribune, August 4, 1910: "I also saw the book written by Mrs. Eubanks after her release and return to Illinois."

Is the Eubank surname really Eubank or Eubanks?

This question is often debated by historians and referenced in non-fiction publications. Eubank family ancestors are traced back to the *Eubank Entries in the Caroline County, Virginia, Court Order Books*, 1732, and through Revolutionary War Patriot records. The Eubank family moved to Kentucky in the early 1800's and were silversmiths. The name Eubank was stamped on their work. Eubanks, the plural form, was often substituted for the actual name Eubank.

Who was the oldest Eubank daughter?

Hannah is often cited as the eldest daughter living in Nebraska Territory with the Eubank family. However, Hannah Eubank was born in 1838, married Daniel Walton in 1855, and lived in Illinois and Missouri. Mary Eliza, the mother of Ambrose Asher/Conrad Eubank, was the eldest daughter born in 1834. In the 1860's, she is found living in Illinois and was contacted in Kentucky at the time of Ambrose's release. Facts suggest Sarah, born in 1843, is the daughter who worked at Liberty Farm, Nebraska Territory, in 1864.

Was Joseph Eubank, Jr. really a stagecoach driver, one of the Overland Boys?

Yes. A complete list of drivers can be found in: *The Overland Stage to California: Personal Reminiscences and Authentic History of the Great Overland Stage Line and Pony Express from the Missouri River to the Pacific Ocean* by Frank Albert Root.

Was Wild Bill Hickok a family friend?

Evidence suggests James Butler Hickok and Joe Eubank, Jr. worked for the same stage company, lived at the same station, and drove the same route during the same period. We extrapolated the relationship from there.

What happened to the bodies of the Eubank family?

During the visit to Oak in 1964, Beatrice Eubank Ellis was informed that Eubank bones were found and at rest in the Hastings Museum in Hastings, Nebraska. The kind Curator of Collections and Program Director at the museum, Teresa Kreutzer-Hodson, retrieved a box filled with skeletal remains from the 1864 raids and presented them to C.J. for viewing. Analysis of bone remains matched the genders and ages of several Eubank family members.

Was George Bent present at the Eubank Ranche during the raid?

Probably. Eyewitness accounts place him there. The readers can draw their own conclusion.

> I do not intend to give a detailed account of the raids that were made during July and August. They were terrible affairs, but after all, the Indians were wild people in those days; they had been attacked again and again by the troops without any cause, and they were retaliating in the only way they knew how.
>
> George Bent

An interesting letter from George Bent to W.M. Camp dated September 1, 1917, was found in the Colorado College Special Collections MF 0018. See a reproduction of the actual letter on pages 472-473.

Is there still a tree at the Narrows where Lucinda and the children hid during the Indian attack?

Yes. The Narrows Bur Oak tree saw significant activity during the western migration of the 1860s. It is located 150 feet from the site where Lucinda and the children were captured at the Narrows on the Oregon Trail. In 1929, Laura Roper Vance returned to the Narrows to verify the place of capture. The bur oak is over 200 years old, received state distinction, and is officially known as the Narrows Bur Oak Tree.

Did Grandfather's dog really follow the captives into the Indian camp?

Yes. The mention was a tragic tidbit the authors found to be personal, and it enriched the story.

Did Alights on the Cloud really give Ambrose the ledger of drawings?

Yes. Artwork credit is also attributed to Lame Bull, Medicine Water, and possibly eight other unknown artists. Sotheby's Arts of the American West sold the ledger at auction in 2013 for $185,000. The provenance connected to the item confirms it was given to Ambrose Asher in Black Kettle's village on the headwaters of the Smoky Hill River, Kansas, during his August/September 1864 captivity. He and Danny Marble stayed with the Lewis and Sarah Giberson family in Denver City after their release. The ledger itself indicates Sarah Giberson acquired it in 1864 when Ambrose returned to Illinois to live with his grandmother. Margaret Giberson added an inscription to the notebook, parts of which are as follows: *1929, Ambrose Asher, Coonie Pokins as called by Indians.* The Giberson family preserved the ledger until it was sold. It is the oldest documented collection of Cheyenne Ledger Drawings, and the authors hope this important piece of Cheyenne history is returned to the tribe.

Was Lucinda present at the Sand Creek Massacre?

Yes. Lucinda told family members she was at Sand Creek during the attack. Firsthand accounts also place Lucinda at this infamous event, a disgrace to Colorado history. In reference to Sand Creek, John Ellenbecker wrote in his Indian Raids of 1860-1869:

> Mrs. Wm. Eubank and child were with the Indians here, held by Chiefs Two Face, Doc Billy & Big Thunder. But during the battle these three chiefs with their captives and a small band of Indians got away and headed north of Cheyenne agency and the mountains.

According to a deposition taken at Denver, Colorado, on November, 9, 1891, Oliver P. Wiggins said:

> Roaring Wind, Two Face, Doc Billy, and Big Thunder. They were the ones that made the raid that took Mrs. Eubank's family, and came back up to Sand Creek; three weeks after that they got back to Sand Creek and Col. Chivington came in and got the whole outfit except Doc Billy and Big Thunder and Two Face, and they took Mrs. Eubank and run away.

The following article was found in the Anaconda Standard, Anaconda, Montana, dated August 13, 1897:

Massacre at Sand Creek

> Mr. Wiggins once told the Record correspondent that the testimony of Mrs. Eubank was to the effect that she as the captive of Two Face, was at Sand Creek. With characteristic cunning Two Face had his teepee some distance from the camp, and when the attack was made Mrs. Eubank had no chance to escape or make herself known.

Walter M. Camp wrote the following from an interview with O.H.P. Wiggins dated January 20, 1913:

> When Mrs. Eubanks came down to Alkali on her way from Laramie, Wiggins talked with her and she told him the whole story of her capture and release.

It is our desire to present the massacres of our family and the native families with respect and honor for the innocent victims.

Did Lucinda actually meet Crazy Horse?

Perhaps. Native sources place her in the same Sioux/Cheyenne village as Crazy Horse and Sitting Bull on both the Powder and Tongue Rivers in Northern Dakotah Territory (now Wyoming). Crazy Horse commanded the wild Indians in the Battle of Horse Creek, so the association is based on real events. The fun part was describing the man.

Was Baby Willie really thrown off a cliff?

Probably. Accounts shared around the dinner table and found in tiny notepads are special to the authors. For example, their grandmother, Beatrice Eubank Ellis, often shared the story of baby Willie's toss off a cliff—found in the chapter "Forty Warriors." It seemed unbelievable until Gladys Hamilton, the granddaughter of Hannah Walton, substantiated the *same* tale.

Were Indian papooses thrown into the river by soldiers?

The event is documented. Also, verbal family lore entwines the interesting supposition that Lucinda herself became an advocate for the Plains Indians and was appalled by their treatment. Lucinda told her family about her sympathies for them. In a letter, her niece stated that Lucinda never spoke an ill word against those who harmed her. The authors' grandmother, Beatrice Eubank Ellis, recounted how Lucinda was mortified by soldiers throwing Indian babies into a river.

What happened to Lucinda's Indian baby?

The authors developed a theory based on census reports, the family's geographical movements, and a family photo. If their supposition is correct, Lucinda's child conceived by Big Crow had a blessed childhood, married, and had five children. Because the descendants of this person may not have this information, it seems inappropriate to reveal the child's identity at this time.

Was there a connection between Lucinda and the Sioux Chief Two Face?

Yes. Two sources provide evidence suggesting an association between Two Face and Lucinda: the testimony of Lucinda herself and O.P. Wiggins' statements. Two Face saved Lucinda and Willie on more than one occasion. Whether he actually placed himself at the Eubank Ranche on purpose is left to conjecture. "A Little Hasty" describing Two Face's death was probably one of the most difficult chapters to write. The authors still choke up when reading it. An interesting twist in Two Face's story was found in a recent Rapid City Journal article dated December 31, 1998. A relative of Two Face, Connie Fast Horse, was part of an effort to repatriate the remains of Two Face and forty-one other Sioux from the Smithsonian Institution repository. He was laid to rest on the Pine Ridge Indian Reservation.

Were there true heroes and villains?

TWO FACE: The character research of Two Face deepened as the authors deduced he was possibly the real reason Lucinda and Willie survived their captivity. He had a knack for rescuing them when the fires grew hot. If indeed he had a hand in their survival, the authors are grateful for it dawned on them that without his intervention, Baby Willie might have perished, and they would not exist today.

NED WYNKOOP: Major Edward W. Wynkoop of the First Colorado Cavalry attempted to secure a lasting peace on the plains and was thwarted by Colorado's first territorial governor and others. Many in powerful positions viewed the natives as expendable obstacles to the unending resources and potential wealth production of the plains. Wynkoop continued his efforts toward a peace agreement and became a trusted friend of Black Kettle. Frustrated by planned attacks on the Indians, Wynkoop resigned his commission as brevet lieutenant colonel in November 1868, and became an Indian agent.

LEFT HAND: Not surprisingly, a few notables developed into dual characters—holding the double distinction of hero and villain. Gina grew up near Left Hand Creek and was in the first graduating class of Niwot High School, Colorado. Holding a special affinity for the Arapaho chief, Niwot (translated Left Hand), she admired him as a man of peace whose fluency in English lent a voice to his people. One of the jarring consequences of historical research occurred. Gina's idealistic vision of the man was tempered by Laura Roper's deposition statement that he and Black Kettle were present at the Roper Ranche on the day of the raid. It is quite possible they were among those who murdered the Eubank family just one mile away.

> Left Hand and Black Kettle seemed to have absolute control as the two chiefs over the party and they were, as Left Hand told me, present at the time my father's house and property were destroyed. Left Hand told me frequently that he did not want to kill my brother but that Black Kettle did.
>
> Laura Roper

The following is according to Wikipedia contributors: "Chief Niwot." *Wikipedia, The Free Encyclopedia*, 31 Dec. 2021. June 2022:

> Over the years, reports filtered out of Oklahoma that Chief Niwot did not die at Sand Creek, but rather was alive and well on the reservation. Since he made it off the battlefield alive after the Sand Creek Massacre, official accounts never confirmed his death. Photos of an Arapaho named Niwot appeared in the late 19th century, which only fueled the rumors of Chief Niwot's survival.
>
> But historians agree that Niwot did not go with his people to Oklahoma. A younger warrior named Niwot, possibly a distant relative, did emerge as a leader of the Arapahos in Oklahoma, but it is now believed he was confused in news reports with the legendary chief who first welcomed the white man to the Boulder Valley.

THUNDER BEAR and BLACK SHIELD: Blackfoot's son Thunder Bear and Two Face's nephew Black Shield (a.k.a. Calico, Minihuha) became judges on the Indian Court at the Pine Ridge Reservation.

JOHN EVANS: In July 1865, Governor Evans was notified by the Secretary of State in the following letter:

> To John Evans, Governor of the Territory of Colorado, Denver City.
>
> Sir; I am directed by the President to inform you that your resignation of the office of Governor of Colorado Territory would be acceptable. Circumstances connected with the public interest make it desirable the resignation should reach here without delay.
>
> I am, Sir, Your obedient servant, William H. Seward.

JOHN CHIVINGTON: In January 1865, Chivington mustered out of the army avoiding prosecution for his abhorrent acts. One source says he was already out of the army before his attack and had no right to command anyone.

The documented actions of the villains in this story speak for themselves.

Is the Hailstorm a real drink?

The Hailstorm is an Old West inspired drink. In the 1830s, fur traders and trappers at Bent's Fort and Trading Post near La Junta, Colorado, would gather hailstones and prepare the delectable drink in a mason jar. During the writing of FIRE-HAIR WOMAN, the authors raised a jar… or two. For those who wish to try it, here is the recipe:

Hailstorm Frontier Drink

3 oz. Tin-Cup whiskey or your favorite bourbon
2 tsp. confectioner's sugar or vanilla bean honey
2 sprigs of fresh mint

Combine ingredients in a 16-oz. mason jar of hail or ice, secure lid, and shake vigorously 50 times. The mint will bruise and release its flavor. Drink from the jar for an authentic Colorado experience.

George Bent Letter

Colony Oklahoma

Sept 1st 1917

W. M. Camp

My Dear Mr Camp

This reason I had not written to you sooner. About Capture of Mrs Eubanks on Plum Creek or Little Blue in summer of 1864. Sitting in Lodge Old Woman of our 80 years with Mo Heap of Birds now dead Captured her. Heap of Birds gave Mrs Eubanks to his Sister "Mower". Mower was living with the Sioux. Mower gave Mrs Eubanks to Sioux Indian name "Black Feet I knew this Sioux well. He called Mr to his Lodge Many times this was in 1863. I was away when Mrs Eubanks was brought into Camp. on Solomon River. but got in few days after. Black Feet, Big Crow Cheyenne Indians and another Sioux Indian took Mrs Eubanks Child and another White Woman not was Captured on South Platte River in winter of 1865 I was present at the time. She was Captured by Sioux Indian by name of Opera Belly. Black Feet Big Crow and Sioux Indian took them to Fort Laramie on North Platte River. to turn the Women over to Commandery Officer Col Moon Light the Officer

Colony Oklahoma
Sept 1st 1917

W.M. Camp

My Dear Mr. Camp

The reason I had not written to you sooner. About capture of Mrs Eubanks on Plum Creek or Little Blue in summer of 1864. Setting in Lodge Old Woman of over 80 years tells me Heap of Birds now dead captured her. Heap of Birds gave Mrs. Eubanks to his sister "Mouci. Mouci was living with the Sioux. Mouci gave Mrs. Eubanks to Sioux Indian name "Black Feet. I knew this Sioux well. He called me to his Lodge many times this was in 1863. I was away when Mrs. Eubanks was brought into camp on Solomon River but got in few days after. Black Feet, Big Crow Cheyenne Indian and another Sioux Indian took Mrs. Eubanks child and another White Woman that was captured on South Platte River in Winter of 1865. I was present at the time. She was captured by Sioux Indian by name of Opero Belly. Black Feet Big Crow and Sioux Indian took them to Fort Laramie on North Platte River to turn the woman over to Commanding Officer Col Moon Light. The officer hung them after taken the white woman to the Fort. All the Sioux told these three men (Indians) to not to take them to the Fort but Black Feet thought they would get big pay for the woman. William Robideaux told me Col Moon Light was drunk when he hung these three Indians. I wanted to find out for sure What Cheyenne captured Mrs. Eubanks then Old Woman just came in and told me all about it.

Yours Truly
George Bent

About the Authors

C.J. Pierce received a Bachelor of Science degree from Bellevue University. She worked as an executive in the nonprofit service industry for over twenty-five years before her retirement. She is a member of the National Society of the Daughters of the American Revolution Organization and a member of the Oregon-California Trails Association. Her debut novel, FIRE-HAIR WOMAN, co-authored with her cousin Gina Ellis, has bestowed her the gift of cultivating the rich history of their Eubank ancestors. She resides in the Midwest with her husband of forty-four years.

Gina Ellis is a fifth generation Coloradan. The Parker and Ellis families arrived in northern Colorado during the mid-1860s and by the 1870s, three homesteads existed in northern Larimer County. She grew up spending time on those ranches hunting, fishing, and riding horses. Running around the hills and mountain forests in cowboy boots as a child fueled her pioneer imagination. She always wondered if she was born a century too late. Gina graduated from Niwot High School, Colorado, and received a Bachelor of Arts degree from the University of Northern Colorado in Greeley. She is a western history buff and pursues her interests as a member of the the National Society of the Daughters of the American Revolution Organization and the Oregon-California Trails Association. Gina is forever grateful to C.J. for the gift of the process and the culmination of a joint purpose.

The combination of researching events, exploring genealogy, and writing this novel has been a great pleasure. Gina and C.J. spent years in business and education while raising families but soon discovered each held within their hearts the story of great-great-grandmother, Lucinda Eubank. The cousins speak to the theory that they share an ancestral, DNA-inspired, memory for the story. And so, the book has become a collaborative reality. May it stand in good stead for future generations.

C.J. and Gina
Walking toward the Narrows,
at the Eubank ranche site.
Authors' Collection

Acknowledgements

Our heartfelt gratitude is extended to husbands, family, and friends for their enduring support.

With deep appreciation to Patty Henrichs for her friendship, encouragement, and expertise in the editing of the manuscript.

To Greg and Jean Stichka, Jody and Dan Wolford, and the Werner family—you truly enrich our lives.

We are grateful to Gladys Hamilton for Hannah Walton's photo album, the Eubank/Frogge personal diaries and letters, and the shared memories.

Thank you to the following individuals: Chris Mathers, National Park Service, Fort Laramie NHS; Tom Mooney, Curator of Manuscripts, History Nebraska; and Teresa Kreutzer-Hodson, Curator of Collections/ Program Director, Hastings Museum.

The following resources were invaluable: Oregon-California Trails Association; History Colorado; History Nebraska; Lily Library, Indiana University; Denver Public Library; Bent's Fort National Historical Site; National Archives, Library of Congress; Colorado College Special Collections, Sand Creek Papers MF 0018; and Heritage Museum, Oak, Nebraska.

We are appreciative of the following books, authors, journals, newspapers, periodicals, and websites: *Roughing It* by Mark Twain; *Silas Soule, A Short, Eventful Life of Moral Courage* by Tom Bensing; *The Great Platte River Road* by Merrill J. Mattes; *Forgotten Heroes & Villains of Sand Creek* by Carol Turner; *Massacre along the Medicine Road, A Social History of the Indian War of 1864 in Nebraska Territory* by Ronald Becher; *Tragedy at the Little Blue, The Oak Grove Massacre and the Captivity of Lucinda Eubank and Laura Roper* by Lyn Ryder; *The Overland Stage to California: Personal Reminiscences and Authentic History of the Great Overland Stage Line and Pony Express from the Missouri River to the Pacific Ocean* by Frank Albert Root; *Daughters of the American Revolution, Nebraska Pioneer Reminiscences: Stirring*

Events Along the Little Blue by Clarendon E. Adams; *Frontier Spirit, The Story of Wyoming* by Craig Sodaro and Randy Adams; *Mollie, The Journal of Mollie Dorsey Sanford in Nebraska and Colorado Territories, 1857-1866* by Mollie Sanford; *Boggsville, Cradle of the Colorado Cattle Industry* by C.W. Hurd; *Mochi's War* by Chris Enss and Howard Kazanjian; *Pump on the Prairie* by Musetta Gilman; *With My Own Eyes, A Lakota Woman Tells Her People's History* by Susan Bordeaux Bettelyoun and Josephine Waggoner; *Fort Laramie and the Sioux* by Remi Nadeau; *Fort Laramie and the Pageant of the West, 1834-1890* by LeRoy R. Hafen and Francis Marion Young; *Fort Laramie, Visions of a Grand Old Post* by Robert A. Murray; *Fort Laramie, Military Bastion of the High Plains* by Douglas C. McChristian; *Boss Cowman, The Recollections of Ed Lemmon 1857-1946* edited by Nellie Snyder Yost; *Massacre at Sand Creek, How Methodists Were Involved in an American Tragedy* by Gary L. Roberts; *The Sand Creek Massacre* by Stan Hoig; *A Wild West History of Frontier Colorado, Pioneers, Gunslingers & Cattle Kings on the Eastern Plains* by Jolie Anderson Gallagher; *The Arapahoes, Our People* by Virginia Cole Trenholm; *Voices of the American West, The Indian Interviews of Eli S. Ricker, 1903-1919* edited by Richard E. Jensen; *Narrative of My Captivity Among the Sioux Indians* by Fanny Kelly; *The Fighting Cheyennes* by George Bird Grinnell; *Halfbreed, The Remarkable True Story of George Bent Caught Between the Worlds of the Indian and the White Man* by David Fridtjof Halaas and Andrew E. Masich; *Life of George Bent, Written from his Letters* by George E. Hyde; *Destination: Denver City, The South Platte Trail* by Doris Monahan; *The Tall Chief, The Autobiography of Edward W. Wynkoop*, edited by Christopher B. Gerboth; *Ned Wynkoop and the Lonely Road from Sand Creek* by Louis Kraft; *Indian War of 1864* by Captain Eugene F. Ware; *Captive of the Cheyenne, The Story of Nancy Jane Morton and the Plum Creek Massacre* by Russ Czaplewski; *The Capture and Escape: Life Among the Sioux 1870* by Sarah Luse Larimer; *Finn Burnett, Frontiersman* by Robert Beebe David; *The Saga of the Pony Express* by Joseph J. Di Certo; *Road Ranches Along the Oregon Trail 1858 to 1868 Between Marysville, Kansas and Fort Kearny, Nebraska* by Lyn Ryder; *The Sand Creek Massacre, A Documentary History 1865-1867* by John M. Carroll (Sol Lewis original); *Crazy Horse* by Mari Sandoz; *Black Kettle, The Cheyenne Chief Who Sought Peace but Found War* by Thom Hatch; *Pioneer Tales of the Oregon Trail and of Jefferson County, Volume 1* by Charles Dawson; *A Fate Worse Than Death, Indian Captivities in the West, 1830-1885* by Gregory and Susan Michno; *Indian Raids and Massacres, Essays on the Central Plains Indian War* by Jeff Broome;

The Southern Cheyenne by Donald Berthrong*; Cheyenne War, Indian Raids on the Roads to Denver 1864-1869* by Jeff Broome; *Brigham and the Brigadier: General Patrick Connor and His California Volunteers in Utah and Along the Overland Trail* by James F. Varley; *Chief Left Hand, Southern Arapaho* by Margaret Coel; *Circle of Fire, The Indian War of 1865* by John D. McDermott; *The History of Wyoming From the Earliest Known Discoveries* by C. G. Coutant; *Women and Indians on the Frontier, 1825-1915* by Glenda Riley; *Indian Depredation Claims, 1796-1920* by Larry Skogen; Denver Republican; The National Tribune; Sunday World Herald Magazine; Daily Mining Journal; The Quincy Whig; Omaha Daily Bee; The Marysville Advocate; Marysville Enterprise; Nebraska History Magazine; The Trail, Plain Tales of the Plains, Julia Lambert; Lincoln Journal Star; Rocky Mountain Daily News; Big Blue Union, Marysville, KS; Wild West Magazine; Quincy Weekly Herald; Anaconda Standard;

https://www.ancestry.com

https://www.american-tribes.com

https://www.newspapers.com

Special thanks to the early pioneers, freighters, and soldiers who penned their recollections: *The Captivity of Laura L. Roper* by Virginia N. Leasure; *Autobiography of M.A. Alexander and Letter* by M.A. Alexander*; The Oak Grove Massacre* by John Ellenbecker; *Pioneer Tales of the Oregon Trail* by Charles Dawson; *Nancy Morton's Own Story of the Plum Creek Massacre of 1864* by Nancy Morton, History Nebraska, RG3467.AM*; The Trail: New Light on Mrs. Lucinda Eubank's Experiences and Plain Tales of the Plains* by Julia S. Lambert; *Incidents of the Indian Outbreak, Freighting on the Plains-Plum Creek Massacre* by James Green*; The Powder River Indian Expedition 1865* by H.E. Palmer; *Indian Raids Along the Platte and Little Blue Rivers, 1864-1865* by Leroy Hagerty, History Nebraska. *"My Diary"* by Mollie E. Sanford, Brand Book of the Denver Posse of the Westerners.

www.ingramcontent.com/pod-product-compliance
Lightning Source LLC
Chambersburg PA
CBHW030747030726
47497CB00001B/166